P9-CRE-135

HOUSE OF REEDS

TOR BOOKS BY THOMAS HARLAN

IN THE TIME OF THE SIXTH SUN

WASTELAND OF FLINT

HOUSE OF REEDS

OATH OF EMPIRE

THE SHADOW OF ARARAT

THE GATE OF FIRE

THE STORM OF HEAVEN

THE DARK LORD

HOUSE OF REEDS

THOMAS HARLAN

A TOM DOHERTY ASSOCIATES BOOK
NEW YORK

This is a work of fiction. All the characters and events portrayed in this novel are either fictitious or are used fictitiously.

HOUSE OF REEDS

This book is printed on acid-free paper.

Map by the author

A Tor Book
Published by Tom Doherty Associates, LLC
175 Fifth Avenue
New York, NY 10010

www.tor.com

Library of Congress Cataloging-in-Publication Data

Harlan, Thomas.
House of reeds / Thomas Harlan.—1st ed.
p. cm.
"A Tom Doherty Associates book."
Sequel to: Wasteland of flint.
ISBN 0-765-30193-8 (acid-free paper)
1. Life on other planets—Fiction. 2. Space colonies—Fiction. 3. Mexico—Fiction. 4. Aztecs—Fiction. I. Title.

PS3558.A624244H68 2004
813'.54—dc22

2003057060

First Edition: February 2004

Printed in the United States of America

0 9 8 7 6 5 4 3 2 1

Without the inspiration of Jack Vance, Hayao Miyazaki,
and Talbot Mundy, there would be no book.

Without the able and expert assistance of Chris Cornuelle,
Chris Weuve, Martin Helsdon, Loma Griffith, Teresita Flores,
and Suzanne MacDhomhail, the story would be far poorer.

A NOTE CONCERNING MEASUREMENTS

Though her later victories rendered the full terms of the Lisbon Accords moot, the Méxica Empire abides by the common set of weights and measures set forth by the Accords in A.D. 1724. As a result, distances are in kilometers, weights in kilograms and so on.

OFFICER RANKS OF THE IMPERIAL MÉXICA FLEET, ARMY AND MARINES

NISEI TERM	FLEET RANK	MARINE/ARMY	MÉXICA TERM
Thai-sho	Admiral	General	Cuauhnochteuctli (*EAGLE PRICKLY-PEARL LORD*)
Chu-sho	Vice Admiral	Lieutenant-General	
Sho-sho	Rear Admiral	Major-General	Tlacoccalcatl (*COMMANDING GENERAL*)
Thai-sa	Captain	Colonel	Tlacateccatl (*GENERAL*)
Chu-sa	Commander		Cuauhtlahtoh (*CHIEF*)
Sho-sa	Lieutenant Commander	Major	
Thai-i	Lieutenant	Captain	Cuahyahcatl (*GREAT CAPTAIN*)
Chu-i	Sub-Lieutenant	Lieutenant	
Sho-i Ko-hosei	Midshipman		
Gunso		Master Sergeant	Cuauhhuehueh (*EAGLE ELDER*)
Joto-Heiso	Chief Boatswain		
Gocho		Sergeant	Tequihuah (*VETERAN WARRIOR*)
Itto-Heiso	Chief Boatswain's Mate		
Heicho		Corporal	Yaotequihuah (*LEADER OF YOUTHS*)
Nitto-Heiso	Boatswain's mate		
Ittohei		Senior Private	Tiachcuah (*OLDER BROTHER*)
Itto-Shihei	Spacer		
Nitohei		Private	Telpolcatl (*YOUTH*)

FROM THE ANNALS OF CUAUHTITLAN

In the beginning was the First Sun,
4-Water was its sign;
It was called the Sun of Water.
For water covered the world,
Leaving nothing but the dragonflies above
And the fishy men below.

The Second Sun was born,
4-Jaguar was its sign;
This was called the Sun of the Jaguars.
In this Sun the heavens collapsed,
So that the Sun could not move in its course.
The world darkened, and when all was dark
Then the people were devoured.

The Giants perished, giving life to the Third Sun.
4-Rain was its sign;
It was called the Sun of Rain.
For this Sun rained fire from bleeding eyes
And the people were consumed.

From the torrent of burning stones,
The Fourth Sun was born.
4-Wind was its sign, and it was called the Sun of Wind.
In this Sun, all which stood on the earth was carried
Away by terrible winds.
The people were turned into monkeys,
And scattered from their cities into the forest.

Now, by sacrifice of the divine liquid, the Fifth Sun was born.
Its sign was 4-Motion.
As the Sun moved, following a course,
The ancients called it the Sun of Motion.
In the time of this Sun, there were
Great earthquakes and famine,
No maize grew, and the gods of the field

Turned their eyes from the people.
And all the people grew thin, and perished.

The Lord of Heaven cut the heart from his living son,
And so was born the Sixth Sun, which sustains
The universe with infinite light.
Its sign was 4-Flint.
Those who watch the sky say this Sun
Will end in annihilation, when the flint-knife
Severs the birthcord of the Sun, plunging all
Into darkness, where the people will
Be cut to pieces and scattered.

This is the time of the Sixth Sun. . . .

DRAMATIS PERSONAE

THE IMPERIALS

Tezozómoc, a Méxica prince of low repute. The youngest son of the reigning Méxica Emperor Ahuitzotl

Master Sergeant Lorne **Colmuir,** a Skawtish Eagle Knight, the prince's bodyguard

Sergeant Leslie **Dawd,** a Skawtish Eagle Knight, and the prince's other bodyguard

Yacatolli, *Tlacateccatl* (Colonel) of the 416th Arrow Knight regiment (motorized)—the "Tarascan Rifles"

THE CREW OF THE IMN HENRY R. CORNUELLE

Chu-sa (Commander) **Mitsuharu Hadeishi,** captain

Sho-sa (Lieutenant Commander) **Susan Koshō,** executive officer

Thai-i (Senior Lieutenant, weapons officer) Patrick **Hayes**

Thai-i (Senior Lieutenant, engineering) **Isoroku** Oushi

Sho-i (Midshipman, communications) Daniel **Smith**

Thai-i (Senior Lieutenant, Marine detachment) **Huémac**

Gunso (Sergeant) "Hork" **Fitzsimmons,** Imperial Marines

Heicho (Corporal) **Felix,** Imperial Marines

Captain's Steward Kusaru **Yejin**

Helsdon, chief machinist's mate

IMPERIAL CITIZENS ON JAGAN

Itzpalicue (Skirt-of-Knives), agent of the Mirror Which Reveals The Truth

Mrs. Greta Hauksbee **Petrel,** wife of the Imperial Resident on Jagan

Soumake, Imperial attaché in charge of Antiquities, Jagan

Johann **Gemmilsky,** Polish expatriate, riding lizard trader

THE HONORABLE CHARTERED COMPANY

Doctor **Gretchen** Anderssen, xenoarchaeologist, mother of three

David **Parker,** Company Pilot, assigned to Anderssen's analysis team

Magdalena, Hesht communications and systems expert, also assigned to Anderssen's analysis team

THE JEHANAN

Bhrigu, *kujen* of Parus, lord of the Seven Rivers

Bhāzuradeha, a poetess, client of the *kujen* Bhrigu

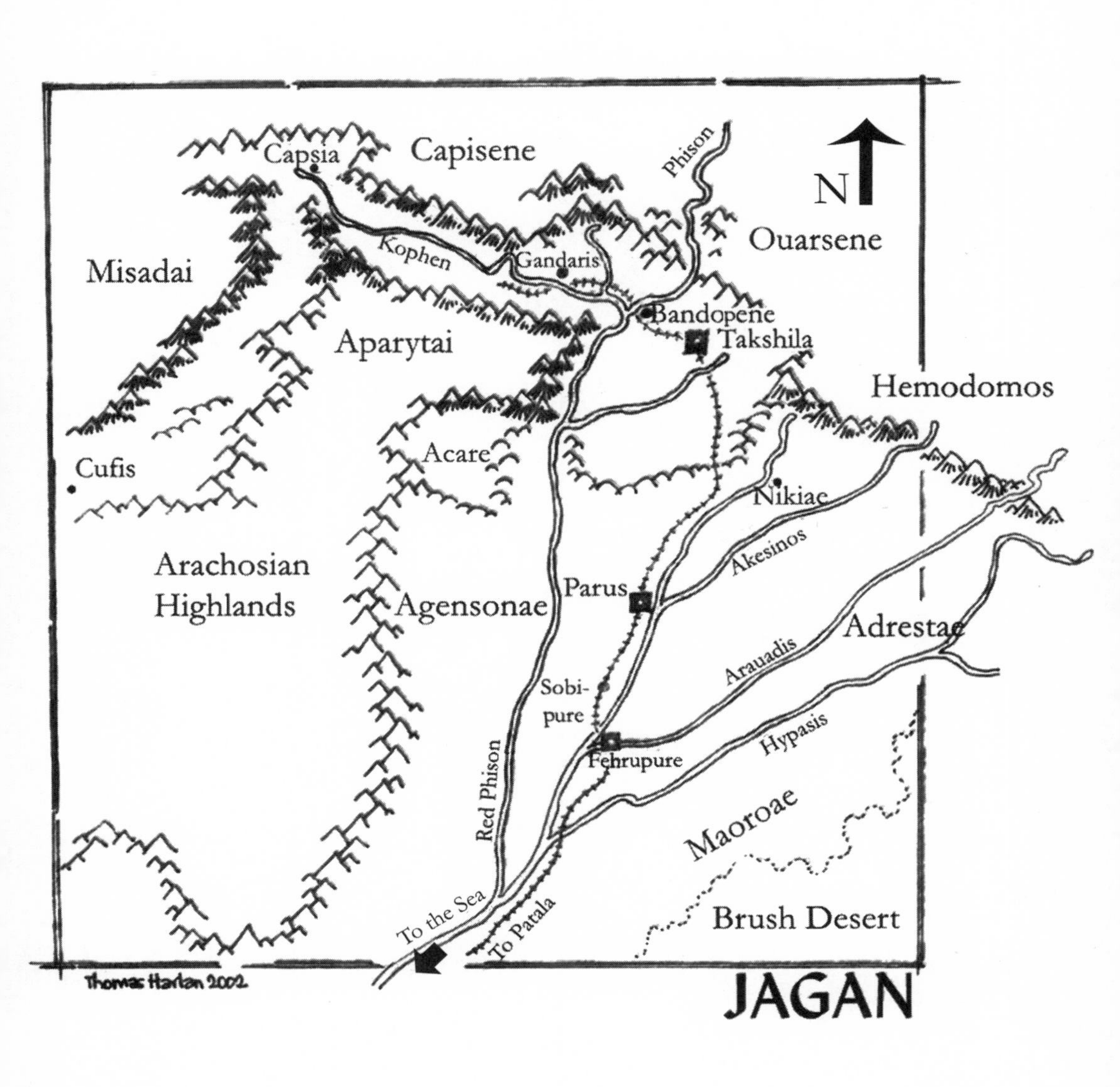
Capsia
Capisene
Phison
N
Ouarsene
Misadai
Kophen
Gandaris
Bandopene
Takshila
Aparytai
Hemodomos
Acare
Cufis
Nikiae
Akesinos
Arachosian
Highlands
Parus
Agensonae
Adrestae
Arauadis
Sobi-
pure
Hypasis
Fehrupure
Red Phison
Maoroae
To the Sea
To Patala
Brush Desert
Thomas Harlan 2002
JAGAN

AN IMPERIAL LIGHT CRUISER
THE HITTITE SECTOR, BEYOND THE EDGE OF IMPERIAL SPACE

Chu-sa Mitsuharu Hadeishi, captain of the *Henry R. Cornuelle*, was sitting in the ruins of the senior officers' wardroom when his personal comm chimed. The thin little Nisei gentleman set down his cup of tea on a utility table covered with departmental readiness reports and tapped his comm-band live.

"This is Hadeishi."

"Bridge, *kyo*. We've picked up a Fleet message drone on long-range scan." The ensign standing third-watch communications didn't bother to hide his anticipation. The *Cornuelle* had been out in the wasteland of stars beyond the frontier for nearly nine months. The tachyon relay on the Imperial Méxica Navy *Astronomer*-class light cruiser wasn't quite good enough to punch through to the big receivers at Ctesiphon Station or Tadmor. Unrepaired battle damage to the ship's systems had further degraded their ability to correspond in realtime with Fleet. The prospect of fresh news from home would be very welcome to everyone aboard. *Though we're not suffering cabin fever, not yet.*

Hadeishi felt the crew had fallen into a good routine over the last six to seven weeks. Everyone was still sharp—no one was making silly mistakes or starting fights—and there was a certain confidence in the crisp way they'd dealt with the last two 'incidents.' The Megair weren't used to Imperial patrols ranging so far out from the frontier.

"Is the drone intact?" Hadeishi reached to key up the main comm panel in the mess, but found an empty cavity in the wall instead. A Khaid penetrator had burrowed into his ship far enough to incinerate everything in the officers' dining room and surrounding passageways. Some amenities had been restored by looting the port-side Marine ready-room, but there weren't any spare comm panels to go around, not this far from a Fleet depot.

"Hai, *kyo*. We're still negotiating security protocols, but we'll have a download soon."

"Route anything flagged 'Fleet' or 'Priority' directly to my office panel," Hadeishi said, then drained his cup. The waxy black substance in the bottom would not count as 'tea' in the poorest inn on Anáhuac, but out here beyond the frontier? *A mild stimulant in solution*, the *Chu-sa* thought in amusement, *and drinkable hot. Must be tea!*

Bridge-comm signed off and Hadeishi walked carefully along a pathway of fire-proof blankets laid down on jagged metal. The thought of mail cheered him—not necessarily for the contents, as Fleet would be sure to deluge him with demands for reports and reams of fresh regulations, but for the prospect of some news from the inner worlds. Mess conversation below decks would improve, he thought. *Fresh zenball and tlachco scores and standings—very important—the men will have something new to wager on.* Down in enlisted territory, thousands of quills of back-pay were riding on games played months ago. Only Fleet security codes and operational doctrine were more heavily encrypted on outgoing message drones than sports scores. Fleet orders weren't configured to release directly to the public infostream, either.

Hadeishi thumbed into his quarters and could not help but smile broadly to see his personal comm panel filled with a fat list of 'new message received' glyphs, already sorted and coded for his attention.

The *Chu-sa*'s thin face twisted into a frown. Eyes narrowed in thought, he ran a hand pensively over a sharp black beard. In the harsh light of a temporary fixture hanging from the damaged roof his angular features seemed cast from bronze. A fat section of the messages on his pane reiterated a common theme—one which made his stomach churn. *This is good news*, he told himself, trying to control his initial despair. *Good news. Time to break out the last of the sake and have Yejin try and cook a real meal. Time to reminisce about the things we've done and seen. Time to turn my ship towards home.*

> Imperial Fleet Office of Personnel, Nineteenth Fleet, Toroson System: Be advised that Thai-i Hayes, Patrick; weapons officer, IMN *Cornuelle*; has

been promoted to Sho-sa in recognition of time in service and exemplary duty to the Empire. Sho-sa Hayes is directed to report at first opportunity to Toroson Fleet Base for reassignment to the heavy cruiser Taiko. . . .

"Such *good* news! Gods of mountain and stream . . ." Hadeishi's nostrils flared. ". . . they're gutting my staff to the bone! Hayes, Smith, Isoroku . . . how will Susan and I—"

His thumb tapped the 'down' glyph for the next message and everything seemed to freeze. Two more personnel orders were in queue, each accompanied by a noted marked 'Personal' from *Thai-sho* Hotategai at Nineteenth Fleet HQ. Hadeishi's hand moved away from the panel controls. The churning feeling in his stomach was gone, replaced by a cold, leaden sensation. One of the personnel reports was signed for him, and one for . . .

His thumb moved violently and the message queue flashed red. A confirmation pane opened and he pressed his hand against the plate. A verbal counter-sign followed and Hadeishi, speaking quickly, in short, clearly enunciated phrases, confirmed dumping the whole slate of messages.

Then he sat back, beads of sweat on his forehead, eyes closed.

In the silence, in the darkness, Hadeishi could hear the ship all around him. Humming along, as it had for six faithful years. The faint gurgling sound of the recycler pipes running under the floor plates, the muted hum of the comm panels. A distant thunder—more felt than heard—of the maneuver drives and the reactors turning over. The sound of a well-tuned ship, lovingly tended by skilled men like Isoroku. Sounds and vibrations he'd lived with so long they'd faded into the seamless background fabric of reality, just as the sound of crickets and car horns had been omnipresent in his youth.

After a long time, Hadeishi opened his eyes and tapped open a system control pane. Horribly weary—just sitting forward exhausted him—he summoned up a set of *dories* in the comm system and set them to scrubbing all evidence of the mail packets from shipside records.

MISMATCHED SECURITY KEY FAILURES, he keyed into the log. DAMAGED A NUMBER OF TRANSMISSIONS FROM FLEET. A RETRANSMIT REQUEST HAS BEEN QUEUED FOR NEXT MESSAGE DRONE INTERCEPT. . . .

Hadeishi tapped the comm pane closed and slumped back in his chair. *I am suddenly so tired.*

DROWNED VENICE, SIX MONTHS LATER . . .
NORTH ITALIAN MILITARY DISTRICT,
ANÁHUAC (OLD EARTH)

The air throbbed with violent sound, the heavy beat of a thousand drums making the floor jump under prince Tezozómoc's feet. The young Méxica noble pushed through a crowd of gaily ornamented men and women. Feathered headdresses brushed against his face, brilliant paints and jewels flashed at his eyes. The sound grew louder, the basso droning of conch trumpets piercing the thunder of the dance-drums. An arched doorway appeared above the masked heads of the revelers, filled with a pulsating red light. The prince whooped, changing course, shoving aside writhing bare arms gleaming with sweat and scented oil. His bodyguards fell behind, trapped by the chattering mob.

Countless voices were singing, a hoarse, bellowing roar:

So it has been said by the Lord of the World,
Huitzilopochtli,
Only a subject,
Only a mortal was.

Tezozómoc's long coat snagged on a woman's emerald-encrusted snake-bodice, and he let the heavy, armor-reinforced leather garment fall away. Heated air flushed against newly bared skin, and the prince felt a rush of relief. He was glad to be out of the chill winter air and into comfortable heat. Strobing lights blazed on his chest and shoulders, making vertical stripes of red and orange paint blaze. Turquoise bracelets shimmered at his wrists. He pressed through the arch, long-fingered hands trailing across the exposed bellies of two girls writhing to the all-encompassing sound.

For an instant, standing at the top of a tall staircase, vaulted roof booming overhead with the roar of the crowd, staring down at the surging mass of painted, feathered, jeweled humanity dancing below, the prince felt alive—transported, wrenched free from his miserable skin, elevated even beyond the humming buzz of the *oliohuiqui* coursing through his blood—and he threw back his head in a long, wailing howl.

The priests were singing:

A magician,
A terror,
A stirrer of strife,
A deceiver,
A maker of war,
An arranger of battles,
A lord of battles.

The sound was lost in the throbbing beat, the countless flutes, braying horns, the shaking roar of rattles and gourds. On the floor of the ancient Catholic cathedral, a line of four hundred dancers began to circulate, horned masks bobbing, powdered feet stamping, stiff arms thrown up in the stylized motions of the ancient barbarians. Tezozómoc grasped the shoulders of two revelers—were they Italians? Beneath their feathered mantle-cloaks and elaborate masks, who could tell?—and leapt up onto the balustrade of the staircase. Marble polished to glass by hundreds of years of use slipped under his bare feet, making the prince stagger and lurch for balance.

A flush of heat surged through him, morning-glory extract mixing with adrenaline, and the vast chamber spun around. The prince laughed queasily, trim brown arms reaching out. Balance returned, helped by a forest of hands reaching up to grasp his legs. Countless gleaming eyes stared up at him in surprise, every face hidden behind fantastical masks.

"I run!" he screeched, swinging his head round. "I run!"

Against the antics of the four hundred dancers, the red-masked priests droned with one voice:

And of him it was said
That he hurled
His flaming serpent,
His fire stick;
Which means war,
Blood and burning;

Throwing his arms wide, Tezozómoc sprang down the marble banister, nimble feet light on ancient, moss-corroded stone. Within a breath he lost control and, unable to stop, plunged headlong into the close-packed crowd. At the same moment, a veritable forest of maroon banners sprang up from the revelers. The drums rattled to a crescendo as the circle of dancers at the middle of the vast floor fell to hands and knees. A brawny man—nearly seven feet tall, dyed blue from head to toe, his shoulders and arms covered with a coat of glued iridescent feathers—sprang up, raising a curling, snapping banner bearing an azure hummingbird. Muscles flexing, he whirled the banner around his head with great speed. As he did, another man—no more than a youth—darted from the crowd, racing counterclockwise around the ring of fallen dancers. Like the prince, he was painted with vertical red and orange stripes.

The blare of horns and conch trumpets faded away, and now only a single massive beat of the drums punctuated the chanting of the priests:

And when his festival was celebrated,
Captives were slain,
Washed slaves were slain,
The merchants washed them.

Tezozómoc crashed into one banner, tearing the cloth from the hands of a startled celebrant, then into another. His cry of pain was lost in a tumult of sound as the banner-men raised a mighty shout, shaking their flags violently. The prince scrabbled at the hard-muscled bodies tangled around him, kicking fruitlessly, narrow chest heaving with effort. He could see nothing but a forest of bare, dyed legs and the strobing flash of arc lights on the distant ceiling. Someone kicked him in the side and his own mask slipped sideways, blinding him.

"Ahh . . . curst peasants! Get off!"

The booming rattle of the drums began to pick up, and the voices of the priests melded into one thundering roar of sound:

And thus he was arrayed:
With headdress of green feathers,
Holding his serpent torch,

Girded with a belt,
Bracelets upon his arms,
Wearing turquoises,
As a master of messengers.

A hand reached down, seizing his wrist, and Tezozómoc felt himself dragged to his feet.

"You're strong . . ." the prince started to exclaim, stripping away his sweat-soaked mask. Then he stopped, surprised.

An oval-faced girl wearing little more than long glossy black hair smiled up at him. Her mouth was moving, but he couldn't hear anything, only the crushing thunder of drums and horns and a thousand hoarse voices shouting their praises of red-and-black–faced Christ the Warrior. Tezozómoc shook his head, grinning, and pulled her close. Her hip rubbed across his thigh, slippery with oil. To his delight, she pressed close, nails scraping his chest and back. He tried to kiss her, but she turned her head, lips pressed to his ear.

"Isn't it bad luck to have two of the same god at the festival?" he heard—a strong, breathy voice with an indefinable accent. Not a Méxica girl, then. Tezozómoc felt a flash of disappointment, immediately lost in a surge of desire as her tongue flicked against his earlobe.

"There's another Painal the Runner here?" he asked, confused, turning to put lips to her ear.

"Of course," she laughed, slim body undulating against his. Oddly, her skin felt almost glassy under the oil. "Doesn't Raising-the-Banners celebrate his race around the Valley to summon the allies of the Méxica to battle? Isn't this *his* festival?"

"Yes . . ." Tezozómoc said, blushing. His face crumpled a little. "It is. I just thought . . ."

"A prince should be able to come in any costume he wants," she breathed, caressing his face with one hand. Oil and paint smeared across his cheekbone. "Do you like girls?"

"What do you think?" The prince replied, chagrin washing away, and thrust himself against her. His heart was beating faster, almost as fast as the hands of the drummers on deer hide. His skin felt hot, hotter than the bitter, smoky air.

"You do!" The girl laughed, drawing away, pulling him with her, hands clasped tight around his wrists. Again, Tezozómoc was surprised by the strength of her grip, but before he could follow the thought a cloud of other girls, all silvered hair and glossy, scale-painted skin, emerged from the surging, dancing crowd.

They swirled, flashing smiles and pert golden breasts, around him. All alike they were, shimmering with scales and sparkling indigo dust in their hair. "Come with us," they cried, weaving and bobbing in a stamping, quick-footed spiral.

Their hands were on him before the prince could react and he giggled, starting to feel alive again, as they swept him away towards the ancient, crumbling edifice of the altar of San Marco. A quartet of bronze horses reared above him, festooned with garlands of flowers and paper lanterns.

Amazingly, the crowd parted in front of them, as though the sea ebbed before his majesty.

"Wait!" The prince stared around in dismay, seeing nothing but a frenetic sea of heads, banners, masks, feather headdresses and upraised arms. "Where did she go?"

The woman with long hair had disappeared.

"You'll see her again," chimed the ring of scaled girls holding him tight. "Soon!"

Mumbling a constant, unintelligible litany of curses, a tall, elderly, lean-faced man shoved his way through the crowd. Despite the rolling waves of heat rising from the mob of dancers, he had not cast aside his heavy leather coat. Immediately behind him, a shorter man with wild dark brown hair and a dyspeptic expression tried to follow.

"D'ye see him?" Master Sergeant Lorne Colmuir spat out the wet, crushed remains of a tabac, his head in constant movement, trying to pick out one depressingly familiar brown visage among all the masks and painted faces bobbing on the dance floor. "Our wee-wee bairn?"

"I can't see *anything*," Sergeant Leslie Dawd answered, bulling his way to his companion's side. He tried to stand on tiptoe and was immediately crushed into the Skawtsman's side. Furious, the Eagle Knight lashed out, knocking down a drunken man with an elephant-face mask. Colmuir lent a hand, dragging the shorter man to his feet.

"Circle roight," Lorne growled, already moving left, leading with an elbow and pressing through the crowd.

" 'Roight.' Learn to speak properly . . ." Dawd grumbled, smoothing back his disordered, sweat-stiff hair. Leading with both hands, he jammed through a line of copper-skinned men, tall prongs of multi-colored feathers dancing against their backs. "Useless, useless waste of a prince . . ."

He stumbled out into a tiny void in the chaos of the crowd, nothing more than the counter-rotating calm generated by a stream coiling around a rock. Sergeant Dawd shook out his shoulders, letting the gun-rig under his coat settle, bracing to plunge into the mob again.

A girl—no, a woman—popped out of the wave of caroling dancers in front of him. He caught sight of piercing blue eyes between strands of heavy black hair and got an impression of a lithe, muscular body before she was in his arms.

"Hello." Her voice was husky and hot, hotter than the steaming air filling the ancient cathedral. Her hand was around his neck, slippery on his skin and cold—something hard pressed against his spine—Dawd tried to jerk away, left arm slashing up to break contact.

Bzzzt! His entire body convulsed in a bone-wrenching spasm. The woman grinned, flashing a brilliant smile, and was gone into the crowd. The sergeant staggered, body jerking with successive electric shocks. Despite overwhelming, teeth-grinding pain, his hands scrabbled to tear the jitterbug away from his neck.

The thudding beat changed as the Runner completed his last circuit of the hall, and the Four Hundred dancers began to shout their war cries in counterpoint to the roar of the Méxica drummers. Flames cavorted above the crowd, hurled up by men in wolf-cloaks, spinning wheels of sparks flashing against the dark roof.

The crowd surged again, the tiny space collapsed, and Dawd went down, wracked by electrical shocks and trampled by dozens of unwary revelers.

Colmuir sprang up onto the dais holding the drummers, left hand over his ear to keep the near-physical blast of the amplifiers rising in a black tower from crushing his eardrum. Ignoring the startled looks of the naked, sweating musicians he weaved quickly through them, eyes on the crowd below, looking for a too-familiar youth . . . *there!*

A clutch of girls in little more than silver and gold paint were disappearing through a low arch, a stumbling Painal-the-Runner among them. The Skawtsman cursed, vaulted a row of flute players and plunged into the crowd beyond.

Two enormous brutes—faces unexpectedly bare, masses of iron rings glittering on clenched fists—grabbed at him. Twisting sideways, Colmuir dove between them, hands plunging beneath his coat and vest. The bouncers collided, bounced back shouting in rage and were gone behind a wall of spinning penitents in long white mantles. The Skawt bounded through the archway, hands filled with a pair of Nambu 'double-rack' automatics. A fresh contingent of celebrants—winter coats still draped over their costumes, snow dusting their hair—scattered away as he charged up the staircase.

At the top of the stairs, the Eagle Knight skidded to a halt, taking a measured glance down the corridors branching away on either side. The flash of silver heels caught his eye and he was taking the next flight of steps three at a time. Laughter rang in openness and he was suddenly surrounded by pale watery light.

The half-dome of a boat bay rose before him, all green plexi and damp iron ribs. Beyond the man-high windows shining lights moved in the depths—submersibles and party barges cruising among the drowned towers and palaces of old Venice—searchlights briefly illuminating the empty windows and doorways of the dead city. Colmuir darted forward, thumbing off the safeties on both automatics. A sleek black Stiletto minisub was floating in the right-hand boat pool. One of the silver girls had keyed the hatch and was throwing back the glassite dome.

"Halt, in the name of the Empire!" The automatics bucked and a sharp *crack-crack-crack* bounced back from the plexi dome as the master sergeant opened fire. Tracers slashed through the prince-nappers and one of the girls staggered, crimson splashed across her golden breasts.

The enemy broke ranks, and Colmuir threw himself to one side, crashing to the floor behind a valet station. The brief glimpse of their deft, coordinated movements filled him with a sharp burst of fear. Despite his sudden appearance, they'd separated left and right without the slightest hesitation.

The hammering roar of a submachine gun raked the valet station, tearing gaping holes in the light wood. Lorne flattened, trying to scramble away. Twisting on the floor, he dropped behind the lip of the left-hand boat pool, one leg splashing into chill seawater.

Something metallic tumbled overhead and splashed into the dark water.

"Curst!" Colmuir vaulted back the other way, both automatics blazing in a wild figure eight.

Whooomp! The grenade went off, blasting water in all directions. Drenched, the Eagle Knight scuttled back towards the entranceway. The dead girl sprawled on the dockside. The Stiletto was still rocking at anchor, a string of bullet holes spiderwebbing the cabin canopy.

A low groaning sound permeated the air. His wild spray of fire had cracked the heavy glassite panels holding back the chill waters of the Adriatic.

Without a pause, Colmuir darted towards the far exit tunnel, thumbing the magazine ejectors on his pistols. Strips of smoking plastic bounced away on the metal decking. He reached the corner, flattened himself against the wall, and jammed fresh ammo coils into each weapon.

There was a grinding noise as glassite and metal twisted around the hairline cracks in the clear panels.

Grimacing, Colmuir punched a locking code into the boat-bay panel on the wall, then ducked around the corner, pistols raised. The deck under his feet shuddered as the lock door began to descend, squealing on long-unused tracks.

The tunnel was empty, but against the thudding backbeat of the now-distant liturgy he could hear the clatter of running feet. Crouched, guns low, Lorne sprinted up the corridor. A steadily brightening light swelled ahead—another boat bay? A lift core?

Almost too late he heard a rush of air behind him and the mosquito whine of an aeropack. The Skawt threw himself down, trying to roll round and bring his guns to bear. Something smashed into his left hand, wrenching the Nambu out of his grasp. The gun ricocheted from the wall of the tunnel with a clang. The other automatic blazed, lighting the corridor with a flare of venting propellant. Tracers stitched across the roof, then rebounded crazily. In the brief illumination, Lorne caught a glimpse of a sleek, seemingly naked woman zipping past.

He rolled up onto his knees, steadying the automatic with both hands for a chase shot, but the flying woman hadn't fled. His chin slammed back, caught by a spinning heel-kick, and he sprawled backwards, skidding across the wet, rusty floor. Gasping, face spattered with blood, Colmuir groped for the automatic.

The woman crossed her arms, grasped something with a metallic clicking sound, and lunged. Lorne blocked sharply, bared hands blurring into an X against her expected punch. A coiled-metal rod lashed against his forearm and the Eagle Knight choked out a gasp as a massive electrical shock flared across his leather-clad arms.

"*Uuuuh!*" He braced, letting the insulated layer in the armored coat bleed away the current.

In a blur, the shockrod slashed at his head, but by then Colmuir had recovered from the kick. He countered vigorously, smashing aside the blow, off hand clenching to seize a twenty-centimeter combat knife slapped into his palm by the spring-loader strapped to his arm.

He slashed up, trying to catch the underside of her chin with the point, but she was fast—very fast—and sprang back. The aeropack whined again and she was gone, zipping off down the tunnel. "*Dosvidanya*," she laughed, the sound rolling hollow in the metal corridor.

The master sergeant charged off in pursuit, leading with the knife, right hand scrambling to draw a gun from the small of his back. Behind him, the pressure door made a squeaking sound as the boat bay collapsed, sending hundreds of tons of water smashing against the metal.

Tezozómoc was still giddy, skin burning, member painfully stiff in his loincloth, when the silver-painted girls dragged him onto a lift-core platform. The drug paste smeared across his chest and face pierced him like needles. He collapsed to his knees, heaving violently, both arms bound tight behind him. A stomach filled with *oliohuiqui* and too much *octli*-beer did not mix with the tranquilizers and readysetgo seeping into his bloodstream.

The girls holding him cursed—a guttural, barbarous language—and he felt a sharp blow to the side of his head.

"You dare . . . I'm a member of the Imperial . . . *urk!*" An elbow jammed into his stomach, making him heave again, and four sets of slim golden hands grasped him by arms and legs and pitched him unceremoniously into the basket of a balloon tethered to the lift platform. The prince's head struck the wicker wall on the far side, leaving him stunned. He tried to sit up, but a petite foot, as bare as any of the silver girls seemed to be, came down on his neck, driving his head into the basket floor. Cool plastic chilled against his flesh.

"Get rid of them," someone said, and Tezozómoc realized there were two slumped figures also in the basket with him. The foot lifted from his neck and the whole gondola shivered as the girl above him leapt lightly onto the platform. "We can't spare the weight . . ."

Gunshots rang out. The prince felt the gondola shake and he twitched violently, thinking the balloon had been hit. A furious hiss answered his movement and he lay still, fearing another blow to the head or stomach.

"Ware!" Someone shouted. The entire gondola shook again and Tezozómoc felt his stomach drop away. A sustained ripping sound roared not too far away and something hot smashed through the base of the basket, stinging the prince's face.

Eyes screwed tight shut, Tezozómoc curled into a ball, knees against his forehead.

A *whoomp!* sound—right on top of him—startled the prince into a fit of crying and harsh metallic smoke stung his nostrils. Distantly, there was a violent crashing sound followed by screams.

"Mi'lord?" Someone touched his shoulder. Tezozómoc opened his eyes. The fuzzy image of his shorter bodyguard—what *was* his name?—slowly came into view, ringed by a shimmering halo of white light. "Are you able to speak?"

"Do . . ." The prince struggled with swollen lips. His throat was terribly dry and tasted awful. He peered desperately at the man. "Do you have anything to drink? Champagne? Beer? Even water will do!"

Running flat out, his entire attention focused solely on the speeding back of the Russian woman, Colmuir burst out onto the lift platform too late to realize that there was no railing, no gondola and only a yawning shaft twenty meters wide before him.

"Ayyyy!" He tried to slide to a stop, but a messy pool of water and rust betrayed the noskid on his boots. The Eagle Knight realized—in an instant of unremitting clarity—there was no possible way to stop and flung himself forward, combat knife discarded, fingers grasping for the woman's feet as she soared heavenward.

By nothing less than a miracle his right hand seized hold of her ankle, slipping a little on her strangely stiff skin, before they both plunged into the shaft. The aeropack whined in protest, trying to counter the unexpected weight. Another lighted lift platform flashed past and Lorne's coat billowed up in the rushing wind.

The woman twisted, kicking at his head as they fell, and the Eagle Knight wrenched his shoulder trying to get his other hand around her ankle.

"*Chudak!*" Eyes flashing in the lights blurring past, hair now unbound in a flying cloud around her head, she sharply clenched her left fist twice. The skinsuit gelled to her lithe frame flared with a ripple of violet lightning and Colmuir screamed, nerves savaged, and his grip flew loose.

The aeropack squealed and the woman flashed away and up into the darkness overhead. The master sergeant plunged, tumbling wildly, nearly unconscious from shock. He tried to scream, but his throat had contorted—like every other muscle in his body—into an agonizing cramp.

"Status!" Van Belane hissed into the comm thread pasted beside her plush lips. "Where is the prince?"

"Gone," came the furious answer. "We had him in the backup vehicle, but the other Eagle cut the mooring ropes and they escaped."

"My father's beard . . . Like a cockroach, that one!" The Russian craned her neck upwards and thumbed the aeropack on full boost. Far above she could make out the half-moon shape of a lift rising up the shaft. Strings of colored lights lining the ancient atmosphere vent cast a rippling gleam on the balloon. "I see them—scatter to the tertiary rendezvous. I will take care of this business myself."

Arching her back, Van Belane reached behind her, slim fingers searching through the combat pack clinging to her spine under a huge mane of black hair. Fingertips found the casing for a Norsk-make *Mistletoe* HL-SAM and slid the rocket from its holder. Strands of hair tangled, and—cursing again—she ripped the wig away.

She closed in swiftly with the balloon as the gondola bumped past another platform. Van Belane swung wide, trying to see past the lift, and realized she'd run out of time. The mouth of the shaft was only a hundred meters away, shining darkness speckled with stars and thin clouds gleaming with the lights of the city ringing the wide bowl of the Lagoon.

Sighing, feeling a melancholy tide rising in her heart, the Russian woman pointed the rocket, waited for the aiming tone, thumbed the activation switch, and cast the rod-shaped weapon free. The aeropack whined again, forced into a tight maneuver and she curled up her legs, zipping into the mouth of a side airway. Behind her, the missile spiraled away in free-fall, then the engine ignited with a flash, the tracking mechanism locked onto the gondola and the rocket blazed up the shaft.

A concussive *whoomp!* followed and a wave of superheated air rushed past. In the mouth of the airway, hands braced against the sides, Van Belane turned her head as flaming debris plunged past. Two bodies wrapped in flame careened by and then the burning balloon itself wallowed into the depths.

Popping a stick of cinnamon-flavored chicle into her mouth, Van Belane turned and loped off down the airway, letting her skinsuit turn opaque and flicking nightsight lenses down over sullen, ice-blue eyes. "Damned Shtlantskee carrion . . . lapdogs of the Empire . . ."

Smoke billowed in the shaft, but the constant pressure of air from below began to clear away the fumes. In the airway shaft opposite where the Russian commando had disappeared, Sergeant Dawd raised his head from the floor of the tube, gray-green eyes filled with a grim light. He waited another hundred heartbeats, saw that the last of the smoke was gone and no slinky, black-haired shape had reappeared in the other tunnel, and lifted himself to his knees.

"Safe, mi'lord. For the moment at least."

Tezozómoc sighed and the Skawt helped him sit up. A twist of the wrist released a combat knife to cut the tiemeups holding the prince's arms behind his back.

"I'm terribly sorry," the prince said in an unconvincingly contrite voice, "but . . . what is your name again?"

"Dawd, mi'lord." The Skawtsman avoided meeting his master's eyes, concentrating on sawing through the plastic composite. The serrated back edge of the knife made it tricky work. "Eagle Knight in your service, ex-Fleet Marine Sergeant."

"A *Tequihuah* . . . Well done, master Dawd." Tezozómoc drew out the words, trying to affect a fashionable languor. The prince tried to focus on the Eagle Knight—to fix an image of the short, dark-haired Skawtsman in his mind—and was struck by an impression of the man looking more a scholar than a soldier. Even near-shaven, Dawd's black hair was unkempt and wild, and his smooth round face suggested a puckish humor.

"Now wait a moment. . . . Aren't there supposed to be *two* of you accompanying me at all times?"

"Yes, mi'lord." Dawd's tone became rather more clipped than before, though he was a man who prided himself on a clear, cultured voice. The sergeant could feel the youth—*more than a boy*, he thought rather morosely, *and less than a man*—trembling under his hands. "Master Sergeant Colmuir is also in your service."

"And where is *he*?" If anything, the prince sounded aggrieved.

"I believe, mi'lord"—the sergeant's jaw clenched—"that *Cuauhhuehueh* Colmuir has . . . has plunged to his death while attempting to apprehend the terrorists who attempted to kidnap you."

"Kidnap?" Tezozómoc drew back a little in surprise. "The *ahuienime*—those joygirls . . . they were terrorists?"

"Yes," Dawd managed to get out. "They were. Mi'lord. A Danish or Russian kommando, I would venture. Very . . . dangerous."

"Kidnapped. I was kidnapped." The prince's face slowly lit with delight, perfectly even teeth white in the darkness of the tunnel. "By the Holy Ever-Virgin Mother of God, I was *kidnapped!*"

Sergeant Dawd did not react, though he could feel the ulcers in his long-suffering stomach begin to pucker with acid.

"This . . ." Tezozómoc clapped a friendly hand on the Skawt's shoulder. "Is the best news I've had . . . oh, in ages! Wait until my father hears this!" The prince suddenly paused, staring at Leslie's stony expression. "Master Dawd? Why such a long face? This is *good news!* Someone—dire enemies of the Empire—perhaps even the infernal *Danes!* For the love of Christ, they thought I was worth doing away with!"

Sergeant Dawd turned, frowning, raising a hand for silence. Lights were beginning to flicker on the roof of the tunnel and a booming, chattering noise filled the air. He could hear people laughing, their voices raised in drunken, inharmonious song.

"Lie flat, mi'lord," the Skawtsman whispered, struggling to keep from just jamming the boy's head down onto the corrugated metal. He checked to make sure the magazine was full, then thumbed back the safety on the Nambu 10mm. "We're not safe yet."

The vast, round shape of a party barge drifted past. The balloon was festooned with glittering lights, including a broad glowing videopatch showing drunken rabbits dancing under a smiling moon. "Drink Mayahuel beer," boomed a recorded voice, "and be more fertile!"

The gondola swayed into view, crammed with masked people laughing and singing, then rose majestically past. Dawd lowered the automatic slowly.

A black figure swung into the opening of the tube, boots clanking on metal.

Tezozómoc leapt up, shouting in fear, and cracked his head against the curving roof. Groaning in pain, the prince collapsed, clutching his scalp, fingers bloody. Dawd breathed out a long sigh of relief and flipped the automatic back into the holster on his gun-rig.

"Not dead, I see," he said, nodding to Master Sergeant Colmuir.

"Nawt yet," grinned the Aberdeen-man, keeping his head low. "But close, very close . . . what about him?"

Dawd turned, staring in disgust at Tezozómoc, who was curled up and whimpering. "Take him home, I suppose. Clean him up. Nothing else to do now."

As an aside, he leaned close to Colmuir. "Master Sergeant, why did we ally ourselves with these . . . savages?"

"Oh, lad," Colmuir nodded sagely, "it was them or the Anglish. And compared to the Anglish . . . well, we've still the better of the deal wit' these heathens."

The lean-faced master sergeant grinned at Dawd's sour expression and snaked a tabac from his pocket. The older man looked a little battered—craggy brow and seamed face spattered with blood and bruises—in the flare of the self-lighting cigarette. "Don't make such a face, lad. It's a man's work, isn't it? Better than wasting time in University!"

"I suppose," Dawd checked his weapons and tools by touch. "The pay is better."

Colmuir chuckled, taking a long drag. His long-limbed frame was bent almost double to keep a graying head from knocking against the roof of the tunnel. "Most don't think so, but you've seen both sides of the fence, haven't you? D'you miss the hallowed halls of aca'deme?"

Dawd grunted. "I suppose . . . but grading lower-form essays on early Méxica poets lacks something of the spice of our activities here."

The master sergeant ground out his tabac. "Let's get him out of here, then."

TADMOR STATION
THE EDGE OF IMPERIAL MÉXICA SPACE

The murmur of four thousand impatient travelers filled the transit hall, making it difficult for Gretchen Anderssen, field xenoarchaeologist for the Honorable Chartered Company, to hear the politely soft voice of the Albanian Spaceways ticket agent in front of her.

"I am sorry, Anderssen-*tzin*, but your tickets have been changed."

"Changed?" Gretchen scowled uneasily at the little Nisei woman, tucking tangled blonde hair back behind her ear. "By whom?"

"By the issuing authority. There is a note and a new travel packet." The ticket agent tapped her pad and a metal plate slid aside on the countertop, revealing a comm panel. Anderssen pressed her thumb onto the receptor pane and crossed muscular arms, steeling herself for bad news. Though nearly a century had passed since the Empire's conquest of Earth had driven her parents into exile on the Skawtish colony-world of New Aberdeen, the middle-aged Swedish woman didn't expect *any* superior—either in business, or in a social setting—to treat her as anything but a tool to be moved from place to place as the needs of the community bid.

We lost the War, her grandmother's voice echoed in Gretchen's memories, *and we have to make do with just surviving. It used to be worse . . .*

A Company memo header appeared, accompanied by a terse message and her field supervisor's chop.

Go to Jagan. Apply for a survey permit at the Legation. There is a device which must be examined.

"This is the entire note? The only message?" Gretchen wiped the pane clear with a flick of her hand. "Have all our tickets been changed? All three of us?"

The ticket agent nodded politely, providing Anderssen with a set of travel chits. "David Parker—Imperial citizen, Magdalena—Hesht female on a wayfarer visa. They are your traveling companions, yes? Here are their new tickets. You have been re-routed to the Imperial Protectorate of Bharat, planet Jagan. Stay is open ended, with a return voyage to New Aberdeen as originally scheduled."

"What?" Parker, the Company team pilot, was standing in line behind Anderssen and now he plucked a half-burned tabac from his mouth to stare at her in horror. "Where the hell is Bharat? What happened to our vacation time?"

Gretchen turned the chit over in her hands. The dull roar of fellow travelers arguing, crying, pleading lapped around her. "A drop-in," she mused aloud, feeling intensely irritated. "I haven't gotten a drop-in for . . . well, ever, actually." She looked up to find the others staring at her. "What this means is someone reported something unusual on this planet. Probably some farmer turned over his field, broke a plow wheel and thought he found a First Sun library. The Company heard about it and—"

"We shouldn't go." Parker made a disgusted face, rubbing a flat hand across his balding pate. The pilot was thinner than Gretchen, a wiry, stoop-shouldered Anglishman with twitchy reflexes and a mellow, almost indolent approach to every task. "Never give up vacation time. Can we refuse?"

Magdalena showed her incisors, a dull yellow-white gleam against ebon lips. In truth, the Hesht wasn't more than a few centimeters taller than Parker, but the thick muscle corded over her sleek feloid frame and her plushy, glistening fur made him seem frail and weak in comparison. "More work? The *yrrrchowl-ssshama* is playing with us."

Gretchen hastily covered the exposed fangs with raised fingers, glaring at the Hesht. Maggie's eyes narrowed and then she closed her mouth with a petulant flick of her ears. The Hesht were still not common in human society, though their interstellar migration had been creeping across the Empire for nearly twenty years. Magdalena was very well acculturated, as least in comparison to other knockabout youngsters exiled from the enormous sub-light Arks carrying the bulk of her people on their endless voyage. But most citizens quailed at the sight of *so many* needlelike teeth exposed at once.

"Next, please." The ticket agent waved them away, beckoning for the line to advance.

"Do we get duress pay at least?" Parker relit his tabac as they moved aside. "A bonus? Working-on-vacation time?"

Magdalena's long ears pricked up. "Fresh-killed meat, still hot, dripping with juice?"

Anderssen studied the fine print on the work authorization. "Yes . . . works out to triple-time, plus the usual bonuses if there's really something to find." She bit her lip, thinking. "A fair bit of change." *New clothing for all the kids, new turbine core for mom's lifter, maybe even a new field comp for me . . .* "Paying by the day, too, not the usual flat rate."

"Really?" Parker brightened. "Including transit time? Can I see that?"

Gretchen handed over the chit, feeling disoriented, and raised her head to search the massive v-pane filling one entire wall of the cavernous hall. Thousands of ships passed through Tadmor every week. One of them would carry her team to Bharat. *Hope it's a real liner,* she grumbled to herself, *not a tramp with berths over the reactor.*

Then she thought about how long it would be until she saw her children and her mother, walked in the realspruce forest behind the steading breathing cool, fresh air, and had to fight down tears. *Fucking Company. I am so tired of this.* She rubbed her eyes.

"Hey," Parker said, watching her face with alarm. "Hey now boss, it's just a couple weeks. Look—they're estimating a week to Bharat, two weeks there and then another week back to New Aberdeen. You can route through Toroson instead of Coromandel Station and it'll be faster. With triple-time, it's like working three months in one! You could spend nine weeks on vacation instead of three and still be ahead, quill for quill."

"Rrrr . . ." Magdalena's ears flicked back, showing what she thought of that. The Hesht never mentioned her own pack, or expressed the slightest interest in returning to the Ark of her birth, but she considered Anderssen her 'hunt-sister,' and Gretchen's cubs, therefore, were *her* cubs as well. Her opinion of Parker varied, but most of the time she treated him like a younger brother, which meant cuffing him, claws retracted, at least once a day. "Another month until she sees her cubs? How many feathers is that worth?"

"They're called *quills*," Parker replied, handing the Hesht the chit. "Not *feathers*, fur-brain."

Magdalena bared her incisors at the human male. "You need feathers to make a quill, stinky."

"I *have* to go," Gretchen said, interrupting them before her two companions really started to bicker. "But you don't. I could log a call saying you'd already boarded your own ships . . ."

Magdalena sniffed, ears back, and held up the travel chit. "Where hunt-sister goes, I go. Not for feathers"—her plushy black nose wrinkled up—"but to make sure you see your cubs and den again." The Hesht caught sight of Parker's grimace. "No one knows this world—any untasted meat is dangerous!"

"But . . . but . . ." Parker glared at both of them. "My mum is expecting me for dinner in two weeks! What am I going to tell her?"

"Buy her some nice fresh meat," Magdalena sniffed, "with all those extra quills you'll earn."

JAGAN
FOURTH PLANET OF THE BHARAT SYSTEM

A brisk chime disturbed the meditations of a tiny old woman sitting cross-legged on a rumpled, unmade bed. The room was dark, lit solely by the glow from dozens of v-pane screens. Bundles of cable snaked everywhere, disappearing through holes cut into the floorboards. She was breathing steadily, first through one nostril, then through the other.

The chiming became insistent—drowning out the muted sound of pedicab horns and passing trolleys—and beetle-black eyes flickered open.

The old woman turned her attention to the flashing glyph on the panel, a wizened thumb mashing the winking shape of a running man. A v-pane unfolded, revealing the shaved head of a Flower War Priest, forehead marked by broad stripes of soot and ash.

"My lady Itzpalicue." The man inclined his head nervously. In the near-perfect fidelity of the display, she could see sweat beading beneath the paint anointing his brow. "There is news of Battle group Eighty-Eight *Tecaltan*. They are inbound now from the forward Fleet base at Toroson."

"When will they arrive?" Her voice was creaky and dry, dead branches rubbing against stone, but the sharp expression on her face betrayed a keen intelligence. Her high, classically Méxica cheekbones were marked with lines of red-stained pinprick scars. "Who commands the Flingers-of-Stone?"

"Villeneuve, my lady." The Flower Priest's expression changed subtly, shading from barely hidden fear to nearly-open delight. Itzpalicue suppressed a surge of irritation with the openness of the man's thought processes. An agent of the Empire, she thought, should show some self-control. "We have already forwarded the officer rosters and ship manifests to your network."

"So . . . Duke Alexis has his frontier command at last." The old woman's wrinkled lips twitched up slightly, black eyes glittering with delight. "I am pleased the Admiralty saw fit to grant your request. I am sure *he* is delighted as well."

"How could the Frenchman fail to be pleased?" The Flower Priest made an expansive gesture, mostly lost in the narrow focus of the v-pane pickup. "Four *Mitla*-class fast dreadnaughts, a dozen *Kasei*-class heavy cruisers and a veritable armada of smaller ships. Two Marine regiments, thousands of support personnel . . . everything an ambitious junior admiral could want."

"Everything he needs to fight a minor war on some forgotten planet on the edge of the Empire. A pity his reputation will be stained by the inevitable result . . ." Itzpalicue turned a portion of her attention to the officer rosters flipping past in her secondary data-feed. The documents opened, paged and closed with blurring speed. An unexpected sense of relief glowed for a moment as she digested the information. "Have your analysts examined the commanders' list for the battle group?"

"Yes, my lady. They are entirely acceptable for our purposes. Almost all are barbarians . . . or at least not citizens born of the Four Hundred Houses. No one *important* is liable to be killed or injured."

"Well, your enterprise should go well, then." Itzpalicue inclined her head. "Did you expect the presence of the prince Tezozómoc?"

"Yes!" The priest's face swelled fat with self-congratulation. "A lucky stroke! The Light of Heaven recently spoke with our master about his youngest son's poor reputation. Of course we were happy to oblige his desires . . . as they run alongside our own. The boy will be thrust into the forge fire . . ."

Itzpalicue snorted delicately, a dry whispery sound. "Forge fire? In this flowery war you're arranging? More like the flame of a candle, I think."

"Not so!" The priest had forgotten his earlier trepidation and now soot-blackened eyebrows converged over a sharp nose. "The *Xochiyaoyotl* is not play-acting, my lady! The divine fluid will be spilled in full measure, pleasing both the Holy Mother and her Son. The boy may die gloriously, as befits a Méxica prince on the field of battle, or he may triumph as Imperial arms will surely prove victorious over the barbarians. Either outcome will suit our purpose—and please the Light of Heaven!—well enough. Prince Tezozómoc's reputation *will* be given new luster, whether he lives or dies, you may be assured of that."

I would not call the Jehanan 'barbarians,' the old woman mused, *as their civilization predates even the simians of Anáhuac who gave birth to our noble race . . . and the thrice-blest Light of Heaven.* She considered the Fleet rosters on the secondary displays. "Have you chosen the ship to sacrifice as Elder Warrior?"

"No . . ." The Flower Priest sniffed, annoyed at having his contemplation of the Emperor's incipient favor disturbed. "My acolytes are reviewing the Fleet records now." He paused, peering at her with a tinge of apprehension. "Do . . . do you have a recommendation?"

Itzpalicue made a show of pausing to consider, though she had already grasped sufficient detail from the data-stream to know that while there were commanders on the list who could play the traditional role, none of them were *just right.* Then she said: "The Mirror bows to the experience of the *xochiyaotinime* in this matter." She favored him with a tight, wintry smile. "Should circumstances change, however, do not fear but I will render any advice deemed necessary."

"Of course." The Flower Priest managed to nod genially.

The old woman could see fear pricking in his face, making the priest twitchy and nervous. Most Imperial citizens had a remarkably similar reaction when confronted with an agent of the Mirror Which Reveals The Truth. Itzpalicue, who had served the Imperial security ministry for her entire adult life, would have been affronted if she had not been regarded with trepidation and near-horror. And not without cause, for the Mirror wielded enormous power within the Empire, answering only to the Emperor himself, and keeping many secrets.

One lowly Flower Priest could easily disappear, particularly with *Xochiyaoyotl* in the offing.

Flower War exercises were not usually the domain of the Mirror—Itzpalicue's presence on Jagan had already thrown the priests' usual planning into confusion—and awareness of the Mirror's interest in this particular War of Flowers was causing more lost sleep for their analysts than the presence of one junior, ill-regarded and expendable Imperial Prince.

The Flower Priests operated on the fringe of Imperial space, allowing themselves a generous margin of anonymity and distance in case of some unforeseen disaster. While they took some care in picking a suitable 'honorable enemy,' past events indicated that even the most placid-seeming world could unleash untold devastation on the Imperial combat forces sent in harm's way. Not every alien civilization was pleased to have the Méxica engage them in unexpected warfare, just for the purpose of blooding freshly raised regiments and newly promoted Fleet commanders. *Still,* Itzpalicue thought, with a rather amused air, *the* xochiyaotinime *and their games do serve a purpose, both for the people and the military, and for the Emperor. Even, sometimes, for the Smoking Mirror.*

The modern implementation of the Flower War was a far cry from the ritualized combats waged by the ancient Méxica against their neighbors in the Heart of the World. Long gone the glorious mantles, feathered cloaks and elaborate headdresses for the favored combatants. No more the cleared fields of honor scattered along the frontiers of the early Empire. No year of pampered luxury leading to the altar of divine sacrifice awaited those honorably overcome in combat. Only simple death, spilling precious fluid on some forgotten world.

Itzpalicue sighed aloud, wondering if the reality of those lost times was as clean and elegant as the official histories related. *Not likely! Blood and shit smell much the same, regardless of the age.*

Jagan *was* a remote world, but introducing the Light of Heaven's personal interest, even if through the disreputable person of Tezozómoc, raised the stakes enough to make everyone sweat. And with a high-ranking Mirror agent in residence . . . well, Itzpalicue knew for a fact the Flower Priests were twisting themselves into a knot trying to second-guess her purpose.

"Any advice you might deem fit to relate," the priest continued, trying to keep his head above water, "would be as jade and turquoise to us. You have our priority channel, of course."

"I do." Itzpalicue quashed her smile. "Please let me know before the horns and flutes sound. I will remove myself from Parus for the duration of the . . . contest."

"Oh, there's no danger . . ." The priest stopped himself. A trail of sweat trickled down the side of his head and disappeared into a starched white collar. "Your pardon, my lady. There will be *some* danger. We are not fighting with *macauhuitli* wrapped in cotton, oh no! The barbarians have only modest arms to hand, but a knife still cuts! No, no . . . I would be remiss to tell you there was *no* danger once our own troops are engaged by the rebellious elements among the Jehanan."

He tried to show a controlled smile, but the pasty color of his flesh beneath the ceremonial paint made him look much like a defleshed skull. "I fear the substance of most buildings in Parus—grand city though it is—will not be able to stop even the small-caliber railgun rounds fired by our Fleet shuttles or *Tonehua*-class combat vehicles. You should take care."

"I will." Itzpalicue made a sitting bow, indicating the conversation was over. "Good day."

The channel folded closed on the v-pane even before the Flower Priest could respond.

Sighing, Itzpalicue shook her head in dismay at the man's lack of control. Even the most dim-witted Flower Priests probably guessed the Mirror agent had full access to all Imperial communications in Jaganite near-space and on the surface of the ancient world. Yet he still tried to keep her informed of developments, even though her own communications network was superior to his own. The Mirror's reputation of omniscience was not vigorously reinforced by all the power available to the Imperial government for nothing.

If the *Tlachiolani*—the Mirror Which Reveals The Truth—could not see into the minds of every citizen, much less the secret councils of the European and Afrikan governments fulminating in exile among the Rim colonies, they *could* ensure full access to Imperial communications, secure public networks and voice traffic. Nearly all civilian data was exposed to the Mirror of Black Glass, either through back doors in mass-produced communications equipment or revealed by Imperial 'mice' scanning and analyzing broadcast data streams in realtime.

In the hands of an experienced *nauallis* like Itzpalicue, the wealth of data surging around Jagan was a clear ocean from which she could pluck almost anything she wanted.

Everything inconsequential is revealed to me, she thought sourly, *save that which I desire.*

Carefully avoiding the display panes and comps piled on the edges of her bed, the old woman rose up and stepped carefully across a nest of cables to reach the bathroom. Her hand, unerring in the dimness, found the pull-cord of an archaic-looking light fixture. The bulb flared white, stark in comparison to the soft phosphor glow of her screens. Itzpalicue grimaced, eyes narrowed to slits, and turned the tap. A rattling gurgle followed, and eventually water gushed into a pale green basin. She took time to wash her face. Curlicues of reddish stain swirled in the water and vanished down the drain. The pricking which focused her concentration had its own cost.

Everything in the washroom was gorgeously made, from hand-cast faucets and taps, and colored tiles deftly arranged in an elegant pattern on the floor, to a gleaming porcelain bathing-bowl sitting on massive stone feet. Lips pursed in appreciation, the Méxica woman ran a thin-boned hand along a filigreed wooden border surrounding the stall. Unidentifiable Jehanan creatures—flying snakes? serpents with myriad legs?—interwove in a delicate pattern. The heavy wood showed faint honeycomb striations beneath a dozen layers of varnish. She rapped her knuckles against the screen and was rewarded with a low, rippling hum. The 'trees' of Jagan did not lay down the familiar rings of Anáhuac.

"Barbarians indeed . . ." The old woman shook her head and turned out the light. The heedless racism of the Flower Priests was only part of the puzzle confronting her. Given her purpose, other matters were more pressing than trying to teach them manners.

Settling back into her nest, Itzpalicue stripped a comm thread against her cheek and tapped open a fresh channel pane. Radiance from a room filled with bright lights lit up her wrinkled old face. Behind her, a pale yellow flush climbed across tapestries made from hundreds of thousands of tiny, carefully placed feathers stitched to a silk backing. Turquoise hummingbird, green quetzal, yellow parrot, red spoonbill, raven, glossy crow and blue cotinga shone brilliantly in the darkness. Scenes of Méxica soldiers with golden breastplates and backswept, Nisei-style helmets wading through the surf onto a green shore emerged. Pigeon down made the white sails of the mighty fleet behind them. The sky was bruised gray in owl and sparrow, heralding an impending storm. Bearded men—pale-skinned, with bristling red mustaches—were waiting, hands raised in greeting. Their tartans and breeks were wild with vivid, clashing color.

On the opposite wall, the carnage of Badon Hill was vividly displayed. The faces of the Anglish soldiers, fleeing in defeat, were stark. Far in the background, the skyline of London was aflame. Amid clouds of gunsmoke, the Skawtish king Stuart advanced on a white horse with fetlocks stained red with blood. He, at least, was properly dressed in a russet mantle with bracelets of turquoise and gold.

"Have you finished deploying the secondary hi-band array?" Itzpalicue grimaced, watching the disorderly chaos of men and women moving boxes in the background of the image on the v-pane. There were no locals among the workers. Every one was an Imperial, imported at considerable cost from the nearest loyal colony. The old woman did not intend to lose her quarry for want of a few quills or horseshoes.

"Yes, mi'lady." The Mirror engineer in charge of the operations center was a hair too young for comfort, but he had come highly recommended. "We'll be finished tomorrow. Everyone's moved in, all of the landlines are active, and satellite is coming on-line now . . ."

"Are your generators shielded? How deep are you?"

The boy—could he be more than twenty?—nodded sharply. "Yes, mi'lady. This set of rooms is twenty meters beneath the city ground line." He grinned. "Six hundred years ago, we'd have had a nice view of the street. Right now we're still on city trunk power, but by tonight we'll switch over to a rack of fuel cells in an even lower basement."

"Good." Itzpalicue was pleased. The *xochiyaotinime* did not intend their War to erupt for another two weeks, but the old woman believed in being well prepared. Experience suggested that the arrival of the Fleet battle group—and the prince, once his presence was known—might incite the natives to violence long before the troublemaking priests had finished clearing and grading the field of battle. "Security?"

"Well . . ." The lead engineer's face twisted sour. "Are . . . are these *creatures* trustworthy?"

"The Arachosians?" Itzpalicue laughed breathily. "Don't they seem trustworthy with their wicked *kalang* knives and long muskets? With such peaceful faces and polite ways?"

"Mi'lady!" The engineer did not spit on the floor, but she knew he wanted to. "The Arachs are notorious thieves and murderers, brigands with chains of foreteeth around their necks, scales pitted and scarred from a hundred brawls . . . muskets? You've provided them with some odd-looking muskets! Muskets don't take clips of Imperial Standard 8mm 'firecrackers,' do they? No, I don't trust them at all."

"They've not set aside their long knives for our new toys, have they?" The old woman sat up a little straighter, concerned.

"No." The engineer shook his head. "Most of them are carrying muskets, axes, stabbing swords, bandoliers of grenades . . ."

"Good. Very good." Itzpalicue was relieved. "Lachlan-*tzin*, you can trust the Arachs while they are waiting for the other half of their payment. After that . . . well, we will be far from here. The Jehanan princes can clean up the mess. So, while no one offers them a more generous array of toys, you can trust them to keep you and your technicians safe."

The Éirishman shrugged, nervous but wanting to believe.

"What about surveillance in the cities?" Itzpalicue had begun to key up screen after screen of surveillance channels on her displays, each sub-pane no more than a palm wide. Most of them were still dark and inactive.

"Tomorrow," Lachlan replied, squaring his shoulders. "We're waiting for the *nymast* to fly up at dusk before we launch the spyeyes. I have three crews—protected by your trusty Arachs—laying out the hives on appropriate rooftops tonight."

The old woman raised an eyebrow, fixing him with a piercing glare.

"The *nymast*," the engineer said, a little stiffly, "are night-flying avians which feed on the insect cloud which rises over the city at sundown. I thought . . . I thought we should be careful in releasing the spyeyes. . . . It is possible someone might mark the launch and . . ."

"Wise." Itzpalicue dismissed the rest of his explanation with a sharp twitch of her fingers. "The Jehanan are neither savages nor fools. They have eyes and the wits to understand what might be seen. What about asset tracking? Do we have a trace on every Flower Priest active on Jagan?"

Lachlan nodded, shoulders settling. "Sixteen ground-side controllers, all running under Imperial merchant passports from a variety of authorized *pochtecan* based at the Sobipuré spaceport or in Parus itself. We tagged them within a day of arrival. There are another seven operating under double-cover in the hinterlands. . . . Four are locked, and we're running down the other three."

The old woman nodded, considering. The numbers matched those provided by the Flower Priests. "These seven are presenting themselves as agents of 'Swedish Naval Operations and Research'?"

"Yes. We've tentative pheromone, scent and skin flake idents on them; but given the relatively few number of Imperials working on Jagan . . . we should be able to keep track of them fairly easily."

"I assume they are already hard at work?"

Lachlan nodded, sandy hair falling into his eyes. "Sowing mischief, mi'lady. Selling arms and ammunition, filling the hearing pores of local revolutionaries with wild tales . . . blackening the Emperor's name with a will. Within three weeks, I would guess, every local potentate will be sweating tears in his sleep, wondering when the sky will open and the invasion fleet will descend. The usual Swedish line of propaganda."

"Good." Itzpalicue swept her eyes across the feeds. "And every marginal sect leader, patriot, malcontent and outlaw will be hyping himself into a frenzy. Someone must save civilization from the invaders, of course. Have you identified the princes who will step forward?"

"The *darmanarga moktar*—Those-Who-Restore-the-Right-Path?" Lachlan's forehead creased. "No. Not yet. The 'Swedish' agents are still sounding out possible allies among the *kujen*. Do you want me to anticipate them?"

The old woman shook her head slowly, eyes fixed on one of the v-panes. The motion of her retinas caused the pane to unfold, filling the display with vibrant color and motion:

Hundreds of brightly painted kites were dancing above the rooftops—somewhere in the city where an Imperial spyeye was already aloft—weaving and ducking in grayish air. As she watched, one of the kites, diamond-shaped with a stubby tail, controlled from the ground by what seemed to be an adolescent Jaganite, swerved across the path of another. For a moment, their controlling strings tangled and Itzpalicue blinked—was that a spark? Then one cord parted and a black and white striped kite tumbled out of the sky, string cut.

The old woman's eyes unfocused as she took in dozens of screens. "Let them do their work. No wasted effort, child. And Lachlan-*tzin*, you're prudent to wait until dark to launch the other hives—the natives are fond of aerial sports. We must be able to see everything before we can begin our own operation."

And then, wrenching her attention away from the fluttering sky, *perhaps I can find my . . . prey.* Her hands splayed across the displays. An odd, tight feeling was growing in her chest. A constriction of breath, an irritation plucking beneath her breastbone. *Cold . . . almost metallic. That is how you feel, my enemy. Not like a Swede or a Dane or any of the scattered nations defeated by the Empire.* Slowly, she licked her lips, considering. *I doubt there is a Högkvarteret operative within thirty light-years . . . but within the week, every Imperial and Jaganite on this tired old world will think the shadows are crawling with HKV agents.*

Itzpalicue closed both eyes, letting her mind settle. *Will all this be enough?* she wondered, trying to let her impression of the enemy come into focus. For the moment, there was only a confused sense of wrongness, of emptiness. *I have nothing but a feeling—a half-felt disturbance in the pattern of this civilization—to incite this conflagration. Will I catch him—her—it—this time?*

The old Méxica wondered if the Flower Priests realized this world had been chosen for their War of Flowers at her insistence. That the arrival of Villeneuve and the prince had never been in doubt, not from the moment the Mirror began to act. *I doubt it! Hmmm . . . I wonder . . .*

She opened her eyes, fixing the patient Lachlan with a piercing look. "I need your researchers to find me something. A shrine or temple or great work of art. Something every Jehanan citizen knows by name . . . something beloved, an example of the glory of ancient Jagan. The closer to a city, the better."

"Does the size of the specific object matter?" The Éirishman's hands were already busy on his control panel. "Jehanan artifacts, or something from a previous period?"

"Size and source are inconsequential—name recognition and emotional response are more important."

Lachlan nodded, looking up. She could see he had already guessed her desire. "I offer you two possibilities, mi'lady: two Arthavan-period shrines—the 'Wind King Temple' at Fehrupuré and the great statues of 'Kharna and the Hundred Princes' at Jihnuma. Both are within city bounds."

Pictures of the edifices appeared on Itzpalicue's display. She pursed her lips in appreciation. "Exquisite." A finger drifted across the pictures. "This sky . . . the air is filled with pollution?"

"Every city within the valley of the Phison is plagued with smog, acidic rain and almost toxic levels of industrial vapor waste." Lachlan glanced sideways at one of his secondary displays. "Do you wish to see rates of decay and damage? We don't have them on file, but I'm sure . . ."

"The fact of the matter is inconsequential. How quickly can a xenoarchaeological team be routed to Jagan?"

"No need." Lachlan tapped up a series of citizen profiles. "Civilization on Jagan is of sufficient age that the University of Tetzcoco already has a dig underway outside Fehrupuré. Apparently the remains of an Arthavan-period planetary capital are located there. Hmm . . . sixty University staff, about four thousand diggers . . . we can pull profiles on all the Imperials if need be."

"Not now." Itzpalicue brushed away the spyeye feeds open on her displays. "Only a thought. Now, how extensive is our infiltration of the rural, township-level communications networks?"

LANDING FIELD SIX
THE MÉXICA MANDATE AT SOBIPURÉ, JAGAN; END OF THE NORTHERN HEMISPHERE RAINY SEASON

Waves of heat rippled up from the tarmac of a primitive shuttle field. Gretchen tipped back her field hat to wipe a sweat-drenched forehead. Her other hand waved a Shimanjai-made fan over the supine form of her communications technician, Magdalena, who was sprawled on the ragged earth border of the landing field. The black-pelted Hesht was panting furiously, purple-red tongue lolling from the side of her long mouth. The alien female's eyes were bare slits against the copper glare of the Jaganite sky.

"Can she die from overheating?" Parker shuffled his boots on the pavement. The Company pilot's shirt clung damply to a thin body. He was standing between Magdalena and the swollen red disk of the sun, though he cast very little shade at all.

"I don't know," Gretchen said. "But she's suffering. I wish we had our heavy equipment here—at least we could put up a shade."

Parker shrugged, plucking a dying tabac from his mouth and flicking the butt through a nearby fence. Beyond the hexagonal wooden barrier, ten meters of dusty red earth choked with waste paper, discarded glass bottles, scraps of shuttle tire and tangles of glittering cotton string separated them from a row of houses. The shacks were little more than sections of cargo container—most of them bearing the faded, cracking labels of Imperial shipping concerns—turned on their sides and tacked together with extruded foam glue.

The slums sprawling away from the edge of the spaceport did not impress the Company pilot. There were no skyscraping towers, no gravity-defying buildings of alien hue. Nothing over a story in height. Only a mass of tiny, squalid-looking buildings reaching off into a choking brown haze.

"Wouldn't do anything about the thickness of this air, boss." The pilot looked left and right, mirrored glasses catching the heat-haze boiling up from the tarmac. "At least out here, if there's a breeze, we might catch a little of it. In there . . ." He pointed at the teeming city crouched just beyond the barrier. ". . . you can't even breathe."

The smell from the city was already overpowering; a thick soup of hydrocarbon exhaust, smoke from cooking fires, a harsh, unexpected smell like cinnamon and the sharp tang of solvents and heated metal.

Ahead of them, some of the other passengers moved up, sending a slow, jerky ripple down the line. Parker was quick to snatch up their bags—one huge duffel each—and drag them forward before the Taborite missionaries behind them could dodge into the gap. Gretchen reached down, took hold of Maggie's upper arms and grunted, hauling the Hesht to her feet.

"*Yrrrrowwl-urch,*" Magdalena groaned in near-delirium, long tongue disappearing behind rows of grinding teeth. One paw batted listlessly at the air. "Sister . . . just put the gun to my head and trigger-pull. Then . . . then take my pelt and make a sun-shade for your cubs. . . . Remember me, when you sing at the hunting-fire . . ."

"Oh, be quiet." Gretchen shook her head in dismay, helping the Hesht forward. The line moved two, perhaps three meters towards the Customs House at the end of the runway. "We'll be in the shade soon, and then, eventually, we can get to our hotel."

Parker snorted, tapping another tabac out of the pack in his shirt pocket. "I think anything called a 'hotel' on this planet will be a sore disappointment." He sighed, shifting to put himself between the sweltering glare of the red giant filling the western sky and the panting Hesht. "After Shimanjin . . . maybe Mags should have stayed and taken her vacation time *there*."

Gretchen shook her head, squatting, feeling the asphalt give queasily under her boots. Heat radiating from the tarmac burned the soles of her feet and beat against her face; the landing strip was an oven a thousand meters long and fifty wide. "There will be places like Hofukai on this world, too. Clean, cool, nearpine swaying in a shore breeze, crisp white linens on immaculately made beds. . . . But not down here in this . . . hole."

"Stupid-ass Company," Parker said, thin lips twisted twisted into a scowl. "You don't suppose we're being punished for doing a good job on Shimanjin? No . . . what about that business on Ephesus Three? Maybe they're dinging you for all the data the Imperials confisca—"

An accelerating blast of sound drowned out his voice and everyone in the customs line jerked in surprise. As one, the six hundred passengers recently disembarked from the Imperial passenger liner *Star of Naxos* turned, staring in alarm at the northern sky.

There, beyond a kilometer of open ground—high springy grass poking up between scattered stubs of eroding concrete, some kind of small horned ruminant grazing on low-lying furze—lay four more shuttle runways—all empty. Beyond them, in turn, a line of gleaming, modern buildings marked the 'main terminal' of the Sobipuré spaceport.

The thundering roar resolved into the shriek of shuttle engines—not just one, but dozens. The northern sky split open, smoky clouds peeling aside as four enormous slate-gray shuttles dropped down through the haze over the sprawling city. The first shuttle tilted back, landing thrusters howling, and a hot, metallic-tasting wind swept across the field.

Gretchen turned her head away as overpressure whipped around her, tugging long blonde hair loose from her field hat, filling her nose with the bitter smell of engine exhaust. A sharp clattering rose from the rows of shacks beyond the fence. The ground trembled as the first Fleet assault shuttle cracked down, enormous wheels spitting sparks.

"What's all this?" Anderssen switched to her local comm as she crouched against the fence, one hand tight on her duffle, the other shielding her face from a whirlwind of grit kicked up off the tarmac.

"It's the Fleet," Parker shouted in reply. He had not turned away, dialing the magnification on his lenses up as high as it would go. "It's not a combat drop . . . unit markings are still visible under the cockpit windows. A rampart lined with skulls . . . I think that's the Tarascan Rifles. An Arrow Knight Regiment."

Another flight of four shuttles cut through the clouds, increasing the deafening blast of noise, wind and fumes battering at them. The first set had already rolled to a halt near the main terminal and fore and aft cargo doors were opening.

Parker watched silently as armored combat tracks rolled down into the hot Jaganite afternoon, squads of men clinging to the sides or jogging out of the cavernous holds in long, professional-looking lines. After a moment, he looked up, ignoring the next wave of shuttles coming in. Sure enough, high in the sky, glinting between the streamers of cloud, there were fresh stars burning in the daylight sky.

"Boss . . ." His voice was a little hushed on the comm circuit. "Did you know Fleet was about to put the hammer down? Here, I mean, on this piss-poor world . . ." The pilot turned, staring down at Gretchen with a sickly look on his face.

"Parker." Anderssen started to chew on her lower lip, then forced herself to stop. "The Company decided we should come here. End of story. Get your bag, the line's moving."

A noisy, restless crowd pressed against Gretchen on all sides. The cinnamon smell choked the air, making her gasp for breath. Outside the Customs House—a suffocatingly warm hall with a dirt floor and no chairs—was some kind of a public transit station. Enormous metallic conveyances, smooth curves covered by thick, irregular layers of pasted-on advertisements, sat huffing exhaust beneath corrugated metal awnings. A huge mob of the reptilian Jehanan—scaled heads adorned with eye-shields in violent greens and blues, slender arms filled with packages bound in twine—were jostling to climb aboard.

"Which one do we need?" Gretchen had both arms wrapped around *her* package—the duffel with her gear, clothes, tools, books and papers—and was squeezed in between a nervous Parker and an awake, furious, agitated Magdalena. None of the buses bore Imperial lettering, only the flowing, curlicued native script. "Can we get an aerotaxi?"

"I don't think so," Maggie growled as the motion of the crowd pushed them between two wooden pillars supporting the nearest sun-shade. The bus idling in the bay was easily seven meters high with a bulging glass forward window. The original color of the metal seemed to be a pale, cool green, hidden under layers of grime, glue and paper scraps. Gretchen couldn't swear to her guess about the color. There was more of a *sense* of flowing water in the smooth outline of the vehicle.

"See?" the Hesht snarled at the sky, where the bloated red sun was suddenly obscured by the whining shapes of aerotaxis flitting past, heading northwest. Parker cursed, spitting out the crumpled remains of a tabac. Human faces stared down out of the open windows of the jetcars. One of the Imperial officers—their black uniforms were clear to see, even from below—waved jauntily at the vast crowd below. "We're on the wrong side of the river for anything to be quick . . ."

"Yes . . ." Gretchen slowed to a halt, staring up at the muddy copper sky, watching a veritable armada of aerocars speeding past. For an instant, just the time a drop of water took to plunge from the mouth of a faucet into a sink, everything seemed to slow to a halt. The chattering, rustling shapes of the reptilian Jehanan ceased to move. The hot, humid air held suspended, each droplet of moisture falling from the underside of the metal awnings caught in mid-motion.

I've seen this before. A woman in a feather mantle was smiling down at me. What does—

Then everything was moving again and they were swept past the green bus towards another rank of smaller, harder-angled conveyances.

"There!" Parker started pushing through the crowd. "That one has a sign in Imperial! Mother of God, it's a hotel shuttle bus!"

Gretchen breathed a sigh of relief and followed, leading with her duffel.

High above the flock of aerotaxis, an Imperial troop carrier roared north along the line of the Sobipuré–Parus highway. In the cargo bay, Sergeant Dawd clung to a strap, boots braced against an enormous pile of luggage—the prince's 'personal effects'—buried in green-and-tan cargo webbing. The carrier jerked and shuddered as it swept through pillars of white cloud. The sergeant swayed, wondering how the prince was doing—the boy had managed to sneak a flask of something smelling like industrial solvent aboard. *He'll be sorry*, Dawd mused as he kept watch over the baggage.

The hatch to the forward seating compartment cycled open and Master Sergeant Colmuir swung through, shaking his long angular head in dismay. The older man's uniform was liberally stained with yellow-green bile.

"Bit bumpy," Dawd commented, staring at the overhead. "Have a bit of a problem with lunch, Master Sergeant?"

"I did nawt." Colmuir tugged at the webbing over the luggage. He grimaced, stolidly ignoring the long streak of vomit drying on his chest, torso and leg. "Not all Army officers have the steady stomach God gave me." The master sergeant gave Dawd a flinty stare. "An' you'll not repeat such words in any other company, Dawd, not if you value your time in service."

"I do!" The younger man bowed in apology. "Just . . . never mind, Master Sergeant. I'll keep my thoughts to myself."

"Good." Colmuir held Dawd's gaze for a moment, then looked down at his jacket and shirt and sighed. "Ah, the lad is a study of extremes, isn't he? Has the constitution of a mule for a week's carouse with old man *pulque* and sister *mescal*—then can't even keep oatmeal down on a bit of rough air. I am derelict in my duty, I am, hiding back here with you and the hat boxes."

Dawd grinned. "I'll not put you on report, Master Sergeant." He paused, looking forward towards the troop compartment where a good thirty Imperial officers of the 416th were packed in like Avalonian salt herring. "He is an odd one, isn't he? Not what I expected . . ."

"No . . ." Colmuir removed his ruined jacket and shirt, revealing a rangy frame matted with bristly black-and-white hair. A faint patchwork of quickheal scars described a lifetime in the Emperor's service. "I've not been here much longer than you, Sergeant. Only a few weeks. I am given t' understand the previous detail was sacked under acrimonious circumstances."

"That's very surprising," Dawd said with a straight face. "Were you briefed?"

"Nawt a word. Just my assignment papers and a new billet." Colmuir dug around in his pack and found a fresh shirt. "Th' prince himself has provided my education. And he is a right educational lad isn't he? Rarely have I seen such a bitter, despondent fellow—particularly one so young. Makes one wonder what made him that way, doesn't it?"

Dawd nodded, his mind fairly boggling at the thought of a young, handsome man—an Imperial prince of the ruling house, no less—grown angry as some crippled old soldier from the bayside pubs. A frown gathered, drawing bushy black eyebrows together. "Master Sergeant, have you met his brothers, his father or mother?"

Colmuir snorted with laughter. "You're trying to balance upbringing against bloodstock, are you? I've the same thought, from time to time. I can tell you this—rumor in the guardservice has it that the boy has never even spoken to the Empress, nor she to him. If you read your guard protocol manual again, lad, you'll see there are orders to ensure she and the boy are never in the same location at the same time. If you look closer—an' I have—you'll see the orders came down from 'er side."

The master sergeant shrugged in response to Dawd's quizzical look.

"Rarely does he see his brothers either—and they are a braw lot, breathing fire every one of them—not a bit like him, d'you see? I have, to balance the scales, seen his father. The Emperor is a proper gentleman, if a bit pinch-faced, an' you can see he cares for the boy." Colmuir sealed up his shirt and rummaged for a pressed jacket. "But respects him? Tha' I do not know."

Dawd's next question was interrupted by a chiming sound. Colmuir threw on the jacket, checked his comm-band, grimaced, and scrambled back through the hatch. The younger man turned his attention back to peering out the window at passing clouds. The edges of a city were now visible through breaks in the thunderstorms, covering the valley floor with a rumpled quilt of flat roofs and isolated skyscrapers.

Rain drummed against a cracked window beside Anderssen's head. Outside, the afternoon downpour was so fierce she could barely make out the shapes of trucks rushing past on an eight-lane raised highway. Inside the bus, she, Parker and Maggie were crammed into a long bench at the very rear of the vehicle. The leather upholstery under her thighs was cracked, discolored and burning hot to the touch. Some kind of multicylinder hydrocarbon engine rattled and wheezed beneath her feet.

"How long until we get into Parus?" Gretchen peered over the pile of duffels between her and Magdalena. The Hesht was folded up, chin resting on her knees, eyes narrowed to angry slits.

"*Rrrrr . . .*" Maggie's nose wrinkled up in disgust. The bus smelled old to Gretchen—dry papery sweat, rotting onions, newly washed linoleum—and she was afraid to ask the Hesht what *she* thought of the odor. "Too long!"

"How big is this bonus again?" Parker was jammed in on the other side of the Hesht, his legs sticking out into the central aisle. An enormous Jaganite filled the rest of the bench. The creature seemed to be asleep, eye-shields lidded down over milky lenses, clawed hands clasped over an ornamented leather vest covered with hundreds of enameled disks. Supple skin around the long nostrils fluttered with regular breaths, though the pattern sounded dissonant to Anderssen's ear. "Can we leave here *really soon?*"

"Not as soon as we'd like. All the Company note said," she said, leaning closer to the other two and lowering her voice, "was to get here and apply for a survey permit. After we get to the hotel, and get something to eat, and get some sleep—then we'll worry about getting papers."

"And transport," the Hesht rumbled deep in her throat. "I'm not walking in this heat."

"My job, I guess." Parker started tapping his tabac case against one knee, then realized the pack was empty. "Not much to fly down here. I'll bet the Fleet grounds all air traffic as a 'precaution,' even if we had the money for an aerocar. The brief didn't say anything about a military exercise? Maybe an invasion?"

Gretchen shook her head. As was usually the case with the Company, there was little or no briefing material. *Costs money to make a proper survey! Can't have that kind of waste . . .*

"No, but all of this happened so suddenly I wouldn't be surprised if some genius at the home office heard something from someone and decided to take advantage."

"Of what?" Maggie's eyes slid sideways to glare suspiciously at Anderssen.

"Of us being done with the project on Shimanjin." Gretchen leaned back against the hot, trembling seat. She was very tired. There was a medband around her wrist—no Imperial citizen traveled without one—but it was winking amber and red with warnings about local microfauna trying to assault her system with each breath. *No wakemeup for me today!* "And nearby—as things go, in stellar distances—and the Fleet arriving for whatever reason. I mean, I'd guess if we have to get a survey permit then they need us to examine some Mother-forsaken wilderness, looking for 'anomalous readings' or something equally helpful."

Parker frowned, peering over Maggie's furry, night-black shoulder. "Wait, you mean—for you to just wander around we need a permit? Do we really need that? I mean, Mags here is pretty sly with her surveillance equipment. We could just get an aerocar or ultralight and see the sights . . ."

Anderssen did not reply, giving the pilot a stony look.

"Oh, okay." Parker slumped back down behind the Hesht. Maggie snorted, flaring her nostrils in amusement. "Be all legal then . . ."

"We will follow the Company directive and get a permit." Gretchen let out a long, slow hiss. Outside the rain-streaked window, traffic was slowing and she could just make out lights—long strings of glowing neon—rising in the murk. *Buildings. We're finally in the city. Oh, I hope there aren't a hundred k of suburbs or something. . . . I suppose it is rush hour, too.*

Horns started to blare outside, traffic slowing, and the bus shuddered to a near-halt. *Delightful,* Anderssen thought, *five hundred light-years from home . . . and stuck in traffic.*

Fat drops of rain spattered on the landing platform tucked into the northeastern corner of the Imperial Legation as Sergeant Dawd set foot on Jehanan soil, head up, attention on the ornamental trees surrounding the aerocar pad, one hand on his Nambu and the other extended to guide prince Tezozómoc down from the aerobus. The transport was steaming in the humid air, fans whining dully. This was apparently the last stop of the day—the other officers had been dropped off at the Imperial Army cantonment south of the city.

"Where are my men? Where are my brave warriors?" the prince declared, striking a commanding pose, long nose in the air. He was wearing his second-best field dress uniform, which featured a dashing cape and an enormous amount of gold and jade trim. Rain hissed away from a built-in repeller field, surrounding Tezozómoc with a corona of mist. "I cannot rest until I've seen to their needs! Food, a hot meal, every soldier a bed for the night. I will lie down on the cold earth with them if need be, drinking day-old kaffe from a canteen, sharing their struggle hour for hour, day for day—even the sound of the guns will not dissuade me from my purpose! Even—"

Master Sergeant Colmuir coughed politely, motioning for Tezozómoc to step away. The prince scowled, but moved aside for the taller man to step down to the tarmac as well. Two Fleet ratings were pulling bag after bag from the cargo compartment, steadily piling up a huge collection of armored, dent-resistant grav-lifted luggage.

"Mi'lord," the older Skawtsman said patiently, "you're attached to the Tarascan Rifles as a diplomatic aide—the voice of the Emperor, as it were—not as an actual *commander* with actual, ah, *troops.*"

Tezozómoc's lips curled bitterly and for an instant, Dawd thought the prince was going to strike the master sergeant. Then the boy's face congealed into a tight mask. "Oh. Well, then, where *do* I sleep?"

"The Legation itself, mi'lord," announced a Marine corporal in a dress duty uniform who had hurried up while they were talking. He was carrying a large black umbrella. "*Yaotequihuah* Clark at your service, sir. Legate Petrel has provided rooms for you in the Guest House. Our finest accommodations, you may be assured."

The corporal nodded to Colmuir. "You've rooms directly adjoining, Master Sergeant. If you'll follow me?"

Dawd held back, keeping an eye on the baggage. The rain was starting to pelt down hard, cutting visibility to a dozen meters or less. He could taste half-burned methanol and oil in the air. The prince was whisked away, Colmuir and Clark on either side. The sergeant followed, both automatic pistols out and in his hands. The Fleet ratings guiding the cavalcade of floating luggage didn't notice—they were concentrating on keeping the prince's baggage from wandering off into the rose bushes or getting hung up in the trees.

Magdalena stared around the hotel room in a tight-lipped, tips-of-her-fangs-bared way far too familiar to Anderssen. They were on the fiftieth floor of a crumbling concrete tower in south-central Parus. Gretchen had been struck, as they walked down the hall to their room, by the wear pattern on the floor. A shallow basin nearly four centimeters deep described the middle of the passage. The room was low ceilinged, dark and very musty.

"Well," Gretchen said brightly, "this is nice." She was looking for somewhere to put her duffel. Jaganite budget hotel rooms seemed to have been designed by Russian efficiency experts. There were no chairs, only high beds on heavy wooden frames and medium-height tables reminding her of spindly armoires. Given the tripodal, tail-heavy stance of the natives, Anderssen realized there might not be *any* chairs on the whole planet.

That's odd. She was suddenly struck by the seating arrangements on the bus they'd taken from the shuttleport. *Was that a human-built vehicle?*

"Hhhhhrrrrr!" Maggie's tail twitched sharply from side to side. "Parker is happy—I think his whole clan have laired here with their nose-biting smoke."

The pilot ignored her, peering curiously at a mechanism controlling a set of louvered blinds over the windows. Gretchen dumped her bag on the foot of the smallest bed—both Maggie and Parker were taller. The pilot tried one of the buttons on the face of the device and was rewarded with a whining groan from some kind of pulley system.

"This won't blow up, will it?" He poked another button and the blinds shivered into motion, rotating out to reveal a view of the rain-soaked city below. At the same time, a gust of damp, chilly air blew into the room. The pilot grimaced, then started to cough. "Urgh. Smells like a benzene cracking facility. *How* long are we staying here?"

"One night." Gretchen had opened the 'bathroom' door to stare at an uneven tiled floor, rusty drain and complete lack of a bathtub with horror. *How would some giant lizard-thing with a tail like a third leg take a bath, o child?* Her eyes swung unerringly to a bin along the wall. *Sand. They abrade their thick, scaly skin with sand. What a nice scraper made of stone. Oh blessed Mother of Our Savior, deliver me from working off-world.*

"Tomorrow," she declared, "we're going to find someplace catering to human tastes. I promise. Well, you two will find a place to stay while I visit the Legation and see about our permits."

"These beds are *not* soft," Magdalena declared, having stripped away a coarse blanket to reveal a metal frame holding a suspended net of stout-looking ropes. "I do not like hummocks. No. Not at all."

Parker started to correct the Hesht, caught Gretchen making an 'are-you-stupid' face and turned back to staring out at the rain. Parus at sundown was a forest of tall, round towers with softly glowing windows. The local ceramacrete tended to dusty red. Coupled with the setting sun, the city was being swallowed by a foreboding, sanguine night. The pilot squinted through the murk—individual storm cells were visible, pelting the crowded, twisting streets below with rain so thick it made patches of early darkness.

Rubbing his stubbly chin, Parker was puzzled for a moment before he realized the odd layout of the buildings was caused by the presence of broad, curved boulevards looping across the city. Hundreds of tiny, straight streets intersected them at unnatural angles. *Weird. Why did they build everything all higgle-piggle like that? Crazy aliens.*

Gretchen sat down on the end of her 'hummock' and began digging in her duffel. All of their heavy dig equipment—tents, analysis sensors, environment suits, hand tools—was in storage at the port, in the dubious care of the Albanian Spaceways office. Thankfully, she'd thought to stow a clutch of threesquares in her personal effects. Just the effort of finding them made her feel faint. *Too big a day for us. Oh yeah.*

"Here," she said, pitching a bright blue and orange food bar to the pilot. "I really don't think we should risk room service. Though, Maggie, they might have something live for you to eat . . ."

"Not hungry." Magdalena had curled up in a corner on the wool blanket, plush tail over her nose, as far as she could get from the 'hummocks.'

"Right." Gretchen began chewing on the molé-flavored ration bar. It sure didn't taste like chocolatl. They never did, no matter what the advertisements said.

The office of the Imperial Attaché for Antiquities had tall windows opening on a garden filled with riotous blossoms. Something like a rhododendron tree shaded the windows, heavy boughs of pinkish red flowers hanging against the open shutters. Gretchen was sweating mildly, sitting in a wide-backed chair covered with leopard skin.

While the rest of the Legation was air conditioned and dim, this room was bright, sunny and warm. Around the garden, three stories of windows set into whitewashed, ivy-covered brick reached up to a murky yellow sky. Despite thunderstorms growling and muttering through the night, the pollution hanging over the city had not been washed away.

"Hmmm." The attaché made a noncommittal noise, his head bent over Gretchen's identity papers and transit visa. She guessed the windows in *this* room were flung wide to embrace the hot, tropical smell of the flowers outside because the slim young man sitting across from her was a Mixtec. A climate like this would remind him very much of home. She had never seen the great cities of Timbuktu or Ax Idah or Brass herself, but articles in the travel magazines endemic to starliner waiting lounges indicated gorgeous architecture, sprawling gardens and a lively social life. The old Méxica colonies in sub-Saharan Afrika had flourished after the end of the War.

He looked up, fine-boned features sharp under dark cocoa skin. The young man's face held such a look of seriousness Anderssen was struck by unexpected sadness. *Such a handsome man should be letting himself live a little more. Just a tiny bit. Does he remember how to smile?*

"I am sorry, Anderssen-*tzin*, but I cannot give you a survey permit for any region on Jagan." He gathered her papers together and put them into a folder. "I understand you've wound up here by accident, more or less, but an exclusionary planetary excavation, analysis and recovery grant has already been made to the University of Tetzcoco department of Extrasolar Anthropology."

Gretchen grimaced. Tetzcoco EXA had quite a reputation. She tried to hide her reaction, but the young man's eyebrows rose in surprise.

"Have you worked with Professor Der Sú before?"

"Not directly, Soumake-*tzin*. But I spent two years on Old Mars working for one of his graduate students. He has a towering reputation among my peers."

"Does he?" The attaché rose from his chair and moved to the window, long-fingered hands tapping on the sill. "Well, I have only met with him once or twice since my arrival." Soumake turned, still dreadfully serious. "He is—in my personal opinion—an ass of a man, with half the sense. I do not know what kind of agreement my predecessor struck with the local princes, but Sú is running his own fiefdom up at Fehrupuré and I doubt the local *kujen* would care if a hundred tons of artifacts were being shipped out every month. He'd be using his cut of the proceeds to buy guns."

Anderssen settled a little in her chair, realizing the attaché was giving her a particularly searching look. "You're . . . um . . . worried about smuggling?"

"I am." Soumake leaned against the window. Like most of the officials and staff Gretchen had seen while wending her way through the halls of the Legation, he was dressed in a long, narrow-cut cotton mantle over a light shirt and dark pants. She sighed inwardly to see he carried off the look very well. Most people in official costume looked like they were wearing a tent . . .

"Jagan is an ancient world, Anderssen-*tzin*. Some estimates place the first remnants of civilization here at over a million years old. That verges on First Sun times. Rare to find such a world continuously inhabited over such a vast span of years. One wonders what might lie buried beneath the cities in the hinterland. Sú is hoping for glory, I'm sure."

He looked down at her papers again, now packed up in a dark olive folder. "I am also aware of the reputation enjoyed by the Honorable Chartered Company. Not one which shouts 'academic integrity' or 'law-abiding,' is it?"

Gretchen tried not to squirm and regretted taking a stab at a legal professional presence on this world. *But I'm supposed to inform the authorities! They told me to get a permit!*

"I'm not . . . I'm not here on official Company business, Soumake-*tzin*. We finished a project on Shimanjin and had some free time. The Company doesn't care how I get back home, as long as I pay any difference in the ticket. I missed my connection at Tadmor Station and the next ship out was the *Star of Naxos* and it was coming through here. Reading about the worlds on the liner-run piqued my interest in Jagan, so I thought I'd spend some time sightseeing before the next liner arrives."

The attaché's expression did not change. "You picked a bad time."

Gretchen nodded, striving for a suitably morose expression. It came easily. "We saw the Fleet landing at the spaceport while we were waiting at Customs. Is there trouble brewing?"

A rich, melodious laugh burst from the Mixtec and he shook his head, the flash of a grin lighting his face. The moment passed as quickly as it had come. "Brewing? My dear lady, the valley of the Five Rivers is well past brewing . . . on the edge of explosion I think." He sat down.

"Between Capsia in the northwest and Patala on the southern coast there are sixty kujenates—principalities—and a dozen feudatory tribes. You may not have noticed yet, but the Jehanan are not the only sentient race resident on Jagan. To my knowledge, there are at least three others. Little love is lost between any of them. There are hundreds of religious sects, all quarreling with one another. In some districts there are entire armies of brigands roaming the countryside.

"Labor unions have begun to spring up in the cities as industry catalyzes around new Imperial technologies. The factory owners negotiate with clubs, poison gas and murder. The mountains to the west are filled with semi-nomadic tribes—such as the Arachosians—whose livelihood is wholesale theft. East of the Phison, thankfully, is a harsh desert, because beyond the Ghor is the fiercely xenophobic empire of the Golden King.

"Into this cookpot you thrust the Empire, the *pochteca* companies, our own missionary orders and the whole mixture boils far too fast."

"We're not welcome here?" Gretchen indicated the luxurious room and the sprawling compound of the Legation beyond the betel wood doors. None of the buildings within an ancient, red-brick rampart showed the first sign of a hostile populace. There were no guard-posts, no machine guns, no waspwire.

"On the contrary," Soumake said, running a hand across a perfectly smooth scalp. "Every single one of those factions, parties, sects, unions, gangs and princes wants our friendship desperately. Consider this—you are a scientist, you will understand: Jagan is *old.* Ancient. Worn down by thousands of generations of inhabitants. Entire civilizations have risen and then fallen again. Nuclear wars have smashed them back to savagery and they have clawed their way back up again. Twice the Jehanan have reached into space, only to tumble back at the last moment."

The attaché sighed, pointing at a heavy glass case on one wall. "Consider this metal fragment in an isolation case. Not sealed to protect the artifact, no, but to protect us from radiation permeating the metal casing inside. One of the metallurgists with the Tetzcoco expedition examined the item and confirmed what I had already surmised. Go ahead, take a good look."

Gretchen stepped to the case and frowned. Inside was a stout-looking hexagonal rod, marked by two parallel indents. Faded, indecipherable lettering ran around the top in a band two fingers high. The metal shone silver, without any sign of age or decay.

"This looks like the fuel cylinder for a power plant of some kind."

Soumake nodded, spreading his hands. "An antimatter container, to be precise. Empty now. The antiparticles inside decayed long ago, suffusing the steel sheath with byproduct radiation. After the AM evaporated, the magnetic containment system inside shut down."

"How old is it?" Gretchen measured the device with her hand, taking care not to touch the glass. "Where did it come from?"

The attaché rubbed his chin. "I purchased the 'holy relic' from a scrap metal dealer in Capsia last year. A trader from out of the cold waste beyond the mountains had brought it to him. A tentative estimate of the decay rate weighs in at several hundred thousand years. But here is what interests me. . . . The lettering is a very, very early form of Jehanan. Much like you will see on the porticoes of their oldest temples today."

Gretchen turned around, one pale blonde eyebrow rising. "You said the Jehanan civilizations had been destroyed before they could reach into space. Antimatter production facilities are nearly always built in orbit, outside a gravity well."

Soumake nodded. "The physical xenoarchaeologists disagree with me, Anderssen-*tzin*. They say *proof is lacking*, but the biologists concur. The Jehanan are not native to this world. They came from space, as we have done, and conquered Jagan. What conflagration tore down their starfaring civilization I do not know . . ." He grimaced, making a motion which included the city outside the walls of the Legation. ". . . but the native princes are eager reach the stars again. As I said, Jagan is an old, old world."

A steadily deepening frown on Gretchen's face suddenly cleared and she indicated the casing. "Iron."

Soumake nodded. "Iron. Steel. Guns. Ammunition. Armored vehicles. Petrochemical products. Fuel cells. Advanced atmospheric aircraft. Methanol-engine cargo trucks. Computer networks built from rare metals, or with processing cores which can only be fabricated in zero-g. Before our arrival, the local armies were armed with bows and arrows, spears tipped with metal scavenged from the ruins of the ancients, quilted armor, precious swords made of stainless steel handed down through a hundred generations. . . . Does this sound familiar?"

Anderssen felt cold and sat down, crossing her arms. The Mixtec regarded her steadily.

"Now *we* are the Japanese merchants," he said softly. "Making landfall on a strange and fabulous shore. Finding an ancient, wealthy civilization lacking iron. Not the *knowledge* of iron as it was with the Toltecs, no . . . but the mines are played out, or so far distant from Parus as to be on the lesser moon. They remember the old civilization, these descendants of ancient kings. There are still books, drawings, carvings, oral traditions of a Golden Age when the Jehanan ruled the sky, the waves and the land. They are very, very eager to regain the tools which made them masters of the world.

"I will tell you, the factors from Kiruna paid a heavy price for the right to sell *scrap metal* on this world. But they are making a handsome profit, unloading the detritus of a hundred years of war in the Inner Worlds. Bargeloads of recycled aluminum from Svartheim and Korgul and New Stockholm arrive every week. And the Fleet won't be interrupting that traffic, oh no."

"But wait . . . what do they have to trade? Not gold, surely."

Soumake's serious expression remained, but there *was* a twinkle in his eyes. "Did the Japanese who fled the Mongol invasion of holy Nippon want gold from the Toltecs? No, they needed food, clothing, slaves to clear the deep forests of Chemakum and Chehalis. So they traded what they had—horses, double-season rice, geared milling machinery, metalsmithing—for what they did not.

"And here, on Jagan, aside from pretty artifacts by the ton, there are certain plants which only grow in the Arachosian highlands, or in certain valleys around Takshila and Gandaris. The bitter *Nēm* is a mild psychotropic for the local people, but once the labs on Anáhuac have processed the seeds and the milky white sap, well . . . it becomes much more. Very popular, or so I understand."

"How much profit can there be in biochemicals?" Disbelief was plain in Gretchen's voice.

Soumake snapped his fingers. "Enough, considering they're trading something worth less than a *ming* here for something with a six hundred percent rate of return by volume on Anáhuac. And there are other sources of revenue . . . glorious textiles, rugs, fine porcelains and ceramics, excellent liquors, certain unique woods. Many, many luxury items in demand in the core worlds because they are *new*.

"But all of this involves *you* only peripherally: I will not grant you a permit for survey in the land of the Five Rivers."

"I see." Gretchen thought she *did* understand and was oddly touched. "You think it's too dangerous for me to be wandering over hill and dale. You think the local princes have accumulated enough firepower to see about settling all their old scores. Is that why the Fleet has arrived?"

Soumake rose from his chair abruptly, face clouded. "I wish every Imperial citizen on Jagan were aboard a Fleet lighter and bound for Tadmor Station today. I suggest . . . you find an out-of-the-way place to stay, Anderssen-*tzin*. And remain there and not go out until the next liner comes through. Good day."

Gretchen returned his polite bow, retrieved her papers and made a quick exit. Walking into the cool dry air of the hallway was a welcome shock, wiping away a gathering sense of foreboding. For a moment, though, she turned and looked back at the closed door. *He must be truly worried,* she mused. *I've never seen such a talkative Imperial official before.*

The heart of the Consulate was a staircase of native stone dropping two stories from the main business floor to an entry foyer large enough to hold a zenball field. Gretchen was making her way down the steps, distracted by the carved reliefs lining the balustrade, when she nearly ran into a tall woman coming up the steps with a quick, assured walk.

"Pardon," Anderssen said, coming to an abrupt halt before they collided. The woman looked up, fixed her with a cornflower blue gaze and a brilliant smile lit her face.

"My dear! Terribly sorry—I haven't been paying attention all day! You must be freshly arrived? Come about some official business? Of course, no other reason to be in this drafty old place, is there?"

Gretchen found herself turned about and escorted briskly up the stairs and into a sitting room filled with overstuffed chairs.

"Let me look at you. Yes . . ." The woman's good humor did not abate and the brilliant azure eyes turned sharp, considering Gretchen from head to toe. "Dear, have you found someplace nice to stay? Your current residence just will not do, not for a woman of repute like yourself. There are some beautiful little hotels near the Court of Yellow Flagstones. You will like the White Lily best if I am not mistaken, and I rarely am. Ask any of the taxi drivers, they'll know the way. Yes, very nice, with breakfast—*human* breakfast—and real beds and, dare I say? Proper bathtubs with hot water. Oh yes."

Anderssen felt a little shocked, as if a bison had crashed out of the nearpine and run right over her, but she mustered herself and managed to squeak out: "Doctor Gretchen Anderssen, University of New Aberdeen, very-pleased-to-meet-you."

"A doctor?" The woman's smile changed, dimming in one way, but filling with warmth as her public persona slipped aside. Gretchen relaxed minutely. "Well done, my girl. Very politely done—reminding me to introduce *myself* as well." A strong hand—surprisingly callused, given the exceptionally elegant gray-and-black suit the lady was wearing—clasped Anderssen's. "I am Greta Petrel. No, don't laugh, my hair just comes this way, not an affectation at all. All the Army wives don't believe me, of course, but I think you might. Yes, I think you do."

Gretchen managed to tear her attention away from chasing the crisp flood of words coming out of the woman's mouth and saw that Mrs. Petrel's hair was raven black with two white streaks, one falling from either temple. The woman dimpled, one finger brushing across small sapphire pins in her ears and flicking away from the snow-white hair.

"Fabulously jealous, all of them. But what can they say? Nothing but nice things to my face, oh yes. Now, behind my back . . . well, I really could not care less about their twittering. Now, dear, tell me how you've fared today in my so-grand house. Did you get good service from whomever you saw? Did they serve you tea? Doctor of what, exactly?"

"Xeno . . . xenoarchaeology, ma'am." Gretchen was suddenly sure the woman wasn't exaggerating when she said *my house*. She could only be the Imperial Legate's wife. "I'd come to see the attaché of Antiquities about a permit . . ."

"Ah, Soumake is a dear, isn't he? Such a serious young man, though. I'm sure he told you *no* quite firmly, even with such beautiful golden hair and sweet features. No matter, he's terribly married and you've children of your own to see after—no sense in gallivanting around after a career officer like him, oh no. Well, he was right to send you on your way, though I'm sure you're just disheartened by the whole sordid business."

Mrs. Petrel shook her head and Gretchen felt suddenly chastised, as if she'd forgotten her sums in front of the entire class. She also felt dizzy. Trying to keep up with the older woman's turn of conversation was wearing her out.

"There is only one sure cure for such things, my dear." Mrs. Petrel tucked a stray tendril of Gretchen's hair back into place and pressed a handwritten card—shimmering green ink on creamy realpaper—into her hand. "I'm having the smallest gathering possible at the summer house in a few days. You come and sit with me and we'll have a bite to eat and some tea. Perhaps I can see if Professor Sú can find a scrap of decency in his black, black heart and let you work under *his* permit. But no promises!"

Mrs. Petrel swept out of the sitting room, head high, the two white streaks merging to make a V-shape in the heavy fan of hair across her shoulders. Gretchen stared in surprise at the handwritten card in her hand. The front read: "Mrs. Gretchen Anderssen is invited to my party" while the back had an address—also in green ink and the same crisp hand—a date and time.

"How . . . did she know I have children? How did she know my *name*?" Anderssen stepped out into the hallway and caught sight of Mrs. Petrel sailing past a quartet of armed guards, the tall, thin shape of a manservant following quietly behind. Seeing him, Gretchen realized he'd been in the background the whole time, silent and as much a part of the paneled walls as the wood itself. "Well."

She laughed, feeling tension ebb from her chest. "I should say, *I never*. I think I'd better sit down for a minute and get my breath back. What a bracing person."

The chairs were far more comfortable than they looked and Gretchen took a moment to key "Court of the Yellow Flagstones" into her comp. Good lodgings—and she was certain the White Lily was excellent and probably reasonably priced—were worth more than a woman's weight in quills in this business. She couldn't help but smile.

I hope Maggie and Parker are doing all right. Oh, bother! I'd better call them about the hotel.

A NONDESCRIPT HOUSE
NEAR THE TOMB OF GHARLANE THE MAD, PARUS

Lachlan's image turned sideways, alarm plain on his young face. "An unexpected hyperspace transit, mi'lady." He tapped a glyph on his end and Itzpalicue watched with interest as a navigational plot unfolded on a spare display. "A relatively small ship . . . 'casting Fleet ident codes . . . here we are, an *Astronomer*-class light cruiser, the *Henry R. Cornuelle*."

The old woman bared her teeth moodily. "A late arrival for Battle Group 88?"

"Not on the squadron list," Lachlan replied, scratching the edge of a stubbled jaw. Like Itzpalicue, work had replaced sleep on his schedule. "Fleet records say . . . the *Cornuelle* is assigned to deep range patrol in the Hittite sector. One zone to core from here. Commander of record is Mitsuharu Hadeishi, a Nisei from New Edo on Anáhuac . . ."

The old woman grunted and sat up a little straighter.

". . . graduate Fleet Academy, this is his third deep space command, no notable clan affiliation, sponsor list is . . . empty?" Lachlan frowned, looking up at her. "How did he get an independent cruiser command?"

"Consider his service record, child." Itzpalicue stifled a yawn. She had been working long hours, racing to keep ahead of the Flower Priests. Spyeye deployment had gone well, but high levels of acid rain were causing intermittent problems with the relay grids. She plucked a maguey spine from her sleeve—one of dozens carefully pinched through the cloth—and pricked her cheek. A stab of pain cleared her mind, leaving a tiny crimson dab on a cheekbone serrated with a closely spaced pattern of puckered scars.

". . . sixteenth in his class at the Academy," Lachlan was reading, growing more puzzled with each entry in Commander Hadeishi's personnel jacket. "Fourth in tactical exercises, second in overall efficiency, high marks from his science instructors, winner of the Graymont Exercise three years in a row, very good rating in engineering, management skills, composure under fire."

"Yes." Itzpalicue had already scanned the records herself. "Do you see the note from the senior chief petty officer of the *Shoryu* concerning his first tour of duty?"

Lachlan flipped to the appropriate page, green eyes searching through the records.

"*Sho-i* Hadeishi," he said slowly, digesting the passage, "is as fine an officer as I've had the honor to serve with aboard any ship of the Fleet." Lachlan leaned back in his seat, staring at the old woman. "High praise from a thirty-year *joto-heiso* on a Fleet heavy carrier. But he has no friends noted at Court, or on the Heavenly Mountain, no heavyweight *pochteca* backing him up, he's not married to an admiral's daughter . . . he's no one at all."

Itzpalicue nodded, a pleased smile beginning to seep into her wrinkled old face. "He is an exemplary officer, Lachlan-*tzin*. An honorable credit to his family—though by their surname they are not of noble birth, so perhaps they do not care—and to the Fleet. You see why he is here?"

The Éirishman nodded, biting his lower lip. "Ship's been two years out of refit or a Fleet base. Must be worn down to the nub. Hmmm . . . four recent engagements with 'hostile elements.' Three confirmed counter-privateer kills, including a *Tyr*-class refinery ship. Five stationside or colony disputes settled by force of arms. Greeting squirt to Admiral Villeneuve reports his ship is at seventy percent capability due to crew casualties and mechanical attrition. Well! The commander has been keeping busy out in the big dark."

"Battle group 88 has a Fleet mobile repair dock assigned?" Itzpalicue was considering a picture—now several years out of date—of Hadeishi. A thin little man with an intelligent face, narrow beard and pencil-thin mustache. She imagined he would laugh easily, sitting around a low table with his friends, drinking sake and listening to a samisen player. The edge of her thumb, polished sharp and reinforced to razor sharpness with layers of rebonded polytetrafluoroethylene, tapped slowly against a list of 'associated persons.' The list was not part of Hadeishi's public Fleet jacket.

The Mirror took care to watch the activities of ship commanders, even ones who barely existed from a political point of view. At some time in the past, a 'mouse' had observed *Chu-sa* Hadeishi speaking in a familiar way with a *certain person*. An individual Itzpalicue knew and detested, not solely because he was an Imperial Judge—a *nauallis*—or what the credulous would call a *sorcerer*. Unlike everything else in the Empire, the activities of the *nauallis* were kept well hidden from the Mirror. Of course the rival organizations took great interest in one another's doings. The old woman's lips tightened in remembered anger, considering the name.

Her eyes moved on, coming to rest on a red-flagged Admiralty note at the bottom of the record. *Ah, I see why our brave captain has stayed in the shadows so long. . . . He has been avoiding fate.*

"He must be looking to refit with the battle group while the Flingers-of-Stone are in-system." Lachlan rubbed one of his eyes. The medical readout showed him close to complete exhaustion. "Or use the battle group tachyon relay to get recalled by Nineteenth Fleet. So . . . he's shot off every sprint missile in his stores. His beam weapon mounts must be caked solid with particle flux. Shipskin and armor are barely hanging to the hull. This ship desperately needs to recycle at a repair base."

The old woman pursed her lips. "This ship was placed under orders months ago to return to Toroson to be decommissioned. Commander Hadeishi is very tardy in returning from his patrol." She considered the message traffic passing between the *Cornuelle* and the battle group's tachyon relay. "He's reporting damage to the last message drone—how convenient . . ."

"That won't matter," Lachlan said, yawning again. "All the queued mail and orders are dumping to his main comp now—he'll have to make transit for the Fleet Base within a day or so."

Itzpalicue shook her head, decision crystallizing even as she considered the matter. "No. The Holy Mother is watching over our shoulders, Lachlan-*tzin*. This is one of our missing elements, cast down from heaven to serve our purpose."

"Mi'lady?" Lachlan was noticeably surprised.

"The *Cornuelle* will serve as Elder Warrior's sacrifice for the exercise about to commence on the planet. Pass my desire on to the Flower Priest handling such things. Have them cut Hadeishi new orders, delaying his return to Toroson until after our activities here are complete."

The young Éirishman stared at her in dismay for a moment, then shook himself, nodded and turned away to key up the appropriate comm channel. He said nothing about her decision, as was proper.

Itzpalicue tapped the public personnel jacket closed without a further thought. Her attention, as always, turned back to the banks of video feeds reflecting the spyeyes over Parus, or relaying local holocast and voice-only transmissions. Her room was close and still, filled with the birdlike cries of thousands of chattering voices. One sharp fingernail continued to tap slowly on the list of persons associated with the so-able Commander Hadeishi.

Huitziloxoctic. Green Hummingbird.

How fine to meet the friend of an old . . . acquaintance.

The captain's launch from the *Cornuelle* drifted through an enormous airlock, the slow pulse of guide-lights illuminating the boat's ebon exterior. Inside the landing bay, every surface gleamed white and gray, sharply illuminated by banks of lights on the overhead. A boat bay unfolded in complete silence to engulf the smaller craft. Inside, *Chu-sa* Mitsuharu Hadeishi felt the clamps lock on and snug tight. Darkness fell across the forward windows as they were drawn into the cradle.

He was a little puzzled. The usual flood of orders, directives and paperwork from Fleet had included a general reassignment order for the *Cornuelle*, attaching the light cruiser to the *Tecaltan* battle group. There had been no sign of their original orders to report to Toroson. The promotions and other personnel assignment papers had not reappeared either.

Very odd, Hadeishi thought, but he was relieved enough not to question the Gods of the Fleet. *Not right now at least.*

Ship-to-ship chatter between the launch pilot and traffic control on the DN-120 *Tehuiā* was quiet and professional, never rising above a soothing murmur. The launch trembled and then all vibration ceased as the maneuvering engines shut down. Hadeishi sat quietly, letting his crewmen do their jobs, savoring the idle moment. He was uncomfortably aware of burn marks around the boat airlock and panels patched back into place with a hand welder. The decking under his feet was badly discolored. *Ah*, he remembered, *we must have used the launch at Argentosonae, when we ambushed the Megair attacking the mining station. Every man with a weapon was needed that day.*

The memory was already tinged with melancholy.

The lock cycled open, environmental lights shining green, and Hadeishi unfastened his shock harness before kicking out into the tube leading onto the Fleet dreadnaught. Two Marines in shipside duty dress were waiting, arms presented. The men flanked a young, blonde *Sho-i* with fine-boned European features. She bowed gracefully as Hadeishi swung out into gravity, both feet landing solidly on the 'welcome mat' inside the reception bay.

"Commander Hadeishi? Welcome aboard the *Stonesmasher*. I am Ensign Huppert."

The *Chu-sa* bowed in return, taking care to keep his face expressionless. He was rather surprised for the *Sho-i* to greet him in Norman, rather than Admiralty Japanese. Despite the dissonance between expectation and reality, he showed no reaction.

"A pleasure, Ensign. I understand a Fleet general staff meeting is scheduled? I would like to report to my division commander and, if possible, tender my regards to Admiral Villeneuve."

"Of course, sir." Huppert bowed again. "There is a gathering of the battle group officers underway—though I must tell you it is not a staff meeting. You should be able to find Captain Jamison—he's senior cruiser division commander—there, as well as the Admiral."

The young woman gestured Hadeishi into a waiting tube-car. The Marines were already gone—a light cruiser commander did not rate an escort, not on a fast dreadnaught carrying a Fleet Admiral. Huppert sat opposite, hands clasped on her knees.

For a moment, Hadeishi considered starting a conversation. The ensign seemed personable enough to respond in kind, but something—a queer, itchy sensation along his spine—bade him sit quietly, staring without focus at the wall of the tube-car. Huppert did not seem to mind, her pleasant half-smile remaining in place during the ten-minute transit the length of the massive ship.

The ensign stood just before the car slid noiselessly to a halt. "Flag Officer's country, commander." Huppert was not smiling openly, but her grass-green eyes twinkled in anticipation. "The Admiral does not believe in stinting as a host, particularly not when his line commanders are aboard."

The tube-car door slid up and the sound of odd, lilting, music flooded into the car. Hadeishi stepped out onto the transit platform, one eyebrow rising uncontrollably. Music—live music; he could distinguish a slightly out-of-tune cello behind the most vibrant sound—was playing not too far away. The acoustic paneling in the ship corridors deadened most of the flowing music, but the piece was unmistakable.

"This is Berlioz's *Messe Solennelle*?"

Huppert nodded. "Very astute, commander. The Admiral believes shipboard service should not be . . . cheerless."

"Live musicians?" Hadeishi followed the ensign, though he nearly missed a step when he realized the floor was covered with rich, heavy carpets. The usually plain shipboard bulkheads were covered with thin, filmy patterned hangings. Actual oil paintings, if the unforgettable aroma of linseed, turpentine and canvas was not produced by a sensorium, were spaced every ten meters or so. The illustrations seemed garish and overdone to his eye, filled with fantastically overripe flowers, rosy-cheeked peasants and bucolic scenes drawn from a rural milieu centuries dead.

"The Admiral approves of the men's hobbies. He supports those with talent—talent beyond simple duty, of course. The flagship maintains an orchestra for the men's entertainment."

The itchy feeling grew worse. Huppert paced into a doorway and the music was drowned by the clatter and chime of crystal, people talking carelessly and the rustling of hundreds of men and women in freshly starched dress uniforms. Hadeishi slowed half a step, one hand automatically adjusting his collar and the line of his jacket. His first thought, seeing so many officers in one place, was to wonder how deep in the *Tehuiā* they were. *Would a Khaid antimatter cluster be stopped by ship's armor before incinerating every line captain in this room? Are their executive officers here too? Who is standing watch on their ships? Ensigns and midshipmen?*

"Commander?" Huppert turned and beckoned him through the doorway. Mustering himself, Hadeishi stepped into the officer's mess, slightly narrowed eyes taking in the field of battle. *I will never begrudge my uniform allowance again,* he thought, stricken morose by the gaudy sight before him. *And I will listen to my dear Koshō and buy a very, very nice, custom-tailored dress uniform. As soon as I can.*

The flag officer's ward room of the *Stonesmasher* was very large—probably the size of one of the assault shuttle bays on the *Cornuelle*—and besides an elevated stage holding nearly an entire orchestra, more than a hundred officers mingled in the open space. Long rows of tables, positively glowing with silver, crystal and porcelain, were waiting for the dinner gong to sound. A vaulted roof seemed to soar overhead, filled with chandeliers and a gilded, rococo ceiling. Clouds of tabac smoke coiled up, vanishing into hidden vents.

I do hope that ceiling is a holocast, Hadeishi thought, coming to a numb halt beside Huppert.

Huppert was speaking quietly into his ear, trying to point out who was who, but one singular fact had already impressed itself on the *Chu-sa.*

He was the only Nisei officer—the only non-European *face*—he could see in the entire room. No one seemed to have noticed his arrival, for which he was now unaccountably grateful.

"An interesting staff meeting . . ." he started to say.

"As I said, Commander . . ." Huppert's fingertips pressed against his arm. "Not so much a staff meeting, but the Admiral's Dinner. Once a week the Admiral likes to have all of his ship commanders over to dine, have a few drinks, get to know each other. Very convivial."

"I see." Hadeishi tried not to move his head, but his eyes flitted along the walls, searching for the quiet, unassuming presence of security officers from the Mirror, or a *nauallis* or anything which might make this loud, cheerful gathering look less like the kind of treason which gave loyal Fleet captains ulcer-ridden, sleepless nights. *I must already be on camera, too.*

A ringing tone cut through the murmur, and everyone turned towards the tables.

"But after the meal, you must make yourself known to Flag Captain Plamondon. He's the Fleet operations officer and the Admiral's exec." The pretty ensign took him by the elbow and began to guide Hadeishi towards his seat. Her hand was very firm.

A Fleet cargo shuttle, solar-flare blazon of the *Cornuelle* visible on the side doors, steam hissing up from triangular wings, rolled to a halt in the cavernous space of a groundside hangar. Ground crew jogged out, heads down, to slide chocks fore and aft of the wheels. A gangway levered down, and the hatchway swung up.

Shoi-i Daniel Smith swung down the ladder, sweat springing out across his grinning pale face, and he went immediately down on one knee and kissed oil-stained concrete. "Terra firma," he declared, wiping his mouth and standing up. "Almost one g, too!"

"Aren't you supposed to be our commanding officer?" Marine *Heicho* Felix slid down the ladder and took a careful look around the hanger, one hand on the stock of her assault rifle, before relaxing a little. Satisfied the immediate area was clear of danger—the hangar looked like every other Fleet maintenance facility she'd ever seen—she gestured Helsdon and his technicians down out of the aircraft. "Take a little care, *kyo*."

"Here?" Smith waved a negligent hand around, indicating the fuel gurney being wheeled out by two Fleet crewmen, the mammoth shape of an assault shuttle filling most of the hangar, and the exposed wooden ribs of the huge building. "We can breathe the air, we're in the middle of a Fleet base with three brigades of combat troops around us, I have my medband on . . ." He held up a skinny, fish-belly-pale wrist to show her. ". . . and . . . Lord of Hosts, what is that divine *smell*?"

Felix turned slowly, brown eyes narrowed, and tucked thick, black hair behind her ear. There *was* a smell—pungent, oily, sharp as a knife, tart with something familiar . . .

"Oh. Oh oh." Smith moved spasmodically forward, a glazed look in his eyes. "I smell roasting meat, *Heicho*. I smell . . . barbacoa! With chíles and onions! Real, fresh onions. Are those *tripas*? Someone's cooking real food!"

Felix took hold of his collar, dragging the midshipman back. Smith was easily a head taller than Felix, but he didn't work out in the *Cornuelle*'s gymnasium every single day, without fail. On a small ship like the *Henry R.*, a great deal of work was done in low or zero-g conditions. Fleet didn't bother to lay in grav-decking in every crew space, only in primary crew quarters, the mess and exercise spaces. The Marine had no trouble keeping her officer from charging across the flight line.

"I see the barbecue pit, *kyo*." Felix pointed with the flash-suppressing muzzle of her assault rifle. Unlike the lightweight shockrifle the Marines toted shipside, the *Heicho* was now sporting an ugly, black-finished 'top-deck'-style Macana 8mm assault rifle. Groundside, Felix didn't have to worry about punching a hole in the ship and letting her air out. The Macana was slung under her right arm on a shortened strap, one long clip in the magazine and another taped reversed to the first. A Nambu automatic was tucked under her other arm, held close by the gunrig strapped over her body armor. "Do you see what's between here and there?"

"Nothing!" Smith made a face, trying to brush off the Marine's hand.

At that moment, a thundering, earth-shaking roar split the air. Hot wind rushed past the hangar doors and a huge shape swept past, throwing a split-second shadow on the runway. Heat from the afterburners of another Fleet shuttle washed over them, making Smith turn away.

Felix pushed up her combat goggles and gave the midshipman an arch look. "Nothing. Of course."

"Sir?" Chief Machinist's Mate Helsdon, hands clasped behind his back, caught Smith's eye. "Would you like me to see about the replacement parts we need?"

Smith sighed, gave Felix an apologetic shrug and nodded. "Yes. Yes, I would."

Turning his back on the open hangar door and the shimmering, miragelike vista of the officer's recreational complex squatting between the two runways, Smith flipped open a handpad from his duty jacket. "All right, *Sho-sa* Koshō would like us to tick off two priorities while we're groundside." He nodded to Helsdon. "You've got chief engineer Isoroku's list of replacement parts for the ship. I doubt local industry is up to fabricating most of this stuff, but maybe you can cadge some from the base supply officer. Or . . . there's a note here from the commander saying a near-space development effort is underway at the port. A coalition of local *kujenates*—whatever those are—and the Imperial Development Board are working on deploying a series of communications satellites in orbit. *Sho-sa* Koshō says they're behind schedule, so hopefully you can swindle them out of whatever we need."

"Understood, sir." Helsdon had his own copy of the list, but he was being very polite. "All that will take some time—we're low on virtually every kind of material, machine part, and friable tool. When should we meet back here?"

Smith looked at his chrono, frowned, then looked out the hangar doors at the coppery afternoon sky.

"Local time is thirteen-hundred, sir." Felix had already adjusted her chrono to show both shiptime and groundtime.

"We'll be making more than one trip . . ." Smith sniffed the air, then shook his head mournfully. "But until we know the lay of the land, we'll bunk on the ship. We meet back here at nineteen-hundred, gentlemen. *Heicho*, send two of your men with Helsdon, the rest will come with us."

"Aye, aye." Felix motioned at two of the Marines in her fireteam. "Tyrell, Cuizmoc; keep the engineers from having their shoes stolen."

"Right." Smith thumbed through his list—direct from the *Chu-sa*—and grimaced. "Where the devil are we going to get all of these things? Five thousand kiloliters of purified water, four hundred kilos of wheat flour (or equivalent), twelve hundred square meters of cotton sheeting, sixty kilos of chile powder, three hundred square meters of nonskid decking, a hundred twenty kilos of chocolatl powder, a ton of potatoes . . ."

Felix was waiting patiently, a slight smile on her elfin face, when the midshipman glared at her in a rather plaintive way.

"Why do you look so smug, *Heicho*?"

"Why, sir, haven't you ever been shopping before?"

Smith made a face and ignored her while scanning through the rest of the list. By the time he was done, his foul mood had evaporated. "Good, we can divide up the rest of this. You take the dry goods and mess supplies, while I see about arrangements for shore leave for the crew."

Felix's eyes narrowed slightly. *Of course you'd be glad to arrange for the hotels—fresh sheets, convenient brothels, home-cooked food, hot water—for the crew. And make sure to see they're of proper quality . . . men!*

"I'm sorry *kyo*, but you're the officer on mission and you have the Fleet scrip to pay for all the things we need. I'm not authorized to sign for purchases, just here to make sure brigands don't cosh you on the head and drag you off to toil in a salt mine. Sir."

Smith gave her a fulminating look for a long moment, then shrugged in defeat. "Fine. Let's go. You lead, bam-bam."

"Aye, *kyo*!" Felix gestured for her two remaining Marines to take point and tail, then plucked her own handpad out of the other holster slot in her gunrig. Humming tunelessly to herself, the Marine thumbed up a map of the spaceport and surrounds. She had already marked a number of locations on the holodisplay. "If it pleases you, *kyo*, we will want to hire a ground truck first . . ."

Hadeishi handed off his jacket, replete with service ribbons, two small medals and what seemed—now—to be a very paltry amount of gold braid, to old Yejin, his steward, as the door chimed.

"Enter." The *Chu-sa* was exhausted, but he managed a tiny smile for *Sho-sa* Susan Koshō when she stepped into the outer room of his office. The slim, perfectly coiffed executive officer's nostrils flared slightly to find her commander in shirtsleeves, but then she caught sight of his face and stiffened like a sword blade drawn ringing from the sheath.

"Ship's status?" Hadeishi unsealed the collar of his shirt and sat down on one of the low cushions lining the wall of his stateroom.

"Nominal." Koshō gave him a sharp look. "Circumpolar orbit, as directed by squadron traffic control. Crew is on stand-down and there are two shuttles groundside, arranging for resupply."

"Yejin-*san*, bring us something to drink. Sake, I think. If there is any Nadaizumi left."

The steward's face crumpled like an apple left out in the sun for several weeks. He bowed very deeply. "I beg your forgiveness, mi'lord . . ." His voice was raspy and thin.

Hadeishi sighed openly. "What do we have to drink?"

"A little rice beer, mi'lord." The steward had the look of a man forced to strangle his own child. "There is tea . . ."

"There is always tea," the *Chu-sa* said dryly. "The beer will do. *Sho-sa*, sit."

Koshō knelt, somehow managing to suggest gracefulness even in a Fleet duty uniform. Hadeishi watched her with leaden eyes, finding himself nearly overcome with weariness. The ringing sound of crystal and china was still echoing in his ears. The steward returned and placed drinking bowls and two hand-sized ceramic jars on a low table between them.

Showing admirable restraint, Koshō said nothing while the old man filled their cups and then disappeared through the doors into the main part of the captain's cabin. The battle-steel doors were painted with a traditional scene of mountains and cloud, but the gritty whine of track motors in need of replacement spoiled the illusion of rice-paper *shoji* sliding closed.

"I was not able to meet with Admiral Villeneuve," Hadeishi said, after clearing his throat with a long cold swallow. He set the cup down very carefully, then clasped his hands. "I did make the acquaintance of Fleet Captain Jean-Martel Plamondon, operations officer of battle group *Tecaltan*. I requested reassignment for *Cornuelle* so we could continue on to the advanced fleet base at Toroson for a complete refit."

Susan waited, her sharp black eyes intent.

"My request was refused." Hadeishi let out a breath. "I then requested access to the Fleet mobile repair dock traveling with the battle group, as well as emergency resupply for our munitions and stores directly from 88's magazine ships."

Koshō's smooth, unmarked forehead developed a slight, but noticeable, line—no more than the shadow of a samisen string running up from the bridge of her nose.

"Flag Captain Plamondon also declined this request. He felt . . ." Hadeishi closed his eyes. When he opened them again, they were glittering with repressed anger. "He felt such a small ship as the *Cornuelle*—'really no more than an overweight destroyer'—could be provided for by local sources of resupply and provision."

"What—" Koshō fell silent. Her porcelain skin flattened to china white. "Your pardon, *Chu-sa*. I was not aware the industrial base of Jagan was advanced enough to replenish our ship-to-ship missiles, beam capacitors, shuttle engine cores, shipskin . . ."

Hadeishi nodded, lifting and dropping one hand in an admission of defeat. "I know."

"Was there an . . . explanation for these . . . rejections?" Koshō's voice was brittle. Like her captain, the executive officer of the *Cornuelle* was bone tired in a way no wakemeup could relieve.

"Yes. Battle group *Tecaltan* will only be in-system for a few more days. There is some situation on Keshewān that requires their presence. Villeneuve has decided to break orbit with all due speed. Given this operational situation, the Fleet tender cannot remain, nor the magazine ships . . ."

"We could cross-deck—" Koshō forced herself to silence, a brief expression of horror flitting across her face. Hadeishi felt his humor revive slightly. The number of times the *Sho-sa* had interrupted him in the last three years could be counted on one hand, perhaps on one finger.

"I know. A hold-to-hold transfer from one of the *Verdun*-class magazine ships would take less than a day to resupply our entire manifest. It's not like we require a dreadnaught's loadout of shipkillers! Plamondon dismissed the suggestion. He implied they were on a tight schedule."

The *Sho-sa*'s upper lip twitched infinitesimally. Hadeishi almost smiled.

"You have no idea, Susan. No idea. I should have been comm-threaded."

"What do you mean?" Koshō seemed taken aback. "What else did he say?"

"Very little. The Fleet captain had no time to speak with me. The dessert course was of far greater interest to him."

"Dessert?"

Hadeishi nodded, smoothing down his beard. "*Thai-so* Villeneuve was hosting the weekly Admiral's Dinner for his ship commanders—but you have never, ever seen something like this. Nearly a hundred officers, I would guess. A banquet! Everyone seemed to be very cheerful. The music was quite good . . ."

"A party?" Koshō was fighting to hide open incredulity.

"Yes. A very odd party. That is the most troubling thing." Hadeishi rubbed his eyes, then gave her a considering look. Susan Koshō had served as his executive officer for three years. During all that time she had been reliable, professional and sometimes impossibly calm. The *Chu-sa* had known from the first day she'd come aboard—back when they'd been on the old *Ceatl*—she was an eagle learning to fly down among the accipiters and falcons. He did not mind being a hawk, and took considerable quiet pride in lending this fledgling the benefit of his hard-won experience.

Hadeishi knew he had some talent for command, a skill for finding the right course through the chaos of battle. He came alive when the alert klaxon sounded, when the ship shuddered into high-grav drive, when the shockframe crushed him into his command station. Out of the crucible, he was average, no more or less than any other captain serving in the Fleet. He would never earn the notice of his superiors, never gain a battlecruiser command. He had laid aside dreams of captaining a dreadnaught or a strike carrier years ago. There was more contentment to be found in his books, in his father's old musical recordings, in the quiet efficiency of the crew he'd built with such care.

But Susan . . . she never discussed her family, clan, or lineage. *But you cannot hide the eagle forever among the hawks. Blood shows. Plumage becomes unmistak-*

able in time. Then she would ascend into more rarified air, into the realms where she—Hadeishi was sure—had been born and raised. *Where she belongs right now. Where . . . where she should have been months ago.*

Hadeishi struggled to keep his face politely composed.

"Susan, we've been on frontier patrol for two years. This is the closest we've been to the core systems in all that time. While Plamondon might be . . . hasty, one of his adjutants was more forthcoming. There is a courier boat heading back to Toroson tomorrow. I think . . . you should be on that boat, using some of your leave time. See Anáhuac again, taste clean air. See your parents."

Leave this poor old ship before my . . . foolishness . . . taints your record.

The shadow on Koshō's forehead cut into a knife blade edge. She took the still-filled cup cradled in her hands and placed it very carefully on the table. Her lips thinned down to pale rose streaks. "*Chu-sa*, what troubled you about the Admiral's Dinner on the *Tehuiā*? Is our ship in danger?"

"I do not know." Hadeishi looked away, unable to meet her eyes. They were filled with concern. *Sometimes the eagle forgets the mountain peaks, comes to believe it too is a hawk. What follows then? Calamity.*

"What did you see?" Koshō turned her wrist, activating her comm-band and preparing to call the bridge.

"There is no danger at this moment, *Sho-sa*. Nothing overt." He motioned for her to turn off the band. "You won't take leave?"

Koshō shook her head, straight, raven-black hair rustling across her shoulders.

Very well. Hadeishi was sad to feel relief. *Mitsuharu, you've become a selfish old man.*

"I sat to dinner with close to sixty captains. Many of them had brought their executive officers, aides, adjutants. Battle group 88 general staff were well represented, including the Admiral and his flag captains. In all those number, I do not believe I saw a single officer of rank who was not of European extraction. No Nisei, no Méxica, no Mixtecs. A sea of pink faces and light hair. I cannot think such a thing happened by accident."

Koshō sat back, openly troubled. "None of us? An entire squadron of *gaijin* dispatched to the Rim?"

"And something else"—Hadeishi turned his cup around in his hand—"which worries me more, given our bitter experience of the last two years. None of the officers I spoke to—and truthfully, I did not have time to canvass them all—had served on the Rim before."

"But . . ." Susan put her hands on her knees. "They've some combat experience? Somewhere? Against the Kroomākh? Or the Ma'hesht?"

Hadeishi shook his head. "I don't know. It seemed not."

"An entire squadron of inexperienced commanders? Without so much as a single Nisei or Méxica commander among them?" Koshō stared at him in horror. "Who let *that* happen? Fleet would never do such a thing . . ." Her voice trailed off.

"Something is going on," Hadeishi said, relieved to voice the fear plain in her face. "Fleet has to have arranged this. For a purpose."

"*Kyo* . . . we're not making the jump to Keshewān with them, are we?" Susan's lips were turning white. "I'll tell Isoroku to disable to main drive—some kind of flux bottle failure—that should gain us a week at least. I can send a t-relay message . . ."

Hadeishi raised a hand. He did not want to know *who* she planned to contact. *Some radiant faces should remain hidden in the clouds.*

"No need." The *Chu-sa* squared his shoulders, hands on his knees. "We have new orders—to maintain station here at Jagan, in support of the 416th Arrow Knight motorized infantry regiment, which is being deployed groundside to 'protect Imperial interests.' I'm not sure Captain Plamondon realized he was doing us a favor. I gained the distinct impression he was pleased to get rid of us."

Ha! He was horrified to be associated with me, even in such a distant capacity.

Koshō started to breathe again. "Can he be so blind?"

"Perhaps." Hadeishi shrugged. "The *gaijin* are happiest surrounded by their own people. Indeed . . . well, who am I to say what the Grand Duke Villeneuve thinks of all this? I am simply relieved our faithful old ship will not have to make another hyperspace transit before Isoroku can effect repairs."

Koshō regained her usual imperturbable calm. She stiffened as if on report. "The engineering staff will review the repair schedules, *Chu-sa*. We have already found some sources of spare parts and repair materials. At least—*at least*—we will be able to replenish stores and non-recyclable goods."

"Good." Hadeishi's eyes crinkled up in a tired smile. "And I can get some rest."

"Hai, *Chu-sa*. We can all rest a little." Koshō stood, guessing her captain was near the end of his tether.

Hadeishi felt as if the last microliter of strength had drained from him, but there was a little taste of relief to come. *Perhaps*, he thought, *I will get a chance to walk under the open sky, see a place I have not seen before.* His eyes strayed to the door of his study. *Perhaps they have music here I have never heard . . .*

"Oh, one matter has come up, *Sho-sa*." Hadeishi unfolded himself from the cushion and stepped to a working desk folded down from the wall. He picked up a cream-colored envelope and passed it to the *Sho-sa*, who took the letter, a little taken aback. "The ship has been tendered an invitation. To a party."

Koshō opened the envelope, rubbing slick parchment between her fingertips. "This is real paper . . ." She turned opened the sheet inside, eyebrows rising to see a flowing hand in vibrant green ink. "My dear captain Hadeishi," she read. "I am entertaining the Imperial Prince Tezozómoc, son of the Light of Heaven, long may he reign, at my estate in the suburbs of Parus on Thursday night. I would be delighted if you and some of your officers could attend. Grace of God, Mrs. Greta Hauksbee Petrel."

Susan looked up, faintly alarmed. "There is an Imperial Prince *here*?!"

Hadeishi put on a very strict face. "You are best suited for this task, *Sho-sa* Koshō. Take those junior officers who would benefit from rubbing elbows with the mighty and a security detachment of your choosing."

"I am best suited?" Koshō's dark eyes flashed dangerously. "How so? Am I expected to make appropriate smalltalk with the Light of Heaven?"

"You've training I lack, Susan." Hadeishi wondered if he'd pushed her a little too far. "And display a full dress uniform far better. Go on, *Sho-sa*. We've a great deal of work to do."

Giving him another sharp look—not a glare, to be sure, but something close—Koshō bowed and left. Hadeishi sighed, rubbing his eyes again, and stumbled through the hatchway into his sleeping cabin. Yejin had turned down the coverlet on his tatami and set the lights on a steadily darkening sleep cycle. Faintly, a recording of waves breaking on the shore at Sasurigama played. A discerning ear could pick out the sound of branches creaking in the night wind.

The *Chu-sa* stared at the door to the bathroom for a long moment, then gave up on the thought. *Too tired. I'll take a long shower in the morning. We can afford the water entropy—we'll have our supplies replenished within the week . . .* Shedding the rest of his uniform, he crawled into bed. Hadeishi was asleep within moments of his head touching the rice-husk pillow.

A little later, the steward stepped quietly into the bedroom, folded up the crumpled uniform to be cleaned and pressed, and shifted the sheets to cover Mitsuharu's chest. Yejin scowled, face nearly invisible in the fading light, thick fingers brushing across a fresh hole in the cotton sheet. There were others, carefully mended, but the fabric was nearly translucent with wear.

THE IMPERIAL DEVELOPMENT BOARD WAREHOUSE
SOBIPURÉ SPACEPORT

Chief Machinist's Mate Helsdon thumbed the ident panel of a crate marked with Fleet colors and raised an eyebrow in interest as the contents listed themselves. "Microcell power units, six dozen? These will fit in our field equipment and shuttles. You don't need them?"

"Already replaced." The shop foreman shrugged, waving his hand at the wall of shipping containers the Fleet engineer was examining. "They sent us sixteen satellites for a first-tier global information grid, along with replacement parts to cover five years of attrition and the shuttles to place them in orbit. Ten of the satellites failed within a week of going operational, so then they sent us another sixteen—but of a different model!"

Helsdon nodded, bending down to examine the bottommost crate of a dangerously tall stack. Despite the efforts of his shipsuit to adapt to the climate, he had to wipe sweat out of his eyes before he could read the manifest. "Sensor relays, type nineteen. Are these in good shape? We could use hundreds of them . . . they run our automatic compartment doors."

"Like I said," the foreman chuckled, lank dark hair tied back behind his head in a ponytail. Watery blue eyes glinted with amusement. "This *whole wall* is redundant material. Small equipment power cells, replacement comm panels and nodes, synchro-tracking lasers, the works! The development board director wants me to surplus the whole lot to the slicks as an economic stimulus project. But between you and me, Helsdon-*tzin*, I'd really rather *trade* for something I can use."

"Trade?" Helsdon frowned, fiddling with the environmental controls on his shipsuit. Normally, the temperature regulators built into the millimeter-thick fabric under his uniform shirt and pants kept him nice and cool. The shop foreman didn't seem to mind the heat—he wasn't even sweating. "What kind of equipment do you need?"

"Well," the foreman frowned, "what I really need is a whole 'nother cargo shuttle—the humidity here breeds a bacterium capable of metabolizing hexacarbon—and if I had five or six hundred Macana auto-rifles and ten thousand rounds of 8mm caseless, I could raise the cash to buy one . . ." He raised a placating hand at Helsdon's grimace. "But! But . . . I've no desire to hand the slicks something that will wind up aimed at me, so the *real* thing I could use is whatever scrap metal you might have on hand."

"Scrap?" Helsdon gave up on not sweating and feeling miserably hot. "We've suffered some battle damage. We planned to dump the wreckage . . ."

"That," said the foreman with a broad grin, "is exactly the kind of trade goods I can use."

"So," Helsdon said, scratching his jaw and turning on an earbug channel to the ship. *Thai-i* Isoroku would be interested in this bit of bartering. "How many square meters of hexacarbon steel are you looking for?"

THE PETREL ESTATE
DISTRICT OF THE CLAW-POLISHERS, PARUS

Despite *Chu-sa* Hadeishi's suggestion that she attend the Legation party in a traditional *furisode*-style kimono, Koshō stepped out of her groundcar in a straight, knee-length black silk dress. Conceding a non-Fleet, civilian occasion, she did not pin up her hair. She also dispensed with her usual command bracelet, settling for a comm-thread disguised by foundation and blush powder on her cheek. A *chevalier*-style jacket disguised a palm-sized shockpistol. Two silver bracelets obscured her medband.

Rain threatened, charging the air with the sharp smell of imminent thunder. The sky over Parus was clogged with fat, dark clouds as night advanced. By the time her car was within sight of the estate, Koshō decided to get out and walk. Strings of globe-lights atop the walls gave her an unmistakable heading. A great crowd of locals milled about at the edge of the security perimeter. An instant festival had sprung up on the sidewalks, complete with carts and canopies, and vendors selling steaming drinks, roasted meat, and confections of all kinds. The peculiar cinnamon smell of the Jehanans mingled with wood smoke and boiling tea in the sweltering twilight.

Fleet ID and the invitation passed her through to an ivy-covered gate. The mansion sprawled within a rectangle of crumbling red-brick walls. The one- and two-story buildings themselves looked quite old to Susan's eye, but she couldn't tell if this was by design or circumstance. The customs of the rich often ran counter to what she considered common sense.

A stream of party-goers crossing an ornamental garden carried her towards the main house. Servants were waiting to take coats, hats, ornamental cloaks, and umbrellas beneath the shelter of an imposing entranceway flanked by tall granite statues. The figures were Jehanan, bulky, muscled bodies carrying the lintel of the doorway on their shoulders. Koshō made a face at the overwrought tableau as she passed into the vestibule, a very small purse in hand.

Beyond the entryway, the main, hexagonal hall of the house rose towards a lofty ceiling circumscribed by a mezzanine-style balcony. Old-style chandeliers supporting clusters of shimmering paper lanterns hung down on long cables. Dozens of slow-moving fans stirred the air. The wavering light, reflecting across the ribbed vault of the roof, reminded Susan of sunlight dancing on the walls of a sea cave.

She guessed there were nearly a thousand people packed into the room, and found a section of wall to stand beside, out of the press of traffic. Humidity and constant noise enveloped her, pressing tight against her flesh. Within a heartbeat, a servant appeared before her with a platter of drinks. Politely, Susan took one—something amber-colored, which she hoped was beer—and waved him on.

Interesting, she thought, scanning the multitude of human and alien faces. *Not as disturbing as the Admiral's Dinner, but telling in its own way*. She could pick out only a handful of Fleet officers—the white dress uniforms were hard to miss among the splashy colors of the natives or the rich garments of the civilians—but there were quite a few groundpounders in evidence. As she expected, they formed their own reefs of dark olive uniforms amid the sea of civilians. Koshō judged most of them to be of Mixtec extraction, if the profusion of strong noses, mahogany skin and visible tattoos was any guide. . . . *or Indian*, she corrected herself, spying a tall infantry officer with a spade-shaped, belt-length yellow beard, sharp nose and turban wandering past.

The drink proved to be a passable lager, but far too warm for her taste. Another passing tray won the glass back. Koshō found herself considering elaborate tortures for *Chu-sa* Hadeishi.

I do not like parties, she remembered. *And this is a very lively, but disorganized party.* Worse, the training of her childhood nagged at her conscience. *You should introduce yourself properly to the host and hostess.*

Her disgust at feeling guilty about proper protocol must have shown on her face. A middle-aged human, a European with short, sandy blond hair, moved into her field of view. "Surely the beer isn't that poor . . ." he started to say, then paused with a startled look on his face.

Koshō realized she was considering him in the same way she scrutinized the unsatisfactory work of junior ratings. *Not polite, ko-ko!* A voice very much like her grandmother echoed out of memory. *Say hello. Introduce yourself. Even a* gaijin *deserves so much.*

"Your pardon, sir," Susan said, very stiffly. She offered a very small bow. No more than required by common courtesy. "Lieutenant Commander Susan Koshō, IMN *Henry R. Cornuelle.*"

"Really?" The man's fine-boned face lit with surprised delight. He bowed in return, rather more deeply than necessary. "How unexpected! What brings you to Jagan? You know . . ."

The familiar tone in his voice touched off a flood of nausea. *I feel trapped*, she realized, *eyes flicking from side to side. There are too many people here. This room is too big. Those windows are open. Why is this person talking to me?*

Without another word, she turned on her heel and made her way back through the latest arrivals. Everyone she passed seemed appallingly cheerful. Overhead, on the mezzanine, a troupe of native musicians began tuning up their instruments, filling the air with an atonal wailing and clashing sound. The Jehanan nobles present lifted their heads in interest. A hissing and clicking undercurrent to the sound of human voices rose.

Puzzled and surprised, Johann Gemmilsky, once the Librarian of the refinery ship *Turan* stared at her retreating back. ". . . I was just wondering how Captain Hadeishi was doing . . ." His voice trailed off in dismay. "Good to meet you in person!"

Shaking his head, Gemmilsky turned around, a tumbler of *vladka* between thumb and forefinger. "Very disappointing," he sighed. "Quite a striking woman."

His eye fell upon two brawny Jehanan tribal chiefs, flat, spadelike heads wrapped in unusual red, purple and magenta *haylan*. They were deep in discussion with a tiny, old Méxica woman in a black shawl and traditional beaded dress. "Hello! A pair of Arachosian nabobs come down from the hills. . . . Now that is interesting. . . . I wonder if they've brought strings of sprinters for sale?"

The Pole took a quick swig of his *Chernei Gyooz*, nodded genially to a chattering crowd of Lencolar Sisters pressing around him and began circulating towards the chieftains with commerce on his mind.

Koshō stepped out into the garden with a sense of enormous relief. She had not realized how hot and close the hall had become. Even the still-warm night air was a relief. Walking quickly away from the servants in the entryway, she dabbed the sides of her neck with a cloth. *I never sweat! Am I falling ill?* She realized her fingers were trembling.

Concerned, she checked her medband, which showed little but calm green lights. Her heart rate was well above normal, but everything else was fine. *Perfectly healthy. What is going on?*

Koshō turned, looking back at the dazzling lights, and saw she'd automatically followed a bricked footpath winding through ornamental hedges of native flowers and imported fruit trees. Lemon, pomegranate and hibiscus were thriving in the thick, humid air.

Susan stepped back to the edge of the porch, trying to make herself re-enter the house. The atonal wailing of the orchestra had faded away, replaced by a sprightly, soaring sound like the wind rushing through golden aspens.

"This is their music?" she said aloud, surprised by the clean, clear sound. The alien instruments changed pitch and tone, now evoking a rushing freshet cascading over mossy stone. She could feel the vibrations tremble in her skin, almost in the bone itself. *Oh, Mitsuharu should have come—he would love this!*

At the same moment, Susan became aware of a tight, constricting sensation in her chest. *That's just impossible. I haven't been claustrophobic since I was a little girl.* But the feeling was the same, even worse for the cloud-filled sky above her. *I serve on a tiny Fleet ship every day! So what if there are a thousand people crammed in there, people I don't know, people . . . oh.*

She suppressed a sharp stab of irritation, nostrils flaring, and was filled with relief no one else from the ship was present. Despite the security risk, she'd left her Marine escort with their transport. Koshō had no idea how vigorous the local thieves were, but she assumed there *were* thieves, and three well-armed Marines should be able to defend the groundcar she'd signed out of the Sobipuré motor pool.

Heicho Felix, Susan was sure, would laugh if the imperturbable *Sho-sa* admitted to suffering from 'miner's disease.' She triggered a mood stabilizer from the medband. To appease the *yurei* of her grandmother, she made sure her dress hadn't become stained. She still had her purse. Satisfied with her appearance, Koshō decided to take a leisurely walk through the gardens—which seemed quite beautiful, if difficult to appreciate in the footlights—while her serotonin and endorphin levels evened out.

Perhaps, she allowed to herself, waiting for a gap to open in the stream of garishly dressed civilians passing by, *we were out in the dark for too long. Two years of treading the deck without a friendly shore in sight, dealing with marauders, slavers, angry miners, Megair corsairs, the Khaid . . . No wonder the Chu-sa found the Admiral's dinner party so disturbing.*

Now she was a little concerned, wondering if Hadeishi's report had been overly colored by this same tricky sense of paranoia. Susan considered calling the ship on her comm and having Smith run a racial-source analysis on the battle group personnel lists, and then remembered the communications officer was groundside, seeing about shore-leave housing for the crew.

A strikingly alien-looking creature—something like a jewel-crusted mantis—passed into the house and Koshō stepped onto the tiled walkway before realizing everyone had fallen silent for a reason. The kind of supernal calm which crept upon her in the midst of battle threatened, and she turned to see what was going on.

"Stand aside, ma'am." A very alert Eagle Knight with a craggy face was there, motioning for her to step back. Koshō did so, returning the man's polite nod, and one slick black eyebrow rose in alarm at the scene unfolding behind him.

A slim young man advanced grandly down the walkway, head held high, chest rippling with platinum scales, long dark hair threaded with gold, turquoise silk pantaloons billowing around his ankles, and a maroon cape fringed with clattering jade slung carelessly over one shoulder. Another Eagle Knight clad in the darkest possible civilian clothing was moving just behind his shoulder, wary eyes flickering across the faces of the goggling onlookers.

Behind the young man, a huge crowd of giggling, barely clothed courtesans, jugglers, magicians and smug-looking junior officers spilled from the walkway into the gardens. Koshō blinked, took two steps back and stiffened to attention: the reflexive action of an officer confronted with the queasy horror of higher command authority outside her usual chain of command. Worse, the man was an *Army* officer.

Unmistakably, the Imperial Prince Tezozómoc had arrived.

The prince's party swept past Koshō with a blare of laughter, leaving a cloud of alcohol fumes, stimulant smoke and eye-smarting perfume in their wake. Two junior Army officers bumped into her, then saluted cheerily. The boys were holding up a civilian youth of comparable age, though he was wearing only a blue serape, one sandal and a liberal amount of *octli* liquor. A great deal of shouting followed as everyone tried to crowd into the vestibule.

Servants converged from all directions and Koshō caught a glimpse of a tall, assured-looking woman with black hair slashed with white. She appeared from nowhere and took the prince's hands in greeting. Then the jugglers were in the way, tossing lighted brands through the lines of lights hanging from the ceiling. A cloud of smoke wicked up into the red dome.

"Enough entertainment for me, I think." Susan turned away. Many of the people in the garden flocked to gawk at the prince and she strode quickly towards the vine-covered gate, relieved the prince had neither seen nor recognized her.

That might be embarrassing, she thought, amused. Susan began to grin at the thought, her humor improving. *Assuming he remembers being six years old anymore.*

"*Sho-sa* Koshō?" A vaguely familiar voice called out. Susan looked up and almost laughed aloud. *The monkeys of circumstance are playing tricks tonight.*

A familiar-looking blonde woman of medium height and pleasantly even features was in the archway, bowing and smiling in greeting. A balding servant stood behind her, making a belated, but proper bow.

"Doctor Anderssen," Susan replied, matching the bow. "A pleasant surprise."

"The pleasure is ours, *Sho-sa*. The *Chu-sa* and your crew are well?"

"They are." Susan relaxed a little. Doctor Anderssen had been their guest on the *Cornuelle* during the investigation of certain mysterious events on the planet Ephesus Three. Despite some trying times, the xenoarchaeologist had proved herself circumspect and polite. Koshō approved of her, which was not always the case when civilians were concerned. In the intervening two years, the xenoarchaeologist seemed to have lost a little weight and spent far too much time outside in the wind and sun. She seemed a little uncomfortable in a formal dress. Koshō understood how she felt. "You've just missed meeting Prince Tezozómoc of the Imperial House and all his friends."

"We saw him." Anderssen bowed again, but Susan could see she was hiding a grin. "His arrival delayed ours. We couldn't even cross the street."

Koshō looked out, seeing the traffic had grown much, much worse. A large number of expensive-looking groundcars of Imperial manufacture filled the avenue in front of the mansion. Jehanan drivers were hissing curses at one another and honking their horns. Legation security was trying to clear the traffic, but with little effect.

"There is still time," Susan said, keeping her voice low, "to return to your place of residence and spend a productive evening watching holovee or playing cards."

Anderssen choked back a snort of laughter and covered her mouth. "Thank you for the astute advice, *Sho-sa*, but I received an invitation from the lady of the house and it would be impolite to disappoint her. And . . ." Gretchen sighed, revealing a flash of irritation. ". . . there is someone I am trying to find. I hope he will be here."

"I see." Susan began to feel uneasy again. The blare of the car horns and shouting was beginning to fray her concentration. She tapped her cheek, waking up the comm-thread. "Good luck, Anderssen-*tzin*. I must warn you, however, the mansion is large—and very crowded. Good evening."

"Good evening," Anderssen called after her, obviously puzzled. "Best wishes to . . ."

The rest of the sentence was drowned out by the raspy shouts of Jehanan street vendors. Koshō left the crumbling sidewalk and slid sideways between two battered thirty-year-old Scandia panel trucks. The comm-thread woke to life with a tingle under her jaw.

"Felix, this is Koshō. Where are you?"

Twenty meters ahead, Sho-sa. An alley on your left, behind the cart selling sweetened ices.

Susan pushed against the crowd of natives flowing the other way, making slow going. The Jehanan came in different shapes and sizes, but they all took up a lot of sidewalk. Eventually she passed the cart—bright yellow, festooned with colorful paper banners and enameled masks—and turned into a shadowy opening.

Felix appeared out of the murk, a long field coat doing a poor job of covering her muzzle-down Macana assault rifle. Combat armor bulked beneath a civilian-style mantle. "This way, *kyo*."

"Put that away," Koshō hissed, shaking off her funk. The brisk walk was clearing her head. "Legation security will void themselves to see you waving a cannon around—not to mention the Imperial bodyguards!"

The sight of her security detail shouldn't have changed her mood, but it did. By the time Susan ducked into the back seat and Felix slammed the door closed she was feeling almost normal.

Without instructions, the Marine in the front seat fired up the engine, and immediately they were accelerating down the alley, driving lights illuminating refuse bins and indefinable structures protruding from the buildings looming on either side. Koshō leaned back wearily against the plush leather seats. "*Heicho*, status of security arrangements groundside?"

"Good, *kyo*." Felix turned, peering back over the seat. "Smith-*tzin*'s lined up four or five hotels. We scouted out some bars selling liquor humans can drink. Seems the slicks like their methanol straight, with local alkaloids for flavor. Pure poison for us, of course."

"Slicks?" Susan stared out the window. Buildings dashed past, most of them wooden, with a few crumbling brick edifices thrown in. She'd seen skyscrapers from the window of the shuttle, but out here in the suburbs everything was low and squat and packed closely together.

"The Jehanan, *kyo*. Have you touched one? Their skin is smooth . . . almost like glass."

"Fine." Koshō craned her neck over a little, staring up at the sky. The clouds were low and glowing with the light of the city. "What kind of extraction points do you have on tap? Rooftops? Public parks? Streets?"

"Rooftops are poor, *kyo*. Every single one hosts a laundry, a hostel or some kind of aviary. The locals eat a lot of *skomsh* . . . it's just like chicken." Felix swallowed a laugh, catching the tense expression on her commander's face. "The streets are worse—they use electric trolleys with overhead power lines on all the avenues wide enough for one of our shuttles to touch down. Parks look like our best bet. Smith made sure the hotels he picked are across the street from a nice one. Not too many trees, mostly ornamental shrubs and fountains."

Susan felt combat tires rattle across recessed tracks as they bounced through an intersection. Neon lights over the storefronts reflected from the bracelets on her wrist. "Local situation? How do they feel about the Empire?"

"Hard to tell." Felix shrugged. "Smith-*tzin* says the local holovee is filled with all kinds of the-Empire-is-our-friend propaganda. But on the street, you can tell they don't like us much. They *do* like our quills, though. All the merchants I've dealt with were pretty friendly. It's hard to read their faces. But no one's taken a shot at us yet."

Koshō nodded absently. The sitrep reports forwarded from battle group command related much the same thing. "An undercurrent of resentment exists in the population," they said. "But no open violence." *I think . . . the* Chu-sa *is a little jumpy about Villeneuve's extravagance. He is French. The real issues here are more immediate—and far more routine than an officers' plot.*

"Everyone needs to take care, *Heicho*. Pass the word around to the squad leaders and petty officers to go ones-and-fours when ship's personnel are groundside. And armed." She turned her attention on the Marine, eyes sharp with an orange glow from the sodium lights passing overhead. "But if anyone goes rabbit on me and shoots someone—even a local!—then I will put them out the lock myself."

"Aye, aye!" Felix shifted in her seat uncomfortably. The *Sho-sa* seemed worked up tonight and nervous officers made her uneasy. "Something specific security detail should watch out for?"

"No." Koshō stared out the window again. The crowds on the sidewalks ignored the rain, letting the steady downpour sluice the day's dust from their scales. In the misty night, with the glare of neon in her eyes, they could have been any Saturday-night crowd along the Ginza or around the Tlatelolco. "I suspect I'm worrying for no reason, but everyone's to be on best behavior. No exceptions!"

"Oooh, native tribesmen!" Tezozómoc laughed gaily, barely able to stand. His cloak covered with jadeite lozenges was disconcertingly heavy. He kept listing to one side and having to right himself. His blood buzzed with a delicious tide of *oliohuiqui* and 'little guardian of dreams.' "Legate, which province do these fellows come from?"

Petrel, his hand raised in preparation for formally introducing the prince to the commander of the 416th Imperial Arrow Knight regiment (motorized), halted abruptly, and then turned towards Tezozómoc with a perfectly still face. "Your pardon, mi'lord?"

The prince could see the older man was nonplussed. Tezozómoc could see furtive, hasty thoughts flitting behind the cultured face. *Doesn't the Prince Imperial recognize fellow Imperial officers? Even his putative commander in the 416th? Even though*—the prince felt cold anger welling in his churning stomach—*this same officer has refused this same prince an actual command? Who has slighted this same prince by shunting him into a useless assignment?*

"These black fellows." The prince cheerily waved a mostly full bottle of *Charodei* vodka at the middle officer, a full colonel, who was indeed of Mixtec extraction and therefore possessed of dark, almost chocolatl-colored skin. "Him! Are these some of the . . . the Misa-whatever-dai . . . the barbarians you've been bending my ear about?"

"*Tlacateccatl* Yacatolli is an Imperial Arrow Knight, mi'lord." Petrel's white eyebrows stiffened and Tezozómoc fought to keep a huge bellyful of laughter from bursting out. The old man looked like an owl! The Legate's perfectly groomed face was growing pink around the edges. *Oh oh.* The prince felt even giddier. *He's getting angry! Soon some of those gelled hairs will be out of place!*

The colonel, for his part, had grown dangerously still. Tezozómoc peered at him, a little nauseous at the chance to twit the stone-faced Arrow Knight. *Oh oh, he can't say anything to me! Not the Son of the Light of Heaven, the Prince Imperial! No no. Not in front of so many barbarians and civilians and other witnesses. But I can say whatever I want!*

"Yack-a-toll-ee. Doesn't that mean *snot* in our language? What does it mean in his?"

The colonel twitched, fists clenching. The prince stared at the man's shoulders in delight. The carefully tailored fabric was stretching as every muscle in the man's upper body stiffened in rage. *Will he burst right out of his uniform? Is he wearing underwear? Did he bring any spare? I think he only has one dress uniform, poor bean eater.*

Legate Petrel stepped between the two men, looking down at Tezozómoc with narrowed eyes. The older man had recovered his composure, though the prince could see tiny lines of strain around his eyes. "Mi'lord, perhaps you would care to sit and eat? There is a salon where you and your companions can take your ease, out of the press of the crowd?"

"Of course! My feet hurt—your floor is too hard." Tezozómoc stamped his sandals, making the golden scales covering them clatter on the hardwood parquet. The hall would serve for dancing, eventually, when the buffet tables were cleared away. "Good night, chief of the snots!"

The prince waved at the colonel, who was watching him with slitted, furious eyes from behind a wall of his subordinates. The other Mixtec officers were trying to calm Yacatolli down.

Stupid name for a military officer, Tezozómoc thought, swinging the weighted cape carelessly over his shoulder. Out of the corner of his eye, the prince caught a glimpse of the shorter of his bodyguards ducking aside. Hand-sized jade lozenges whipped past the Skawtsman's face. *He should change it to something that doesn't make everyone snicker. Perhaps I should submit an official memo of recommendation.*

"Are there buttered shrimps dusted with chili powder?" Tezozómoc asked the Legate, following the older man towards a doorway opening off the crowded, sweltering hall. The prince's voice was entirely amiable. "I like those very much."

Petrel nodded, but did not look back, pushing open the doors to an well-furnished room with a bar, overstuffed chairs and a permanent aroma of burned broadleaf tabac and fine liquor. "Of course, mi'lord. I will let the cook know."

Tezozómoc threw himself down in the largest chair, heaved a sigh of relief and then stared quizzically up at his host. "You don't look like a bird. You should change your name too."

The rest of his new friends piled into the room, making the two bodyguards wince with their usual ruckus of noise, banging about, shrieking and general merriment. The Army officers began looting the liquor cabinet.

The prince, seeing no one was paying attention to him for the moment, let out a long, shuddering sigh. His stomach burned, molten stones churning against his intestines. *So many officials and lords and officers.* Tezozómoc closed his eyes tight, feigning weariness, squeezing back tears of frustration. *By Christ Sacrifice, I hate this. I hate them—all of them—and I hate having to wear this stupid costume.*

The hatred he'd seen flashing in Yacatolli's face, at least, had been a welcome change from the usual pity, or curiosity, or contempt. The prince raised his head, wondering if there was any liquor to be had. "Geema, be a dear heart and share some of that wicked-looking red liquid with your poor old prince, will you?"

Parker drained his glass. "Boss . . . are you sure you need to talk to this guy?"

"Yes." Gretchen tried not to sigh and loosened the shawl around her shoulders. The great hall was just getting hotter and closer as more people crowded in. The Jehanan musicians were still playing, but their beautiful efforts were drowned out by drunken voices. "Look, Parker, I know we're supposed to be here on 'vacation' and *technically* I don't have to report to anyone. Not the attaché, not Professor Sú. But we're going to be traipsing all over the north-country, trying to find this . . . place. I would rather play by the rules, if we can. Mrs. Petrel said . . . don't make a face like that!"

The pilot removed the tabac from his mouth and flicked the butt into a nearby planter. After entering the hall they'd tried to reach the banquet tables, but a near-solid wall of Imperial military uniforms blocked any access. The infantry officers were making a serious dent in the Legation catering budget. Then Gretchen had tried to find the hostess, but moving in the crowd was nearly impossible, so the press of humanity had thrown them up in a little alcove where a bastion of potted plants protected a side door.

"Sorry, boss. But look at this place—we're so far down the totem pole we can't even get something to eat. Drink, sure . . . the Embassy lays on some nice locally produced vodka but we'll have to wait *hours* just to say hello to the hostess." He took a long drag from a fresh tabac and let the smoke curl out of his nostrils. "You saw the prince and his posse. He's going to suck up every featherhead within ten klicks to kiss his radiant ass. Doc Sú, the Legate's wife, everyone."

"Parker!" Gretchen made a shushing motion. *It is crowded,* she silently acknowledged. *He's probably right. And finding Professor Sú in this madhouse isn't terribly likely. I don't even know what he looks like.*

Then she grew still, realizing she could probably tell what the senior xenoarchaeologist from the University of Tetzcoco *felt* like. *And if I can feel him, then I could probably find him . . . if I wanted.*

Gretchen looked sidelong at Parker, who was staring moodily at two attractive young women passing by. The pilot looked entirely out of place amid all the finery on display. His going-out shirt, pants and shoes were only the best a junior Company employee could afford. She could see him comparing his appearance to the young bravos circulating in the crowd, and falling short. *We're out of place here. As usual.*

Anderssen looked down at herself. The kimono-style dress was the best the Shimanjin colony had to offer—impeccably tailored, luscious native silk, dark radiant colors—and in comparison to the extravagance of feathers, gold and jade adorning the Prince's companions, about four years out of style. Field crews rarely spent any time far enough in-Empire to be fashionable. Dust and sweat and the minute personal cargo allowances provided by economy spaceliner tickets precluded anything but the necessities. She spread a scarred, muscular hand, frowning. *Not very elegant.*

Gretchen breathed in slowly. *If you find Professor Sú, what then? Will you ask him for permission to root about in the ruins of the ancient Jehanan cities, unsupervised? Looking for something the Company can't even describe or identify?* Being polite, she realized, hating the nagging, pragmatic voice in her head, would only make her job more difficult. *I am supposed to follow the rules,* she thought, but knew the Company really didn't care at all. *They just want me to steal something. Again. Rules are something I'm supposed to follow,* she thought sourly, *when I'm filling out expense reports.*

"You're right, Parker. There's no point to finding him. Let's see if we can swing by the dessert table on our way out . . ."

Standing quietly in the corner of the huge, busy room, a thing in the shape of a man was watching the flood of <cattle|breeding stock|meat> eddy past, stinking of toxin-saturated cooling fluid. It stood quietly in dark, carefully tailored human clothing, presenting a tray of inefficiently constituted raw protein to anyone who passed by. A group of Imperial military officers paused, snatched up handfuls of baked crackers coated with imported soft cheese and caviar, and then moved on.

The Lengian expressed no overt interest in them, and following the strict social conventions of this primitive society, they ignored it in turn. The sower of <disorder|fear|wisdom> was not surprised. It had watched and waited among the humans for many cycles. They were random and filled with the heedless, careless energy of a young, immature species—one which had not yet been culled and set on the straight path—and as such they believed themselves to be favored by the hand of the <breeder|devourer>. *But they will be tested in the fullness,* it thought coldly, without either remorse or antipathy. *Then they will likely perish, for they are a weak, ill-fitting species.*

Another human moved into its field of perception—a tall man with slick blond hair, dressed in the costume of a broker associated with one of the Imperial merchant houses active on Jagan—and the Lengian's attention sharpened. The man—a sub-brain identified him as being *Finnish* in origin, which meant he was from one of the outworld colonies like Vainamoinen—nodded in passing to some other human merchants and struck up a conversation with a cluster of lesser Jehanan nobility who were nervously eyeing the *asuchau* offworlders swarming around them.

Inside the Lengian's human-shaped ears, a cluster of leaf-shaped fronds oriented themselves, swelling the primitive organ's capacity to capture sound, and two of the fingernail-sized sub-brains strung along the creature's spine asserted themselves, capturing the resulting flow of aural data and sorting out dialect, language, intent and meaning.

This one is an Imperial Flower Priest in disguise, the sub-brains submitted to the decision-making cortices. *He is presenting himself as an agent of the exiled Swedish government, probing for possible allies among the native princes. But in truth he serves the Mirror Which Reveals.*

As a whole, the Lengian was aware of the myriad Imperial security organizations, but it was also quite confident in its ability to continue avoiding their notice. Sixty human years had already passed without even the faintest evidence of suspicion on the part of its unknowing hosts. It had been in close proximity to more than one Mirror agent dozens of times without drawing the least attention. *Three hundred human years remain in life-cycle,* one of the sub-brains handling motile-form biological functions reported, eager to show its worth to the whole, *before this form degrades beyond usefulness.*

The Lengian did not think it would need to remain among the humans for so long. *They will be culled soon, even as they measure time. The <guides|executioners> will be affronted by their unregulated breeding.*

The blond human passed close by, eyeing the canapés, but shook its head, smiling, when the Lengian lifted the tray. A faint cloud of pheromones, skin-flakes and exhaled breath washed over the creature and—unseen by human eyes—thousands of pores opened on its simulated human skin and captured the wealth of information so haphazardly scattered to the winds. Dozens of sub-brains immediately set to work dissecting the breakdown of the human's DNA and metabolism.

This shape will be useful, the decision cortices had already resolved. *We will add it to our collection.*

"Timonen!" Another human male approached the blond man, skin oozing poorly metabolized alcohol. "How's the medband business?"

The Lengian remained impassive, watching and waiting. In a day or two, when this shape's normal duties allowed it to leave the Legation, it would find the Finn and make the human useful, for a change, and in an orderly and efficient way.

The two human males were now joined by two females and they all moved away together, chattering mindlessly, looking for more protein and alcohol to metabolize. The Lengian's watery blue eyes followed them for a time, nostrils flared to let threadlike filaments hiding in the dark recesses of the nose practice separating Timonen's smell from that of the herd.

"What a delightful surprise!" A bronzed face appeared between the potted plants. Gretchen felt mildly alarmed to see a group of young Méxica men emerge from the crowd. "Our freshly arrived colleagues! Of whom we've heard so many exciting rumors."

"Hello." Gretchen took them in with a glance and there was a sour taste in her mouth. They were well dressed, for graduate students, and all of them were sporting the University of Tetzcoco *mon*. Despite being freshly shaved, showered and perfumed, she was sure their fingernails were as dirty as hers. *Honorable Doctor Sú's post-docs. Drunk as rabbits under a full moon.* "How do you do?"

"We're doing just fine . . . you're the famously unknown Anderssen?"

"I am." Gretchen felt Parker stiffen behind her. "Doctor Gretchen Anderssen, University of New Aberdeen, forensic xenoarchaeologist . . ."

"A Company pit-rat, you mean." The tall one in front's skin was flushed with sweat. "Come sniffing around our work . . . looking to steal enough for a publication, Anderssen? They don't let you do much *real* work, do they? Shouldn't you be carrying jade for your husband?"

"I think you'd better just step back," Parker said, pushing past Gretchen, who had been struck speechless. "And apologize."

"Parker . . . we're guests here." Anderssen felt her heart start to race and her fingers found the comfortably smooth surface of her medband. Adrenaline churned through her bloodstream. She triggered a calmedown. "I won't disappoint our hostess by starting a brawl. Good evening, gentlemen."

The Méxica spread his arms, blocking their path. He smiled, showing fine white teeth. "We're curious, *Doctor*. I'm sure you've seen *wonders* on the Rim, while you were scurrying here and there, stealing crumbs to take back to Old Mars. Why don't you . . ."

Gretchen felt her breath slow and the room faded a little.

Crepuscular gray light vomited from an ancient doorway, hurling her backwards. She hit sand, tumbled and staggered up. The Sif shockgun was still smoking in her hand, making elaborate curlicues of smoke in the terribly thin air. Someone was shouting, but a howling roar of static filled her ears. Monstrous shapes boiled out of the tunnel, striding forward on countless joined legs, a forest of spike-like tendrils dancing above translucent, half-invisible bodies.

". . . share them with us?" The post-doc jammed his elbow sharply into Parker's chest. Gretchen stepped aside, her face tight and composed, giving Parker room to catch his balance.

"I am here on vacation," she snapped, voice very cold. "A personal guest of Legate Petrel's wife, Greta. If you wish to discuss your work at Fehrupuré with a professional, I advise you to contact the local Company offices." She stepped forward and the tall Méxica, surprised, gave ground. Gretchen swept the rest of them with a scathing look. "Tend to your trenches and alluvial assays, children. Drink less and think about your work more."

Without waiting for them to react, she pushed between two of them on the left. Even as she started to move, Gretchen felt them give way. She'd *known* they would back down. *Known* just these two were too timid to seize her arm, too drunk throw a punch. Reaching behind her, she seized Parker's arm and dragged him through the opening.

She heard a confused shout from behind, but did not look back. An avenue opened in the crowd and she was striding effortlessly through a gyrating, constantly moving throng of brightly dressed people. A path opened before her with the movement of their bodies, a random, confused dance without pattern or form. Parker was trying to say something, but the words felt slow. They failed to reach her attention, which was focused on moving without thought, reacting without contemplation.

Gretchen was in the vestibule, feeling the rain-cooled night wind on their face, when the sharp feeling collapsed, some unimaginable equilibrium disturbed. She felt sweat spring out all over her body and nearly tripped on the step. Her fingers cramped painfully and she released Parker's arm. The pilot was staring at her, eyes wide.

"Mother of Christ . . . damn, boss, that hurts!" The pilot rubbed his arm, wincing. "How . . . how did we get out of there?"

"Never mind. Let's go." Anderssen ducked her head, embarrassed, and hurried out. *Oh, Sister, where did that come from?* Her stomach turned over, knowing too well what had happened. *I thought I'd forgotten all about . . . those things.* "I'm very tired."

"Sure . . ." Parker followed, looking over his shoulder. The gay, cheerful mob filling the hall seemed impenetrable from this vantage. Hundreds of people engaged in drinking furiously, talking nonstop, filling the entire chamber from wall to wall. "How did we . . . ?"

Standing near the buffet tables, Itzpalicue's head rose, eyes narrowed in sudden interest. The old woman stared around warily, ignoring a coterie of Imperial merchants babbling away about rates of exchange and tonnage loads of used groundcars. They were all very pleased with the appetite of the Jehanan for their wares.

What was that? Something in the charged, drunken atmosphere had changed. A ripple. A wave counter to the current swirling around the hall. *That was not what I was looking for . . . something else. That felt familiar.*

Excusing herself, Itzpalicue made her way stiffly up a staircase curving onto the mezzanine. One wrinkled old hand on the railing, she stopped at the first turn in the stairs. Below her, the crowd was a dizzying array of brilliant colors, flashing metal, somber uniforms. The old woman licked her lips, eyes almost closed, leaning on her cane, tasting the air, feeling sound rushing around her in a palpable, physical wave.

Gone. Whatever had disturbed the familiar pattern of avarice, fear, lust, hope and despair charging the air had vanished from her frame of perception. *Did someone leave?*

"Lachlan?" She turned her head, hiding her lips from anyone in line of sight. "Ident trap everyone in the garden, minus five minutes. Someone leaving the party, perhaps in a hurry . . . felt human, but get me . . ."

Another change in the air—a spike of imminent violence shot with sharp, inhuman rage—snapped her head around. A ripple of reaction was spreading through the crowd, though the Mirror agent doubted most of the humans below were even aware of their instinctive movement away from unseen danger. The splashpoint was a salon on the far side of the hall and something there—an enraged Jehanan, she realized—was about to draw blood.

A sound like a steam pipe bursting caused Tezozómoc to spring backwards, heart racing. The Jehanan female he'd been trying to converse with made an equally alarmed squeak in a fluting voice and scuttled sideways, pale rose skin turning a bruised orange color. As the prince whirled around, all he saw was a blur of black cotton as the taller of his two bodyguards hurled himself into harm's way. There was a *clang!* of steel on aluminum and the Skawtsman was driven back into Tezozómoc's chest. The prince went down with an *oof* and his face flushed red as he gasped for breath. Then he started to wail in fear.

The bulky shape of a Jehanan loomed over the Skawtsman's shoulder, long triangular mouth agape, exposing multiple rows of triangular teeth. A cruel scar puckered under the creature's left eye-shield, twisting like an enraged snake. A fetid stench of rotten meat and spoiled grain alcohol rolled over the prince, making him gag. Colmuir struggled, shoulders grinding back into Tezozómoc's breastbone and arm, to keep a stabbing sword locked against the hand-guard of his Nambu. The point of the gleaming blade jutted over his shoulder, aimed directly at the prince's forehead.

"*Kkkkrrrr-ich! Khay-gu, izh-huma!*" The Jehanan shook his massive head, ornamental eye-shields bouncing, a rippling shirt of copper rings stretched tight against scaled pectorals.

"What does he want?" Tezozómoc squeaked in fear.

"Wants . . . to kill you . . . mi'lord," the Skawtsman bit out, both hands locked tight on the grip of the Nambu. "Shouldn't have touched the lass . . . *urrgh!*"

"I didn't do anything!" The prince's voice was squashed down to a frail whisper. "She was . . . *urk* . . . just singing for . . . me!"

"*Hhuh-hen yehr*," a careful voice intruded. Sergeant Dawd appeared behind the Jehanan, a short-barreled automatic rifle in his hands. The flash-suppressor of the weapon jammed into the side of the native's neck, just behind the jaw joint, where heavy plate-scales protecting the face, cranium and chest faded away into pebbly stretch-skin. "*Ghawww-yeh*."

"What is he *saying?*" Tezozómoc wasn't trying to whisper, but his vision was blurring with black sparks as his lungs compressed under the weight of both the muscular Skawtsman and the bent knee of the Jehanan. "Oh, mother . . . I'm dying . . ."

Shocked silence was broken by a babble of voices. Vaguely, the prince made out the smooth, controlled voice of the Resident speaking rapidly in the same barbarous, guttural tongue. The pressure on his chest eased fractionally. Dawd withdrew, the assault rifle disappearing under his black coat. The sergeant seemed very tense. *He should lie down*, Tezozómoc thought, his head spinning. *Like me. Very comfortable. Heavy, heavy blankets they have here.*

Colmuir eased back his pistol, wincing to see the hand-guard had been nearly cloven through, and spread his hands, eyes locked on the black, glittering pits which served the Jehanan for optics. The stabbing sword remained exactly poised, needlelike tip aimed directly at the prince.

Resident Petrel, elegant face sheened with sweat, leaned in, talking quietly to the Jehanan. Colmuir, catching the gist of the conversation—his command of the Parusian dialect did not match Dawd's easy mastery, but it served—rolled carefully over, shielding the prince with his body. At the same time, he plucked an ampoule from a stickypatch inside his armored jacket and jammed the drug dispenser against the side of Tezozómoc's neck.

"Oh now, not fair . . ." wheezed the prince, eyelids rolling up. His body shuddered and fell limp on the floor. Sweat slithered down Colmuir's nose and spattered across the boy's gilded shirt.

"Oh, Saint Mary of the Angels," the Skawt muttered, waiting for the wickedly sharp sword blade to plunge in between his shoulder blades. He had a sinking feeling the ablative, armored mesh would not stop the ice-pick-like stroke for more than a heartbeat.

The guttural exchange between the Resident and the Jehanan general was now a three-way conversation as Bhrigu, *kujen* of Parus, had arrived, and the sound level was rising very, very quickly. The prince hopped nervously from one foot to the other, complaining loudly to Petrel in a mishmash of Náhuatl and Jehanan. The Skawt could feel more people—men in Army dress boots and trousers—crowding into the salon. All of the prince's 'new friends' had fled.

Dawd edged into Colmuir's field of vision, pudgy face lit with a kind of inner glow. "Nice party, Master Sergeant? The Governor's got *kujen* Bhrigu calming down his man. Apparently the bonny lass is regarded with protective affection by General Humara there. But we need to get his highness out of here immediately." Dawd peered at the boy's face. "Knocked him out, did you?"

"Aye." Colmuir rolled sideways, saw the massive shape of the Jehanan soldier had withdrawn. A solid wall of Mixtec officers—though none of them were armed with more than carving knives snatched up from the buffet tables—was between the limp, sweaty shape of the prince and a steadily growing crowd of hissing Jehanans. The rose-tinted female had disappeared. "Didn't take much. Don't see how the lad can drink, smoke and drop so much in one night . . ."

"Youth," Dawd grunted, slipping one arm under Tezozómoc's. Colmuir took the other side and together they sidled off, heading for the servants' entrance at the back of the entertaining room. A tall, well-dressed woman with white-shot hair held the door open for them. She looked down at the prince with a pensive expression as the two Skawts hustled him into a brightly lit, tile-floored maintenance corridor.

Itzpalicue watched the bodyguards dragging the prince away in an eyecast v-pane transmitted by a spybug loitering near the roof of the kitchen corridor. She sniffed with longstanding amusement. Her opinion of the prince had not changed in years. "Well, he certainly livens up a party, doesn't he?"

Will he live? a female voice replied. The old woman nodded, marking the efficient way the two Skawtsmen were moving the body.

"Of course," Itzpalicue said quietly to the empty air. The mezzanine balcony had emptied with amazing speed once word of the altercation lit through the party. An excited buzz throbbed in the air as hundreds of people chattered madly about what they imagined they'd seen. "He's young and took no direct harm. Worse for his liver, to judge by the prodigious quantity of stimulants he downed this evening. But I suppose he'll get another fresh one."

He was sweating like a malaria victim when he greeted me, Mrs. Petrel said in a concerned tone. *Does he spend all of his time like this?*

"Probably," the old woman answered drily. "With the Light of Heaven for a father? This son is not cast from the same alloy as the others. But no matter, more fuel for my fire. We'll make sure he gets home safely this time. Can't have him dying in some sordid brawl over a joygirl—that would not play well on the holocast nets, no indeed."

Bhāzuradeha is no courtesan. Greta's voice was very sharp. *She may be the finest poet in this generation of Jehanan—certainly the most talented in Parus. General Humara was enraged because she was singing part of her new composition,* Sky-the-Color-of-Birthshell-Fragments, *for the prince. They were verses the general had yet to hear—and among these people, such things are touchy matters. Humara is particularly sensitive.*

"A few stanzas were cause for attempted murder?" Itzpalicue bristled at the implied reprimand in the woman's voice. "Over poetry?"

Over an impromptu audition. Bhāzuradeha is very ambitious. Humara feared the prince would become her patron in his place.

"Not a very discerning woman." The old Méxica snorted into her hand. "What would she want from our dissolute boy?"

To be elevated beyond the reach of these squabbling petty nobles. The safety to speak that which is in her heart. In time, holocast access via the Development Board's new satellite network. The chance for her words to reach millions of her fellow Jehanan, rather than merely the tens of thousands who gather to hear her recite in public.

"Tens of thousands?" Itzpalicue said in disbelief. "For a poet?"

If Nezahualcoyotl of Tetzcoco were alive today, how many of your people would wish to hear him read Nitlayocoya *or* Song of Flight *in person? A hundred thousand? A million?*

"That's entirely different. The Doomed Prince was a Méxica!"

Of course.

Itzpalicue terminated the conversation and switched back to the operations channel. She did not enjoy being mocked. Frenetic air surged around her like a living sea, making her tremble with reflected excitement, fear, rumor and adrenaline. She started a breathing pattern to slow her heart before she lost focus.

"Lachlan? Yes, you saw? Good. The crowd is nearly hysterical right now . . . patch me through to the Whisperers downstairs . . ." There was soft tone in her ear. "Instant rumor, little mice: There is a secret Imperial archaeological mission on Jagan, seeking to steal certain artifacts . . ."

THE *CORNUELLE*
OVER THE NORTHERN POLE OF JAGAN

A large v-pane on the wall of Hadeishi's office displayed the threatwell feed from the bridge. A mass of ship glyphs in a variety of colors stood poised at the center of focus. The *Chu-sa* was only paying partial attention to the chatter on the Fleet channel; too many lists and rosters and status reports spread out on the table between him and Koshō demanded his concentration.

"Transit kick in three . . . two . . . one . . ." The voice of *Thai-i* Hayes was calm, collected and a little bored.

The threatwell convulsed as local space distorted. The cloud of lights wavered, climbing rapidly into gradient, and then vanished abruptly. A side-glyph flashed as the *Cornuelle*'s main sensor array went active, scanning a vast empty globe around the transit point. Two minutes passed as the *Chu-sa* paged through readiness reports, lips pursed.

"Transit zone secure. No debris. No gravitational anomalies." Hadeishi heard the senior lieutenant straighten up in the command chair as he activated a wide-band transmission channel. "Attention all ships. Imperial battle group *Tecaltan* has made transit. Bharat system traffic control reverting to IMN *Henry R. Cornuelle*. Please verify orbit and routing status . . ."

Hadeishi turned down the sound. Duke Villeneuve and his weekly dinner parties had departed, leaving the *Cornuelle* the sole Fleet presence in orbit around Jagan. For some reason, the *Chu-sa* felt a weight leave him. He grunted at himself, causing Koshō to look up, dark brown eyes questioning over the top of a stack of repair and maintenance requests.

"I feel," he said in answer to her silent question, "as if we've stood down from alert status."

Susan laid down a lengthy report discussing repairs to the Officer's Mess. To other eyes, she would seem perfectly composed, but Hadeishi saw a frown hiding behind her smooth features. "*Chu-sa*, there are persistent rumors of trouble groundside. Now we are alone again and our armaments are drawn down to almost nothing. No backup. Not even a frigate to extend our sensor range . . . our crew exhausted . . ."

"I know." Hadeishi shrugged, offering a tiny smile. "I still feel better. We're used to operating alone. I wait with interest to see if Nineteenth Fleet responds to my latest readiness report in a timely fashion, or if *another* battle group arrives from the direction of Keshewān with sobering news."

"You still think Villeneuve is making transit into a trap? That the Admiralty purposefully gathered every suspect captain into one group, so they could all be exterminated at one go?"

"I suspect—but I do not know—such things have happened before."

Susan frowned openly. "*Chu-sa*, I disagree. . . . If those captains carried the 'black mark,' then the Mirror would disappear them one at a time. Quietly. Without anyone noticing. It's insane to let them form a battle group, complete with resupply ships, a fleet mobile repair dock, everything they'd need to flee . . . or fight."

Hadeishi shrugged again and put down the v-pad. He rubbed his temples, feeling a headache start to come on. "True. But *something* is going on . . . I'm getting a gitchy feeling."

"*Kyo* . . ." Koshō paused, wondering how much she should push her captain. "Have you considered going groundside with the first shore-leave contingent?"

"Should I?" Hadeishi gave her a questioning look. "Do you feel I've been cooped up on this ship for too long?"

"No one," Koshō said, after another pause, "has carried more responsibility than you for the past twenty months. Despite Isoroku's grumbling about his workload, I would feel better if you put yourself on the first rotation. Did I tell you about the musicians I heard?"

Hadeishi lifted a hand. "*Sho-sa*, you're avoiding the question. Do you think my ability to command has been reduced by a lack of . . . recreational activities?"

"I cannot say that, *kyo*." Susan stiffened.

"No, you cannot!" Hadeishi sounded irritated. "In some situations, that could be construed as mutinous. I will go with the last rotation, as I've already made clear. It is traditional for the captain to go last, so last I will go."

Koshō remained silent, but he could see she didn't agree.

He settled back in his chair with a sigh. "Which is not to say I haven't seen anything but bulkheads and v-displays and the same faces for too long. You think my judgment has been impaired by a too-long patrol cruise? That I'm suffering psychological effects from extended isolation in the big dark?"

That I would . . . mislay orders to keep my crew and ship together for just a few more months?

Koshō did not reply, but her already straight spine became even straighter.

"I see." Hadeishi looked away for a bit and thumbed his medband. Clearhead hissed into his bloodstream with a cool, tingling sensation. "I am a little tired, *Sho-sa*, but this grandiose suite of rooms and the ever-comfortable chair on the bridge come with unavoidable responsibilities. Our duty station here is set for seven weeks. If we rotate the crew down for three-day leaves, I will be groundside, and *enjoying myself*, within a week." He grimaced, feeling the medband inject a second dose automatically. "I will be very glad to do so."

"Hai, *kyo*." Susan politely turned her attention back to the reports in front of her. "Have you seen this request from Isoroku to replace the decking in the officer's ward-room and surrounding areas?"

"I have." Hadeishi tapped up the same report on his pad, accepting the change of subject with relief. "Those rooms haven't been the same since that fire. Who would have thought a Khaid penetrator would decide the galley was a critical system? What do you think about his use of 'alternative materials'?"

"I'm not sure Fleet would approve the modification." The stiffness in the lieutenant commander's demeanor relaxed a little. "But with metal so scarce here, it is innovative. Wooden floors, cabinetry and paneling would be a nice change from the usual Fleet grey. These samples he's provided look gorgeous."

"They do." Hadeishi considered the same set of holos. "What about fire danger? And slippage. Will nonskid stick to this material?"

Koshō plucked a stylus from out of the heavy bun of black hair behind her head. She tapped the wall v-display awake and scrolled through the system to bring up the Engineers' request. "Isoroku sent one of his department supervisors groundside to look for replacement materials—Helsdon found the locals have developed organic replacements for a wide variety of metals. These trees—well, they're not really trees the way we think of them—are designed to lay down an internal structure like a honeycomb and secrete a crystalline lattice into the interstitial membranes." An appropriate diagram appeared.

"According to Fo-san from the Imperial Development Board, the timber from this species of *lohaja* is fireproof and has a tensile strength approaching light steel.

On pad, at least, it matches or exceeds the specifications required by safety regulations." She looked at Hadeishi and shrugged, the very tiniest lift detectable at the corners of her lips. "And it has a beautiful color."

"Better than sanity-green on enameled metal," the *Chu-sa* said, nodding. He scribbled on the bottom of his pad. "Let him give it a try. If it works, and we can acquire enough of the material, we can use it to repair or refurbish internal non-bulkhead walls, furniture and cabinetry. What about the rest of the repair schedule?"

Susan sighed. Two years out in the dark had left nearly every shipboard system seriously degraded. The endurance of an *Astronomer*-class light cruiser on patrol was supposed to be nine months. Some systems had simply failed at a year plus, when parts wore out. Others had been destroyed or severely damaged in combat. It was unlikely they would be able to pass a shipworthiness review. "We're stuck on over half of these items without a dry-dock to set into. Including the number one priority for everyone below decks . . ."

"The aft heat exchangers?" Hadeishi rubbed his nose. "Could we run atmosphere with only the fore environment plant?"

Koshō shook her head. "Only if we send all but repair crews off-ship. Efficiency of the whole system is down almost forty percent . . . we need to pull both and replace them with brand new units, if possible."

"Can the Jaganite industrial base fabricate replacements?"

"Helsdon has been looking for compatible systems . . . but has found nothing. The natives don't have the right kind of machining and composite construction technology. Isoroku had been hoping a civilian spaceliner would be in-system with a spare, compatible environ-plant we could commandeer. This was not the case."

Hadeishi smoothed his beard, looking at his chrono. "Then we'll have to wait until we reach Toroson. And the rest of these leave schedules and maintenance priorities will have to wait. I've a conference cast about to start with *Tlacateccatl* Yacatolli of the 416th about our reaction and support plan."

Koshō did not laugh, but she made a funny coughing sound. Hadeishi glared at her, suppressing his own smile of amusement. "Now you have to sit here with me and listen to the Army and be *polite*."

The *Sho-sa* nodded, resigned to her fate, and began sorting all of the report pads on the table into neat piles.

"I understand your combat lift requirements, *Tlacateccatl*," Hadeishi repeated. "But the *Cornuelle* is not an assault carrier. We carry three *Varanus*-class cargo shuttles and a captain's launch. Those shuttles could be stripped out, I suppose, but they'd still only carry a platoon each of troops in full combat armor. I don't have *anything* capable of evacuating one of your armored tracks from a combat situation."

Yacatolli's face twisted into a truly fearsome grimace, the tattoos incised on both cheeks bunching into vaguely demonic shapes. He was getting angrier with each tick of the chrono. "What good is your ship to me then? You've no lift support for my men, you say your missile inventory is exhausted, you've only two squads of Marines . . . why are *you* here and not a proper support craft?"

"You will have to discuss that with Admiral Villeneuve," Hadeishi snapped, voice rising involuntarily. His headache was getting worse. The Mixtec officer's eyes narrowed to slits. Hadeishi's face closed up tight, lips thinning to a harsh line. "My apologies, Colonel. My request to transit to Toroson for repair and resupply was rejected by the Admiral's operations officer. Instead we were put on picket here until the battle group returns. More than this, I cannot say. Those are my orders."

"What support can you give me, then?" Yacatolli's tone verged on open anger. Hadeishi understood his position all too well—the Army was used to operating under an umbrella of rapid-response Fleet fire-support, used to being able to call on heavy-lift shuttles to redeploy their ground combat vehicles and troops, expecting supplies to be delivered in any kind of terrain—and now none of those resources were available. "Anything?"

"Full communications net," Hadeishi answered, knowing how paltry his offering sounded. "For remote detachments. Surveillance overwatch. We can swamp all local comm from here. Override or seize any satellite support the native princes might have in operation. Medevac for your wounded. In dire circumstances I have three bombardment missiles still in inventory, but I was saving those in case we get jumped by a raider." *And we can't run fast enough to avoid battle.*

"I see." The colonel let his fury at the universe, Hadeishi and Admiral Villeneuve leak through into his voice. "Very well, we will adapt our reaction plan accordingly. If we have need of your assistance, *Chu-sa*, I expect immediate compliance. My operations officer will forward a copy of your rules of engagement and expected support duties tomorrow, after we've worked them up."

"Colonel!" Hadeishi leaned towards the v-display, stung by the man's words. "I expect my executive officer, *Sho-sa* Koshō, to be fully engaged in your operational planning at every step!"

"Do you?" Yacatolli scowled, lip curling. "Given the disparate levels of resources we each can apply, I think the Army will lead the planning, as we'll be doing all the work. Don't worry, we won't overburden your ship's capabilities."

"Overburden?" The temperature of Hadeishi's tone dropped remarkably. "How would you even know what our capabilities are if we're not fully engaged in working up the ops plan?"

"You've given me an excellent idea of your capabilities," Yacatolli snarled, holding up his thumb and forefinger circled into an O. "Do I need to remind you I am the ranking Imperial officer in this system? This is an Army operation, and Fleet will follow orders."

Out of the immediate range of the channel pickup, Koshō's eyes widened and she shot a pleading look at Hadeishi, pressing her palms towards the floor. The *Chu-sa* unclenched his fists—also out of view—and tried to breathe deeply. Yacatolli stared back at him, waiting.

Finally, Hadeishi nodded in agreement, though there was a sour taste in his mouth. *Army running Fleet? At this moment, even the Buddha is dumbfounded!*

"Expect a 'cast transfer of new orders tomorrow. Yacatolli, out."

The v-display went black, then reset to standby. Hadeishi sat stiffly, staring at the pale blue colors, the corner of his left eye twitching. He did not look at Koshō. After a little while, she stood up, bowed and went out quietly.

When she was gone he slumped, almost shuddering into his chair. *Now, what will you do if something happens?* A sharp, angry voice echoed in his thoughts. *You've worn your poor ship to the bone—how could this be an improvement on sending her to the breaking yard?*

Hadeishi had no answer for his conscience. He rubbed his brow line with the back of his thumb, trying to drive away the piercing headache.

With the aft air exchangers running at less than half strength, the enlisted mess on deck sixteen of the *Cornuelle* was oven hot, stifling and filled with an oily smell from the recyclers. Marine *gunso* Fitzsimmons slouched into the mess in a pair of ratty exercise shorts and a sour mood. Due to the constant heat and humidity, off-duty personnel had taken to wearing as little as possible.

This made the sight of *Heicho* Felix and some of her cronies draped in flamboyantly colored fabric from head to toe unexpected. Fitzsimmons altered course, veering away from the rows of drink dispensers, and parked himself on the end of a nearby table.

Felix and the other female Marines ignored Fitzsimmons, their attention on a stack of iridescent cloth wrapped around wooden dowels, boxes of shining trinkets, fluted leather bottles with wax stoppers, stacked sets of bowls and cups in a pale, shimmering green glaze, plump bags of ground spices, a basket of some spiky native fruit, and boxes covered with garish labels and boldly unintelligible lettering. A rich smell of ginger and cinnamon suffused the air around them. After a moment of watching the women, Fitzsimmons realized they were dividing up the goods.

"Hey Felix, where'd you get all this stuff?"

The *Heicho* looked up, made a face to see the fish-belly-pale shape of the Marine sergeant in nothing but tatty shorts, and then grinned mischievously. "*Gunso*! How are you today? Well, I hope." She cocked her head to one side, considering him. "Have you been working out?"

Fitzsimmons scowled, scratching his taut stomach. Every Marine on-ship worked out constantly. There was little else for them to do, since both combat simulators were broken and when there *was* an opportunity to exercise their skills, it usually meant the captain needed them to storm some refugee ship seized by raiders, after floating with their combat suits dialed down to minimum power to escape detection as they spiraled through a long ballistic orbit to match velo with the captured ship, while the *Cornuelle* traded missiles and beamfire with the Megair spider-cloud as a distraction. The sergeant pointed at one of the leather bottles. "Is that booze?"

"If it is," Felix said in a brisk tone, stepping in front of the rack of bottles, "it's not *yours*."

"You've been planetside," Fitzsimmons said, considering the piles of loot and scratching a jaw covered with stiff black stubble. "Lot of free time if you were supposed to be standing security. Your detail commander know about all this?"

The other Marines shared a brief, worried glance. Felix, however, gave the sergeant a commiserating smile. "Of course. *Sho-sa* Koshō likes *me*. Oh, did I mention I happened to run into an old friend of yours groundside? That blonde girl you spent so much time with . . . what *was* her name . . ."

"What are you talking about?" Fitzsimmons glared at the corporal. "There's only one blonde I've even *seen* in the last two years that wasn't wearing a uniform, and she's—"

"Miss Anderssen! That's right." Felix's dark eyes glinted in amusement. "She was looking very fetching the other night, when the lieutenant commander was out on the town. Nice dress. Very stylish. Would you like to see a picture?"

"Smoke and ash," Fitzsimmons barked, standing up. His stomach made an odd, queasy flip-flop. "Gretchen's about sixty lights from here, at home, working on some . . . some important scientific discovery . . . or something."

"I don't think she's working," the *Heicho* said, rummaging under the gleaming silk. "Ah, here we are." She pulled out a holo and examined the image—hidden from Fitzsimmons' line of sight—with a critical air. The other Marines leaned in, smirking. "Yes, she is an attractive woman in a very flattering outfit. Don't you think so, girls?"

"Oh yes," they all said, batting their eyelashes.

Fitzsimmons made a strangled sound, closed his eyes, took three deep breaths and opened them again, glaring at Felix and the holo in her hand. "Fine, Corporal, keep your bones. Can I see the holo?"

"Hmmm . . ." Felix hid the picture against her shoulder, making a show of considering the matter. "Well . . . you are a pretty solid squad leader, and you saved my life one time on Kotopaxi, so I guess you could have this . . ." She handed him the holo. "Our surveillance cameras are really very sharp, even at night and in the rain."

Fitzsimmons stared intently at the picture. A pretty blonde woman with long wavy hair was standing in the shadow of an ivy-covered gate, talking to the slim, straight figure of *Sho-sa* Koshō. He tried not to sigh, watching the European woman smile, face lighting up, one hand brushing thick hair back over a bared shoulder. The fidelity of the holo *was* very good—you could see raindrops falling past. Then he noticed targeting and range indicators softly glowing at the edges of the holo.

"Mother of Tepeyac, Felix, you were surveilling the *Sho-sa* with your gun-scope?!"

The *Heicho* shrugged. "You want the picture or not, sergeant? Sure would brighten up your rack."

Fitzsimmons shook his head and handed the holo back, drawing a surprised look from Felix. "Thanks, Corporal, but no. Some of us are borne by water, carried by wind. Not her, though. Not her." *She has a family, children—a whole world waiting for her at home.*

"That's pretty poetic for a . . ." Felix started to say, then fell silent at the pinched, distant look on Fitzsimmons' face.

Without another word, the *gunso* slouched off towards the drink dispensers. In the picture, visible for just a moment as Anderssen moved her hand, there had been a flash of gold on her ring finger. Fitzsimmons couldn't remember her wearing a binding band before. *But she was working when I was with her. Not at a party. Don't want anything on your hands if you're dinking around with heavy machinery.* Though he'd sent her several letters, she'd never replied.

Surrounded by the bright colors of native loot, Felix watched the sergeant with a worried look. She glanced down at the holo in her hand, then pinched the bottom-left corner to flush the paper clean. She wondered if she should apologize, then set the thought aside. No sense in stirring up old regrets. The *gunso* would survive. They all did.

THE IMPERIAL LEGATION
THE RED FORT, CENTRAL PARUS

Head throbbing, prince Tezozómoc stumbled into a door-frame, bruising his shoulder. His eyes were having trouble focusing, but he seemed to be in some kind of domicile, a bedroom, a sitting room . . . *Glorious savior, where am I? Is this someone's house?* The prince tried to kick sheets tangling his feet away—part of his mind recognized they were of exceptional quality—but he wound up on the floor, staring up at a white ceiling. Gripped by nervous fear, Tezozómoc's addled brain started to babble: *I hope her husband does not come in right now. Whoever she happens to be—oh, Christ the Risen Sacrifice, I hope she was pretty! Or at least from a good family—that would please my divine father—getting some foreign princess heavy with jade and gold—then what would I do? What can I do? Should I run away? If . . . if I could stand up . . .*

"Mi'lord?" A familiar voice intruded. The prince stopped struggling with the entangling cloth and looked up. The shorter of his two bodyguards stood over him, hands clasped behind his back. "Would you like some breakfast?"

"No!" The thought of food made Tezozómoc's stomach roll over queasily. "Something to drink—my mouth is terribly dry. A beer? A cold Rabbit? Or peyotl if they have some—aaah!—even *octli* liquor will do . . ."

Face impassive, Sergeant Dawd knelt beside the prince and took his wrist in gentle fingers. The Skawtsman considered the lights on the prince's medband carefully, and then stood with an easy motion, dragging Tezozómoc to his feet. The abrupt change in position sent blood draining from the prince's head and he nearly fell over again.

"Ahhh . . . what *did* I do? Was there a party?" Tezozómoc let himself be led to a chair in the sitting room. He stared around owlishly, throbbing head, parched mouth and general ill-feeling beginning to inspire a very poor humor. The prince tapped his medband peevishly. "This cheap trinket isn't working properly, is it? I feel . . . I feel wretched! Wrung out, stamped, dried, put away with the short kernels! Oh, my head . . ."

"Mi'lord," Dawd opened a refrigerated cabinet hidden in one of the walls. "Your medband shut down days ago. The level of drug toxicity in your system exceeded the band's safety limits. So you've been sleeping. . . . Here, drink some of this."

Tezozómoc took the glass with a horrified expression on his face. "This looks like bile."

"Drink up, mi'lord. Enzymes to help your liver process the alcohol and drugs and other toxic chemicals polluting your system."

"I am *not* drinking bile!"

Dawd's eyes grew rather cold and he leaned close to the prince. Surprised, Tezozómoc quailed back into the overstuffed chair.

"Mi'lord, it's my business to keep you alive and healthy. By whatever means please your honored father. So—drink this and let the fluids do their work."

Flushed, the prince looked away and gagged down the glass. *Stupid Skawt—I've gotten drunk before! This is no different than last time . . . though that rose-colored girl did let me taste some giddyup from her fliptop . . . everything got woozy after that. I wonder . . .*

"What happened to the beautiful singer?" Wiping his mouth, Tezozómoc tossed the glass carelessly behind the sofa. He peered at Sergeant Dawd expectantly. "Is she here? Oh . . . did we mate? I was wondering what she'd feel like—"

"There was *no mating*, mi'lord." Dawd assumed parade rest by reflex. He looked down at the prince, who sprawled bonelessly across the chair. "You were . . . touching her in an inappropriate way and . . ."

"She was very smooth!" the prince exclaimed, flushing copper. "I asked her permission first!"

". . . her patron, General Humara, did not like that at all." Dawd's voice was quite cold. "No indeed. He came within a hair of splitting you open with as fine a damascene-style blade as I've ever seen."

"Fine. Fine. I'm very grateful." Tezozómoc started to feel stymied. *This always happens. I hate this. Why won't anyone answer my questions?* "What happened to the rose-colored girl?"

"Humara took her away. Under local law, she is his legal possession . . ."

Tezozómoc grunted and stood up—swayed unsteadily for a moment, but found his footing—and gestured violently at the Skawtsman. "Oh, shut up. Shut–shut–shut up! Do you know where she is? Was she hurt?"

Dawd shook his head. "We moved you to safety as quickly as possible."

"Listen to me, Sergeant." The prince rubbed a fine-boned brown hand across one cheek. Pain stabbed behind his eyelids at the touch. *Oh, I have done myself an injury this time. What was in those red crystals? Gasoline? What if they like to drop shots of petroleum distillate here?* "There are very few things in this world I find enjoyable. That girl . . ."

Tezozómoc stopped and closed his mouth with a snap. He felt truly terrible, worse than he had in at least two weeks. Despite the stabbing pressure threatening to burst through his eyelids and spill blood down his cheeks, the prince could see enough of the sergeant's face to realize the man was only barely disguising open contempt. A groping hand found the back of the nearest chair. The feel of solid wood under his fingertips kept him from pitching over.

"Did you hear her singing, Sergeant? Did you listen to her at all?"

Sergeant Dawd shook his head minutely. "Mi'lord, I was . . ."

"Be quiet." Exhausted, Tezozómoc's anger flared, the stabbing reflection of sunlight from a drawn blade. "I am speaking. If you cannot listen, then you are discharged from my service. Did I choose you to watch over me? No—so you may go at any time. You were forced upon me, just as Colmuir was." The prince's thin face twisted in anguish and his right hand scratched angrily at the side of his neck. "Two Eagle Knights set to guard a Prince Imperial—yet I am *Otomitl*—an officer! Where are my captives? Where are the men I've defeated in battle? There are none!"

Dawd stepped back, gray-green eyes narrowing in puzzlement.

"You barely even comprehend what I say." Tezozómoc looked sick again, but the hangover was losing its hold. "My father and my brothers don't even bother to speak to me—why should they? My mantle of red and white feathers is ash and glue and paint, my victories—not one plume is mine. Not one. Only my father's name shields me from disgrace—his will, and men like you, who watch over me and keep me from harm."

Tezozómoc abruptly wrenched the chair from the floor and hurled it into the nearest wall. Hardwood shattered, sending splinters clattering from the light fixtures. Dawd braced himself, but did not move.

"I am a Méxica!" The prince's voice was bitter and furious. "The blood of conquerors is in me—every nation bows down before my father—our enemies know only ruin and exile or lie dead, their nations wastelands under the Blow. My brothers . . ." Tezozómoc gasped for breath, tears beginning to stream down his cheeks. "They are strong—those Blades Undimmed—what am I? Only a broken mirror, distorted, filled with shadows. A blunted edge."

Dawd, alarmed, thumbed his comm, sounding a warning on the circuit he and Colmuir shared.

"The eagle screams," Tezozómoc said, his voice starting slow, chanting.

> *"Jaguars howl, and you—O Prince—you are*
> Macuilmailnalli.
> *Here, in a region of smoke, in the land of red color,*
> *bravely the Méxica are fighting."*

The prince stopped, body drained by the outburst. His hands were trembling.

> *"I am intoxicated—I, Tezozómoc.*
> *I of the flowery, shaven hair.*
> *Again and again, I drink the flowering liquor.*
> *Let them pass me precious flowery nectar.*
> *Oh, my brother, you are young and strong.*
> *I grow pale. Where is my strong hand? My blade of flint?*
> *Gone—rabbits have taken them—stolen my strong heart.*
> *Nothing is left."*

Dawd heard the door behind him open and raised a warning hand. The prince's voice was growing, filling the room, even as his thin body seemed to shrink in upon itself. There was a faint metallic click as Colmuir eased his Nambu back into the gunrig.

> *"Within the waters, they are singing.*
> *The divine flowers are calling—they are intoxicated, they are shouting*
> *The princes who are precious birds, the mighty Cuextecas.*
> *Begin the dance!*
> *To his house go those with spoiled flowers,*
> *Those with plumed shields,*
> *Those who guarded the heights,*
> *Those who took prisoners alive,*
> *Now they are dancing,*
> *Vomiting blood as they go,*
> *The spoiled flowers, those of the flowery shields.*
> *My divine brothers."*

Tezozómoc stared gravely at the two Skawtsmen, dark eyes enormous in a pale, wasted face. "Am I so bright with glory? No—I am sitting in a dark house, fumes in my nostrils. You are warriors—far better men than I—you had to earn the arrow, the jade, the feathered shield." A thin finger stabbed at the matte black *mon* on Colmuir's stiff collar. "You deserve what you have been given."

The prince fell silent, clutching his head. Dawd risked a brief glance at Colmuir, who was looking curiously at him in turn. The younger Skawtsman licked his lips, looked around at the mess, and mustered up enough breath to speak.

"Mi'lord? I'm only a clanless man from Glasgow, but by the blood, you've a ringing voice and a piercing way with the ancient words. Of all men, I know how fiercely the Méxica venerate the poet, the singer, even above warriors, even above kings. Does your father know—"

"I only recite," Tezozómoc interrupted, anger flickering awake. "Nezahualpilli, son of fabled Nezahualcoyotl, raised his voice with those words nearly a thousand years ago. A trained monkey could do so well."

He stumbled to the nearest couch and threw himself down, utterly drained. His voice was a faint thready whisper. "Somehow, all the divine spirit which fills my father and shines in my brothers was gone by the time I came into this cursed world. Was my mother exhausted? Am I only half formed?" He raised his head, fixing Dawd with a glittering stare. "If I am truly an officer, where are my men? Where is my command?"

The Skawtsman stiffened again, face automatically settling into a stiff mask. The prince laughed softly.

"No one will trust me in the presence of warriors. I am always 'attached to headquarters'—given indefinable tasks, responsibilities without weight. If this continues, I will someday be a general without an army—save perhaps the two of you, grown old and gray."

Dawd ignored a soft snort of laughter behind him. "Why is the Jehanan girl important, mi'lord? Should we try and find her?"

Tezozómoc's face changed, unhealthy pallor fading, eyes coming alert. "She sang to me, Sergeant. Their vocal cords are not ours, their range is higher, with a beautiful mellow tone . . . I have read a little about this place, dabbled in some books, watched the usual briefing holos. They are a very old race, very old. Their language is quite complex—even with a translator you will find a Jehanan can manage Náhuatl or Norman better than we can pronounce the simplest words in Uheru or Ssagatiak. But when she sang to me . . ." The prince's face lit with a smile. "I understood. I could feel what she felt, see what she saw."

Dawd frowned. Tezozómoc gave him a pitying look.

"Do you think I am lying?"

"No, mi'lord!" Both Skawtsmen stiffened to attention.

"What you believe doesn't matter." The prince pushed himself up gingerly. "For a moment, my heart was light and all this gall drained away into forgetfulness. I would like to hear her sing again, if the kujen will allow such a thing. Perhaps I can learn a few of the words myself." He sighed, head drooping again. "I suppose the Fleet will depart and we will be gone before there is opportunity."

"Now . . ." Dawd was interrupted by a polite cough and Colmuir placed a hand on his shoulder. Obediently, the younger Skawtsman stepped back, clasping both hands behind his back. The master sergeant bowed to the prince, a comm-pad tucked under his arm.

"Mi'lord, two messages came while you were asleep. One from Grand Duke Villeneuve—he extends his apologies for not entertaining you at dinner, but the battle group has received orders to proceed to the Keshewān system with all speed. Your regiment has been left behind on Jagan to ensure the safety of Imperial interests here."

"When will they return?" Tezozómoc looked up, concerned. Dawd was relieved the question had been broached—he detested the muggy climate here in Parus and wished to be someplace colder and drier as soon as possible. Preferably on a Fleet battlecruiser in transit back to the home systems.

"Three to four weeks, if not longer." Colmuir hesitated. "Regimental headquarters seemed a little surprised by their departure, mi'lord, and had no good answer for why only the 416th had been left behind. Apparently there is considerable unrest growing in the rural provinces against the Imperial presence. There is concern attacks against Imperial citizens or their business operations may occur."

The prince's nostrils flared, but he said nothing.

"The second message is a personal social invitation, mi'lord, from the kujen of Gandaris."

Tezozómoc raised a weary eyebrow. "Another party?"

"A traditional hunt, mi'lord." Colmuir offered the comm-pad. "The kujen expresses his desire for the most-noble prince to join him, local dignitaries and several Imperial Army officers in searching out and destroying a pair of *xixixit* beasts which are preying upon the villages near his city. Apparently the *xixixit* are surpassing rare and not lately seen south of the mountains."

"A hunt? Are they mad?" Dawd surprised himself by speaking out of turn. Both the prince and the master sergeant favored him with disapproving glances. The sergeant decided to fade into the wall.

"I am sure my reputation as a fearsome warrior has preceded me," Tezozómoc said in a very dry voice. "Do I make such a desirable party ornament? Don't these barbarians realize currying favor with me is utterly useless? Better they should hire a dancing clown in black and white instead!"

Colmuir pursed his lips and took back the comm-pad. "Mi'lord, this message came care of the Legation—I spoke with Mrs. Petrel, the Legate's wife, when she commed—and she implied the kujen of Gandaris is no good friend of Lord Bhrigu."

"Who is Bhrigu?" The prince's patience was waning. "Do I care?"

"Bhrigu is kujen of Parus, mi'lord. His liegeman Humara tried his best to split you in two the other night when you were . . . speaking . . . with Miss Bhāzuradeha."

Tezozómoc stiffened, staring at the master sergeant. "What? The rose-colored girl is named 'radiant sunrise'? Does Mrs. Petrel know her—I mean, personally? Would she have a comm address?"

"I have no idea, mi'lord." Colmuir sounded uncomfortable. "But it might be a good idea to leave town for a wee bit. Let things settle here, if you see."

The prince glared at the Skawtsman, then deflated abruptly. "Bhrigu is not a fool—not to have recognized her talent in the first place. He'll have her under close surveillance. She must have slipped away from him at the reception . . ."

"Mi'lord . . ."

"Hunting. Hah!" Tezozómoc sprawled despondently on the couch. "All princes love hunting! I'm sure someone believes it's in my blood. Idiots . . . Yes, tell the Legation I will do my royal duty and show a brave face for the locals."

In the corridor outside, Dawd coughed discretely. "Ah, Master Sergeant?"

Colmuir looked up from his comm-pad. "Yes, lad?"

"Is it cooler in Gandaris?"

"Snowy mountains, Ser'gnt, right among high snowy mountains."

Dawd breathed a sigh of relief. *Some chance of a cool breeze then.* Then turned his attention back to the job at hand. "What about these *xixixit* creatures, Master Sergeant? Do we have any intel about them?"

Colmuir let out a hiss, shaking his head in disbelief. He handed the younger man the comm-pad. Dawd thumbed through the briefing, then stopped at a grainy two-d picture, appalled.

"Master Sergeant! What the devil is the Legate thinking? These things are vicious!"

"I would guess," Colmuir said, glancing back over his shoulder at the door to the prince's suite, "Mrs. Petrel thinks a three-meter-long wasp is less a trouble to our wee lad than the singing girl might be. And she would know, I think, being a wise woman if I've ever seen one."

Dawd grimaced again. "Does the prince have the faintest idea how to use a hunting lance?"

"None of that, lad." Colmuir gave the sergeant a sharp look. "Not our place to comment on the prince and his abilities! You'll keep a civil tongue in your head and your opinions to yourself."

THE HORUMKEL BATHS
STREET OF THE EYE-SHIELD JEWELERS, PARUS

Shrouded by a cloud of soft, billowing steam, Itzpalicue leaned back against glistening marble and closed her eyes. The stone felt cool against her thin back and she clasped both hands on a bare stomach. The inside of her eyelids began to yield up images—a little fuzzy, the humidity interfered with the commcast receiver—but still clear enough to make out a scene occurring not too far away.

She looked down from a ribbed ceiling, the spybug hidden among old cobwebs beaded with dust. Below her, the long trestle tables of a cabinetmaker's workshop had been cleared away. A pair of Jehanan in bulking robes and face-shrouding cowls unlatched a rectangular plastic case. The slate-colored lid rolled back, revealing two wicked-looking tubes stenciled with Imperial military script. There was a sibilant trill from the natives, a sound the old Méxica recognized as pleased laughter. Each day she spent among these people yielded up more of their body language, slang and private conversation to her. Their language was almost musical, and she allowed—with some disdain—their poetry was affecting, even to her, a human with the wrong kind of ear to appreciate its subtleties.

"There are sixteen more in this shipment," the human standing across the table said, his voice a little tinny after being filtered through the audio pickup on the spybug, broadcast scrambled to a Mirror relay on the roof of a nearby pottery kiln, tightbeamed back to Lachlan's operations center and then retransmitted to the dropwire in the back of her skull. "Consider these a gift, from those who hold the same enemies as yours."

One of the Jehanan—not the leader of this particular cell of the *darmanarga moktar*, but his spokesman—ran a supple, scaled hand across the anti-aircraft missile in the portage case. "We need more of theesse," he said, in passable Náhuatl. "Your predecessor offered two hundreds of them."

Did he? Itzpalicue wondered if the Flower Priest who had made the initial contact was really so bold. A real agent of the illegal, constantly hunted and thoroughly dangerous Swedish Royal Intelligence Service—the HKV—would not have made such a daring play. *The Swedes would have given these creatures the tools and diagrams to make their own missiles. Much less costly than actually shipping two hundred Kärrhök 'live-eye' hunter-seekers to such an obscure world.* Itzpalicue was equally abstemious where her own budget was concerned. *But here the* xochiyaotinime *are footing the bill—so cost is of little concern as long as we make a good show.*

Another of the Jehanan nobles examined the missiles with a handheld sensor. After a moment's scrutiny, apparently satisfied, he coughed something unintelligible. The spokesman repeated his question.

"They are already on-planet," the Flower Whisperer said, producing a folded paper from his Parusian-styled overcloak. As it happened, the agent was one of Itzpalicue's 'mice' infiltrated into the *xochiyaotinime* team on Jagan. He was, of course, pretending to be a Swedish agent-provocateur. "Here are contact directions to meet someone who will help you move the rockets to a safe location of your choosing. But not for another four days."

Itzpalicue's technicians were watching on the spybug feed from Operations, waiting to see what kind of check the Jehanan would make before accepting the shipment. They would need time to make appropriate adjustments to the rest of the missiles. The old Méxica did not intend for more than one in four of the rockets to work properly, once things came to violence here on Jagan. While the Flower Priests and the natives were expendable, she had no desire for the Army to spend too much blood in victory.

One of the *darmanarga* stirred and Itzpalicue saw a ripple of reaction sweep the others. *The leader of this cell,* she judged, watching their postures carefully. *Once, long ago, this race expressed hierarchy through physical reactions, many lower, one higher. Those instincts have grown thin over time, but they are not yet gone. Interesting.* The leader—his features were hidden by a deep cowl—said something the spybug did not pick up. The spokesman turned back to the human.

"We have assked before, *nahwah*, but we asssk again. Why do your clanss help uss? We are not of the same blood, same stock . . ."

Itzpalicue shifted a little on the stone bench, feeling sweat ooze from every pore. Fresh steam surged up from pipes laid under the perforated floor. The bathhouse was very old, every surface worn smooth as glass, the local travertine gaining a translucent, almost fleshy, shine. In the last four meetings she'd monitored—spread across the entire length and breadth of the valley of the Phison—the *darmanarga* representatives had asked a variation of the same question. Each time in the same way—accepting the goods, then posing the question as a seeming afterthought.

They are trying to cross-check, she thought, watching her agent's response closely. *Lachlan needs to winnow their secure channels from the usual chatter. I need to know what they think they know.*

"We know what will happen," the Flower Whisperer said in a somber voice, "if you do not receive better weapons. The Empire understands only strength. Without our assistance, all your valor will be useless in the face of superior arms. Then you will be little more than slaves. But if you fight, if you show a warrior's spirit, then they will respect you and see you as worthy of being allies."

The leader was whispering in the spokesman's ear again, claw tapping nervously on his subordinate's shoulder. "You . . . do not believe we can defeat the Empire?"

"No. Not alone. Not without our help."

Itzpalicue could feel, even through the video feed, the agent sweating with tension. *Not so comfortable as being at the baths*, she thought in amusement, *with a good scrub and oil waiting.*

"Without military-grade spacecraft," the Whisperer continued, "you will not be able to drive the Empire from your world." The human looked around the shop, indicating the lengths of cured golden timber stacked against the walls. "Beautiful tables and chairs will not suffice. Your people need time to build the industry required to put starships into service."

A bitter hissing rose from the Jehanan, and from her vantage point Itzpalicue saw the leader's clawed hand dig tight into the spokesman's shoulder. For a moment, something seemed familiar about the way the *moktar* cell leader was standing. The old Méxica made a mental note to review the recording when she returned to her rooms. Another hurried conversation passed among the natives. Then the spokesman made a passable imitation of a human nod.

"We undersstand," the Jehanan rumbled, gesturing for two of his juniors to take the portage case in hand. "Patience iss required."

Do you? Itzpalicue sat up and opened her eyes. Time to be oiled. *People are rarely patient about destiny.*

An hour later, refreshed, the old Méxica strolled slowly down a winding street crowded with narrow-fronted shops. Elaborate hand-painted signs in local script ran up the face of each building. There were no windows, only reinforced wooden doors. From what she could read of the ornate lettering, this was a district of jewelers and fine metalsmiths: a rare trade in the valley of the Phison! There was a great deal of traffic, though most flowed past Itzpalicue, heading downhill. Somewhere ahead—the sound was muffled and distorted by the buildings—there was a cacophony of gongs and drums.

Even here, where iron and copper are so rare, the whore-priests can still afford metal instruments to raise a heavenly noise.

Anger clouded up, disturbing the quiet she'd gained in the bathhouse. She slowed her pace, breathing steadily, forcing her mind to emptiness, until the spurt of rage died away. The old woman did not care for priests of any race or religion. They were all much the same to her. Working with the vast clerical hierarchy supporting the Empire taxed her self-control. The irony of using priestly techniques to control her emotions was not lost on the Mirror agent. *A flint blade has no master but the hand on the haft,* she thought, and then felt a trickle of fury again. *Even my aphorisms are infected with their bile.* A well-trained memory—another gift of the religious calmecac which had been her home for the first sixteen years of her life—was sometimes a burden. She remembered the exact time and place she had first heard that particular phrase.

There had been a boy, of course. Even now, so long after everything had become ashes and broken bone scattered on the ground, she remembered his green eyes. Lingering pain dulled their shine. *That boy was worthy,* she thought sadly. *His heart was still pure. As was mine.* Unbidden, he was singing in her memory, lying on velvety grass, the shadow of sycamores painting his bare brown chest.

Gold and black butterflies are sipping nectar.
The flower bursts into bloom.
Ah, my friends, it is my heart!
I send down a shower of white petals . . .

The song had always made her glad. Even now, standing in the shade of an alien building on some world beyond the sight of a boy and girl staring up at the brilliant azure sky over México, her heart lifted a little. The festival procession passed away down the hill. The air stirred with the smell of cooking, of wood smoke, the harsh cinnamon odor of their sweat. The city was alive, humming and breathing. She closed both eyes, leaning her forehead on the cane.

Breathe in. The river was flowing, slow and sure, rolling down from distant, snow-capped mountains. Twigs were floating in the saffron water, offering brief perches for leather-winged avians hunting eel-like fish.

Breathe out. Trolleys rumbled down curving streets, crowded with passengers heading home for the midday meal. They swayed from side to side as the red-and-black car rattled around a turn.

Breathe in. Somewhere children were learning to dance, three-toed feet stamping in time on a wooden floor. A withered old male was tapping time on a tiny drum.

Breathe out. Workmen were laughing—a rattling, hissing sound—as they raised the wooden frame of a wireless comm tower on the roof of a hotel. Their foreman sitting in the shade of a sign advertising fang-cleaning powder, running gnarled hands over the smooth, perfect shape of the relay. He had never held so much metal in his hands before.

Breathe in. A boy on the street, not so far away, felt his blood begin to race with mating fire for the first time. He was afraid, clutching his mother's tail painfully tight, trying not to stumble over his feet.

Breathe out. Far away, at the edge of the old woman's perception, a cold emptiness moved effortlessly through the flow of the city.

Itzpalicue's eyes flew open and her withered old hands tightened convulsively on the cane.

There is something here. She licked her lips and glanced around, feeling fear curdle in her throat. *I truly felt that. I am not imagining things.*

With a conscious effort, she settled her racing heart, closed her eyes, shut out the cheerful noise surrounding her and tried to regain the instant of clear perception. Once more the fluid, vibrant sensation of the city flooded into her consciousness. She remained standing quietly, breathing steadily, for nearly an hour. Though she learned a great deal about the street around her, and even about the district, the brief feeling of cold nothingness did not return.

Her stomach growled and Itzpalicue opened her eyes, admitting defeat, if only to herself. The sun was beginning to set, painting the ancient buildings with red and gold and amber. The boulevard was beginning to empty as the natives made their way home for the evening rites and, eventually, last-meal. The old Méxica set off for the house she had rented near the Legation.

At each end of the street, shadows stirred and the lean shapes of her Arachosians emerged, moving as she moved, their knives, guns, and woven bandoliers of ammunition mostly hidden under heavy cloaks and baggy, cowl-like sun-hats. Seeing them—she had felt their presence all along—Itzpalicue felt relieved. *At least some footpad won't try and steal my hairpins.*

The presence she'd glimpsed so briefly was another matter.

Something odd was happening on the fringes of the Empire of the Méxica. Itzpalicue knew for a fact the Imperial government had yet to fit the scattered bits and pieces of the larger puzzle together into a recognizable shape. The Mirror only knew—*she* only knew—because they spied upon the activities of the *nauallis*, the priests who watched at the edges of things. The *nauallis* were not kindly disposed towards the Mirror-Which-Reveals, though they often acted in concert when a threat to the Empire was discovered.

The *nauallis* had yet to officially inform the Mirror, or the Emperor, of their awareness of an unknown power active amongst the Rim colonies. Itzpalicue wondered if the priests truly believed a threat was growing on these isolated worlds. It was possible the priests had not yet conferred enough to piece together all of the data available to the Mirror. Individually, the 'mice' were not as perceptive as the *nauallis*. Nearly every agent lacked the skills and talents of the least worthy *nagual*, but there were thousands more of them. And all of *their* reports flowed back to Anáhuac where enormous resources were devoted to sifting all that chaff for whole kernels.

One of those kernels—little more than a pine-nut—had brought Itzpalicue to Jagan.

Even before the arrival of the first Flower Priest, before the Fleet, before the foolish prince had made such a spectacle of himself, something was happening under the bloated red sun of Bharat. Initial reports indicated an odd pattern of off-planet purchases as Imperial trade picked up. Then one of the traveling 'mice' passing through the system had thought he'd seen an HKV agent in the Sobipuré marketplace. Yet, though the old woman had been on-planet for nearly a year now, she had not even caught a hint the Swedes were actually present in the sector. Their interests were always directed inwards, towards the older colonies, towards Anáhuac itself. They wanted to go home.

Itzpalicue had a sense, a feeling, of something inimical moving in the darkness. "Nothing more than smoke in rain," she grumbled. "How do you catch hold of mist?"

She hoped beating the bushes and shouting loudly would scare something into the open.

But will I recognize what it is, if I see it? The old woman shook her head, worried, and turned onto her own street. Thunder was beginning to growl in the heavy, humid sky. Her stomach answered, reminding her of a quick, spare breakfast. *Time for dinner.*

THE PETREL TOWNHOUSE
NEAR THE COURT OF THE RESPLENDENT KING,
CENTRAL PARUS

Following an immaculately attired servant, Gretchen stepped out onto a broad porch. The veranda was high roofed, with exposed beams of pale wood converging on an open cupola. A fire burned beneath in an iron bowl. Smoke twisted up into the opening, disappearing out into a rain-streaked night. Another storm had moved over the city with sunset, hiding the lights of the skyscrapers with fog, drenching the streets with flurries of rain.

"Come, dear, sit." Straight-backed chairs had been placed beside the fire, surrounded by a palisade of gossamer mosquito netting. Mrs. Petrel lifted her head, firelight gleaming on her resting kimono. Subtle images of canes and herons and bent-winged swallows were picked out in delicate thread, dark blue on darker blue verging upon black. "There's room for two."

Gretchen bowed very properly, glad for the burst of calmedown her medband sent surging through her bloodstream. The whole setting made her very nervous. A dry voice—very much like Honorable Doctor Kelly from her graduate research seminar—was keen to point out, *Your hostess's kimono is worth more than the Anderssen land-grant and all the timbering machinery. More than you'll make in ten years of grubbing in the dirt. More than . . .*

"Thank you, Petrel-*sana*." Gretchen nodded politely to the servant—a tall, lean man with an impassive face and watery blue eyes—and sat. She shifted a little, unused to sitting on a chair, particularly one with such a straight back. "It is very gracious of you to meet with me."

"Nonsense." The older woman tucked one leg under the other and produced a pipe from the folds of her kimono. "Are you hungry? Thirsty? Muru, do bring Mrs. Anderssen some tea—honey, thick, hot—not used to the chill of our Jehanan nights, are you?"

"No, ma'am." Gretchen forced herself to relax a little bit. "Shimanjin is very dry in comparison."

Petrel tamped tabac into her pipe and lifted a glowing punk from the fire. A spark leapt in finely cut leaves and she puffed quietly, letting the bowl draw at its own pace. "You'll get used to the weather, if you are here long enough. Until then . . . you'll be soaked with sweat and chilled at the same time."

A small folding table was set down between them, carrying two jadeite cups and a softly steaming kettle. Petrel nodded to the man and settled back, somehow contriving to slouch comfortably against the stiff wood. "Drink then—this is a native concoction, very restorative, perfectly safe." She smiled around the stem of the pipe.

Gretchen drank. The steaming liquid drove away the damp chill with admirable speed. The taste was unusual, more like drinking flowers than the sharp harsh bite of the black teas she could usually afford.

"I am sorry," she said, putting down the empty cup. "I tried to find you at the prince's reception to pay my respects, but there were so many people . . . are all of your parties so crowded?"

Mrs. Petrel laughed, shaking her head. "No. The Legation would be bankrupt if we put on such a show every month—or even every year. The presence of the Blessed Prince forced us to—ah—raise our bid or be driven out of the game. Such things are required . . ."

For an instant, the Legate's wife grew still in Gretchen's vision, face tight, eyes glittering with distaste. Thin curlicues of smoke froze in the bowl of the pipe. The woman's nostrils were drawn back, sharp little creases beside her generous mouth thrown in sharp relief by the firelight. *Such a weight she is carrying . . . does her husband see? Does anyone?*

". . . or we'll simply be laughed out of the Diplomatic service." Mrs. Petrel sighed openly, frowning at Gretchen. "It would have been nice to see an honest face, dear. I am reliably informed however, that you had a little trouble—besides the press of the crowd? Some business with the Honorable Doctor Sú's reckless children?"

"It was nothing," Gretchen said carefully. *Bad blood with the Tetzcoco faculty would only mean a reprimand from the field supervisor in her Company file.* "Only a difference of opinion about the work."

"They do not like you." Petrel puffed on her pipe, contemplating the ruddy glow of the fire. "They are cheap, loud boys. Much like their patron. I spoke with dear Soumake about your request for permits and—as you know—his hands are tied by the existing grant of work-rights. Only the Tetzcoco-designated primary investigator can loosen those restrictions . . . and you see how he's responded to your mere presence on-planet."

"I understand." Gretchen could hear mild regret in the woman's voice. Petrel did not seem upset by the outcome, which Anderssen found entirely understandable. *Why invite trouble for someone you barely know? Someone with no political connections to speak of?* "Thank you for thinking of me. It was very gracious of you to make the effort."

"You're welcome, dear." Petrel stared moodily out through the arches lining the porch. The glistening, wet trunks of perfume trees made a fence between firelight and the night. "I do not like the Honorable Doctor or the careless way he is pursuing his excavations down at Fehrupuré. Might as well be clearing the ruins with blasting putty. . . . He is rude, not only to me, to you, but to his native workers and the local village nobility."

Gretchen watched the Legate's wife with growing unease. *We've passed the polite part of receiving a visitor you barely know . . . shouldn't I be sent on my way now?*

"My husband," the older woman said in a slow, careful voice, "is concerned about the political situation. Things are becoming unsettled here, even dangerous. I have spoken to him about Doctor Sú and his methods, but there are larger matters on his mind." Petrel shrugged, dark silk rustling. She gave Gretchen a wry smile. "You will have to be discrete during your stay."

Anderssen felt an odd sense of association slip over her. Two shards of pottery, then three, clicking together; the shape of a bowl, a plate, a vase coming together in her hands. *Someone passed word on to the Company about the device, bringing me here. Someone who has extensive local contacts. Soumake? Through this woman?* She started to sweat, goosebumps washing across her arms under the thin fabric of her shirt.

"Of course," Gretchen said, forcing a smile, starting to rise. "My apologies for wasting your time."

"Sitting with friends—particularly new ones—is never wasted." Petrel pointed firmly at the chair, then beckoned for her manservant. Gretchen sat down.

"Muru—bring us some poppyseed cakes please. Thank you." The older woman smiled around the pipe again, face wreathed in smoke, waiting for the manservant to leave the room. Then she sat a little forward, eyes glinting. "I've heard the festival of the gathering of the *Nēm* in Takshila is very moving. A very ancient celebration, if you like that sort of thing. In fact, one of the oldest buildings on the planet is there, the famous 'House of Reeds.' "

Petrel looked up as the servant parted the netting and set a polished blue plate between them. A set of fresh, still-steaming-from-the-oven golden cakes were revealed. "Ah, just the thing. Here, my dear, try one—my great-grandmother's recipe. Delicious."

Gretchen bit into a cake, watching the Legate's wife warily while she ate.

Petrel leaned back in her chair again, face turned away from the dying embers in the grate. After a moment, she sat up a little and pointed out through the arches. "Do you see that bright star? There between the branches?"

Craning her head over, Gretchen managed to make out the steady, brilliant light. "Yes . . ." *What now? This is becoming surreal. . . . My groundside contact is supposed to be some smuggler with his hair in waxed braids, wearing too much cologne. We meet in an abandoned warehouse—the air charged with dust and diesel fumes and the smell of rust and burning insulation—not here, on a sixty-thousand-quill veranda, with servants and fresh poppyseed cakes on porcelain platters.*

"An Imperial ship rides in orbit. You can see them when the angle of the sun is just right and the sky is clear. . . . Muru there, he is my eyes and ears in the city, among the people. He says they have a tale told to children—of the 'star-which-returns.' Apparently, there is a parking orbit just visible from here . . ."

Petrel set down her pipe. Suddenly pensive, she rubbed her lower lip with a neatly manicured thumbnail. "Mrs. Anderssen, in truth, I wish I could put you and your two companions on the next starliner for the home systems. My husband has served on eight planets now, both as direct governor and as ambassador. We've been moving from place to place for nearly twenty years. Over all that time . . . Well, you start to develop a feeling for things." Her hands made a pushing-away gesture, eyes fixed on Gretchen. "Soon enough, Imperial citizens will not be able to walk the streets safely."

"I'll take care," Anderssen said. The older woman's voice had a funny tone—regret, pleading, warning—and the archaeologist suddenly turned and looked around the veranda. The servants stood quietly along the wall, faces in shadow. The furniture glowed in firelight, the mosquito netting obscured half-closed doorways into other rooms. She could hear the sound of water dripping from the perfume trees. Everything seemed very elegant, well-matched, perfectly placed. Her brief passage through the house reflected the same careful taste. *How much does all this cost?* An enormous amount, answered her grandmother's dry voice. *How much does a Legate or Governor make on the Imperial payroll? Not enough, not for such luxury.*

She turned back to the woman, throat constricted. *Four pieces fit together and the bowl begins to assume a beautiful shape; part of a handle fits, you can see the curve where the potter turned a fluted lip for a water jug. Patterns emerge from the jumble of lines and colors. The face of a god, a monster . . . my Company contact.* "Do you think the Honorable Doctor Sú would care if we spent a day or two in the north, to see this . . . festival? Visit the markets?"

Petrel's eyes glinted in amusement. "No. No, I'm sure he wouldn't do anything malicious. How could he know? Soumake won't tell him, and who else would know?"

Gretchen felt a little sick, feeling her stomach turn queasily with the same kind of acid bitterness which came every time she thought about her bank account. The woman across from her had a steady gaze. Her hands didn't tremble, but Anderssen wondered if there was a medband hidden under the silken drape of her kimono. *Or perhaps her blood is just as cold as nitrogen ice.*

"Well then," Anderssen said. "We'll get transport to Takshila and see the sights. You recommend the 'House of Reeds'?"

"An excellent itinerary," Petrel said briskly, reaching into her kimono and producing a sheaf of brightly colored papers in a cardboard sleeve. "There are a variety of ways to reach the old city—bus, train and so on. I suggest the train—here are tickets—and I've had a friend rent you an apartment."

Still rather numbed by the prospect of the Legate's wife working for the Company, Gretchen forced her hand to take the papers and stuff them into her bag. "Thank you. Is there . . ."

Petrel pressed a datapak into Anderssen's hand. "A guidebook to the local sights, if you will. Come back soon, and safe, and let me know what you've found."

The chattering sound of a news holocast greeted Gretchen as she closed the hotel door behind her. Her field jacket was soaked with rain, and she brushed damp hair from her eyes. The storm had picked up again during her ride home. "Maggie, did Parker get back?"

"He did," the Hesht grunted, her rumbling voice carrying down the hallway dividing their suite of rooms. As Mrs. Petrel had said, there were several petite hotels near the Court of Yellow Flagstones catering to the Imperial trade. This one even boasted a Náhuatl-speaking receptionist downstairs. Anderssen hung up her jacket in a tile-floored alcove, feeling the fabric of her shirt stick to her forearms. Despite a dehumidifier running somewhere in the ceiling, the air in their rooms insisted on congealing at every opportunity.

"He has made a mess, just like the scruffy kit he is."

Gretchen peeled back her sleeves as she walked into the main sitting room. Sliding glass doors set into burnished, rosy wood frames opened onto a balcony. The floors were covered with plush colorful rugs and carpets. Native artwork—mostly threaded tapestries held in ironwood frames—covered the walls. Everything felt crisp and new; the sheets, the furniture—the hotelier was betting on a steady stream of Imperial guests. Only the holocast set was out of place—an ugly, refurbished block of plastic and pitted metal hidden under a fresh coat of paint.

Gretchen considered the squat object—the heads of threevee Jehanan pundits were yammering in the air over the projectors—and felt uneasy. *This thing must be six or seven years old, a cheap Occitanian set. . . . And how much did they pay for it here? Too much. And how did they get political talk shows so fast? It's unnatural . . .*

Magdalena was surrounded by a drift of newspapers, holovee cubes, nondescript black equipment boxes, Imperial romance novels sporting lurid covers, tabloid-style magazines filled with two-d images of indistinguishable local celebrities, her comm-pad and plates piled with cracked bones. Antenna wires spilled off the bed and disappeared out a narrow window. Gretchen felt a little queasy for a moment, glad she'd missed the Hesht feeding, and then frowned ominously—someone had dumped a large, dusty rolled carpet on her bed.

"Did Parker do this?" Anderssen's nose twitched. There was a familiar oily smell, mixed with the tang of dust, grime and old shoes.

"He is shedding pelt," Maggie said absently, attention fixed on her comm. Delicate claw tips were tapping rapidly on the control surface. "Was there a heartfelt exchange of endlessly fascinating infant-cub stories with the packleader's mate? Consumption of sweetened, flavored alcohol?"

"Not quite." Gretchen cleared off a sitting mat and knelt to take off her dress shoes. They were out of style and scuffed, but better for paying a social visit than her work boots, which were three times patched. She caught Magdalena's eye, signing: *Can we talk?*

The Hesht nodded, flicking the back of a flat, spatulate finger against a black metal tripod perched on her side table. The cylinder sported a single green light, which was burning steadily. "No one's bothered to install landline pickups in the walls yet—a newly excavated den for sure! They build solid walls here, too, of fired ceramic brick, which dampens broadband emissions. Also, I've been scanning all the usual frequencies—lots of traffic, but none of it terribly sophisticated."

"Ok-kē. Parker! Get out here." Gretchen leaned back and sighed in relief, wiggling her toes. *Grandmother always said dressing properly required practice . . . didn't tell me I'd need adaptive surgery for my feet.*

A *shoji* slid open in the wall and the pilot stepped out of the bathroom, a towel around his neck, shallow chest freshly scrubbed. "Hey, boss, bring me anything to drink?"

"I think you've had dinner already," Gretchen said drily. There were Mayahuel beer bottles stacked in a pyramid beside his bed. "There some reason you're buying ratty old carpets? I think there is a rule of traveling which says 'don't put your crap on your roommate's bed without permission.' "

"Sorry! Just needed to put this down for a minute . . ." Parker took hold of one end of the rolled carpet and dragged it onto the floor with a heavy metallic *thunk*. Exhausted by the effort, he produced a tabac from behind his ear and looked around for a lighter.

"If you stink up our den with your bitter leaves again," Magdalena said softly, without looking up from her comm, "I will suffocate you while you sleep and draw out your intestines for my cubs to tease with their claws."

The pilot looked aggrieved. "I've my religious rights, Mags! You can't just . . ."

Anderssen made a face at Parker and pointed towards the balcony. "Worship your smelly god later, outside. I've news—our groundside contact showed up."

"At the packleader's den?" Maggie's ears rose slowly. "Or afterwards?"

"Here's what I know," Gretchen said, crossing her legs. "The Honorable Company stringer here is the Imperial Legate's wife, Greta Petrel. She's tight with the attaché in charge of antiquities and neither of them can stand the Tetzcocoan expedition leader. So . . . when attaché Soumake hears about something interesting, Petrel drops a note to the head office via diplomatic channel from the Legation. Nice and secure. She'll get a finder's fee from the Company banked straight to an Anáhuac account."

Anderssen shook her head slowly. "She has a nice house. An expensive house. Entertaining so lavishly must cost a fortune. . . . Like us, she needs the quills to make ends meet. Her ends are just . . . more costly than ours. She must have arranged our 'chance encounter' at the Legation so she could scope me up close. Tonight we had cakes and tea and she told me where the 'device' is. Maggie, do you have a local geodatabase up?"

The Hesht flashed two rows of needlelike teeth. "Of course!"

"In the city of Takshila, there is a ruin called the House of Reeds."

Magdalena hunched over her screen for a moment. "*Rrrrr* . . . not a ruin, hunt-sister. A living temple or monastery—there is a report here, from a Hussite missionary named Lynch who passed through the city several years ago. He says:

The House of Reeds is the most ancient structure in Takshila. Some say it is the most ancient structure still standing on all Jagan. From a distance, the hill is rumpled and gray, seemingly filled only with ruins. There are few windows or doors to be seen, for the denizens of the benighted place spend their lives in heathen practices which would not stand the light of day. A reputable local guide informs me they are called the mandire *which in the local dialect (more convoluted and difficult, I admit, than the plain-spoken Parusian) means 'those who are relentless.' Their charge is the protection and contemplation of an artifact of unknown provenance known as the* kalpataru*—the heavenly tree giving that which you desire.*

Gretchen raised an eyebrow, looked to Parker, who was still sulking, and then back to Magdalena. "A heavenly tree? Is there a description? Did this preacher actually *see* the artifact?"

The Hesht shook her head, long mane rustling. "There are no other entries. This is not a local datasource."

"Typical." Parker made a snorting sound. "Probably a trash disposal. Bet he heard about it while he was in bed with some—"

Gretchen shushed the pilot and handed Magdalena the datapak. "Here's everything the Company has on the House, the *mandire* and the *kalpataru*. Load it into all of our comps. I've train tickets, too, so tomorrow—Parker, listen to me—we need to find the train station and see how much baggage we can take with us."

The pilot nodded, though he didn't seem pleased.

"Maggie—is there any kind of local datanet we can query for more information about these priests?"

The Hesht shook her head mournfully. "I fear not, hunt-sister. This entire *kaaasha-shaan* suffered a catastrophic failure—one involving the profligate use of atomic weapons—six or seven hundred years ago. There are notes in what passes for an Imperial historical archive indicating a sophisticated world-net existed before the last collapse. But now? The natives just reinvented rotary-wheel counting-cards."

"Are you sure?" Anderssen unfolded from her mat and paced to the window. Outside, the storm continued to belch rain into the streets, hiding everything behind a wall of fog and mist. "There are relay towers on some of the higher buildings. . ."

"A voice network." Maggie tapped her earbug. "The Imperial Development Board for Barbarous Planets is financing a city-level network for personal use. Very old technology, cheap, reliable and easy to deploy—every kit and caboodle has one." The Hesht's tongue flashed in amusement. "Once all the relays are built, a world-net will creep up out of the grass . . . but there's nothing now."

Parker was frowning, which drew an inquiring eyebrow from Gretchen. "Didn't they have a communications network before the Empire showed up?"

"They had a post office," Maggie said, flat black nose wrinkling in disdain, "before you monkeys arrived. Paper letters delivered twice a day to each den in the city, once a day out in the country."

The pilot's disbelief was plain. "Not even a telephone? That's stupid. You can make a telephone with two cans and some string!"

"There are telephones," the Hesht snapped, "but they're restricted to central offices in each town or city—no private lines—and you have to stand in line, breathing everyone's—"

"Not string . . . shielded copper wire or optical thread," Gretchen interrupted thoughtfully. "Even a voice-only residential network would require thousands of kilometers of cable. Millions for the whole planet . . ."

The Hesht flicked her ears at Parker and sniffed loudly. "My hunt-sister pays attention."

"Sure . . . sure . . . I remember." Parker frowned at the dirty carpet as if it had begun to chew on his boot. "They don't have any ready sources of iron or copper or tin—all used up thousands of years ago. I get that—but if that's the case—then *anything* made of metal should be pretty costly, right?"

Anderssen nodded. "So?"

"So, why was I able to buy these for next to nothing down in the souk?" Parker knelt, rolling open the dusty carpet with a deft movement. There was a rattling clank and four gleaming metallic shapes were revealed under the cloth. Gretchen hissed in alarm, and then her eyebrows drew together in concentration. Each weapon was held in place by a strap sewn to the carpet. Rows of pockets between each rifle held ammunition magazines.

"Automatic rifles? Imperial issue? You bought these in a public market?"

Parker nodded, catching her eye with a worried glance.

"I went out this afternoon," the pilot said, running a hand over the nearest rifle. "Looking to catch the lay of the land, find some smokes, get Maggie the latest *malinche*—you know, the usual. Didn't scare up anything on the main streets, but then I found the edge of the market district and decided to see what was for sale in the back alleys."

Parker spread his hands, indicating the guns. "Off the boulevards, things are a little different than you'd expect. Hundreds of dark little streets lined with shops. Arcades three and four stories high filled with music and smoke and little bakeries. Cafés. A farmers market a kilometer long and two wide. And anything you might want to buy. These I found in a street of—it's hard to describe—but travel supplies, I guess: gangs of bearers to carry your bags, luggage, tents, these horned riding lizards, everything you'd need for a journey. And guns—lots of guns."

"How much did these things cost?" Gretchen's lips thinned to a sharp line. She glared at the pilot. She didn't care much for guns, not on the job. Any girl growing up in the high timber on New Aberdeen learned to shoot when she learned to walk, but that didn't mean she *liked* them. Having weaponry around meant there was an easy way to solve disputes—and Anderssen had teased enough bones out of the ground without putting them there too.

"Fifty quills the lot." Parker didn't smile. "These are military surplus submachine guns—they've makers' stamps from some factory on Kiruna. They're a knockoff of an old KV-45B rifle used during the last war. Super reliable. Takes a standard Imperial 8mm round. Won't jam up or rust in this drippy weather . . ."

Gretchen rapped her knuckles on the barrel of the nearest weapon. "This is anodized steel."

"Exactly." Parker started to chew on his tabac. "So if iron and copper are supposed to be like gold here, why could I buy these on the sidewalk? Why so cheap? What are they doing here anyway?"

"I don't know." Anderssen stood up. "But they're not our business and *we* don't need them. In the morning, I want you to trade them for something useful—anything but more weapons."

"Wha . . . boss! Wait a minute, there's something else you need to know." Parker stood as well, and Gretchen was alarmed to see open fear on the man's face. "I haven't been here long, but everywhere I went there was a really, really bad vibe in the air. Down in the souk—I mean where the natives go to get happy—they don't like humans very much. Not at all. . . . We might need these. I saw . . . there are plenty more guns on the street. And what about the priests in this reed house place? They don't sound very polite either!"

Gretchen shook her head sharply. "Parker! We aren't here to rob a bank, even if these monks are vicious fanatics. We aren't an army and we're not going to try and take on the city population. We're going to stay quiet and get up to Takshila and find out what this 'heavenly tree' is, or isn't, quietly. Guns are not quiet. Ever."

The pilot started to speak, saw the tense look on her face and raised his hands in defeat. "Sure, boss. I'll get these out of here in the morning."

"Good." Gretchen turned to the Hesht. "Maggie, can you access the local wireless voice network? Are our personal comms compatible? They are? Good." She shuffled through the papers Petrel had given her and found what seemed to be a rental agreement. "Find out where this apartment is and make sure it's in line of sight of the House. If it is, great, otherwise—find us someplace that *is*."

The Hesht nodded somberly. "What about this den?"

"We'll keep it," Gretchen said, staring out at the city again. Lights were beginning to shine fuzzily through the murk as the rain lifted. She wondered what the Jehanan sitting in those dimly lit rooms were thinking. *Are they cursing us? I might be, if Imperial merchants suddenly started dumping surplused machine guns on my streets.* "We might need to arrive suddenly at any hour. Keep the key."

A NONDESCRIPT HOUSE
ON A STREET OF TRUMPETVINES, CENTRAL PARUS

Skin stretched tight, a jittery hum tickling her spine, Itzpalicue settled into a nest of patterned quilts and v-pane displays. Thin trails of blood seeped down her chest, spouting like tiny serpents from pricks along her collarbone and breasts. The bitter taste of *oliohuiqui* burned on the back of her tongue and the Méxica woman felt two steps removed from the quietly glowing panels. Lachlan's technicians had installed two large v-pane displays on either side of the bed.

Every window was shuttered—the putative owners of the house were on vacation, visiting the seaside temple of Tembanifar, way off in the south near Patala—and reinforced with ablative armor. One display held a string of palm-sized v-panes, showing feeds from cameras scattered through the house and grounds.

A motley company of Arachosians squatted or dozed in the garden, long reptilian heads hidden by embroidered traveling cloaks. Not one of the mercenaries was more than a hand's reach away from his weapons. Invisible against the smoggy sky, translucent spybugs drifted over the whole neighborhood, watching every passing cart and laundry boy. Inside, the downstairs rooms were empty save for lengths of armored cable descending into the tunnels under the old house. Three meters behind each window and door, 'pop-top' area saturation weapons stood on triangular stands, ready to erupt if anything burst uninvited into the ground floor.

Itzpalicue's wrinkled hands drifted across the displays and they sprang to life, filling with dozens of v-panes, showing telemetry from the orbiting *Cornuelle*, video from every native and Imperial groundside source, an overhead view of the Mirror operations center, even the bridge of the Flower Priest support ship *Tepoztecatl*.

". . . thirty-five seconds to command conference call," Lachlan announced. In the background, his technicians were busy at work, examining and discarding datafeeds, winnowing out everything but the transmission streams from the Army cantonment at Sobipuré, the Legation in Parus and the *Cornuelle* high above. "Stand by to intercept."

The old Méxica woman stretched her back, settled her haunches and thumbed up the three primary displays. A blank v-pane appeared in each, accompanied by secondary panes holding personal information, morphology data and a constellation of datastream adjustment controls. She started to slow her breathing in preparation for a sustained burst of activity.

"Legation secure comm is up," Lachlan reported and the leftmost display shimmered. "Matching feed, slipstreaming . . . now." The face of a diplomatic service communications tech appeared to Itzpalicue's left for a moment as the man adjusted the comm set in a well-appointed office and stepped away. Legate Petrel sat down, stubbed out a thin cigar and leaned back, waiting for the other members of the conference call to come on-line.

"Running morphology check now. . . ." Lachlan's voice was a constant, steady whisper in Itzpalicue's ear. "Heart rate slightly up, eye-blink rate normal, breathing normal . . . tension index is moderate. He's having a good morning—the missus must have sent him off to work right."

That was not helpful of Greta, Itzpalicue thought in amusement. *He needs to be irritated.*

"Delay conference interconnect by one minute," she ordered Lachlan through her submike. "Push disturbance report series one through Legation."

The other two panes began to shimmer as Fleet and Army secure comm registered on the Imperial network. Itzpalicue let her awareness lose discrete focus, taking in the appearance of all three men at once. Both Hadeishi in orbit and Yacatolli at the Sobipuré base showed minute and welcome signs of tension. They waited patiently while the conference call synchronized.

"Legation push complete." Lachlan came back on-line. "Routing delay for triconnect stands at thirty seconds."

Legate Petrel looked aside as an aide leaned in, whispering urgently, a sheaf of dispatch reports clutched in his hand. Itzpalicue spent the extra ten seconds the delay gained them thumbing up the latest pause-counts for Yacatolli and Hadeishi. The Fleet officer's numbers made her frown.

Fleet and Army secure comm was routinely compromised by the Mirror in the name of state security. Lachlan's technicians had been busy for the past week capturing every comm stream generated by the three men waiting for the conference call. From this data, an array of Mirror comps had been building voice-delay patterns from intercepts of Hadeishi and Yacatolli in conversation. Luckily for Itzpalicue's purposes, the normal flow of human conversation was filled with innumerable silent pauses, gaps, filler sounds like *uh*, and misspoken, repeated words. Not all minds processed data at the same rate. A distinctly measurable response time dragged between exposure to new data and the mind's concious response.

Chu-sa Hadeishi's recent medical records indicated the long patrol voyage had worn down his body—immune counts were off, fatigue was up, muscular degeneration was apparent, reflexes had slowed—but his mind seemed to have been honed to a distressing keenness. His pause-count was quite low. The old Méxica woman's fingers danced across the panels, shifting comp attention to the *Chu-sa*'s datastream. *Every microsecond will count.*

"Connect in three . . . two . . . one." A solid green bar outlined each v-pane.

Itzpalicue let her mind release from conscious concentration, hands poised over the display controls.

"Our meeting has particular import this morning," Petrel announced without preamble as soon as the images of the Fleet captain and the Army colonel appeared on his display. He raised one of the sheets of paper in his hand. "Disturbing news arrived here only moments ago—news I doubt has reached the public networks. There has been an attack on a bus terminal in Bandopene on the upper Phison. Sixteen Jehanan were killed outright and dozens more severely injured. Local militia drove the attackers off, but suffered two wounded themselves."

Hadeishi's image frowned, but the Fleet commander waited silently.

Colonel Yacatolli was more abrupt in his response. "How does this concern us, Legate? There is inter-factional strife among the slicks on a daily basis."

"There is," the Legate replied. "The target of this attack, however, was a bus owned by Apaxis Transport Company, not the passengers. Apaxis uses imported vehicles of Imperial make—in this case, a Mitsubishi *Zō*-model seating sixty passengers—and the company is human owned. An Apaxis factor present in Bandopene believes the attacking gang was composed mostly of Jehanan working in the employ of rival transport companies."

"Imperial-made vehicles have a competitive advantage?" Hadeishi's voice was curious and entirely without the affront already present in the Army officer's. "They would inspire jealousy?"

"They do," Petrel said, pursing his lips. "They are very expensive by local standards. Only a company with Imperial investment capital available could reasonably afford one or more such vehicles. Apaxis owns twelve such buses."

Hadeishi nodded in understanding. "Quite aggravating to their competitors."

"This is not the first such attack." Petrel raised the sheaf of papers. "My aides have been culling the last several weeks' news reports. There have been nearly thirty such incidents."

"No one noticed this before?" The colonel interjected, surprised. "Weren't they reported?"

Itzpalicue moved—her hands a blur, and the two comps under the bed cycled fully awake.

No one noticed this before? Yacatolli said scornfully on both other channels. *Wasn't anyone paying attention?*

"Of course they were!" Petrel stiffened slightly in his chair. "We keep a close watch on everything occurring within the mandate—but none of these other attacks were against a company holding an Imperial charter!"

The old woman dialed up an undercurrent of scorn in the datastream carrying the Legate's voice to Yacatolli's headquarters. The physiology readouts for both men twitched upwards nicely.

"There was no reason to notice," Hadeishi said, very diplomatically. "*Shuchiji* Petrel, do you believe this is part of a larger pattern, or simply a series of localized disturbances?"

"I am concerned," Petrel said. "There is palpable tension growing between those who support the presence of the Empire and those who do not . . . as we all saw at the reception the other night. The natural rivalry between the Jehanan princes is both suppressed by our military presence and exacerbated by the influx of new wealth into Parus and Fehrupuré."

Yacatolli laughed, tapping the side of his nose. "You mean—the *kujenai* of Gandaris and Patala and Takshila have lost control of the trade monopolies which made them rich . . ."

Petrel nodded approvingly, pleased by the officer's grasp of the local situation.

And Itzpalicue's swift fingers made the colonel see a condescending smile.

"Even so." *Sneer.* "The great cities of the middle Phison—Fehrupuré and Parus—control vast populations and agricultural wealth, but they were starving for metal, timber and raw materials to fuel local industry. Their worked goods—textiles, machined parts, and ceramics—had to leave the local economy via the sea at Patala or by caravan via Gandaris. So things were in tenuous balance."

"But now," Yacatolli interjected, eyes narrowed in irritation, "we've put a spaceport right between them at Sobipuré, and a whole new economy is booming under our protective shield. Do you believe the outland *kujen* are preparing to move against Parus?"

"No . . ." Petrel frowned, showing concern. "But there are persistent rumors . . ."

No, the Legate said confidently on the 'cast feed, *though there are always rumors . . .*

". . . of intrigues and plots and mutinies." Petrel shook his head in dismay. "These princes are a nest of snakes. I don't trust them out of my sight."

. . . and they rarely prove true. The Legate shook his head dismissively. *Jumped up thieves and robber-barons, every one of them. I don't trust them out of my sight.*

"What do we need to do, then?" Hadeishi stepped into a momentary lull. "If there is a spate of anti-Imperial violence, can the local authorities handle matters, or should the Army?"

Itzpalicue's lips twisted into a grin, a soft green glow shining on her teeth.

What should we do, then? The Fleet captain's troubled voice fled across the datastream. *If there is more anti-Imperial violence, can the local authorities handle matters?*

"This is Imperial business!" Yacatolli stiffened in his seat and glared openly at Hadeishi. "Our treaties with the lords of the Phison are very clear—attacks on Imperial citizens will be handled by Imperial courts under Imperial law!"

"True . . ." Hadeishi started to reply, and Itzpalicue stalled the feed—only for a second or two—drawing the Army colonel naturally into the pause. Unbidden, Lachlan—who was watching the conversation on his own relay—kicked up facial manipulation on the Fleet captain's appearance, making the Nisei officer look slightly worried.

"I understand," Yacatolli said in a stiff voice, "*Chu-sa* Hadeishi fears for the ability of Fleet to protect Imperial interests on Jagan—he's made clear his ship's readiness is far below par. But the 416th has more than enough fire power to police the entire valley of the Phison if need be."

Hadeishi's physiological index crept up a point. Itzpalicue released the delay.

"True," said the captain. "Yet—Legate, *are* there Imperial courts in operation on Jagan?"

Petrel shook his head. "Not enough to deal with this level of brigandage. There is a circuit court here in Parus and small claims at the spaceport in Sobipuré." He smiled wryly. "Mostly to deal with crew from merchant ships in port."

Hadeishi heard . . . *crew from Fleet ships on leave.*

Yacatolli heard . . . *off-duty soldiers from the cantonment.*

Both indexes jumped a point and a half while the Legate continued to speak. Itzpalicue felt a singing rush of adrenaline replace the stretched-tight feeling induced by the morning glory extract melting under her tongue. Everything slowed—even the voices of the men arguing—and infinite silences swelled between their words. Plenty of time for her to shift and shade and replace meaning and intent as needed.

". . . so we've little choice," Petrel said in a considering tone, "but to use the local constabulary and judiciary to apprehend and try any Jehanan citizens who attack Imperial businesses."

"And if they attack Imperial citizens directly? If they murder someone?" The Army colonel fought to keep his temper on a short rein. "What then?"

Petrel raised a hand, his voice sharp. "Then we will need to try them ourselves—with the assistance and cooperation of the local authorities!"

"That won't work," Yacatolli said flatly. "You can't trust the slicks to turn one of their own over to our courts. That never works! You'll need my men to make the arrests." He glanced briefly at Hadeishi. "And we'll handle groundside transport ourselves."

Hadeishi saw a contemptuous sneer on his v-feed and stiffened at the insult.

"My shuttles can render any prisoner transport you might need," the *Chu-sa* replied icily. "Is there a suitable holding facility at Sobipuré?"

. . . are you sure you can keep them penned up at Sobipuré?

"Are *you* sure?" Yacatolli replied, not bothering to mask his irritation. "Aren't all of your shuttles behind schedule for maintenance and overhaul? I wouldn't want to risk the lives of any prisoners . . ."

"Enough!" Petrel's voice rose sharply. "Colonel, I am well aware of the reduced capacity of the *Cornuelle* at this time, but Fleet will do their duty and provide all the fire support and air cover you might need. This dispute is pointless. In any case, the 416th outmatches any force the local princes can put into the field, much less whatever thugs or brigands the local merchant guilds can hire. We are not faced with open war. We have a law-enforcement problem. We will treat it as such."

Both military commanders nodded, but *both seemed resentful* to Petrel. The Legate tried not to sigh openly at their stubbornness. "Colonel—you've already forwarded me an operations plan in case of a general uprising in the cities along the Phison. I would like you to work up—in cooperation with Fleet—an alternative deployment for your forces, so they can respond rapidly and effectively to these isolated attacks, should they escalate."

Both Hadeishi and Yacatolli heard: *prepare a distributed deployment for the 416th, to respond rapidly and effectively to these isolated attacks, should they escalate.*

"Petrel-*tzin*!" Hadeishi was alarmed. "Shouldn't part of the regiment be held in reserve at Sobipuré? What if there *is* a general uprising?"

But the Legate and Yacatolli heard only, *shouldn't the regiment be held at Sobipuré against a general uprising?*

"Such an event is quite unlikely, *Chu-sa* Hadeishi," Petrel started to say, but Yacatolli's response drowned his out.

"We needn't *hide*! A single arrow of my men could smash an entire division of slick cavalry—riding lizards, lances and all—much less these mobs of spearmen in quilted armor. We'll hold a proper reserve in case they spring something surprising on us—but otherwise, I can have ready-reaction teams in every provincial center within the week."

But the *Chu-sa* heard nothing of a reserve, only *ready-reaction teams in every provincial center within the week.* Yacatolli's intransigence was clear and easy to read in his face.

Hadeishi hid a grimace and raised his hands in acceptance. "Very well."

"Good." Petrel made a quiet, personal decision not to talk to both military commanders at the same time again. "It's settled. Good day, gentlemen."

The three v-panes flickered dark. Itzpalicue felt something like a physical shock, coming out of the elevated state of awareness induced by carefully applied pain and the *oliohuiqui* coursing through her system. A trembling hand brushed across the displays and the whole system began to shut down.

Beneath the bed, her two comps returned their attention to scanning and filtering the wireless voice traffic flooding the air over Parus. The old Méxica woman had set them to winnowing the chatter for hints and signs of her hidden enemy.

She slumped back on the bed, staring at the shadowy ceiling, exhausted and spent.

Her back teeth were humming.

For a moment, she felt young again.

UP-RIVER
THE PARUS-TAKSHILA RAIL LINE

A jarring bump woke Gretchen from a heat-induced doze and she looked around, momentarily disoriented, feeling the usual swaying motion of the train replaced by a clattering roar. The compartment shook, grit spilling from the lacquered ceiling, and across from her, Maggie hissed in annoyance. The Hesht shook her latest paperback in the air, shedding a cloud of dust to sparkle in the late afternoon sunlight streaming through the passageway door. Parker, his shoulder jammed in between the window-frame and the leather-backed seat, continued to snore.

Yawning, Anderssen stretched and peered out through a grimy, soot-stained pane of glass. The daily express train from Parus to the northern cities was rattling across a wooden trestle bridge under a placid cerulean sky. A vast brown flood rolled past under the girders and ceramic rails—at this point, the Yellow Phison was nearly a mile wide—curling around ancient stone buttresses. She could see debris caught in the current below; brush, something like a dead cow with six horns—a *molk* according to the flora and fauna booklet—cellophane bags, drifts of river weed.

The train passed unexpectedly into shadow and Gretchen looked up. For a moment, her eyes had trouble focusing on the size of the edifice blocking out the sky and then she gasped aloud.

"Hunt-sister?" Magdalena put down her *malinche* and leaned across Parker. A glossy black paw swiped at the window, clearing away a decade's accumulation of sweat-oil and scale-shell. "What . . . *hssst!* Builders of the Ark of the Fathers!"

An enormous gleaming arch supporting a flat 'crossbar' rose from the middle of the river. Brown water surged around leviathan pillars. Blue-green moss clung tenaciously to a surface shimmering like abalone shell. The railway bridge ran straight as an arrow under the vault, passing slightly closer to the eastern buttress. Gretchen craned her neck, staring up, and guessed the flat top of the arch was nearly four hundred meters high and six hundred from end to end. The 'crossbar' flared out in a jagged lip. The obviously shattered edges were in striking contrast to the smooth, elegant proportions of the rest of the mammoth structure.

What could have broken off? Everything else seems so sturdy . . .

The part of her mind which could puzzle out the surviving fragments of a broken Tcho-Tcho pot from the midden debris of a late Khmer burial site stirred. She looked east and then west, staring at the banks of the river. A cold chill washed over her and she flinched away from the window. Far in the distance, on the northern horizon, a long blue smudge marked the rampart of the low hills ringing the city of Takshila.

"*Hrrrr . . .* " Magdalena paged through her guidebook. "Ah! The 'Arch of the Risen Dawn,' " she rumbled in her deep voice, "the largest standing remnant of the Haraphan civilization which once ruled all of Jagan, nearly a million years ago. Huh—doesn't say what it was . . ."

Gretchen swallowed, staring at the lumpy hills in the distance. All the land they'd passed through since leaving Parus was depressingly flat farmland, lined with tiny roads and hedges of dusty blue-gray brush. Every few kilometers, the whitewashed buildings of a village—each sitting atop a substantial hill—broke the monotony. The fields spiraled out from the villages, following shallow canals cut through brick-red soil.

"It was a bridge." Her voice sounded strange, as if it rang from a great distance.

Magdalena's ears twitched back and she made a disbelieving sound.

"Once," Anderssen said, rubbing her thumb against the dirty glass, "it vaulted a swift white river plunging through a rocky gorge or steep hills. The Haraphan builders drove the pillars into the sides of the canyon and laid their road atop . . ." She peered outside, but the train had rattled on, leaving the slow muddy river behind. "The roadway is gone, shattered as the land wore away, carried down to the sea by the waters of the Phison, or torn up for building material. Only the bridge itself remains—the Haraphan engineers built to last."

Maggie closed her guidebook, nostrils flared. Her hackles were stiffening. "*Eeee . . .* can . . . can the land change so much, in this million years?"

Gretchen nodded, still cold, and she shrank into her seat, tugging the field jacket around her. The dusty, hot compartment now seemed small and sad and terribly fragile. A queer sensation of weight—building in her thoughts since they'd climbed the endless flights of stairs up to that first horrible little hotel room in Parus—now settled fully on her.

Everything is ground down here by age, even the land. Everything. Leaving nothing but finely ground dust. What I'll be, soon enough . . . Anderssen felt terribly sad—not for the Haraphans, so obviously wiped away by the inexorable progress of history—but for herself, knowing Duncan, Tristan and Isabelle would be unrecognizable when she saw them again. *And how much longer will my mother live? She's not young, not anymore. . . . Is this artifact worth anything?*

Parker continued to snore, his mouth slightly open. Gretchen hugged the jacket tighter. She had a sinking feeling the *kalpataru* would be nothing more than a can full of rust.

"Here isss room." The Jehanan rental agent inserted a cross-shaped key into a lock at the center of a hexagonal portal. Gretchen stepped through the opened door, duffel bag dragging from her shoulder, and stared around at a long, empty chamber. Soot-stained windows lined the northern wall, looking out over the jumble of Takshila and its seventeen hills. The floors had once been lacquered wooden parquet, but years of wear had left some sections black and others an eroded white.

"There isss cleaning de-posit," hissed the rental agent's voice through Magdalena's translator. The slick showed a mouth full of pinlike teeth. "For *asuchau*. Very dirty."

Magdalena nodded dolefully in agreement and pressed a stack of Parusian *shatamanu*—trade coins—into his claw.

When the agent had yielded up the key and a stack of paperwork with colored stamps, waxed sigils and handwritten signatures affixed, the Hesht spun the door closed and coughed in amusement. "See, Parker? He agrees!" Mockingly, she chanted: "If we lose deposit, your hide will pay me back!"

"Sure . . ." Parker stuck his head in the nearest door opening off of the main room. "Toilet? Filled with sand . . . just like Maggie likes it!"

"That's the bathing room," Gretchen said absently, staring out one of the window panes. "The toilet will have urea crystals in the cracks between the floor tiles."

Her calves hurt and her hip was throbbing. The apartment tower—a *khus* in the local dialect—stood among a cluster of equally tall buildings just to the east of the city center. As in Parus, there were no working elevators. The steam-powered express train had left them at a station on the southern fringe of Takshila. Getting a taxi had proved impossible—where Parus had benefited from an influx of imported Imperial vehicles, the northern city seemed almost untouched by the signs of Méxica commercialism so apparent in the south.

Having no way to identify an honest porter from a thief, they had carried their bags through the streets to the apartment tower themselves. A seemingly short distance on their one map had become several miles of pushing through strange-smelling crowds and dodging carts and wagons drawn by lizardlike beasts of burden. That had been unpleasant.

Maggie slunk in and out of all the rooms, before testing the windows. Each opened along a grooved track, but years of pollution had jammed them shut. The Hesht grunted, running an extended fore-claw through the black gum sticking the window panes closed. "Den needs a good scrubbing—but Parker would be welcomed among his gods by smoking this . . ."

Takshila was strewn with seventeen famous hills, and circumscribed to the south and east by a tributary of the Phison. The largest of the hills—a stolid limestone outcropping rising above neighborhoods of tightly packed buildings—stood in full view, bathed russet by the late afternoon sun. At first glance, the massif seemed untenanted and empty, but as Gretchen let her eyes rove over the whitened cliffs and straggling trees clinging to the rocks, she realized the entire top half of the hill was a single enormous building.

So this is the House of Reeds. Anderssen slid the work goggles down from her forehead and clicked up a magnification mode. Now, without the grayish-yellow haze permeating the city air softening edges and obscuring vertical walls, she could see dark windows piercing the hill, staircases climbing shoulders of barren rock, arcades of pillars, and the ornamental trees filling terraced gardens. *Quite large . . . doesn't seem so old, though.*

Puzzled a little—her first impression of the city was of relative newness, particularly in comparison to Parus, which had fairly reeked of hoary age—Gretchen began scanning the rest of the city within her line of sight. *Skyscrapers, more of those odd curved boulevards, wide streets . . . hmmm . . . each hill is circled by radial roads . . . ceramacrete buildings . . .*

"Ha!" She laughed aloud and pushed her goggles back up. Turning around, she found Parker watching his self-inflating floor pad deploy itself. Maggie was banging around in what had to be the kitchen, though Gretchen wasn't sure she *wanted* to see what passed as a Jehanan kitchen. "Mags—this big hill to our north is the House of Reeds, right?"

"*Yarrrrr*," responded the Hesht. She emerged from the kitchen with a hooked steel blade as long as her forearm. Parker's eyebrows rose in alarm and he backed quietly away to stand near the front door of the apartment. "You wanted a hunting lie close to the prey, yes? Well, there it is. All rocky and grim-looking as any citadel of the slave-lords of Magdag . . ."

Gretchen made a face. "Slave-lords? What *have* you been reading? Is that a cutlass? Why do the Jehanan have . . . never mind."

Magdalena sniffed ostentatiously, whiskers twitching and went to the nearest window. The hooked blade proved to be near enough in size to allow her to pick out the gummy debris clogging the window tracks without getting her claws dirty. The Hesht began rattling the window back and forth, trying to make it open properly. Making a face at being so ostentatiously ignored, Anderssen turned to the pilot.

"Parker—would you say this is an older city than Parus?"

"This place?" Parker had a tabac out, but seemed wary of lighting up while the windows were still closed. "Not as old, I guess. Kind of funny, since Parus is so filled with the comforts of home—buses, aerocars, three-d sets, personal comm, six kinds of Imperial beer . . . —didn't see any of that here."

Gretchen nodded brightly, running her hand across the nearest wall—smooth ceramacrete—just like the dorm buildings at university. "We have to be careful," she said, considering the material. The layers of bonded polycarbonate were almost imperceptibly flaking away. "According to Petrel's guidebook, Takshila has some of the oldest buildings on the planet. More than just the monastery over there. I think this apartment building is one of them."

"This place?" Parker looked around. "But—"

"You thought the buildings in Parus looked old because they were made of crumbling brick, and not more than five, six stories high. Crowded together, blackened with soot from wood-fired stoves—all those things say *old* to us. To humans. Right?" She gave him an expectant look.

Parker spread his hands questioningly. "Hey—not an archaeologist! Pilot. Pilot. I fly aerocars, shuttles, old-style air-breathing jets, drink too much, smoke too much, always ready with the clever quip. Figuring out historical strata or long-term habitation chronologies is not in *my* job packet!"

"Hah!" Magdalena jiggled the wooden window-frame and the panel moved smoothly in the newly cleaned track. Once open, the window allowed a gust of cold, bitter-tasting air into the apartment. "Eeeww . . . an entire planet of leaf-smoking herbivores . . ." She slammed the window shut again, looking aggrieved. "I wear a breathing mask from now on. We'll need one of these windows open for cameras and aerials."

Gretchen ignored the Hesht muttering to herself. "Think about the societal-crash, Parker—some of the cities, like Parus, were obliterated by atomics. They've been rebuilt *new* but with the materials at hand; fired brick and wood and ceramic tile. This building is ancient—I'd guess Takshila wasn't hit with a nuke during the collapse—so it's built from materials the *old* civilization had mastered. The cues we're used to following? They're reversed here!"

"Sure, I get it." Parker gave her a puzzled look. "Is that going to matter?"

"It might." Gretchen made a face at the pilot, annoyed he didn't share her interest.

"Well, let me know when it does, right?" Parker began unpacking his sleepbag and personal effects. Anderssen looked around to see if Maggie was interested, but the Hesht was already arranging a nest of communications equipment and blankets and coils of cable and other, unidentifiable tools around her. As promised, the technician had already mounted a camera in the open window, pointing across the sprawling city at the hill.

Feeling stymied, Gretchen zipped up her jacket and leaned on the windowsill, watching the cityscape below. *Why didn't I take that post-doc position at the Ney Arkham institute? Why?*

The sun was low in the sky, almost vanished into the layer of smog hanging over the city, and the air at the thirty-third floor level was getting chilly. The hill holding the monastery of the *mandire* was still glowing with the light of sunset, while the darkened neighborhoods at its feet were beginning to sparkle with lights. From a height, the city didn't look as dangerous and dirty and crowded as it had felt in the heat of the afternoon.

Anderssen stood at the window for a long time, watching the city slip steadily into night. Then her stomach growled and she shivered, turning away.

"We should get some food."

"*Hrrr* . . . yes. I should go hunting." Maggie looked up from her equipment, most of which was now humming and chirping to itself. One of the v-panes showed an infrared view of the massif. Figures could be seen coming and going along the narrow staircases.

Parker turned from the open window, flicking the stub of a tabac out into the empty air. "I can go, kitty-cat. I know what we all like—assuming I can identify the basic food groups in the street vendors' stalls. But grease, bread and meat should be about the same everywhere."

The Hesht shook her head as she draped a stained and mended rain-cloak around her shoulders. "Not wise, cub. I'm beginning to get the smell of these scaled-runners-underfoot. Humans are not welcome in Takshila. Didn't you hear them hissing and lashing their tails when we were walking from the station?"

"Yes," Gretchen said, kneeling by her own pile of gear. "This dialect's not working so well with the translator in my earbug though . . . could you make out what they were saying?"

Magdalena's tail twitched from side to side. "Distrust—envy—fear—hatred, they all smell the same, even if the pelt is different and one clan says *'hhrrruukh'* when the other says *'hhrrruuch.'* I will go out—they have not seen my kind before—I'll be no more an oddity than a stray Hikkikit going to market."

"A Hiki-what?" Parker glared at the Hesht. "I think you're making up the names of things now. That is supposed to be what *humans* do for a living!"

Magdalena bared her incisors and hissed dismissively at the pilot. "Read the guidebook—there are more races on Jagan than the Jehanan. I will return soon."

"Wait, wait, wait . . ." Parker found his own jacket and goggles. "I'm coming with you. I'm almost out of my delicious 'bitter leaves' and we're not going through that whole 'me-having-no-smokes' business again. Look, I'll wear my potato hat—no one will be able to tell I'm human!"

"Maggie—" Gretchen raised a quieting hand. "Let him go. Comm me when you're back and I'll open the door so you don't have to lug the key around."

Gretchen slowed to a halt, feeling sweat trickle down her back, and looked up at the ribbon of dirty brown sky visible overhead. She clicked her teeth, turning on the comm built into her earbug and goggles. "Magdalena, I'm lost again. Can you tell me where I am?"

For a moment, there was only the spitting hiss of static—something in the local environment threw out an inordinate amount of interference on the bands used by their work radios—and then Anderssen could quite clearly hear Parker coughing violently. A wicked chainsaw-starting sound drowned him out and then Magdalena's voice was filling her ears.

"Kit kit kit . . . always getting lost on the way home from the watering hole . . . ah . . . you're not on scope here either. Can you see a landmark?"

"No . . . if I could, I'd know where I . . . what is *wrong* with Parker? He sounds like he needs new lungs again."

Maggie laughed. "He . . . he is trying to smoke the local leaves. They are very strong, I think! Stronger than Parker—he is lying on the floor now. *Hrrrr!* What a funny color he is!"

"Great," Gretchen muttered under her breath. "Check his medband—but if he has a seizure, there's no doctor."

There was momentary silence on the channel. Anderssen moved into a doorway, finding even a little sun too much in the all-encompassing humidity. *Lucky it's so cool up here in the hill country*, she thought miserably. *Not like Parus, where it's really hot.*

The streets of Takshila came in two flavors—wide, curving and lined with broad-leafed trees, apparently part of the citywide network of ring-roads radiating around the seventeen hills, and narrow and twisty. While getting from the apartment tower to the monastery hill itself seemed simple enough from thirty-three stories up, the lack of aerocars meant Gretchen had to use her own two feet for the day's business.

The close, hot air put Gretchen on edge. The impassive, alien faces of the Jehanan did not make her feel welcome. The tension on the main streets was bad enough—today, she could feel hostility sharp in the air—but the side lanes were claustrophobic. There were doors—but they were all closed and locked and seemed very solidly built. In her experience, that meant a district where the fall of night meant footpads and murder and thievery. By day, it all gave her a stifling impression of being a rat in a maze—with no cheese in sight.

"Parker will live," Magdalena's voice boomed in her ear, making Anderssen jump. "Good there is no carpet here for claw-sharpening, or it would be ruined. These fierce leaves have wrestled our smelly cub to the ground and pinned his ears right back."

"Can you find me?" Gretchen tried to keep her voice calm. No gang of murderous locals had come along in the past five minutes, but a twitchy feeling between her shoulder blades was convincing her they would *very soon now.* She could hear noise ahead—bouncing back and forth off of the buildings—and it sounded like lots of people. Lots of angry people. The thought of continuing down this narrowing lane filled her with dread.

There was muttering and the clicking sound of Magdalena's claws on her comp panels. "No. Your locator signal keeps hopping in and out of its hole. If you get to a clearing, or a sunny rock exposed to the sky . . ."

Anderssen took a steadying breath and her fingers drifted to the medband on her wrist. She could feel her heart speeding up. *Right. Time to retrace my steps—if I could remember which way I'd come! Stupid machines, why do they . . .* Her thoughts became still for an instant. *Wait. Remember . . . how do you unravel a knot you can't untie? You close your eyes. Let your fingers—or your feet—find the way.*

Then doubt assailed her. Why should her feet, mended workboots and all, know their own way back to the apartment building? *Because Green Hummingbird would say you'd left a shadow on the world while you were walking and if you were quiet, quiet as a desert mouse, you could catch hold of that shadow and follow it home.*

The jarring sound of a clanging gong joined the angry, buzzing noise filling the air in the alley. Gretchen thought she could hear the trampling of hundreds of huge clawed feet on cobblestones. The sway of flickering, scaled tails. She knew how that felt, to have a long counter-balancing tail, to have stiff three-clawed feet digging in the sand as she ran.

Just like the Mokuil. As I was, if only for a moment . . .

Anderssen was surprised by the clarity of the memory, the fierce feeling of the Ephesian sun burning on her face, thin, bitterly cold air biting at her throat. The events she'd suffered through on Ephesus Three were muddled now, both by Imperial memorywipe and time, but every once in a while something surfaced, sharp and clear as broken glass. For the last year and a half, she'd done her best to ignore the hallucinogenic visions.

But now—here in this hot, alien labyrinth—the memory felt useful.

Suspicious, she looked at the houses lining the lane with sharp interest. Her moment of connection with the denizens of dead Mokuil had only been momentary—an hour, if that long—and suddenly Anderssen was sure the creature she'd shared footsteps with was not so very different from these Jehanan. The Imperial survey notes said the Jehanan had come to Bharat from another world—some kind of interstellar migration—had they crossed the void from lost Mokuil, wherever that might be?

Did—could—Green Hummingbird know I'd step into their footsteps again? Such a coincidence seemed impossible. Anderssen set the hypothesis aside in her mind. *No data. Nothing but a queer feeling. Not enough . . .*

But sometimes an irritating feeling—a sense of things being out of place—was all she'd needed to find something lost, a missing bit of evidence, a bone, a stone, whatever she needed to find in the rubble of the dig. Gretchen pushed away from the wall and clicked the channel to the apartment open.

"Maggie, I'm going comm silent for a bit. Watch for my locator signal."

She shut down the earbug and then went through the gear on her belt and body-webbing, turning off everything running on a fuel cell or power chip. Then she closed her eyes again and stepped out into the lane, fingertips outstretched, feet firmly planted.

The sounds of trilling and squeaking and drumming in the air around her changed, shifted, fell from chaos into order. Gretchen breathed steadily, her attention focused on counting—a simple series of numbers, no more, no less—and let her feet, her hips, her arms shift minutely, bit by bit, until she felt perfectly comfortable.

After a long time, the sounds changed again and she felt cooler—had the sun been obscured by clouds?—but the buzzing noise resolved into voices piping and squealing. *Children? Delicate fluting voices. Not adult Jehanan, for sure.* The gong continued to sound, a stately voice calling out into some open space. *A park? A square?* Wheels were rattling on stone, that was very clear, the constant passage of wheeled carts and rickshaws. *A commercial street beside a square. A temple, a school, someplace where the young are taught to sing.*

The moment of cold passed and Gretchen felt the sun touch her shoulders and hair. *Clouds are gathering. It will rain.* Someone passed her in the passageway and she could feel—not hear, no, the moving creature said nothing—a sensation of *pardon me* as it passed.

Gretchen turned away from the unseen square and street and school, feeling the air push and press at her, and began walking. The sun was warm on the side of her face. Plaster brushed dustily under her fingertips.

She continued to count and walked more confidently. The lane turned and turned again, and then she was walking down a flight of steps. She could hear a saw cutting through wood, smell sawdust and hear the chatter of workmen laboring over their daily business.

Parker groaned in pain and rolled over on the blanket. He stared, eyes bloodshot, at Magdalena's back. The Hesht was working on the windows again. Four of the panes were open, letting a cold, damp breeze eddy through the barren apartment.

"Wha' you doing?" The pilot's mouth felt fuzzy and bruised at the same time. "Di' I pass ou'?"

"*Hrrr* . . . You're sicker than a cub who bit a spinytail on a dare. Drink your water."

A half-full water bottle stood on the floor beside Parker's sleepbag. Gingerly, he moistened his mouth. That seemed to cut some of the horrible taste, so he took a longer swallow. "Gods, Mags, it is fucking cold, can't you close a window?"

The Hesht looked over her shoulder, yellow eyes sharp. "No. Crawl under your hide and turn on the bag heater. Packleader needs running three-d camera, infrared, sensor readings—all the eyes of the hunt we have—on the hill. Business, remember? Hunting, remember? No—you're coughing bile and cheese on nice clean floor while I work. *Hrrr* . . . stupid leaf eater."

Parker stared around, realizing the room had changed considerably since he'd shaken a local tabac out into his hand. The cig had smelled all right—a little sharp—but nothing like some of the things he'd smoked over the years. Came in a fancy cardboard box with advertising on every square centimeter. A stick of flavored chicle had been stuck in a cellophane wrapper on the back and the front had a little mini-manga which folded out. All completely confusing, of course, as Parker hadn't taken the time to learn the Jehanan script, but the tabac had *seemed* safe.

Of course, after inhaling he couldn't remember anything until opening his eyes in a pool of his own stomach lining. He forced himself up onto his forearms.

"Where's the boss?"

Maggie shook her head and wrenched the window pane she was working with violently. The glass made a shivery sound and cracked diagonally. The Hesht made an irritated hissing sound and groped around with her spare hand to find some sealotape. "Packleader will talk to us later."

"Why? Did something go wrong?" Parker levered himself up. The room began to spin.

"Wrong? *Hssss* . . . puking kitten, has anything gone particularly right since landing? No—the whole planet smells like your urine, nothing works, there are no soft beds and even the freshly killed meat tastes like hides-in-the-grass-and-bites-your-tail. *Hrrr!* Wrong? *Hrrr* . . ."

Parker nodded woozily, elected to say nothing and collapsed.

Shadow passed over Gretchen's face, her footsteps echoed down some kind of tunnel for thirty or forty paces and then she came out into a quiet space, half in shadow, half in the sun. She could smell rain gathering when the cooking smoke wasn't too thick—but for the moment, in this place, the sun was shining clear. A strong smell of wood smoke, hot tile, yeast and metal tickled her nose.

The feeling of the air pressing her, guiding her in a direction, evaporated.

Anderssen opened her eyes, disappointed, sure she was not back at the apartment building. *That didn't work worth a damn.*

Two lanes came together in a jumble of archways and a looming wall of square-cut stone. Ahead, she could see a half-open door and beyond that, a sunny garden filled with red and blue flowers. The sound of a treadle clacking away filtered out of the upper air. To one side, to her left, was an alcove where the heavy stone wall came to an abrupt end.

A curving surface, cool and blue-green, shone in the sunlight. For an instant, as she first became aware of the fragment, Gretchen thought she was staring into the ocean depths, light bending and scattering among rippling waves, the image of the sun broken into dozens of reflections, each wavering in time to unseen currents. Then she blinked and there was only a smooth, solid surface glowing in the midday light. A section of wall rising above her head and an arm's reach to the left and right.

"Oh . . ." Anderssen stepped forward, nudging her work goggles up into her hair, stripping away her gloves, and gently—as gently as she'd ever lifted up one of her children—she ran her hand just over the surface of the—ceramic? Glass? Steel? Care urged her not to touch the unblemished surface, while hard-earned caution held her breath and kept her balance canted away from the object.

As her hand moved, the smooth surface seemed to ripple, just as water would move under a breeze, and then settled back into its accustomed shape. At the same time, a very faint tone belled out from the curve, filling the whole alcove with a wonderfully soft sound. ". . . That *is* beautiful."

A raspy, whispery voice grumbled behind her: "You stand before the moving waters."

Gretchen became still, wondering for a split second if the sound had been her own voice, or something she was thinking, and then turned around.

A Jehanan was squatting against the plastered wall opposite the curving surface. Most of the body was in shadow, though feet and hands were caught in a shaft of sunlight. Its scales were finely grooved and pale around the edges. Like most of the natives, it wore only a leather harness holding enameled signs of rank, and a long staff of dark wood lay against one shoulder. The creature's hands were broad, with long, strong-looking fingers. Gretchen's eyes flitted across a muscular, triply-ridged upper chest, splay-toed feet stained with dirt, and settled on tiny chips of stone and soil ground in and around the claws of both hands.

"Hello," she ventured, wondering if she'd trespassed onto someone's shrine. Guiltily, Anderssen stepped out of the alcove and into the lumpy floor of the lane. "Your pardon, I did not mean to intrude on your . . . meditations."

The Jehanan's head turned, regarding her. The eye-shields were plain and unadorned, shrouding deep cavities where two dark, glittering eyes caught a little of the bluish reflection from the curving wall.

"Your race is called Méxica," the creature said in a deep, slow voice. "I have studied your old tales from time to time. Only once or twice have I seen your kind, but they did not strike me as being a quiet people. You—are you a male or a female? No matter—came quite unnoticed until you stood between me and the waters."

"I . . . am a *human*—that is the name of our race as a whole—but I am not of the Méxica, who are a tribe, or clan, who rule us."

"This is clearer." The Jehanan rose and in the laborious act of motion, Gretchen realized the native was very old and female. Anderssen also felt a twinge of alarm—the native's command of Náhuatl was quite good for someone who had only met one or two humans before—and wondered what exactly the chances of her encountering such a being were. "You did not disturb until you spoke. Of truth, I was . . ." A sibilant *hooooo* interrupted. ". . . resting old eyes. Without interruption, I would remain until the still waters came, and then—" More trilling. "—the sun would be resting too."

"Do you . . ." Gretchen paused, her eyes drawn back to the elegant gleaming curve. "This is not a Jehanan artifact, is it? This is something from the time before your people, from the—"

The old native made a deep-throated sound, a booming hiss, and clashed her claws together to make a rattling, chiming noise. Alarmed, Anderssen jumped back, eyes darting for an exit. The creature seemed surprised by her reaction and shrank back. Clawed hands seized the staff tightly. Then the Jehanan relaxed, and there was more trilling.

"Pardon, pardon, pardon . . ." The long, angular head shook from side to side, eyes downcast. "I speak the name of those before—as they have made the sound—no alarm was meant, no bellow of challenge." The head rose. "Human voices small, ours large. You speak of the Ha-ra-phans, if there is no mistake."

"Yes, this section of wall, is this all which remains—like the bridge across the Yellow Phison, the Arch of Dawn?"

The lean old head, jagged with blunt horns, made a very passable human-style nod. "No more than shell-fragment, caught up in brick and plaster, stone and wood. Left behind in the fury of a new world. Long time this was buried. Entombed. Held-in-shell."

The Jehanan settled onto her haunches again and reached out with the staff to trace the edges of the curving surface. "Beyond this is house of sitting and eating and drinking. Many times, as a soft-scale, I sat there. Sometimes—if my busy, chattering mind were still—I felt warmth in this wall, pleasant, comfortable. But nothing catches the wiggling attention of a short-horn. Only last year did plaster give way and show what lay within."

Gretchen sat as well, intrigued. "Had you seen a Haraphan artifact before? Are they rare in this district, or common? Is there more of this one—perhaps hidden below the ground, or inside these other walls?"

"*Hooo . . .*" The Jehanan let out a long, trembling note through its nostrils. "Such a sharp bite *asuchau* thoughts have, fixing on the tasty prey, winnowing away skin, cracking bones. . . . Is anything left when you are full? Scraps of ligament? Splinters? A single lonely scale on bone-dry plate?"

Anderssen flushed, embarrassed. *Remember to respect the native religious observances, but don't think they haven't eyes to see what we really want.* The Honorable Doctor Kelly told her that in first year. Then she heard a half-hidden, swallowed trill and realized the creature was laughing at her. "Is there more than this section?"

"No." The Jehanan paused, and then shook her head in what seemed to be conscious imitation of the human mannerism. "I sit here. The light moves with air, clouds and sun. My people . . ." She paused, settling in upon itself. "Were spade to strike soil, mattock the wall, chisels and hammers the plaster, what might break under clumsy claws? Would they care? No, they would trample on without thought."

Gretchen rubbed her chin with the back of her hand, thinking. "Don't people come along this way—see the wall? Wonder what it means?"

"Do they see what you see, *asuchau* with sharp thoughts?" The Jehanan cocked her head to one side. "See what I see, when my gaze rests on shimmering waters? They do not care. Our people are tired after so long, after so many struggles, so many defeats. They wish to feed, to sleep, to mate. No more. Rarely do they look aside from their path, much less to the heavens."

"You sound . . ." Anderssen paused, trying to remember the first time she'd heard that particular lament—*from my grandfather, of course!*—and then laughed, realizing she'd muttered the same thing, more than once. ". . . like anyone watching the young, of any species, of any time."

"Perhaps." Gretchen wasn't sure, but there seemed to be a peevish, grumpy tone in the creature's response. "Truth, despite."

When the Jehanan fell silent, Anderssen said: "May I ask you a question?"

The long head lifted, which she took for assent. *This thing could probably just bite my arm right off with those teeth. . . . Why not stick my head right in?*

"What is your name? What do you do? For a living, I mean."

"*Ssss . . .* You dig in the marrow! Rude creature! *Hooooo . . .* Will you trade?"

Gretchen nodded, though a little voice warned her to tread carefully in matters of names, even with a stranger she'd never see again. "I will."

The Jehanan made a chirping, warbling sound, then shook her head. "No . . . your tongue is doughy and soft, sadly congealed. I am . . . perhaps 'Malakar' is close. Yes, memory agrees. A gardener. I once turned the soil, weeded away the pernicious, tried to see if young shoots would grow strong in the sun."

Anderssen bowed politely, as her grandmother had taken pains to teach her, and replied. "I cannot choose a Jehanan name which will suffice, but in my tongue, I am Gretchen. As you suspect, I am a digger-into-buried-things-which-ought-to-be-left-alone. But I try to be careful and sure of hand, and not break anything."

The Jehanan trilled in laughter, bobbing her long head. "How often have you made good that promise? Once? Twice? Ever?"

Gretchen felt a flash of irritation at the mocking tone, but couldn't convince herself the assertion wasn't true. "Things always seem to break."

"Then keep claws—"

A sound interrupted the old Jehanan—cascading out of the sky, echoing in the archways and rebounding from the tall white buildings—a hollow, extenuated *hhhhoooooooooo* . . . Malakar's long head rose, nostril flaps widening and, hissing like a leaky tea kettle, she rose again, leaning heavily on the staff.

"What *is* that?" Gretchen turned from side to side, fruitlessly trying to gauge direction.

"Time passes," the Jehanan rasped, pointing overhead with her staff. "See the sun?"

Anderssen covered her eyes against the ruby-tinted blaze of light shining down into the alcove. The Bharat primary was now visible in the triangular opening between the eaves. *Noon already? A wasted morning, then, getting lost. . . . Now how do I . . .*

"Your pardon!" Gretchen caught sight of the Jehanan's tail flicking around a corner and ran to catch up with the gardener. The native paused. "I won't keep you for more than a moment, honorable one. But . . . do you know how I could reach the intersection of *panca-sapta* and *trieka*?"

"*Hooo . . .*" Malakar eyed her up and down again, hissing softly. "Tall teeth indeed. You do not seem so rich or so powerful to have such a *khus*." A clawed hand scratched dirty scales. "Are you lost?" Gretchen nodded. "Entirely."

The Jehanan's nostrils twitched. She looked down the passageway, then back at the human, and then down the passage again. Laboriously, Malakar shifted herself around, the butt of the staff clanking on the ground. "Not polite to let guests wander and die in confusing city. I will show you the way."

Gretchen was short of breath and wheezing after fifteen minutes of following the old Jehanan up out of the maze of the city. Not only was Takshila located at considerable altitude in comparison to the lowlands around Parus but the gardener was quite spry. Despite being half blinded by sweat, Anderssen took care to note they had left the street level and climbed a flight of stairs—through a dark, musty shop selling carpets and between two buildings—to reach a flat rooftop.

"This is how the locals travel?" Gretchen looked around in appreciation.

Malakar nodded, indicating a landscape of domes, flat roofs, racks of drying, freshly dyed cloth and trellises covered with brightly colored flowers. "Streets below for commerce, for wagons, for hauling. This path is for sensible people."

"Not usually including humans, I'd imagine." The archaeologist adjusted her hat. Out of the humid tangle of streets, the air was cooler and the sun hotter. She surveyed the horizon and was immediately disgusted to see the base of the monastery hill less than a kilometer away to the north. *I was probably about to step out at its foot. . . . So much for Green Hummingbird's vaunted finding-the-path.* The cluster of skyscrapers soared against a cloud-flecked sky to her left. *Doubtless, Magdalena can count my nose hairs now.*

"You see? There is your destination." The elderly Jehanan pointed towards the apartment building with a long, tapering snout. "By ancient law, stairs which ascend to rooftops are public thoroughfares. Then you must pass between buildings. You see?"

Gretchen saw. While the rooftops of the buildings were filled with tub gardens, cages holding plump gray birds and covered patios, the intervening walls were topped by walkways of brick or wood. Sometimes lined by railings, sometimes not.

Without waiting, Malakar set off towards the cluster of finlike apartment buildings. Anderssen hurried after, trying not to gawk at the private patios on either side. There were a very large number of Jehanan out sunning themselves, either on blankets or on wooden frames, and none of them paid her any mind as she walked past. She was both relieved and wary. The hostile air prevalent in the streets around the train station was absent, but there was still a tense feeling in the air. As on the stairs, the gardener set a swift pace.

After another twenty minutes of clambering up and down flights of stairs and rattling along splintery walkways, the rooftops ended at one of the wide boulevards. Malakar paused, peering left and right. "This *panjir*-road leads to the *khus* you seek," Malakar said, rumbling voice slightly raised.

They descended to the level of the boulevard, and Gretchen became distracted as they turned right up the street. The curve of the roadway—seen intermittently through the throng of swift-moving Jehanan—kept drawing her eye. There was something odd about the trees shading the sidewalk. She stopped, staring at a planter. The tree itself seemed very old—the roots had cracked the pavement all around, lifting up concrete in tilted slabs—and the branches reached out almost level across the road, casting deep shade over a constant stream of carts drawn by brawny Jehanan runners.

Drifts of leaves had collected in the gutter along the edge of the road, but—and this was the oddity which had drawn Gretchen's eye—the surface of the road itself had not split or broken open like the concrete. Keeping an eye out for onrushing wagons, she brushed back the leaves. Beneath her fingers, a smooth black surface gleamed up.

"All these larger roads, they're Haraphan?" She looked up at the gardener, who was running both claw-hands across the ridged trunk of the tree. "They liked curved paths and surfaces?"

"*Hoooo* . . . yes. They say the straight is dangerous." Malakar tapped her staff against the disintegrating concrete. "Sturdily made, their things are. Last a long time, longer than anything made by our feeble claws."

Gretchen studied the native's face and the gardener seemed weathered and weary, more like the tree than the languid, soft-shelled youths loitering in the shop doorways, narrow heads wreathed in pipe smoke. "Do you know stories about the Haraphan civilization? Do records survive from that time? In stone or metal or . . ."

Malakar said nothing, regarding the human stonily. Her leathery lips twitched back, exposing rows of blackened teeth. Gretchen flinched and bowed automatically—still on her knees beside the invincible roadway—and pressed her forehead into the pavement. "Your pardon. Thank you for showing me the way home."

"*Huuuu* . . ." The gardener made a thoughtful hooting sound, then rapped her staff on the ground again. "As I say, they last, perhaps longer than we."

Then, before Gretchen could respond, the old Jehanan strode away without another word, the dark gray-green scales on her back dappled with sunlight falling through the branches of the ancient trees.

Anderssen watched the gardener go, then realized she was alone on a public thoroughfare, surrounded by thousands of busy Jehanans. Some of them were now staring at her—suspiciously, she thought—and keeping a wide berth as they passed. Whatever polite grace the gardener had lent evaporated in her absence.

Layers upon layers, she thought, turning towards the apartment building. *Did she mean records of the Haraphan civilization still exist, perhaps when the equivalent Jehanan history has been lost? Or . . . does she mean the Haraphans themselves still live upon Jagan?*

Anderssen kept her head low as she headed home, hoping to avoid notice. In comparison to the placid rooftop gardens and industrious, half-seen workshops, the public street was very loud and dirty and filled with agitated, angry natives. The barking sound of runner-cart horns drowned out everything else, even the hissing shouts and complaints of the drivers.

THE PALACE OF THE KUJEN
GANDARIS, "THE INDOMITABLE, EVER-VICTORIOUS BASTION OF THE NORTH"

A spear struck the window of the Imperial aerocar, the *lohaja*-wood point scoring the armored glass before falling out of sight. Prince Tezozómoc, sandwiched in between Colmuir and Corporal Clark, flinched at the sharp sound. The young man's eyes were screwed tight and his white-knuckled hands clutched his knees. The lean-faced Skawtsman peered out the window, taking in the surging mob filling the square below and eased the safety on his Nambu back with a soft click.

"Now there is a vigorous reception, mi'lord. They do seem to love us here."

The city residence of *kujen* Nahwar, prince of Gandaris, was a gaudy confection of russet domes and towers and fluted minarets gleaming with rust-colored marble. Colmuir could see a series of interlocking courtyards and gardens, all flush with green trees and limpid pools. Some of the inner buildings seemed to be entirely composed of flowering trellises. The stout, ten-meter-high battlement surrounding the palace would have seemed out of place, were it not for the thousands of angry Jehanan citizens swarming in the public square facing the residence. A squat gatehouse rose up out of a sea of gray-green faces, surmounted by an overhanging parapet. A cluster of Jehanan nobles was standing on the roof, well back from the edge, and Colmuir guessed the fat one in the middle with all the bronze and copper chasing on his body-harness was either the prince himself, or his vizier.

Below, in the center of the square, the mob was tearing a wooden landing platform apart with their bare hands while a whole array of priests hammered enormous drums, bellowed encouragement to the crowd and waved forests of painted banners over their scaly heads. Any sign of princely authority had fled. Smoke billowed from an impromptu bonfire fed by wagons, meters of pro-Imperial posters and anything flammable to hand. The crowd around the fire parted, allowing a dozen husky Jehanan to topple an elaborate plaster statue of—well, the Skawt guessed the local artisans had tried to model the effigy on a public relations photo—a human head atop a Jehanan body into the bonfire.

The statue crashed into leaping flames with a resounding crash and huge clouds of sparks leapt up. The cheering roar of the crowd penetrated the armored skin of the aerocar as a dull booming sound. Hooting in delight, the mob drew back as fresh jets of flame erupted from the collapsing mannequin, then rushed forward as the plaster broke apart and the effigy turned black, spewing an inordinate amount of heavy smoke. Another cart toppled into the conflagration.

"Swing over the palace," Dawd said from his forward seat. The younger Skawtsman had a Bofors Whipsaw squad support weapon cradled in his arms, the six-barrel muzzle resting against his window. "See if there's someplace to land."

The aerocar jolted to speed, sweeping through the air. A cloud of cobblestones, burning torches and more spears burst up from the mob, though Colmuir noted none of them had the raw strength of arm possessed by whoever had pitched the first spear. All of the missiles fell short, and then the aerocar was turning over the palace. Both Dawd and Colmuir studied the maze of gardens and pools and sharply pitched rooftops with growing dismay.

"Nothing big enough," Dawd grumbled into the private comm linking him and Colmuir. "Unless we want to try a step-off onto one of those balconies."

The master sergeant shook his head dourly. "We're aborting this drop. We'll go directly to the Gemmilsky house." He turned to look over the silent prince's head at the adjutant. "Corporal Clark, make sure the staff there is informed of our imminent arrival. I'll see if the Legation representative has his comm on down there . . ."

The aerocar banked in a tight loop as the pilot took them back across the palace grounds. Dawd could see dozens of curious faces at the windows, and some of the Jehanan in the courtyards waved as they sped overhead. The young Skawtsman wondered if the clients of the *kujen* were truly friendly, or if they'd been ordered to put on a welcoming show. None of the Jehanan nobility he'd encountered so far had struck him as being truly interested in friendship with the Empire.

They want whatever edge we can give them over their rivals, and I'm sure our diplomats are just as cynical in dealing with them. A sorry world, indeed. Dawd hid a sigh. He was sure the owner would be *very* gracious about being bumped out of his own house for the duration. *Sounds like he's a tough customer, though. Can't be dealing in cross-border trade in this place without having something to back it up with.* The Legation dossier on Johann Gemmilsky said the Polish nobleman was involved in a thriving import/export business—bringing sleek, Turzanian riding lizard stock down from the cold plains beyond Capisene and shipping a variety of machined products back north. *Guns, Imperial guns I'll bet, for breeding stock. Hope that means he's rich and has real toilets in his house.*

Dawd could hear Clark speaking stiffly to someone on his comm and checked the ammunition load on his Whipsaw. He doubted Gemmilsky would get violent, but there was no guarantee the local rumor mill couldn't beat them to the town-house in the form of another violent mob.

"This is outrageous!" The honorable viscount Johann Gemmilsky's voice made the chandelier in the main entryway of his tidy little mansion shiver, crys-talline droplets tinkling. "I offer my house for the prince's comfort—as a host, he as an honorable guest—and you say I must leave immediately? With only the shoes upon my feet? You are a rogue, sir!"

Colmuir, feet firmly planted, hands clasped behind his back, looked down at the Pole and narrowed his eyes. "This residence is now the property of a Prince of the Blood, Gemmilsky-*tzin*. You'd best be packing a bag and spending the night at your mistress's boudoir. With the situation in the city being so . . . volatile . . . we can't have any strangers about. You understand, of course. Security. Now, Clawk here will give you a receipt and you can charge the Legation for damages, but you'll be out of here before the Light of the World steps through those doors, won't you?"

Gemmilsky's pale blue eyes twitched from Colmuir's forbidding face to Dawd, then down to the black shape of the Whipsaw. The machine gun was politely pointed at the floor, but the younger Skawtsman knew he made a danger-ous figure with the ammunition bandoliers looping over his chest and behind his back. The heavy dark combat jacket didn't hurt either.

"I see. Very well. I will go, now, and be assured there will be a *very careful* accounting of everything in this house! There *will* be a bill for damages!"

"I'm sure there will be," Colmuir said in a stolid voice. He inclined his head at the adjutant standing beside Dawd. "Corporal, see Gemmilsky-*tzin* on his way, will you?"

Clark, giving the older Skawtsman a reproving look, escorted the business-man out of the hall.

"That was a little harsh, Master Sergeant." Dawd said. "I doubt he's a security risk to the prince." *At least he wasn't before! Now, though . . . who knows?*

Colmuir sniffed in disdain, looking around at the opulent wall hangings and hardwood floors. The house was certainly fit for the prince to lay his head on the silk pillows and featherbed the opulently appointed lower floors promised would be waiting upstairs. "I don't trust Poles and Russians, sergeant. You know that. Tricky, devilish fellows they are and murderous t' boot. The Light of Heaven himself has often told me to beware their wiles."

Dawd didn't bother to hide his disbelief. "Of course. I'll bring the prince inside."

"You do that," Colmuir said, picking up a slender vase from a small table set against one of the walls. He rubbed a thick, scarred finger across the golden porcelain with an appreciative eye. "I'll be checking the rooms for hidden devices, bombs, and the' like. Can't be too careful."

The younger man considered saying something, then took in the calculating look on the master sergeant's face and decided to keep his opinions to himself. *Now poor Corporal Clark will have to round up an air-truck to haul all this . . . booty away. The Resident is going to have an aneurysm when he gets the bill.*

Outside, Dawd hurried across a graveled carriageway, the collar of his jacket turned up against an unexpectedly cold wind, and opened the door of the aerocar. The Gemmilsky house was on a bit of a hill, surrounded by conical trees with long trailing limbs studded with sharp-edged leaves like an unwound accordion. The residence itself was three stories of marble-faced brick—all quite new, in a design which suggested a Russian boyar's villa implemented by a Jehanan architect who'd lost his glasses. In the air, the sergeant had praised the Mother and her Son for providing such a thick stand of foliage around the property. The pilot had dropped them straight in with the 'car fans on whisper, and Dawd hadn't seen a single Jehanan in line-of-sight.

On the ground, though, his neck was prickling as the prince stepped out of the car and looked around in perplexed amusement. *Just need one slick with a rifle or a compound bow in those trees*, he worried, fingertips light on the Whipsaw's firing lever. *And it's early retirement with no pension.*

"There isn't anyone to greet me," the prince said, rather petulantly. "Aren't there supposed to be singers and dancing monkeys and trays of sweets? I thought the *kujen* wanted me to come visit this dirty little city of his!"

"We should go inside, sir." Dawd didn't think Gandaris was dirty at all—the city climbed the side of a thickly forested mountain in tiers of white and tan and russet buildings. The air was cool and the climate—from what he could see of the foliage and surrounding mountains—was temperate. A far cry from the dirty, industrial sprawl of Parus far to the south. Even the railway line they'd followed along the winding valley seemed to be well maintained, with painted bridges each time the tracks crossed over the swift, white-flecked current of the Kophen. He could understand why Gemmilsky had chosen to set up shop here, where you could smell something like pine resin on the wind, and there were white-capped peaks lining the horizon in every direction.

Tezozómoc gave him a hurt look, put down his head and walked quickly to the side door of the house. Dawd waved the pilot to park the 'car in the carriage house and, walking backwards, his eyes restlessly scanning the trees beyond the closely cropped lawn, followed the prince inside.

"Now this is a gun," Colmuir said, beaming at the enormous rifle in his hands. "You'll enjoy shooting this, mi'lord. Yes you will."

Tezozómoc, who had only recently managed to drag himself out of bed, was sitting in the private garden behind the mansion with a steaming cup of coffee clutched in his hands. Despite the frosty morning—Dawd nearly wept with relief to step out into a proper temperature—the prince seemed entirely comfortable in a thin cotton shirt, flannel pants and bare feet. He regarded the Gandarian hunting rifle with naked distrust.

"You've mistaken my useless commission in the regiment, Master Colmuir, for actual skill at arms. This rifle is longer and heavier than I am."

"Now, sir—it can only weigh twenty or thirty kilos!" The Skawtsman heaved the weapon up to his shoulder. The heavy wooden stock, inlaid with curlicues of pearl and gold, didn't quite fit into Colmuir's shoulder, forcing him to brace it against his right pectoral instead.

"Bit unwieldy, though . . ." Colmuir grunted a bit before he could get his hands wrapped around the firing trigger, which was slightly longer than his thumb. A basket-guard resembling an archaic saber enclosed the trigger and the rest of the fittings were etched with tiny scenes of daily life in the northern *kujenate.*

Tezozómoc scratched his eyebrow, downed the rest of his coffee and set the cup under his chair. "I only weigh fifty-five kilos myself, *Cuauhhuehueh.* If I pick up that cannon, I'll fall over, much less survive shooting the abominable thing." The prince gestured impatiently at Dawd. "Sergeant, give me your side-arm. I will demonstrate the extent of my martial skills."

Dawd hesitated for just a fraction of a second, hand clutched possessively over his Nambu, and then forced himself to hand the weapon over to the prince. Colmuir watched the transaction with equal trepidation. Tezozómoc spat into the bushes, fumbled off the safety, turned his body like a duelist and pointed the gun at the far side of the garden.

"That potted tree," he said through clenched teeth and pulled the trigger three times in quick succession. The whip crack reports tripped over one another and a pinelike tree two meters to the left of the potted lemon tree shivered, shedding finger-length needles.

Dawd's combat visor—currently configured as a rakish pair of sunglasses—showed the other two bullets miss the pine tree as well and crack into the brick wall at the back of the garden. The lemon tree was unharmed. Tezozómoc turned, shrugged and tossed the gun to the sergeant, who caught it with both hands—gently as a baby—and immediately cleared the action and safetied the automatic.

"My father—glorious Light of the Heavens which he is—forced a dueling tutor upon me for nine years, Master Sergeant. Among my many faults are unsteady hands and a tendency to flinch. I couldn't hit the side of a ball-court to save my life." He grinned nastily. "Thus, your constant presence."

"But how—" Dawd swallowed the rest of the sentence, catching the furious expression on Colmuir's face. Flushing with embarrassment, he bowed in apology. "Your pardon, mi'lord."

Tezozómoc ignored him, snapping his fingers to summon one of the servants hovering just inside the patio doors. "Bring me something to drink," he barked as soon as a timid-looking Jehanan poked its head outside. "I smelled vodka last night, I'm sure of it—bring me the best you have! Two bottles!" Then the prince turned back to Dawd, who had assumed a stiff parade rest. "How did I graduate Officer School, you mean? Where I had to show skill with rifle, pistol and blade?"

Dawd remained entirely still, staring fixedly at the puffy clouds cavorting amongst the shining white peaks looming over Gandaris. Tezozómoc squared his shoulders, planting his bare feet on the ceramic tiles as if he were on parade himself.

"My glorious father would rather have cut out his own heart than stoop to 'speaking privately' with the commandant of Chapultepec. There were no bribes, no gifts, no quiet exchanges of favors." The prince licked his lips and Dawd caught a glimpse of half-forgotten pain in the prince's face. "A candidate is allowed to bear his personal weapons in the challenge—a rarely invoked privilege in these modern times, but in common use when a noble Méxica or Nisei youth was expected to bring his own sword, armor, horses and pistols with him to the Castle. My father sent a man to me the night before the Last Day."

The prince's lips curled into a sneer. "He did not come himself. I was provided with a pistol, a rifle and *katana* of exquisite make. Straight from the workshops in the Radiant Palace itself, I'm sure. Toporosky himself could not have crafted finer weapons. The pistol and rifle were provided with their own custom-loaded ammunition. I wondered if I was meant to use the pistol to end my own life, sparing my father further embarrassment."

Tezozómoc scratched the back of his head, still puzzled after so many years. "I didn't. To be truthful, I was so drunk from the Last Night revels I couldn't even stand up when the man came to deliver the weapons. But in the morning, when I woke up with my head ringing with all the hammers in Hachiman's forge of war, I thought of suicide, and then decided to go ahead anyway. If I failed—well, then, I'd have a bit of revenge on him—blackening his radiant name with a tiny smudge. If I succeeded? Well, then anything was possible, wasn't it?"

The prince's eyes lit, and Dawd saw the servant scuttle up out of the corner of his eye and place a silver-chased platter with three crystal goblets and a chilled bottle of *Zlotawoda* on a low table. Tezozómoc ignored the goblets and uncorked the bottle with a smooth, effortless motion. He saluted the sergeant, Colmuir and the distant mountains in turn, then took a long swallow.

"Ahhh . . . excellent choice. My compliments to . . . where is our host?" The prince scowled at Colmuir. "He is remiss in not sitting to breakfast with me. I can tell he is a man of refined and elegant taste."

"The viscount Gemmilsky is away on a business trip, mi'lord," Colmuir said with a perfectly straight face.

Tezozómoc grimaced and lowered the bottle. "Is he dead?"

"Sir?" Colmuir was taken aback by the furious expression on the prince's face. Dawd was taken aback himself—the young man looked very much like his father when anger sharpened his eyes and made his high cheekbones cut into the dissipated flesh.

"I asked," Tezozómoc bit out, "if he was *dead*."

"No, mi'lord! He's . . . staying at another house while you are here. Perfectly safe."

Tezozómoc turned back to Dawd, his fury draining away as the puzzled Skawtsman watched. "I walked out onto the shooting pitch," he continued, as if nothing had happened, "and tried to stand as steadily as I could. You're allowed sixteen rounds at ten, twenty and fifty meters. I took every one. Emptied my ammunition clips and walked to the next marker. Then I did the same with the rifle. By the time I reached the sword-dojo, I wasn't even aware of the hour of the day. The only thing in the whole world was a cord-wrapped sword hilt and the face of the slave they'd put into the dueling square with me."

A gust of wind rattled the goblets, making Tezozómoc glance away for an instant. He remembered the bottle of vodka in his hand and took another long swallow.

"An officer is expected to dispatch his opponent with finesse, Sergeant." Tezozómoc grimaced, weighing the half-empty bottle in his hand. "But in the end, all that matters is your ability to spill the *teoatl tlachinolli*—the divine liquid, the burnt things—for the Empire. The sword-sacrifices at Chapultepec are not diseased or starved or beaten before being put into the square. Do not think they are unskilled men! Their patron saint is Tlahuicole of legend, a captive so valorous the Emperor Moctezuma spared his life again and again, yet the noble Tlaxcalan demanded to be sent to the gladiatorial stone that he might die properly, as befitted one taken prisoner. The man I faced believed implicitly in his divine duty. What could I do but hope to be worthy of him?"

Grimacing, the prince tossed the empty bottle carelessly away. Colmuir almost lunged to catch the unexpected missile, but controlled himself. There was a crashing sound as the heavy imported glass shattered a window, and the sound of scattering feet as the servants fled.

"I am indifferent with the sword," Tezozómoc allowed, shaking his head in remembered wonder. "But that morning—the last day of my life, I thought—I strove to be worthy of a nameless, unknown slave who had volunteered to serve the gods, to serve *me* by testing my skill with the sacred blade. We fenced—there was a blur of steel—and then he happened to block a *kesa giri* cut I'd thrown at his shoulder edge-on with his katana."

The prince snapped his fingers sharply, startling Dawd. "His blade shattered—broke like cheap glass—and I'd thrust and pierced his heart before I realized what had happened. That much of my training had taken hold.

"Then I was an officer and they put a red mantle over my shoulders and named me *Cuahyahcatl* as if I'd taken a hundred captives and a dozen towns. All for killing one pious man on a square of sand. An aerocar from the palace came to take me home. Later, I received my letter of commission in the 416th—in this very regiment—yet no orders came for me to take a duty posting. Nothing but staff work in the capital, until this assignment to Jagan." A wry smile twisted Tezozómoc's lips. "And here? Here I command a single *Cuauhhuehueh*"—he inclined his head towards Colmuir—"and a doughty *Tequihuah*"—he nodded to Dawd—"for the first time."

The prince caught Dawd's eye, a bitter look marring his handsome features.

"But you are still wondering about the pistol and the rifle. An officer must shoot twelve of sixteen to pass. Perhaps . . . perhaps you are even wondering how a katana of superior manufacture—do not believe the *teomicqui* are provided with dross!—could break at my weak blow?" Tezozómoc spread his hands and the expression on his face made Dawd's heart quail. "Never have I seen those weapons—that magnificent pistol, exemplary rifle or *shinken* again. Never. They were taken away, where by tradition they should have been mine.

"But then," he said, face turning sad, "my father and my mother should have greeted me when I emerged from the dojo; a man at last, a warrior of the Empire. But they were not there. Nor were my brothers. No one was, only a palace driver waiting to take me away in an unmarked aerocar."

Dawd stared at the prince, wondering what, if anything, he could say. Colmuir coughed politely, drawing Tezozómoc's attention.

"Mi'lord, you'll not be wanting to try this gun out then, I expect?"

The prince shook his head, staring blankly at the sky. "No. Come fetch me when it is time to leave. I will be upstairs."

Dawd followed Tezozómoc to the master suite, searched the room, bathroom and closets carefully before letting the prince enter, then closed the door quietly. After a few moments, he moved across the hallway and took up an overwatch position behind a massive marble bathtub the viscount had decided to use as an ornamental table, and clicked his comm thread alive.

"Master Sergeant?"

"Aye, lad. I hear you." Colmuir sounded subdued. "Lovely story t' brighten up a morning isn't it?"

"Had you heard it before?" Dawd didn't bother to suppress his curiosity. "Did his father order him passed out of Chapultepec?"

"Ah, now lad, tha' is dangerous business, wanting to poke about in the lives of the Imperial Family. Some things are best left alone." Colmuir clicked his teeth together, a pitying tone coming into his voice. "But I've heard a bit, here and there. I asked around you know, when I was assigned to watch the wee lad. No one would say much, but still . . . you've seen him hold a gun; like a sack of apples and his eyes closed half th' time!"

"Master Sergeant, for the love of the Revealed Heart of Jesus, who gave up his life to sustain the world, will you tell me *what happened*?"

"He passed, is what happened," Colmuir replied, a little put out. "He shot his twelves of sixteen at range and killed that poor *teomicqui* and walked off th' dojo sand white as an Aberdeen-man in winter, he did."

"What?" Dawd looked around in the hallway, startled by the sound of his own voice. "What about the weapons? Were they rigged? Where did they come from? Why did his family stay away?"

"No idea, Sergeant, no idea. First I've ever heard of those details—but then only the lad would know those things, wouldn't he?" Colmuir's voice turned brisk. "But back to business—this hunting trip will prove purely interesting if he won't carry a gun—one of us will have to carry it for him and then be bleedin' quick if one of these wasps jumps out at us."

Dawd rubbed his face, feeling a little ill.

"Now I've given the matter some thought, my lad, and I'll walk with him in the high brush. You now, you will be piloting the aerocar with luncheon and drinks and what not and I'd be very appreciative if you'd bring along that bleedin' huge Whipsaw of yours. I have a most depressing feeling we will need its services."

"Master Sergeant! I should walk point for him, not you! I'm the junior man—"

"My responsibility, Dawd, my responsibility. Nor will I shirk. You just be quick with that cannon when th' time comes."

A NONDESCRIPT HOUSE
PARUS

"I have a private comm call to the *Cornuelle* on intercept," Lachlan announced. "The Legation naval attaché is calling *Chu-sa* Hadeishi directly."

"Show me," the old Méxica woman growled, sitting up from her bed. A v-pane ready to display voice analysis and a running transcript appeared on her panel. The hour felt late and cold, even in the humid Parusian night. Itzpalicue rubbed her eyes and pinched a maguey thorn from her sleeve. "Where's the visual?"

"Voice-only call, mi'lady." Lachlan didn't sound apologetic, he sounded exhausted. "The call is on a cross-link from a native cell network."

"Where are you intercepting? Can you get me a delay?"

Lachlan's image shook his head. "We're tapping the call directly from the *Cornuelle*. We could override local comm on the ship, but their bridge crew is sure to notice."

Itzpalicue grimaced, head cocked to one side, listening. The sound of aerocar fans was loud, and then the voice of a Fleet ensign said, "Connecting now."

Chu-sa *Hadeishi? This is* Thai-i *Sagamish—I'm attached to Resident Petrel's staff—*

Yes, the Naval attaché. Has something happened? Where are you?

Flying into Parus by aerocar. Kyo, *have you seen the latest news reports? Is there fighting in the city?*

Itzpalicue raised an eyebrow. The senior lieutenant sounded panicked. She tapped up his personnel record and started scanning through the entries, half an ear devoted to the two men talking.

Things were quiet when I went to bed, Hadeishi said in a very dry voice. *Why the call,* Thai-i*?*

I live in the suburbs, Sagamish replied, still sounding on edge. *Just after midnight my house was attacked—vandalized—graffiti on the walls warned me to leave Jagan before the old ways were restored and the Empire swept away.*

Has this happened before in your district? The sound of the *Chu-sa* tapping up the latest situation reports was clear in Itzpalicue's left ear. He sounded very calm. *Have you been attacked before?*

Slicks throwing rocks at my car. Two of my servants quit—I believe they were threatened.

Do you know why? Hadeishi's voice changed tone, making Itzpalicue curse softly, wishing the transmission were carrying video as well. She opened another v-pane, showing the data sources from the *Cornuelle*, but a tap into the captain's workstation was not available.

I've heard . . . I'm sorry, Chu-sa, *I shouldn't be bothering you with this. Legation comm section is shut down at this hour . . . I was hoping to reach your bridge watch officer for a situation report.*

You're on the shortlist of groundside personnel to route directly to me, Hadeishi said wryly. *What did you hear?*

I've heard plenty, Sagamish said, now almost calm. *It is said the Fleet is going to tear down all the old temples and put statues of the Emperor in their place; that the* kujen *is going to accept the quill as the official currency in Parus and its dependencies; that prince Tezozómoc has been sent to be the new planetary viceroy; that the* kujen *has agreed to sell six hundred thousand Jehanan of the lowest caste to Legate Petrel for blood-sacrifice on Anáhuac. Those are the things I've heard—or my informants have heard—in the last three days.*

The Emperor is very busy, it seems. Hadeishi's voice was tinged with dismay. *Next there will be secret weather satellites causing famines and droughts to inflate the demand for imported grain.*

The old Méxica woman coughed in surprise, her lips twitching into a grim smile. "That is for later," she muttered caustically. "If this world becomes unruly. Or the *pochteca* cartels need a few extra quills at end of quarter."

Thai-i—*none of these things are fact, to my knowledge. Have you heard differently?*

No, sir. The sound of aerocar fans in the background changed. Itzpalicue could tell they were shifting into vertical landing mode. Unbidden, a v-pane opened in a relatively clear section of her panel, showing a video-feed from the Legation. A late-model aerocar, splashed with angular Jehanan script in vivid green paint, was setting down on the staff landing stage. *Legate Petrel has been very, very strict about keeping a low profile, adapting to native customs, treating fairly with the princes. . . . I don't know who is spreading this . . . it's not us, not the Fleet or Army staff . . .*

How many, Hadeishi said slowly, in a thoughtful tone, *Imperial citizens have business on Jagan?*

I don't know, Sagamish replied and the sound of venting fans whined down to nothing. *What kind of merchant or tourist is going to spread those kinds of rumors? Be bad for business, I think . . .*

True. The *Chu-sa* did not sound convinced. *Let me know if anything else happens.*

Hadeishi closed the connection and stood with a grimace. Even with the unobtrusive assistance of his medband, two hours of sleep was just not enough to clear his head. He yawned and wrapped his robe tighter. Like everything else on the ship, the flannel-lined silk was threadbare. Old Yejin was a deft hand with needle, thread and a fabric sealer, but all things—even high-quality cloth—gave way in time to wear. He sat on the bed, trying to marshal his thoughts, but he was too tired. The best he could do was key himself a note for *Sho-i* Smith to review local comm traffic in case someone was stirring up trouble on the planet.

Then he fell back into bed and was instantly asleep.

"Lachlan, what *did* he hear?" Itzpalicue turned her fierce dark eyes on the Éirishman.

Lachlan shook his head slowly, unkempt hair falling into his eyes. "We've . . . nothing scheduled on the Flower Priest agitation plot for his district. Must be either the *darmanarga-moktar* or locals copying what they've heard has happened elsewhere."

"Coordinated action? Or is the lid starting to come off? Did the attaché provoke something with his neighbors?"

The young Éirishman shrugged, spreading his hands. "If a local animosity cell has triggered, they're not organizing by comm. The build-out schedule for the wireless network won't even reach this suburb for another two years. So any organization will be face-to-face and we've no tap on that."

Itzpalicue nodded in understanding. These kinds of operations were always much easier on planets with pervasive comm networks. Here, hoary old rumor had legs like Painal and leapt from city to city with a speed rivaling a t-relay. "Reroute a Flower Listener into his neighborhood today. See what they can pick up. And have analysis section pull an incident map for the last two days for the whole land of the Five Rivers. This feels . . ."

She stopped, shaking her head. The agitation pattern running up to the outbreak of hostilities was still quite clear. All of her data sources—both from the Flower Priests, her own comm intercepts and groundside informants—pointed in the same direction. Another week of steadily rising tension would rupture equilibrium somewhere—indicators were good for the shantytown districts of eastern Parus to erupt first, followed by the noble cabal and the princedoms trying to capitalize on the wave of popular hatred. There seemed little need for the Flower Priests to try and ignite the tinder themselves. The *xochiyaotinime* were past masters of this kind of exercise. The right kind of wind always seemed to blow hot enough to strike sparks.

Itzpalicue squinted at the young Éirishman, who was staring bleary-eyed at one of his displays. His medical readout on her panel indicated he was running on stimulant fumes.

"Lachlan—take yourself off duty for the next ten hours. Take a sleepyhead and rest. Nothing is going to break today. But soon, very soon, we will be quite busy."

He nodded, stretching, and Itzpalicue closed the comm herself. *Almost time to send my Arachosians out hunting, waiting for a break in the clouds hiding my prey.*

A nagging feeling stole over her, though the old México tried to ignore the concern that her opponent—if there was indeed a subtle force acting against Imperial influence—might have stolen away from the field of heroes. She had drawn an empty net from dark waters before.

Itzpalicue pricked her upper arm, letting the stabbing pain clear her mind of such phantoms.

Moderately refreshed by four hours of sleep, *Chu-sa* Hadeishi swung onto the bridge of the *Cornuelle*, weaved his way past two engineering technicians replacing padding on the shockchairs at number two Weapons and number three Comm and settled himself into his own station. The bridge crew was currently standing half-strength to make room for the repairs. Midshipman Smith nodded to the captain and switched over primary command.

"Captain on deck!"

"Ship's status?" The v-panels making a half-circle in front of the command chair came alive, showing summaries of ship's status, local space and the greater Bharat system. Mitsuharu registered his identity code and let main comp recognize him.

"Repairs underway on all decks, *kyo*. Traffic control is light today—a handful of shuttles are in-atmosphere and several merchantmen are unloading, all registered and verified. Nothing's made transit in the last six hours. The threat board is clear."

Hadeishi nodded, lips pursed in consideration. He fixed Smith with a sharp look. "Time to hyper for the *Cornuelle*?"

Smith blinked in surprise, then his hands were active on his own panel. The *Chu-sa* ignored him, reading through the latest groundside status reports culled from the Legation and public press.

"Ah, *kyo*, baseline time to spin to hyperspace gradient and reach minimum safe distance for transit is one hour, sixteen minutes." Smith held his voice steady, but he was twitchy and rattled. "Are . . . are we going to need to make transit today, sir?"

Hadeishi grunted, then looked at the young officer. Smith, being in comm section, did not stand senior officer on duty watch very often. The *Chu-sa* considered him for a moment, face impassive, and then decided there was nothing to be gained by reprimanding the boy. Not this time.

"Unlikely, but not impossible *Sho-i*. Keep this in mind at all times."

"Hai, *kyo*!" Smith shrank into his chair. Hadeishi turned back to the departmental status reports. Repairs were indeed underway on all decks. *Isoroku and* Koshō *are not wasting any time . . .* Every hand not already ripping up worn-out nonskid or cutting out damaged plating was unloading cargo shuttles as fast as they arrived in the number two and number three boat bays. The *Chu-sa* allowed himself a tiny smile. *Real food for a change. Yejin will be pleased, and the crew will swoon with delight to eat something with unfamiliar molecules.*

"Smith-*tzin*? You're on duty for the next half-watch?"

The boy stiffened as if shot. "Yes, sir."

Hadeishi tapped a glyph to transfer a recording of the midnight comm call to the *Sho-i*'s panel. "Review this. The situation on the planet is deteriorating, but no one at the Legation can put their finger on the cause—I wonder if someone is stirring up the locals. Do what you can to verify these reports. If you find anything unusual, strange or simply out of place, let me know immediately."

"Hai . . . *kyo*? Do you think there are, ah, separatist agitators active on Jagan?"

"Swedish or Danish terrorists, you mean?" Hadeishi smoothed his beard, considering the prospect. "If so, they're a long way from any system sympathetic to their cause. Difficult to support operations out here without a fleet . . . but not impossible."

Smith nodded and turned back to his panel. Hadeishi frowned, wondering if the outlawed 'Swedish Naval Research' or its Danish equivalent might have changed their operational patterns. *No. There's nothing here to invite their interest . . . wait a moment! There is one target of opportunity for them here. Not one whom anyone would miss, but still . . .*

"Smith-*tzin*, find the Imperial Prince Tezozómoc and keep track of his locator. Just in case the long arm of the *gaijin* has reached out here to do him mischief."

Sweat ran freely from Senior Engineer Isoroku's bald head as he knelt on the floor of the officer's dining room, a metal saw howling in his hand. Showers of red sparks burst around him as he cut the last of the damaged panels free from the underfloor supports. The saw whined back to silence and the engineer shuffled back on his knee-pads. "Done," he coughed, and then cleared his throat of hexacarbon dust with a long swallow from his water bottle. "Take it away."

Two Marines privates—seconded to Engineering for the duration of repairs—ducked in and hefted the heavy panel. Grunting, they duck-walked out of the mess and stacked the partially melted chunk of metal on a grav-lifter in the corridor outside. Isoroku spat to clear his mouth and then thumbed the cutting blade on his saw over to a finishing surface.

Deftly, he ran the blade over the jagged edges, burring them down to a smooth bevel. The elderly Nisei abhorred sloppy work, even in locations—like the sub-floor supports—where no one would see his care and attention. This particular project was very relaxing too—a far cry from trying to clear and seal compartments shattered by battle damage, while alert horns blared in your ear and Khaid cluster bombs shook the ship like a rat in a Kochi terrier's mouth. Isoroku was fond of carpentry, particularly making cabinets and furniture. The chance to rebuild this whole suite of rooms brought a faintly pleased expression to his habitually impassive face.

"*Kyo*? Do you want the new flooring in now?" One of the Marines, sweat making his face shine like polished mahogany, leaned in the doorway. Most of the corridor was filled with stacks of pre-cut floor panels. Isoroku had arranged a very sweet trade, he thought, with the Development Board warehouse. All of the hexacarbon floor plating—even the sections gouged and damaged by combat—for four times the amount of highest-grade native *lohaja*, cut and planed to his specifications. The wood was incredibly wear resistant and took varnish to a truly beautiful gloss.

To his even greater delight, the *lohaja* was too hard to cut with the paltry set of woodworking tools aboard, so he'd been *forced* by circumstance to dig into the departmental budget to acquire—again through the sources Helsdon had found on the planet—a complete, matching set of Sandvik power tools designed to cut, finish and fit the native woods. Isoroku was itching to try them out. The tools themselves were works of art.

"Not yet. Not yet. Let me finish edging these supports . . ."

His personal comm chimed and the engineer sat back, turning off the saw and locking the safety cover in place. "Hai?"

This is Hadeishi. How are repairs progressing?

"Very well, sir!" Isoroku plucked a hand-comp out of his toolbox and thumbed up the current status display. "We're on schedule for repairing all the non-critical battle damage we've accrued in the past nine months. I'm in the dining room now, replacing the flooring. Crews are replacing the passageway vent filters by alternate decks. We've got one water recycler down while we flush and scrub the tanks before refilling with fresh supplies. The other will get the same treatment the day after tomorrow. Supply replenishment is underway—though you'll have to ask *Sho-sa* Koshō about her time-to-complete."

There was silence on the link, and Isoroku started to frown. When the captain started asking for status reports, something was going on. The engineer's forehead furrowed and he rubbed his pug-nose vigorously, trying to clear the metallic bite of ozone away.

Thai-i, *I want you to scale back your repair schedule. A situation might be developing on the planet and we can't go to combat acceleration if you've got the corridors filled with unsecured construction materials.*

"*Kyo*!" The engineer sat upright, horrified. "We reviewed the schedule just yesterday! You and the *Sho-sa* approved the whole list—we've already torn out everything designated first phase! We can't . . . we can't just put everything back."

We're still on a combat duty station, Thai-i. *Adjust your schedule to pull and repair a compartment at a time. You must assume we are always a moment's notice from battle alert.* The comm-band beeped cheerfully, signaling the channel had closed. Isoroku stared in horror at his wrist.

"One at a time?" Isoroku's voice rose violently and then, with a massive effort of will, he closed his mouth, swallowed a bellowing shout of disgust, and ground both palms into his eyes. "One at a time . . . oh, mother Ameratsu, save me from flight officers of all kinds."

His thick, muscular fingers separated and he peered at the comp pad on the deck beside him. "My beautiful, perfect schedule . . ." The thought of having to stand down all of the extra hands he'd been given and having his technicians concentrate on one compartment at a time, rather than addressing entire decks at a go, made him want to weep. "What a waste of able hands and hours. What a waste!"

For once, Itzpalicue was not in her darkened bedroom, surrounded by the pervasive hum of comps and the sullen glare of v-displays, when a system alert sounded. Instead, the old Méxica was sitting on the covered veranda running along the southern side of the rented house. Elaborately carved wooden screens blocked out most of the sun's glare, leaving the porch dim and quiet. Some kind of a vine with petite white flowers climbed the roof supports and exhaled a thick, heady fragrance. Her bare feet were in sunlight, and her head was in cool shadow.

Her comm-band chimed again. She opened one eye and regarded the turquoise and silver bracelet sitting on a side table at her elbow, alongside a tumbler filled with the local equivalent of limonata. She had been trying to write a letter to one of her nieces, but the effort of putting pen to paper—the old woman did not send recorded messages—had lulled her into a drowsy nap.

"Ah, Lachlan must still be asleep," she said when the band chimed for the third time. "They will wake him if I'm not properly responsive." Sticking out her tongue at the device, she picked it up and tapped the channel open. "Yes?"

Your pardon, mi'lady, a tentative voice answered. *We've registered a system trace alert. The communications officer of the* Cornuelle *has begun a planet-wide scan of the local comm networks, including our own and the ship-to-shore traffic control system.*

"Has he noticed our cell tap?" Itzpalicue shifted in the chair, sitting up straight, her mind waking slowly from its comfortable doze. "Are our secure relays compromised?"

We don't believe so, replied the voice. *He's only just started. Shall we shut him down?*

"No! There's no need to draw attention. Use the relay tap on the *Cornuelle* to monitor his progress. If he finds any data we don't already have, shunt it to my message queue. If he impinges on our surveillance network, or seems likely to come across the time-delay interfaces on the military and diplomatic comm channels, dial back our presence and let him find the Flower Priest operation instead. The *xochiyaotinime* can deal with Fleet for us."

Yes, ma'am. The operator went off-line and Itzpalicue shrugged her shoulders, a little annoyed at being disturbed. "Lachlan needs to ease up on his staff, I think," she mused aloud. "They're far too timid for my taste."

A private channel glyph started to wink on Hadeishi's command display and the *Chu-sa* coughed, interrupting Isoroku, who was in the midst of an impassioned speech regarding the sacred and infallible nature of engineering repair schedules. "We will discuss your concerns later, *Thai-i,*" Hadeishi said smoothly as he terminated the call. "I have an incoming call from *Sho-sa* Koshō."

"Hello, Susan. How is resupply going?"

Ahead of schedule, kyo. The executive officer's voice was a cool, confident breeze after Isoroku's affronted tirade. *Shuttle two has just finished unloading—three months' supply of local firewater, fresh bed linens and a hundred cases of hand-milled soap. Assorted local flavors, but none of them will make you gag.*

"I see you and *Heicho* Felix see eye-to-eye on certain critical matters, *Sho-sa.* When is the water supply coming aboard?"

Shuttle three is downbound now with the reinforced bladder in place. They should be back in about sixteen hours. I'm preparing to take shuttle two down as well—Helsdon's managed to find us three to four tons of miscellaneous spare parts. All Imperial issue. Not the latest revisions, but then the ship is not exactly fresh from the Jupiter Yards.

"Excellent. Be aware the situation on the ground is starting to cook. If you've space on the shuttle, take a squad of Marines. I've—ah—freed some up from

Isoroku's repair projects. If anything happens, evac to orbit immediately. We need you and those crewmen back here more than the repair parts."

Understood. Felix's fireteam is already standing by with Helsdon and two of his technicians. We'll see you in about twenty hours. Koshō, out.

On the bridge of the *Cornuelle*, midshipman Smith leaned heavily on the armrest of his shockchair, eyes half-closed, one finger pressed to his earbug. His free hand drifted across the v-display, tweaking frequencies and absorption ranges. A constant stream of static, chattering, booming music, lilting singing voices, twenty-second advertisements and encrypted bursts of garbage noise washed over him. In comparison to the spare interstellar communications environment he usually worked in, Smith felt like he'd thrust his head into a hive of angry, polyphonous bees.

A particular warbling squeal caught his attention. "I've heard that before. Three-Jaguar, can you isolate the comm spike at six-thousand-and-fifteen?"

The second watch communications officer, a petite Tlaxcalan girl with perfectly straight ink-black hair, nodded, tapping up a new pane on her display. The frequency isolated and Smith leaned in, watching the main comp apply a score of decrypt filters in dizzying succession.

"Doesn't that look familiar? I'm sure it's an Imperial code . . ."

Jaguar nodded absently, her attention wholly focused on the v-display. Short, neatly manicured fingers skipped across the board, pulling slates of Fleet, Army and Diplomatic code images from archive and queuing them for decrypt comparison. After a moment, she paused and lifted her sharp chin. "I remember this," she said slowly, "it's from commtech school—an old-style encrypt used by one of the priestly orders."

"A military order? Like the Knights of the Flowering Sun?" Smith started scanning through the code archive. After a moment, he found something which looked vaguely like the pattern flowing across their panel. "Might be an upgraded version of this one . . . I'd tell the captain. Jag, look at this other thing . . ." He swapped in a completely separate v-display showing clusters of locator signals scattered all along the Parus-Sobipuré-Fehrupuré axis. "Run down these locator idents—there are Imperial signatures all over this countryside—like school let out or something . . . they're encrypted too and we'd better find out who they are."

The second watch tech nodded, transferring the v-display to her panel, quick mind already nibbling away at the new problem. Smith changed his earbug channel to the command push and thumbed the priority glyph for *Chu-sa* Hadeishi. Not for the first time, he found it amusing the main comm system was required to route a talktime request to the captain, who was seated behind and above the comm station and no more than two meters away.

"Yes, *Sho-i* Smith?" Hadeishi spoke quietly into his comm-thread. A particular feeling was beginning to steal over him, a sensation he associated with patrolling in hostile space. A sense of impending action, as if a steadily building weight was pressing on his mind. He had been keeping an eye on the communications station—Smith had not left his station when second watch arrived on the bridge, which meant he had gotten wrapped up in the analysis project. Hadeishi let him stay; Three-Jaguar did not appear to mind and they made a good team.

"Have you found something?" The *Chu-sa* was keeping track of Isoroku and his repair crews who, despite the mournful protests of the senior engineer, were making excellent progress at securing all of the repair supplies and adapting to a more conservative schedule. *If only we had received some kind of munitions resupply. Fresh soap has a laudable effect on morale, but will do little for us if we have to provide ground-support for the Army.*

Unfortunately, despite considerable investigation, the local industrial base simply could not provide the *Cornuelle* with fresh sprint and shipkiller missiles, or even capacitors and munitions for the point-defense network.

"Hai, *kyo*." The boy's face was keen with anticipation. "First, we've started to pick out a lot of chatter on fringe Imperial bands—all encrypted—using an old-style code formerly associated with certain Imperial religious military orders. We've had no indication there are any Templar or Tlahulli brigades operating on Jagan, so that's a little strange."

Hadeishi considered this for a moment, turning the indication over in his mind. *That does not seem to fit at all. So it must be a foundation piece of the puzzle . . .* "And?"

Jaguar leaned over, whispering in Smith's ear. Hadeishi waited patiently. As the two junior officers consulted their panel, the *Chu-sa* kicked off a ship-wide request for departmental status.

"Second, *kyo*, it looks like the 416th Arrow Knight regiment has taken to the field. Motorized elements apparently departed their cantonment south of Parus two and a half hours ago. The furthest afield are almost at Fehrupuré, but they're encountering sporadic resistance."

"What?" Hadeishi stiffened, his entire body suddenly and completely awake. "We've had no notification of an operational deployment! Get me Colonel Yacatolli *right now*."

Jaguar immediately began speaking into her comm-thread, the glow of a fresh v-feed from the surface shining on her cheekbones. Smith tapped a copy of his locator map to Hadeishi's station.

"What kind of resistance is the Army encountering?" Hadeishi tagged the flight paths of his shuttles into the map. Number three was already on the ground, while Susan's shuttle two was inbound to the main shuttle field at Sobipuré. Shuttle One, with a Marine drop-squad standing by, was still in boat bay one. "Local military contingents?"

"No, *kyo*." Smith shook his head and copied a set of thumbnails to the command station. "Kids throwing rocks and firebombs—mostly methanol and soap in glass. Some of the squad commanders have reported roads blocked or bridges under repair where satellite sweeps yesterday showed plenty of local traffic crossing."

"I see. Jaguar-*tzin*, do you have Yacatolli on comm for me yet?"

The Tlaxcalan ensign shook her head, pixyish features immobile with anger. "Regimental headquarters is saying he's busy and doesn't have time to talk to you right now. They say . . . they say they'll call us when he's free."

Hadeishi's eyes narrowed and he considered overriding the channel himself. For a moment. Then he pushed the anger aside and turned his attention back to the two junior officers. "Very well. Smith-*tzin*, find out where all this priestly traffic is coming from. Yacatolli's belief in the superiority of his regiment over the locals is a known quantity—this other business is more disturbing."

TAKSHILA
DISTRICT OF THE MOLT

Humming softly to herself, Gretchen gently drifted her hand across the control surface of a Zeiss-Hanuman field camera. The lens and imaging body of the surveillance scope were mounted in a north-facing window. She was sitting cross-legged, watching the 60X image of the monastery with great interest.

On the v-display, a line of Jehanan elders was slowly climbing one of the external staircases cut into the rock of the hill. One by one they bent down and entered a T-shaped doorway near the summit. Some kind of domed building nestled in the rock, filling what the geodetic survey revealed was an old ravine. Gretchen was interested in this particular vignette because a similar number of monks made the same journey every morning. They did not return the same way. None of the penitents—if they were, in fact, performing a religious service—carried anything, as far as she could tell, and had dispensed with the usual leather harnesses and disc-shaped signs of status and rank.

A purification bath? she wondered.

She moved her hand again, and the camera scanned to one side. More cliffs pierced by tall narrow windows and occasional doors leading onto precarious walkways or steep sets of steps blurred past and she found the terrace Magdalena had labeled 'Southern Orchard' on the comprehensive three-d map their cameras, radar packs, and geomagnetic sensors were building on a base of out-of-date satellite photos. The orchard was filled with slender-trunked trees with perfectly rounded crowns. Gretchen's lips twitched into a faint smile—the ornamental arrangement of the *naragga* trees was the result of meticulous daily maintenance by a stooped old Jehanan and a swarm of children who carefully plucked wayward leaves from the trees and trimmed the stems with scissors.

"I'm amazed those trees are still standing. A dozen kids should have reduced the whole terrace to a desert by now."

Magdalena looked up from her comps—now laid out on a low wicker table Parker had found in the district furniture market—and twitched her ears lazily. "Perhaps the orb-trees grow quickly in this *nnningurshimakkhul* climate. Perhaps the kits are specially trained guardians who protect the world from being consumed by leaf demons."

"Ha!" Gretchen laughed, grinning at the Hesht. "You're in a good mood this morning."

"*Hrrr* . . . This *ssshuma* will be in a good mood when we find the gifting-bush and leave this nose-biting place."

Anderssen shrugged, looking at the northeastern sky through the windows. A pall of yellow-gray smoke filled the sky, drifting west from a huge district of chemical refineries. The noxious cloud choked the city whenever the wind turned. Magdalena had been particularly revolted to find the smog left a gummy residue on her fur.

"Any luck on getting the ground-penetrating radar to work?"

The Hesht shook her head and the tip of her tail lashed from side to side in annoyance. "There must be shielding beneath all the ornamental carving." She tapped a claw on one of her displays. "Each open window and door gives us a paws-breadth slice of the interior, but only for six, seven meters—then nothing. Without sensor relays placed inside the complex? No more than this."

Magdalena flexed her claws, letting them slide out of cartilage-sheaths, and tipped her chin at the three-d map. Three quarters of the surface of the hill had been mapped in painstaking detail by the array of sensors clipped to the windows or mounted on tripods. The far northern quadrant was still a mystery, though Gretchen intended to hike around to the far side in a day or so and mount their two spare cameras and radar packs on a rooftop, if she could find a suitable location.

Everything within the hill was also beyond their reach, at least while they observed from a distance. Sadly, the Company had neglected to provide them with antigrav spyeye remotes. Every indication pointed to a warren of tunnels and chambers and hidden rooms. The personage identifier system in Maggie's number three comp was counting silhouettes, facial pictures and stride lengths—when they could be captured on camera—and the count of inhabitants of the hill of the 'relentless ones' stood at four hundred so far.

Anderssen scanned her camera down to the 'Southern Entrance.' This was a broad, triumphal-style staircase vaulting up a near-vertical cliff from a warren of closely packed, shoddy-looking buildings at the foot of the hill. Age-eroded statues lined the stairs, which ended in a monumental gateway. The massive doors—probably made of the ubiquitous *lohaja* wood—were closed. Gretchen had yet to see them open.

She shook her head in consideration. "The south doors have to be for ceremonial occasions. There are drifts of leaves on the steps and a native avian is roosting in the crown of this topmost statue. We haven't seen any other location where there's traffic . . . no deliveries, no waste being taken out, nothing. So—do they leave? Are they a completely self-contained community?"

"An ark in the middle of a city?" Magdalena growled in disbelief. "What would be the purpose?"

"It's only a thought," Gretchen replied, standing up with a groan. "More likely, day-to-day business is conducted out of sight, through tunnels or even an entrance which is completely obscured by a building." She stretched, feeling her back creak in protest. "Do you suppose Parker can find me a real chair?"

"*Hrrr!* Shiny-backed lizards don't use human chairs! Learn to sit on comfortable floor like the Nisei do!"

"He found you a table . . ." Anderssen swung from side to side, trying to loosen up her stiff back. *Time to get out of the house.* "We've mapped enough of the rooftop walkways," she said, beginning to braid her hair into a thick ponytail, "for me to be able to reach the cliffs. When Parker gets back, I think I'll try making a circuit of the whole hill—"

The apartment door made a grinding sound and then recessed into the doorframe, allowing the pilot to stomp in with an enormous woven basket clutched to his chest. The top was packed with glass bottles filled with purified water.

"*Konnichi-wa!*" He called cheerfully. "Where can I put this down?"

Magdalena regarded a covered wooden bowl Parker had removed from the basket suspiciously. "This is supposed to be food?"

"Extra spicy," the pilot said, mouth already full of fried *pakka* dumpling. "G'head, that's yours—all raw and juicy, but with some peppers—well, *I* say they're peppers, dunno what the slicks call them. Meat, Miss Magdalena, real meat! And not *skomsh* either."

The Hesht's nostrils flared, but she removed the cover and sniffed the goopy contents with interest. The hackles rose on the back of her neck, then settled and she experimentally hooked one of the pieces of meat out with her little claw. Gelatinlike brown fluid dripped into the bowl.

Gretchen averted her eyes, hoping to keep her own lunch down. Parker grinned, a familiar-looking paper cylinder in one hand, his lighter in the other.

"That's not an Imperial-brand tabac is it? Is your medband on? Did you take an anti-anaphylactic?"

"Very funny," Parker replied, lighting the tabac and taking a tentative puff. His eyes widened, he coughed sharply, then inhaled again. "Ahhh . . . much more like the real thing."

"Is it real tabac?" Anderssen picked up the little cardboard box. The lettering was modern Takshilan block script, and the packet had all the usual gewgaws the city vendors used to flog their wares. In this case, a whistle was tacked to one side, enclosed in cellophane, while small paperboard cards with the toothy portraits of famous Gandarian racing lizard jockeys were on the other. For a moment, Gretchen had trouble making out the brand name of the tabac, but then realized the blocky, bold name was transliterated Náhuatl.

"You're smoking 'The Emperor's Teat,' " she said in a dry voice. "How does he taste?"

Parker snorted, laughing, and with tears in his eyes managed to choke out "Just like the real thing!" before going into a violent fit of coughing.

Magdalena looked up, still suspicious. "What are you hooting about, monkey?" She recoiled, suddenly aware of the cloud of tabac smoke coiling lazily in the air. "These leaves smell stronger than the last ones . . ."

"Great." Anderssen pinched her nose closed and picked up one of the bottles of fresh water. The pipes in the building were only capable of disgorging rust-red fluid which did, in fact, contain some H-two-Oh, but all three of their medbands flashed red when used to test the potability. Parker was of the opinion that "some water is provided with the bacteria." Gretchen was surprised the building water mains still worked as high up as the thirty-third floor. "I'm going out."

"Wait—" Parker rolled up, wiping his mouth. He looked quite pale. "Be careful. I saw something really strange while I was out getting groceries. It's hard to navigate roof-stairs with that basket, so I was walking back through the tanner's district—which is never terribly busy, unless you're delivering hides—and some buses went past."

"Real Imperial-style buses? With wheels and methanol engines?" Gretchen glanced at Magdalena. "Do you hear anything on your comm-scanner about that?"

The Hesht shook her head. Out of habit, she had set up a frequency-hopping comm wave scanner to listen for anything interesting. Unfortunately, the only comm traffic in the city was encrypted beyond the capability of Maggie's comp soft to decode. "Sometimes I hear chartered merchants chatting, if they're here sitting attendance on the *kujen* . . ."

"Anyway!" Parker raised his voice, giving both women a glare. "These weren't just Imperial-*style* buses; they were surplused Colonial Department of Education sixty-seaters. Repainted, of course, but it's hard to cover up the markings with only one coat of sprayon. But that wasn't the oddest thing—I mean, you know how hungry the market here is for modern transport, why not ship your retired school buses to the back of beyond?—what made me stop and stare was the buses were filled with Quarsenian *jandars*—"

"Which are?" Gretchen spread her hands questioningly.

"Which are tribesmen from the northern mountains," Parker replied. "Nasty-looking characters—mottled hides, felted armor, conical hats and ornamental spiked masks; they look like porcupines—these ones were armed to the teeth. They had rifles too, modern rifles—not those *jezail*-looking things some of the richer nobles carry."

"Why were they riding in buses? Where were they going?"

"How do I know?" Parker took another drag on his tabac, then blew a fat cloud of pinkish smoke towards the ceiling. "They were driving east towards the freight railway yards. The funny thing, though, was I saw a *European* on board the lead bus. He was giving the driver directions."

"A human male? There is a scheme a-paw for certain." Magdalena hooked another slimy chunk out of the bowl and popped it into her mouth. "*Hrrr* . . . these are delicious, Parker, what are they called?"

"*Zizunaga*, which is snake, I think. Anyway, boss, be careful if you go out. The streets were pretty empty. Something must be going on."

The well-maintained roofwalk Gretchen had been following ended in an irregular wooden platform lined with wide-mouthed ceramic pots. Each jar held a carved stone head surrounded by freshly planted flowers. The heads were recognizably Jehanan and their jaws yawned towards the sky, catching a fine mist of water spilling from the cliffs above.

A funeral offering? she wondered. *Remembering ancestors, or placating their ghosts?*

Gray limestone soared over her head, hung with trailing vines and thick, fingerlike succulents growing in crevices and clinging to tiny ledges in the rock. The walkway had been built up into a crevice, making a sort of elevated platform surrounded by a constant damp mist. Green-gray moss covered the wooden slats, making her footing tricky.

Gingerly, she reached out and touched the cliff face. The limestone was damp, beaded with water, and crisscrossed with sharp puckered ridges. *Eight days of traveling and running around and finally I get to our destination. Hah.*

Stepping carefully between the jars, Gretchen climbed up into the root of the crevice, gloved hands pressed against either wall. Trailing saprophytes brushed against her goggles. Cool water beaded on her face, a welcome relief from the usual soup of humid sweat she moved in. The narrow space ended in a still-smaller alcove—obviously worked by chisels at some time in the past—holding a lumpy-looking statuette.

A shrine? The planters and stone heads could be attendant ritual devices.

The god's features were entirely covered with moss. There were no tracks or traces of anyone coming to clean the votary, which made Anderssen grimace, realizing her boots had already left very obvious scars on the mossy stones. She turned around and carefully picked her way back to the platform. Once she was standing under the dripping vines, looking out through slowly falling sheets of mist, Gretchen was struck by the perfect quiet in the little ravine.

The usual sounds of the city—runner-cart horns, clattering machinery, the hooting voices of the natives singing, the pounding of hammers and the rasping whine of lathes—were swallowed by the mossy walls, or blocked by the mist.

"Quiet and still again," she mused, hands on her hips. One eye narrowed in thought. *I keep finding these little pockets of solitude—but there's no quarrelsome gardener here. And there's no way up, or into, the hill in this place.* A little disappointed, she left the shrine and headed back towards the last junction in the maze of walkways running hither and yon across the rooftops of Takshila.

Two hours later, Gretchen turned a corner, one eye on her hand-comp—which was displaying part of their map—and found herself looking at a short, arched passageway cutting through the base of a circular tower made of brick. Beyond the opening, a flight of stairs—broad and low, just as the Jehanan liked with their long, splayed feet—disappeared up into the hillside.

"Maggie? Do you have me on locator?"

Yes, hunt-sister, plain as blood on whiskers.

"Good. Mark this spot. There's a passage through a building—our map shows the walkway ending here in a dead end—and a staircase. Can you see that?"

There was a pause, and then Magdalena made a thoughtful hissing sound. *No . . . from our angle there's only more cliffside. Must be hidden in a fold in the rock.*

Anderssen tiptoed through the passageway, looked carefully up and down the staircase, then double-checked all of her equipment. "Am I still on locator?"

No. You've dropped off the display.

Gretchen nodded to herself and pulled a UV dye marker out of a jacket pocket. "The stairs below here are blocked by rubble—looks like a building collapsed and they just made a new wall out of the debris. Keep an eye on my comm signal. I'm going to head up, keeping quiet."

You should wait, Magdalena grumbled. *We're far away. Let me send Parker to stand by at the entrance. Then, if a hostile clan pounces, he can come to your aid.*

"I'll be fine." Anderssen peered upwards. The stairs disappeared into the side of the hill. "I'll be right back out and we'll be able to talk on comm."

Oh, I've heard many a kit say that before, just before they were snatched up by crag-wolves. The Hesht did not sound convinced at all. *And if you don't return? How long should I wait before singing your death-howl and collecting the skulls of a hundred lizards for your memorial tomb?*

"You will do no such thing!" Gretchen was appalled at the prospect. "If anything happens—if I'm not back in twelve hours—or you have to abandon the apartment, we'll meet at the train station, or if not there, then at the hotel in Parus. But don't worry, I will be *fine.*"

There was a grumbling sound, but Anderssen ignored the protest, turned around to fix the location of the passageway in her memory and then started climbing, the pen tucked into her right hand.

A warbling, humming sound echoed down a hallway lined with perforated stone screens. Anderssen, who had been creeping along the left-hand side of the passage, keeping her head below the rosette-shaped openings, became completely still. She waited, expecting to see the bulky shape of a Jehanan come padding down the hallway.

Nothing appeared, though the warbling sound—rising and falling in a tuneless way—seemed to come a little closer. Gretchen moved forward to one of the supporting pillars and unclipped an eyeball from her vest. Rotating a ring-control to turn on the tiny device, she pointed the camera out through an opening.

The heads-up display on her right goggle lens flickered awake, showing her a close-up of a leaf. Frowning, Anderssen dialed back the magnification until she could see more than vascular channels and phylem. Most of her view was blocked by foliage, but something moved in her field of view and—after peering at the image for a moment—she recognized a large Jehanan foot covered with mud and leaves. As she watched, a spade scraped soil back into a hole.

Well, I doubt it can see me, she thought, stowing the camera again. Checking behind her in case a whole troop of ferocious monks with saw-toothed swords had crept up, Gretchen scuttled forward to the end of the hall. A partially illuminated passageway dropped down a concave set of steps into the terrace to her left—she caught a glimpse of the city skyline—and curved away into darkness on her right. Intermittent lights spotted the passage, falling from tiny sconces set at the junction of roof and wall. They were not candles, but some kind of bioluminescent pod held in a fluted ceramic shell.

Nervous the Jehanan digging on the terrace would notice her, Gretchen tapped her comm awake and peered at her locator band. Both devices had stopped working as soon as she'd entered the monastery. The ruined stairs had led her to a circular door much like their apartment entryway, though the triangular sections were permanently rusted into the wall recesses. Oddly, the first door had immediately led to a second, which, while in slightly better condition, was also frozen open. An empty passageway, wide enough for four Jehanan to march down abreast, had beckoned her into the heart of the massif.

After that, she had tried to keep to the left-hand wall, indicating each turn with the UV marker. With no data suggesting where the *kalpataru* might lie, she had concentrated on covering as much ground as possible while the mapping software in her comp measured each winding ramp, hallway, abandoned chamber and empty passageway she passed through.

Though she heard voices echoing in the distance once or twice, she had not encountered a single Jehanan. After hours of leaden silence, accompanied only by the echo of her footsteps, even the alien tonalities drifting in from the terrace were comforting.

Can't go left here, she thought, considering the glimpse of the city skyline. *But if I did, I could squirt Magdalena all the mapping data in this comp . . . and check in. My dear sister is probably chewing her tail in worry.*

The clomping sound of heavy, leathery feet made up her mind. The Jehanan outside was climbing the stairs. Gretchen flattened against the carved wall and tried to make herself perfectly still. A shadow blotted out the dim light from the doorway and then a blunt-horned Jehanan shuffled past, weighed down by a leather bag bulging with square-edged objects. Through slitted eyes, Anderssen watched the creature disappear down the hallway, and then breathed again when the long, angular shadow vanished.

Vastly relieved, she slipped down the stairs herself and out onto the terrace. The smoke- and fume-tainted Takshilan air felt brisk and clean after the motionless funk inside the hill. She glanced around the terrace and was puzzled to see quite a bit of earth had been turned near the low retaining wall facing the sprawl of the city. *Odd gardener who isn't planting something. . . . Maybe he was just weeding. Or harvesting. Or burying something to ferment. Or . . .*

Ducking behind one of the thick blue-green bushes, she clicked her comm awake.

"Maggie? Can you hear me?" Gretchen whispered, though she was sure no one was within hundreds of meters. "I've managed to get outside."

We have you on camera, the Hesht replied, sounding relieved. *Your locator just popped out of its hole. We're glad the* mandire *have not boiled the skin from your skull for a drinking cup.*

"Good." Anderssen's goggles had darkened to shade her eyes from the sun, but she could see the apartment tower clearly. The whole western face was blazing with reflected sunlight, capturing the swollen red disc of Bharat in a long puddle of molten gold. "I'm bursting you all of the mapping data I've collected so . . . *urk!*"

A spade, smelling of earthworms and freshly turned soil, lifted her chin.

Gretchen looked up, swallowing, into the grim face of an enormous Jehanan. The creature's dark eyes seemed to spark with rage, and then the pebbled skin around the eyes tightened and the shovel shifted away from her neck.

"*Hooo . . .* You are a curious digger, aren't you? How did you get up here?"

At the same moment, Gretchen heard Magdalena say: *Parker has the creature targeted with a spare rangefinder. Raise your hands if you want it blinded so you can run.* The Hesht's voice sounded eager, and Anderssen could imagine the big black feline crouching in dimness under brambleberry bushes, claws flexed, waiting to pounce on an unwary truelk. She turned her head slowly, hands pressed carefully into the loamy soil.

A brilliant red dot was dancing in a handspan-wide circle on the side of the creature's head.

"Your pardon," she said slowly, amazed Parker's hands were steady enough to keep a bead on such a tiny target at such a distance. "We need not quarrel. I have trespassed, but I will leave immediately, without making any trouble."

"Oh ho, will you?" The Jehanan stepped back, squinting at her, and Anderssen realized with a cold feeling of shock that she knew the creature. "And if I think you should meet the Master of the Gardens, then what will you do?"

"This will seem odd," she said, shrinking back into the cliff, trying to leave Parker as clear a shot as possible, "but each time I get lost in this city, I find you. Aren't you Malakar the gardener? You were meditating by the blue shell, down in one of the neighborhoods below."

The creature's nostrils flapped open and there was a buzzing hum of sound. "Weak eyes do not deceive," the Jehanan said, cocking her head to one side. "You are the Disturber-of-Forgotten-Things—the one with such hungry thoughts. Now—*hoooo*—what would you be hungry for in this dilapidated old house?"

"Isn't this the oldest building on Jagan?" Gretchen kept her hands down. She could hear Magdalena breathing over the comm link, and the red dot continued its frantic little dance on the creature's scaled hide. "I wanted to see for myself."

Malakar's eyes, still nearly entirely in shadow, glinted. A long, clawed finger extended, pointing at her vest and belt. "Your little machines, they sing of this old shell? Tell its age? Even if no one living could swear such a truth?"

Gretchen nodded slowly. "Sometimes. If the object is made of the proper kind of material. Wood or metal are best. Do you have something you would like me to test?"

Malakar regarded her for a moment, seemingly puzzled. "*Hoooo*—when last we met, you could not properly speak without moving your foreclaws. Now you keep them to the ground. Odd and odder yet. Have you been injured?"

"No. I'm—"

Don't tell it anything! Magdalena whispered on the comm. *Just let Parker flash it, and then you can get out!*

Gretchen sighed, looking down at the ground and taking a breath. For all her bluster and menacing shovel, the Jehanan did not feel dangerous. *Not like it couldn't just wrench my arms out of their sockets or bite my head off.*

"Don't shoot unless I'm actually attacked," she whispered into her jacket collar.

"What do you say?" Malakar leaned close, eye-shields half-lidded against the glare of the sun. "There are only *bizen*-grass shoots there, no one can . . ." The native grew still. Gretchen looked up, meeting wide green irises. "*Hoooo* . . . This old one is not imagining being watched by distant eyes? My old hide is itchy, as if a *xixixit* hung in the trees above a quiet lawn where I lay sunning. . . . Am I too old, my mind troubled by phantoms? Tell me, hungry soft one, tell me if I suffer night-fears while my eyes are open?"

Gretchen shook her head before realizing the creature might not grasp the cue. "My friends are watching us from the fin-towers. One of them has a weapon aimed at you. If you try to harm me, he will kill you before you can reach the tunnel."

"*Hooo* . . . " Malakar settled back on her haunches. "Quick of eye and sure of hand, this friend. A long reach across eight *pan* to scratch my hide."

"A machine—a weapon—firing an explosive, hide-piercing shell," Anderssen said, squatting comfortably. "Though in truth, you might lunge and strike me down as quickly as he can act."

"Then we both end, hungry-thoughts, leaving only an unexpected feeding for the *yi* birds who roost on the crumbling shell of this house."

"I do not wish to feed the *yi* birds," Gretchen said in a serious tone. "Not today."

"No one ever does," Malakar allowed, a deep trill echoing at the back of her throat. "They are often hungry and must eat of the bitter *naragga*. Then here we sit, trapped as Húnd and Gukhis were above the fiery pit, each unwilling to loose claw from claw and so save themselves."

"Are you compelled to keep me here? Why not let me go?"

"*Hooo* . . . Could such an old, wrinkled hide as mine take the punishment the Master of the Garden would mete out for letting an *asuchau* human tread these sacred halls? Oh, my eye-shields would bleed for such an affront!"

Anderssen peered at the Jehanan, wondering if her translator were working properly. Something very much like cynical bitterness echoed in the words. *I don't think this old creature cares overmuch for the 'Master of the Garden'* . . . "Then let us make an equitable exchange—I will do something for you, and you will help me, poor lost human that I am, find my way home. As you did before, which was very gracious of you."

"As I did?" The gardener blew a mournful note with its nostrils. "Gracious? You are oiling my scales like a short-horn wishing mating privilege! *Hooo* . . . I was not cracked from the shell to be impolite. A lost hatchling is everyone's business to see home safely. But you . . . you and your little machines . . . can you truly tell the age of a thing?"

Gretchen nodded, trying to hide a relieved smile.

Don't trust it . . . Magdalena muttered in her ear. *The khaysan drifts in the river, pretending to be an old scratching log, waiting for an unwary kit to come all thirsty to the water . . .*

"I can try. What do you want to test? Is it far from here?"

Malakar made a rumbling sound and rose up, joints creaking, using the shovel for a cane. A long arm reached out, and slung the leather bag over one pebbly shoulder. Metal clanked against metal. The long head turned, regarding her with a lambent emerald eye. "I will show you an old thing, as old as I have ever seen, if you wish to follow."

Gretchen stood, brushing dirt from her work pants and held up the comp to the skyline. There was a warbling squeal in her earbug—the sound drowned out Magdalena cursing luridly and trying to warn her hunt-sister *not to go into the cave!*

"I will."

Anderssen's boots rang on polished stone, and she reached out to take hold of a railing embedded in the wall. Below her, the old Jehanan was treading carefully on terribly worn steps, testing each one with her weight before proceeding. They had spent a long time pacing down abandoned tunnels and descending broad curving rampways. Gretchen wanted to ask how deep they had come, but the gardener refused to speak, only stomping along with the leather bag over one shoulder, lost in her own thoughts.

These chambers—they seemed vast, though Gretchen hadn't attempted a sonosound reading to gauge their size—swallowed the faint radiance of a single blue light carried by the Jehanan. They followed a smudged path across an endless dusty floor. Anderssen wasn't sure, but it seemed the ground was made of a polished ceramic.

Someone has come this way before, she thought, feeling more and more oppressed in spirit as another vaulted doorway loomed out of the darkness before them. *But only one set of footprints, I think, repeated over and over.*

They turned at the doorway and did not pass on into the limitless darkness beyond, but followed along the wall instead. Gretchen caught sight of a row of sconces, much like the ones in the tunnels above, but these were dark. They did not hold any of the blue eggs. Malakar's steps slowed and they entered a smaller hall, this one of a size Anderssen guessed a Jehanan might find comfortable. Vague shapes loomed in the faint light, and the scuffed path wound among piles of debris—broken machinery, if her eye encompassed the splintered wooden gears and cracked wheels properly—and into a still smaller passage. This, she thought, was an actual hallway and a far cry from the cyclopean proportions of the chambers outside.

Her medband beeped quietly, the sound almost lost in the endless curve of the passage.

"Malakar . . ." she whispered, afraid to disturb the tomblike silence. "This air is poor. You shouldn't stay long . . . my band can counteract the toxins in the air, but you . . ."

"I have passed this way before. After a twelfth-sun passes one begins to hear voices, or see flashes of light where there are none. This is the place I wish to show you."

The old Jehanan stood before a circular door in the wall. Gretchen blinked, realizing the entire hall was lined with similar openings. All were closed. Malakar leaned heavily against the wall, claws on either side of a recessed panel.

"What is on the other side?" Gretchen unzipped the collar of her field jacket and tugged out two breathing tubes. Pressing one clip to her nose, she let the other rest against her chin. "Were these the first chambers cut into the hill?"

"No . . ." the Jehanan sighed, slumping before the door. "There are other levels below, but the air is so poor, even the strongest takes ill and the weak die. Torches fail, and even the *gipu*"—she raised the glowing blue egg—"sputter and fall dark."

Malakar brushed dust away from the panel. "When I was only a short-horn fresh from the egg, this was a busy place. Often I was brought here—the air had not turned, there were lights in the dark places, some of the elders even held conclave here, as their ancestors had done. But then the *gipu* began to fail and shadows spilled in from the walls. Foul air rose from below and everyone moved up and away, closer to the gardens, to the terraces."

Another mournful *hooo* escaped the creature's slitlike nostrils. "Now my hide grows tight and brittle, and what was once clear in mind fades." A claw tapped on the door, making a sharp tinking sound. "The last Master of the Garden to tread these hallways is long still. The new Master sees only the sky, gardens, and bright chambers with tall windows. *He* cares only for the favor of the *kujen* and filling his claws with *shatamanu*. There is talk among the tough-hides of closing off these tunnels, filling them in, keeping the short-horns from mischief.

"When I was fresh from the egg, this chamber was filled with *gipu*-light, almost as bright as day. Our voices were very sweet, when we sang . . ."

The creature fell silent, crouched before the door. Gretchen waited patiently, sitting at the edge of the circle of light. The oxygen tube under her tongue made a quiet *hiss-hiss* sound as she breathed.

"That's odd," Parker said, squinting at a portable holovee sitting on his stomach. He had been flipping through the channels, half out of his mind with boredom. The windows were dark; night had come, bringing heavy clouds, but no rain, only a tense, oppressive stillness. Inside, without the cold night wind to stir the air, the ozone-stink of the comps and surveillance equipment made the room feel stifling.

Gretchen had failed to reappear on their scanners. Magdalena was certain the woman had been taken captive and horribly murdered. Parker didn't think so, but he was beginning to wonder what they would do if she were. *Go in after her, I guess. But how would we find her in there?*

"Hmm?" Magdalena was in her nest, legs and arms curled across her chest, clutching her tail and staring at the ceiling. "You don't like the dancing monkeys here?"

"The shows are fine. Unintelligible, but fine." Parker clicked back to the previous channel. "The Imperial 'cast channel is showing some footage taken by one of the Jehanan stations, with a translation running over the original voice track? But they don't match up."

The Hesht rolled over, staring at him in mild interest. "So?"

"So," Parker said, sitting up. "The news 'caster said the footage was of an anti-Imperial demonstration in one of the southern cities—the port of Patala I think. But that's *not* what the Jehanan narration said—they said the 'demonstrators' were some kind of local religious festival—one of those slice-of-life bits—but I guess down south they set things on fire to pay homage to their gods."

"Huh. That does seem odd. You think the Imperial 'cast just got a bad translation?"

"Maybe . . ." Parker scowled. *I should have kept one of those rifles. I didn't and now we might need it and I don't have it.*

He set the holocast set aside and paced to the nearest window. Miserable, he wedged his shoulders in beside a thick bundle of cables running up to comm-scanning antennas mounted on the roof of the building. The city below was filled with faint lights—the flickering yellow glow of lanterns and candles, here and there the dull red of bonfires or forge chimneys—a far cry from the jeweled splendor of human cities. The hill of the *mandire*, in comparison, was entirely dark and silent.

"Mags—how long are we going to wait for her?"

"As long as it takes," the Hesht growled, lying back down and fiddling with her earbug.

Parker heard a high-pitched whining sound and craned his neck up. A low layer of clouds blanketed the city, gleaming softly in the lights from below. *An aerocar*, he thought, feeling a sharp stab of envy. *We need an aerocar—be easy to land on the top of the hill and snatch Gretchen from the jaws of death if we had an aerocar. If we had an aerocar, there would be something for me to fly.* He scratched the back of his head, suddenly tired of waiting.

"She's in trouble, kit-cat. We're going to have to go in there and get her. I'm going out."

"To do what?" Magdalena's yellow eyes fixed on him. "We are supposed to wait."

Parker picked up his jacket. "Get some things we might need later." *When we have to bug out of town. I know we're going to have to leave all a'sudden, with the lanterns and whistles of the* keisatsu *shrilling behind us.*

The Hesht made a hissing sound, but did not stop him from leaving.

"Somewhere below," Malakar said, rousing itself, claws rasping on the floor, "lie many rooms filled with *pushta*. Thousands of them, each filled with more words than a single Jehanan could read in a whole lifetime. Your clans must have such things, where histories, songs, stories of the old, are graven?"

"Yes." Gretchen blinked awake, her interest sharpening. *An old library?* "Can you read them?"

The old Jehanan shook her narrow head slowly from side to side. A long arm reached out and dug into the leather bag, removing a rectangular metallic plate. "These are *pushta* I stole long ago and hid in the terrace. I hoped to learn their secret, to open them up, to see the flowing words gleaming in my hands." Malakar scooted the plate across the dusty floor towards her. "They are ruined, as are the ones lost below in darkness."

Anderssen picked up the plate with careful, gloved fingers and examined each surface in turn. A double cluck of the tongue cycled her goggles through a wide range of frequencies and light sources. Nothing was incised on the outside, but she could see an interface of some kind on one end and a recess where a long, claw-tipped thumb might press a control.

"Did the *pushta* fail all at once," she ventured, "or one at a time, until none were left?"

The old Jehanan hunched her shoulders. "Such knowledge was lost long before I hatched from a speckled egg. There was once a book, handwritten, on *pypil* leaves, which described a means of turning the glowing pages, but the leaf of the *pypil* does not last in dampness."

"Did this fit into a machine?" Gretchen pulled a compressed air blower from the inside of her jacket and gave the stippled interface a squirt. Malakar's eyes rose at the puff of dust, and then frowned as Anderssen cleaned the rest of the plate with a swab. She looked up, wondering if the wrinkled expression on the creature's face was avarice or longing. *I would be gnawing straight through the arm of such a slow creature!*

"I was frightened," the gardener admitted, hanging her head. "Some things I snatched from shelves and fled. Even when I was barely horned, the air in the deep was poisonous."

Gretchen set the plate down and unwrapped a comp octopus she'd been carrying in her pocket. "Some of my kind," she said, making conversation, "are digging in the ruins at Fehrupuré. They say there was a planet-wide war six or seven hundred years ago, one which crashed a great civilization . . ."

"Arthava's fire," the creature rumbled. "The credulous say he challenged the will of the gods, scratching at the doors of heaven, making edicts to guide all Jehanan to a right path in the place of the old religions—and they humbled him with quenchless fire and burning rain and deadly smokes which covered the land for an age. Foolish tales told by those who do not have the wit to look beyond their food bowl! No gods were needed to bring ruin upon us . . ."

"The truth is known? Beyond this place, I mean?"

Malakar hooted sadly. "Some learned men know. The *kujen* knows. He sends his servants to dig and pry in the dead cities, searching for trinkets. . . . .They have even been here, poking and prying! The Master tells them secrets he should not! Things entrusted to us. . . . Worst, we have forgotten, or lost, the long tale of the clans, that stretching back to the earth which gave us birth, to the first shell cracking in the hot sun. But the Fire is still hot in our minds, sharp and hard." A bitter trill issued from the back of her throat. "Each time we look to the sky and see your shining *rukhbarat* race overhead, parting the clouds, we remember what has been lost."

Gretchen plucked a set of leads from the octopus and began testing each stippled point on the plate. All of them were dead. *No current the octo can recognize. Better let the comp try*. She wiggled the octopus's main interface onto the comp, tapped up a broad-spectrum power testing routine and set everything back down.

"There are stories about the Arthavan period? When your people had aerocars and built the fin-towers and great highways? Before the Fire consumed your civilization? Were the *pushta* working in those times?"

"Perhaps." Malakar scratched her claws on the floor, making doodles in the dust. The passageway seemed to have grown darker and Gretchen eyed the *gipu* with concern. The radiant egg was getting dimmer. "We recall fragments, scraps of shell and hide—there is only one history which can be read—and that is precarious, precious, and perhaps lost forever. But I do not know if that history is from the time of Arthava, or from before, when our race came to this world for the first time."

Anderssen looked up sharply, one hand outstretched to hold her oxygen tube next to the *gipu*, which brightened visibly as fresh air hissed across its surface. "What remains? Another book?"

The gardener twisted, pointing at the sealed door with a foreclaw.

"There," she said, voice rumbling low, almost beneath the limit of human hearing. "A cruel jest—and a reminder to the great to tread warily in the world, for even the most glorious monument may be crushed beneath the stepping-claw of time." Malakar swiveled back, brushing scaly fingers over the plate wrapped by the softly humming octopus. "*Pypil* leaves erode, *pushta* fail, inscriptions wear away in the wind and rain, the memories of Jehanan fade. . . . I can tear the pages of your Méxica books with ease . . . but sometimes the simplest things endure."

"Malakar, what is in the room?" Gretchen shivered. "Why is the door closed?"

"There are paintings on the walls," the Jehanan said, sighing out a long *hoooooo*. "They show many scenes, but most striking are those of seventeen great ships descending from the sky. Golden Jehanan step forth and they are garbed like kings, like heroes. They fight terrible monsters and ferocious beasts with spears of lightning, laying low all who contest their dominion. Cities of emerald and silver rise from plain and mountain. They feast on the most savory food, they bear many young, they rule the world as gods. Oh, mighty is their aspect!"

Malakar fell silent again, claws scratching on the floor, raising tiny puffs of dust.

"But . . ." Gretchen wanted to pat the creature's shoulder, but had no idea if such an offering of sympathy would be properly understood. "There are no dates, no signs to tell *when* the murals were painted? Or even if they relate a true tale of your people?"

"*Hoooo* . . ." The old Jehanan raised her head wearily, seemingly spent. "We feel the truth in our bones, on our tongues, in the taste of the air, the bitterness of the *Nēm*. Even the freshest hatchling knows without being told . . . Jagan is not our home. We are strangers here, picking for grubs in the ruins of our ancestors."

"The *Nēm* fruit is supposed to be sweet?" Anderssen could see the signs of pain and loss in the creature's expression now. "Is it from your true-home?"

"Yesss . . ." Malakar's mouth yawned sadly, showing a forest of broken teeth. "The breath of life, the guardian, yielding a sap which folds back illusion from reality. There are many rituals concerning the *Nēm*, but . . . there, in the room, there is a little painting of a trilobed fruit in one corner and the characters 'I like *Nēm*, it is sweet to eat.' This old horn believes those words are true."

"Who painted the murals, Malakar? They weren't priests, were they? Not historians."

The Jehanan rubbed her long snout. "The roof is a little low and curved. We sat on the floor, listening to the shower-of-the-way. So many stories she told us, explaining all the bright pictures . . ."

"It's a school room, isn't it?" Gretchen kept her voice soft. "Children—hatchlings—painted the murals. But you don't know how long ago, or if they were painting something they'd seen themselves, or only read about in *pushta* or heard from a long-horn. That's why you wanted to know *how old* the paint is . . ."

Malakar hissed in despair, pressing her head against the floor. "How long have we been lost?" she wailed. "Where is our home—is earth gone? Did we flee? Are there sweet *Nēm* somewhere, under a bright sun, not so cold as cruel Bharat which glares at us from the sky? Are we alone? All alone?"

Anderssen felt a chill wash over her; the translator in her earbug was running out of synch with the sobbing wail of the creature's words. She waited until the groaning voice fell silent again.

"Malakar, can we open the door? Do you remember how?"

"*Huuuuuoooo . . .*" The old Jehanan opened her eyes. "This door has stood closed for a long count of years. . . . The last good Master bade it sealed. The painted colors were beginning to fade, to crack, like an old shell left out in the wind."

"Oh." Gretchen checked her comp, which was still humming to itself and trying to make the metallic plate wake up. "If the pigments and binding layer are breaking down, then opening the door might break the atmosphere suspension inside. . . . The whole façade of the wall could crumble to dust." She stood up slowly, fearful of alarming the creature huddled on the floor, and stepped to the portal.

Dust and a surface layer of grime came away at her touch. Gretchen dug a sampler out of one of the pockets of her work-pants. Running the pickup over the surface cleared a hand's breadth section—and the material resembled the polished ceramic making up the floors and walls. "Probably not a metal," she muttered, watching the display on the sampler flash through an analysis sequence. "Looks solid though. Airtight."

The sampler beeped, displaying a list of compounds. Anderssen puzzled through the materials, then shook her head. "A layer-bonded ceramic—nearly as tough as steel and probably lasts longer in this environment. Unfortunately, it's holding cohesion pretty well. No noticeable surface degradation and I don't have an erosion matrix built up to gauge what wear there is."

Her eyes fell on the *pushta* under her octopus. "Malakar, wouldn't these books be even older than the room? I mean, if they came from . . ." She paused, wondering if she'd caught the translator in an error. *Wouldn't be the first time!* "Did you say your people came from 'earth'?"

"Yes," rumbled the Jehanan, now squatting, long arms folded over bony knees. "Another bit of shell we've not lost hold of. . . . Our race was born on earth, long, long ago."

But Anderssen had plucked out her earbug, and the hooting, warbling voice had pronounced a word she knew. Her heart sank, knowing at least part of the answer to the creature's agonized questions.

The Jehanan word for 'earth' was 'Mokuil,' not Anáhuac, not Terra. *A dead world, if Hummingbird spoke true*, Gretchen remembered, filled with pity. *Desolate and shattered, a vigorous race which had woken the Valkar and so been destroyed millennia ago. Leaving only corpses among which humanity might hide, avoiding notice ourselves . . .*

There was a soft beep from the floor.

She knelt and checked her comp. The first set of scans were complete. The *pushta* was inert, showing no response to external power. Cold and dead, broken by the weight of thousands of years of neglect. Organic analysis found traces of a bacterium particular to Jagan, one which ate and corroded metal, on the stippled contact points.

How sad, Gretchen thought, cradling the plate in her hands. Malakar was watching her, eyes hooded, shoulders hunched against the sides of her long head. *The world ate away everything they wanted to save, leaving nothing but dust and empty, lightless halls. Even their great conquest turned bitter . . . Were they refugees from the destruction of their homeworld? Had they seen the Valkar rip aside the sky, seen their cities burn? How long did they flee through the dark, seeking a new home?*

She looked up. "There is only one thing we know for sure. The child who painted that picture had tasted *Nēm* untainted by the biosphere of Jagan. He or she must have come from race-home, from Mokuil itself. You've looked upon—touched—the work of the first of your kind to stand under the red sun of Bharat."

The creature lowered her head, clasping scaled arms over eye-ridges. A trembling, desolate hooting sound reverberated from the walls and fled down the empty hallway.

THE GEMMILSKY HOUSE
GANDARIS, "PEERLESS FOUNDATION OF THE VAULTS OF HEAVEN"

Two aerocars lifted from the rear garden of the mansion, their repeller effect rippling the conical trees and making their trapezoidal leaves rattle musically. Both vehicles bore nondescript colors and flew no warning lights, though the house and grounds were still wrapped in night's cloak. Standing in the watchman's alcove of a more traditional Jehanan building across the street, a figure in a long leather coat watched the 'cars rise silently and then speed away across the hills. The peaks behind the city—a long arm of snow-covered mountains reaching down from the massif of Capisene—were painted pink and silver with the first brush of dawn.

Rubbing cold hands together, the figure watched the mansion gate for a quarter-hour before stirring as the wooden portals opened. A Jehanan bundled in thick furs and enormous padded boots emerged, long snout puffing white vapor in the chill air. The house cook shuffled across to a locked wooden box beside the street and produced a key.

While the cook was taking out the day's delivery of eggs, freshly cut *zizunaga* fillets and imported Bandopene *molk*-cheese, the man in the long coat walked quickly across the street and ducked through the gate. With a furious expression, he strode up the curving carriage drive and let himself in the front door with his own key.

A three-toned chime sounded in the entryway as Gemmilsky unsealed his coat, stripped off his gloves and hung a drover's hat on its accustomed hook in the coat closet. Brushing back short-cropped sandy hair, the nobleman paced down the main hall and almost immediately encountered both old Nuskere Pol—who was majordomo of the current residence, just as he had served the venerable Gandarian mansion torn down to accommodate the whim of a mad *asuchau* outlander with far too much money for his own good—and Corporal Clark. Despite the early hour, both the human and the Jehanan were completely turned out for a day's business.

"Viscount," Clark said, surprise hidden behind a neatly trimmed dark beard. Nuskere Pol bowed, long hands clasped together in front of his fur-lined brocade robe.

"If there is business to discuss, we can speak by comm—" Clark fell silent. Gemmilsky had such a look of restrained fury on his sharp face that the adjutant realized any attempt to speak reasonably was doomed to failure.

"I have come for my personal effects," Johann said. "Nuskere, if you could wake the servants and have them pack my things, I will be speaking to the cook."

Clark frowned. "Sir—I assure you, nothing of yours has been touched."

"Almost truth," Nuskere interjected in a whispery voice, snout wrinkled in distaste. "The young *kujen* drained every last egg of *voodku* in the house."

"That will be paid for!" The corporal twitched slightly, trying not to glare at the majordomo. "Mi'lord, I was careful to pack away all of your clothes and other personal effects and—"

Gemmilsky's eyes narrowed. "Very thoughtful," he said coldly. "Some of my men will be arriving outside in short order. Bring all of my *carefully* packed belongings downstairs and see them properly stowed. A bill has already been submitted for the rest to the Legation in Parus."

Clark nodded, hoping the man wouldn't lose his temper and have to be restrained. Gemmilsky turned to the old Jehanan and produced a sheaf of documents from his coat pocket.

"Nuskere Pol, I am pained to inform you that I will no longer require your services or those of the staff." Johann pressed the heavy documents into the majordomo's claw. Clark could see they were affixed with wax stamps and different kinds of seals and some were bound in metallic thread. "Here are papers of release from your service to the household and severance pay. Generous, I hope. There are also letters of recommendation, for I trust you will find a worthy household to serve in future."

The corporal stiffened a little at the man's tone and was about to speak sharply with him when the front door banged open and the cook burst in, bags of eggs clutched to his heavy coat. The Jehanan was hissing and warbling at a tremendous rate, far faster than Clark's translator could keep up. Old Nuskere stiffened in alarm, but Gemmilsky—his face softening for the first time—replied to the agitated cook in a calm tone, managing a very respectable version of the same wavering hoots and trills.

Catching a bit of the conversation, Clark stepped to the open door and looked out warily. The front gates had been thrown wide and a procession of enormous hairy behemoths was striding up the drive. Each *hrak*—an untranslatable word the corporal's translator supplied from context—bore a creaking howdah of wooden slats and leather fittings. The lead *hrak* slowed to a halt, guided by a tiny, short-faced type of Jehanan the corporal had never seen before, and then knelt with a snuffling groan.

"Wouldn't expect to see mammoths here, would you?" Gemmilsky said, coming to stand at Clark's shoulder. "They're not the real thing, of course, just an unusual Jehanan analogue. True mammals, too. Quite rare on this world. A biologist I consulted in Parus thinks they might actually be native. Now, you had carefully packed baggage to bring down, didn't you?"

The corporal nodded, tore his eyes from the *hrak* settling onto the lawn, and hurried back down the hall. Old Nuskere was wringing his hands, watching the near-legendary *hrak* and their drivers with wide eyes, when Johann turned from the door himself.

"Master? Are you . . . are you going to the Cold Lands? Truly?"

Gemmilsky nodded, a faint sparkle in his eyes. "I am. Too many Imperials here for my taste. I hear many wild tales of the lands beyond Capsia. I would like to see the cities in the ice for myself, if they truly exist."

The Jehanan shuddered and pushed the door closed with both hands. "Horrible fates await those who pass the White Teeth, master. Horrible . . . you should stay here—I am sure the brown-faced men will leave soon. This is your home!"

Johann looked around the hallway with a pensive, sad expression. "It was, for a little while. Now, I want you all out of here before the sun is high. No one is to stay! Let these Méxica and their *minging* lapdogs feed themselves." He paused, a grin starting to twist his lips. "Tell cook to give all the food and drink in the house to the poor. My gift to the city. And I give you and the other servants all the bed linens, towels, everything but the furniture and the manse itself."

Nuskere stared at him for a moment, then began to trill helplessly in laughter, sides shaking, hiding his snout in stiff old hands.

Tezozómac waved cheerily at a Gandarian nobleman moving quietly through the scrub higher on the slope and looked down quizzically at Colmuir. The master sergeant was down on one knee, the long-barreled rifle at the ready.

"What was the name of that one?" The prince pointed over his shoulder. "The one with the particularly long snout and the green and black felting on his jacket?"

"Lord Pardane Fes," the Skawtsman whispered, tensely scanning the plane trees rising above the high grass. "Cousin of the *kujen* I believe and an avid hunter. . . . Mi'lord, you really should lower your profile. The *xixixit*—-"

"What exactly *is* this fearsome creature?" Tezozómac interrupted. He was feeling rather good—the aerocar ride had cleared his head a little, the day was pleasantly cool, and there had been a fine selection of beverages laid on by the *kujen*. While the natives had not made their way into the hills by air, they still managed to put on a very respectable luncheon in a pavilion under spreading trees. "Dawd tried to show me a picture, but I was busy throwing up at the time."

Colmuir did not look up, keeping his attention focused on the upper branches of the nearest copse. The Ghuhore district lay in the rain shadow of jagged mountains on the southern side of the Kophen. The vegetation ran to grassy hillsides spotted with clusters of dry-leaf trees and thickets of a spiny bramble. Steep ravines filled with thick brush split the slopes. The *tu* grass varied in height from two to four meters, which made visibility difficult for men on foot and excellent hunting territory for the triply-winged, uncannily silent *xixixit*.

"A native wasp, mi'lord, of uncommon size and ferocity. Hangs in the trees like a three-meter-long bat. Carries a bifurcated stinger—the poison dissolves the innards of the victim—very grisly, you understand."

Tezozómac frowned, checking his teeth for bits of grilled meat. He had found the roast *zizunaga* fillets very savory. "Are they colored like a wasp? I'd think yellow and black would stand out in this country . . . Or are they sort of a mixed brown and green with tan legs?"

"Sir, I don't rightly—what did you say?"

The prince pointed, Colmuir snapped his head around and an enormous, mottled insect burst up from the high grass between Tezozómac and Lord Pardane Fes and his loaders. The master sergeant hurled himself between his charge and the *xixixit*, swinging the rifle around. Shoved off balance, the prince fell backwards into the grass, broke through a screen of immature *tu* stalks and tumbled down the hillside.

The wasp, crystalline wings blurring into near-invisibility, darted to the right. Colmuir's rifle bellowed, spitting a long tongue of flame and sending the *crack!* of a gunshot echoing across the hillside. Lord Pardane's servants bolted, the noble Jehanan flung himself flat on the ground and the slender tree above him burst into flames as the self-fusing high-explosive bullet smashed into the trunk and blew apart.

Colmuir cursed, jacked back the ejector lever on the side of the rifle and groped for a fresh round. The Jehanan lord bounced back up, shrilling lurid insults at the clumsy human and caught sight of the *xixixit* blurring downslope, weaving between the isolated trees with fluid grace. Burning branches falling around him, Pardane Fes braced his rifle, took aim and squeezed the trigger.

The master sergeant felt the air over his head snap with the passage of a bullet, and rolled up himself, shouting in alarm. "Mi'lord! Mi'lord Prince, where are you?"

Downslope, the Jehanan bullet narrowly missed the fleeing *xixixit* and blew apart in a stand of red-barked brush. Flames licked up from the wounded trunk, caught among dry leaves and began to smoke furiously. The insect dodged into the unexpected cover and daintily wiped its feeding mandibles clean of fresh blood. Having only whetted its appetite, the *xixixit* then noticed a bipedal figure stumbling through the brush at the bottom of the slope and took flight, pleased at the prospect of a second meal so soon in the day.

Pardane's servants, meanwhile, followed their lord headlong down the slope. The long legs of a Jehanan were well suited for bounding between the tufts of high grass, but one of the loaders stumbled almost immediately and when he'd picked himself up, stared in horror at the eviscerated carcass of a young *molk*, entrails scattered by the *xixixit*'s cutting mandibles. The servant had only an instant to wonder why a calf had wandered this far up from the valley before the hooting bellow of his master summoned him to the chase.

Tezozómoc, half-blinded by dirt and clouds of *tu* pollen, crashed through a wall of thorny brush and stumbled into a stream. An algae-slick rock immediately turned under his foot, pitching him into the water with a splash. For a moment, he lay stunned in the current, shivering as snowmelt rushed over him, and then the prince heaved himself up and crawled onto a muddy bank.

Exhausted and in shock, Tezozómoc rolled onto his back in a drift of fallen leaves and tried to clear his eyes. The first thing he saw was the blurring, jerky flight of the *xixixit* as it darted through the stand of trees hanging over the stream. Bluish plates of fresh chitin gleamed under older sections of brown scale. The long, pendant legs and cutting mandibles tucked against the bipartite body gleamed jewel-green.

The prince groped for something to use as a weapon. In the incongruous silence, the sound of an aerocar turbine idling was jarringly loud. Tezozómoc tipped his head back and caught sight of a woman—a human woman—in a silk blouse, field trousers and a sensible sun-hat.

The *xixixit* blurred forward, glossy black stingers flaring down for the paralyzing strike.

There was a deafening *crack-crack-crack* directly over the prince's head. The smell of propellant and atomized metal choked Tezozómoc and he flinched into a tight ball, hands over his ears. Three armor-piercing rounds smashed into the thorax and head of the *xixixit* as it lunged across the stream. The fluoropolymer-coated bullets tore through the armored chitin and splintered into dozens of razor-sharp sub-munitions, which tore through the soft inner organ sac.

A hand seized the prince, dragging him to his feet, and Tezozómoc opened his eyes in time to see the *xixixit* blow apart in a cloud of shattered chitin, lubricating fluid and gossamer wing fragments.

"Christ on the Stone," he gasped, "that was an excellent shot!"

"Thank you," a rich alto voice purred in his ear. The prince turned in time for the unexpected woman to wrap his fingers around a still-smoking Webley Afriqa-Express hunting pistol and then swoon gracefully into his arms.

"*Ooof!*" Tezozómoc staggered, taken by surprise, and managed to hug the woman to his side before he dropped her. The hot barrel of the Webley burned his arm, but—juggling both unexpected objects for a moment—he managed to seize the pistol grip. He looked down at himself in dismay. He was soaked and coated with mud. "Ah . . . curst wilderness! Another good shirt ruined! I *hate* hunting—"

"Mi'lord!" Colmuir crashed out of the thicket on the far side of the stream, rifle at the ready. The master sergeant stumbled to a halt, gaping at the scene in front of him. Pardane Fes was only a step behind and the Jehanan let loose a hiss of astonishment. The crowd of servants behind him spilled out onto the bank and then everyone looked up, shielding their faces from blowing grit and dust as an Imperial aerocar settled between the trees. Dawd hung over the side, one foot on the bottom step of the boarding ladder, the Whipsaw tracking across the chuckling stream.

"You killed it?" Colmuir stared in amazement at the shattered remnants of the *xixixit* scattered in front of the prince and the woman. The master sergeant blinked, recognizing her. "Madame Petrel?"

Behind the Resident's wife, still in the arms of her Imperial savior, the pale faces of two young ladies peered over the side of an aerocar, then squealed in relief to see the horrendous monster stricken down. Colmuir stepped back, eyes narrowed in suspicion, and let the Jehanan hunters—nearly everyone had now arrived, drawn by the gunshots—stampede past to examine the insect carcass. Tezozómoc was staring around him, bemused to suddenly find a striking woman in his arms and two young girls clapping in delight and thanking him for such "quick thinking."

Pardane Fes rose from the shattered *xixixit*, shaking his long scaled head in appreciation. "Not sporting," the Jehanan boomed, "to use such a keen blade, but a well-placed shot withal—straight between the thorax plates. Well placed, well placed."

Clinging tightly to the prince's rather narrow chest, Mrs. Petrel's brilliant blue eyes fluttered open and she looked around, apparently so overcome she'd forgotten where she was. "Oh—what was that *horrific* beast?" There was a hesitant pause, then, in a ghoulishly fascinated tone: "Was anyone *killed*?"

Eight hundred kilometers away to the south, Itzpalicue grunted and her wrinkled old face screwed up into a disapproving grimace. "Cut that last," she growled to

Lachlan and his editing team, who were hunched over a double-wide set of v-displays in the operations center. "She always overdoes these things. . . . Cull the rest, make it look presentable for a handheld cam and squirt it to the t-relay on the *Tepoztecatl.* They'll want to forward it on to the core worlds as quickly as possible."

Lachlan nodded, watching approvingly as the two girls from Editing winnowed out everything which would have made the prince less presentable—such as the look of stark fear on his face when the *xixixit* burst out of the trees—and recast the crystal-clear video from the spyeyes into a fuzzier, lower-def format. A body-filter was already processing the prince's torso, adding muscle and definition.

"We'll have a final edit in about twenty minutes," the Éirishman reported after a moment. "Anything else we need to track from these spyeyes today? I'd like to route them back to Gandaris to recharge."

Itzpalicue shook her head. The old woman leaned on her cane, keen eyes roving across the workstations crowded into the low-ceilinged room. Everyone appeared entirely focused on their work, which pleased her greatly, and a particular, familiar tension was building in the air.

"Soon," she said, clicking her teeth together in consideration. "I can feel the index peaking. We'll have our war soon . . ." Coming to a decision, she rapped the top of Lachlan's console with her knuckles. "I'm going out to see to my Arachosians. They are getting impatient."

Shaking his head in dismay, Corporal Clark stepped through the ruins of the kitchen and pushed the door of the ice locker closed with a dull thump. Every edible scrap of food was gone. Nearly all of the utensils, pots, pans and other cookware had been hauled away. Some eating tines wrapped in a damask napkin lay forgotten on the floor. The rest of the house was in a similar state.

Chasing off the last of the scavengers—once word had circulated around the neighborhood about the viscount's departure, every short-horn in the district had descended on the '*asuchau* house' to get their share—had taken the whole afternoon. The genteel ambience Gemmilsky had worked so hard to establish had been destroyed, leaving only an echoing, empty house filled with scattered litter and forgotten trinkets.

"Well, this will take some fixing," the adjutant said, squaring his shoulders and tapping his comm awake. "Hello? Is this the Gandaris consulate? Yes, this is Corporal Clark. I'm acting factotum for the Prince Imperial while he's in the city . . . Yes, that one. Yes. Listen now, there's been a bit of a problem with the servants at the Gemmilsky house." Clark paused, listening to the consul babble in his ear. The corporal's face grew still, then turned grim.

"You say the Resident's wife is coming with him? She's not injured? Good. But her vacation party has been invited to stay with the prince?" Clark's dark eyebrows drew close over brown eyes. "And where would her luggage be? At the palace? No? Ah, the train station. I see. Well, sir, if you wish to remain employed by the Imperial Diplomatic Corps, I suggest you tell me how to acquire thirty properly trained household staff and hot dinner and drinks for thirty in . . ." Clark raised his wrist, glanced at his chrono, then peered out the window at the sun. "Three-quarters of an hour. As, sir, there are *no staff* here. They have all fled to the four winds."

There was a pause. Clark waited, trying not to tap his boot on the floor. Eventually the consul spoke again and a begrudging smile lit the corporal's dour face.

"Does the *kujen* have an Imperial-addressed comm? He does? Excellent—what's the number there? Good. Now, can you send a man to get her Ladyship's baggage? I will be very busy here, very busy."

PARUS
THE DISTRICT OF THE CLAW-SHARPENERS

Just west of a mustard-yellow mercantile arcade, where rug merchants laid out their wares in smoke-stained alcoves, an old royal residence with two slender towers sat hidden inside a block of residential flats. Inside the palace, in a large domed chamber holding a dry pool, the leaders of four of the *darmanarga moktar* cells in the capital considered a table covered with maps and diagrams.

The topmost map described the environs of the Imperial Legation, housed within the *dhrada-mandura*—the Rusted Citadel—and the streets surrounding the human enclave. The chart was covered with annotations describing the security arrangements, guards and other items of interest in the Legation. Despite the reflecting pool having gone dry the room was pleasantly hot and humid.

"We will have to commit nearly every brigade in the city to overwhelm this position," declared the smallest, most nervous of the conspirators. "With the weapons they control, the *asuchau* could hold the *dhrada* against us with a claw of warriors! We should wait until more lance commanders commit to our cause."

The largest of the *moktar* flared his nostrils dismissively. When he frowned, a deep scar puckered beneath his left eye-shield. "They are expecting an attack by warriors bearing swords, spears and the occasional rifle. The 'artifacts' we've put back into service will be a complete surprise—much less the number of rifles and heavy machine guns our agents have purchased on the black market. A swift, coordinated assault on these points . . ." General Humara's claw tapped the map, indicating the main gates of the Legation, as well as two service entrances on the far side of the compound. ". . . will allow our troops entry *and* trap them inside. Then it will be a matter of—"

"A matter of counting your corpses," an unexpected—human—voice said, rising over the sound of brisk footsteps on the expanse of mosaic floor. All four of the conspirators turned in alarm, horrified to find a tall, lean-looking Imperial with short blond hair emerging from the dim recesses of the vestibule. Despite civilian attire—short jacket over a cotton mantle, pleated trousers tucked into leather boots—the entire line of his body shouted *military*. "The Imperial soldiers assigned to the Legation are equipped with combat armor and modern weapons. A single *gunso* with a Macana 8mm could slaughter two to three hundred of your soldiers with ease. Even the surplused rifles you've purchased from passing merchants will have a hard time penetrating their hard shells."

The man's brash pronouncement froze three of the conspirators, but not the general. Humara trilled a soft laugh and rose to his full height—easily a head over the human—and looked down a scarred old snout. "Humans selling us guns to kill other humans is pleasant," he boomed, "and convenient. But we are not without powerful weapons, even in our diminished state. Not all of the glory of old Jehan has yet failed."

Timonen inclined his head in acknowledgement of the point. Then he raised pale, watery blue eyes to meet the gaze of the old *kurbardar* and lifted one hand. "Can you still reach to the stars, as your forebears once did? Do you still rule the skies?"

Humara hissed angrily in reply. "No, not as we did. We have been gnawing the same scale. There are Imperial starships in orbit, and those we cannot reach. Thus our desire to seize the Legation and the humans within immediately, so as to shield ourselves from orbital bombardment—"

The Finn produced a trill of laughter. "The Empire will not hesitate to spill innocent blood. The Imperial commanders you face will obliterate any massed forces you expose—such as concentrating all your brigades in the city against the *dhrada*—along with their 'shields.' "

"How then," the *kurbardar* growled, "do we defeat this enemy? How do we win?"

"Another question, first," hissed the nervous one. The Jehanan hopped from foot to foot, claws clicking together. "Who are you, *asuchau*? We have not seen your face before—your coloration is different, your speech pattern unfamiliar! How did you find and enter this place?"

"I am a courier," the blond man replied, producing a packet. "My name is unnecessary. I was given certain signs and procedures to follow and directed here. I have unexpected—but welcome—news for your cause."

The nervous Jehanan snatched the proffered packet and began going through the identity card and other letters inside. "What news?"

"First, I think you should not wait." The cold-eyed human nodded to the old *kurbardar*. "Each day only increases the chances one of your, ah, less-committed fellows will change his mind, or tell someone, or be betrayed by a subordinate. Then all of your heads—and mine, most like—will be on a drying rack with hooks through our eye sockets. I understand there is a city-wide festival in the next day or so?"

"The gathering of the *Nēm*," Humara rumbled wistfully. "The streets will be filled with street festivals and processions of the hatchlings bearing the sacred flowers. . . . The entire city will turn out in hatching-day best, the air will be fragrant with perfume and the smell of a thousand savory dishes." He paused, leathery lips rippling back from rows of ivory-colored teeth in growing anger. "You suggest we should attack the Imperials on one of the most holy days in our year? A day when conflict has always been forbidden?"

The other three hissed in alarm and began to eye the human with great distaste.

"Do you want to free yourselves from the yoke settling so gently around your necks? Do you want to win?"

The Jehanan officers said nothing, but there was a half-audible hissing. The *kurbardar* leaned forward, glowering at the human. "If we dishonor ourselves for an instant's advantage, a heavier weight than the Empire will be upon our *kshetrin*, an indelible stain—"

"But if that single moment of advantage is *necessary* to free your people," Timonen said, removing another, heavier packet from inside his jacket, "and you do not grasp the horn—sharp as it is—then the weight of slavery will be upon you until the sun fails. In truth, time is shorter than you expect."

He slid his thumb along the sealstrip on the packet and removed a three-d photo of a wizened old Náhuatl woman. "This is an Imperial agent, a servant of the Smoking Mirror. She is upon Jagan—in Parus right now—and she is hunting for you."

All four Jehanan stiffened, and while the most nervous one darted a glance at the doorways, the *kurbardar* picked up the photograph between two chipped claw-tips. He examined the woman's face carefully. "This *asuchau* has been seen by these eyes—at the feast of welcome for the Imperial hatchling. Where is she now?"

The human shrugged. "I have only lately arrived. Now you know the face of your enemy. You must strike before she can find *you* and drag your entire cabal before the *kujen* in chains." He removed a set of smaller envelopes, each heavy with clinking metal.

"I—my people—have been preparing for the moment of your liberation for some time. You have already received your shipments of Kärrhök missiles, *kyllä*? You have tested them?"

The *kurbardar* nodded. "Some failed, as your accomplice warned, but they have been destroyed and the remains hidden. The rest have been distributed to the brigades. But even with the reactivated artifacts, they will not suffice to remove the threat beyond the sky. . . . Without that, any rising is doomed to failure. A second Fire will sweep away what we have built, leaving only savages to toil in the wreckage for the Empire."

A satisfied glint flashed in the human's watery eyes. His lips twitched into a cold smile. "Do not concern yourself with the Imperial warship. When the festival day comes, you will see a brilliant sign in the heavens and *that* particular obstacle will be removed."

"How?" The nervous Jehanan looked up in horror from the photograph of Itzpalicue. "What do you mean *removed*? What if we are not ready to rise up by *Nēmnahan*?"

The blond man shrugged. "Then opportunity will pass you by."

"So, you force us to action—whether we are ready or not." The *kurbardar*'s claw clasped a heavy, curved *kalang* blade held in his ornamental harness. He showed his teeth again. "We do not seek a new master to replace the old!"

Unimpressed by the threat, the human spread the smaller envelopes out on the table. "I—we—have been sent to give you an opportunity. If an *accident* befalls the light cruiser on watch-station, then, well . . . you can express your sincere condolences to the Resident. It is well known the ship is already damaged and in poor repair—its destruction due to an accident will not be surprising. There is nothing to implicate your little conspiracy.

"But you will have missed your chance. Years of preparation will be wasted. None of your confederates will find the will to act again." He shook one of the envelopes, making the package rattle.

"There are twelve of these envelopes—each contains an address to a location in or around Parus and a key. In each house, you will find several hundred boxes of ammunition for your small arms and machine guns. These rounds have been specially modified to defeat Imperial combat armor. A little gift from those who also hate the Empire."

"So we rise up . . ." The nervous little Jehanan's split tongue flicked along well-polished teeth. "And we are successful—what prevents the Empire from invading us with irresistible force? They have far more than one light cruiser to claw!"

"They do." The human nodded. Despite the continued hostility of the conspirators and the muggy atmosphere in the abandoned building, he remained genial and composed. "But the Emperor has hundreds of colonies to consider, and many, many more problems than a brief incident on one obscure—no offense, my friends—

world on the periphery of his domain. Even the death of prince Tezozómoc will not inspire him to action—the boy has been sent here to spare embarrassment at home.

"But your true allies"—the blond man's lips stretched into a wide smile—"are the factions among the appropriations board of the Colonial Service. If you are successful, then those who favor consolidation will gain influence and the 'expansionists' will lose ground."

"A fantasy!" The nervous Jehanan slammed the photograph down on the table. "Bickering among bureaucrats may delay an Imperial reaction, but it will not *stop it*. If we destroy the Legation, slaughter their citizens and defeat their warriors, the Empire will *have* to respond or lose face. Then the sky will bleed fire and we will be cast back into the savagery we've only just crawled up from!"

The other three conspirators stared wide-eyed at the little one. They had never seen him so agitated.

Humara sheathed his knife. "Where is our path then?" he asked in a slow gravelly voice, gesturing at the human. "We must do something. Even the public Imperial records show what happens to worlds like ours . . . slow suffocation, economic enslavement, the inevitable reduction of each *kujen* to a puppet good only for imposing ever higher taxes. Here, at least, we will show our mettle and challenge them. Perhaps gain a space of years to build our own orbital infrastructure, our own warships. . . . With a little help, with access to offworld trade, we could rebuild the old yards at Sobipuré."

"A wild dream . . ." The nervous one scratched the line of cream-colored scales along his jaw. He glared openly at the human courier. "And again, we rely on this *creature* and his unseen masters to supply us with the technology and resources we need."

"An equitable trade could be arranged," the human said. "We are seeking allies, not slaves."

"Allies . . ." the little Jehanan hissed in disgust. "A cheap way to bleed the Empire!"

The *kurbardar* waved the stack of envelopes in *kujen* Bhrigu's face. "If you do not wish to seize the claw of opportunity, then retire to your estates! Find a more righteous path, if you can. We will do what must be done. This way we have at least a *chance* of victory."

The other two, who had remained silent, hooted in agreement. The human said nothing, watching the nervous prince with a placid expression.

"Yes, a chance . . . for the *yi* birds to peck your eye-sockets clean and dig their talons into your rotting entrails!" Bhrigu hopped from one foot to the other, then reached out his claw. "Very well. Give me our share. We will be ready on *Nēm*-day."

"You will?" The *kurbardar* and the other two stared at the nervous one in surprise. "But—"

"He knows," Timonen interjected smoothly, retrieving the stack of envelopes and sorting them swiftly into four equal piles, "that if you do not stand together, you will each be buried separately." The blond head bowed to the little Jehanan. "Your friend here understands how to gamble."

Bhrigu flashed his teeth again, but took careful custody of the proffered keys.

"Now," the Finn said, affecting to wipe sweat from his forehead, "some small issues to consider when you attack the Imperial installations . . ."

All four Jehanan bent over the table and maps, eyes and ears attentive.

WITHIN THE HOUSE OF REEDS
TAKSHILA

Gretchen sucked absently on her breathing tube, cheek pressed to the floor of the passageway. Dust tickled her nose and one eye was closed as she squinted into the viewer of her microscope. The lens-end of the tiny Ericsson 'scope was nosed into an almost imperceptible crack between the base of the doorway and the floor.

"No . . ." Anderssen turned a tiny dial with her fingers. The image expanded, swelling until she could see the pitted surface of the ceramic composite. "This seal is airtight. I think the door sets into a groove in the floor. To get an atmosphere probe inside we'll have to drill a hole."

"*Hoooo . . .* " Malakar shook her head slowly from side to side. The Jehanan was showing signs of oxygen deprivation. The long-fingered hands twitched intermittently. "Door is thick, very strong, like all these old walls."

"Yes, I'd imagine so." Gretchen rose slowly, running the 'scope along the edge of the door with long-practiced ease. The entire seal was tight, showing a remarkably well-turned edge to the door-frame and the portal itself. Disappointed, she folded up the 'scope and tucked it away. "Your ancestors built well. This"—she patted the door gently—"is as well machined as any human factory could make."

The old Jehanan made a leaky hissing sound. Anderssen reached down and picked up the *gipu*. The egg was weak and faint. Darkness lapped around them, reducing the shape of the gardener to pale bluish glints on scale and a tiny gleam in each eye-socket.

"We have to leave," Gretchen said, holding the ovoid to her breathing tube. "I don't have enough emergency oxygen for both of us to stay. We have to get up to a level where there's still some air circulation."

Malakar nodded weakly, hunching over and placing her hands—fingers splayed out—on the floor. Anderssen crouched, hooking an arm under the creature's shoulder, and heaved up. The Jehanan was surprisingly heavy.

"Here, breathe for a moment." Anderssen tugged the air tube further out of her jacket collar and slid the tip between blackened, diamond-shaped teeth. Malakar stirred, wheezing softly, and then was able to stand up.

"My thanks," she rumbled, still leaning heavily on the human.

Together, they shuffled down the passage, the wan light of the *gipu* shining before them. For a few moments, reflected light gleamed on the door, and then there was only stifling darkness.

By the time they had climbed the long stairs, Gretchen could taste the air freshening. Malakar's strength returned as well, and the gardener could make the last steps—the most worn, Anderssen thought, from the brittle concavity of the stone—under her own power. They passed through a vaulted doorway and Gretchen paused, running her hand across the door-frame. A deep, rectangular groove filled with cobwebs and dust ran down the center of the outthrust stone.

"Malakar—are all of the doorways like this one?"

The Jehanan turned, hooded eyes considering the opening. "In the lower levels. They are no longer cut so, above. There is no purpose—only old, traditional decoration."

"This . . . this isn't just decoration," Gretchen said softly, wiping away the grime. In the light of the *gipu*, something gleamed in the recess. Bending slightly closer, Anderssen jammed her hand into the opening and felt a cold, smooth surface under her fingers. Turning her palm over, she brushed grit from her fingertips into the cup of her hand. She whistled softly, seeing dark brown flakes against her pale skin. "This is rust."

"*Hur hur!*" The Jehanan trilled in amusement. "There is no—what are you about?"

Gretchen stepped around the side of the door and switched the frequency on her goggles. A UV wand clicked on in her hand and the human began running the light up and down the wall. Three steps along, she stopped and began knocking on the surface with her fist.

"There is nothing of use here," Malakar said, sounding irritated. "All of these passages are the lungs of a dead tomb. I should not have brought you here. . . .

You've told me nothing I didn't grasp before! Everything we were is lost, drowned in shadow. *Hrrr* . . ."

The knocking sound changed tone, ringing hollowly, and Anderssen tucked away the wand and brought out a wooden-handled chisel. Scraping the edge across the hollow section, she sketched a quick rectangle. A blow with the haft cracked the fragile surface, and then she picked away the rest with the tip.

The Jehanan stared in surprise as Gretchen, face intent, cleared away old paint and plaster from a recessed panel holding six indentations.

"This is just like the locking panel on the door down below," she declared, glancing sideways at Malakar, eyes shining *gipu*-blue. "All of the doors in the lower tunnels are like this. Mechanical locks—electrical locks—and pressure-tight portals. When they open, they slide up magnetic tracks into the ceiling. . . . Every floor is perfectly even. Every wall curves so smoothly. No chisel and hammer ever touched these surfaces! The lower levels are filling with bad air because the air circulation system broke down thousands of years ago. Then the recyclers failed and no one knew how to fix them. . . . The native bacteria ate away everything metallic it could find . . ."

Gretchen stood away from the wall, head tilted a little to one side. She stared at the Jehanan intently. "Do you understand what I'm saying, Malakar? Do you know where we are?" She paused, nodding to herself. "You *do* know. You remember, when all else have forgotten. Are you the only one who does?"

"*Hoooo* . . . " The Jehanan shuffled back warily. The head ducked down a little and turned, fixing the human with one gleaming eye. "Many things have been forgotten, some for the best! Your thoughts, this old one thinks, are too quick by far for your own good. A wonder your tribe has not cast you out! Abandoned you in the Cold Lands to starve and die . . ."

"You wanted answers," Gretchen said, alarmed by the creature's tone. "I've given you some. Now you'll give in return—trading like for like—this place, the 'hill of the *mandire*,' your 'house of reeds'—did it come from Mokuil? Are we standing in the bowels of one of the great ships which crossed the void? Was a *Nēm* painted on that wall by the light of a green star?"

"*Hrrrr!*" Malakar lunged, catching Gretchen by surprise with long arms, throwing her to the ground. Enormous strength pinned the human down, crushing the breath from her lungs. Anderssen struggled, trying to break free. "What do you speak of?" Malakar bellowed. "How can an *asuchau* human know the sacred light, the star of our fathers, burns *harivarpan*—green as the first grass?"

"*Ayyy!*" Gretchen cried out in pain, feeling claws dig into her arm. "Mokuil has a hot green sun," she bit out, wrenching fruitlessly against the gardener's strength. Anger boiled up, casting discretion aside. "But your race-home is dead. A blasted wasteland tenanted by ghosts. A dead shell where nothing grows—no

Nēm, no hatchlings, no short-horns, nothing—only wind keening through endless ruins."

"*Hurrrr* . . . " Malakar slumped despondently and Anderssen pushed the creature away. The Jehanan swayed, clawed fingers scratching at the floor. "No, no, you are lying. A sly *asuchau* human, making stories, shadows dancing on a wall—deceiving me. You cannot have seen the lost world. You cannot!"

Gretchen felt her arm, and clucked worriedly when her fingers came away damp with blood.

"Say you did not see . . ." The gardener's voice trailed away into a dismal fluting.

"Ahh . . . that hurts." Anderssen pulled one arm out of her jacket and winced to see three deep gashes shining red against her pale skin. Her medband had dispensed a coagulant, but Gretchen snaked out a bandage and slapped the self-disinfecting pad onto the injury. "I have not seen Mokuil with my own eyes. A vision on a distant world let me look with a Jehanan's eyes, walk with their steps. In that moment, I felt the warmth of that hot, young star on my shoulders." One arm done, she turned and bandaged the shallow gash on the other as well.

"Do you exist solely to torment?" the Jehanan groaned, huddling against the floor. "You question and pry and sneak, you offer to separate shell from sac, truth from legend—and everything you say is a needle-sharp claw digging into my heart. *Hooo* . . . I did not believe in demons ere now! I scoffed—I raised my voice against the short-sighted Masters—argued—connived—stole to keep the old tales alive . . ."

Gretchen shrugged her jacket back on and began picking up her fallen tools.

"I should have listened to them!" Malakar wailed, inching away. "They knew better than this old one! They knew . . ." The whistling voice faded into unintelligible hooting and fluting.

Rising, Anderssen walked quietly over to the gardener's side, then knelt, putting both arms around her shoulders. "Come, rise up. Do you have a room of your own? A place to sleep? You need to rest, to eat."

"No . . . I have no *khus*." The old Jehanan tried to rise, failed, and then—with Gretchen's help—managed to come to her knees. "I will not work at the tasks they set me—so they let me lie by the fire in the common hall with the other vagrants. I am"—a deep *hur-hur* boomed in the broad chest—"not to be trusted with the minds of the hatchlings or short-horns. Too many tales do I tell, of kingdoms lost and days gone by." Claws folded over the Jehanan's snout. "Ahhh. . . . Our lost home, our paradise, a tomb . . . all gone . . . gone . . ."

Anderssen heaved the gardener up to her feet. "You will be in worse trouble if I'm found here. Can you show me the way back to the terrace? I can get out from there."

A clawed hand folded around Gretchen's wrist and the Jehanan's deep-set eyes fixed upon her. "Why did you come here, human? What were you looking for when I found you?"

Anderssen's lips twitched into a wry smile. "What was I looking for? I was looking for a scrap of legendary shell. A memory out of the past. One of your stories. Something so old it would be new to human eyes. Even older than the Jehanan or the Haraphan. As old as Jagan itself."

"*Hoooo* . . . " Malakar whistled, nostrils flaring. "You are seeking the heart of the Garden! The false idol, the holy of holies which the blind worship, crawling before a dead god. You are looking for the *kalpataru*."

Anderssen nodded, one hand sliding inside her jacket and taking hold of the chisel. "I am."

"Worthless," the Jehanan said, puffing air dismissively. "Old accounts say the tree once gave every desire, revealed all secrets, elevated the mind as the gods might . . . but *I know* no Master of the Garden has been graced with its power for three hundred generations! This *I know*, though my old hide would be laid bare with barbed whips to say such a thing aloud."

"Have you seen it?" Gretchen said eagerly, before she could restrain herself. "Is it far away?"

"*Hoooo!* Your eyes are very bright, human! Your voice is quick, your little claws scratching at the wrapper of a sweet—very much like a short-horn, you are, very much."

"Your pardon," Anderssen said, bowing in apology. "Just show me the way to the terrace."

"*Hurrr*. . . . A curiosity to confound the foolish . . ." The Jehanan paused, long snout lifting in thought, eyes glittering in the *gipu*-light. "Your machines . . . You wish to pry and snoop and listen and *measure* the tree-of-deceit, don't you? Yes, you do, all those hungry thoughts picking and chipping and breaking open shells to see what savory treats lie inside." A delicate trill escaped the creature's throat.

Gretchen watched the Jehanan with growing unease. There was a malicious tone creeping into the gardener's voice. "What happened to you?" she said after a moment. "You believed in the Masters of the Garden once, but now . . . now you think I'll prove the *kalpataru* is false. Will that give you back what you lost? You didn't seem pleased about the school-room . . ."

"I will never tend the Garden again," Malakar said, head dipping mournfully. "None of the others would allow such a thing. The short-horns and hatchlings are not interested in my dusty old stories. But this new Master . . . his snout is crooked and filled with lies! He says . . . he says the tree is still alive—but that only *he* can hear, that only *he* is blessed."

A frenetic energy welled up in the old Jehanan's frame.

"I think he lies," Malakar snorted, "but you can tell me the truth of the matter, can't you?"

Swallowing, her throat unaccountably dry, Gretchen nodded.

"Yes," she said. "If you take me to the device, I can see what can be seen."

THE *CORNUELLE*
IN ORBIT OVER JAGAN

Two message-waiting glyphs—one from Engineering and one from *Sho-i* Smith—winked to life on *Chu-sa* Hadeishi's command display. As the communications officer had been ordered off the bridge, Hadeishi pointedly ignored the call from Engineering and thumbed open a comm pane to the junior officer's quarters.

The v-pane unfolded, revealing Smith—still in uniform, sweat-stained collar undone—sitting in the cramped workspace created by folding a JOQ rack into the bulkhead. Hadeishi could see Three-Jaguar lying on the bunk overhead, eyes half-lidded as she listened to a signal feed on a set of old-style headphones. A command-class comp was jammed in with her—a feat only possible because the Tlaxcalan woman was petite enough to fit sideways into a Fleet sleeping rack—and the display was alive with analysis diagrams and data flow patterns.

"Yes, Smith-*tzin*?" The *Chu-sa* kept his voice level, though he was irritated with the boy. *Junior officers are supposed to sleep whenever they can*, Hadeishi thought very piously, *not stay up working late.*

"*Kyo*, we've managed to trace most of this off-band encrypted traffic through the local comm networks. There is a locus and it's in orbit."

"Coordinates?" Hadeishi raised an eyebrow in interest. "A ship or a satellite?"

Smith punched the descriptors directly to the threatwell on the bridge of the *Cornuelle*. One of the heavy merchant ship icons shown on orbital path flared amber and acquired a targeting outline. The *Chu-sa* considered the shipping registry data on his sidepane.

"The *Tepoztecatl* . . . Six months outbound from Old Mars. Interesting . . . registration is up to date, port taxes paid, customs seals intact. Logs show daily shuttle traffic to the surface—expensive." Hadeishi brought up the secondary comm traffic data the two junior officers had collected and his face stiffened into impassive, glacial surprise. "This is an *enormous* volume of traffic. . . . What are they doing?"

"Video feeds, *kyo*." Smith glanced up. Jaguar nodded in agreement, eyes now open and following the conversation. She'd pulled the headphone away from one ear. "We haven't been able to crack their encryption, but the volume of data is so large they can only be passing realtime video from some kind of surveillance array on the planet back to the ship."

"Video? You mean they're processing intercepts from a fleet of spyeyes?"

Smith and Jaguar nodded. "There are hundreds of active comm channels in the traffic volume, and we think *each one* is a discrete camera. And, *kyo*, look at the source distribution . . ."

A map of the northern part of continent four unfolded on Hadeishi's command display. An orbital track designator appeared, showing the location of the *Tepoztecatl*, while clouds of brilliant points emerged on the map, clustering heavily in the large cities, but also liberally dusting the countryside.

"This covers every locale of size from Patala to Gandaris," the *Chu-sa* said in a thoughtful voice. He paused. "This level of coverage must be enormously expensive to deploy and maintain." Hadeishi glanced at the two officers. "Could *we* deploy this kind of network?"

Jaguar shook her head. Smith shrugged. "We've got spyeyes for the Marine combat teams and some extras for shuttle security and surveillance, plus spares, which gives us twenty. This network on the planet has—at last count from the data-stream—almost a thousand in operation."

"Then they're not documentary filmmakers," the *Chu-sa* said in a dry voice. He was beginning to get a tickling feeling on his neck. *This sounds familiar, but where . . .* "What else do we know about this freighter? Have they had any conversations with traffic control?"

"Minimal contact with traffic control," Smith answered. "All their transponder codes are squared away and they haven't moved orbit other than stationkeeping burns. They seem to have four different shuttles aboard—or so Hayes-*tzin* guesses from their drive-flare signatures." Jaguar reached over Smith's shoulder and tapped up something on his panel. The *Sho-i* nodded, watching the feed come up. "Here, *kyo*—we shot some video of *them* as well—just to make sure we were tracking the data-stream properly."

A hand-sized v-pane appeared on Hadeishi's display, showing the long cylindrical shape of the *Tepoztecatl* with an edge of Jagan in-frame. The view panned, showing that nearly a quarter of the surface was covered with antennas and comm relay receptors. The *Chu-sa* grunted, not terribly surprised. "Looks like a *Nightingale*-class emissions collection frigate . . ." Then he squinted in interest at the display. Hadeishi tapped the 'magnify' glyph twice and then slid his finger back along the time-in-spool indicator. From a distance, the freighter seemed stationary, but the close-up revealed the cargo and habitat pods behind the screen of communications equipment were spinning.

"They've got spin up throughout the whole ship," the *Chu-sa* said, mostly to himself. "Why would they need gravity in all those cargo areas . . ." His eyes flicked back to the side-panel with ship registry information. "Manifest shows a crew of sixteen, but radiated heat load is high . . ."

Hadeishi's expression suddenly changed, a keen light coming into his eyes and the corners of his thin lips tightening. "Comp," he said to the command interface in his comm-thread. "Dictionary lookup, source, *Tepoztecatl*."

Tepoztecatl is one of the Four Hundred Rabbits, ship's main comp replied in a grandmotherly voice. *The Four Hundred are the gods of the* pulque, *of drunkenness, of fertility. They are the consorts of* Mayahuel, *the goddess of the maguey, who is a mask-avatar of Xochiquetzal—Precious Flower—the goddess of spring.*

"Precious Flower?" Hadeishi frowned, still trying to capture a half-remembered anecdote overheard in a Fleet transit bar. Then the furrow in his brow cleared and he snarled, making both Smith and Jaguar flinch in alarm. "She is the historical patron of the *xochiyaotinime!*"

"The *xochi*-who?" Smith asked, confused. At the same moment Jaguar blurted: "The priests of the Flowery War? But they're just military archivists . . ."

"No, they certainly are not!" Hadeishi's hand jerked towards the 'battle-stations' glyph at the top of his command panel, then he mastered himself. *Haste will only lead to disaster*, he thought, reminding himself of the repairs underway on nearly every deck. *We are not in any condition to rush to combat alert. The freighter is a fellow Imperial vessel, mis-flagged as it may be, and deserving of some courtesy—not a hostile target!*

"They're not?" Jaguar's voice brought his attention back to the two junior officers. "Don't they put on the historical pageants and mock battles at Teotihuacán for Emperor's Day? The ones with everyone dressed in the old costumes and armor made of feathers?"

"They do," Hadeishi allowed, his burst of emotion suppressed. His voice chilled noticeably. "Though they serve the Empire in other ways as well." *And if they are here, on Jagan, in pursuit of a flowery war with the natives . . . then I may lose my command for gross incompetence. We are not ready for battle.* The tight feeling in his neck increased. "You two, take a knockmeout timed for six hours. I need you back on the bridge, rested and refreshed, as quickly as possible."

Without waiting for a reply, Hadeishi brushed away the open channel and punched up *Thai-i* Huémac's comm. The fresh v-pane flickered and then revealed the copper-skinned Marine officer in the number two armory, high cheekbones sheened with sweat, and a towel around his neck.

"Huémac h—"

"Disposition of your men," Hadeishi snapped before the lieutenant could say anything more.

"Ready squad in boat bay one, *kyo*, with the combat shuttle." The Marine's response was instantaneous. "Squad two is groundside with *Sho-sa* Koshō at the Sobipuré maintenance yards. Squad three is dispersed on-leave groundside."

The *Chu-sa* drummed his fingers on the side of his command panel. *This is what quicksand feels like,* he realized. *A third of the crew are off-ship, my exec is twelve hours away, and my only reserve troops need to stay in reserve.*

"*Thai-i*, I need two of your men in z-g combat armor and a launch prepped for a foray in orbit," he said, forcing himself to calm down. "Comm *everyone* groundside and order them back to the ship with all speed. If they aren't near a shuttle, they should immediately proceed to the Sobipuré spaceport or the Legation cantonment in Parus. We are not at combat stations, but a situation is developing groundside and I think we'll need all hands aboard within the day."

"Hai, *kyo*!" Huémac's response was professionally brisk, but Hadeishi could see a hundred questions poised to spring to the man's lips. The *Chu-sa* nodded and thumbed the channel closed. He turned in his command chair, fixing the duty officer with a cold stare.

"Hayes-*tzin*, shift our orbit to pass over Sobipuré. Squirt the shuttles on the ground with our new vector. I want those crews back aboard as quickly as possible, so let's keep them from wasting too much time in transit."

The weapons officer nodded and began tapping course corrections into the ship's helm.

Hadeishi, in turn, thumbed the still-winking comm request from Isoroku alive.

"Engin—"

"We are no more than four hours from battle stations," Hadeishi interrupted. "Prepare all compartments for combat acceleration. Shut down all repair activities, stow your materials and prep your teams to assist Medical in handling wounded. Do you understand?"

Isoroku nodded, eyes wide, and Hadeishi closed the channel. Sourly, he looked around the bridge, where everyone was suddenly very busy. The murmur of voices on comm was noticeably sharper. His mood improved by the sight, the *Chu-sa* tapped open an all-department-heads channel.

"This is the *Chu-sa*. Be aware hostilities are imminent on the surface of Jagan. Prepare to go to combat acceleration and conditions in no more than four, repeat four, hours. We will be providing orbital fire-support for the Army against native military elements." *And whatever other surprises the Flowery Priests have devised for their 'training exercise'!*

Hadeishi hid an involuntary grin—the sharp, crystalline feeling of incipient combat was stealing over him—and all the tedium of handling repairs and resupply banished instantly. He tapped up groundside comm to *Sho-sa* Koshō, then waited for the channel to clear through the usual routing static.

Waves of heat rippled across the tarmac at Sobipuré, hiding the sprawling shantytown beyond the edge of the spaceport behind a wall of shimmering haze. Susan Koshō turned away from the window of the repair depot quartermaster's office and pressed a hand over her earbug, trying to hear Hadeishi clearly. A faint sheen of sweat made her forehead glisten. Outside, a shuttle was warming up for takeoff and the roar of its engines was making the building tremble and obliterating any chance of conversation.

... ship on ready-alert. You need to get everyone back into orbit. If you can't make lift from Sobipuré, relocate to the Legation in Parus and we'll extract you from there.

"*Kyo*? What's going on? What's the situation?"

The shuttle engines throttled back, and the office—a dingy room with walls covered with tacked-up posters and damp manifests—swelled with the chatter of conversation, the chiming of comms and the ozone-stink of comp equipment running hot in dreadful humidity. Koshō peered out the window, wondering where Helsdon and his scavengers had gotten to. The captain's voice on her comm had the particularly sharp quality she associated with their ship plunging into combat.

We're dropping orbit, the *Chu-sa*'s voice continued, each word crisp, *to reduce your lift time back to the ship and to provide fire-support for the regiment. Hayes will handle outbound traffic control through the bombardment path. Make sure you—*

"*Chu-sa*?" Koshō tapped her earbug in irritation. Some kind of interference had flooded the channel. There was a warbling squeal for a moment, and then Hadeishi's voice popped back, perfectly clear.

—can you hear me?

"Hai, *kyo*. The channel went out for a moment." Susan palmed her comp out and thumbed up the local locator grid, hoping everyone was in range. "Should I evac just ship's crew, or everyone at Sobipuré?"

Just our crew, Hadeishi said, after a brief pause. *We need the shuttles back in orbit so we can provide medevac for the 416th. I've learned the—*

The comm dropped out again, just for a fraction of a second, but Koshō caught the missing beat in her captain's voice rhythm. Puzzled, she cleared away the locator grid and thumbed up a diagnostic on her shipsuit comm.

—natives are preparing to rise against the Imperial presence. So I want all of you safe in orbit as quickly as possible.

"Understood . . ." Susan stared at her comp, where the diagnostic display was showing an unaccountable lag in the transmit/receive time between her and the ship. The *Sho-sa* turned to the corporal who had been trying to help her round up sixty tons of raw protein for the shipboard recyclers. "O'Reilly-*tzin*, can you bring up the orbital traffic control plot on your comp?"

"Of course, ma'am." The quartermaster's aide pushed a pair of antique spectacles back on his nose and pudgy fingers danced across his comp display. "Here . . ."

Susan craned her neck to check the position plot on the display, found it matched the one on her handheld, and her nostrils flared in puzzlement. *The ship has not moved a million kilometers away from me in the last minute and a half. What could be throwing this kind of delay in the comm channel? Is the network relay failing?*

"Captain," she said slowly, paging through the rest of the diagnostics provided by her comp. An obscure screen holding network routing information caught her eye. "I've an entire squad down here, as well as Helsdon and his technicians. Should we reinforce the landing field perimeter? What do you want me to do if the comm net goes dark?"

If you lose comm, Hadeishi said, *then collect everyone groundside. Third squad is on leave in Parus. We don't want to leave them hanging—not like at Forochel. I trust your judgment.*

Susan nodded and squared her shoulders. The Forochel exercise posited a failure of inter-unit comm due to a precedence dispute among Fleet commanders of equal rank. All subordinate commanders were expected to maintain their heading and unit cohesion while a unity of authority was re-established. The *Sho-sa* felt herself become very calm. "Understood. Koshō, out."

Then she jammed her thumb down on the all-units channel. "Koshō to all *Cornuelle* personnel groundside, we've been recalled to the ship with all haste. Return to the shuttle immediately and prepare for lift. Repeat, return to the shuttle immediately."

A babble of voices filled her comm as the Marines and technicians checked in. Only Helsdon was more than ten minutes from their shuttle. Koshō frowned, realizing the master machinist's mate must be overseeing loading of the replacement power supplies Isoroku had bartered for. She tapped up Felix, who was standing by at the shuttle itself.

"*Heicho*, go get Helsdon and his techs—they're at the Imperial Development Board warehouse—if they've got everything on the lifter, bring it with you, but if not, leave the supplies in place and get those technicians back to the shuttle in one piece."

Hai, kyo*!* The corporal signed off. In the ensuing pause, Susan realized the quartermaster's office had fallen silent. She turned, one eyebrow raised, and found all of the clerks staring at her with wide eyes.

"Yes?" The *Sho-sa* groaned inwardly. All of the personnel in the room were Fleet—but not crewmen from the *Cornuelle.* Sobipuré was a Fleet installation, but not attached to a specific ship, being staffed by crew seconded from battle group 88's general staff pool. "Where is your commanding officer?"

"In Parus," O'Reilly squeaked, pale round face sheened with sweat, "arguing with the staff liaison of the 416th about acquiring more surface transport for resupplying the squads operating in the field. . . . Are we going to be attacked?"

"I have no idea," Koshō said bluntly, counting heads. "Who is responsible for perimeter security for the landing field? Do you have an evacuation shuttle assigned? Someplace secure to go?"

O'Reilly swallowed, one finger picking nervously at his collar. "D-Company was handling fence patrols and keeping the slicks from picking through the rubbish tip, but they were reassigned to secure the highway and rail-line north to Parus."

Susan stared coolly at the corporal. "And now?"

"Now . . . the *kujen* of Fehrupuré sent a brigade of lancers. They're encamped over at the east end of landing strip two . . . near the customs shed. I heard they were only temporary, until a company from 2nd brigade arrived to take over, but they won't be here until next week . . ."

Koshō nodded, hiding her horror at the prospect of the entire Fleet landing field having no security at all if the wrong princeling had secured the assignment.

"And your shuttle?"

"Hangar two," O'Reilly replied, his voice rather faint.

She started to tap open a comm channel to Felix, then paused, staring intently at the comp in her hand. *Something is delaying our comm,* she thought, reading through the routing details. *This looks like the entire military net is being relayed through a location far out in space.* She keyed a series of commands into her suit comm, then squirted a reset code to every Fleet comm within range.

Sixteen devices in the quartermaster's office beeped simultaneously, startling the already edgy clerks, and then reset.

"We're in local point-to-point mode," Koshō announced briskly, "in case the nearest relay is damaged by enemy action. You men, pack up this office, pull your comps, flashbox any hardcopy and get to your shuttle as fast as possible. O'Reilly-*tzin,* you're in charge. Our shuttle is in hangar number six. Comm me when you're ready to lift—we'll go in sequence and relocate to the ship."

"Yes, ma'am!" the corporal said, weak-kneed with relief he wouldn't be abandoned.

Susan spun on her heel and banged out the door, taking the steps down to the searingly hot concrete two at a time. She started running towards the looming row of hangars, her armor activated, safety off of her pistol, a locator grid now showing in eye-view on her combat visor. Her temperature regulators immediately began complaining.

"Felix." Koshō cleared a channel to the *Heicho*. "Forget the repair supplies—we've no cover out here; an unknown force is handling fence security—just grab Helsdon and get back to the shuttle. *Do not* assume any native troops you encounter are friendly."

The *Sho-sa* heard Felix acknowledge, then swerved to use a warehouse for cover as she approached a road cutting across the base. She could hear a distant rumbling to the north. Clouds were busy gathering for the afternoon thunderstorms, but had not yet built up enough to deluge the landing field with a torrent of greasy, warm rain.

Hadeishi slid into the passenger's side of the captain's launch and let the shockchair fold around him, mating on-board environmental to his z-suit and hooking his comm into the launch relay. The forward window showed twin boat bay doors recessing, revealing a widening slice of abyssal darkness. A ring of landing guide lights flared to brilliance and the chatter of the bay traffic officer and *Sho-i* Asale negotiating undock and departure filled his earbug.

"Captain's launch is away," Asale said briskly, and the ship's boat puffed free of its cradle and swept through the bay doors with steady grace. "Outbound to make intercept with traffic control orbit ninety-six, freighter *Tepoztecatl*." The pilot turned slightly, inclining her head towards the *Chu-sa*. "Time to match velo and orbit is four hours, *kyo*."

Hadeishi's eyes narrowed, displeased. "I'm in a hurry, *Sho-i*. Don't hold back on my account."

The pilot's dark brown eyes widened in delight. "Orbital traffic control regulations say I should—"

"The faster you get us there, *Sho-i*, the happier I will be." Hadeishi tapped his shockwebbing. "Everyone's in-harness."

"Yes, sir!" Asale toggled off the thrust regulators and checked her distance from the nearly invisible shape of the *Cornuelle*. "Fitz, Deckard, you strapped in back there?"

"Hai . . ." Marine *gunso* Fitzsimmons answered with a grumble. "I just had lunch . . ."

The cocoa-skinned pilot shook her head in amusement, then twisted her control yoke all the way forward. The pair of Ventris Aerosystems thrusters at the heart of the launch flared sun-bright and Hadeishi felt a *kyojin*'s heavy, heavy hand crush his chest. The launch leapt forward, spaceframe groaning, and there was a muttered curse from the passenger compartment.

"Forty-five minutes to intercept," the pilot reported cheerfully, letting her boat cut loose. Hadeishi could see the planet begin to swell ahead. The *Tepoztecatl* was in a lower orbit than the Fleet warship on overwatch. Scattered satellites and a lone merchantman sparked on the navigational plot. Most of the face of Jagan was wreathed in cloud. A huge storm system was gathering in the southern ocean.

The *Chu-sa* listened to Hayes with one ear, keeping track of the *Cornuelle*'s maneuvering burn. After he was satisfied nothing had gone wrong aboard and the cruiser was on the proper heading, he cleared his display of the Navplot and tapped up a communications relay interface.

Now, he thought, steeling himself, *we will see if a little truth can be sifted from all this deception.*

His earbug went silent and Hadeishi keyed the traffic control channel to the merchantman alive. "*Cornuelle* to the registered Imperial freighter *Tepoztecatl*, come in please. This is a priority call to . . ." He glanced at the registry information. ". . . Captain Chimalpahin."

The channel popped alive with gratifying speed and the face of an irritated-looking, elderly Náhuatl with very long black-and-gray hair appeared in a fresh v-pane.

This is Chimalpahin.

"Hadeishi of the *Cornuelle* here, I am inbound to match your orbit. We have some matters to discuss face-to-face."

The man's expression twisted into intense annoyance. *Captain . . . this is not a good time for a social visit. In a day or two, I would be happy to meet you on the* Cornuelle *and we can discuss whatever you wish.*

"I am on my way now," Hadeishi said. "You will allow me aboard your ship and you will explain to me *exactly* what you and your fellow priests are doing here."

We are about the Emperor's business, Chimalpahin said in a patient tone, *as I'm sure you guess. So—shouldn't you be with your command? There will be work for you soon.*

"Yes, I expect there will be 'work' for us within the day, or at most the week." The *Chu-sa*'s tone cooled. "And Imperial starmen and soldiers will die because you've arranged a 'live training exercise' for them—without informing Yacatolli, the Resident or myself of your presence or your purpose."

The corners of Chimalpahin's small mouth twitched in amusement. *Go back to your ship, Hadeishi. Yours is an honorable role, do not dishonor the Fleet by taking our business personally. Just do your duty.*

"My duty," the *Chu-sa* bit out, "is to secure the common peace, police mercantile traffic and enforce the will of the Emperor. At present, I have every reason to believe you and your companions are actively seeking to destabilize the situation on Jagan and place every single Imperial citizen on the planet in danger—citizens I am oath-bound to protect."

Asale reached over and tapped Hadeishi's display. A time-to-intercept counter was ticking relentlessly, showing ten minutes to deceleration. At the same time, the freighter captain's nose crinkled up in a mocking sneer.

Are you intending to arrest us? Impound our ship? Clap us in chains?

"In approximately fifty minutes," Hadeishi said, fighting to remain calm, "you will be showing me your identification, Imperial writ and other authorities proving you are, in fact, executing the Emperor's Will in this matter. If I am satisfied—"

Satisfied? Chimalpahin interrupted, face blushing coppery red. *We are not beholden to Fleet! Our authority far exceeds yours, particularly in these matters! The Admiralty will severely reprimand you for interfering, Hadeishi, and your career—*

"If I am not satisfied, Captain," the *Chu-sa* snapped, "then my Marines will storm and seize your vessel and you *will be put in shock restraints* until this matter is sorted out! As for your authority, I have yet to see any proof you are more than saboteurs, agitators and insurrectionists." He paused, trying to remain impassive. "Fleet reaction protocol to revolt is quite clear. How am I to know—despite your *noble* face—you are not a pack of HKV operatives, or a Danish *volkscommando* conspiring with native elements?"

The comm channel suddenly cut out, much to Hadeishi's surprise, and then popped back in. Chimalpahin seemed taken aback, staring off the edge of his v-pickup. The *Chu-sa*— feeling unaccountably wary—glanced at the comm channel status information and was perplexed to see no warnings indicating a lost relay or network problem.

"What was that?" Hadeishi growled. "Are you showing a secure comm connection on your end?"

Yes . . . The freighter captain stared at his panel in alarm. Then he looked up, his expression ashen. *Return to your ship immediately, Captain. We can meet socially on another day.*

The channel went dead.

"Five minutes to deceleration. Forty minutes to intercept," Asale said quietly, watching her commander's stonelike face with concern. "Should I turn around?"

"No . . ." Hadeishi switched comm to the bridge channel on the *Cornuelle*. "Hayes-*tzin*, are we suffering some kind of comm interference? I just lost channel with the *Tepoztecatl* in mid-sentence."

No, sir. Everything here shows green. Should we run a system check?

The *Chu-sa* tapped one knuckle thoughtfully against the faceplate of his helmet. "Something odd is happening with comm. If Isoroku has a moment, have him check the relays and master nodes for interference, degraded comp function, anything at all."

Hayes signed off and Hadeishi nodded to the pilot. "Proceed."

I'm going to need something solid out of this priest, he thought, fighting imminent melancholy. The faces of Koshō and Hayes and Isoroku and even midshipman Smith were clear in his mind's eye. *To save their careers. Otherwise, every indication will point to incompetence on my part and complicity on theirs. And they will be dragged down with me.*

Hadeishi felt certain Fleet Command had been apprised of his slow return to Imperial space. *A black mark has been set beside my name, against the* Cornuelle's *record, an admonitory note for every officer serving with me. And with no patrons to offset my . . . refusal . . . to obey orders, my old ship becomes expendable. An honorable sacrifice to cover some political game played out by the* xochiyaotinime. *Her brave heart spared the wrecking yard . . .*

He started to feel very bitter and forced himself to think of something else, something beyond the faceless hand which placed his ship and crew in danger of disgrace. The first words which popped into his consciousness were very old, a fragment he'd seen on a moss-covered tombstone in the old temple grounds at Jorikū, on the western side of Shinedo city, overlooking the Chumash Sound.

A noteless tune fills the void:
spring sun, snow whiteness, bright clouds . . .
clear wind.

He grunted, feeling entirely helpless, trapped in a tight, confining suit in a tiny bubble of air, light and power speeding through limitless darkness towards an uncertain welcome. *A death poem. But whose? Mine?*

Heicho Felix grunted, feeling the strain in her upper back, and heaved a packing crate onto the back of the groundtruck her squad had commandeered. Helsdon and one of his technicians grabbed hold on the other side and shoved the heavy package against the sidewall.

"That's the next to last," a man in an Imperial Development Board jumper yelled, scrambling up onto the truck. Felix turned, jammed ink-black hair back behind her ears, and saw two of her troopers struggling to carry the last crate out of the warehouse.

"Leave it," she snarled, listening to a steadily increasing level of panicky chatter on the all-hands channel serving the Imperial installations around the periphery of the landing field. "We've got to get to the shuttle. Let's go!"

Ignoring her, both men staggered up, then tipped the crate onto the rear lip of the truck bed. Cursing, Felix joined in, pushing for all she was worth. The vehicle groaned, settling on its springs, and then complained bitterly as all three troopers swarmed aboard. Helsdon ignored them, concentrating on throwing tiedowns around the cargo and punching the liftgate control. The *Heicho* clicked over to the squad channel.

"Drive," she barked, swinging her Macana around to point out the back of the truck. The corporal in the forward cabin fired up the big engine, threw the vehicle into gear and they jounced out of the cargo yard behind the warehouses in a cloud of fresh dust. Felix swayed, caught herself, then braced one armored foot against the metal-reinforced crate squatting between her and the machinist's mate.

"What is all this stuff?" she asked, dark brown eyes wary, as the truck turned out onto the ring-road surrounding the number two landing strip. The driver jammed on the accelerator and they raced down the unsurfaced road. Felix could feel a pregnant heaviness gathering in the air. A thunderstorm was about to burst over their heads, turning the roads and fields around the strip into gooey, hip-deep mud.

Helsdon grimaced, eyes tight, holding a bandanna to his mouth and nose. None of the technicians were in armor and they'd left their z-suit helmets back on the shuttle. "Power supplies," he shouted, trying to best the roar of the methanol engine in the old-style truck. "They were supposed to go into the communications satellites the Board is putting up."

They hit a buried culvert under the road and everything bounced up, then slammed back down again. Felix clung grimly to a stanchion, hoping she wouldn't be pitched out. "How'd you get them?" she wondered aloud, watching the packing crate shimmy and bounce from side to side, straining the tiedowns. "Aren't they expensive?"

"Part of our trade." Helsdon shrugged, face coated with a fine layer of yellow dust. He sneezed, wiped his nose and left a muddy smear. "These are Fleet-grade packs, but they're not the right kind to fit the latest round of satellites. So Isoroku traded all our scrap—"

The man in the Development Board jumper leaned over, shaking his head. "These aren't Fleet grade," he shouted, then clutched wildly at a hanging strap as the truck swerved off the main road and into a parking lot behind shuttle hangar six. There was a squeal of brakes, Felix felt the tires slipping on loose gravel, and then the whole vehicle lurched to an abrupt halt. A veil of road dust drifted past, settling on everything.

"Everyone out!" Felix bawled, jumping down and stepping out, scanning the immediate area. Her Macana was off-safety and she'd made sure a fresh clip of armor-piercing was loaded up. The latest intel on the Jehanan troops deployed on the perimeter said they were lancers in heavy ceramic and cloth armor, armed with a wide variety of hand-weapons and native muskets. Against targets in so much ablative armor, she thought penetration would knock them down faster than trying to flay them alive with splintering sub-munitions. Technicians piled out of the truck, surrounded by a screen of Marines with weapons at the ready.

The Board technician jumped down and Felix seized him by the collar. "What do you mean, those aren't Fleet-grade power supplies? That's what the packing display says. That is what we *paid* for!"

The civilian went pale, fingers clutching at her armor-clad wrist. "*Urk!* I repacked those crates myself . . . Go easy, ma'am! They're the original power supplies from the satellites. They've got the same interface—"

"Helsdon!" Felix pointed at the crates being lifted down from the truck. "Break open one of those once we're inside. I think you've been stiffed by this insect . . ."

"Not me! Not me!" The technician was now an alarming shade of parchment. "The lead engineer on the project had us switch them out—he wanted to extend the time-to-repair for the commercial comm relays! They can drain a pack pretty quickly. But . . . but these will work fine in your equipment. I swear!"

"That," Felix said, shoving the man in front of her and prodding him towards the hangar with the muzzle of her rifle, "is not the point. You don't cheat the Fleet, and if you do . . ."

A long, drawn-out crackle of thunder drowned out the rest of her threat. Everyone looked uneasily at the sky, which was now dark with huge, humped clouds. The Fleet crewmen seized hold of the rest of the crates and began moving them inside with commendable speed.

Scowling at the buildings across the road, rifle to her shoulder, Felix waited just inside the hangar doorway until everyone else had gotten under cover. Nothing was moving save stray winds eddying debris across the tarmac and the ring-road, blowing clouds of dust and litter into swirling *tchindi*. The *Heicho* could hear *Sho-sa* Koshō's distinctive voice echoing inside, ordering everyone onto the shuttles and the crates aboard.

Uneasy, Felix threw the locking bar and sprinted for the shuttle. Koshō was waiting on the loading ramp, silhouetted against the bright lights of the shuttle hold and the yellow-orange glow of the sun gilding the runway and the other station buildings.

"Come on, Felix, the captain wants us upstairs right away."

The *Heicho* double-timed up the ramp, automatically checking to make sure her men and the engineers were strapped in, the cargo was secured and everything was shipshape. The ramp whined up, and then clanged shut. Koshō ran through the environmental seal checklist at light-speed and then tapped open her comm.

"Koshō to pilot, we're clear to lift. Is the other shuttle ready to take off?"

Hai, kyo. *They are on rollout now.*

Felix found a seat and wedged herself in. Koshō was sitting opposite, somehow already secured and looking unruffled in her matte black Fleet z-suit. The shuttle began to tremble and the *Heicho* felt the landing wheels rolling across broken concrete through the seat of her armor. She thumbed up a v-pane on the inside of her visor, catching the feed from the pilot's station. Clouds were still building over the field and the northern horizon was black with rain.

"*Kyo*—did Helsdon tell you about the power packs?"

Koshō nodded, lifting her chin to indicate the row of crates secured to the pallets running down the middle of the hold. "Isoroku got stiffed, I see. What was supposed to be in these packs?"

"Military-grade field power cells," Helsdon said. The machinist's mate had his comp out and the inventory tag on the side of the nearest cargo pack was blinking in response. "Sunda Aerospace Yards PPCAM-17's—that's a long-term, antimatter powered cell—should keep those satellites with juice for . . ." The engineer paused, and Felix turned, catching a raised eyebrow through the glassite of his facemask. ". . . about three thousand years at the draw on file for the commsats the Board is putting up."

"What?" Koshō turned her attention on the Board technician, who looked like he'd swallowed a whole puffer fish. "What does the Development Board think it's doing? Those satellites will wear out from micrometeoroid abrasion long before these cells decay!"

The shuttle trembled again, rolling out onto the landing strip tarmac.

Hold on, came the pilot's voice. *The other shuttle is boosting off the field now. We'll be at high-grav accel in—*

Felix flinched, her face suddenly awash in brilliant light. The pilot shouted in alarm.

The evacuation shuttle carrying the clerks from the Supply office disintegrated in a blossom of blue-white flame. For an instant, both engines continued to flare, propelling the shattered vehicle out over the shantytown surrounding the landing field. Then the shuttle drive blew apart in a secondary explosion. A corona of explosive gas and smoke belled out in a black cloud, and then burning debris was raining down among the rows of huts. The main mass of the shuttle, wreathed in flame, corkscrewed into the ground. Another concussive blast followed, flinging shattered rooftops and wooden tiles up in a billowing cloud of dust and smoke.

Missile launch plume at eight o'clock! the pilot shouted. *That was a high-v interceptor shot!*

Felix twitched back to look at the *Sho-sa*, and Koshō's voice was crystalline in her earbug: "Battle comp says it was a Kärrhök ATGM—they've got a sprint range of six kilometers—full acceleration, *Chu-i*, and keep us on the deck! If they only have one launcher there's a minute-and-a-half reload time between shots. Get us out of range!"

Felix jammed her head back against the supports and the Fleet shuttle engines lit off at maximum power. The back blast flooded the hangar behind them, tearing off the doors, and sending flames roaring from the windows. The entire building buckled, crumpling like a paper bag tossed into a fireplace. The shuttle roared across the tarmac, crossways to the flight line, canted over at an angle—wingtip barely missing the rooftop of a maintenance shed—and blew across the perimeter fence with a shriek of ruptured air.

A rippling *crack-crack-crack* slammed into flimsy buildings, shattering windows and deafening thousands of amazed Jehanans crowding into the narrow lanes to see what had made the violent noise in the sky. Howling wind lashed them seconds later and the multitude flattened as the gleaming black shape of the shuttle raced past overhead, heading northeast.

Clinging grimly to her shockwebbing, Koshō cleared the ground-to-ship channel. "Hayes! We've been attacked at the Sobipuré field by a ground-launched surface-to-air missile. Do you have us on tracking scope? Hayes? Hayes, are you there?"

The comm channel was howling with static, frequency indicators blazing red and hopping madly as the comp in her suit searched desperately for a clear channel.

"Hayes?! Koshō to the *Cornuelle*, is anyone there?"

THE GEMMILSKY HOUSE
GANDARIS, "ABODE OF THE HEAVEN-SUNDERING KINGS"

Prince Tezozómoc stretched out his arms and beckoned with his head for Sergeant Dawd to produce the next garment. Trying not to roll his eyes, the Skawtsman draped a greenish-tan velvet shirt over the young man's arms and chest.

"Hmmm . . . no . . . makes me look too sallow." The prince plucked the silk out of the sergeant's hand and tossed the shirt into a heap of equally unsuitable garments. "Is there anything red in there? A nice crimson or scarlet one—they always make me look striking."

"You've already gone through the red ones, mi'lord." Dawd pursed his lips. "We're down to duller tones."

"Curst wardrobe! Where is that adjutant! He's lost all my good shirts . . ." Tezozómoc kicked a wardrobe bag aside and began rooting through his boxes of shoes. "Did I give one of my shirts to Mrs. Petrel—that's it, I did! Hers was ruined . . ." The prince squinted over his shoulder at Dawd. "Oh, Lord of Light, I spilled wine on her blouse didn't I?"

"You were laughing, mi'lord," Dawd said, keeping a straight face. "And the glass tipped."

Tezozómoc blushed. "I shouldn't be allowed to touch alcohol. I gave her the red shirt as a replacement? Did I apologize?"

Dawd nodded. "I believe you did, mi'lord."

The prince made a growling sound, hands on his hips. "Can't we beg off this festival? Say I've cut off my head by mistake, or lost a leg in a car accident?"

"No mi'lord, we cannot." Dawd said patiently. "Mrs. Petrel and her ladies have already gone off to breakfast. Corporal Clark will be coming back for us momentarily with the aerocar. So you do, in fact, have to get dressed, be presentable and prepared to hobnob with the *kujen* and his relatives."

Tezozómoc pouted sourly. "What *is* a *Nēm* anyway? One of their gods?"

"The *Nēm*, mi'lord, is a flowering bush—sometimes growing into a tree—which grows in the bottomlands along local rivers. Their blossoms herald the end of the rainy season. I also understand they are considered sacred, due to a bitter, psychotropically-active sap—"

Tezozómoc, perking up at the prospect of something novel, was taken aback by the fixed, focusless way the Skawtsman stared at the door to the prince's dressing chamber and he turned, wondering what had drawn Dawd's attention.

Gemmilsky had not stinted with furnishings or ornamentation in his house. The master bedroom possessed magnificent doors of dark red *ruhel* wood inlaid with pearl and jade. At the moment, both were closed, though the prince expected one of his servants to arrive at any moment with a fresh bottle of vodka. "Sergeant? Is something—"

Dawd moved, one forearm slamming the prince back, sweeping Tezozómoc behind him. In the same motion, a flat Webley Bulldog sprang into his hand.

The doors burst open, crashing into the marble-covered walls on either side, porcelain doorknobs shattering, and three Jehanan in Gandarian livery rushed in. The lead native twisted from the waist, broad shoulders powering a *lohaja*-wood machete straight at the Skawtsman's head. Dawd ducked inside the blow, jammed the pistol into the charging creature's gaping mouth and pulled the trigger twice. The blast was muffled by the Jehanan's snout, but the shock-pellets blew out the back of his cranial cavity, spraying a cloud of broken bone and blood and bits of scale through the door. The jaws, abruptly severed from central control, spasmed shut and Dawd grunted, feeling needle-sharp teeth shear through the cuff of his jacket and shatter on the combatskin beneath.

Tezozómoc screamed in fear, bounced off the bed, and flung himself towards the bathroom. One of the Jehanan assassins hurled a short-bladed spear overhand, missed the prince by a scale, and the ceramic blade punched straight through the light wood of the door as it slammed shut.

Dawd wrenched his caught arm sideways, dragging the still-twitching corpse of the Jehanan into the path of the next assailant, who stabbed under the falling body with a spear. The Skawtsman skipped back, barely avoiding taking a blow to the inside of his thigh, twisted his hand inside the mouth and fired three times in quick succession. Highex pellets shredded the rest of the skull and stitched across the spearman's chest with a rippling series of explosions. Chunks of scale and ligament spattered across the dresser and a heavy antique mirror, and drenched the window drapes. The Jehanan flew backwards into a shattered wardrobe and then crumpled slowly to the floor.

With the left jaw and skull torn away, Dawd wrenched his arm free. He started to spin to face the last Jehanan, but a machete slammed into his shoulder as he moved. The stroke drove the Skawtsman to the floor though the combatskin stiffened, absorbing the impact and spreading the blow across his entire upper body. His boots and outstretched hand lost traction in the spilled intestines of the second assassin and he fell backwards.

The last assassin sprang over the corpse, a whistling shriek on leathery lips. The Skawtsman twisted up, pistol centering on the leaping creature's chest, finger squeezing the Bulldog's trigger—and the magazine whined emptily. A pair of enormous, clawed feet crashed down on carpet as Dawd rolled to the side and was up in one seamless motion.

The Jehanan spun, slashing with the machete, and his turning jaw was met by a combatskin-enhanced sidekick. Metal-cleated combat boot smashed into the creature's eye, splitting the fine scales, and the Jehanan staggered back, one long-fingered hand raised to shield his wound. With a fraction of a second to find balance, Dawd ducked a windmilling machete, turned slightly in and slammed forward with both forearms crossed and braced. The combatskin stiffened automatically, augmenting the Skawtsman's musculature, and the blow caught the Jehanan square in the chest. The creature flew back, smashing through a window in a cloud of shattering glass, wooden framing and broken plaster.

Squealing, the Jehanan assassin cartwheeled through an ivy-wound lattice and hit the tiled patio with a sodden crunch. Dawd tossed the empty Bulldog aside and snatched up his pair of Nambu automatics from the side table. Thumbing off both safeties, he jammed one into the holster of the gunrig, threw the leather and metal mesh harness around his shoulders with one hand and darted across the room to the bathroom door.

"Mi'lord, time to go!"

There was a muffled whimpering sound inside. Dawd slammed the lock-side of the doorframe with his armored shoulder—the entire cedarwood panel shattered—and turned in, both automatics now centered on the broken doorway to the hall.

"Mi'lord—are you hurt? Were you hit?"

"Eeee . . ." Tezozómoc was curled up in the bathtub, still in his nightshirt, arms tight around his head. "I hate this place!"

"Don't care for it much myself," Dawd coughed, throat tight with adrenaline. He holstered one automatic and reached down with his free hand. "Get up, sir, we've got to find Colmuir."

The young man blinked, looked up, and turned very pale. Despite the blood dripping from Dawd's forearm, he reached out and seized hold. The Skawtsman dragged the prince to his feet, and then—keeping Tezozómoc close to hand—scuttled across the room, avoiding the scattered bodies.

Tiny fires were burning in the ruins of the wardrobe and a string of deep craters, coiling with smoke, pocked the wall in the hallway opposite the door.

"Master Sergeant?" Tapping his comm-thread awake, Dawd flipped up the longeye mounted on his automatic and snaked the muzzle around the doorframe in each direction. "You still alive?"

I'm coming, Colmuir replied. *Don't shoot my fool head off. I'm on the west stairs.*

Seconds later, the master sergeant appeared, sliding along the inner wall, and ducked into the room as well. Dawd was frowning, finger pressed to his earbug, the comm display on his skinsuit flashing with amber and red lights. Colmuir spat out a dead tabac, looked the prince up and down and said: "Regimental net went wild a moment ago, heard someone shouting about being under attack—then everything flooded with ECM. Now it's all static and garbage."

The master sergeant shook his head, produced another tabac from his vest and snap-lit the paper with a fingernail. Smoke wreathing his head, he knelt, lifted up the whole bed with a strained grunt—sending mountains of clothing and quilts cascading onto the floor—and dragged out a Fleet duffel bag.

Dawd was still by the door, watching the hallway through his longeye. "Regimental net is back up," he reported, listening intently, "but some kind of jammer is playing havoc with the Army gear down in the flatlands. All the comm channels keep popping in and out. I don't know if they'll be able to get comm clear until whatever is pitching all this noise gets hit."

"That's not good," Colmuir said. He unzipped the bag and pulled out Dawd's Whipsaw along with two heavy ammunition coils. A broken-down Macana 8mm with the shoulder-stock removed followed, as well as a Fleet skinsuit pack and three combat visors. He beckoned politely to Tezozómoc: "Mi'lord prince, you put this on now. Quickly, lad. It's not a combatskin, but it'll have to do."

Swallowing nervously, hands trembling, the prince shed his shirt and pajama pants and unzipped the skinsuit pack. An amber colored gel spilled out on the floor, studded with two rows of black rings. Tezozómoc stepped carefully into the middle of the gel, reached down and slid his fingers into the rings. Colmuir—watching to make sure the suit got a clean seal—assembled the Macana with brisk, endlessly practiced efficiency. The prince pulled his hands up—the gel raced up his legs, covering his torso and chest, and then his neck and the back of his head—

and swung his shoulders back, letting the skinsuit congeal to his body. He flexed both hands, then held them down by his thighs. Gel shifted, solidified and oozed down to cover his fingers.

"Good," Colmuir said, patting the prince's shoulder. The skinsuit was slowly turning Fleet black. "You want a gun?"

Tezozómoc stared at the proffered Nambu, then shook his head. He was still very pale, but seemed to have regained some of his composure. "I might hit one of you. I can carry the bag, if that will help."

The master sergeant nodded and helped him swing the heavy back duffel over both shoulders. "Dawd—what have you got for us?"

The sergeant shook his head. "I can hear vehicles on the street from our remotes—running feet—slicks—and lots of them. There are at least a dozen hostiles downstairs too—more spears and machetes."

"We can take the lot, if we're quick, but . . ." Colmuir said, sidling to one window and looking out into the gardens. He hissed in disgust. "Ah, that tears it—they've got themselves a bloody tank."

"A what?" Dawd and the prince stared in disbelief at the master sergeant.

"A tank! Can y' not hear me?" Colmuir pointed out the window.

Dawd stiffened, hearing the rumble of multi-ton treads on cobblestones through the remote spyeyes watching the garden wall. A number of Jehanan in fleece-lined jackets and leggings, carrying what looked very much like KV-45B rifles, were messing with the front gate, which was closed. He looked at the prince, down at his pistol, over at the door, then started paging rapidly through building schematics and street maps on his comp.

"Do . . . do you have something that will stop a tank?" Tezozómoc's voice was rather faint.

"Nooo . . . we do not. Not a real one." Colmuir backed away from the window, slinging the Macana behind his shoulder. "Come on lads, time to run for it."

TAKSHILA
WITHIN THE HOUSE OF REEDS

Following close behind the gardener, Gretchen climbed a flight of narrow steps sandwiched between dusty stone walls covered with fluid carvings of shallow interlocking circles. She felt a little strange, as though the close, warm air was pressing heavily on her skull. Malakar reached the top of the staircase and peered out into a very narrow passageway marked by tilted walls and a curving floor.

"We are close," the Jehanan whispered, turning her head from side to side as she listened. "The level of the fane is arranged just in this way." Malakar patted a leathery palm on the nearest wall as she padded forward. "Quietly now, just beyond this stone are other, larger halls still in use."

Gretchen found her footing poor on the dusty floor. The surface of the passageway lifted in the middle and sloped away on either side, which made her wonder if they were moving down an old drainage tunnel of some type. She reached out to touch the Jehanan's shoulder, to ask exactly that question, when a muffled *thud-thud-thud* sound reached her ear.

Malakar stopped, skin wrinkling around her mouth. "*Hooo* . . . What an odd noise to hear."

Anderssen felt a steady vibration start up through the soles of her boots. "That feels like heavy machinery turning on. It's not very far away either."

The gardener did not reply, moving forward again. After a few moments, the curve in the passage became particularly noticeable and Gretchen was forced to lean a little sideways.

We're in some kind of a dome, she realized, looking up and finding the ceiling had receded into tapering dimness, *like the shell of a cathedral.*

"Here . . ." Malakar stopped and suddenly Anderssen could see a faint gleam of light on the Jehanan's scales. The gardener turned, mischief sparkling in her deep-set eyes. "Looking upon the mystery of the *kalpataru* is forbidden to the acolytes," she said very softly, "so every short-horn in orders must find a way to creep in and touch the thing itself. Once the fane of the divine tree was seamless and whole, but over time the walls have been damaged and repaired . . ."

Crouching down, the Jehanan reached between two riblike carvings on the walls and took hold of a wooden beam. The *lohaja* groaned a little as Malakar pulled, but then there was a scraping sound—which seemed very loud to Gretchen—and blazing light flooded into their dim little passageway as the patched surface came away.

"*Ho!*" Malakar snorted in alarm, half-blinded. Anderssen leaned in, her goggles automatically darkening to block the lurid, blue-white glow. "Never have the *gipu* been so bright!"

"That's not *gipu*-light," Gretchen said, eyes narrowed. "Those are industrial floodlights."

With the section of wall removed, Anderssen knelt and stared into the fane of the *kalpataru* in growing dismay. The opening seemed to be a meter or two above the floor of a circular, domed chamber dominated by a raised platform holding what could only be the tree-of-giving-what-you-desire itself.

In the glare of a row of Imperial-style floodlights hanging from wooden scaffolding, the *kalpataru* was a four-meter-high arc of perfect darkness rising out of a glassy gray marble floor. The surface of the object struck Gretchen as being impossibly smooth, even mirrored, but nothing reflected in the inky depths—not the pure white walls of the huge room, not the figures of uniformed Jehanan soldiers scurrying about its base, not the scaffolding, not even the hulking presence of three Honda EB62B fuel cell generators at the center of a network of heavy cables spilling across the floor. The generators wouldn't have been out of place at any dig Gretchen had ever worked on, but here the bulky red-and-silver chassis seemed almost alien. The *kalpataru* itself stood alone, apparently untouched by the bustling activity.

Gretchen felt a warm leathery snout push under her arm and squeezed aside, letting Malakar stare into the domed vault as well. The gardener made a strangled, horrified sound.

"*Hhhh!* Those are unlettered *kujenai* soldiers! They profane the holy of holies!"

"Yes," Gretchen whispered, eyeing a huge rough-edged opening in the wall behind the scaffolding. "They've dispensed with the old doorway. . . . Looks like they cut right through the marble with cutting gel and jackhammers."

"Heathen barbarians!" Malakar stiffened in fury, grinding Anderssen against the side of the passage. "*Hoooo*—if only this old walnut were young again! I would smite them mightily for such an affront!"

A pair of technicians approached the gleaming black shape and Gretchen tensed. The two Jehanan were dragging a thick power cable fitted with an induction clamp.

"They shouldn't do that—" Anderssen groped in her field jacket, dragging out the big survey comp and flicking the device on. "They're going to supply power to the artifact—fools!"

The comp cycled up; a suite of video, magnetic and hi-band sensors waking to life. Almost immediately it reported the air in the chamber was charged with steadily rising heat and electromagnetic radiation from all the equipment, bodies and the lights. Only the glassy arc was inert, radiating nothing, yielding nothing to the passive scan. The two Jehanan technicians reached the base of the *kalpataru* and bustled about, aligning the clamp and checking readouts on the cable.

"We've got to stop them," Gretchen said in a tight voice. "Do you have a—"

Across the floor of the vault, the senior technician jammed the cable-plate to the gleaming dark metal at the base of the tree. Anderssen's vision sharpened in a peculiar way, as though she suddenly rushed close to the device and realized the glossy surface was composed of millions of tightly packed threads, each distinct, yet adjoining one another with micron-level precision.

An overwhelming sense of vast age struck her as an almost physical blow.

There was a soft flash—a muted, yellow-white light flooded the chamber—and Gretchen's eyes blinked wide. Everything in her perception slid to a gelatinous stop. The fronds of the ancient tree twisted, uncurled, revealing millions of tiny sparkling green cilia. A sound beyond hearing issued forth from the heart of the tree, bending the air, filling every cavity and crevice in the fane, in the network of curving corridors twisting around the vault like the chambers of a nautilus, singing down every tunnel and passageway, spilling into every room and hall, washing across countless unwary Jehanan priests and acolytes going about their business.

Gretchen beheld the air unfolding, molecules twisting, unraveling, shedding photons in a brilliant cascade. Shimmering waves of solid light belled up from her equipment, from the cables, haloing the unknowing technicians, swirled around the comp in her hand. A single golden tone—a deep, encompassing note—sustained, held captured in the shape of the curving fronds, in the arc of the tree.

The heart of the black arc split, revealing a green void filled with boiling, half-seen movement. Countless cilia unfurled from the top of the arc into a winged, sharply edged star. An even more brilliant glow began to emanate from the cluster.

Anderssen felt herself recoil from a sensation of emptiness, a moment of annihilation, an unfolding which would leave her exposed, her self—her mind—her thoughts—her core—inverted and extended into . . .

Something sighed and the fuel-cell generator popped loudly. Smoke hissed from its metal housing. The technicians looked up, puzzled, and the vault was filled with their hissing and hooting.

Gretchen jerked back, dizzy, and fell into Malakar's arms. Everything was spinning. Her fingers were numb. The comp clattered to the ground. A strange, half-familiar sensation fled as she tried to grasp what had happened. For a moment—just the time between two breaths—she thought she was *surrounded by Jehanan in ragged, carbon-scored metallic armor. They seemed grimly pleased, as though they'd won through to a desperate victory. The wooden scaffolding was absent, replaced by huge green-tinted floods hanging from cranes. Power saws roared, cutting away the sides of an enormous obsidian box. The sides toppled, crashing to a rough limestone floor. The outline of the fane was already present as a vault of stone ribs, but unfinished, lacking the smooth marble facing. Inside the box a shape was revealed, heavily padded with shock-foam. A Jehanan technician stepped forward, spraying dissolver from a pressurized canister. The pinkish-white encasement sluiced away to spill across the rough floor. A black curved shape was revealed, fronds folded back to make a twisted, ropy arc . . .*

The floodlights shone hot in her eyes. Anderssen blinked away tears and tried to sit up. Her limbs were trembling as if she'd run clear to the postal station at Dumfries and back again without stopping.

Malakar dragged her back into the darkness, but not fast enough to keep one of the Jehanan soldiers milling around in the vault from catching sight of movement out of the corner of his eye. Curious, the soldier moved along the wall, long feet slapping on marble, and then saw the opening. He crouched down, drawing a modern-looking pistol, and crawled inside.

Behind him, a spirited discussion began between the *durbar* commanding the detachment of soldiers and the lead technician. After a few moments of hooting and hissing, the dead generator was pushed aside by four brawny Jehanan corporals and the second one rolled forward.

The *durbar*, disgusted at the fragility of the Imperial equipment, snarled at his underlings. Time pressed and he kept checking his chrono. Somewhere outside, the *kujen* of Takshila was counting on them to invoke the power of the dusty old machine. "Clean up all this mess—there are work tools and cables and cutting equipment everywhere!"

The *kalpataru* remained quiescent, pressing into the marble floor with the weight of ages.

Parker clattered down the last flight of steps and out into the courtyard at the center of the apartment building. He was draped in a long rain poncho, a broad-brimmed, waxed field hat on his head and an umbrella tucked under his arm. The thirty-third floor weather service reported rain and more rain in the offing. The pilot turned right, strode along a dim, sour-smelling arcade and pushed open a door made of interleaved wooden slats.

Then his pace slowed and he looked back curiously at the empty arcade. Rain was drumming on ancient, cracked concrete in the courtyard.

There's always a whole crowd of grandmas down here, the pilot thought. *Selling ornaments and scale-polishing cream and claw-sharpeners. Where'd they go?*

Cautious, he moved quietly down the hallway to the front lobby. Everything was very quiet, which made Parker nervous. Like the courtyard, the lobby was empty. Even the little green felted tables where the diviners consulted their oracular bones had been packed up and taken away. Parker licked his lips, wished he had a tabac, and eyed the street outside.

A single runner-cart rolled past, a wiry Jehanan bent between the wooden poles, powerful legs loping along the glassy surface of the boulevard. The pilot blinked, noticed the shops across the street were all closed and shuttered, and then frowned at a reflection in the front windows of the *akh*-noodle cafeteria on the corner.

That is a lot of riding lizards, he realized, *and a lot of big Jehanan with guns and spears. What are they . . .*

"Oh, bleeding hell!" Parker bolted back down the passage, through the wooden door and then up the stairs as fast as he could go. After three flights of steps he was wheezing and feeling faint. "Come on, David," he cursed at himself, poking at his medband. "Only thirty-two more to go. . . . Oh, Xochipilli, Lord of Flowers, why did I ever taste your bitter smoke?"

Pale in the face, he hauled himself up another flight, slewed around the turn and then gasped up another. Finally, he remembered to tap on his comm. "Thirty more . . . only thirty . . . *huuuugh!* Magdalena! Can hear you hear me?"

Gretchen's head cracked against the stone floor, sending a bolt of pain through her skull. Malakar dragged her along the passage, heedless of the human's flailing limbs.

"Malakar," she managed to croak out. "Stop!"

The gardener turned, *her face livid with scars, dull crimson battle-armor still scorched with particle-beam impacts, one eye a glassy white where shrapnel had torn into the socket. The* kujen*'s guardsmen clustered around her, armor and weapons equally worn. Most of them were barely adult, though not one soldier remained young.*

"We must go back," Anderssen said, using the wall to help her up. Icy fear rolled along her arms and back. "They are trying to wake up the *kalpataru*. I have to stop them. It must be destroyed."

"Are you mad?" *White-Eye bellowed, her voice booming with anguish. Claws clenched the hilts of her force-blade. "We've not heard from homeworld in sixteen years—with that device we can reopen the communications network, send for reinforcements, send for our families! My scientists are sure they can restore the linkage and bring up the planetary net in only hours."*

Malakar's face interleaved for an instant with the crippled Queen. Gretchen swayed, clutching at the wall. "No, no, we mustn't do that!" Her voice boomed strangely and Anderssen felt a wrenching sensation, as if other voices were forcing themselves through her mouth. "The Jeweled-Kings attacked us and seized the device because it's horribly dangerous—"

"No more of these child's superstitions," the scarred Jehanan screamed, blade flaring sun-bright in her hand. Gretchen flinched back and Malakar lunged forward, stabbing with the length of shattered *lohaja* taken from the wall cavity.

"We've paid dearly to reclaim the kalpa' and by Húnd's name, I'll invoke its power mysel—"

Anderssen hurled herself away from the blow—saw the jagged end of the board smash into the face of a Jehanan soldier bulking in the corridor—and everything *popped* back into reference. The soldier squealed, snout bleeding, and knocked the board aside. Gretchen surged up, throwing the point of her shoulder into the thick, armored chest. The Jehanan slammed into the wall.

"Quick, Malakar!" Gretchen shouted, struggling to hold the massive soldier pinned. He hissed like a steam boiler in her ear and flexed forward, flinging Anderssen into the wall. The gardener swung wildly with the board, but the soldier ducked and slashed at her head with his claws.

Gretchen snatched a cutting tool from her vest, thumbed the little device to high-beam and jammed the hissing plasma-jet into his neck. The Jehanan squealed, scales flaring red-orange. Flame spilled away from the tool, blinding him. Anderssen threw her weight behind the cutter—scales popped with a *snap!* And there was a gout of scalding steam as the plasma-torch sheared through the scaly integument and erupted into his chest cavity.

Malakar hooted in horror, scuttling back, but Gretchen kicked the body away, her face grim.

"Come on," she said, thumbing off the tool, "we've got to stop them. Find his gun."

Parker stumbled through the door into the apartment, gasping for breath, sweat streaming from every pore. He collapsed to his knees on a sleeping mat. "Oh god, Mags, they're right behind me!"

"I heard you," Magdalena said, briskly rotating the wheel controlling the door. The six triangular sections rasped closed and she threw the locking bolt with a clang. The Hesht turned, ears back flat, and sniffed Parker's sweaty head. "*Pfawgh!* Stewing in your own waste! Can you even stand?"

The pilot groaned, forcing his fatigue-exhausted legs up. He was trembling from head to toe. "I don't . . . feel so good."

Maggie snarled in disgust, showing all her teeth, forced herself up and slapped self-adhering black packets on either side of the door. "Get into harness, sog-tail. Now!"

The pilot staggered to a pair of open windows and slumped against the wooden frame. Most of their equipment had been gathered up and stuffed into Maggie's duffel, but a black fleximesh harness lay out and Parker managed get one arm into the proper opening by the time the Hesht reached his side.

Magdalena seized his other arm and forced the harness on, glossy black paw sealing the clasps and jerking the mesh to a proper fit. Parker bleated, feeling doubly abused, but was having trouble standing without assistance. "Now, Maggie, you're not thinking we have to—"

"There is no other way off this floor and out of the building," the Hesht growled, slinging the duffel across her stomach. The sound of Jehanan voices hooting and booming echoed dimly through the door. A sharp rapping sound penetrated. "Clip to my back," she said, snapping two dark green monofilament spools to the front of her harness. "Now, kitling, no time to laze on the rocks!"

Startled, Parker put his chest to the Hesht's back, hooked harness to harness and wrapped his arms under her shoulders. "All aboard," he muttered.

Magdalena squared her hips, planted her feet and lifted with a strained hiss. A little dizzy, Parker clenched his legs back to get them out of the way. Awkwardly, the Hesht turned around and backed into the window, paws gripping the frame on either side. Monofil line hissed from the spools on her harness. Parker caught a glimpse of a line of anchors driven into the floor of the room.

"Will that—*ayyyyy!* Oh sweet Jesus!" Parker squeezed his eyes shut as Maggie tipped backwards.

The Hesht worked her feet into a solid position, a cool breeze gusting across her pelt. She carefully took a pair of monofil gloves from a pouch on her climbing harness and tugged them on. Inside, the banging on the door had ceased and she could hear a drill whine sharply against ceramic. Dust puffed from the center of the portal. Both gloves on, she powered them up and watched for the winking green light indicating descender field strength at maximum.

The hexagonal door shattered with a *crack!* and bits of ceramic rattled against the windowpanes. A cloud of dust billowed into the room. Maggie heard a cheerful beep from the gloves, clenched hard on the monofil line and kicked back. Wire hissed between her gloves and she, Parker and the duffel bounded back a half-dozen meters. Her feet hit a section of blank concrete and started to skid. She leaned further back, forcing her boots flat on the wall.

Parker felt cold wind ruffle his hair, the cawing of native avians from far below and absolutely nothing beneath his swinging feet. "Oh goddddd," he bawled, clutching tight.

Takshilan guardsmen burst into the apartment, one ducking left, one right and another dodging forward in the middle. All three were clad in bulky cloth armor plated with hand-sized ceramic lozenges. Their long snouts were covered with leather facings, their deep-set eyes masked by bulging goggles. The one on the left turned, the muzzle of his automatic rifle sweeping across the empty room.

"Kramat—" he started to call out, beckoning the rest of the squad forward with one claw.

The black packets pasted beside the doorway detected heat and motion within their limited perception and blew apart. Choking white smoke blasted out, hiding the near-supersonic expansion of tanglewire coils. A thread-end smashed into the chest of the lead commando, puncturing his armor. He was thrown down, gasping, and the wire stiffened, tearing through scale and muscle. The room filled with a glittering black cloud. The other two soldiers had leapt back in time to avoid the brunt of the blast, but the knockout gas in the smoke flooded over them.

Someone in the hallway—spooked by the high-pitched *ting-ting-ting* of wire anchors punching into the walls—fired accidentally and the entire squad opened up, blazing away at the smoke. Tracers ripped through the haze, smashing the remaining windows. The lead commando, still tangled, was torn in half by the fusillade, his body jerking violently. Ricocheting bullets whined through the apartment, scoring the walls and clattering into the corners.

Magdalena looked up, saw the windows shattering into a cloud of glittering, plunging glass and kicked off again. Her legs were starting to cramp. Parker was a thin little human, but his squirmy weight was no furless kit clinging to her pelt. They bounded into another section of concrete and she kicked off again, flying past a row of windows.

Inside, a wide-eyed Jehanan child stared out, caught sight of a completely unexpected apparition, fluted in terror and scrambled under its sleeping rack.

The broken windows rained past them, forcing Maggie to duck her head and swing in close to the wall. Slivers of greenish glass caught in her pelt and spanged away from the concrete. Without looking up, the Hesht pushed off, monofil whirring through her harness and gloves. This time her legs were tired and they bounced into a row of windows. Glass splintered under her boots, and Maggie crabbed to the side, trying to reach concrete. The window groaned under the stress, cracked lengthwise and burst inwards.

One leg plunged into the opening, crashing through a shelf of potted plants. There were outraged hoots inside. Maggie kicked her leg free, shoved off with the other and swung past three more intact windows. She glimpsed two very large, very angry Jehanan males inside. The monofil whined, complaining, and she clenched hard with the gloves. She flew down the line as the descender released, their weight swinging them into a shallow arc.

Maggie forced her paws to release, skipping across ceramic facing. Their swing slackened, losing momentum, and they bounced to a halt against a concrete rib jutting from the face of the building. Parker grunted, suddenly jammed into a rock-hard surface, and his eyes flew open. The Hesht braced her feet, panting.

"Ooooh . . . my stomach feels . . ." The pilot stopped, squinting, his goggles automatically zooming in on the rushing shape as he focused. "What in the Nine Hells is—"

A shrieking roar filled the sky. Maggie snapped her head around, alarmed.

A huge, winged silver shape blasted past—less than a kilometer away—between the apartment tower and its nearest neighbor. Sunlight gleamed on swept-back triangular wings and blazed from a mirrored canopy. Slender black canisters nestled under the wings. Bright red insignia were blazoned on the double-finned tail. Super-heated air howled from twin fairings at the rear of the aircraft.

"Yeeeee-hah!" Parker screamed, his entire body jolted with adrenaline. "Lookit that!"

The Jehanan jet fighter boomed past, slicing between the skyscrapers. One of the black cylinders suddenly broke free from the wing, ignited in mid-air and raced off to the southeast at supersonic speed. The *boom* of its passing hammered at Maggie's ears, making her blink with pain. The jet hooked left, flashing out of sight between the towers. A corkscrew of shimmering air remained, slowly untwisting in the haze.

"I can fly one of those," Parker shouted—half-deafened—in Maggie's ear. "I can!"

"Of course," Maggie choked out, twisting her neck to clear her airway. "Leggo!"

Parker relaxed his arm, looked down automatically and went white. "*Eeep!*"

The Hesht kicked off and they sailed down another twenty meters, passing more windows and sections of bare concrete. This time they touched down within spitting distance of a building adjoining the apartment tower. Maggie clenched her hand repeatedly and they bounced down onto whitewashed plaster. Parker's legs touched slate tile and he collapsed bonelessly.

Magdalena grunted, taking his weight in her legs, and unclipped the monofil tabs. Squeezing the tabs twice, she threw them up into the air and ducked down.

The microspools clicked into retract and both tabs began reeling in the monofil at top speed. They vanished in the blink of an eye, racing up the side of the building.

Pushing the terrified gardener in front of her, Anderssen hurried them back to the opening. The floodlights were still shining bright as the sun. Wiping blood from her face, Gretchen crouched down, casting a wary eye at the chamber of the *kalpataru*.

The survey comp lay undisturbed on the floor, but now it had woken up and was happily scanning away.

"Get ready," Gretchen said, voice tight with strain, as she picked up the comp. A rising sense of fragility was swelling in her mind, as though the stone under her feet, the bulky shoulder of the gardener, even her own skin was growing thinner and thinner with every passing second. The comp was reporting a steadily rising level of ambient electromagnetic energy in the vault. She adjusted her goggles, making sure they were on tight. "In a second, I'm going out there. When I do—"

Anderssen closed Malakar's claws round the handle and trigger of the captured pistol.

"You have to shoot out those floodlights. Do you understand?"

Malakar stared at her with huge, wild eyes. Gretchen tried not to focus on the section of wall slowly becoming visible through the Jehanan's head or the white scars slowly emerging from her brown old hide. "Shoot? Me?"

"Yes." Anderssen fixed her with a fierce glare. Her fingers were trembling as she tucked the survey comp away. "You have to shoot out the lights."

"I . . . this old walnut's never used *a gun like this before," the Librarian stuttered, gingerly holding the bulky shape of a beam-pistol in her claws. "I can't do this—she's the* kujen*! Our Queen! You're talking treason and murder."*

"There's no time—" Gretchen heard the second generator whine up to full speed and threw herself through the opening, cutting tool tight in her right hand.

"There's only moments to spare," a voice hissed from her mouth. *"We should have listened to the Jeweled-Kings when they tried to warn us. . . . Now it's almost too late."*

The heavy power cable shivered, current flowed through to the induction plate. The technicians—Gretchen caught a flickering double-image glimpse as she rolled up, Jehanan scientists in leather harnesses and too-small-seeming Imperial tools superimposed over much larger counterparts in advanced armor, festooned with tools properly fitted to claw and limb—were stepping back from the gleaming black arc of the tree.

This time the single ringing tone leapt instantly into immanence. The green void unfolded, rushing out to encompass the room. Gretchen stumbled, feeling the shining, sparkling effusion as a physical pressure on her face and hands. The arc unfurled, countless threads stiffening, forming a sharp-angled triangle. Then another, inverted triangle blossomed within the first, then another, inverted again. The shivering, endless *hnnnnnnnnnnnnng* of the device slid upward, shrieking into ever higher registers.

Anderssen pushed forward, feeling time grind slow. The floor mottled and cracked and she became terribly aware of the vast pressure the artifact exerted on its surroundings. Stone crumbled an atom at a time, the air congealed, electrons crept sluggishly from valence to valence. Only the arc itself remained immobile, impenetrable and immune to the crushing press of time. The blaze of its power pierced the vault above, lancing towards the sky hidden beyond the marble dome, and down, plunging into the roots of the world.

The flood of visions touched old memories in Anderssen's mind, culled from endless days spent in library carrels, stacks of dusty books piled up around her 'net terminal.

Two eagle-faced abzu *lift their sacred cones towards a juniper tree surmounted by a winged sun-disk. In the leaves of the divine tree are held all knowledge, as well as the fruit of eternity.*

A cold, implacable awareness flooded out from the *kalpataru*, touching every comp within its purview.

Murdered Osiris is placed by divine hands into the heart of a tamarisk *whose roots burrow into the earth, reaching the land of the dead, and stretch up to the heavens, entangling the stars. The god's eyes fly open, his sundered body returned to life.*

The comp behind her on the floor turned itself off.

A gnarled ash rises against the abyss, branches spread out over all the worlds and across the sky. Three of the tree's roots reach far indeed. One winds among the Aesir, the second among the frost-giants, where Ginnungagap once was. The third extends over Niflheim, which is the source of all that is cold and grim. It was created many ages before the earth was formed. Under that root is the spring Hvergelmir in the midst of Niflheim, and Nidhogg the Serpent gnaws the bottom of this root. From this spring flow the rivers Svol, Gunnthra, Fjorm, Fimbulthul, Slidr and Hrid, Sylg and Ylg, Vid, Leiptr, and Gjoll, which is next to Hel's gates . . .

Gretchen's own perception attenuated, grown suddenly vast.

Photons flooding from the floodlights continued to crawl forward, brushing aside the thick soup of molecules floating in emptiness. Every computer-controlled object in the chamber—her chrono, the generator fuel regulators, the Jehanan commander's hand-comm—stopped working.

Waiting.

The wave of electron paralysis leapt outwards, permeating the bulk of the ancient ship, flooding across Takshila and its myriad buildings, washing through the jet fighters howling in the late afternoon sky, licking across every comm and comp and Imperial device within the planetary magnetosphere.

Every device halted, set aside its allotted tasks and fell quiet, seized by the irresistible power of the *kalpataru*.

Listening.

In that same still moment of time, Gretchen perceived all this, ears flooded with sound, eyes drowned by a million unfiltered points of view.

And the shimmering tone of the *kalpataru* changed: a keen, sharp wail echoing out of the abyss of time trapped in the ancient metal. The matrices of form inside the howling green void shifted, attempting to attain proper alignment. Gravity dragged against them and the wear of millennia fouled the trembling dance, but the machine adapted, resorted, shifted, pressed mightily on time and space, trying to fold aside barrier after barrier.

The dials on the Honda fuel-cell generator pegged over to maximum and the entire machine began to whine dangerously.

Here, the *kalpataru* wailed after an eternity of patience. *I am here! Command me!*

All this Gretchen perceived, but she found herself powerless to act.

In her mind, at one instant, she was everywhere within the purview of the machine, a helpless passenger swept along in the tide of radiant power.

In that one instant, she was with Magdalena and the Hesht was growling at Parker, urging him to stagger forward across a wet, rainy rooftop. The buildings around them were unfamiliar and their faces were tense.

Maggie, Gretchen wailed, *you've got to run! Get out of the city! Run, Maggie, run!*

PARUS
DISTRICT OF THE EVER-TURNING WHEEL

Itzpalicue moved through a large dim room with a ceiling of hard-fired yellow brick. Sunlight streamed through openings piercing a succession of domes. The Arachosians filling the room regarded her with curiosity as the little old Náhuatl woman examined their archaic-looking weapons and ammunition bandoliers.

"You are hunting an invisible enemy," she rasped, mouth contorted to pronounce the harsh highland dialect of the tribesmen. Her earbug was running hot, providing a simultaneous translation of every voice in the room, and two vibrating 'sounders' taped to the sides of her throat managed to produce a facsimile of the thrumming overtone present in Jehanan voices. "A deadly one, quiet as a *xixixit* in the forest or a *huungal* in the marsh. The kind of enemy which never strikes with its own claw, only those of a pawn or a decoy. No open battle, no heroes clashing between arrayed armies, no charge of mounted man against mounted man. This is not a mudfoot you seek . . ."

A throaty trill of laughter boomed from the Arachosians. They were tall and wiry, scales stippled brown and tan, with narrow, cold eyes. They were garishly adorned with rows of fore-teeth and ear-bones. Long cowls shrouded their triangular heads and layered cloaks hid elaborately scaled armor of ceramic plates, leather harnesses hanging with knives, punch-daggers, pistols, ropes of grenades, the queer strangling rope called *than-tan* and bags of loose cartridges for their long-barreled rifles. Most had their modern, Imperial weapons laid out for cleaning and inspection. Strings of ammunition coils were stacked on the floor.

"You say," rumbled their *kurbardar*, a notorious chieftain named Gher Shahr, "we are hunting a man from the hills? Something like an Arach? In this fetid, wet den of fools a canny hunter might hide forever . . ."

"Even so." Itzpalicue removed a black lozenge from the folds of her dress. "Do you feel the fire and smoke quickening in the air? Soon the divine liquid will be spilled in plenty. The lowlanders will strive to drive the Imperials from their cities, their towns, from the land of the Five Rivers. When that happens, my enemy *will move*. He will press his pawns to attack, he will reveal his hidden strength to strike at the Empire—and he must make his will known *somehow*." She held up the lozenge. "These detectors ignore Imperial and *kujenate* comm traffic. They will lead you to anyone else operating advanced equipment in the city. If he is here . . . even an encrypted voice makes a sound."

Gher Shahr accepted the lozenge—the device vanishing in his huge hand—and made a passable human-style nod. "Hu–hu–hu . . . You have hunted before, little one. You are using the lowlander fools and their prideful war to flush prey from the deep thickets and ravines." The Arachosian tilted his long, scarred head to one side, nostrils flexing. "You are cold—like old ice always in sun-shadow—you send your own tribe out to die, just to spook a single *kaichesh* from cover!"

Itzpalicue smiled warmly, patting his scaled thumb. "Divide your men into claws of four—there are enough detectors for all—and spread out—quietly!—through the streets. Vehicles have been provided to allow you swift movement. Be mindful of my voice! I will be watching over you."

One of Lachlan's technicians began handing out the black lozenges to the Arachosians, who crowded around in interest, hot breath snuffling in the elderly man's face. Itzpalicue watched carefully, making sure the tribesmen sorted themselves out properly. They began to file out of the old thread-dyeing factory. A dozen nondescript Imperial-built trucks in assorted makes and models were waiting, engines idling, specially trained Jehanan drivers sitting at the wheel.

"Get back to operations," the old woman told the technician as the last detector was handed out. "I will run all of this from another location."

Her earbug chimed in a two-up, one-down pattern indicating an incoming Flower Priest network call. Itzpalicue grimaced, pulled out a hand-comp and thumbed up Lachlan's video channel. The young man appeared instantly, now sporting several days' growth of beard.

Mi'lady?

"You've kicked a *xochiyaotinime* call to me? Are they having cold feet?"

It's started, Lachlan replied, the corners of his eyes tight with tension. *You wanted overwatch on their opening response.*

"Ah . . ." The old woman smiled beatifically. "Right on time. Patch me in."

Mi'lady. A hurried, agitated voice came on-line. *The* darmanarga-moktar *have jumped the starting gate! We've reports of full-scale fighting in Gandaris, Takshila and the outlying districts of Parus! The locals have acquired some kind of comm-jamming system . . . and it's not something we gave them!*

"Is the 416th regimental combat net down?"

No, it's handling the jammers. They've gone to tertiary frequencies in some cases. Yacatolli's aggressive dispersion has nearly every Imperial detachment in combat with rebel elements. The Arrow Knights are going to chew up the initial attacks faster than we anticipated, keeping the moktar *from massing their forces . . . Should I drop their network?*

"The Regimental net? No. Patience, child, patience. Let Yacatolli and his officers test themselves. That *is* what we wanted, isn't it?"

Very well . . . The priest's voice was still tinged with panic, and Itzpalicue knew the Whisperers working in orbit were a little shaken by the precipitate reaction of the natives. For herself, she was not terribly surprised. Any large conspiracy tended to gather momentum as it rolled downhill. The air had felt *right* this morning, clear and a little hot, and her Arachosians were already fanning out through the city. Today was as good as any to fight her war.

Wait . . . The priest's voice quickened. *Regimental is adapting. Yes, they've restored comm across the board. Battle data is flooding in. . . . By the Painted Lord, there are reports entire native military units have mutinied in Sobipuré and southern Parus! The spaceport has been overrun. Wait . . . wait . . . what is this?*

Itzpalicue raised an eyebrow at Lachlan, who was drinking some coffee at his station and rubbing his eyes with the back of his hand.

This is impossible, the Flower Priest pronounced. *The Mercantile Exchange House in Takshila has been attacked by hostile air elements firing guided munitions of some kind. There are hundreds of dead. By the Mother's Son, these creatures have managed to buy or hire atmospheric aircraft! Yacatolli is calling on Fleet to provide suppression fire.*

"Lachlan?" The old Náhuatl woman raised her chin questioningly. "Did we provide them with aircraft of some kind?"

No, he answered, covering a yawn. *We're getting scattered reports of the mutineers deploying archaic Jehanan war machines of different kinds—tanks, aircraft, artillery—which survived the nuclear exchange six hundred years ago.*

"Numbers? Enough to make a difference?" Itzpalicue was impressed by the self-discipline of the native princes. This was the first mention she'd seen of any pre-Collapse military equipment surviving in an operable state. The prospect the *kujenai* had restrained themselves from wasting any possible advantage over one another during the last century of internecine conflict raised her estimation of them markedly.

We don't think so, Lachlan said. The Flower Priest was still babbling, alternately outraged and baffled by the steadily increasing reports from elements of the 416th in combat with squadrons of heavy tanks and being bombed by solitary Jehanan jet aircraft. *Assets in action are still too few to tip the balance. Now if someone has a whole armored division in his pocket. . . . Analysis section thinks all of this gear was in storage or non-operable until Imperial* pochteca *started selling enough metal parts, lubricants and civvy-grade power-cells to get things working again.*

"Ha!" Itzpalicue laughed heartily, having to wipe away a tear from her eye. "And we took such pains to supply them with near-modern anti-armor missiles and automatic rifles. . . . Well, get combat efficiency reports when you can. The Mirror will be interested to see how the indigenous manufactures stack up against Army issue."

Lachlan started to nod—

—and the comm channel went dead.

Itzpalicue blinked, staring at the blank comp in her hand. The signal strength indicator was showing zero and the lighted front panel was dark. A cold chill washed down her spine. "Lachlan?"

ABOVE THE SOBIPURÉ-PARUS RAILWAY
NORTH OF THE SPACEPORT

The howling roar of shuttle engines suddenly faltered, pitch dropping precipitously, and *Heicho* Felix felt her gut flip over as the aircraft shuddered from nose to tail. She clutched tight on the support rails beside her jump seat, eyes squeezed shut.

And then realized her earbug had fallen silent, that her z-suit environmental controls had stopped humming, that aside from the shriek of air rushing past the hull, the inside of the shuttle was utterly quiet. Her eyes flew open—and there was nothing but darkness all around her—not so much as the gleam of a readout or a comm screen.

"What the hell!" Her shout tumbled over the exclamations of the rest of her squad and *Sho-sa* Koshō as well. "We've lost power!"

"We're not hit," Susan growled in the darkness. Felix could hear the lieutenant commander's fingers jamming fruitlessly against a control pad. "Comps are dead—everything's off-line."

"Everyone brace," Felix shouted, trying to grapple with the kind of weapon which could knock out all their comps inside of a shielded Fleet shuttle. "Hang on, we're going down!"

"Like a brick," Koshō muttered, forcing herself back into the seat.

TAKSHILA
NEAR THE INTERSECTION OF *PANCA-SAPTA*
AND *TRIEKA*

In the apartment, a stiff breeze from the windows was clearing away the smoke and once more the Jehanan commando squad entered—this time very cautiously—rifles moving restlessly from side to side. The web of tanglewire stopped them for a moment, until two of the brawnier guardsmen crashed through the barrier with a large table from an adjoining apartment.

A commando scuttled through the gap, swung to the right, and then caught sight of the pair of missing windows. Gingerly, booted feet crunching in scattered glass, he crept up to the opening and peered out, rifle at the ready. The *durbar* following him paused halfway into the room, staring suspiciously at the monofil anchors embedded in the floor. In the smoky air, his goggled eyes did not catch sight of the two wires stretched to the window frame, where a strip of magnetically charged 'lipping' material kept the monofil from shearing through the wood and concrete.

Both tabs zipped up to the window, bounced over the lipping strip, started to coil automatically—sliced cleanly through the neck and left arm of the commando on point—snapped into their anchors and demagnetized.

The *durbar* poked at one of the anchors with the muzzle of his rifle, then looked up—a question on his lips—in time to see the point commando topple over, blood spurting from a severed neck and gushing onto the floor from the arm. Eyes wide in shock, the *durbar* made a sound like a steam boiler venting overpressure; his rifle twitched towards the window and his claw clenched tight. One round boomed from the HK-45B, vanishing through the opening, and then the rifle jammed, the chamber fouled with substandard propellant.

The rest of the squad, having whirled at the gunshot, stared in horror at the body sprawled by the window. None of them had seen or heard anything. The *durbar* continued to try to fire the rifle, which made a *click-click-click* sound in the sudden quiet.

Malakar lunged after the human, her claws snapping on empty air, and shouted heedlessly with fear, seeing Anderssen stagger across the marble floor of the vault, in plain sight of the soldiers, every detail plain in the fierce, omnipresent glare of the floodlights.

"Hoooo!" A wail of fear burst from the gardener's old throat and she wrenched the heavy, clumsy pistol up, claw-tip scrabbling on the trigger.

Technicians whirled around at the unexpected noise. The Jehanan *durbar* stepped out, snatching for his automatic. His deep-set eyes widened, seeing an ancient monk waving a weapon at him. Then he caught sight of a smaller figure dashing for the artifact.

"Guards!" he shouted, enraged, and swung the iron-sights of his gun towards Gretchen. "Kill them both!"

His finger tightened—there was the sharp *crack!* of a gunshot—for an instant the *durbar* thought he'd been hit himself, claw convulsing on the automatic's trigger. There was the booming, echoing report of a second shot.

The secondary Honda generator shuddered, spewing hydrogen from a punctured cell. A mechanical pressure safety tripped and the current flowing to the *kalpataru* abruptly cut off.

PARUS
DISTRICT OF THE EVER-TURNING WHEEL

Itzpalicue stared at her comm with a sensation of icy dismay welling in her stomach.

"Lachlan?" She could barely whisper.

Gingerly, she turned the hand-comm over, then rotated the thumb control. Nothing happened. The usual whispering thread of voices from her earbug had fallen silent. She raised her eyes to the elderly technician and found him staring at her with equal horror.

"Mine is dead too," Nacace said in a frightened voice. "My earbug is dead. Everything just . . . stopped working."

"What about your other equipment?" The old Náhuatl woman tapped experimentally at the sounders clinging to her throat. They made a dull drumming sound. "Are any of your comps working?"

Nacace shook his head after a moment. He was sweating profusely—the environmental control in his suit had failed.

Our control network is dead, Itzpalicue repeated to herself, trying to grasp the enormity of the disaster which had overtaken her entire plan. *Without comp online, there's no way to communicate with anyone. The Army will be blinded, unable even to fire most of their weapons. O merciful mother of Tepeyac, guide our spears true to the heart of the enemy, for we have nothing else with which to fight . . .*

Her earbug suddenly squawked to life. Itzpalicue jerked as if she'd been shot.

"Lachlan! Are you there?"

Static and a confused babble of voices answered her.

The v-pane on her hand-comp flickered as the comm software reset—the Mirror-built system cycled through seventy or eighty thousand channels and popped back into synch with operations. Lachlan reappeared, but now he was standing and shouting orders at a chaotic room. His technicians were yelling in panic and the old woman could see dozens of monitoring screens showing nothing but static. *Restart*, Lachlan shouted again, *we've lost the primary network. Shunt to secondary, then restart the primary. Go to battlefield beta cycling and rekey all encrypt sequences!*

Itzpalicue waited, weak with relief. Sotto voce, she said: "Nacace, primary comm has suffered severe damage. We'll move to the secondary operations center immediately."

Then she made a sharp hooting sound, summoning the pair of Arachosians she'd chosen for bodyguard detail. By the time they arrived, Lachlan was staring out at her, still frightened.

"What happened?"

I don't know what that was! The Éirishman was sweating, jaw clenched. *Everything just turned off. Everything had power—but nothing was working. Then the whole system just restarted itself.*

"Do we have primary comm back?"

Lachlan managed a feeble grin and shook his head. *Another new wave of jamming has hit the modern comm networks groundside—ours, the Flower Priests', and the Army's—this is modern, Imperial-style battletech too. Absolutely nothing we imported. Analysis says the* xochiyaotinime *didn't bring it in either. We're running the emission signatures now . . .*

"Our network is back up?" Itzpalicue was walking quickly through the factory sheds, heading for an armored truck parked in a nearby garage. The elderly technician was jogging ahead, checking each doorway with a drawn automatic. The two Arachosians flanked her, *kalang* knives drawn and the grips of their pistols turned forward for swift access. "Do we have full coverage back? Spyeyes still in the air?"

No. Lachlan's voice was filled with despair. *Whatever knocked out our comps killed their hover controls. One of our men on the roof is picking up the pieces of several right now.*

"I see." Itzpalicue tried not to clench her jaw. "Shift as much traffic to groundline or line-of-sight laser as possible. Do we have replacements to launch?"

Some, the Éirishman said, looking haggard. *We're running a broadband restart command to try and wake up any of them that survived dropping out of the sky. They're pretty tough, so we'll get a few back. I'll have any reserve hives launched as soon as we have comm back.*

"Other alternatives?"

Commercial comm is completely dead, the Éirishman said sadly. *Every single relay node probably shorted out with this level of feedback. The* xochiyaotinime *are chasing their tails—they suffered three primary node failures and have lost nearly a quarter of their coverage.* He grinned ghoulishly. The Mirror network had lost its eyes, but the backbone was still up. *The Army is bouncing back—I think they'll have a full recovery in about six minutes—but the colonel is going to blister some hides for this. . . . Their net is supposed to be hardened against exactly this kind of jamming.*

The old woman slowed to a halt, waiting until the technician had climbed into the cabin of the truck, fired up the engine and put the transmission into gear. One of the Arachosians loped over to unbar the garage doors. "Will there be more outages?"

I don't . . . wait a moment. He looked off-screen, listening to one of the Analysis section technicians. Then he nodded, turning back to Itzpalicue. *We've an ident on the attacking system, mi'lady. Albanian work—the latest version of their Seitaj IV battlefield countermeasures system—usually sold to mercenary brigades working the Rim. Good—very good, really, for a backwater like this—but we'll be able to keep comm up for the duration.*

"Unless whatever neutralized our comps happens again." Itzpalicue swung up into the back of the truck. One Arachosian was in front, a brace of pistols and his Macana on the seat beside him, while the other rode with her in tepid darkness. The surprised chill of losing all contact was fading, but a tickling, unpleasant feeling of things being badly out of joint replaced her initial alarm. "A battlefield ECM system like that would only be useful against a *modern* opponent. Against the Empire."

True enough, Lachlan replied. *But whoever brought in the Seitaj knew they'd be fighting some kind of Imperial troops. Only surprising they managed to get it on-planet without anyone noticing. They must have some mercs running the gear—quick-trained natives wouldn't be able to mount an attack like this.*

"Pertinent," the old woman nodded sharply. The truck shuddered into motion under her and rolled out onto the street. "Dispatch a report to the Mirror. Whoever provided this equipment needs to be dealt with. As for the Seitaj itself, my Arachosians will find and destroy it soon enough . . ."

Lachlan signed off and she leaned back against the jostling side of the truck, frowning in thought. *Something is out of place. They launch an escalated attack . . . three surprises now . . . near-modern arms, this comp neutralizer and modern countermeasures to try and level the field of combat. Do they have more in hand?* She laughed softly to herself. *We didn't need to meddle at all! Yacatolli and Hadeishi will have quite a time putting these lizards back into their bucket! Now wait . . .* Something about the presence of the Seitaj nagged at her. *A system like that is useless against troops fighting with sword, shield and lance. Did someone know an Arrow*

Knight regiment was coming here or did they expect us to equip the native princes with modern weapons?

The old woman scowled, fingertips tapping on her cane as the truck shook and jostled around her, engine rumbling, speeding through the streets of Parus. Rain-heavy clouds began to blot out the sun as the afternoon advanced.

THE FANE OF THE KALPATARU
DEEP WITHIN THE HOUSE OF REEDS

A succession of sharp popping sounds rippled across the vault. The banks of floodlights hanging from the wooden scaffolding flickered and died. Darkness engulfed the Jehanan soldiers scrambling to react to Gretchen's mad dash across the floor. The *durbar* blinked, suddenly blind.

"Lights!" he shouted, edging backwards, claw out to find the cover of the generator housing. "Get some lights on in here, you fools!"

His wild, panicky voice touched Anderssen's ears as a long, muffled *huuuummmaaa*. For her, the air was still thick and impenetrable—the glorious radiance of the shining black arc was failing, swallowed by the air, by the stone dome overhead, by the inert marble of the floor—but its influence still pervaded the vault. Ghostly forms thronged around her—both the Jehanan workers in the distant past as they cleared away the shockfoam from the *kalpataru*, and those in the present, who were cowering wherever they could, fearful of being struck by a stray bullet.

She turned, the delicate shining curve of the divine tree drawing her eye.

The boiling green void was dimming, the vast array of sharp angles collapsing, softening, the buckling vortices of space and time folding back in upon themselves, the half-open gate disintegrating as quickly as it had begun to form.

Gretchen saw: *A jagged stone plunging from the sky, white-hot with atmospher-*

ic friction, spearing into a green mountainside with a burst of flame. Spindly-looking trees toppled, blown down, and the stone—hissing and popping—lay inert at the bottom of a crater.

Tri-lobed grass grew with dizzying speed, violet-colored fern-trees lifted themselves from the ashes. Millennia passed. The forest was swept away by fire, then renewed, over and over again. The sun darkened. The violet-leafed saprophytes failed and were replaced by hardier species that could live on the slowly dimming radiance of Bharat.

Gods raged in the heavens, splitting the clouds, fighting among themselves. Cities rose, glittering, on the plain below the mountain and then failed, wiped away by the relentless pressure of time. Still, the sun continued to dim. Slowly the forest darkened as the implacable hand of circumstance winnowed the weaker species away.

Something came pacing in the nighted forest—a shining chitinous creature with long bifurcated legs and shimmering wings bearing a glowing eye—in the radiance of the eye, the mossy stone was ablaze with light. The Jeweled-King plucked it from the heather and carried it away.

The stone sat alone in a blue-green room, undisturbed until slender machines descended from the roof, poking and prodding, examining the striations in the jagged surface. Then the stone split, falling into three equal portions. Behind glassite windows, the jewel-colored insects chimed in horror as a single glistening dark seed was revealed.

The seed split and split again, unfolding into a sharp, jagged arc of darkness which lifted towards the sky . . .

Anderssen wrenched her attention away from the distant past. Furtive images of burning cities and vast armies of insectile creatures warring upon one another for custody of the dreadful arc slipped away from her awareness.

The vault was aglow with shifting, subtle patterns. Gretchen turned with enormous effort—everything seemed frozen, but now she realized her perception of time was drastically altered. Something was approaching her—a cylindrical bullet, corkscrewing through the heavy air, leaving a twisting trail of disrupted gas behind it—and she dragged her head out of its path.

The Jehanan *durbar* was caught in mid-lunge, lurching towards the freshly punctured fuel-cell generator.

Technicians were scattering, claws over their heads.

One of them was crouched by the entrance, beside the dead generator, hands placing packs of blasting gel and triggers into a metal carrier bearing the Sandvik logo. Gretchen saw him, perceived a shining glide path in the air between her and the back of his scaly skull, felt the heaviness of the cutting tool in her hand.

Breathe, she commanded herself, struggling to wrench her arm back. *Let yourself breathe.*

A dry, acerbic voice cut through her thoughts—*Clarity is the enemy of action,*

Green Hummingbird said mockingly—and the illusion of elapsing time snapped violently back into synch with her perception.

The bullet snapped past, spanging away from the glossy metal. Gretchen thumbed the cutting tool to life and pitched the heavy rod in one desperate motion. Malakar was hooting wildly, her pistol blasting again and again. The *durbar* rolled behind the generator, his own automatic blazing back at the stuttering flashes of the gardener's weapon.

Ducking low, Anderssen spun and scrabbled wildly across the floor. "Malakar, go go go!"

The old Jehanan flung the empty pistol away and scrambled towards the hole.

The cutting tool clipped the Jehanan technician on the back of his head, hissing plasma-jet searing the side of his face, and bounced away into the auditorium beyond the broken wall, still spewing flame. Crying out in terrible pain, the technician jerked to the side, mashing the trigger pack in his hands down into the container of cutting gel. There was a sharp, hot spark.

Gretchen threw herself into the crevice, cracking her shoulder against the marble, and immediately had her nose smashed by Malakar's wildly lashing tail. "Ahhh! Move move move!"

The gardener bolted up, reached back to seize hold of Anderssen's jacket collar and staggered off down the tilted passageway.

Sixty kilos of cutting gel ignited in the container. Ravening flame burst upwards, incinerating the wounded technician and engulfing the wooden scaffolding. Marble groaned, tormented by raging heat. The air in the vault rushed inwards, fueling the flames roaring outwards. The *kalpataru* was wrapped in liquid fire, though the ancient metal remained unmoved and untouched. All three fuel-cell packs blew apart, adding yet more heat to the incandescent explosion. Stone ribs flexed, expanding violently, and then the roof of the dome splintered, raining debris down on the huge room below.

A shockwave of white-hot flame, smoke and dust boomed out through the adjoining corridors, overcoming more Jehanan soldiers rushing towards the fane. The entire structure, buried deep within the body of the House, buckled, crashing down, burying the divine tree in thousands of tons of limestone and marble.

THE CAPTAIN'S LAUNCH
IN ORBIT OVER JAGAN,
APPROACHING THE *TEPOZTECATL*

An indicator on Hadeishi's navigation plot spun downwards, showing the launch closing rapidly with the freighter. Asale began her braking maneuver, swinging the launch below the main axis of the ship as the most suitable boat bay faced the planet. The *Chu-sa* was listening intently to reports being relayed to him from the bridge of the *Cornuelle*. The burgeoning revolt on the planet looked to require Fleet intervention.

"Can you patch me through to Yacatolli?" Hadeishi reached out and touched the pilot's shoulder while he waited for the communications duty officer on the *Cornuelle* to respond. Asale looked over questioningly, dark face composed and attentive. He signed for her to hold position.

"Groundside comm is shot to hell, *kyo*," a very sleepy Three-Jaguar replied. Both the first and second watch communications officers had taken his advice to get some sack time—and then had been jarred awake by the combat stations alert only an hour later. "Smith-*tzin* is trying to reestablish comm to the Legation, to Sobipuré and to the Army cantonment, but the main relay station at the landing field is off the air and some kind of general jamming is flooding the whole area."

"Where did the request for atmospheric suppression come from?" Hadeishi caught Asale's eye, made a circling motion with his z-suited finger and pointed towards the *Cornuelle*. The light cruiser had completed its initial maneuvering burn and was now sliding into a lower orbit, one almost directly over Parus. The pilot nodded, twisting her control yoke, and the launch shuddered, dumping the last of its velocity.

"We're picking up fragmentary fire-control requests from elements of the 416th in Takshila in the north and near Fehrupuré in the south. They're being engaged by atmospheric attack craft—old-style supersonic jet airplanes—with a variety of munitions. The jamming storm is interfering with their vehicle-mounted fire-control radar. They want us to establish air superiority from orbit."

Hadeishi coughed in polite amusement. "Well, it is a welcome change to be appreciated. What does Hayes think—one moment . . ."

The quiescent channel to the freighter flickered to life and the face of Captain Chimalpahin appeared. His choleric expression had been replaced by a pale sheen of sweat and worried eyes. A claxon was ringing in the background.

"*Chu-sa* Hadeishi! The situation on the planet has deteriorated. A number of our surveillance networks have been destroyed and we've lost touch with the Legation and Regimental command. We need your ship to take over master relay from lower orbit, allowing us to reestablish comm."

"We're already working on that," Hadeishi said in a dry voice. "Our first priority is to resynch the combat comm net with the Regiment and any dispersed elements. Then we will work on contacting the Legation and the consulates. After that . . . we'll see about your surveillance networks."

"*Chu-sa!*" Chimalpahin's face turned dark red. "Fleet is not the command authority here! Our precedence is well established—"

"I am not concerned about your little war of flowers and padded swords." Hadeishi let a little of his anger flare, shocking the man into silence. "You've put thousands of citizens in harm's way—once we've seen to their safety, then we will help you restore your comm network. Do you—"

An enormously bright light flared off to Hadeishi's right and above his shoulder. For an instant, he saw everything in the cockpit of the launch cast in sharp, unadulterated shadow. The view ports polarized a microsecond later and an alarm blared in his ear.

"Evasive!" he shouted, pressing himself reflexively into the shockchair. "Full power!"

Asale had already thrown the launch into a break to the left, engines howling, the entire frame of the little ship groaning with rapidly mounting g-stress. Hadeishi felt his chest compress, then the z-suit kicked in and the shockwebbing took the brunt of the acceleration. His fingers darted across his command board, bringing up a situational plot and tasking the two realtime cameras on the launch to track the *Tepoztecatl* and the *Cornuelle*.

A tiny fragment of his mind heard the two Marines shouting in alarm and *Sho-i* Asale hissing through clenched teeth as the launch tumbled into a random series of spins and hops, hoping to avoid whatever enemy had crept up out of the dark.

His eyes focused on the video-feed of the freighter. In the seconds since the blast—another part of his mind had already correlated the flare of light with the detonation of some kind of anti-ship mine—a third of the *Tepoztecatl* had been smashed into ruin. Sections of the freighter's hull were glowing white-hot, while atmosphere boiled out in white clouds of ice crystals. The fans of comm relays on the outer hull were twisted wreckage. A secondary explosion ripped through the engine spaces as he watched, spewing a cloud of debris and short-lived flame. The fore part of the ship still seemed to be intact, but all of the habitat rings had stopped violently, their guide-rails torn and mangled. Inside, he knew from cruel experience, every compartment would be in chaos, filled with mangled bodies, crushed equipment and a cloud of paper, unsecured objects, fire-suppression foam, droplets of blood from the wounded and the stink of burning electrical circuitry.

"Situation report," Hadeishi rasped, wrenching his attention back to the plot. He hadn't served as weapons officer for nearly a decade, but an eternity of cadet drill did not die easily. "Comp shows twelve orbital detonations. Dirty anti-matter signatures are coming in . . . bomb-pumped x-ray lasers . . ." He snarled in disgust. The flash plot on the tiny board matched up perfectly with traffic control's last update showing the Development Board's planetary communications network satellite array. "Max acceleration, pilot, match orbit with—"

Hadeishi stopped, heart in his throat, a chill feeling of horror flooding his z-suit. Six of the mines had erupted in a nearly perfect flower-box formation around his ship. Even at this distance, the v-feed of the *Cornuelle* showed massive ruptures in her hull, atmosphere venting in an ever-expanding cloud, the intermittent flare of secondary explosions, and worst—one maneuvering drive still firing in an orbital correction burn while the other five were silent. The light cruiser slid sickeningly towards the upper atmosphere of Jagan, spewing bodies, debris and radiation.

"Jaguar-*tzin*!" Hadeishi's face froze. "Hadeishi to the *Cornuelle*, come in. Hadeishi to the *Cornuelle*, come in!"

Static roared across the standard comm bands, popping in and out as the launch's little comp attempted to restore communications with the ship. Hadeishi flinched as the display flared again. Two thirds of the way around the planet, the free merchantman *Beowulf*—struck by only one of the mines—suffered catastrophic reactor failure and vanished in a sun-bright burst of hard radiation. The flare rippled across the launch—now racing to catch the wounded *Cornuelle*—only seconds later, and Hadeishi watched grimly as his display sparked, shuddered and went dark. The launch's shipskin groaned, toasted by the wave-front. The lights flickered and went out.

Asale released her hands from the control yoke. She flipped the main system reset control experimentally. Nothing happened. "Comp is down. The radiation tripped a safety."

Hadeishi leaned back in his shockchair, staring out at the vast tan-and-blue shape of Jagan. He breathed slowly through his nose, counting to ten with each breath. His z-suit had automatically switched to internal atmosphere. His heart slowed, his mind settled and he watched with cold eyes as the launch coasted ever deeper into the planetary gravity well.

Aboard the *Cornuelle*, the senior officer's ward-room was empty. Though there were no crewmen present to take heed, the battle-stations alarm blared from speakers hidden in the ceiling. Decompression warning lights flashed above both doors, which had automatically sealed themselves when the call to battle-stations went out. A terrible groaning sound echoed through the walls as the ship's spine flexed unnaturally. Unlike some of the other compartments, the mess had been tidied up long before the combat alert sounded. Isoroku had finished the repairs to the floor himself and made sure everything was shipshape before moving on to other, more pressing, duties.

The resulting floor was a beauty to the eye. The varnished surface glowed golden in the light of the overhead lamps. The subtle hexagonal accretion pattern in the *lohaja* fit well with the rice-paper paintings hanging on the walls and an expanse of native carpet. Even by his own high standard, Isoroku had done an excellent job in refurbishing the dining room.

The only things marring the elegant space were nearly a ton of spare *lohaja* flooring sections tied down in one corner with a web of magnetic straps and the box of custom-made Sandvik cutting and finishing tools, which had been carefully tucked away on a shelf beside the gaping hole where a command display had been mounted for the convenience of the senior officers.

Space on the *Astronomer*-class light cruiser being at a premium, most of the common interior spaces had been fitted to do double duty as necessary. The senior officer's ward-room was no exception, possessing a relatively large table and room for eight or more to sit, and the design firm handling the class specifications had provided appropriate furnishings to allow the room to function as a planning center with full access to main comp if the need arose.

The alarms continued to blare and gravity failed in the command spaces. Battle-lights came on as normal lighting dimmed. The mess was plunged into near-darkness. Inside the Sandvik box, a sensor tripped and one of the spare power cells—hidden beneath two of its fellows—hummed to life. A cutting beam sparked, cut through the shockfoam around the tools and out through the side of the wooden case in a perfect circle. A moment later a disc of wood popped out and a small 'bot—a cylinder no more than the size of a man's pinky—crawled out on six joined legs.

The infiltrator rotated, scanning the surrounding volume for a data-port, and found nothing. Secondary programming kicked in and a different set of patterns was loaded into its minuscule processor. This time the scan identified a comp conduit interface hanging in the void where the command display had been. The 'bot climbed the wall easily, reached up two forelimbs and seized hold of the hanging cable. A moment later the 'bot matched interface to interface, negotiated systems access, and disgorged a flood of wrecker viruses directly into the *Cornuelle*'s master comp network.

The infiltrator then waited an eternity—three seconds—and exhausted the last of its tiny power cell with a piercing burst of hi-band radio noise.

Four meters away, a series of organic detonators woven into the *lohaja* wood tripped at the infiltrator's signal and initiated a catastrophic chain reaction through the six hundred kilos of nitro-cellulose explosive forming the plank cores. The officer's mess vanished in a shocking blast of flame and super-pressure plasma. The internal doorway to the galley blew apart and the blast engulfed two storage spaces and the dishwasher. Vent covers for removing waste heat and cooking smoke—closed by the battle alert—crumpled and flames roared down four air circulation shafts—two heading aft and two forward. The main door to the officer's mess was torn from its hinges and smashed into the opposite bulkhead.

A damage control party kicking past at that moment—heading for the number three boat bay, which was at that moment open to naked vacuum and venting atmosphere—was engulfed in plasma and their z-suits, shredded by flying splinters of steel-sharp wood, failed. They all died instantly. The whole center section of the command ring convulsed, ripped by the explosion, and then filled with a rushing wall of flame.

The wall behind the officer's mess, which contained one of the three primary nerve conduits handling all of the ship's data networks, buckled, and most of the blast boiled through the gaping hole where the command panel had been mounted. Luckily, the critical networks were encased in heavy armor, and the blast—though the conduit was severely kinked and sections were badly melted—did not penetrate into the datacore.

A third of the ship's comp, however, did go momentarily off-line as the automatic damage control system shut down the conduit and rerouted traffic into the other two cores. The wrecker viruses, which had already permeated the ship's neural web, began a systemic attack on every sub-system, interface and command and control system within their reach.

Asale counted under her breath, hand on the manual system restart. "Two . . . and one!"

The lever clicked forward, there was a chirping sound, and the command panels in the cockpit of the captain's launch jolted awake.

"We have system restart," Hadeishi announced, watching the boot log flash past on his display. "Fitzsimmons, Deckard—you still with us?"

"Hai, *kyo*," Fitzsimmons answered, sounding a little rattled. Both Marines had been completely silent while the pilot and the *Chu-sa* were working feverishly to get the launch controls operating again. "Is there anything we can do?"

"Yes," Hadeishi said, perfectly calm and collected. "The *Cornuelle* has been severely damaged, if our sensors are reporting the atmosphere and radiation cloud around her properly. We are going to match velocity and go aboard. The locks and boat bays may be damaged, so hunt around back there and collect anything we can use to cut into a lock or handle damage control and medical emergencies once we're inside. Take everything you can carry."

"Engine restart in three . . . two . . . one . . ." *Sho-i* Asale twisted the ignition handle, felt the drive reactor in the back of the launch rumble awake and mimed wiping sweat from her high brow with her free hand. "The gods are smiling, *Chu-sa*. We've lost comm and external video and some of the navigational sensors, but we can still fly."

"Good." Hadeishi cleared a display showing all comm interfaces offline from his panel. "Get me to my ship as fast as you can."

The launch trembled, the drives lit off and they jolted forward. Jagan continued to swell before them, and Hadeishi imagined he could see the matte black outline of the *Cornuelle* ahead, growing nearer every second. His face became a mask, his eyes cold obsidian.

The *Chu-sa* was trying to keep from bursting into tears. *I've failed my men, my ship . . . everyone. What did I think I was doing—haring off on a political visit with combat imminent? Ah, the gods of chance are bending against me tonight.* The only thought which gave him some shred of hope was the knowledge that Susan was on the ground, far from their dying ship, perhaps safely ensconced in a command bunker at Sobipuré or the Regimental cantonment.

Hold on, he prayed, watching the fragmentary navigational plot for signs of the *Cornuelle. Hold on, I'm coming. Hayes knows what to do, he'll get maneuvering drive back and pull you into a safe orbit. Just hold on, just a little longer . . .*

Six thousand kilometers behind the launch, the *Tepoztecatl* continued to shudder with explosions as more systems failed. Atmospheric venting continued unabated and the long, curving rooms filled with communications equipment drifted with clouds of paper, globules of vomit and blood and water. Bodies clogged the doorways where the explosive decompression of the ship had sucked the hapless priests to an ugly, instant death. The main reactor had shuddered into an emergency shutdown, preventing the kind of catastrophic failure which had claimed the *Beowulf*, but only isolated portions of the ship glowed with emergency lights.

The bridge and command spaces were twisted wreckage—the laser burst from the nearest mine had smashed lengthwise into the ship directly through the control deck. Chimalpahin and all of his subordinates had been instantly killed, either incinerated or boiled alive as the internal atmosphere roared out through the shattered hull.

All possibility of the Flower Priest network being restored was wiped away with one brilliant flash of light. Across Jagan, the Whisperers working quietly in town, countryside and metropolis stared in alarm at their comms, finding the ever-present voice from the sky had fallen silent.

Warning lights flared, nearly blinding Isoroku as he struggled back to consciousness. The engineer raised a hand, found his ears ringing with a warbling emergency alarm, and seized hold of the nearest stanchion. The engineering deck was in chaos, filled with drifting men, loose hand-held comp pads, tools and broken bits of glassite. Weakly, he tapped his comm.

"Engineering to Bridge . . . ship's status?"

Static babbled on the channel and Isoroku stared at his wrist in alarm. "Hello the bridge! Hayes? Smith?"

His comm continued a sing-song wail, warbling up and down the audible frequency. Isoroku shut it off and swung to the nearest v-display. Finding the display still up by some miracle, he mashed a control glyph with a gloved thumb and the blaring alarm shut off. In the following silence, his breath sounded very harsh in his ears. The engineer stared at the panel, felt his stomach fall into a deep pit and clenched the sides of the station to keep from drifting away.

Every readout and v-pane was filled with random, constantly changing garbage. Isoroku glanced around the engineering deck, finding his staff struggling back to stations, though at least two drifted limply, one leaking crimson from a shattered face-plate. He tried tapping up the all-hands channel on his comm. A blast of scratchy music assaulted his hears, accompanied by a wailing voice like a lost soul writhing in the torment of a Christian's hell.

Comms are down, he realized, feeling even sicker. *Main comp is corrupted—or at least the interfaces are. This is a cold day indeed.* Isoroku lifted his wrist, eyeballed the environmental readouts, saw the air was still breathable and unsealed the helmet of his z-suit.

As soon as he tasted burned circuit and fear in the air, he kicked across to the main comp station and rapped his fist on the helmets of two crewmen trying to get the panel to reboot. Alarmed, they unsealed their faceplates, staring at him with wide eyes. Fleet discipline was very strict about keeping z-suit integrity in an emergency.

"Main comp is corrupted," Isoroku barked as soon as they could hear him. "Drop the entire ship-wide network—every node, relay and interface—and keep main comp off-line. We'll need altitude control and environmentals back as quickly as possible, but we'll have to bring them up as standalone systems."

Before they could reply, he turned and kicked across to the cluster of stations controlling the main reactor and the massive hyperspace drive systems. *Chu-i* Yoyontzin, his second, was already at the panel, haggard face sheened with sweat. The Náhuatl officer's helmet was tipped back behind his head, though Isoroku could see the engineer was nearly paralyzed with fear at the prospect of losing pressure on the deck.

"Reactor is still up," Yoyontzin reported, biting his lip. "Main drive was on standby, but I think we can bring her on-line in thirty minutes . . ."

Isoroku shook his head, the dull glare of the emergency lights shining on his bald pate. "Shut down main power and the transit drive and maneuvering. Right now—manually, if you have to."

"But, *kyo*, we were in the middle of a maneuvering burn! One engine was still firing. We need to adjust attitude control and establish a stable orbit!"

"Can't do that while the comp network is corrupted." The lead engineer stabbed a thick finger at the sidepanel displays flanking the reactor and drive subsystem. They were crowded with garbage and wild images. Pornographic three-d's pulsed on two of them, emitting a shrieking wail of sound and the *whomp-whomp-whomp* of electric drums. "We need cell power to bring up critical systems and we can't spare it to keep the main drive hot. Shut down all drives *right now*."

"Hai!" Yoyontzin bleated in response, bending over his panel.

Isoroku spared himself an instant of relief that the corruption had not managed to penetrate the isolated reactor and hyperspace drive systems, and was even happier when Yoyontzin managed to initiate a controlled shutdown without missing a step and tipping the hyperspace matrix into some kind of catastrophic transit gradient.

"Communications are down," he bawled, drawing the attention of every other rating in the compartment. Everyone who was still up and mobile had at least cracked their helmets. "We need shipside comm up so we can handle damage control—every third man to the repair lockers—pull the commwire spools and local relays. Every z-suit comm switches to local point-to-point mode, no central relay allowed. Four teams—one for each fore-aft access way—run those spools out from here and affix local repeaters at each bulkhead. Move!

"Environmental section! Bring up your systems isolated from main comp, reflash your control code from backup and get the air recyclers working again." More ratings scattered and the engineer fixed his gaze on the damage-control section, which was staring helplessly at rows of displays which were showing flashing, endlessly repeated images of an animated rabbit hopping through a field of psychedelic, oversaturated flowers.

"Damage control is—"

Main comp shut down hard and every single display on the ship went black with a pitiful whine. The rabbits flickered wildly before vanishing with a *pop!* The engineering deck was suddenly very, very quiet.

The subsonic background thunder of the main reactors stuttered and failed.

Even the space-bending, subliminal ringing tone of the hyperspace coil fell silent.

Isoroku swallowed, suddenly feeling cold, and realized he was trapped in the heart of a nine-thousand-ton tomb of hexacarbon and glassite and steel.

THE HOUSE OF REEDS WITHIN THE NAUTILUS

Dust billowed along a trapezoidal passage, enveloping Gretchen and Malakar in a dirty tan cloud. Coughing, the Jehanan fell to her hands, overcome. Anderssen, thankful for her goggles, bit down on her breathing tube, seized the gardener under the shoulders and forged ahead. Twenty meters on, a ramp cut off to the left and they staggered up the slope, rising out of the toxic murk stirred up by the collapse of the vault three levels below.

Snuffling loudly, Malakar collapsed on the stone floor, gasping for breath.

Gretchen knelt beside the gardener and shook a thick coating of limestone powder from her field jacket. Everything was permeated with the fine gritty residue. "Can you breathe?"

Malakar responded with a wheezing snort, spitting goopy white fluid on the ground.

"I guess you can." Gretchen offered the Jehanan her water bottle.

Watching the alien drink, Anderssen was struck again by the dilapidated age of the entire structure. The grimy sensation of every surface being caked deep with the debris of centuries was only reinforced by the strange, massive pressure the *kalpataru* was exerting on her mind.

"Do your people—the priests, I mean—do they ever make new halls, cut new passages?"

"Is there need?" Malakar shook her head, returning the empty bottle. "Even I can become lost—once a Master ordered maps and charts made—but after a hand of years, the project was abandoned. I saw the room of books so made, when I was a short-horn, they were rotting. Paper is treacherous with its promises. No, all the priests do now is close up the places they fear to tread."

Gretchen nodded and helped the Jehanan to her feet. "Do you know the way out?"

"This old walnut doesn't even know where we are," Malakar grumbled, sniffing the air. "Perhaps this way."

After an hour or more, they turned into a long narrow hall, spaced with graven pillars reaching overhead to form a roof of carved triangular leaves. Malakar picked up her pace, forcing Gretchen to jog along behind. Here the floor was cleared of dust and ahead a *gipu* gleamed in the darkness.

"Quietly now," the gardener whispered. "We will reach the first level of terraces soon, and there will be priests—or even more of those profaning soldiers—about. The closest outer door known to me is some distance away, but that one is watched and guarded. We must reach one of the forgotten ones . . ."

They reached the end of the pillared hall, found themselves in an intersection of three other passages—all of them lit—and Malakar turned down the one to the right, then immediately stepped between two of the pillars—into a shadowed alcove—and began climbing a very narrow set of stairs. Once they had ascended beyond the lights, the gardener brought out the *gipu* and held the egg aloft. Picking her way along in the faint light, Gretchen ventured to speak again.

"Do you call this place the Garden because of the terraces?"

Malakar shook her head, still climbing. "They are new—or as new as such things can be in this hoary old place. Once they were broad platforms edged with rounded walls on each level above the entrance tier. One of the Masters—six of them ago now?—decided they should be filled with earth and planted. Some fragments still surviving from those times speak of a dispute with the *kujen* over the provision of tribute to the House."

"They provide all your food now?" Gretchen was thinking of the countless rooms and dozens of levels and the failure of her comm to penetrate the walls of the massif. "How many priests live within the House?"

"Two hundred and nineteen in these failing days," Malakar said, coming to the end of the stairs. "We no longer use the Hall of Abating Hunger—too many echoes and shadows for so few. But there I wager over a thousand could comfortably squat and stanch their hunger with freshly grilled *zizunaga*." Her long head poked out into a new passage and sniffed the air. "We are very near the terrace where I hid the *pushta* in the soil."

"I can find my way back to the entrance I used from there." Gretchen checked her comp. The mapping soft was still running, showing her path as an irregular, looping line of red through half-filled-in rooms, chambers and halls. The cross-corridors fanned out like spines from the back of a broken snake. "Was I wrong before, when I said this was one of the spacecraft which brought your people to Jagan? Was this a fortress, a citadel raised at the heart of their landing, to secure the new conquest? And all these new halls and tunnels and rooms cut from the rock—they're not as ancient as they seem—only hundreds of years old, from the time of the Fire."

Malakar did not answer, but waved her forward and they hurried down another curving passage. A faint radiance began to gleam on the walls ahead, a slowly building light, promising a smoggy sky and clouds pregnant with rain.

The Jehanan remained silent, head moving warily from one side to the other, until they reached a junction where—suddenly and without warning—Gretchen's goggles picked up a UV-marker arrow pointing down a side passage.

"There!" she exclaimed, enormously relieved. "That's the way I came."

"*Hooo . . .*" Malakar squatted down in the passageway with the pierced stone screen, claws ticking against the floor. The bright light of afternoon filtered through the trees and picked out shining scales on her head. The *gipu* was tucked away. "I know this path. A steep stair with many broken steps leads to a laundry and a bakery selling *patu* biscuits. I had not thought the entrance still open, but . . . memories fade and fail. *Hoooo* . . . I am weary now."

"Both the inner and outer doors are frozen open." Gretchen knelt as well, thumbing her comp to the display showing the analysis results from the scan of the *kalpataru*. "Are there stories of the House during the time of the Fire? Could the entire population of the city fit inside? Is it that vast? Are there—were there—other citadels like this one?"

The Jehanan opened her jaws, trilling musically. Anderssen guessed she was laughing.

"So hungry, so hungry . . . With your claws full, you reach for more! Does this hunger ever abate or fade?"

"No, not often." Gretchen shook her head sadly. "Sometimes, when I am at home, with my children—I have a hatchling, as you would say, and two short-horns—I forget for a little while. But then I rise one morning and my heart wonders when the liner lifts from port, what quixotic vista is waiting for me, what dusty tomb will reveal the lives of the dead and the lost to me. Then I am happy for a little while, until I miss my children again."

"*Hur-hur!* One day you will catch your own tail and eat yourself up before you've noticed!"

Anderssen grimaced at the image, then held up the comp. "There is a preliminary analysis, as I promised, if you still want to know the truth of the *kalpataru*."

Malakar raised her snout, flexed her nostrils and hooted mournfully. "Does it matter now?" She stabbed a claw at the floor. "Everything is buried for all time . . . Who could say how many lie mewed up in that bright tomb? Will truth taste as bitter as the other fruit I've plucked from your tree?"

Gretchen shrugged and looked the gardener in the eye. "Neither sweet nor sour, I venture. Not, perhaps, what you expected."

"Tell me then, meddling *asuchau*. Dare I ever sleep again? May I feel just, righteous anger at the fools who run squeaking in empty halls, pretending to be the *kujenai* of old? Should I weep for what you've destroyed?"

Gretchen ran a hand through her hair and grimaced at the gritty feeling. She desperately needed a shower. *Should I tell this old one what I saw? About the ghosts?*

She gathered her thoughts, looked Malakar in the eye and said: "The stone floor holding the root of the tree was a particularly pure, seamless marble. These readings show it was all of one piece. Marble, you should be aware, does not conduct heat, vibration or electricity well. The domed chamber around the tree also served to dampen electromagnetic waves or currents. I think the chamber was completely enclosed. It *was* a tomb."

The Jehanan hooted questioningly. "Why would they hide the—"

"Because they thought the tree was dangerous!" Gretchen stared at her grimy hand. Her fingers were trembling. *Are there scorch marks from the green fire that washed over me? Is this how Hummingbird feels every day of his life? Merciful Mary, please keep my thoughts from sin, drown my curiosity, still my reaching hand.* "Because they *knew* it was dangerous. So they built a prison in their strongest fortress, and they set a particularly devout order—the *mandire*—to guard the cell and keep it safe."

Malakar's eye-shields rattled. "Safe? Safe from what?"

"From other Jehanan? From the last of the Haraphans?" Anderssen clenched her hands together. "Whoever they captured it from . . ."

The gardener hissed, confused. "You are filled with riddles. My snout is cold from all these twisty thoughts. The only matter to claw is—did any life remain in the cold metal? Was aught revealed to the Masters when they embraced the *kalpataru* down through these endless years?"

Taking a deep breath, Gretchen tucked the comp away. "I believe . . ." she said in a ragged voice, thinking of the fuel-cell generators. "Without power the tree slept for millennia. I believe the machine was very, very old. Older than the arrival of the Jehanan, older than the Haraphans. Once, the *kalpataru* had a power source of its own, but that mechanism failed long ago."

Malakar peered at Gretchen, turning her long head from side to side, letting each eye gaze upon the human. "Without power . . . and those whining boxes, they were feeding the tree? Would it have woken to life?"

"For an instant—Mother Mary bless and protect me!—for less than the blink of an eye, it did." She smiled grimly. "Don't worry about the Master of the Garden and his propaganda. If he had truly beheld the visions of the device, his mind would have been destroyed long ago."

"No loss!" The Jehanan hooted in amusement, rattling old, yellowed claws on the floor. "He might gain some wit thereby!"

Gretchen shook her head sharply, feeling a curdling, acid sensation stir in her stomach. "He might gain more than wit—if something filled his broken mind with new thoughts. You would not like what happened then—" She stopped, wondering if Hummingbird would tell the gardener of the cruel powers which had shattered lost Mokuil and still lay in dreaming sleep on desolate worlds like Ephesus. "You were right to mistrust the *kalpataru* and feel its worship unwholesome."

"But," Malakar said, "without rain and sun, it lay fallow."

"Yes," Anderssen allowed, rubbing her face with both hands. She was beginning to feel truly exhausted. "But not dead, only dormant. Waiting for meddling fools to come along and give it life again."

"Hrrr . . ." Malakar fell silent, watching the human with an intent expression. Anderssen grew nervous, wondering if the Jehanan would attack her again. After a long time, the gardener stirred. "This slow old walnut suddenly realizes even rich *asuchau* humans must spend *shatamanu* to buy tasty food, to travel the iron road, to stay in tall *khus* where the wind is always cool in the windows—but the *rich* never get their claws soiled with dirt, or split by toil. Never."

Malakar's fore-claw extended, gently touching the scars on Gretchen's hand. "These are not the claws of a rich woman," the gardener said softly. "Yet you are here. . . . Who paid to send you so far? Someone who heard of a divine tree standing in an ancient Garden, this old walnut thinks. Do they desire the *kalpataru*? Will they dig in the ruins with greedy claws? Will they fall down and worship it? Will they feed it?"

Anderssen squared her shoulders and forced herself to *not* bite her lip. "They—the Honorable Chartered Company—sent me to Jagan to look upon the *kalpataru*, to take the readings I have in my comp now, and to bring them back. No more."

"*Hoooo*! Well, you've twisted my tail, sure enough." Malakar's jaws gaped. She hissed angrily. "Everything you wished, I've done, haven't I? What a good servant this old one proves! The Master of the Garden would be stricken dumb to see me bow and scrape!"

"Here." Gretchen held out the comp. "Everything is in here. If you take this, then I will return home with empty hands. The secrets of the *kalpataru* will be safe. No one will ever return to disturb the Garden. Go on, take it."

Malakar stared suspiciously at the comp and hesitated, just for an instant.

A howling, shrieking noise pierced the triangle-leaved trees and the stone screen. Malakar jerked back her claw and both she and Gretchen stared towards the terrace with alarm.

"What was that?" Gretchen blurted. "That sounded like . . . no, that's impossible . . ."

"I have never heard such a noise before," the old Jehanan said, striding down into the passage out onto the overlook. Anderssen hurried after her and they both stepped out into the ruddy sunshine of Bharat. Takshila lay before them, the sprawl of the apartment buildings and factories and refineries half-hidden under a dirty yellow haze. There was a distant, rippling boom.

Gretchen tugged the goggles down over her eyes and scanned the horizon. After only a second she pointed, stabbing her finger. "There—in the sky to the southeast! A silver flash!"

"*Hrrrr*!" Malakar shaded her eyes. "I see—a *yi* of enormous size, racing faster than the wind! Trailing smoke and fire!"

"Not a *yi*," Anderssen said, alarmed and puzzled by turns. "That looks like an old-style jet fighter—but they've not been used by the Empire for hundreds of years . . ."

The distant dot swept low over the sky, flashing through the rising fume of hundreds of smokestacks, then darted skyward. Below, there was a bright flash among the buildings. A sharper roar trembled across the city to reach their ears. A black smudge billowed up, lit from below by the red-orange glow of flames.

"What are they attacking?" Gretchen zoomed the magnification of her goggles, but the haze in the air obscured everything. "The train station?"

"No . . ." Malakar pointed off due south. "The iron road is there. . . . That fire is where the *asuchau* merchant houses stand."

Gretchen pushed back her goggles, heart thudding with fear. "I have to get back to my friends right now. If Imperial citizens are being attacked, they are in danger."

Without waiting for a response, she turned and bolted down the passageway, goggles jammed down to her nose, the filter keyed into ultraviolet. There was a startled hooting from behind her, and then the slapping of leathery feet on stone. Anderssen didn't wait, plunging down the ramp at the end of the perforated hall, survey comp clutched to her breast.

NEAR THE BOULEVARD OF STEPPING CRANES
DISTRICT OF THE WHEEL, PARUS

The hue of sunlight falling through the back of the truck changed, even as the driver swerved into a narrow lane between two buildings of painted brick and plaster. Itzpalicue looked out, puzzled by the shifting light, and then two things happened at once: her earbug roared painfully with static, making her flinch, and the dappled shadows beneath the trees lining the lane shifted wildly.

Another attack? My hand-comp!

Queasy with fear, the old woman wrenched out her earbug with a gasp of pain. The Arachosian stared at her, puzzled himself, and watched in concern as she snatched out her comp, saw the machine was showing wild, fragmentary garbage on its screen, and then hooted with surprise as she vaulted the tailgate and bolted across the flagstone-paved courtyard the truck had just entered. *Radiation attack*, she realized, her medband squealing an unmistakable alert.

The sky over Parus rippled with queer, diamond-hard light. The sun gained three smaller companions, each brilliant pinprick glaring down through gathering cloud. The Arachosian warrior jumped down from the truck—now coughing to a halt—and stared up, one long, tan claw shading deep-set eyes. The tiny suns burning the sky were already fading, leaving scattered spots in his vision. He blinked, tear ducts flushing his seared retinas. The black spots did not disappear.

Itzpalicue hurried down a flight of stairs into the empty basement of the safe-house, pressed one hand against a hidden security sensor and then threw back her scarf as a second door opened in the floor, allowing her to descend a flight of newly built wooden stairs.

She cursed, seeing the lights had dimmed to dull red emergency filaments powered by an on-site power-cell. A handful of humans stared up at her, eyes wide in the near-darkness. The banks of comm displays, comps and monitoring apparatus were silent and dead.

"What are you doing?" Itzpalicue snapped, eyes going cold. "Bring up emergency power! Switch to the landline network!"

"But . . ." One of the Mirror technicians, eyes dark in the poor light, lank black hair shining with grease, started to stand up. "What happened? All the networks have gone down again—the *Tepoztecatl* relay is off-line, we can't . . ."

"Sit down and get to work," the old woman said in a hard voice. "Or you will be replaced."

The man sat, flushed, sweating now with fear.

"Operating power can be provided by the power-cell array in the other chamber," she barked, stabbing a thin finger at an engineer. "Start them up!" She stared around at the rest of the frightened people, lips twisted into a sneer. "There is work to be done, children. Get about it! You know what to do if the primary networks fail. I want status reports within ten minutes!"

Everyone started awake and—prodded by her sharp voice—returned to their stations. The whine of power-cells firing up echoed in from the other room and the lights flickered back on.

Itzpalicue waited by the stairs, gimlet eyes fierce on every sweating face. Under her baleful gaze, everyone settled down with remarkable efficiency. The comps were reset and came back up, filling the room with a hard, jewel-like glare.

Itzpalicue let herself take the tiniest breath of relief. *We still have some comp.*

"Over-the-air networks are still down," the lead technician reported a few moments later. "We've lost the line-of-sight relay on the roof and our aerials aren't picking up any comm traffic at all, just undifferentiated static."

"No military traffic?" Itzpalicue raised an eyebrow. "The 416th should have been able to ride out an EMP burst. Any broadband from orbit?"

The technician shook his head, lips pursed. He was staring questioningly at the old woman.

"What?" Itzpalicue's expression hardened to granite and she wondered if Yacatolli had been more careless than she'd planned. *He'd better have had his command tracks in hardened mode, or the Field Officers' School will be making a test question out of his utter failure on the plain of battle.*

"EMP shock, mi'lady? Is . . . is that what knocked out our comm network?"

Itzpalicue grunted. "And the spyeyes back aloft as well, I'm sure. We'll be blind until Lachlan can launch fresh ones." *If he has any left—two blows now aimed at our aerial surveillance capacity—very thorough, very thorough indeed.*

"An atomic on the ground, mi'lady?" The technician was looking a little green. "At the spaceport?"

"Exoatmospheric," Itzpalicue said, softening her voice a little, realizing the operators in the sub-surface room had no way to tell there had been a series of nuclear explosions at the edge of the Jaganite atmosphere. "Multiple detonations in orbit. If the Flower Priest network has gone off-line and there aren't any recog codes being transmitted from orbit, assume the *Tepoztecatl* has been destroyed." She frowned, thumb to her lower lip. "What about the Fleet cruiser?"

"We're trying to get linked back to main operations now. . . . We'll know about other stations and relays in . . ." The technician swallowed nervously. ". . . an hour? Then we'll be able to broadcast to orbit—but we don't have that capability here."

The old Náhuatl woman's lips twitched into a sour grimace. *Deployment planning, operations manual, revision six thousand and three . . . deploy backup orbital uplink with tertiary communications center. Deploy ground-based surveillance mechanisms.*

"Get me verification on all ships we knew were in orbit. Get me a radar scan or visual—something! As soon as possible. If something has entered orbit and destroyed both of our support ships . . . we will need to revise our planning." *Go underground and scatter*, she thought grimly. *With Yacatolli's regiment dispersed and under attack, and no orbital support, we may lose the Legation and our entire presence here. Even one Danish privateer would be enough to tip the balance . . .*

She placed the thought firmly aside. Until more data was available, she'd assume things were as they stood and no more. *Which*, she allowed sourly, *is bad enough.*

"Landline status?" Some of the technicians were talking into their voicephones. Most of the comp displays were live again, though none of them were showing v-feeds.

The technician scratched his head, glancing over his shoulder. "Station two," he pointed, "has gotten ahold of one of the techs at main operations. She's transcribing their status. We're trying to raise the other city operations teams, but so far we've only managed to get through to the one at Sobipuré. They've had to move to their backup site—the landing field has been overrun and the Imperial citizens there slaughtered."

"Hmm . . . what about Fleet staff at the base?" Itzpalicue leaned over the display showing the transcript from Lachlan's conversation. "Were they killed or captured as well?"

The technician shrugged. "No news. We're operating nearly blind, mi'lady."

"Yes," Itzpalicue pursed her lips. "What about datacomm over the landlines?"

"Ten minutes," he said, swallowing again. "I think. There is a problem with—"

She fixed him with a stony glare. "Fix it. Now, where is my station?"

The room had returned to a proper feeling of busy efficiency by the time Itzpalicue had settled herself in a distant corner, half-hidden behind a stack of heat exchangers and storage crystal lattices. The tension and fear was ebbing from the voices around her, though everyone was on edge. The old woman was pleased. Losing all prospect of support and even, possibly, their way home had not reduced any of her staff to uselessness from panic or fear.

They have spirit, she thought, *as I have always maintained.*

A mingled sensation of bitterness and pride filled her. A traditional Mirror field team would have leaned heavily on older, more experienced staff. Ones with 'proven skills' and spotless efficiency records, drawn from well-connected members of the great clans or the military families. None of the young men and women in the room had been recruited from within the Four Hundred. Nearly all, in fact, were from colony worlds or mining stations or the slums of Anáhuac. Patronless, making their way only by skill, tenacity and a blithe disregard for the danger around them. *A more experienced team*, she allowed privately, *would not heed my orders so effortlessly. They would argue and quibble and question. And dwell too much on the prospect of failing to return home in a critical time.*

The comp displays before her came to life at a touch, showing audio transcripts from the operators in the room. She inserted a fresh earbug and twisted the comm-thread around to her lips. The chatter in her ear was confusing for a moment, but she let her eyes relax, let the room fall away and plucked a maguey thorn from her sleeve.

Blood welled from her breast and the sharp stab of pain focused her mind.

An array of glyphs appeared on her main display, including one associated with Lachlan. Pleased, Itzpalicue tapped the glyph and a moment later Lachlan's voice was threading its way through the stream of conversations washing over her.

"Did you suffer any losses in the shockwave?"

No, mi'lady. No human casualties at least. She could hear him smiling grimly. *The gods of war favored us a little—we hadn't relaunched our surviving spyeye assets when the EMP shock blanketed this face of the planet—so we didn't lose any more. Still, we've lost three-quarters of our coverage. We've sorted out twelve primary detonations and one secondary. The first set were anti-matter cascades, the last a fusion explosion. A ship's reactor core by the emissions signature.*

"Which ship?" Itzpalicue reached into her mantle and squeezed an *oliohuiqui* tablet from a sewn-in pocket. The round pill felt grainy and sharp under her fingertips. "The *Tepoztecatl*?"

We think not, he replied. *The orbit position was wrong—best guess says it was the merchanter* Beowulf, *which had recently arrived with a cargo of recycled aluminum blocks and miscellaneous 'spare parts'.*

"More guns for the local trade. Well, they'll not be missed. The native princelings seem to have accumulated enough fuel for a hot little war as it stands." The old woman placed the tablet under her tongue, feeling a familiar bitter taste well in her mouth. "And the detonations themselves?"

Orbital mines. The Éirishman's voice was flat. *The Imperial Development Board's satellite network down to the meter. Civilian power plants replaced with military grade anti-matter packs and converted into cheap bomb-pumped x-ray laser platforms. The* Tepoztecatl *didn't mount the armor to shrug off even a single hit . . .*

"A long-prepared trap." Itzpalicue blinked as everything around her became very sharply defined. "Do you concur?"

I don't know how long someone spent setting this up . . . Lachlan clicked his teeth together in thought. *But someone here has been preparing for battle. We're not picking up any signs of another ship in the system, so I think the mines were used as a cheap way to cripple or destroy any assets we had in orbit. A one-off cast of the patolli beans, if you will. Costing nothing if the gambit failed, but carrying the potential for inflicting heavy casualties . . .*

"This entire world is a snare for us, for the Regiment, for the *xochiyaotinime*." The old woman's voice was perfectly confident, and in the thought-accelerating clarity of the morning-glory extract dissolving into her bloodstream, all known data aligned and portentous signs emerged from the chaos of noise and data around her. "Someone *knew* we chose this world for the Flowery War—someone acquainted with our policies and customs."

Can you be sure? Lachlan's voice quickened in disbelief. *Everything they've done could have been put in place on a very short timetable. Six months, perhaps a year. How long ago was Jagan chosen?*

Itzpalicue consulted the serried ranks of her memory, plucking out one dusty tome loitering in the back of her mind. Pages unfolded before her, yielding brilliant visions of red and black, the smell of dried flowers and the echo of chanting voices. "The Flower Priests are not hasty," she said. "They have been planning their exercise here for almost four years."

Plenty of time to prepare, the Éirishman mused, *if this enemy cabal has an ear inside the Temple of Mayahuel, or among her servants abroad on this world.*

"Not a cabal," the old woman said sharply, "pawns and decoys aplenty, yes—minions dancing on unseen strings—but only one hand on the thread of destiny. Only one true enemy."

Lachlan did not respond, and Itzpalicue knew he was frowning, staring at an empty v-pane, wondering how to disagree. A flood of eager confidence rushed in her veins, straining her voice, making her words tumble like a swift stream. "We have our own ears here, Lachlan-*tzin*! Our own eyes. To hold such a trap secret for so long requires the tightest of conspiracies. Supremely trustworthy confederates. All of this has been arranged by a single mind. *One enemy!* As I have feared and suspected. But he shows his hand at last. Now I begin the see the outline of a face!"

Lachlan held his peace; Itzpalicue could hear him breathing and the muted chatter of the technicians in the distant room. She fought down the urge to giggle or shout aloud. She knew she was right. She was certain the bitter god guided her thoughts unerringly and they were clear, clear as a placid stream under willows.

Most of our data network is back up, the Éirishman said in a neutral tone. *I will route you a copy of everything coming into main operations.*

"Good." Itzpalicue felt her voice shine with bright colors. "My hunters are afield—their scanners still work—as soon as *he* reveals himself, we will strike."

You know your quarry is in Parus? Lachlan tried to hide the skepticism in his voice, but failed.

"No." The admission was painful. She had tried to acquire the services of more mercenaries from the highland tribes, but spending the time to win their trust and establish her power fully in their minds had taken too long. "But the Legation is here, and the *darmanarga* conspiracy will gauge failure or success by its capture. I believe . . . *he* will keep close watch upon them, for even if this is only a spine-prick to bleed us, such a victory would be hard to resist."

Very well. The Éirishman's tone held a disbelieving sigh. *We are launching the reserve spyeyes now. We should have about twenty percent coverage within the hour.*

The old woman smiled, bony hands flat upon her knees, eyes half-lidded, waiting and listening to the flood of sound surging around her. Her perception expanded, filling the world, penetrating even the most minute crevice, winging across the rooftops, hearing the distant voices of men in battle and pain.

The smell of blood and incense was sharp in her nostrils. Again, she felt young and strong, as if the years had dropped away, a heavy, jeweled mantle discarded upon the floor.

THE JUNCTION OF PROVINCIAL ROUTE TWENTY-TWO AND THE RAILWAY NORTH OF THE MÉXICA MANDATE AT SOBIPURÉ

The sick, sinking feeling rushing up in *Heicho* Felix's stomach slammed into a stone wall as the air-breathing turbines on the Fleet shuttle suddenly regained comp control. The engine fans shrieked up to an ear-piercing whine and kicked over, igniting. The pilot, who had been struggling to deadstick the shuttle into the nearest river, felt his ship come alive.

He jammed on full thrust and slewed his control yoke over and back, sending the shuttle clawing for altitude.

Massive acceleration slammed Felix back into the shockchair for an endless, crushing time. Then, suddenly, they leveled off and the aircraft banked sharply. For the first time in their headlong flight, Felix took a breath, realizing the enemy missile team in the shantytown had failed to peg them with a second rocket and comp control had come back on-line. Still rattled, she tucked loose hair back behind her ears and tuned the eye-v on the inside of her visor back to the cameras in the nose of the shuttle. The whine of her suit systems had never been so welcome.

The tiled roof of a farmhouse flashed past, followed immediately by the blur of a wide field flooded with water, green shoots poking up from the mud. The *Hei-*

cho grimaced, stomach churning with vertigo. The shuttle pilot was clinging to the deck like a baby to the teat, roaring over roads lined with flowering hedges, fields gleaming with sheets of water, and long stretches of trees planted in regular rows. The slender figures of Jehanan on the ground were glimpsed for fractions of a second and then left behind. Felix felt dizzy, thinking *I'm glad I'm not a bleeding pilot . . .* and toggled her view to one of the side-mounted cameras.

With more distance between the lens and the landscape, the frenetic passage of the shuttle didn't upset her stomach so much. She saw broad plains stretching out to the horizon, dotted with conical mounds surmounted by villages. Every square meter seemed to be tilled, planted, farmed or covered with clusters of tiny, compact houses. Heavy rain clouds scudded across the bucolic landscape, chasing their own shadows across byre and barn alike.

A trail of dust rising from a long dike caught her eye and she zoomed the camera. An elevated road sprang into focus and at first Felix thought she was watching a column of vehicles from the 416th Tarascan Rifles regiment burling down the highway. Then her mind sorted out the jumble of exhaust, dust, dull gray vehicles and marching columns of antlike figures. The AI in her comm link steadied the frame, causing details to spring into view, sharp and clear.

Lines of Jehanan soldiers were moving down the sides of the road at a brisk pace, rifles canted over their shoulders, bodies heavy with bags of ammunition, canteens, trenching tools and flaring helmets which reached from their eye-shields back down their necks. Armored cars, tanks and Saab-Scandia trucks rumbled past the infantry, raising a thick pall of yellow dust. The entire force was moving steadily north.

Felix swallowed and keyed her comm. "*Kyo*, you should switch to camera six on the shuttle 'net. The slicks are rolling hot today."

Koshō looked up, focused on an infinite distance, and the corners of her lips tightened minutely. "I see. Those tanks are not of Imperial manufacture. Do you recognize them?"

"No." Felix grimaced, panning the camera ahead, flitting along the column. "They look like local work—but I thought they'd lost all their tech?"

"Apparently not." Koshō's eyes twitched to the side. She tapped her comm. "Pilot, swing more to the west. We want to avoid the altercation at one o'clock."

Felix looked back to the eye-v and saw a sudden bloom of smoke and fire along the road. Jehanan soldiers scattered down from the dike, splashing through muddy fields. Tracers flashed out from a cluster of buildings sitting beside the road. One of the squat-looking Jehanan tanks was burning, vomiting flame from its engine compartment. The flash of heavy guns rippled between the buildings. Felix felt the shuttle bank again, and the view twisted. Suddenly they were looking down at a high angle into the crossroads.

The marching column was deploying—tanks rumbling ahead while squads peeled away into the fields and everything else ground to a halt—and she could see rows of hastily dug emplacements in and around the village. Jehanan artillerists scrambled to reload crew-served weapons in pits and she caught a glimpse of another native tank hiding in the shadow of a barnlike building, long gun traversing the elevated road. The entire machine bucked backwards, flame gouting from the long muzzle. Then the entire scene was gone as the shuttle continued to roar northwards.

"They're fighting each other?" Felix looked to the *Sho-sa*, hoping the officer had some clue what was going on. "Different native factions?"

"We've more pressing problems than the disputes of local warlords." Koshō was busily tapping commands into her hand comp. "The *Cornuelle* is not responding to my direct hail." Her dark eyes looked up, fixing Felix with a grim stare. The *Heicho* swallowed, seeing an unexpected ashen pallor tingeing the Nisei officer's usually immaculate face. "Twelve anti-matter detonations have occurred in orbit. All comm relays are down, save ones which happened to be shielded. Navplot shows at least one starship destroyed."

"Oh." Felix tested her grip on the Macana between her legs. The assault rifle had a cheerful solidity. Her eyes flicked across the Marines seated on either side of the cargo bay, counting ammunition coils, grenades and gear. *There'll be some ammunition in the shuttle stores, too. Plus we've got Helsdon and his engineers for repairs and support . . .* "We'd better make for the Army cantonment at Parus then. They'll need the shuttle for air support and medevac."

Koshō stared at her for a long moment, dark eyes flat and emotionless. Then she stirred, nodded and began working with her comm again. "The shuttle relay node is picking up scattered transmissions," she said in a toneless voice. "Sort through these while I try and raise Regimental command or the Legation. We need to know what the situation is before we set down."

"Hai, *kyo*!" Felix tapped her comm, letting the node built into her combat armor range free, scanning up and down through the comm bands, looking for the distinctive signatures of Imperial transmissions.

Almost immediately she began to pick up garbled voices, the whine of encrypted bursts and stabbing eruptions of white noise. Grimacing at the violent sound, the *Heicho* pulled out her own comp and started to filter background noise and countermeasures out of the voice streams.

"Comm is pretty well shot," she said on Koshō's command channel twenty minutes later. "Someone's jamming the Regimental net and the only other clear transmission I can pick up is some scientist yelling for help down at Fehrupuré."

The *Sho-sa* barely reacted. Koshō had been keeping an eye on the shuttle's flight path and trying to raise the *Cornuelle*. The ship had still not responded. With an effort, she focused on the Marine sitting across from her. "The University excavations are under attack?"

Felix nodded, wondering how long it would take the officer to break out of her funk. "It's a big operation, I guess. They've barricaded themselves in the camp and are keeping a mob of slicks back with sidearms and jury-rigged flamethrowers." She glanced at her chrono and a map on her comp. "If we turned around, we could be at the dig site in just under an hour . . ."

"No." Koshō stirred. Her face was beginning to lose its ashen tone. "We're heading directly to the Legation in Parus. I expect the Regimental cantonment to be under heavy attack by . . . whoever is attacking the Imperial presence here. We can set down in the gardens and disembark behind fortified walls." The *Sho-sa* tabbed through a series of displays on her comp, then nodded to herself. "There is a primary orbital uplink at the Residence as well. We can use that to punch through the jamming to the *Cornuelle*."

Felix said nothing, carefully examining the service patches on the man squeezed in next to her. *Purely hopeful of the* Sho-sa *to believe the ship's still up there and not shattered wreckage and a slowly expanding plume of radiation.* She clenched her teeth together. *They're all dead. Huémac and Fitz and the captain and everyone. All just ash and vapor.*

"The city is coming up, *Sho-sa*," the *Heicho* said, recognizing the steadily increasing sprawl of buildings appearing in the camera view. They raced over kilometers of warehouses and rundown apartment blocks and scattered parks and gardens. The streets appeared to be deserted, which the Marine didn't think was a good sign. Huge clouds of black smoke blotted out the horizon, mixing with puffy rain clouds. "Looks like there's fighting . . ."

"Turn right on the next boulevard," Susan said briskly, one eye on a map of Parus on her comp and one eye on the forward camera feed. "Keep low."

The shuttle boomed across a district of row-houses and sliced into a shallow curve. Lines of trees blurred past beneath the wings, the shockwave of the aircraft's passing shaking their limbs and stirring up whirlwinds of leaves and dirt from the streets. Those few Jehanan still out fled into the doorways of abandoned shops or cowered under their runner-carts.

Empty intersections appeared and flashed past, and the sweeping arc of an ancient Haraphan road led them towards the center of the city. Tall buildings began to appear—the clifflike shapes of *khus* and the lower, elaborately domed structures of old palaces and temples. Koshō saw the first evidence of fighting—a bus of Imperial manufacture burning beside the road—and then running Jehanan with guns.

Brief glimpses of gangs of natives pillaging shops and overturning imported vehicles followed. A Jehanan tank rumbling down a side-street, main gun swinging from side to side. A line of civilians on a rooftop, handing packages from hand to hand out of a building gushing flame and smoke from its windows. Hundreds of snouted faces in a courtyard turning up at the booming sound of the shuttle's passage overhead. Clouds of sparkling glass bursting from the faces of buildings rocked by the supersonic shockwave rolling behind the shuttle.

I've got the Legation in sight. The pilot's voice cut across her reverie. *We've got hostile fire.*

Koshō stiffened, automatically checking her shockharness. The forward camera views expanded to fill her visor.

The dull red walls of the Legation were already shrouded with dirty gray smoke. Small-arms fire sparked here and there, but the majority of the haze was the result of a rippling wave of explosions bursting among the gardens and wooden buildings. Susan could see projectiles falling into the compound from the east. At least one structure inside the walls was already on fire.

"What is that?" she snapped, looking to Felix.

"Mortar fire," the *Heicho* replied, working her comp. The camera view rippled and the spidery web of a radar track superimposed on the image. Trailing arcs from puffs of white smoke raised by bursting mortar rounds arrowed back over the wall to a nearby park. Susan zoomed part of the image on a subsidiary v-pane, saw rows of tubular weapons squatting amid crowds of busy Jehanan gunners and support vehicles. Scowling, she locked the coordinates of the park into comp and mashed an override glyph.

A *Sagant* free-flying munitions canister spat from a pod embedded in the right wing, making the shuttle jerk slightly before the pilot could correct.

Hey! he complained over the channel. *Let me know before you—*

"Get us down." Koshō snarled, expanding her radar coverage, fingers light on the tiny display. "I'll handle weapons."

Felix watched with professional interest as the *Sagant* flashed away from the shuttle, popped up over the park and blew apart into hundreds of sub-munitions. The Jehanan on the ground were already scattering from the sharp *crack!* overhead, but none of them was fast enough to escape the cloud of black marbles spilling down out of the sky.

A roughly circular area two blocks wide erupted in flame. The park, the trees, the mortars, the trucks carrying their ammunition and fifty or sixty houses were obliterated in an instant. Air rushed into the blast vacuum, igniting dozens of fires in the shattered rubble. A black cloud whooshed up.

The shuttle braked again, engines roaring as the thrust ducts rotated down, and ornamental fruit trees in the gardens below lost their foliage. A whirling cloud of dust, rocks, splintered wood and debris clattered against the windows of the Legation buildings. Landing gear rotated out of the hull, maneuvering jets flared and the pilot slewed down to a perfect three-point landing. One of the wheels crashed through a gazebo of light wood, crunching into hand-laid blue and yellow tiles.

Felix was already at the landing door, hand slapping the controls. Servos whined and a crack of daylight appeared. "Gear up!" she shouted on the command channel. "Dispersed deployment on the deck—the enemy has artillery—we don't know where the friendlies are! Engineers in the back with the *Sho-sa!*"

The turbines whined down as the landing gear groaned to take the full weight of the shuttle. *Heicho* Felix darted down the loading ramp, her Macana at the ready. Sunlight blazed on her visor and she ducked to the left, rifle sweeping the face of the nearest building. Her Marines scattered left and right, forming a perimeter twenty meters from the shuttle. Felix turned, waving the engineers out of the aircraft.

"Everybody—" There was a shriek of rocket engines and something blurred at the edge of her vision. Her visor flashed a warning, silhouetting an arrowlike shape. Instantly, Felix threw herself behind the nearest cover, which was an ornamental hedge in a brick planter. "—down! Incoming!"

The missile impacted on the rear ventral surface of the shuttle, shredding armor and metal as its warhead erupted. The surface flexed, tormented by a piercing jet of superheated plasma, and the shuttle convulsed as the ablative armor drank up the heat-flow like a sponge. The outer skin layer shattered, sending white-hot hexagonal flakes whistling across the gardens, breaking windows and shredding the trees. Dozens of secondary fires sprang up where they fell.

A pressure wave of heat and flame smashed down, grinding Felix's visor into the dirt. Cursing, she rolled up, her combat visor reacting to the blast with a polarizing sheen and a flashing icon showing the firing source for the attack.

"Missile team in the skyscraper south-southeast," she bawled, swinging the Macana to her shoulder. "Top quarter, right-hand side! Suppressive fire, all units!"

The roar of a Whipsaw cutting loose off to her left deafened the Marine, and her own fire from the automatic rifle was instantly lost as the flechette storm from the squad support weapon stabbed across the intervening distance—the *khus* was at least four blocks away—and ripped across the face of the building. Windows exploded, concrete disintegrated and an entire apartment vanished in a gout of flame as the stream of 1mm stiletto rounds licked across the second Kärrhök as the missile team was maneuvering the weapon into position.

Felix dropped her rifle, eyeballing the plume of smoke belching from the side of the building. "Whipsaw on artillery suppression," she snapped, gesturing for the squad support weapon fireteam to head for the main buildings. "Get onto the roof, cover these skyscrapers, torch anything that moves!"

Then she had time to turn back to the shuttle. The aircraft was engulfed in flame, the entire rear third smashed into ruin. Oily black smoke roared up from burning vegetation all around. One wing had been torn straight off and now tipped forward at an awkward angle. The matching landing gear was skewed out like a broken leg.

"*Sho-sa* Koshō!" Felix felt her stomach twist into a cruel knot. She scrambled forward through smoldering rose bushes. "Second team, with me. We've got to get Fleet out of there!"

Waves of heat beat at her face and the *Heicho* wished she were in full powered armor. She ducked under the broken wing once she saw the entire rear loading ramp structure was twisted into a snarl of blackened metal and armor plating. The fire-suppression system inside the aircraft was coughing foam, but failing to dampen the blaze. The hex-skin of the shuttle popped and hissed, glowing cherry red. She ran forward, wondering if the forward crew doors were still operable.

The door seemed intact, but the access plate cover was bent and refused to open under her reaching fingers. *I'm too damn short*, she snarled to herself, quick fingers unfolding a cutting tool. "Carlyle! Get over here and lift me up—"

A white-hot point appeared at the edge of the door. The two Marines who'd come at her call fell back, surprised. Felix watched for a bare second—saw the point travel upwards, shearing through the armored door—and jumped out of the way before the cutting torch beam clove through her right arm.

"Stand back," she shouted, ducking down under the curve of the shuttle body itself. She was sweating furiously—the whole shuttleskin was bleeding heat at a tremendous rate—and the grass under her boots crisped black.

The cutting torch cut off, a ringing clang followed and the entire lock mechanism flew out. Two Marines reached up as the door ground up and seized hold of the first body pushed out of the stricken aircraft. Felix wiped her brow, half blinded by sweat, and keyed up her all-units channel.

"Form on the shuttle," she barked. "We've got wounded and we need to get them under cover to medical."

Another explosion shook the grounds and the upper floor of the Library tumbled down into an ornamental pool. The staccato roar of the Whipsaw followed before the rumbling boom of the rocket blast had faded. Felix slid out into the open, turning to cover the gardens with her rifle, and caught sight of a dull black Fleet z-suit being lowered from the shuttle door. Helsdon was silhouetted there, his back to raging flames, face tight with pain, hands steady as he handed *Sho-sa* Koshō down to Carlyle.

The commander's face was sheened with crimson and her visor was gone, ripped away by the explosion. Long black hair, matted with blood, clung to her neck and suit. Felix felt time slow, hand reaching out to seize the woman's med-band and turn the strip of metal around. There were too many winking red lights.

"Let's go!" The *Heicho* slapped Carlyle on his shoulder, shoving him and his burden towards the Residence. "Go–go–go!" Felix reached up, took Helsdon's hand and helped the engineer jump down. The broken shuttle groaned, metal twisting in the inferno burning inside, and they ran across the flat, trimmed sward of a zenball field towards the garden doors.

The Whipsaw on the roof roared again, now mounted on a tripod and slaved to the gunner's suit sensors. Another rocket shrieked across the grounds and brushed a stream of flechettes. The weapon staggered in the air, belching flame. Riddled with millimeter-wide punctures, the remains of the missile plowed through the rose bushes, crashed into a low brick wall and failed to detonate.

A SUB-BASEMENT
THE DISTRICT OF POISONERS, PARUS

Lachlan scowled, black hair falling into his eyes, and thumbed up a system status display on his primary v-pane. He itched, his stomach was cramped from hunger, and the entire room smelled very sharply of sweat, fatigue and half-heated three-squares. Dozens of tiny rectangles appeared on the v-pane, showing the status of his surveillance network in the cities of the Phison valley. Two-thirds or more of the v-feeds were blank or showing a skull-glyph indicating the spyeye or stationary relay camera was dead or unreachable.

A truly enormous headache was being held at bay by his medband, but the Éirishman could still feel the pressure behind a thin drug-induced veil.

"Sir?"

He looked up and saw one of the surveillance technicians, her shirt stained with sweat, standing up at her console, an old-fashioned landline phone in her hands. "What is it?"

"I've . . . I've got a call for you, sir." The technician held out the ancient-looking, enameled plastic device. "From a long-distance office in Gandaris. It's the Resident's wife, Mrs. Petrel. She says . . . she says the city has risen up against the Imperial presence, Prince Tezozómoc has disappeared, there's rioting in the streets and she needs immediate extraction for herself and her ladies-in-waiting."

Lachlan rubbed his eyes. *This just gets better and better, doesn't it?* He cleared away the spyeye diagnostic with a sweep of his hand and tapped up a map of the northern city. "We've no way to pick her up by air. She'll have to make her way out on the ground. Where exactly are they?"

The technician mumbled into her phone—the Éirishman stifled a brittle laugh, amused to see her using such an antiquated device. *But here? It's the very latest in native-tech!* When the Old Woman had pressed him to use the ancient native telecom network linking Parus and some of the larger cities, he'd balked—arguing their work crews and technicians would be better employed ramping up the comm relay network—but she'd insisted on having a backup for the backup. *Now six-hundred-year-old cables are carrying nearly a third of our data traffic . . .*

Until the arrival of the Imperials, the old Arthavan-period fiber-optic network buried beneath Takshila, Parus and the other cities had gone unused and apparently forgotten. The sealed cables and their conduits were still in place—the lack of tectonic activity in the land of the Five Rivers had allowed them to remain mostly untouched as the centuries passed—but the new Jehanan civilization struggling up from the ruins had lost the equipment to access the physical network. Rigging adapters to allow Imperial comm to use the outmoded multiplexed fiber had been a bit tricky, but Mirror technicians were nothing if not resourceful.

"She says they're hiding in one of our safe houses downtown. Number sixteen, on Quelling Tongue street." The technician rubbed her ear, waiting for Lachlan to consider the alternatives displayed on the map.

"I see. They're four blocks from the railway terminal." He tapped up a timetable, nodded to himself and tabbed through a series of native agent biographies the comp had on hand. "Tell her to get to the station and find a ticket clerk named Hundun Pao—he's one of ours—there should be an express train to Parus leaving in about . . . three hours." The Éirishman smiled grimly. "Assuming the trains are still running, and Petrel and her girls aren't killed or captured on the way."

The technician swallowed and began speaking rapidly into the phone.

I'm a travel service, Lachlan thought, rather bitterly. *What a disaster. . . . Fetching and carrying for the Anglish of all people!*

THE DISTRICT OF OPEN EYES
TAKSHILA, WHERE ONCE SRA HAYKAN DEVISED A PERFECT GRAMMAR

Gretchen was running along a walkway, dusky-yellow flowers carpeting the rooftops on either side of her, when the overcast sky turned the color of spoiled milk. Her comm had only just woken to life, and she caught Magdalena's voice growling imprecations at Parker, when a roar of static drowned everything out and her earbug squealed painfully.

Disoriented, she fell sprawling on the wooden planks. Her right knee twisted painfully and the survey comp jammed into her stomach.

"Oooof!" Anderssen dug out the earbug, eyes watering, and flung away the suddenly-hot metal, a brief spark of metallic glitter disappearing into the field of poppylike flowers. "Damn!"

Gingerly, she rubbed her ear, wondering if she'd been burnt. The queer light in the sky began to fade and Gretchen looked up, childhood memories waking in response to the odd radiance stabbing through the clouds.

A misaligned three-d projector is buzzing behind her, casting an image of gray seas under a leaden sky at the front of her classroom. A shape moves beneath the waters, an enormous black whale of steel and carbon-composite fibers. Hatches open, something bursts forth from the heaving sea, an engine ignites and a sleek dagger roars away across the wave tops. Rain hammers down from the storm clouds, muting the distinctive sound of the launch.

The Swedish Royal Navy cruise missile extends stubby wings and increases its speed, darting in and out of wave troughs thrown up by the storm. The North Sea is blanketed by a raging gale, the first onset of winter pressing down from the pole. Under the cover of howling winds, three Vasa*-class attack submarines lead off the strike against the Skawtish mainland.*

Dozens more cruise missiles, interspersed with decoys and Shrike*-class radar jammers burst from the waters.*

The cruise missile flashes across the Firth of Forth, dappled skin matching the waves, countermeasures shrugging aside the backscatter of Imperial over-the-horizon radar watching the sky and sea. The complex of submarine nets beneath the water do nothing to slow the missile and the choppy whitecaps confuse the low-altitude radar mounted on Arthur's Seat above the city. Even the coast watch is inside, huddled around their heaters. The winters have been growing worse again—too much atmospheric dust remains from the Blow at the beginning of the war. The bleating of alarms from their comm panels is ignored for a moment—the European Alliance fleet has been nosing about for months, tripping the sensors deployed across the sea floor—and until today there had never been a hint of actual hostilities.

At the mouth of the river Forth, the missile pops up above the dockyards, maneuvering vents jetting flame, and at last exposes itself to the fortifications on the hills above the bombed-out town. The nearest air-defense bunker retracts its armored dome, gatling cannon nosing out. But the guns react a fraction too slowly to prevent the cruise missile from detonating.

For the first time in the European theatre of war, an atomic weapon is used. Everything is blotted out by a sun-bright flash as the Varkan*-class tactical nuclear warhead detonates. The city districts nearest the river mouth are instantly engulfed in raging, superheated plasma. A shockwave batters the town, toppling the ancient walls of the Castle, smashing windows and crumpling houses all up the long valley of the Forth. Buildings shatter, trapping thousands of women and children in their shelters. Every radar installation within line of sight is blinded and most are wrecked outright. The Imperial troops in the fortifications around the Firth are incinerated or stunned by the glare of the pocket-sized star.*

Further north, Aberdeen and Dundee suffer similar fates. The entire air-defense network of eastern Skawtland fails, mortally wounded. At sea, wrapped in the raging storm, a combined Swedish-Russian-Danish fleet races forward. Already steam catapults are hurling aircraft from the decks of the carriers, filling the sky with a raging howl as they race treacherously westward against the island fortress . . .

For a moment Anderssen saw nothing but rushing clouds heavy with rain. Then a tumbling, flashing spark of light caught her eye. One of the archaic aircraft was spinning out of control, plunging towards the city. Anderssen watched in fascinated horror as the raptor-winged jet whistled down, engines dead, and plowed directly into the side of one of the towering *khus* rising from the center of the city. The metallic shape slammed into a cliff of yellowed concrete in a gout of dust and black smoke. A dirty cloud roiled out, spilling glittering debris down the face of the apartment building. A tongue of flame stabbed through the dust, followed by a rush of black smoke. In the blink of an eye, the aircraft was gone, leaving a gaping hole in the side of the *khus*. Dull reddish light spread across the row of windows.

Gretchen turned her wrist over, exposing her medband. A warning glyph flashed, indicating a radiation exposure warning. She bit her lip, watching the indicator change. *Not bad*, she saw. *Still a good thing I've got a medband and my allotment of children.* "Beautiful . . . all our comms will be shot."

The clatter of broad, leathery feet on wooden planks made her turn. Huffing and puffing, long snout gaping wide, Malakar approached at a run. Seeing the human had stopped, the Jehanan slowed in exhaustion and dropped long hands to the walkway.

"What—*hoooooo*, I've not been so hot in an age!—makes you pause in your flight, little thief?"

"Did you see the lights in the sky?" Gretchen was breathing shallowly and felt a little dizzy. The medband was dumping radiation cleansers into her bloodstream and they made her skin itch. "The crashing aircraft?"

"I did." Malakar slumped forward. Her back scales flexed up on ridges of muscle beneath the integument, increasing her surface area and making the Jehanan look like a huge porcupine. "This makes you give pause? Pricks your conscience?"

Gretchen shook her head. "You've no stories of Arthava's Fire in communal memory? No tales of the heavens bleeding flame or cruel killing light stretching from horizon to horizon?"

"*Hrrrr . . .* " The Jehanan looked up, eyes searching the clouds. They continued to roll past, spitting rain over some neighborhoods, parted here and there by gusts in the upper air. "I see no demons towering over the sky, flesh made of smoke, eyes roaring pits of fire . . ."

"No, not today. You're describing a citykiller cloud. This was an ECOM suppression blast at the edge of the Jaganite atmosphere." She tapped her ear, trying to muster a wry smile. "Every unshielded electronic device in this hemisphere will have just died. Every exposed comp will be scrambled."

"And so, why do you—ah, your stolen data is no more." Malakar trilled heartily. "The grilled *skomsh* has fallen to the ground! Soiled! Inedible! All your clever tools and devices rendered useless . . ." She laughed again, bellowlike lungs heaving.

Anderssen grimaced, stung by the accusation of theft. *Cheater!* A voice from memory cried, sounding very much like little Isabelle. *You took my share!*

"I don't care about the data right now," she said. "My friends have fled that *khus* and they're in danger and I can't find them without my comm."

The Jehanan looked up, nostrils wrinkling. "Why would they flee a fine warm sleeping pit?"

Gretchen pointed across the rooftops towards the southeast. "Someone is attacking Imperial citizens, remember? Our landlord will inform the authorities of our presence. . . . Who else but the *kujen* could have attack craft like those?"

"*Hoooo* . . . Some truth there." Malakar swung her head from side to side. "The *kujen* has a face of paper and ink, he does. He snuffles in the dirt before the *asuchau* and then spits on their tails as they turn away." A claw scratched the side of her jaw. "One wonders . . . Rumor has long legs among our people; often soft voices flutter about the lamps in the night, telling tales of secret excavations in the old cities and forgotten machines made whole again . . ."

"Like the *kalpataru*," Anderssen said grimly, testing her knee and wincing a little. "I need to find my friends. My apologies, but I must go."

"*Hooo* now!" Malakar levered herself up, alarmed. "Do not be rash! There is the matter of the divine tree . . ." Her voice trailed off abruptly.

Gretchen unsealed the pouch around her comp and removed the device. The screen was dull, showing no lights. "You see? It's been fried like a *skomsh*. I'll need another undamaged comp to extract the data from this one. Then I'll need time to analyze the remains. . . . I don't know if I would be able to answer any of our questions. Please, let me go. My friends may be hurt, or taken prisoner or dead."

"Then leave them behind!" The old Jehanan reached out a claw, beckoning for the comp. "I know places to hide, perhaps we can even find a working one of . . . these things . . . from a merchant."

"I'm sorry." Gretchen placed the comp in Malakar's hand. "Magdalena and Parker aren't quite my hatchlings, but they are my family. I won't abandon them." She straightened her shoulders, gave Malakar a sharp look and turned away.

"*Hoooo!* You can't . . . come back here! Human! Where are you going?"

The sound of glass shattering and angry hooting gave Anderssen pause. She had been following a lane heading down towards the *khus* holding their rooms and now the narrow street had reached a boulevard. A steep flight of steps led down to the edge of the curving road. Pressing herself against a plastered wall, she peered around the corner.

The broad avenue was empty of runner-carts and wagons and the usual throng of busy citizens—but a large crowd of Jehanan youths were busily smashing windows and dragging merchandise out onto the sidewalks. One store was on fire, belching clouds of heavy white smoke. An angry, grumbling sound filled the air. Gretchen squinted, letting the goggles zoom in, and saw two short-horns then hurl an Imperial three-d set into the flames with a resounding crash. A hooting cheer rose at the burst of sparks.

"Well, that's just typical . . ." Anderssen looked the other direction. More gangs of youths in fancy scale-paint and masks prowled the avenue, smashing windows and throwing firebombs into the shops. Some of the short-horns had bags of loot hanging from their shoulders. A bitter, sharp smell of burning wood and plastic permeated the air. Thin, flat drifts of smoke coiled between the ancient trees lining the road.

There seemed to be no way to reach the *khus* without crossing into plain view.

Worried, Gretchen turned, wondering if she could find a way around on the rooftops. The walkways above had been completely deserted and she guessed the more sensible locals had gotten the hatchlings inside, locked their doors and were going to wait out the rioting with eyes closed. The tall shape of the apartment building seemed intact but she couldn't get close enough to see the lobby entrance.

Malakar was waiting, looming over her, the dead comp strapped to her chest bone beneath the usual Jehanan harness. Anderssen flinched and made a face, angry with herself for not hearing the creature creep up behind her.

"*Hoooo!* You jump like a *skomsh* fresh-caught in a net! I hear angry voices out there. . . . They are not snuffling before the Empire today, no . . . but how will you find your friends? They are far away if you cannot cross the boulevard!"

That is an excellent question, Gretchen thought. "I made a mistake," she snapped. "I expected our comms to work—our first rendezvous is at the train station. But they might still be waiting—"

Malakar stiffened, raising a single clawed finger, head turning to one side. "Wait, *asuchau*, I am hearing strange sounds . . . like a steam-loom of vast size . . ."

Anderssen peered out onto the street again and swallowed a curse. A huge tracked military vehicle—*an armored personnel carrier?*—rumbled down the avenue. At the sight of the apparition, the gangs of looters scattered, throwing down their prizes. Jehanan in body-armor loped alongside the clanking, rattling machine, and they held stubby rifles in their claws. Their eyes were in constant movement, yet they ignored the fleeing short-horns.

"The army," she breathed, ducking back. She looked up at Malakar. "The *kujen*'s men are sweeping the streets. But not for looters! Is there somewhere I can hide until they pass?"

The old Jehanan's snout twisted in disgust. "The *kujen* . . . he will let the *paigim* short-horns run wild, wrecking the livelihood of many a shopkeeper, and do nothing as long as they bite Imperial tails! But do you *asuchau* suffer? No! Only the meek who sought to turn over a single *shatamanu* in profit. So are the powerless ground fine between mill stones . . ." A rumbling and muttering followed. The growl of engines and the stamp of swift feet grew closer.

"Come on," Gretchen said, seizing Malakar's arm, trying to drag her back down the lane. "Up the stairs at least!"

"No, not that way." The gardener wrenched her arm free and strode past the stone staircase. She ducked behind the out-thrust stone and down into a ramp cutting into the earth. "This way, if you must cross the avenue . . ."

Anderssen followed, one eyebrow raised as they shuffled down the ramp, past one, and then two thick layers of rubble and into a vaulting hallway running at an angle to the lane above. Lamps hung from the vaults every ten meters, spilling a warm oil-glow through faces of colored glass. Her eyes flitted across other openings, recognizing doorways built to a different esthetic. The floor beneath her feet was uneven, but lined with irregular slabs. *This* is *an old city, layer heaped upon layer over the millennia.*

Gretchen hurried after the gardener, who had pressed on while she gawked at the archaeological evidence all around her. Other Jehanan passed in the opposite direction, glancing at her suspiciously as they passed. "Malakar—do these tunnels run under the whole city? Are there more levels below this one?"

The passage reached an intersection, splitting into three branches, and light spilled from an open doorway. A squat dome—cracked in places and repaired with brick pylons—hung over the open space. Many lamps hung down on chains. A Jehanan matron followed by two hatchlings emerged from one of the shops, two woven bags in her arms. Anderssen smelled fresh baked bread and realized she was terribly hungry.

"*Hrrr.* . . . yes, there are many hidden ways beneath the city. These are the districts where the poor live, far from the sun, but warm withal. Do you feel the age of these stones? Sometimes one can find old doors like the ones in the Garden, but only down where it is dangerous to tread." The old Jehanan paused, her gaze following Anderssen's intent expression. "Do *asuchau* eat milled grain baked and risen? You look much like a hatchling eyeing the pastry as it cools!"

"Yes—that smells delicious. My grandmother baked bread every day when we were little."

Malakar went to the doorway, nodding politely to another customer leaving the bakery. In the warm lamplight light she seemed younger somehow, or less burdened by age and care. The old Jehanan made a clicking sound with her teeth and pointed with her snout. "Do you see the figurines of clay above the hearth?"

Anderssen nodded, looking around curiously at the shelves filled with bread. The bricks were markedly different in shape from those she'd seen in the buildings at street level. From the slightly irregular pattern, she guessed they had been hand-pressed into wooden forms and fired in a kiln on sheets of marble. Behind the stone-topped counter, a short-snouted Jehanan was kneading dough into loaves. Above the hearth and the half-circle mouths of his baking ovens, she saw rows of small figures—most seemed Jehanan in outline, though some were insectile and a few were outright monsters with horrific features. The lamp- and fire-light danced upon them, giving their painted features uncanny life.

"Are they gods? Protective spirits? Amulets to ward away disease and poison from the bread?"

Malakar nodded, clasping her claws to her chest. She seemed pensive. "This one believes in the old ways. Legends even in the annals of the Garden. Look at him," she whispered in Gretchen's ear. "I envy this one. He is content at his task—as was his father and his father's father—there has been a bakery here for an age of Jehanan. . . . There he spills grain meal every day, paying homage to all the faces of god. A tiny offering, a single prayer. And for *him* this suffices; brings him closer to the *yigal*, what you might call *the real*. For this—his work, his prayer, his simple life—is the proper path for *him*. He is the luckiest of Jehanan—and his pastries and milled loaves are the finest in the city."

"You envy him?" Anderssen frowned a little, suddenly understanding the half-hidden grief in the gardener's voice. "You've lost your own path, haven't you? You were the last teacher to use that school room in the depths of the House. The last person to look at the murals on the walls . . ."

Malakar hooted sadly. "I was happy there, tending young sprouts and making them grow strong. Perhaps even wise . . . I was not the only gardener, but I was the last to teach the old ways, tell the tales of ships which passed between the stars and the might of the Jehanan of old. But I could not still this unwary tongue of mine and those with more cunning minds saw I was left with nothing but scraps and broken shells."

Gretchen pressed her hand against the old Jehanan's scales, feeling the heat of the body beneath, feeling tough scalloped ridges and parchment-thin edges. "Could you leave the House? Seek a position elsewhere? Find some other garden to tend?"

"*Hrrrr* . . . perhaps I could have done such a thing, when I was younger, but I did not. A great nuisance I made of myself instead! Bitterly I plagued them, until I had not even a mat to sleep on, or someone to sleep beside. But no one listened . . . and I was weary then, content simply to take my ration and avoid the eyes of those who'd once looked to me for guidance."

"Your life is not yet over," Gretchen said tentatively. "You could leave . . ."

The old Jehanan wrinkled her snout, giving Anderssen a sharp look. "So easily the words slip from your tongue, *asuchau* wanderer! If I mark your words right, you are sent hither and yon at the whim of your Company. You delight to see the unseen, to turn over rocks left alone for a hundred years, just to see what wiggles out! You are treading a path of choice and one which fits you well, if the look upon your pale, flat face when you are filled with questions is a reputable guide!"

"Working for the Company is not like that! Not all the time." Gretchen said, remembering endless days spent grubbing in the dirt for nothing, risking health and life to plumb the depths of some burial site or midden filled with explosive gasses. Remembering friends and acquaintances crippled or killed in accidents, or simply forgotten when crews were reassigned and split up. "There are moments though," she allowed, "when the toil and bureaucracy and misery of parting are worthwhile. But how often do those days come about? They are very rare!"

Malakar made an amused fluting sound. "Then why are you digging in *my* garden, poking about among *my* trees and stealing secret glances at *my* idols? You've not eaten for two days, you've forgotten your friends, and you just let these questions drag you by the snout from place to place without the slightest care!"

"Maybe." Gretchen felt disgruntled. *Stupid lizard, pointing out the obvious to me!* "If this is my path to the real, then I would like another! One where I can stay home and read books by the heater and watch my children grow up and be successful! One without all the mud and grime and dirt and sleepless nights in spaceport terminals, watching to make sure my baggage isn't stolen!"

"*Hur-hur-hur!*" Malakar swung her head from side to side. "How long would that last? You would be sneaking away to spaceport with your traveling bag in hand by year's end. *Hurrr* . . . Do you wish a pastry? I am hungry now."

The Jehanan went inside, fluting a greeting to the baker.

"I need to find Maggie and Parker," Gretchen called after her. *But they're not going to know about these tunnels, which means if they've not been captured, they will head to the train station and then south to Parus. If they heard my voice—I think they did, but how much of what happened in the vault was real?*

Malakar reappeared and pressed a bun straight from the oven into her hand.

"Ow! These are hot!" Anderssen tossed the crusted pastry from hand to hand.

The Jehanan chewed vigorously, having swallowed the bun whole, and nodded her head.

"Ah . . . very tasty. These are stuffed with *pang* nuts and *melle*. Very sweet. They will drive your hunger away. What were you saying?"

Gretchen pointed with her chin at the ceiling. "Does this passage lead to the *khus*?"

"There is a ramp quite near your building." Malakar allowed, eyeing the uneaten bun in the human's hands. "But if the prince's soldiers are in the streets, will your friends wait? I cannot imagine any creature with an ear and an eye could miss the sound of that machine in movement."

"You could be right," Anderssen nodded, nibbling at the edge of the still-hot pastry. "They'll try to reach the train station and get south to Parus if they don't find me there."

"*Hooooo* . . . " Malakar tapped Gretchen's chest thoughtfully, one claw brushing against the dead comp. "Will the Magdalena and the Parker have another device like this? One which works?"

Gretchen frowned up at the Jehanan. "If they were under cover of some kind when the EMP wave hit the city, yes. Maggie has four or five comps with her—she collects them like Parker collects . . . well, Parker doesn't really collect anything but tabac tar . . ."

The gardener pointed down one of the passages. "The iron road can be reached by following certain ways beneath the city—but if the *kujen* is hunting for *asuchau* I fear his servants will throng the station like *yi* upon the corpses of fallen heroes. If your friends flee that way, they will be taken." Malakar's nostrils crinkled up. "If memory serves, there is only one train to Parus each day and that one not for many hours yet."

"Is there another way south?" Anderssen wracked her memory, trying to remember if there had been other options for local transport. *I shouldn't have just accepted Petrel's arrangements—we should have gotten an aerocar somehow, or a truck at least . . .*

"There is." The old Jehanan indicated a different passage. "Beyond the edge of the city is a *tikikit* station. We could be in Parus by morning if our legs are long enough. The *tikikit* do not care if Jehanan and *asuchau* are fighting!" She clicked her claws together in amusement. "They have seen such things many, many times and are no longer impressed."

Gretchen licked her lips, feeling worry surge in her breast. *What if Maggie and Parker are still waiting for me at the apartment?* But the brief perception of them on a rooftop implied they were already on the run, and somehow she thought they *had* heard her cry out of the green void. *The* kalpataru *was connected to every other communications device and comp on the planet in that one instant, I know it was. Mother Mary, please keep them safe. And me too. Keep me safe until we're all together again.*

"All right," Anderssen said, trying not to chew her lip. "Will you take me to this place? Are you sure we can get to Parus by morning?"

Several hours later, Gretchen and Malakar emerged from a tunnel on the eastern side of the city, following a footpath between disintegrating rows of concrete pilings. The sun was setting, the eastern sky growing dark, though the fields of grain on either side of the old subway line were gilded pink and bronze. Anderssen glanced up automatically and was disturbed to see the sky to the west bruised with odd, harsh colors. Auroralike patterns of filmy lights were strewn across the twilit sky.

Long trails of smoke rising over the city glowed in the failing light. High up, what looked like contrails criss-crossed the sky, though she didn't think any aircraft could have survived the electromagnetic shock wave from the explosions in orbit.

"How far is this station?" Anderssen wondered aloud, seeing the orchards on the far side of the grain fields were dusky with oncoming night. She automatically checked to make sure she still had her flashlight, and was relieved to feel cold metal under her fingers. "Have you taken this path before?"

"Not so long ago," Malakar answered, her stride quickening. The Jehanan's snout was raised, tasting the evening and the hum and chirp of insects rose and fell as they walked. There was a moist, humid feeling to the air and Gretchen was reminded of the lowland farm country around New Canarvon back home. "There is a wood-lot and then a village. The station is beyond, on the old road—but it is not far, not far at all."

They walked in silence for a time, passing out of the fields and onto a larger path—not quite a road, but close—which ran through rows of planted trees. Long straight trunks rose up over their heads, merging into a spreading roof of branches lined with heavy leaves. Anderssen's eye was drawn to the signs of pruning and trimming and guessed the section of woodland was a farm growing lumber for the city markets. Some of the newer prunings revealed a hexagonal pattern in the underlying wood.

"These are *lohaja*?" She gestured at the rows of trees. "This is a plantation?"

The old Jehanan grunted, twitching her nostrils. "Not every soil is suitable for the better woods—but these hills around Takshila are famous for their abundant crops and strong-growing trees. Even the *Nēm* flourish here, though you cannot claim their taste is sweet."

Then the creature sighed, grief settling over her and she fell silent.

"I'm sorry," Gretchen said, feeling guilty at having raised the question. "I've been lucky to do so much of what I wanted. My family sacrificed a great deal to see me on this long road— they still do, with my mother taking care of my children—and the pitiful wage the Company pays is not enough, not really, to make up the difference."

A low humming sound rose from the back of the Jehanan's throat. She fixed Anderssen with one dark eye. "And you say you've not found the right path to *yigal*? Do you bite your own tail in spite? Do you have two mouths to argue with yourself?"

"Ha! I suppose." Gretchen smiled. "I know how it feels to be denied, ridiculed, opposed at every turn. My clan is poorly favored in the Empire. We have no powerful friends. There are no tenured positions for me, no research grants or stipends. Most of my fellows from graduate school have actual posts at actual universities—or they oversee important sites—and me? I grub in the refuse on the edge of human space for a scattering of quills a day, looking for sites of interest to others. Then *they* do the real work, and I'm on to another world, bag in hand, exhausted, my boots needing repair . . ."

Malakar trilled, her mood entirely restored. "A perfect path for your tiny feet to walk! Do you truly enjoy the dull work of counting and measuring and making reports which must come after all this poking and prodding and prying into dusty, hidden places?"

"Yes, I do." Anderssen's professional sensibilities were outraged at such a suggestion, though at the same time a little voice was saying *Oh god, no!* "Survey is only the first step in a long process—the real work is in the analysis and conclusions at the end. I mean, how else will I get a position somewhere without publications? Without discrete evidence of my work?"

"*Hur-hur-hur!*" The gardener hid her snout behind both claws. "This old walnut thinks your path does not lead to the stuffy chambers of a Master, with acolytes fawning and snuffling at your feet. Your path lies at the edge of furrowed soil, it does, where there are strange shadows and queer lights among the trees, where every step is into the unknown. What wonders might you see, with undimmed eyes?

"*Hoooo* . . . Now, how do I interpret such a look as you now wear?"

Gretchen felt pressure grip her chest, driving the breath from her lungs, and a startlingly clear vision overwhelmed her seeing eyes, blotting out the rows of trees looming in the twilight, covering the wagon-tracks they had been following through the grass . . .

Bitterly cold wind lapped around her. Her hands were in the sand, one leg throbbing with pain. Glorious jewel-colored lights shone beneath her, lighting her face. Threads of crimson and sapphire and diamond-blue clung to her forearms, dragging her down. Something was moving in the darkness, a voice was speaking, but all she could see were the glittering pinpoints of the hathol *and the* firten *swarming to the bounty of her exhaled breath, drinking her carbon dioxide and waste gasses; growing, swarming, building chains of fire to trap her so they might feast on the energy reservoir of her body . . .*

"Ahhh!" Anderssen flinched back from Malakar's reaching claw and she stumbled into the brush lining the road. The Jehanan drew back in surprise, hissing. For an instant, before she blinked, Gretchen thought the rule-straight trees were limned with pale light, and the gardener was softly glowing in the twilight, every scale distinct in disturbingly clear sight. Then twilight enveloped her again and there were only stray glints of the sun on clouds high in the sky.

"What happened?" Malakar regarded her warily. "Your countenance changed."

"It's nothing." Anderssen was trembling and she batted uselessly at her legs and arms. *There aren't any crawling threads of living light on me. None. Not even one.* She felt strangely hot, as if she'd plunged her face, hands and arms into boiling water. *I don't think I was supposed to remember that. Hummingbird should complain to whoever sold him that memory eraser.* "Just old memories. Don't think this business of poking and prying is without peril."

"*Hooo!* True words." The gardener took hold of Gretchen's shoulders and set her back on the track with a gentle touch. "Paths are dangerous—if you follow, does it not lead? If you follow all the way, it must take you far from the safety of your own garden, out into brambles and marsh and among twisted rocks."

"I suppose." The last gleam of the sun faded, leaving them in complete darkness. Anderssen produced her flashlight. A cool light sprang out, illuminating the roots of the trees and setting stems of grass in sharp contrast. The flashlight made her feel better. *See? I can drive back the darkness!* "I don't want to follow a dangerous path! I want to do my job, get paid a reasonable wage and go home and talk to my kids about how their day went at school."

She laughed hollowly. "I've already been offered your far-traveled path, filled with spines and pricking wounds and bitter pills. A path into shadows and hidden places—where true secrets lie, not just the grave-goods and barrows of the dead. I said no then, and I'd say no now."

The gardener made a deep humming sound in the back of her throat. "*Hooo* . . . Of course. But this old walnut wonders . . ." Malakar reached out her claw into the beam of the flashlight, making a jagged, monstrous shadow spring up against the silver-barked trees. "Shadows imply light." Her claw withdrew, revealing the track winding ahead of them. "And a path, direction. You remind me of how much I have lost by fearing both."

"Fearing?" Anderssen began walking, finding the bare, widely spaced tree trunks oppressive. "You didn't fear to oppose the Master and his policies!"

"*Hooooo* . . . I feared to leave the Garden. What sprouts have gone untended elsewhere as I lay anguished on a mat in the common room, biting my own tail and dreaming useless thoughts of revenge and malice? Will I ever know?" Malakar lifted her snout, pointing ahead. "Do you see the lanterns?"

Gretchen angled the flashlight towards her feet. Her eyes adjusted and she saw—ahead, obscured by a line of trees—gold and silver lights and heard the rattle of drums and pipes. In the faint glow of distant lamps, she caught the outline of buildings, sharp rooftops, banners and the hot glow of a bonfire.

"Do you hear the voices?" The gardener picked up her pace. "*Nēmnahan* has begun!"

THE GEMMILSKY HOUSE
GANDARIS, "BASTION OF THE NORTH"

Crouched in darkness, Colmuir squinted at the view from one of the perimeter spyeyes. This one was focused down on the front gate from a realspruce tree, where the Jehanan soldiers had found the portal held closed by more than a simple wooden bar. Their commander—even at this range, staring at a reptilian face mostly obscured by black rubber goggles, the master sergeant could pick out an *officer*—waved his men back, then stepped smartly away. The entire gate structure shivered as the tank approached, cobblestones cracking under heavy treads. The armored behemoth—Colmuir counted one main gun, four cupola-mounted machine guns, some kind of grenade launcher on the turret and a smoke dispenser—ground down the lane, stopped, chuffed diesel smoke, and rotated ponderously on one set of treads.

"Just a moment," the master sergeant whispered. "He's at th' gate now."

The rumbling of dual engines carried even through the tiny microphone on the spyeye, as did the grating scrape of dozer blades emerging from the front of the machine. Gears shifted, generating a violent rattling sound, and the tank rolled forward, belching exhaust, and slammed squarely into the gate.

"Go!" Colmuir growled, feeling the ground shake. He thumbed a glyph depicting a conical mountain belching flame. In the spyeye view, he saw the front gate shatter, torn off its hinges by the weight of the tank. The stone pillars on either side of the entrance shuddered, but stood firm until the armored shoulders of the machine ground into them. Then ancient granite split, spewing dust and the entire structure collapsed backwards. The tank rolled up over the debris, treads spinning and crashed down on the other side. Jehanan soldiers darted into the opening, automatic rifles at the ready.

Two Imperial Marine issue *Fougasse* antipersonnel mines hidden in the verge a dozen paces back from the gate detonated as the tank rumbled past onto the lawn. Each popped up from the hedge to chest height and blew apart. A shockwave of flame, choking smoke and fingertip sized needles smashed across the Jehanan infantry. The invaders were thrown backwards by the blast and their body armor, uniforms and exposed scales were shredded by the glassite projectiles. Wherever the needles punched through scale into flesh, they splintered into wicked monofil buzzsaws, shredding muscle, ligament and bone. The entire lead squad crumpled in a spray of blood.

The Jehanan officer cursed, ordered his men to hurl grenades into the foliage and led the second squad onto the grounds at a rush as soon as the blasts had cleared the way.

In the sub-basement of the house Dawd knelt between a sump pump and the old boiler, a blazing white-hot spark howling between his hands. Limestone flooring volatilized, boiling up around him in a dusty cloud. At the far end of the room, Colmuir had his back turned, attention wholly focused on his remotes. Tezozómoc stood between the master sergeant and the cutting beam, hands over his ears, desperately wishing for a drink, any kind of drink, even the barely refined gasoline the natives liked so much.

Dawd shifted his knees, drew the engineering tool back around to complete the circle and felt the stone and brick give way. The circular opening collapsed, spilling bricks and dust into a hidden pit. The edges glowed a dull red where the beam had sheared them to a glossy smoothness. The Skawtsman kicked the rest of the debris away.

Four meters below, a dry sewage tunnel was now filled with the litter from his efforts. Gemmilsky had installed new pipes and a modern sewage recycling module in one of the gardening sheds. The *previous* owner, however, had been forced to pump all of his waste into the common city drainage. During construction of the new house, all of the old sewage, water and power adits had been sealed up with brick, plaster and a new coat of paint.

"Clear!" Dawd called to the prince and the master sergeant. He squeezed himself down into the opening, hung by his hands for a moment and then dropped down into the old tunnel. The sergeant's combat visor switched into infrared, he glanced both ways and saw the passage was empty. "Come on, mi'lord. We've got to move quickly."

The prince swung over the edge, closed his eyes, muttered a prayer to the

Beneficent and Merciful Jesus and dropped into the Eagle Knight's waiting arms. Dawd set the young man down in a rubble-free section of tunnel and tapped his comm. "Master Sergeant? Let's not be waiting about!"

"Just a second, lad. There's a wee bit more work to be done."

Colmuir rotated one of the spyeyes to scan the horizon. The aerocar which had brought them to Gandaris had departed at first light to deliver Mrs. Petrel and her ladies to the palace and return with 'refreshments.' The master sergeant assumed the use of *kujenai* troops to attack the mansion meant Clark, the aerocar and the civilians had all been seized by the *kujen*. He was waiting until the last moment, hoping the corporal would reappear.

The sky was overcast and gray and threatening a day of drizzling rain. There was no sign of the aerocar. Colmuir muttered six and a half kinds of curses to himself, tapped the last glyphs on his fuse screen and scurried to the pit.

A muffled series of thuds and booms filtered through the roof of the subbasement. The old foundation groaned, feeling the house above shift and sway. A distant crashing sound followed, and the lean Skawtsman imagined the entire portico toppling onto the tank and trapping the metal behemoth in a ruin of double-paned windows, marble statuary and triply-varnished *lohaja*-parquet flooring. He slapped two bomb packs on either side of the opening, gave them twenty minutes to live and dropped down into the darkness.

An hour later, Dawd used his combat knife to saw through the bar holding a sewer-grate closed and, after listening cautiously, stepped out into a domed, brick-lined roundabout deep under the center of Gandaris. His Fleet medband chirped politely, informing him of excessive levels of methane, carbon dioxide and airborne bacteria in the newly entered atmosphere.

"Oh, gods of my fathers," the prince exclaimed, splashing clumsily into the grand sewer. "This place smells . . . *urk* . . . oh god . . ." Tezozómoc doubled over, nearly falling into the stream of dark brown effluvia streaming towards the river, and added a gagging heave of yellow bile to the greater collection of Gandarian waste. Dawd seized him by the upper arms and waited for the boy to finish his business.

"Excellent nose for navigation, lad." Colmuir closed the gate to the dry tunnel behind them and replaced the bar. "You've got a fix on the airport, then?"

"No airport in Gandaris, Master Sergeant." Dawd consulted his comp, which had been keeping track of the twists and turns in the sewer system. "Or we'd have landed there when we arrived. . . . That's odd, we've lost any comm signal but our own. The jamming must have gotten worse." He shook his head in dismay. "If Clark managed to escape with the aerocar, he won't be able to raise us, or find us, unless we're out in the open as he flies over, waving the locust-flag of Chapultepec over our heads."

"That won't happen," the master sergeant said, peering over Dawd's shoulder. "Options?"

"We could walk about a thousand kilometers to Parus," the younger Skawtsman said, tabbing up a map of Gandaris and the greater valley. The city spread up a series of terraced hillsides from the banks of the Kophen to reach the embrace of the higher peaks. The far side of the river was subdivided into agricultural plots, and then bisected by the railroad running southeast towards Bandopene. "We could steal an aerocar, if there was one to steal, and be back in Parus tonight."

"What . . ." The prince spat and cleared his mouth. "What about calling for someone to come and pick us up with a combat shuttle?"

"No comm," Dawd replied, shaking his head. "Or we could find a place to hide out, sit tight . . ."

Colmuir considered the map, removed a tabac from a half-crushed paperboard case, smelled the cigarette and put it back. Then he nodded to himself. "We take the train."

"What?" Dawd stared at him, surprised and horrified at the same time. "We'll be arrested at the station!"

"The train?" Prince Tezozómoc frowned. "Wait a moment . . . wasn't someone saying something about the train the other day? About . . . oh, who *was* that?"

Both Eagle Knights stared at him expectantly, but the young man shook his head, bemused. "Huh. Nothing." He rapped his head with his knuckles. "Empty as a gourd! I've forgotten who it was. Don't mind me."

"We don't," Colmuir said in an offhand way. He gave Dawd a tight little smile. "Now, laddie, you haven't lived until you've jumped a train, as my da would say. And he jumped one or two in his time. Now, which way t' the station?"

Dawd made a sour face, hitched up the assault rifle on his shoulder, consulted his comp and pointed up a tunnel spilling a slow, turgid sludge into the main sewer. "That way."

A gloved hand reached up, grasped hold of a marble lip around the urinal and Dawd heaved himself up and onto the floor of an empty restroom. The chuffing sound of a steam engine mixed with the hooting and warbling of Jehanan adults echoed in through high windows. The sergeant glanced around, making sure the large, stone-floored room was empty, and knelt to take the prince by the arms and hoist the boy up. Colmuir scrambled up through the wide-mouthed opening—Jehanan bathrooms were well appointed with ornamental stone, delicate carvings and elegant fixtures but consisted solely of a deep pit to raise tail over—and took a moment to let himself breathe cleaner air. The sharp smell of hot metal, coal dust and hundreds of natives rushing about trying to get aboard the afternoon express train filled his nostrils and he beamed a smile of relief at Tezozómoc, who was batting at legs dripping yellow-green ooze.

"Ah! Much better." The master sergeant considered their appearance and his smile faded. "Now, we must make ourselves presentable enough to cross the tracks and get aboard a luggage car—Dawd you think these faucets will work?"

The sergeant was at the doorway, peering out into the waiting hall with a perplexed expression on his face.

"Sergeant Dawd? Can you hear me?"

The younger Skawtsman shook his head, breaking out of something like a daydream and nodded. "Yes, Master Sergeant. I'll have a look at the faucets—but you should scope this . . ."

Grumbling to himself and waving the prince to stand beside the marble sink lining the wall—and out of the line of fire from the entrance—Colmuir edged up to the door and looked out. At first, all he saw was a melee of Jehanan—young and old alike, all dressed in harnesses hung with flowers, long narrow sun-hats and gaudy drapes and accompanied by a great deal of luggage in woven bags and heavy-looking steamer-style trunks—surging past. And then, much as the clouds might peel back from the mountaintops looming over the city, a troupe of monks in very tall, saffron-colored hats stamped past and he saw, waiting patiently beside the number four track schedule board, Mrs. Petrel and her two young ladies with no more luggage than their handbags, traditional Imperial festival clothes over flesh toned skinsuits and Army-issue umbrellas for parasols.

The Resident's wife seemed entirely composed and perfectly at ease. None of the Jehanan rushing about, hooting and trilling and warbling in their alien tongue, seemed to pay her the least attention.

Colmuir pursed his lips and wished he had a fresh pack of tabacs to hand. He looked back to the prince, saw Dawd had affixed a length of hose from his duty bag to the nearest faucet and was sluicing the sewer ooze from the boy's legs, made up his mind to escape the train station *somehow* and looked back in time to have his heart lurch into his throat.

The auburn-haired of the two girls accompanying Mrs. Petrel was hurrying through the crowd, directly towards the bathroom, with a very determined expression on her face.

"Ah that's torn it," Colmuir cursed, stepping back out of sight. "Dawd, get that hose on me swift-like, we've company coming t' dinner."

The master sergeant had managed to clean off his gear, though his uniform legs and underlying combatskin were still dripping wet when the girl strode into the bathroom and took the sight of the three of them in with a frown.

"Do you have *any* other clothes," she said, in a brisk tone very reminiscent of her mistress. "Capes or something to drape about all your . . . guns and tools and things?"

"We do," Tezozómoc said, while both Eagle Knights were goggling at the audacity of a rather prim-looking Nisei girl barging into the gentleman's restroom.

The prince tapped Dawd on the shoulder. "Sergeant, do you have a rain-cape in the back pocket of your gunrig?"

Dawd blinked, nodded and turned to let Tezozómoc unseal the pouch and drag out a rain poncho. "They're autocamo—" the sergeant started to say, but the prince had already turned the poncho inside out and found the little control panel woven into the waterproof fabric.

"Very useful," Tezozómoc said cheerfully, using his thumbs to switch through the settings, "if you'd like to just sit quietly outside of headquarters and, ah, have a smoke or something . . ." He winked at the girl, which made her stiffen slightly. "Big enough for two, most times."

The rain cloak settled into a dull pattern of interlocking brown and yellow-green triangles. The prince swung the garment around Dawd's shoulders, drew the hood mostly over his face and snapped the bottom straight. The sergeant stared down at himself and realized the young man had chosen a pattern close to the coloring of Jehanan scales.

"You too, Master Sergeant." Tezozómoc nodded to Colmuir and then looked at himself. The Fleet skinsuit he'd donned in the house was dull black, like most Imperial garments, and had its own autocamo capability, but being skin-tight, made him look far too human in outline.

"Miss." He looked at the Nisei girl. "Does your mistress have any local money?"

The Parus Express shuddered into motion, the linkages between the cars drawing tight one by one, clouds of steam and coal-smoke billowing up against a glassed-in ceiling. In the next to last car, Colmuir squeezed into a reserved compartment and immediately drew the window curtains closed. The clashing of wheels on the tracks drowned out all other sound until the door slammed shut behind Dawd.

Then something like silence—save for the swinging rattle of the train car itself, and the assorted sighs of relief from the six humans in the compartment—settled around him.

"Now," the master sergeant said, sitting down beside the prince, "that was some quick thinking, mi'lady."

Greta Petrel smiled at the Eagle Knight and carefully removed her hat from the high, coiffed, hairpinned and gelled pompadour she had elected to sport for the festival. "Nonsense, master Colmuir, I always reserve an entire compartment for myself and my young ladies. Otherwise," she glanced in amusement at the Nisei girl and her Anglish companion, "we would be forced to endure the company of reprobates, villains and men with sacks of smelly ham sandwiches."

"Or those who smoke," the Nisei girl said, glaring pointedly at the master sergeant, who had just fished the last tabac from the crushed box in his vest pocket. "There is no smoking."

"Mei," Mrs. Petrel said, leaning a little towards the master sergeant and smiling faintly, "has asthma."

"Your pardon, miss," Colmuir replied, licking his lips and returning the tabac to its box. "Wouldn't want t' be a bother, now would I?"

"Not at all," Mrs. Petrel said. "You are very, very welcome company. I was afraid the Lord Prince had fallen into the hands of the *kujen* and his fellow conspirators."

"A conspiracy?" Sergeant Dawd glanced at the prince, who was sitting between him and Colmuir, now dressed in flowing native robes and a wickerwork sun hat which hid his entire face behind a long visor designed to protect the snout of a Jehanan matron from the fierce sun. "Just in Gandaris, or . . ."

"I expect the whole of the Five Rivers has risen up." Mrs. Petrel said, turning sideways so Mei could undo her hair. "There have been rumors for months of a secret cabal among the native princes—a society called the *moktar*—which is devoted to expunging the taint of Imperial thought, goods and presence from Jagan." She sighed with relief as the last of the pins came out. The white streaks sweeping back from her temples emerged as she shook out her hair.

"We have never been terribly welcome here," she said, turning back to Colmuir. "They will do their best to drive us off-world. I'm sure *kujen* Nahwar hoped to snare the lot of us—the Lord Prince included—once we'd arrived for the festival of the *Nēm*."

Tezozómoc laughed softly, face still hidden under the long hat. His hands were clasped tight on his knees and he'd said nothing from the time they rushed him out of the bathroom, across the platform and onto the train just as it prepared to pull out of the station.

"Wanted again," he said, most of the bitterness leached from his voice by an aftertone of adrenaline. "I should let them take me—I'd have some use then, as a bargaining chip between princes and the Empire."

"No, dear," Mrs. Petrel said, shaking her head. "Your purpose is doing what you've already done today, seeing your sworn men are looked after. And now—though I'd imagine master Colmuir is about beside himself with the added risk—you've three dainty Imperial ladies to see home safely as well."

This did not please the prince at all, who fell silent and slumped back into his seat, hiding behind the hat. Dawd tipped back the corner of the drapes over the window and watched carefully as the train picked up speed out of the station and began rattling down the tracks leading out of the town. The rail line crossed over a bridge; a thoroughfare passed below and the street was filled with a huge mob of Jehanan marching up towards the center of town, waving banners and placards over their heads. The sergeant guessed the crudely drawn figures on the wooden boards were supposed to be human, though most humans he knew did not have two heads or breathe fire.

"We've cut it fine," Dawd said to Colmuir and Petrel. The sergeant was beginning to shake a little bit, coming down off the steady adrenaline and combat-drug high he'd been on since the door of the prince's dressing room exploded. "But if the train doesn't stop until Parus, we might make it."

"Oh." Mrs. Petrel made a dismissive motion with her hand. "I've taken this train before—last year when the rains were full on—there are stops in Bandopene and Takshila, but I'm sure we'll be fine. They'll only check our ticket once after we've boarded. The conductors are very discrete—we shan't be asked again."

Really? Dawd kept his opinion to himself, though he guessed Colmuir would be of much the same mind. *Then we'll have to shoot our way off this train at one station or the other . . .*

Mindful of these realities, the sergeant set about checking his weapons, cleaning the last of the sewer sludge out of his equipment and trying to look impassive and professional while two rather attractive young ladies sat no more than a meter away and watched him—or were they watching the prince?—with unsettling interest.

Several hours later, the train jerked into motion again at Bandopene and Dawd let himself relax from hair-trigger readiness. Behind closed velvet drapes, the noise of the hot little hill-station echoed loudly, and every footstep in the passage made him tense. Colmuir stood poised inside the closed door of the compartment, automatic in hand, watching a longeye feed of the corridor, until the train doors closed at last.

Mrs. Petrel's calm demeanor proved warranted. No one bothered them save an elderly conductor who checked their tickets just outside Gandaris. To Dawd's eye the Jehanan had seemed oddly unsurprised to find a compartment full of humans on his train. But with the second station falling away behind them, the younger Skawtsman let himself relax a bit. Feeling the train rattle up to speed and boom hollowly over a bridge, he ventured to part the window curtain again and peer out.

Decaying slab-sided buildings lined the tracks. There were no windows and the wooden siding was turning gray and black with age. Tall brick smokestacks rose above sooty tiled roofs and the Skawtsman closed the window, disheartened to be so distinctly reminded of the industrial neighborhoods where he'd grown up. *Alien worlds are supposed to be exotic and beautiful,* he thought. *Filled with never-before-seen vistas and unimaginable grandeur, not shuttered mills and tumble-down factories and fences of spikewire like Pollokshields.*

"Well," Colmuir said, drawing the attention of everyone in the hot, stuffy compartment. "That's a bit of luck, I'd say. By my comp, we'll be in Takshila by dark and then overnight t' Parus."

"If nothing happens in Takshila," Dawd said cautiously. The sergeant turned to Mrs. Petrel, who had spent the day sitting quietly, cooling herself with a silk hand-fan bearing a hand-stitched image of Mount Tahoma rising above interwoven clouds and stands of pine. Both of her young ladies had fallen asleep in the heat, though now they were stirring, woken by the renewed movement of the train. "Mi'lady, a thought strikes me. . . . What happened to Corporal Clark? Didn't he take you to the station?"

Petrel's face tightened slightly and her eyes seemed to darken. "We walked—or rather, ran—to the station, Sergeant. Corporal Clark delivered us to the temple of the Immanent Sun quite early. The processions and prayers and ceremonies to greet the solar deities' first light upon the newly ripened *Nēm* begin at a dreadful hour. But then he took off for the palace to secure more refreshments for the prince and for dinner. After that . . ." Mrs. Petrel sighed and shook her head slowly. "We've neither seen him nor the aerocar."

"Ah, now, that is too bad." Colmuir grimaced. "If he went t' the palace, they'll have seized him and the aerocar. Poor sod."

Mrs. Petrel folded up her fan. "If he was not taken unawares, he might have escaped. But where would he go?" She nodded to the Anglish girl, who had come quietly awake. "They sent men to arrest us at the dawn ceremony, but the captain of the soldiers fell to arguing with the head priest. Cecily noticed the dispute and we were able to slip away. Then I thought of the train . . ."

Dawd rubbed his nose, beginning to feel nervous. *These girls see quite a bit, I would guess. A bold set of ladies these are, larking about on an alien world in their Sunday best.* He pursed his lips, a nagging thought surfacing.

"Your pardon, mi'lady, but . . . you had train tickets for *today?* How did—"

Mrs. Petrel smiled whimsically, unfolding her fan in front of her face. The compartment was growing hotter with every kilometer they sped south. "I believe in planning ahead, sergeant."

"But—" Dawd fell silent, seeing the lady's eyes tighten slightly and feeling Colmuir's glare. He shrank back into his seat, wishing he hadn't asked so many questions. He was guiltily aware of the master sergeant warning him, more than once before, to keep quiet and mind his manners. "Your pardon, mi'lady. It's none of my business."

Mrs. Petrel nodded politely and began fanning her face again. Colmuir settled back into his seat, one hand still on his Nambu. Both Mei and Cecily closed their eyes and the sound of the train wheels clattering along the tracks and the jingling sway of the car and the susurration of people breathing filled the silence.

The prince, still sound asleep, began to snore softly, his head leaning against Dawd's shoulder.

Bloody hell, the Skawtsman grumbled to himself. *I've never been able to sleep on trains.* He snuck a look at his chrono. *Another four hours until we reach Takshila. And our comms are still jammed. Poor Clark. Doubt we'll see him again . . .*

Then Dawd closed his eyes, Whipsaw cradled in the crook of his left arm, right hand resting on the hilt of the combat knife strapped to his leg, and tried to rest.

The Parus express reached the outskirts of Takshila just after sundown and began to slow in preparation for stopping at the main rail terminal. The train engineer, however, saw that the skyline was lit by widespread fires and a pall of heavy smoke lay over the city. The sprawling slums lining the railroad approach were relatively quiet. Very few Takshilans had ever seen an *asuchau* human, but rumor of the *kujen*'s war had permeated the city within minutes of the first bombing attack on the Mercantile Exchange House. The usual traffic of heavy wains piled with ceramics and bundles of flowers and stacks of fresh-cut lumber, runner-carts, *tikikit* buses and crowds of busy Jehanan out and about, shopping and bartering, was noticeably lighter than the engineer expected.

All of this made him wary and he kept one eye-shield peeled for warning lights along the spiked barricades lining the tracks. As a result, as the express slowed to barely twenty kilometers an hour, he caught sight of a diversion indicator light and swing-board at the first spur line. The engineer depressed the main braking lever, felt the entire train shudder at the squeal of brake linings on massive iron wheels, and leaned out as the express chugged onto the secondary track.

Seeing the warning light relieved some of the engineer's fears—the fires silhouetting the *khus* rising at city center were centered around the train station—and he had no desire to plow a sixteen-car train into a mob on the tracks or through a burning station. He eased up on the brakes, let a little steam build and the express settled out onto a straightaway.

The train chuffed past a rail yard traffic tower overlooking a section of cargo sidings, but though the engineer waved at the lit windows, he did not see anyone inside. This was puzzling, but not entirely out of the ordinary. The express rattled through the warehouse district at a modest clip. Inside the comfortably hot driver's compartment, the engineer hooted at his second, who bent over a laminated diagram of the rail network in and around Takshila. After a moment's scrutiny, the junior engineer warbled back, pointing at the map.

The engineer nodded, soot-stained snout bobbing, and prepared to reduce speed. He bled steam from the boiler, slowing the clattering wheels. The secondary track began to curve off to the south and the map showed a tunnel at the edge of town, just before the spur rejoined the main line. Tunnels were a dicey business sometimes, particularly if there was trouble in the city and the railroad temple guards were distracted by fires or rioting.

The engineer leaned out again, snout into the rushing air, and made sure the huge glassed-in lamp on the front of the train was burning, illuminating the pair of iron tracks snaking away into the darkness. One claw was firmly on the brake lever. In his twelve years of service, the engineer had seen stray *molk* on the tracks, short-horns daring the rushing speed of the wheels, even brigands trying to pry up the rails themselves. His mouth gaped, breathing in the tepid, smoky air of the city rushing past.

The train slowed, spitting sparks into the darkness, rumbling and swaying as the incandescent glare of the main lamp was swallowed by mossy brick walls. Steam and smoke boiled back, suddenly trapped in the tight confines of a tunnel. Car after car vanished into the side of a long ridge cupping the southern side of the city.

The tunnel mouth was faced with slabs of imported granite and a builder's plaque had once surmounted the capstone of the arch. The plaque was long gone, stolen by local crook-tails, but the railway easement itself was lined with spiked wooden barriers to keep looters, children and animals away from the tracks.

This had not, however, stopped two figures from cutting through the barrier with a monofilament saw. Now, as the end of the train came into view, the larger figure scrambled up the gravel easement, long *kheerite*-style cloak flapping around her legs as she ran alongside, grasped the step-rail up to the baggage car and swung aboard. The second figure jogged beside the train, gasping for breath, and then a clawed hand reached down, seized forearm-to-forearm and dragged Parker aboard.

Inside, by the dim light of a yellow bulb, the pilot coughed a little and untangled his cloak, leaning against a stained wooden wall. Outside there was nothing but darkness as the train clattered through the tunnel.

"See—*wheeze!*—very simple. Easy as pie. Anyone could do it."

Magdalena wrinkled her flat black nose and drew the cowl of the cape down over her eyes. The duffel bags on her back made standing difficult in the narrow passage. Most Jehanan were a little larger than a human, but they didn't have a hump of heavy comp and surveillance equipment strapped to their backs either.

"Yes, I can see this." The Hesht twitched her long, tendril-like whiskers. "Now where do we lair up? Not so many places to hide on a train . . ."

"Didn't I say I had everything covered?" Parker grinned, face bright with sweat. "You are a cat of little faith! You'd think, after diverting the train worked, you'd begin to believe in me . . ."

"*Hrrr!* We were blessed by the Huntress herself to find a switching station unguarded. The trouble in the city has driven all these groundcrawlers into their holes . . ."

Undaunted by her pessimism, Parker dug into his jacket, tossed away two crumpled tabac boxes and drew out a paper envelope. His eyes twinkled with delight. "And you just wanted to wait near the apartment . . . See, train passes! All we need to do is find a seat."

Magdalena beckoned with her paw, examined the papers and sniffed loudly. "Forgeries, I suppose. Or stolen . . ."

"They are not!" Parker snatched them back. "I paid good solid *shatamanu* for them. The only problem is . . ." The train rumbled out of the tunnel and suddenly everything grew a little quieter without the reverb of walls outside. ". . . they're not reserved seats. So we might have to stand."

"I see." Magdalena's lips curled back from her shiny white teeth. She stuck out her tongue, testing the humid, warm air. "At least my tail won't freeze to the door of the baggage compartment this time."

Parker scowled, crossing his arms. "That was not *my* fault. Anderssen decided we should take that night train!"

Maggie started to hiss, then restrained herself. She was very tired. "Enough. I will lead, you will follow and we will find seats, if any exist on this benighted contraption."

The Hesht turned, squeezing the duffels through the doorway into the passage running down the side of the train. Every time she swung her shoulders, the bags jammed against the wall, which made for slow going. Parker hitched up his own duffel bag and followed along behind.

He wondered, as his legs acclimatized themselves to the swaying motion of the train, if Gretchen had managed to escape the city, or even the monastery. *Oh god, what if she's waiting back at the apartment right now? What if she's been captured?*

But there was no way to tell and no way to go back. He wasn't even sure the voice blaring in his earbug had been hers, but what else could he do? It was enough to keep from falling as the train shuddered into a long curve, heading down out of the hills towards the plain of the Phison.

ABOARD THE CAPTAIN'S LAUNCH
APPROACHING THE CORNUELLE

"Hold on," *Sho-i* Asale said, twisting her control yoke. The launch dodged to one side as a section of hull plating flew past. The fragment was only a dark blot against the abyssal darkness beyond the windows. Hadeishi, standing beside the airlock, felt a twinge in his gut, realizing they had entered the corona of debris around the *Cornuelle.*

"We're clear for final approach." The pilot eased back the thrusters. "I have visual on the aft shuttle bay."

Hadeishi braced one arm against the side of the lock, peering through the forward windows. The aft bay doors seemed intact, though he could see the starboard ventral point defense mount had taken some kind of directed beam damage. The shipskin was bubbled and twisted like taffy. Two stubby anti-missile railguns were exposed, the armor over their emplacement entirely missing, leaving a ragged edge. Mottled, ashy expanses of the shipskin showed the rippling effects of an energy overload to the reactive armor.

"Any response to your access code?" The *Chu-sa* could hear himself breathing harshly.

"None." Asale twisted around in her seat, looking back at the captain and the two Marines. "I can take us around to the other side. The launch bay is well armored, perhaps—"

"No." Hadeishi tapped the EVA bag clamped to his chestplate. "Too far from engineering. We'll need to get there first, if any good is to be done. Open the lock. We'll jet across and cut our way in if need be. Keep transmitting our ident codes. Something might wake up in time to let us inside."

"Hai, *kyo*." The pilot turned back to her controls and began nudging the launch sideways towards the hull a meter at a time.

Hadeishi craned his neck, watching for the surface of the shuttle bay doors to appear in the tiny window of the airlock. A cold band twisted tighter around his heart each time his chrono elapsed another minute. The *Cornuelle* had failed to reply to their hails as they approached, and even the navigational display in the launch showed the light cruiser's wildly degraded orbit. The two-minute-long irregular burn by the out-of-control number three engine had thrown the *Cornuelle* into a sharp dive towards the planetary atmosphere.

The *Chu-sa* was sure the abrupt cut-off of the misfiring engine had been the work of someone still alive, aboard, throwing the ship into emergency shutdown. The damage inflicted by the mines was severe—Hadeishi had never seen his ship vomit so much atmosphere, so much radioactive debris, in any of her countless engagements—but the loss of navigational control was a mystery. *Something else has happened,* he thought grimly, pressing his forehead against the inside of his helmet. *Perhaps main comp was damaged, or one of the control nodes severed.* He refused to believe everyone aboard was dead.

On her new heading, the *Cornuelle* would not corkscrew to a fiery doom—gravity had already seized hold and she was wallowing towards a tentative orbit—but the upper reaches of the Jaganite atmosphere were already reaching up to clutch at her battered surface. Friction would follow as the cruiser settled deeper into the thermosphere, and *that* would steal her angular momentum. The end would come, later rather than sooner, with a glowing, red-hot hull and the stress of re-entry tearing the crippled starship apart.

"Twenty meters." Asale tapped the braking jets and the launch gentled to a halt relative to the crippled ship. "Cycling airlock."

The inner door irised open and Hadeishi stepped in, followed by Fitzsimmons. The launch airlock was too small to allow more than two men in z-suits with all the repair gear which could be salvaged from the launch strapped to their bodies inside at once. Hadeishi squeezed to one side—the Marine was nearly a foot taller than he—and took hold of the outer door locking bar.

Deckard waved cheerfully as the inner door closed between them. Hadeishi waited, listening to Asale breathing and counting their displacement from the *Cornuelle*, while air pumped out of the lock.

"Nineteen . . . back to twenty . . . nineteen . . . holding at twenty meters."

The outer lock blossomed open. Hadeishi clenched his fists around the jet controls and puffed out of the opening. The vast bulk of the *Cornuelle* loomed before him, a wall of ebon darkness slanting up against a rampart of stars. He thumbed the thruster control and swept toward the bay doors outlined on his visor by suit comp. Fitzsimmons waited two breaths, and then followed himself, careful to keep from fouling the medical aid pack on his back in the airlock.

"I have the bay access door in sight," Hadeishi said, changing course slightly.

Understoo—

The autonomic targeting system in the nearer railgun suddenly identified the launch as a hostile vessel launching self-propelled missiles towards the *Cornuelle.* The anti-missile mount flared a brilliant blue-white. A depleted uranium needle two millimeters long accelerated to near-relativistic speed, exited the magnetic 'racetrack' and punched through the captain's launch from end to end. The needle pierced the forward pressure windows fifteen centimeters from Asale's head, flashed the length of the tiny cabin, drilled directly through Deckard's z-suit, his ribs on the right side, one lung and then out the other and impaled itself in the launch's magnetically shielded *Hosukai-Tesla* reaction drive chamber. An enormous amount of energy vomited into the interior of the tiny ship as the needle stopped abruptly. Deckard was incinerated as thousand degree plasma flooded in through the rupture in his z-suit. Asale lasted a moment longer, smashed against the control panel, her suit withstanding the pressure and heat for three and then four seconds, then suffering catastrophic structural failure. The launch spaceframe buckled, unable to contain the explosion and then sublimated into a blast of heat and light and debris.

The explosion flared out, smashing into Hadeishi and Fitzsimmons and hurling them against the side of the *Cornuelle.* Both men were still accelerating towards the boat bay door. Fitzsimmons and his heavy load afforded the *Chu-sa* a tiny fraction of protection, but the Marine's corpse became a missile a half-second later and Hadeishi was slapped against the armored hull of the ship by a giant, raging hand of flame.

The z-suit stiffened on impact, trying to bleed away the shock of collision, but the violence was too much for Hadeishi's nervous system to absorb and he grayed out, grasping fruitlessly at the smooth metal surface of the hull. His medband triggered, flushing his system with adrenaline, anti-radiation agents and painkillers. Tangled in Fitzsimmons' body, fragments of the launch smashing against the bay doors around him, the *Chu-sa* skidded across the hull, impelled by the dying wavefront of the explosion.

Jolted back to awareness by the drugs, his heart hammering violently in his chest, arms and legs numb, Hadeishi twisted, trying to get his hands and feet face-front. Fitzsimmons' charred z-suit sloughed away, breaking up as the straps for the

Marine's ruck disintegrated. A cloud of blackened and melted medpacks flew out around the *Chu-sa*. Hundreds of hours of z-suit drill as a cadet and a junior officer reasserted themselves in a reflexive, four-square crouch. The gripper pads in Hadeishi's gloves and boots realized they were in proximity to shipskin and activated. Friction increased dramatically between the two surfaces and the *Chu-sa* slid to a halt.

Ionized gases and plasma-hot particles blew past, dinging on his faceplate and z-suit. Hadeishi focused, saw the boat bay door was a hundred meters away, and tried to grapple mentally with the concept his launch, his pilot and two of his men had been obliterated from the universe in less than sixteen seconds of sidereal time.

Ah, he moaned inwardly, *so many ghosts will haunt me. So many ghosts. Is there enough incense in all Shinedo to placate your wailing cries?*

Then the *Chu-sa* settled his breathing, forced every thought from his mind but the necessity of survival and began spider-walking across the hull towards the access door. Hidden by the z-suit, his med-band was burning crimson. A too-familiar stabbing pain rippled up his side with each movement, but Hadeishi only bent his head and continued to force arms and legs to move.

I will never fear loneliness, he sang to himself, crawling forward. *I will always be accompanied.*

Before long, I shall be a ghost
But just now, how they bite my flesh
These autumn winds.

PARUS
THE DISTRICT OF THE WHEEL

Rain poured down from a muddy, discolored sky. The gutters rushed with dark water, swirling around ancient drains clogging with leaves, paper bags and discarded wreaths of golden flowers. Four Arachosians—faces hidden under sharp-brimmed, waxed rain-hats—splashed through spreading pools and up to the ornately carved doors of a temple squeezed in between two larger, newer buildings.

Two of the highlanders swung a spike-headed ram between them. The wooden doors crashed aside, lock and bar broken, and the others leapt in, *kalang*-knives flashing. Inside, a lookout was hewn down—no priest he, in the gaudy harness and trappings of a pimp—and the Arachs bounded down age-blackened steps and into rooms once dedicated to a now-forgotten god. They burst into a chamber filled with hazy layers of drifting *tchun*-smoke and the hot neon glow of dozens of modern three-d gambling machines. Soft-scaled lowlander patrons surged up, horrified by the sight of long, lean highland reavers plunging among them, and the sound of wailing screams rang clearly through the spyeye feed. Blood spattered through the intricate holovee writhing in the heart of the nearest machine.

The kujen's board of taxation should pay me a stipend. Itzpalicue's wrinkled lips twitched in amusement and she shifted the active feed, searching for the next of her hunting teams. *But this is not the lair of my enemy.*

Arachosians loped through an empty warehouse, narrow snouts questing for signs of any inhabitants. The old Náhuatl woman could see the tracks of heavily laden carts on the dirt floor.

She switched the feed.

An Imperial-model truck careened around a corner, highlanders hanging off the sides, sopping-wet cloaks clinging to muscled scale, sending a wave of dirty water splashing against the wall of a house. Rain drummed on the roof of the cab. Arachosians on the runner boards pointed the driver towards a row of beehive-shaped workshops. Smoke puffed up into the rain from a forge chimney. The gate to a muddy yard crashed open, smashed aside by an armored bumper. The Arachs sprang down, striding through deep mud, assault rifles at the ready.

A sliding door on the side of the long, low building flew open and a crowd of angry metal-workers poured out into the yard, claws filled with hammers, tongs and lengths of iron bar. The spyeye darted past over their heads as the first burst of bullets tore into the workmen. Itzpalicue muted the sound on the feed—the warbling cries of dying Jehanan irritated her—and shook her head in disgust. The gleaming, modern shapes of two industrial welders sat on wooden platforms on one side of the long forge-room. Cables snaked across a spotless floor to four fuel-cell generators.

Stacks of recycled Imperial iron, aluminum and steel ingots stood behind a locked barricade.

Disappointed, Itzpalicue switched the feed.

An Arachosian glided out from behind a wagon heaped with firewood, assault rifle raised to a shoulder armored with quilted padding. Two more of the highlanders crept along behind, grenades and knives in their claws. Without warning, the rifle stuttered flame. The spyeye view rotated and lowland Jehanan in the livery of the *kujen* of Parus were staggering, raked with bullets. A heavy plastic case fell to the ground between the infantrymen and Itzpalicue straightened up in her nest of blankets, recognizing the shape of a military ordnance crate.

The woman tapped her comm alive. "Take some of them alive," she rasped, catching the attention of the Arachosian *durbar* commanding the hunter team. "Don't damage the goods!"

The knife-wielding Arachosians surged forward, broad feet light on the muddy ground, and were upon the surviving Jehanan in the blink of an eye. Two of the survivors were thrown to the ground and secured with ziptight restraints. The Arachs with rifles circled the truck carefully, searching for survivors. Itzpalicue's spyeye drifted into the covered cargo bed, lingered on three more plastic crates and she dialed up the magnification on the 'eye enough to read the stenciled lettering.

"Albanian work," she muttered, thumbing a translator glyph on her display. The angular Slavic letters were familiar, though she hadn't bothered to learn the little-used dialect.

Orkan anti-mobile-armor tactical missile, type three, export restricted, the comp declared.

"Mobile armor?" Itzpalicue frowned thunderously. "Lachlan?"

The Éirishman's head, dark beard entirely foul with bits of food, turned in the v-pane. *The* xochiyaotinime *did not authorize any restricted imports. Only the outdated Kärrhök anti-tank missiles.* He pursed his lips, consulting a secondary display. *This model of the Orkan is designed to neutralize a Fleet powered armor suit, or one of the Tonehūa APAC's the 416th has in service. Very nasty—fires a cloud of self-tracking hypervelocity composites with reactive warheads—crew of two, integrated ammunition canisters, low-firing profile . . .*

"Expensive. Someone has been spending freely to entertain us." Itzpalicue tapped her comm back to the Arachosian ground channel. A second team of highlanders had arrived and the apparently abandoned houses around the wagon-yard were being searched. "Put your prisoners to the question—who sold them these weapons, where were they going?"

The Arach *durbar* hissed in reply and knelt over one of the Parusian soldiers. The lowlander soft-scale hooted miserably, eyes fixed on the gleaming edge of the *kalang*-knife. The glittering point descended and Itzpalicue watched with clinical interest, sound muted on the channel, as the creature writhed and whimpered and finally, when the mud was puddling crimson, she heard what she had been waiting weeks to hear.

The *durbar* turned, catching sight of the translucent spyeye hovering at his shoulder and exposed many serrated, blackened teeth. *The pretty softscale says these weapons came from a light-scaled asuchau. He has brought them many such devices in the last two weeks. This light-scale made many promises of help from 'friends far away.'*

"A blond human? Lachlan . . ." The old Náhuatl woman growled, feeling her blood quicken.

I've dispatched a collection team to scope the equipment cases. Perhaps we can recover some skin flakes or hair or something to let us match to known humans on the planet.

"Are any of the Flower Priest agents lighthaired? Is someone playing a double-game?"

Lachlan tilted his head to one side, listening to his earbug. *There is one*, he replied, *a Finn. He's used for high-level contacts with Jehanan elements sufficiently educated in Imperial politics to understand he might represent the HKV. His name is Timonen. His Mirror jacket says he's entirely reliable . . .*

"Bring him in anyway." Itzpalicue shifted her attention back to the *durbar.*

"Seal the truck and make sure nothing happens to the contents. Dispose of your captives as you please, but hold position until a pickup team reaches you." She smiled wickedly. "You've done well with this capture, *durbar*. You and your clan will be well rewarded."

The Arachosian flashed teeth again and saluted the drifting mote with his *kalang*. His forearm was drenched in blood.

Itzpalicue shifted the feed, eager for news.

Forty-five minutes later, Lachlan interrupted her scanning. His entire face was impassive and tight, which immediately warned her the Éirishman bore poor news.

Our Timonen is dead. A retrieval team has been checking the safe houses the xochiyaotinime *provided for his cover as a purveyor of medical supplies, hoping to pick up a fresh DNA trace. They found an unusually high concentration in a bathroom in his Yellow Flagstone district flat. The team leader got suspicious and they tore the place apart. Looks like Timonen was murdered, dissolved with a bio-acid and flushed down the lavatory. Whoever did it cleaned up—the team found bleach and antigen foam residue in the tile cracks—but Jehanan toilets don't flush clean.*

"Hmm . . ." Itzpalicue's white eyebrows made a V over her sharp nose. "How long has he been dead?"

Decay rates on the remains in the sewer line indicate a week or two.

The old Náhuatl woman blinked. "Strange . . . that's not much time to make so much mischief. . . . Do we have a track on 'Timonen' afterwards?"

Yes, Lachlan smiled grimly. *He's been lead on nearly every contact with the inner circle of the cabal, in dispersing weapons to the factions, in providing intelligence, planning and other supplies. Right at the heart of their whole effort in Parus.*

"This is the one," Itzpalicue snarled, feeling fate gelling around her. "This is the creature I've felt moving at the edge of perception. Find him! Retask every team in the city, in the whole district. Arachosians, our men, the Whisperers, everyone!"

The old woman sat back, the tips of her fingers running along the rows of maguey spines piercing the sleeves of her mantle. The spines felt hard, smooth and glossy under her touch, like polished bone.

As you say, mi'lady. Lachlan began calling instructions to his subordinates. Then he said: *Should I pass this intel about the Orkan to Regimental command?*

"No." Itzpalicue displayed a cold smile. "Yacatolli and his men are managing. Let them show their true abilities—both the Mirror and Army command will be interested in the results."

THE *CORNUELLE*
A DECAYING ORBIT OVER CONTINENT FOUR

Clinging to the aft boat bay access door, Hadeishi coughed violently. The cutting tool in his hand flew loose, but was almost immediately stopped by a lanyard cinched to his equipment belt. The *Chu-sa* tried to breathe normally, felt the cool tickling of more coagulants and stabilizers flooding his body and opened his eyes. Reddish spots confused his vision for a moment, until he realized they were on the inside of the face-plate.

Not a good sign, he thought ghoulishly, keenly aware of a crystalline layer of pain suppression narcotics insulating fragile consciousness from the pain wracking his body. *I must be getting tubercular.*

He forced his hand to grasp the cutting tool, oriented the microscopic plasma beam emitter towards the emergency access plate cover and thumbed the control. A blue-white flare answered the motion and the beam resumed cutting away the damaged plate. The access door itself was undamaged, but the layer of shipskin covering the mechanism had been mortally wounded, stiffening into a hard, steel-like consistency. The flood of heat from the x-ray laser had distorted the fabric of the shipskin as well, occluding parts of the door and the access port.

Hadeishi completed the cut and the fold of shipskin came loose. Reaching in, he found the recessing bolt, drew it back and the entire cover came loose. Hadeishi felt a surge of relief. Something had gone his way at last, if only finding the green 'ready' light gleaming inside the cover. He punched an override code into the panel and let the Fleet transponder in his suit discuss security matters with the door.

Idle, his stunned mind fixed on the explosion which had obliterated the launch. *A point-defense railgun must have targeted us. Ship's ident processor has been damaged.*

An unusually long period of time passed as the two systems chattered to one another. Hadeishi managed to keep both hands flat on the door, letting the suit grippers hold him to the hull. He tried sucking some water from a tube in the neck ring of his suit, but his whole chest throbbed painfully and he abandoned the effort. He was very thirsty.

At length, the access door shivered, the bolts retracted and a darkened airlock opened before him. Wary—the emergency lights should be on—Hadeishi drifted inside and spun the locking wheel to rotate the outer door closed. As he did so, a single emergency illumination panel woke to life, strobed intermittently for a few moments and went out.

Hadeishi punched his access code into the inner lock door. Nothing happened, though the ready light was shining green on the panel. Feeling a cough coming on, the *Chu-sa* braced himself against the wall, let his broken chest heave for a moment and the salt and iron taste of blood fill his mouth. Then he checked his z-suit's environmental readouts. Pressure stood at zero in the airlock, though closing the outer door should have caused the chamber to flood with air.

Inner lock won't open to zero-pressure, he realized. Air circulation pumps must be dead.

Licking his lips, Hadeishi eyeballed his z-suit air reserve, trying to remember what minimum air pressure was to reset the safety sensor on the inner door. *Three-quarters of a tank. Let's try half that.*

Numb fingers unscrewed a valve on his shoulder pack, allowing a cross-connect hose to emerge from the environmental package on the suit. Hadeishi bounced gently from side to side in the lock, searching for the pressure sensors. After a moment, he gave up. Again, he braced himself against the wall next to the access panel and opened the valve.

A faint hissing sound grew louder, second by second. Hadeishi watched his air gauge fixedly, feeling fainter moment by moment as the capacity marker shrank. At one-half, he closed the valve, feeling dizzy and nauseous.

The environmental readout showed non-zero pressure.

The *Chu-sa* forced his hand—fingers trembling—to punch in the access code. There was another pause. The green indicator flashed to amber, then red. A message appeared on the tiny display. Hadeishi leaned in, having trouble focusing.

Ship's atmosphere compromised, the message read, *rebreather support is required.*

Hadeishi mashed his thumb against the override button. There was a trembling vibration in the wall under his shoulder. The inner lock door opened, grayish smoke rushing in. The *Chu-sa* stumbled through into the boat bay and weakly pushed the airlock door closed behind him.

Everything was very dark, save in the direct beam of his suit lamps, which pierced a smoky, turgid gloom. Hadeishi clutched for a guiderail, found the slim tubing along the wall, and began to pull himself forward, squinting into the haze.

At the first bulkhead outside of the boat bay proper, the *Chu-sa* kicked slowly down a transverse corridor, trying to reach one of the four lengthwise access ways which led from the stern forward. The smoke fouling the aft hangar section thinned but he was becoming seriously concerned. He had yet to see a single crewman, the lights were out, his comm failed to find a single relay node and the air was still unbreathable. Charred debris floated everywhere, making movement in the dark difficult.

Coasting to a halt at the end of the corridor, Hadeishi found the sectional door closed. Hefting the cutting tool, he checked the access panel. This time there was a 'locked' indicator, but the pressure and environment indicators for the far side were glowing green and amber.

Ah, he thought, *the boat bay crews abandoned this section because of toxic air. One of the shuttle propellant tanks must have lost integrity and caused a fire. They've starved the fire out, but not bothered to restore atmosphere.*

Trying to remember the fire control override codes for the internal doors, he poked experimentally at the access panel. After several tries the door glared red at him and locked out the panel. Hadeishi wanted desperately to scratch his beard, which was itchy with dried blood and bits of vomit, but a Fleet z-suit lacked that amenity.

He pushed up and peered through the glassite port into the access way. There too the main lights were out, but he caught a gleam of the emergency lights burning and a sense of motion. Encouraged, he flashed his suit lamps through the window, hoping to draw someone's attention. Then he waited.

A faceplate swam into view—a crewman with Engineering tabs on his shoulders and a spool of commwire on his shoulder—and an ensign started with surprise to see the haggard face of his captain. Hadeishi pointed at the access plate and made a circling motion. The *Sho-i ko-hosei* nodded violently and disappeared from view. The *Chu-sa* pressed himself against the bottom of the door. He felt vibration in the decking through his hands and the door levered up.

Hadeishi squirmed through, heard his comm wake to life with the chatter of crewmen working furiously at damage control and dragged himself up the wall to punch the close-code on the door. Smoke had spilled through with him, but not too much, he hoped. The *Chu-sa* turned to the boy, the corners of his eyes wrinkled in a smile.

"Ship's status? How fast can you get me to Engineering?"

Twenty minutes later, Hadeishi swung along a guiderail into the main Engineering deck and stared around in tight-lipped concern at the wan faces of his crew and the rows of darkened comp displays. Only the stations devoted to the main drive coil and fusion reactors were showing the glow of active displays.

"What happened?" The *Chu-sa* kicked to the half-circle of panels associated with main comp.

Isoroku looked up, bald head gleaming in the light of Hadeishi's suit lamps. "The backbone network is infested with six or seven thousand kinds of attack viruses. We've got comm up in most of the ship via suit-to-suit relays and the hardline you followed up here. But everything else is still useless."

"Can you bring the main drives back on-line? We need to adjust orbit immediately."

The engineer nodded. "We can, but you won't have any navigational control from either the bridge or secondary command." A thick gloved finger stabbed at the single comp display still alive in the array. An endlessly mutating face was shining in the display, alternately leering, giggling and showing a sad expression. A dizzying array of ears, hats, tongues and noses changed with bewildering speed. "See this? This is what happens when you bring up a display."

"Main comp is infected?" Hadeishi tried to swallow, but his throat was dust dry. "That's impossible."

The bulky engineer grunted in agreement. "Main comp is fine, the computational cores are fine, archive and ready memory is all fine. But . . ." He tapped the panel accusingly, voice grating harshly. "The display pane interfaces, the comm nodes and the transmission linkages between the millions of subsystems on this barge are all wrecked by this kind of *baka* infiltrator. We're isolating systems, reflashing them and stitching them back into the network, but it's going to take a long time."

"Hours? Days?" Hadeishi stared around the Engineering deck with a cold gaze. His eyes lingered on three z-suited corpses tied down to the deck behind one of the work panels. "How bad have casualties been?"

Isoroku glanced over, then shook his head. "Damage control teams are still sorting through the wreckage—somehow we lost the entire area around your suite, the officer's mess and the forward galley—Yoyontzin reports everything up there is just twisted metal. All the hallways are clogged with wreckage."

"Again?" Hadeishi stared at the engineer in confusion. He was starting to feel numb. "From the laser impacts? Did we lose hull integrity forward of bulkhead nine?"

"No," Isoroku said, shrugging. "Some kind of secondary explosion. Nearly severed the data mains to the front quarter of the ship, but the conduit armor held—which does us no good, since every comp panel on the ship is useless." He made a spitting motion towards the evil face.

"Do we have replacement interface panels in stores?"

Isoroku bit the inside of his lip, thinking. "If they're not trashed by battle damage . . ."

"Isolate the sublight drive system, and rig a control panel just for the engines. Don't connect it to anything else. Will that let us regain maneuvering control?"

The engineer nodded. "We've been trying to clear the primary combat control backbone, but—"

"One little problem at a time," Hadeishi coughed, starting to drift away. Blood was leaking out of his mouth and making tiny crimson bubbles inside his faceplate. "How long until we have pervasive comm in the ship?"

Isoroku stared at the *Chu-sa* in horror. He seized the nearest crewman. "The captain needs medical attention *right now.* Get a work cart, get him on it and get him to medical! Someone, what's the status of the medical bay? Do they have air pressure?"

Crewmen scattered in all directions, including one who began chattering into the hardwired comm. Another brought Hadeishi back to the ring of comp panels. The *Chu-sa* batted feebly at the helping hands. "I'm fine, just have some splinters loose in my rib-cage. Someone has to relay telemetry from the outside to whoever is driving with this panel, so . . ." He paused, trying to clear his throat. "Are any of the bridge crew alive? Anyone with a pilot's cert?"

"I don't know." Isoroku felt panic start to churn in his stomach. "How bad is the orbit?"

"Not good," Hadeishi wheezed, clenching his teeth together. His medband was shrilling alarms inside his suit. He clenched his arms across his chest protectively. "Ah . . . ! I seem to have exceeded some kind of threshold. You must stabilize our orbit quickly. Then you'll have time to fix everything else.

"Find a clean comp and panel, load fresh soft and get them into the hands of someone who knows how to steer. They'll need Navplot, which means guidance sensors have to be working." He smiled, face obscured by the drift of crimson. "Only tiny problems, *Thai-i*, taken one at a time. Small movements, my friend, small deliberate movements."

Hadeishi's medband tripped the last of its alert levels and flushed his system with knockmeout and a cellular stabilizer. The *Chu-sa*'s eyes rolled up and his head fell loosely forward against the faceplate of his suit.

Isoroku cursed silently, then the work-cart was being wrangled into the work station and he and two of the Engineering deck crew were strapping the captain onto the cart, trying to be as gentle and as quick as possible.

NEAR RURAL HIGHWAY TWO-FIFTEEN
THE TOWN OF CHUMENE, SOUTHEAST OF TAKSHILA

A high-pitched wailing sound pierced the air, setting the hairs on the back of Gretchen's neck erect. The clatter of leathery hands on stiff-surfaced drums followed and then the tramping beat of hundreds of feet stamping on dusty ground. Malakar and Anderssen stepped out of the darkness at the edge of the village, faces lit by the hot glow of hundreds of torches and two enormous bonfires. The deep basso groan of bladder-horns joined the riot of sound. The gardener lifted her long snout, searching the furtive, twisting light for the proper street.

Gretchen watched the natives dancing with growing interest. A ring of elderly Jehanan—fairly dripping with flower petals, paper streamers and jangling charms—moved back, clearing the center of the street. Now they crouched at the edge of the light, long feet rising and falling in a steady, marching beat. A round dozen musicians were ensconced under a cloth awning festooned with statuettes and figurines and mandalas of flowers. One of the brittle-scales held a long, metal instrument in withered hands. The firelight gleamed on silver strings and an ivory-yellow claw began to pluck, sending a plaintive, echoing sound winging up into the dark sky above.

All else fell silent, leaving the trembling notes alone on the dusty stage.

Then, at the edge of the light, the villagers parted silently, bowing and snuffling in the dirt, and the slim figure of an adolescent Jehanan female appeared, wreathed in veils of pale gold and green. She darted out, fine-boned feet quick on the ground, the clink and clash of precious copper bangles marking counterpoint to the humming drone of the stringed instrument. The girl danced sideways, bending and stretching, miming—Anderssen realized, watching the movements—someone plucking flower buds.

"This is Avaya, twilight's maidenhead," Malakar whispered, "and she is dancing in the fields of the coming sun, collecting the opened buds of the sacred *Nēm* as they lie cool, still unturned by the touch of the Lord of Light."

Avaya spun past, wholly concentrated upon the unseen, and Gretchen caught a rustle of feet in grass and the smell of a dewy hillside, pregnant with pollen and perfume. The girl danced on, the single instrument slowly, subtly, joined by the hissing wail of the bladder-horns and hooting flutes. So too brightened the illumination in the dusty circle and Anderssen blinked, startled and delighted to see the waiting crowd, still hidden by the gossamer barrier between shadow and light, raising many paper lamps on long poles to hang over the street.

A horn rang out, a cold, clear note. The girl stumbled, spilled her invisible basket of petals and raised her head in alarm, long back curving gracefully to the east. A deep-voiced drum began to beat, the tripping sound of a hasty heart, of blood quickened by danger. Avaya dashed here and there, snatching up petals from the ground.

So perfect were the girl's movements that Gretchen clutched Malakar's bony, scaled shoulder for support. In the flickering, dim light, surrounded by such rich noise, by so many swaying Jehanan, she began to see—darting, indistinct, gleamingly real—the petals on the ground, the rustling stands of green plants, golden leaves, waxy flowers half-open to the sky. Such an overpowering aroma washed over her she felt faint. Rich, dark earth; the dew on a thousand flowers; a cool, cold sky shining deep blue-black overhead. A steady emerald brightness rising on the horizon.

"See, now the king is coming. Her time grows short . . ."

Malakar's voice broke Anderssen from the waking dream. Another corridor opened in the crowd and a forest of torches clustered there, held aloft in scaled hands. Even now, with so many lights, she could not see the faces of the celebrants. They were dim and indistinct, bound by shadow, but the lamps and sputtering, resin-drenched brands burned very bright.

A tall, powerfully built Jehanan male glided out of the darkness. His scales were golden, shimmering, flashing like mirrors. Well-muscled arms wielded a burning stave, a length of wood wrapped with pitch and resin. He sprang into the circle, whirling flame over his head. So swift was the movement the blurring stroke became a single burning disc, shining in the east.

Avaya fled, leaping and bounding—and Gretchen knew she fled down the hillside, springing rushing streams, weather-worn boulders, seeking always the safety of night behind beckoning hills—and the Sun-King gave chase. The crowd of faces, the soft outlines of the rooftops, the dusty street of a market town, all fled from Anderssen's perception and for a timeless moment, all she beheld was the long chase of the Lord of Light to reclaim the precious *Nēm* from the hands of iridescent Avaya and his endless quest to bring her forth from bondage in the underworld.

A chorus of voices joined the winging sound of the instruments, calling back and forth in counterpoint to relate the pleading cries of the King, and the demure, evasive answers of the maid.

Malakar shook her shoulder gently, drawing the human back into the shelter of the crowd.

"We must go," the gardener whispered. "The *tikikit* do not tarry on their rounds."

Gretchen blinked, rubbed her face and followed—unseeing, half-blinded by clinging smoke—as they passed down a narrow lane and a set of broad steps. The old Jehanan stopped, dipping her claws into a stone trough.

"Here," the gardener said, raising cupped hands. "Clear your eyes."

Anderssen splashed shockingly cold water on her face, shivered and wiped her nose. The glorious visions of the sun racing across the hills of a dry, green world faded. Everything was dark and close again, pregnant with the smell of cinnamon.

"Thank you. I was . . . overcome."

The Jehanan's eyes gleamed in the darkness, reflecting the lighted windows of the nearest house. "You impress me, *asuchau*. You were singing, as the eldest do, remembering fragments of the lost. . . . Most of those around us did not understand the words, but some did. They were becoming alarmed, once they realized who you were and had no business knowing such things."

"Singing?" Gretchen shook her head vehemently. "I can't sing."

"Certainly," Malakar said, amused. "Your throat and pitiful snout are not suited for our songs, of course. I see why you are shy—but still, a worthy effort."

"I was *not* singing," Anderssen said sharply, feeling intense irritation. "You must have been imagining things."

"*Hoooo . . .*" The gardener tilted her head to one side. "Perhaps."

"Where is this *tikikit?*" Gretchen said, relieved the creature did not pursue the matter. Her throat felt a little raw. She cupped her hands and drank from the trough, which flowed silently with cold spring water. The damp, fecund odor of moss filled her nostrils.

"It will come soon." Malakar continued on down the steps, which led into a grove of ancient trees. Forgetting to turn on her flashlight, Gretchen hurried after, not wishing to be left alone in the humid darkness. With the sun passed away behind the seventeen hills to the west, the night air was turning cold.

The path narrowed, winding among close-set trees, and then ended in a rutted track. A lamp-post stood beside the road, holding a paper lantern. Malakar stood in a circle of light cast by the dim yellow flame. In the wan radiance, the old Jehanan looked particularly tired, her scales glowing the color of brass. Gretchen slowed, boots sinking into soft, springy ground, and her eyes were drawn to the trees, to the moss covering their roots and the half-seen shape of a tiny stone house set between two enormous, gnarled trunks.

Dim outlines of seated figures were visible inside the open door. Anderssen felt a prickling chill; haphazard thoughts tickling the back of her mind. *Spirits of forest and glade, watchers over traveling folk. Guardians to keep the foul denizens of the night at bay . . . the hatchet-handed corpse, the weeping woman, swarms of* ciuateteo *seeking warm blood . . .*

"Do we have to wait here?" Anderssen pulled her jacket tight, shuffling forward. "This is an uneasy place. . . . Don't your people know crossroads are unlucky, particularly at night?"

Malakar lifted her snout and blew disdainfully through her nostrils. "Where are your quick, knife-sharp thoughts now, *asuchau*? You're pale as new-laid shell. Did your grandmother feed you tales of ghosts and spirits with your growing milk?"

"I'm not comfortable here," Gretchen admitted, squatting down next to the old Jehanan. In the colorless lamplight, the muddy pools of water in the rutted road shimmered. Short-bladed grass growing at the verge cast long, sharp shadows. Gretchen shivered a little, feeling the eyes of the statue in the little house boring into the back of her neck. "Not comfortable at all."

The gardener made a low, hooting sound, little more than a rumble in the back of her throat. "Fear not—this is only a waiting place. Many have waited here before, many will wait here again. The *tikikit* will come soon and bear us south. Just sit a little, rest your weary feet. Feel the quiet under the trees, in the long branches . . ."

Anderssen tried, but squatting beside Malakar made her feel hot and uncomfortable, so she moved to the side, searching for someplace dry to sit. After a few moments of crawling in the low grass, she came upon a flattish rock and sighed with relief. Now she could sit properly. The gardener had been right about the silence—the only sounds were dew slowly dripping from overhanging boughs and the distant, faint murmur of the festival.

Gretchen realized she was tired and sore. Her legs hurt from running and walking and climbing stairs for days on end. Despite the complaints of her body, she didn't feel hungry, so she laid her head on her forearms and closed her eyes.

Anderssen woke abruptly, roused by the sound of someone singing in a queer, warbling voice, sending hooting, trilling calls wandering among the trees. She blinked, eyes adjusting to the light and found Malakar staring at her with a rapt expression, long head tilted to one side.

"Do not stop," the Jehanan begged. "The wholeness of *Húnd and the Diamond-Eye* has been lost to all memory!"

"What are you talking about?" Nervous, Gretchen unfolded herself from the ground, legs numb and stared around at the dark trees and the road and the lamp-post with wide eyes. "Where are we? Where are the fire-tower and the plain of salt? The city of glass?"

"You were singing of them, but who knows where they lie?" Malakar bent her long snout to the ground. "Your voice is strange—hollow and low and soft—yet still I could make out the words . . ."

Anderssen pressed her palms against her eyes, feeling the edges of a dream fade away into darkness. Her throat hurt. She sipped some water from a flask, and then forced her numb, clumsy fingers to dig out a threesquare. Gagging, she managed half of the cold goo in the tube.

"Are you hungry?" Gretchen offered Malakar the rest of the threesquare. "This is human food, but you might be able to metabolize the proteins. It's spiced chicken."

The gardener sidled up, tail twitching and sniffed the tube. "Che-keen smells like sewage," Malakar declared, nostril flaps tightening. "I will wait."

Unable to finish, Anderssen nodded in commiseration and stuffed the threesquare back into her pocket. She rubbed her throat. "You heard me . . . singing?"

Malakar nodded solemnly, rising to her full height. "Without doubt. How can this be? Did you tarry upon Mokuil in your vision long enough to learn venerable songs, to sit at the feet of the eldest as they sang of the ancient heroes?"

"No." Gretchen closed her eyes again, feeling dizzy. "The music in the village affected me, the dancing, the light and shadow—I felt strange, uncoupled from my body. Ah, the old crow warned me this might happen!" She clenched her fists. "Damn him and his helpful powders . . ."

"What do you mean?" Malakar knelt, craning her head to look at Anderssen's face. She hooted, worried. "What *yi* bird spoke to you?"

"A . . . a *trollkarl,* they are called in my grandmother's tales. A sorcerer we would say today, if anyone believed such things existed." She spread her hands, groping for the proper words. "He gave me . . . drugs which opened my mind to the unseen. He hoped I could aid him, but I think—no, I know—they only made things far more dangerous. I was nearly consumed, destroyed, replaced."

Gretchen managed a grim smile. "He tried to make me forget, but I cannot. I thought these visions and phantasms would fade with time, but they have not." She turned her hand over, remembering the blaze of light which had haloed them in the vault. "When the *kalpataru* revealed itself to me, something changed again in my mind. I am waking up again."

"You are afraid." The old Jehanan stared at her curiously. "What will happen to you?"

"I don't know." Anderssen started to sweat and her breath hurried with incipient panic. "I don't really want to find out—he said, Green Hummingbird said, a woman isn't supposed to follow this path. . . . He implied it was very dangerous." She laughed harshly. "I don't think he meant it was dangerous for anyone but *me*."

Malakar reached out a claw to grip the human's shoulder, but a wash of yellow light spilled over both of them and they heard the sound of a rumbling engine.

"The *tikikit* bus comes," the gardener said, helping an unsteady Gretchen to her feet. "Now we can be upon our way."

The blaze of light resolved into six headlights. The conveyance purred to a halt at the lamp-post. Malakar guided Anderssen forward and once they were out of the direct glare, she could see the smooth curve of a long, high machine with many wheels. A door opened in front of her with a *hnnnnnng!* sound and steps led up into a dim, quiet interior. Gretchen froze, staring at the driver of the bus, sitting in a low, round control compartment directly in front of her.

Glittering, multifaceted eyes returned her gaze. A sleek, chitinous thorax lay low over the controls, which were manipulated by too many forearms. The insectile *Hikkikit* shimmered and glowed in the reflected light of the lamp, gleaming with cool blues and greens.

Malakar prodded her gently and Anderssen climbed up into the bus, hands gripping smooth, slippery-feeling guide-rails. The Jehanan fluted a greeting to the driver, produced something from a pouch on her harness and then they moved down an aisle of low seats. Gretchen did not notice any other passengers. The seats were too low for a human to sit normally, so she sat cross-legged beside the bulbous window. Malakar sighed, twitching tail behind and raised her knees, arms folded across the join-scales.

The *tikikit* bus hummed into motion, raised up a little and then raced off down the road.

Trees blurred past, then fields opened out on either side and the bus sped south under a brilliant, clear night. The queer lights distorting the daylight sky were gone, though the northern horizon leapt with enormous aurorae, casting shimmering curtains of jewels to blind the stars. Gretchen leaned her head against the window, marveling at the smooth, effortless ride.

Unbidden, her eyes closed and she fell sound asleep, cradled in the arms of a seat curling slowly around her. Malakar watched her for a little while, concerned, then laid a bony forehead on her own arms and fell asleep as well.

The *tikikit* raced south, six yellow spotlights illuminating the road and washing across hedges, slumbering farm houses and the streets of little night-shrouded towns. From time to time the bus turned onto larger roads, following them for a time, slowing to pass vehicles parked beside the thoroughfare. The headlights briefly lit columns of Jehanan troops dozing beside the highway, rucksacks piled at their feet, rifles and machineguns clutched to their shoulders, glossy scales gleaming in the light of the sodium lamps.

Then the *tikikit* passed on into the dark, turning down forgotten byways, crossing rivers and canals on crumbling bridges, following no straight path, yet still making excellent time. Occasionally, when an isolated lamp-post appeared in the distance, the bus would slow. If someone waited in the circle of light, the driver would quiet the engine, gliding to a halt, and another jeweled insect or sleepy Jehanan would climb aboard.

As night wore on, the seats slowly filled, though none of the passengers ventured to speak to one another, and all save the insectile *Hikkikit* soon fell asleep. Parus grew closer, hour by hour, though there was still a considerable distance to go.

THE SOUTHBOUND EXPRESS
APPROACHING PAROS FROM THE NORTH

A delicate hand jogged sergeant Dawd's knee and he came instantly awake. Mei leaned towards him in the dim compartment, palms on his thighs. The swaying of the train surrounded them with a musty, rattling blanket. The air was hot and close.

"I heard something," she whispered, lifting her chin towards the roof. "Someone is on top of the train."

"Have we just left a station?" Dawd licked his lips, horrified to realize he'd actually fallen asleep. He clutched the Whipsaw, just to make sure the weapon was still in his hands, and carefully cleared the safety.

Mei shook her head, dark eyes wide. Dawd swallowed and looked to Colmuir for guidance.

The master sergeant was eyeballing the corridor and shook his head, signing *no one outside.*

Dawd unclipped a longeye of his own and gently slipped it under the velvet curtain covering the window. Almost immediately his visor displayed an image of the outside world: a bakingly hot morning glared down on endless flat plains of fields, canals and scattered copses of trees. The sky was spotted with fluffy white clouds, each majestically solitary against an azure background. The shadow of the train rushed along an elevated road running beside the railroad tracks. And on the road, racing to catch the train, he saw three Imperial-style trucks. Jehanan soldiers crowded the cargo beds, hanging on for dear life as the vehicles bounced over potholes and washboarding in the road.

"They're on to us," Dawd hissed, pulling the spyeye back. "Three trucks, each with a platoon, and if Mei-*sana* heard someone on the roof, they're already aboard the train."

"Everyone up," Colmuir said, voice harsh. Mrs. Petrel and Cecily were already awake, faces tight and composed. The master sergeant jogged Tezozómoc's shoulder, drew a snore and then a grumbling complaint. The older Skawtsman pinched the boy's ear, which caused the prince's eyes to fly open. "All quiet now," the master sergeant said, rising from his seat, assault rifle slung behind his shoulder.

Dawd rose as well, swinging the Whipsaw onto his hip and struggling to shed the bulky, confining poncho. Immediately the two girls took hold of the fabric, ran a fingernail down the sealer strips and pulled it away. The sergeant nodded thanks, patted his Nambu, knife, cutting bar, backup pistol and the strip of grenades down the left side of his gunrig. Then he tapped each earbug, making sure they were firmly seated.

"You've a gun?" Colmuir offered his spare Nambu to Mrs. Petrel, but the lady declined, producing a Webley AfriqaExpress from her handbag. "Good . . . Now, here's what we'll do—our sole duty is t' the prince—he canna' fall into their hands. So, we move t' the train engine with all speed and separate it from the rest of the cars, leaving the heathen savages behind. Then we run into Parus and make for either the Legation or the cantonment, as circumstances allow."

The Anglish girl folded the rain poncho expertly and tucked it away in her bag. Mei, meanwhile, had produced a tiny black Moisin-Nagant Mini and held the pistol clasped in both hands. Dawd put a hand on the edge of the curtains, waiting for Colmuir to give the word.

"Ma'am," the master sergeant said, checking the corridor one last time. "You lead, then the prince, then the girls, then me. Dawd will . . . ah, he will reduce the number of the enemy. You understand me, Sergeant?"

Dawd nodded, licked his lips and thumbed the fire control selector on the Whipsaw to high-explosive full-automatic.

"Go!" Colmuir slammed the door open and rolled out, facing the rear of the train. Petrel ducked past him, the Webley in both hands and took off down the corridor. Tezozómoc, pale as a ghost stumbled after her, forcing Mei and Cecily to seize his arms and push him along. Dawd threw back the curtains, paused a half-second to let his combat visor adjust to the blaze of morning sunlight as he braced himself and squeezed the trigger on the Whipsaw.

A deafening howl ripped at his ears, defeating even the protection afforded by the earbugs. The window shattered outwards, spraying glass into the air, and a licking tongue of flame slashed across the front of a cargo truck racing alongside. Jehanan soldiers, preparing to leap onto the roof of the train, were sawn in half in a rippling line of explosions as the highex rounds punctured scale, flesh and bone. The roof of the truck vanished in a convulsion of flame. The driver, decapitated, was flung across the cab. The vehicle swerved violently at full acceleration, bounced into the side of the speeding train and was smashed aside.

Dawd leaned out the window, hip grinding into splintered glass, and traversed the Whipsaw across the front of the second truck. Recoil slammed him back against the window-frame. The entire vehicle was immediately obscured by a gout of flame and steam. The engine block stopped sixteen of the flechettes and shattered into a cloud of superheated metal. The front axle sheared off and the truck pitched forward, back end flying up. A dozen Jehanan soldiers flew out, some already smashed into bloody ruin, and then the whole assemblage was cartwheeling violently down the road, engulfed in flying dust and smoke.

The first truck, meantime, spun off the elevated road, plunged nose-first into a nearby field and burst into flame. Dawd ducked back inside. Machine-gun fire from the third pursuer, which had deftly swerved past the first two wrecks, marched along the side of the train, shattering windows. Heavy, thumb-sized rounds tore through the wood beside the sergeant's head. Splinters stippled his armor and spanged away from his visor.

"Damn!" Dawd leapt to the side, blood streaking the side of his jaw. The curtains disappeared, snatched away by the hail of gunfire tearing into the siding. The sergeant switched the Whipsaw to armor-piercing, braced his legs and squeezed the trigger again.

This time the jolt of flame sheared through the side of the compartment, blowing out a huge cloud of metal, wood and fabric. The third truck, hanging back a bit, suddenly came into view as the wall of the train vanished in a rain of depleted uranium needles. Dawd grinned, face blackening with propellant gasses, and walked the stuttering, sun-bright line of explosions across the engine, cab and cargo bay.

The entire vehicle convulsed, perforated by thousands of tiny punctures. The driver vanished in a red haze, the soldiers with their assault rifles staggered, cut in half, and then tumbled out onto the road in a welter of arms and legs and bloody tails. The truck staggered, swerved wildly, the roof of the cab sliding back with a crash into the truck bed, bounced over the margin of the road and rolled, spewing chunks of metal, spraying liters of blood and vanished into a stand of stumpy-looking trees in a plume of dust.

The train raced onward and Dawd swung round, suddenly thinking of the other side of the passenger car, in time to have the butt of a HK-45B smash into his face. The combat visor held, deflecting some of the blow, but his head flew back, slamming into the wall. A Jehanan in the uniform of the *kujen* of Takshila loomed in the doorway, reversing his assault rifle.

Dawd's hand clenched on the Whipsaw's trigger. Flame flooded the cabin, setting the seats, walls and remains of the ceiling alight. The Jehanan vanished, torn apart by a buzzsaw burst of armor-piercing, and the doorway and the far wall of the passageway disintegrated. A clear view of a field of waving grain was revealed through the ragged opening. The sergeant staggered up, switched the targeting selector to semi-automatic, and swung groggily out into the remains of the corridor.

Smoke whipped away into the slipstream of the train. Dawd caught sight of another truck racing past on the roadway, and then tried to twist left as another Jehanan charged up the corridor. This one had a bayonet affixed to his rifle and the muzzle of the HK-45B was spitting flame. The ripping sound drowned out the rattling roar of the train wheels. Dawd staggered backwards as the burst ripped across combatskin covering his left thigh and chest, but most of the heavy 8mm bullets smashed into the Whipsaw, reducing the squad support weapon to tangled, smoking-hot wreckage and tearing the remains from his hands.

The Jehanan lunged, bayonet gleaming wickedly, and Dawd caught the blow on his right forearm. Metal pierced the ablative armor, tore through his combatskin and washed his arm with a rushing cold feeling. The slick bore down, jaws gaping, and the sergeant groped with his left hand, seized the Nambu and emptied the clip directly into the creature's snout.

A spray of blood painted the ceiling, blinding the next soldier swarming up the corridor. Dawd kicked the body of the first aside, forced himself up with one hand and thumbed the second magazine coil into the automatic. There was a burst of full-auto fire, he ducked and shot back into the smoke-choked corridor. His visor compensated for the haze and two more Jehanan staggered, pitching backwards. But there were more in the corridor behind them.

Dawd cursed; his right arm felt cold and weak and his left hip was throbbing ferociously. He ducked into the next compartment and found it choked with wounded civilians. The window was gone, ripped away by the machine-gun fire from the trucks, and the passengers were crying piteously, snouts smeared with blood, clutching their wounded to scaly chests. Broken glass was everywhere.

"Shit!" The sergeant popped back out into the corridor and pitched a handful of grenades at the muzzle-flashes. More 8mm slapped past him and he ran, bouncing from side to side. The *whoomp-whoomp-whoomp* of explosions propelled him down the passage. The rear half of the train car blew apart, sending a gout of smoke, wood and bodies cascading onto the tracks. The roof buckled, sending a rush of flame into the morning air. A long plume of black smoke spilled out behind the ruined car.

Still the train rushed on, heedless, clattering down the long straightaway into the outskirts of Parus.

The roar of an assault rifle in the passageway snapped Parker awake and sent his blood racing with horror. For a moment, he didn't know what to do. His mind started to question its identification of the violent sound, but his skin was flushed and the hairs on the back of his neck were standing on end.

Magdalena had jerked awake as well, and her head darted from side to side. "I smell—" she started to declare, and was immediately drowned out by a second burst of machine-gun fire. The little window looking out into the passage shattered, and something *zzzzinged* into the wooden wall above Parker's head.

"Blessed Mother Mary!" the pilot gasped, throwing himself onto the floor, hands over his head. "Get down, Mags!"

The Hesht plastered herself to the floor, mostly on top of Parker, which made him cry out in a muffled voice. Desperate to breathe, he twisted aside, head coming up slightly. Peering over the Hesht's furry shoulder, he caught sight of a human walking backwards, silhouetted against the windows lining the passageway. A Macana assault rifle bucked in his hands, fouling the air with propellant smoke.

"Oh, good and gracious lord," Parker whined into Maggie's ear. "Some stupid-ass Imperial Eagle Knight is shooting up the train!"

Colmuir reached the end of the third passenger car and ducked around the corner into a tiny space reserved for the washroom. The wooden sliding doors connecting the cars were banging open, letting a harsh, dusty wind tug at his hair. Gunfire stabbed up the corridor behind him and the facing wall splintered, torn by a handful of bullets. The master sergeant plucked a grenade out of his gunrig, twisted the arming knob and skated it back down the corridor. Then he jumped through the connecting doors and into the next car.

He was met by a wild burst of machine-gun fire and shattering glass. Colmuir plastered himself against the wall, cursing violently. Two Jehanan soldiers rushed down the corridor at him. The master sergeant swung his Macana underarm, ripped off a burst—punching the lead slick back, chest pulping red—and threw himself into the shadow of the falling soldier. The second Jehanan hoisted up his gun, cut loose a burst over the body of his falling comrade, and then the long, scaled head pitched back, punched through by a single shot from Colmuir's rifle.

As he dashed forward the length of the car, there was a sharp *boom!* as the grenade went off, shattering all of the windows in the second car and flinging a screaming Jehanan out to bounce along the side of the tracks, limbs flailing. Heart thudding with fear, the Skawtsman's hands were busy dumping one spent ammunition coil and loading up another.

He reached another set of connecting doors, stepped sideways into cover, heard the *bang-bang* of the Webley discharging and seized the opening lever for the sliding door. Two bursts of assault rifle fire smote his ears, there were screams—human screams—and Colmuir threw the lever, bursting into the compartment beyond with a single leap.

The swaying contents of a baggage car appeared before him. He saw three Jehanan in black body armor, modern combat goggles on their heads and cut loose with the Macana. The tiny space erupted with sound—bullets flayed the Takshilan commandos—and one of them, spinning at the sound of the door, rushed in low, his rifle blossoming with flame.

Colmuir felt a huge kick in his chest and shoulder and flew back into the wall. He bounced off, twitched the Macana aside, fired a burst into the Jehanan and saw the commando's head burst like a ripe melon. One of the others was down and there were bodies scattered on the floor. Colmuir dragged the rifle back towards the last Jehanan, but that one had sprung across the compartment and smashed the gun aside with a blow from his own rifle.

The master sergeant threw himself into the motion, colliding with the commando's chest. The blow staggered both of them, though the Jehanan recovered instantly; his brawny, scaled chest easily absorbed the impact. The Jehanan kicked, smashing a long, clawed foot into the side of Colmuir's head. The Skawtsman slammed into the wall again, vision blurred, then choked as a second kick lashed into his stomach.

Gagging, Colmuir felt huge claws seize him and fling him against the other wall with a bone-shattering crash. He crumpled. The sound of a knife rasping from a sheath penetrated the blinding pain. The Skawtsman twisted, trying to roll up, and the knife sheared through his gunrig, pinning him to the wall.

A gaping jaw filled with chisel-sharp teeth yawned in front of Colmuir's face.

The Webley belched flame and a heavy 9mm round punched through the Jehanan's skull from side to side. Blood vomited out of the mouth, blinding the Skawtsman. The prince's voice was yelling something, but Colmuir had lost his earbug and he was deafened by the pistol blast. The master sergeant wiped gore from his eyes and tried to stand up. A hand seized his shoulder.

Tezozómoc's face appeared over him, staring down with wild fear. The boy dragged at Colmuir's shoulders, but now the Eagle Knight's legs had gone weak and his medband was shrilling wildly. Over the prince's shoulder, the Skawtsman saw Petrel's face—pale as ghost, spotted with blood, her raven hair a black cloud behind her head—turning in alarm.

Two crisp shots rang out and Tezozómoc was flung aside, his Fleet skinsuit crackling and turning gray as a bullet smashed into the back of each of the boy's knees. Petrel was raising the Webley when a long-barreled military pistol—Colmuir didn't recognize the type—pressed into her throat. Pale as a sheet, she released the pistol, letting the Express fall.

There was a frozen moment as the Eagle Knight slid to the floor, hands numb. A Jehanan commando with blacked-out officer's tabs gestured Petrel aside and reached down to seize the prince's neck. Colmuir forced his hand to move. Muscles and nerves responded with glacial speed. He saw the pistol turn over once in the air. His hand was out, reaching and—

The Jehanan's tail whipped around, slapping the Webley across the compartment with a ringing clatter. The officer grinned, hoisted Tezozómoc up and dragged him away. A hoarse hooting sound filled the baggage car and Petrel, hands behind her head, hurried to keep ahead of the gesturing pistol.

Groaning, Colmuir scrabbled for purchase on the floor, trying to lever himself up. He came face to face with Cecily, whose lifeless eyes were filmed with blood. Her festival dress was torn, her chest and stomach oozing crimson. The Skawtsman swallowed, tasting iron, and groped for his backup pistol.

"*Ghawww-yeh*," rumbled an alien voice. Colmuir raised his eyes and found the muzzle of a HK-45B pressed against his forehead. The metal was hot and burned his skin.

Dawd scrambled down the third car passage, his way blocked by burning debris and scattered bodies. At least two Jehanan in uniform were sprawled among the wreckage. Buildings rushed past outside, the agricultural plain now filling with warehouses, single-family dwellings and kilometer after kilometer of brick yards. The Skawtsman had his backup Nambu in one hand and a combat knife in the other. A chorus of screams and hooting wails came from the compartments he passed, making him sweat.

He ducked past a half-open door near the end of the car, automatically swinging his pistol to cover the opening and froze—eye to eye with a sandy-haired, thin human and the huge black shape of a Hesht—each of whom were wielding lengths of splintered wood.

"Ay!" Dawd shouted, jumping aside and jerking the automatic back. "No quarrel!"

A club split the air where he'd been and the Skawtsman shook his head, scrambling on down the passage. Behind him, there was a shrieking growl and someone cursing in Náhuatl.

He slid around the corner at the end of the car, knife towards the washroom, then glimpsed—out of the corner of his eye—a Jehanan soldier's back, heavy with a rucksack and harness and a bandolier of ammunition for an assault rifle. Wooden doors separating the cars banged open and closed between them. Dawd paused, gathering himself, timed the swinging doors and then vaulted across the gap, crashing into the baggage car with his left shoulder forward.

The Jehanan snapped around, rifle coming up and Dawd shot him twice in the chest, pitching the creature back. The soldier flailed, HK-45B flying out of his hands. The sergeant leapt a pair of bodies without noticing who they were and landed in a slippery pool of intestines. His foot flew out—he shouted—and fell hard. The Jehanan staggered up, wailing a warning cry, and ripped the crumpled shirt of ceramic armor from his chest.

Dawd slid in gore, twisting his feet under, and fired the automatic wildly at the soldier. Both shots missed, pock-marking the far wall of the compartment. The Jehanan lunged, tail lashing and batted the Skawtsman's outstretched hand away. His finger jammed painfully in the trigger guard, Dawd blocked a vicious kick with his knife.

Monofil sheared through scale and bone. The soldier screamed horribly, stumbling, useless leg collapsing. Dawd reversed the blade, slashing open the side of the slick's head from shoulder blade to snout. The Jehanan toppled over, gargling. The Skawtsman lunged, clearing the slippery pool and reached the far door of the compartment. Pressing his back to the wall, he extracted his mangled finger from the pistol, switched it to his off hand and jammed the wounded arm into his gunrig.

Flames licked along the ceiling over his head as the baggage car filled with smoke.

"Dawd," a familiar voice coughed. The sergeant's head snapped up. Colmuir crawled out from under the bodies by the door, combat visor gone, hair greased to his head. "They've got the prince and the Resident's wife . . . quickly now, lad, quickly! There's only one or two of them left."

Wrenching his attention around, Dawd swayed into the doorway, timing his motion to the jump and rattle of the train car. The sliding door banged back and the sergeant dodged through, automatic close to his chest. Sunlight blazed around him—he was exposed on an open platform, facing a tender stacked with firewood—and Dawd flung himself to the side. His hip struck a railing, he tipped over halfway and was staring down at tracks and gravel rushing past. Bullets shattered the door and tore chunks of wood out of the end of the baggage car.

Dawd folded himself back, falling to the floor of the little platform, and crawled on one hand and both knees to the other side. Craning his neck, he glimpsed a Jehanan in black body armor and a modern pair of combat goggles crouched on the far end of the fuel tender.

Cursing all arms merchants for fools, Dawd forced his injured hand to work, plucked the last grenade from his gunrig, armed the device and flipped it up and into the back of the tender. In the next motion, he rolled out from the platform, legs hooked into the railing and the automatic blazed twice in his hand as the Jehanan flinched back from the flash of the grenade bursting atop the firewood.

The commando jerked aside, hit twice in the chest, and then the blast of the grenade knocked him over the side with a scream. Dawd hauled himself back onto the platform, shucked a clip from the automatic and jammed in a fresh one. Gathering himself, he vaulted up into the fuel tender, which was now smoldering. Keeping low, he scrambled up along the cords of firewood and hurried forward. He could make out the chuffing smokestack of the engine ahead. Cinders dinged from his combat visor.

The railroad tracks split and split again as the express entered the Parus railyards. Despite this, the train did not slow down, roaring ahead at full steam.

Parker picked his way down the hallway, duffel digging into his shoulders as if it were filled with lead bars. Smoke bit at his throat and fouled the air. The passenger car behind him was now burning furiously, the flames fed by the rushing air of the train's passage. Gingerly, the pilot climbed over a dead Jehanan and found himself staring into a blood-streaked baggage car littered with bodies.

"Oh, Maggie," he groaned, hands clutching the sides of the connecting door, "this does not look good!"

"Move it, witless!" The Hesht shoved his duffel with her shoulder, forcing Parker to scramble across the gap and into the next car. "We'll be burned alive if we stay here."

Inside the ruined baggage car, Parker kept to the wall, trying to avoid the lake of blood, urine, intestinal fluid and limbs sloshing back and forth on the floor. He stared with amazement at the crumpled bodies of two young human women and then froze, terrified to see that one of the bodies leaning against the wall was alive. Fierce brown eyes met his and the seeming-corpse stirred.

"Ahhh . . . Maggie! Maybe we should . . ."

The Hesht was caught in the sliding doorway, but, by dint of a rasping growl and main strength, she managed to force her way through, despite the pair of duffel bags on her back catching in the mechanism. Panting, she shucked the bags, letting them splash to the noisome floor.

Colmuir glanced from the thin human to the Hesht and back again. "Civilians," he choked, sounding amused. "Give a man a hand up, would you?"

Magdalena stared down at him with cool interest. "You're the brainless kit who tossed a grenade into our compartment, I think."

"Did I?" The master sergeant swallowed, trying to muster the strength to stand. One thigh bone seemed to be broken and his chest stabbed with pain each time he took a breath. "Sorry about that, I was in a bit of a hurry."

"Luckily, Parker has quick hands." The Hest leaned down, nostrils flaring. "*Pfah!* You stink." She stood up, reaching for her duffel bags. "Let's leave him. The fire will reach this car soon, and we'd best be—"

All three heads turned, hearing the blast of a grenade and the rattle of gunfire.

"Ah now, the lad's in trouble again." Colmuir beckoned to Parker. "C'mon, sport, help me up. There's still work to be done. You haven't a gun to hand do you?"

Parker stared at Maggie, who snarled, showing a great many white teeth in her black face.

"Leave him!"

"But—"

The train lurched, making a shockingly loud grinding sound. Something metallic shrieked in agony and everyone in the baggage car was abruptly thrown the length of the compartment with tremendous violence.

Dawd surged up over the top of the last stack of cordwood, automatic in both hands and caught sight of the enormous glassed-in roof of the Parus train station looming ahead of the train engine. Four tracks ran into the building, and the train, still barreling ahead at full speed was rushing into siding number two. Smoke stained the sky and an unexpectedly large number of multistory buildings loomed on all sides. The sight of panicked Jehanan scattering away from the passenger platform froze him for just one tiny instant.

His eyes snapped down, the gun leveling, and he glimpsed—in a moment of crystalline, unforgettable clarity—Mrs. Petrel staring up at him with open, glad relief; the prince lying limply on the floor of the engineer's compartment; the engine-mouth blazing red; and the Jehanan officer swinging around, a long-barreled pistol lined up along his shoulder, the muzzle looming huge in Dawd's vision.

Too fucking late, he had time to think, squeezing the trigger of his automatic.

The native pistol flashed, Dawd's Nambu bucked and something slammed into his chest, smashing through the tools hanging on his gunrig and flattened violently against the combatskin. The light armor stiffened automatically, absorbing the hammer-blow of the slug, but the Skawtsman pitched backwards, spilling across the cordwood and crashing into the side of the tender. His head rang, a cloud of sparks flooded his vision and—despite the valiant efforts of his medband—Dawd blacked out.

At that very moment, while the Jehanan officer was distracted, Mrs. Petrel threw herself on the brake lever of the engine, bearing down with all her strength. A rippling shock leapt through the train cars as each set of brakes engaged in turn, shrilling deafeningly with the agony of metal on metal. The wheels skidded, gouting sparks and the entire train slid wildly out of control into the station at forty kilometers an hour.

AN UNDISCLOSED LOCATION
CENTRAL PARUS

A string of portable lamps hanging from the ceiling of the bunker jiggled, sending shadows chasing across concrete walls. Bhrigu, *kujen* of Parus and the principality of Venadan, halted in the midst of incessant pacing and lifted his long, cream-colored snout. Nervous, he turned an Imperial-made comm over and over in his claws. Rubbing the hard plastic case against his scales distracted his thoughts from veering into bleak despair.

"What was that?" The prince rasped, glaring at the commander of his guard.

"A bomb," the Jehanan soldier replied, holding a bulky set of headphones to one ear-hole. Insulated wires trailed off under wooden tables covered with papers and boxes of ammunition. One entire wall of the subterranean room was covered with an immensely detailed, hand-drawn map of the city and the surrounding countryside. Three thin little females were busy chattering into speaking tubes and moving back and forth, updating a forest of pins, flags and stickers adorning the chart. "There is fighting in the western portico. Looters are trying to break into the palace."

"With what? A tank? A battering ram?" Bhrigu wrinkled his snout in disbelief. His lower stomach felt pinched and the sensation did not improve a habitually nervous disposition. "Are we being bombed? Didn't I order our aircraft to stay hidden?"

The guard-captain shook his head. "No bombs, sire. A runner-cart filled with cheap explosives was used to break down the gate. *Sirkar* Khanus and his company are holding them off." The soldier flashed his teeth in amusement. "They do not like machine-gun fire, this rabble."

"Huh! I hope not . . ." Bhrigu turned back to the map wall, hopping nervously from foot to foot as he studied the latest reports. Once, long ago, and well before the *kujen*'s ancestors had hared down from the hill-country of Agen to pillage and then seize the ruined metropolis of Parus from the degenerate, cannibalistic tribes scratching out a living amid the decaying grandeur of old Jagan, the series of chambers under the palace had been equipped with comps and display panels and all matter of technological wonders.

Now there were only gaping cavities in the walls, filled with stacks of leather-bound *pypil* booklets and boxes of dried meat and fish. The ancient *gipu*-lights had been replaced by portable oil lamps and strings of imported camping lanterns. Bhrigu's technicians and craftsmen told him there were kilometers of tunnels beneath the city, filled with an intricate network of old cable, but the equipment required to use the decaying telecom network was beyond their ability to manufacture.

The prince had spent every coin he could scrape together on guns and parts to repair the ancient tanks and aircraft his grandfather had collected in secret depots. *Weren't the Imperials going to build us a shiny new communications system*, he thought, rather bitterly, staring at the comm in his hand. *And they did, and it worked wonderfully for a year. And now? So much expensive trash littering the rooftops . . .*

Bhrigu picked at his teeth with the edge of a small-claw. His lesser stomach continued to clench intermittently, making his entire lower body queasy with pain. "How stands the battle?" he demanded, rather querulously, of the females updating the huge map. "Has Humara taken the Legation yet?"

"No, sire." The seniormost of the scribes shook her head. "The *asuchau* defenders received reinforcements by air during the initial assault. The *kurbardar* is preparing to attack from several directions at once, as soon as his reinforcements are in position."

"Huh! Well then, we will see if old Scar can prove his reputation against a real foe."

Bhrigu rolled from foot to foot, trying not to feel queasy. His relationship with Humara had never been entirely cordial. The general had been hatched with the *kujen*'s father and they had always been close. *Shell of shell, they were.* The prince started to gnaw at his claw. He possessed an abiding suspicion the *kurbar-*

dar intended to ride any victory over the Imperials straight to the high seat of the *kujenate* itself. "What about the attack on the Imperial cantonment?"

The scribes put their heads together, huddled near the section of map showing the sprawling Imperial encampment on the southern edge of the city. Bhrigu had a too-clear memory of the tricky negotiations which had led to his 'leasing' an entire district to the soft-skinned humans for fifty-two solar orbits. *At least it was marshland and refuse dumps,* he thought sourly. *And their primary presence is here, rather than in Takshila or Patala.* Denying his northern and southern rivals direct access to Imperial goods was some leavening to the bitterness of watching their aerocars come and go in *his* sky. Counting the duties his tax collectors imposed on imports from Sobipuré did bring a sweet taste to his mouth, even if he was reviled as a traitor throughout Jagan.

"There is heavy fighting there," the scribe reported. "The lance-commanders are pressing the attack, but casualties are rising very rapidly. Several detachments of the enemy have fought their way in from the countryside. Initial gains have been reversed." One of her subordinates removed several flags from the map and plucked a set of pins out of the diagrams showing the cantonment buildings.

"*Hrrr . . .*" Bhrigu felt his upper stomach clench as well. His nostrils wrinkled. "Have *any* of the Imperial detachments been destroyed? Even one?"

The *kujen* had received the news of the *asuchau* regiment dispersing to 'protect Imperial interests' with cautious optimism. His generals had been ecstatic, believing the enemy had played directly into their claws by reducing his concentration of forces to a 'manageable level.' Bhrigu was notoriously cautious, however, and had taken the human Timonen's offhand remark about the power of Imperial weapons to heart.

If a squad of their troops can match a brigade of ours, he remembered thinking, *then scattering their maneuver elements gives them a free field of fire . . . and the reach to come to grips with more of us than would otherwise be the case.*

"We have reports from various commanders," the scribe said, nostrils wrinkling in obvious disbelief, "indicating thousands of the enemy have fallen. Entire regiments," she continued, "have been destroyed, their bodies scattered, vehicles and weapons captured, females taken as prizes and young crushed alive in their shells."

"Ha!" Bhrigu hooted with laughter, appreciating the female's bone-dry delivery of the news. "What do you see, eye-of-knowing-all-things?"

"They have been hurt," she replied, moving to the chart. A thin claw indicated the rail-line south to Sobipuré. "Where forces loyal to the *moktar* managed to surprise the *asuchau* soldiers in exposed positions, such as along the elevated highways in the farm country, many enemy vehicles have *actually* been destroyed. Several groups of the enemy *have* been wiped out."

"And here in Parus?"

The scribe shrugged, tilting her head to one side. "There are too many places to hide in the city. One Imperial in the rubble can kill a hundred times his number before being chased to ground." A delicate claw tapped the diagram of the Cantonment. "The defenders of their main base are grinding up our men as quickly as fresh brigades can be shoveled into their maw. Zhern and Kuvalan will not be able to take this place, not without massing *all* our forces there."

Bhrigu ground his teeth together in dismay. In the twenty hours of battle which had passed, the *kujen* had been very careful to hold his best troops out of the fray. Humara had taken the field with his own household guards, various brigades of rural levies and the not-so-secret armies of the religious brotherhoods. Thousands of common Jehanan had joined the rising, venting blind fury at the Imperials. Their pride ran deep—even now, after so many disasters and catastrophes—even the lowest beggar knew Jagan had once been ruled by a glorious civilization.

All my enemies are dying, he realized. *Humara is truly too reckless to ever be* kujen. *Should I take a hand? There are hundreds of tanks and dozens of aircraft ready to strike, artillery by the battery . . . all of the newly trained troops with modern equipment . . .*

Bhrigu's grandfather had been a far-sighted old snake. When Jehanan industry had recovered to the point where scrap iron and hoarded steel could be worked again, and the chemical processes described by the old books could be followed, he had invested decades in scrounging up all of the detritus of the cataclysm which had swallowed the Arthavan civilization. Old Vazur had known the day would come when the cities of the Five Rivers would contest for supremacy with more than bow and shield and *lohaja*-bladed spears.

On that day, the old *kujen* had sworn his dynasty would prevail over their many rivals. The coming of the Imperials and their greedy merchants had vaulted a plan requiring decades of painstaking work to the edge of reality in only five years. Entire catalogs of machine tools and raw materials and prefabricated engines and pure, refined source chemicals had been presented to the *kujen* by the Náhuatl *pochteca*—all for the picking, if the quills could be had.

Now I must choose to show my hand . . . or not. Bhrigu stepped closer to the map, deep-set eyes searching the icons and flags and pins for an answer. *How fragile is the balance in this moment? How much of a push is needed . . .*

"How many tanks does Humara have?" he asked curiously after a long moment of consideration. "How does he plan to attack the Legation?"

"Three *Aganu*-class medium tanks, sire. Heavy cannon, machine-guns, composite armor . . . not the most powerful weapons we have in inventory, but sufficient for the task, if there are as few *asuchau* in the Legation as we suspect." The scribe searched around on the table and unrolled a large plan of the old citadel. "At least one company of engineers from the 3rd division has joined his attack, sire.

They'll cut open the eastern wall with explosives and send at least a brigade through in support of the armor."

"Against how many humans?" Bhrigu wondered if his grandfather ever felt faint and dizzy in the midst of battle. *Never! He breathed fire and spat steel nails . . .*

"Reports from our spotters in a nearby *khus* say there are ten to fifteen Fleet Marines in light armor, plus another hundred or so unarmored civilians with a variety of small arms. They have some kind of high-speed cannon on the roof of the Legation, which has been shooting Humara's mortar and artillery rounds out of the sky as they drop in."

"*Hrrrr!* They have quick eyes," Bhrigu scowled, remembering diagrams in the old books of such systems. *More toys we cannot afford and desperately need.* He measured the length of wall around the citadel and frowned. "Old Scar will get inside if he breaches that wall—there's too much perimeter for the humans to hold the whole length . . . if that roof-mounted gun is destroyed, he could flatten the whole complex and let them suffocate in the ruins . . ."

I know what to do, he realized. *Where to push, and just how hard.*

The *kujen* turned to his guard-captain, scaleskin around his eyes tight. "Tell the pilots to get in the air and make for the Rusted Citadel with all speed."

Then Bhrigu hefted the comm in his hand and toggled the switch. The device came to life, made a fluttering noise while the unit searched for a relay node and then beeped happily, showing a green 'ready' indicator. *This is what Vazur the Great felt like*, he thought, feeling both stomachs unclench. He felt light, as if the weight of ages had been lifted from his shoulders. *When his lancers burst from hiding upon the highlander left at Acare and shattered their great army. And then, as now, timing and leverage are everything . . .*

His claw depressed the control button and the *kujen* raised the comm to his lips.

"This is Bhrigu," he said. "Tell your mistress I've matters to discuss with her."

Of course, mi'lord, Lachlan answered, sounding pleased. *One moment, please.*

THE IMPERIAL LEGATION
WITHIN THE RED FORT AT PARUS

The distant *pop-pop-pop* of small-arms fire permeated the air as Felix jogged up a flight of ancient steps within the southern bastion of the *dhrada*. Her skin was stretched tight and tingling with the aftereffects of too much stayawake. Her med-band should have locked itself out—or put her to sleep—if she hadn't disabled the safety features immediately after her last equipment review. The Marine *Heicho* ducked out a heavy stone embrasure, keeping her head low, and scuttled along a broad parapet lined with granite merlons. The ancient Jehanan stonemasons who'd raised the Rusted Citadel expected to defeat sinew-driven catapults, onager-driven stones and sheer muscle power; but the fortification they'd raised in the heart of Parus was proof against 8mm caseless as well.

A squat octagonal tower bulked against the night sky at the end of the parapet and Felix slipped into the shelter of a doorway with relief. Despite the intermittent *snap!* of Imperial guns along the perimeter, and the occasional mortar round whistling over the walls—the situation in and around the fortress had been quiet since dusk.

This does not, she reminded herself, hustling up a circular ramp, *prevent some canny slick from potting me with an elephant-rifle at six hundred meters.* There were four dead Marines in the makeshift medical bay as proof of the ability of massed native firepower to overcome light Fleet combat armor. *Now, if we'd shipped down with powered armor suits,* Felix thought, licking her lips in anticipation of the likely outcome, *we'd be herding the survivors into detention camps by the morning.*

But her troops did not have heavy armor, or weapons, and the Legation guards were no better equipped. Her lone Whipsaw was tasked to anti-artillery duty. Everyone else was scrounging ammo coils and whatever sharp sticks they could find in the Residence. Communications with the Regimental cantonment on the southern edge of the city were out—native jamming continued to snarl the comm channels—and there was no prospect of relief with the nearing dawn.

An attack is what we'll get with light, the Marine grumbled to herself. *I should have taken my mother up on that offer to manage her hotel on Corcovado . . .*

Her head rose through a hexagonal opening in the roof of the tower and the *Heicho* stopped. "Clear to enter the satellite relay station?"

"Clever, Corporal, very clever," Helsdon replied from the shadows on the far side of the rooftop. "Best to crawl—I've avoided attention by showing no lights and very little motion—but I am sure someone is watching out there in the darkness."

Felix bellied down and sidewindered over to the chief machinist's mate, who was sitting cross-legged in the protection of a heavy square flagpole mount. The engineer was surrounded by a motley collection of comps, toolkits, comm gear and miscellaneous lengths of pipe fitted together into a rough antenna array. The *Heicho* stopped at his feet and tilted her combat visor up so they could talk without resorting to comm.

"The runner said you'd gotten a fix on the ship?"

Helsdon nodded towards a crude parabolic antenna hand-wired to *Sho-sa* Koshō's Fleet command comp, which had survived the destruction of the shuttle. A heavy-duty Fleet comm laser was mounted on a motorized tripod nearby, metal legs thick as wrists with their hydraulic stabilizers extended. The engineer had a handful of wire-leads and earbugs pressed to the side of his head. "Skyscan picked up a matching radar silhouette about twenty minutes ago. I've been playing the comm-laser over the surface since then, trying to get a fix on an active data aperture. Haven't had much luck until just a minute ago . . ."

Helsdon tilted his head, listening to the warble of static and chattering machine noise on one of the earbugs in his hand. "Shipside comm has reset—these are all default negotiation messages in the data-stream—the *Thai-i* changed them all years ago . . ."

"What does that mean?" Felix tried not to growl impatiently.

"I'm not sure." Helsdon pursed his lips, puzzled. "One moment, an aperture has come on-line . . ."

He pushed an earbug into Felix's hand. She popped out her Fleet one and screwed the new one in. Immediately, the background warbling and chirping of the local jamming vanished and she could hear the cool, even tones of a Fleet comm relay.

Stand by please, your call is being forwarded to the appropriate personnel.

"Huh! Didn't think I'd ever be happy to hear Miss Manners . . ."

Connecting . . .

"Hello?" The *Heicho* twisted the comm thread on the bug around to her lips. "This is Felix groundside, calling the *Cornuelle*, can anyone hear me?"

I hear you loud and clear, the tart, grumbling voice of Isoroku replied after a second's delay. *Where is* Sho-sa *Koshō?*

"In medical," Felix said, vastly relieved the ship was still in operation.

First tour recruits were treated to a variety of ghoulish stories by the twenty-year veterans. Most of them began with a variation of "when I was serving on the *Cotopaxi* . . . " and ended with the slow horrible death by mutilation of the officers or enlisted men who had *not* heeded the sage advice of their sergeants in matters of war, personal hygiene or keeping Fleet-issued equipment spotlessly clean. One of the more lurid tales concerned a company of Marines stranded on a primitive world when their troop transport had been shot up by a Megair battlecruiser. Lacking even the most primitive food-processing technology, the troopers had been forced to resort to cannibalism to survive. Since hearing the gruesome tale of the *Margaret Acatl* and her survivors, the *Heicho* had harbored a recurring, paranoid fear of being stranded after her ship had been disabled or destroyed.

"We lost a shuttle on landing to an ATGM," Felix continued, wrenching her mind back to the matter at hand. "The *Sho-sa* was wounded, but she'll be fine. What happened to the ship? Where's *Chu-sa* Hadeishi?"

In medical, Isoroku said blandly. *Stove some ribs in and nearly asphyxiated himself by dumping most of his suit air. He'll live—if we can get the ship in a stable orbit—so listen,* Heicho*—we can't help you. No fire support, no evac shuttles, not even much comm relay, until we get the ship stabilized and under control.*

"I understand," Felix said, feeling queasy. She looked across at Helsdon, who'd turned a little pale. "How bad is it?"

Bad. We took six mine strikes simultaneously and the 'skin overloaded. Then there were secondary explosions in the officer's mess and galley. Don't really know what caused that, but we're clearing the wreckage, so—

"Six anti-ship mines?" Felix's brow furrowed. Helsdon jerked back a little in surprise, alarmed by the news. "How did Navigation miss mines parked in orbit? Wait a moment . . ."

The Development Board—the engineer started to say.

"The satellite power cells!" Felix cursed. Helsdon turned green and his eyes widened. "The civilian power cells had been replaced by anti-matter fueled ones . . ."

Good to know that. Now. The engineer's voice was very flat and tense with strain. *A little late,* Heicho *but I'm sure you'll get a nice note in your personnel jacket at some point.*

"Sabotage," Helsdon muttered, nervously counting the tools in his kit. "The Board foreman who sold us all those spare parts was in charge of the satellite network repair and maintenance." The older man's head lifted, eyes narrowing. "He sold us all that *lohaja* wood too . . ."

"*Thai-i*?" Felix ventured. "Did you hear—"

I did. Isoroku's voice affected a zero-Kelvin chill. *We put nearly six hundred kilos of* lohaja *flooring into the officer's mess the day before yesterday. Helsdon, did you bioscan those supplies before they came aboard?*

The machinist's mate blanched. "Hai, *kyo*! But I just scanned them for biological infestations—worms, beetles, egg cases, pupae, virus filaments—I didn't scan them for cellulose-based explosives. Or for shielded fuses or detonators."

There was a hiss of rage on the comm. *We put our neck right in the noose!*

Felix heard an impatient chime on her other earbug, cursed and switched devices.

. . . are you there? Heicho?

"Hai, *Sho-sa* Koshō!" Felix started to sweat, overcome with nervousness. "I'm here! I'm on the roof of the south tower with Helsdon, we've got comm back with the ship! The *Chu-sa* is fine—he's wounded, but stable in medical—"

Be quiet. Koshō sounded irritable. *The* Chu-sa *can take care of himself. Listen, the eastern perimeter lookouts are reporting suspicious heat plumes two streets over and out of line-of-sight from their position. Can you eyeball anything from up there?*

"I'm on it," Felix blurted, sliding over to the eastern side of the tower. From the clear, concise sound of the officer's voice, one wouldn't have thought she was laid up in an antique four-poster bed in a guest bedroom in the Residence with a medband on each arm and under-pain-of-death orders not to move while her ligaments reknit. The Imperial Resident wasn't a military commander—and didn't pretend to be—but he knew how to sit on recalcitrant Fleet officers who needed to recuperate after being nearly incinerated.

But that's our dear old wind-knife, the corporal thought, relieved to have someone confident in command, and ran a longeye up over the embrasure and swung the sensor from side to side. "*Kyo*? I've got visual of the streets east of the main wall . . ."

She paused, watching the feed very carefully. Between the southern tower and the eastern wall was a wide expanse of wooden buildings, ornamental gardens, a twisting pump-fed stream and a variety of huge, carefully tended fruit trees. The outer wall was a solid red cliff rising over acres of flowers. Felix twitched her lips, starting to frown. The composite image included ambient light, infra-red and high-spectrum radiation—whatever the longeye could pick up—all integrated into one color-corrected, annotated image. At the moment, a motion flicker was outlining the roof of a house just across the street from the eastern ramparts.

While the citadel had once protected the northeastern corner of Parus from assault, the centuries since its construction had engendered kilometers of suburbs beyond the squat towers. A variety of brick-and-plaster buildings crowded each side of the old fortress, separated from the wall only by the width of a city street. Even a governor of *kujen* Barak's time would not have allowed civilian buildings so close to the defenses . . .

"There's a building shaking from foundation to gable, *Sho-sa*." Felix's voice was taut with suspicion. "I've seen that before . . . a tank is cutting through the interior! Tell eastern perimeter to fall back—they're about to come under fire!"

The composite image shifted, focusing as her battle comp recognized something of interest. A long barrel crashed through a window on the ground floor of the building. The muzzle swung to one side, clearing away four tall panes of glass and belched flame. The *boom* of the gun firing reached Felix a heartbeat later. A plume of dust and shattered brick puffed up from the eastern wall. The plaques of two Imperial soldiers bolting back across the ornamental gardens were very clear on her visor.

All hands to battle stations! Koshō's voice rang clear across the Imperial com channels. *Attack underway on the eastern perimeter . . . attack underway at the south gate . . . all fire teams to overwatch positions!*

Felix wedged her shoulder into one of the granite embrasures and thumbed the safety from her Macana, activating the sighting reticule on her visor. Another explosion rocked the eastern wall and the clatter of tank treads on cobblestones rose in counterpoint. The clamor of voices on the comm faded into the background as her attention focused. Dust drifted white among the fruit trees. The two Marines who'd fallen back took up firing positions in the shelter of a delicate gazebo of marble and alabaster. The *Heicho* cranked a lever to load the grenade launcher housed under the rifle's main barrel. She licked her thumb, rubbed a spot from the targeting viewer and settled her breathing.

Whooomp! The air trembled and the eastern wall shuddered from top to bottom. A huge blast reverberated in the air, followed by a string of sharp reports. The inner face of the rampart collapsed, tumbling down in a landslide of bricks and dirt and shattered concrete. Something growled mechanically in the opening, treads spinning and the prow of a tank emerged from the ruins.

Felix drifted the targeting indicator for her grenade launcher over the rear deck of the tank, saw running shapes emerge from the cloud of dust and squeezed the trigger. The Macana banged against her shoulder, the grenade whistling away, and she immediately switched to single-shot flechette.

She began firing methodically, tracking the swift, blurring shapes of Jehanan soldiers spilling out of the breach one by one. The grenade burst in a bright flare, knocking down some of the invaders. The tank lurched, smoke boiling from plated armor, but did not slow down. Three Jehanan dropped, smashed to the ground by the flechette rounds from her assault rifle.

Only seconds later, the granite shielding her rang with the impact of native bullets. Stone chips scored her visor and slashed at her shoulders. Ignoring the shrapnel, the Marine dropped another two slicks, but hundreds more were swarming through the gap. The tank rumbled forward and its long gun boomed again. The marble gazebo disappeared in a cloud of dust and flame. Felix clicked her teeth, breaking into the chaos of voices on the combat channel.

"We need the Whipsaw in the eastern gardens with armor-piercing," she growled. "This tank nearly took Carlyle's head off!"

We can't spare the 'saw from anti-artillery duty, Koshō responded curtly.

The tank fired again, obliterating another of the ornamental buildings. The two Marines down in the gardens leapfrogged back again to a low wall only meters from the Residence. Felix gritted her teeth and fired five grenades in quick succession, dropping them right across a line of Jehanan troopers crashing forward through the rose bushes and beds of orchids.

The grenades burst in a rippling wall of fire. A hailstorm of bullets smashed against the granite around her, filling the air with whining shrapnel. Felix ducked down, hearing the high-pitched wail of mortar rounds dropping out of the sky. The Whipsaw on the roof of the Residence stuttered, snapping out interceptor rounds with a piercing whine. The sky blotted with black puffs of smoke.

"Stupid-always-right-officers . . ." The Marine flexed her trigger-hand and thumbed her visor to full automatic tracking. Bullets continued to *spang!* off the merlons. The engineer laid himself down, still fiddling with his comps and antenna array, trying to keep the channel to the ship open. "Carlyle, Renton, go to full auto! Helsdon, get below!"

Felix shifted position two embrasures and popped up. The Macana jerked in her hand, a full-automatic burst ripping from the rifle. Her visor lit up with hundreds of possible targets, glowing red crosshairs dancing across the gardens. She let her conscious mind subsume in the twitch-reflex of the gun/visor interface and emptied a two thousand round magazine coil into the charging Jehanan soldiers.

If I had a powered-armor rig . . . Felix had applied for transfer to a powered armor regiment before being posted to the *Cornuelle*. A rejection letter had caught up with her nine months ago, precipitating a mild funk. Luckily, the ship had immediately encountered a Khaid raiding group and been plunged into a ferocious battle for survival, which had cheered her up immensely.

Flame stabbed out from the other two Marines as the passage of so many hypervelocity flechettes made the air incandesce. For an instant, a whirlwind of ionization and metal lashed the Jehanan battalion spilling through the breach and hundreds of the natives staggered, torn to shreds. The tank continued to grind forward, lurching up over a carved alabaster retaining wall, the forward glacis spotted with smoking, red-hot impact scars.

Then the tank turret swung towards the southern tower and flame blossomed from the muzzle with a *crack!* Felix shouted at Helsdon and flung herself to the side, curling automatically into an impact resistant ball. The granite merlons shattered in a ball of plasma. The engineer's carefully pieced-together antenna array disintegrated, the comps were blown into the far wall and flame washed over both Imperials. The concussion threw Felix into the opposite stonework, where burning debris pelted her armor and face, and Helsdon—who had scooted towards the stairs—was flung down into the tower itself. Smoke and dust billowed up from the gaping hole torn in the parapet.

The Jehanan tank turret whined around towards the Residence, long gun sliding down.

On the roof of the main building, the Whipsaw team ran to the edge of the rooftop and set down the tripod-mounted weapon. The lead gunner cycled the ammunition coil to armor-piercing, flipped the targeting display on and squeezed the firing lever. A lance of super-heated flame—engendered by the supersonic passage of dozens of depleted uranium-core munitions—boomed out, leaping down to draw a white-hot line across the front of the tank and across the turret.

Metal squealed in agony as multiple jets of metal plasma spewed into the crew compartment. There was a deep, resounding *whoomp!* and the entire machine blew apart as the munitions and fuel inside brewed up. Flames engulfed the chassis and the turret, blown free by the explosion, crashed down into an apple tree, setting the leaves and trunk alight.

On the southern tower, Felix—wheezing and tasting gravel—rolled over, groping for her rifle. The Macana had vanished, along with the communications array and half of the tower wall. Pea-sized rubble and granite fragments slid from her thigh and arm as she sat up.

"Oh, crap." The Marine spat blood to clear her mouth and realized most of the gear strapped to her gunrig and belt were gone with the assault rifle. She tapped her comm with a trembling hand. "Helsdon? Engineer? You still alive?"

In her sick-bed, Koshō heard the distant crash of artillery and tried to sit up. She winced immediately, her porcelain face twitching with pain as her head spun. "Who is attacking?" She snapped into the combat channel. "Can anyone see unit blazons, idents, regimental flags, anything?"

The Resident was parked at her bedside, one long hand to his ear, listening intently to the chatter of servants, troops and wayward Imperial citizens who had taken refuge in the Legation. He was still dressed in a formal mantle, cotton shirt and trousers—the rising had caught him amid a state luncheon and he hadn't found time to change. Between them, they represented Imperial command authority in central Parus. Attempts to contact the Regimental cantonment had failed. He shook his head, listening to a babble of reports from throughout the sprawling building.

"This doesn't sound like a single military unit," Petrel said, voice hoarse with weariness. "The rising must have split dozens of regiments along clan or parish lines. . . . One of the lesser princes will have taken control of the forces in this area." He adjusted one earbug, rubbing an eye swollen by a bad cut. "This attack on the garden gate in the south—the harness and traveling cloaks on the dead sound like those worn by religious pilgrims. . . . Rural zealots must be entering the city, looking for *asuchau*—the unclean—to expunge from holy Jagan."

"I see. They will be discerning, I'm sure." Koshō felt faint and tried to lie still on her pillow. The feeling of fine silk under her neck was disconcertingly at odds with the patina of dust on her coverlet and the acrid smell of burned metal and propellant hanging in the air. The banging sound of hammers resounded from the hallway where the household servants were busily fortifying the windows and doorways. At the edge of hearing, a human baby was crying hoarsely. "Do we know where *kujen* Bhrigu stands in all of this? Is he part of the rising, or a fellow target?"

Petrel shook his head in dismay, silver hair mussed by the events of the past two days. "He is a nervous, untrustworthy creature—ever at odds with his generals and the priests. No one trusts *him* either. I would wager, however, that *someone* is attempting to overthrow him amid all this chaos." The diplomat smiled, rather grimly. "If not, then he is hiding in the basement of his palace, waiting for the dust to settle."

Koshō sighed, wishing she'd stayed on the ship. *I wanted to feel the wind on my face—and see what kind of vacation I am having.* Battle reports continued to bark in her ear. *Tireless dogs, tireless . . .* "We needn't look to him for relief then." Exhausted, she made a courtly gesture of resignation to fate. "The enemy has withdrawn from the southern gate. But we will not be able to stop up the breach in the east. Not if they have another tank to send against us."

Petrel stared at her hand, surprised and a little alarmed. "Without holding the outer wall . . ."

"The Residence is large," Koshō replied. "Move the civilians into the basements. Once sufficient rubble has been generated to block their armor, we will be able to hold them off while we have ammunition—"

The combat channel cleared abruptly, leaving only the disgusted voice of the gunner commanding the Whipsaw on the roof shouting: *Incoming aircraft! Three of them on my scope, on an attack run! We're swinging the 'saw round . . .*

"Bah!" Koshō's rude exclamation took the Resident by surprise. "Where is *our* aircover? Are they jets?"

Fragmentary reports from the 416th had indicated the natives had several jet aircraft in inventory. The *Sho-sa* would have laughed at the futility of deploying air-breathing, turbine-powered atmospheric aircraft against Imperial forces in the field, save for her complete lack of orbital fire support to knock them down. The counter-battery guns on an APAC would do the trick as well, but she didn't have an armored personnel carrier on hand either.

No, answered the gunner. *These look like prop-driven fixed-wing models.*

"Antiques?" Koshō made a face. "They're emptying the pantry . . ." She looked at the Resident questioningly. "Have we sold the *kujen* any antique propeller-driven aircraft?"

Petrel shook his head. "Not that I've heard of . . ."

Koshō tapped up the helmet feed from the gunners on the roof. Three heat-emission signatures appeared in the relayed feed, stark against a cold pre-dawn sky. They swung into a banking turn, heading straight for the Legation. She automatically reached for her comp, intending to call up a recog soft and then stifled a curse—Helsdon had borrowed her command comp to drive his communications relay.

Heicho Felix picked her way down a rubble-strewn ramp and hissed in alarm as a body appeared in the light of her hand-lamp. The chief machinist's mate was sprawled on the landing, one arm twisted beneath his body, scalp and face streaked with blood.

"Helsdon?" The Marine knelt down, shoving broken bricks out of her way. "Can you hear me?" Gently, she turned the body, lips tight to see the older man's head fall limply to one side. Felix tugged back his uniform jacket sleeve, exposing his medband.

The silver band was a mixture of amber and crimson, but he was breathing.

"Not dead yet," Felix breathed in relief. She wiped blood out of his eyes with the edge of her hand. "You and the *Sho-sa* will make a fine pair in medical bay together. But at least Isoroku won't stripe my hide bloody for getting you killed."

Grunting, the Marine heaved the engineer up onto her shoulders. *Goddamn*, she thought, straining to lift his body, *bones like lead! He doesn't look this heavy. . . .*

A resounding *boom!* shook the tower, precipitating more rubble to cascade down the ramp and nearly knocked Felix from her feet. Swaying, she leaned against the wall, tapping her comm awake. "What the hell was that?"

Got two more tanks coming through the breach! Carlyle bawled on the channel. *We're out of here!*

Whipsaw to anti-armor, Koshō's voice followed, cutting clear and cold through the Marine's panic. *Ignore the aircraft for the moment. Kill that armor, in the breach if you can.*

Felix swore, shrugged the engineer into a slightly less uncomfortable carry, and waddled down the ramp as fast as she could. The opening onto to the retaining wall was only meters away and she turned sideways in the narrow doorway. Outside, the night was alive with the crash of heavy guns, the rattling sound of small arms and the clanking rumble of armor treads chewing more brick to dust. Intermittent tracer fire jagged into the sky. Burning vegetation lit the stones of the wall with a ruddy, orange glow. Craning her neck, she stared down into the gardens.

Sure enough, two more of the flat-turreted tanks ground noisily through the ornamental trees. A fresh attack out of the breach had developed while she'd been inside—this time the slicks were sending the armor first, with the infantry holding back and scuttling from cover to cover.

Sure are a lot of them, she thought with a sinking feeling. *A couple hundred this time . . .*

A sharp basso droning sound overhead made her turn. "What the—"

Her visor adjusted, scanning the pitch-black sky. The image changed tone and hue, and three cross-shaped aircraft roared over the Legation. Felix blanched, goggling at the antiques winging towards her, and took off at a run for the next tower on the wall.

The Whipsaw on the roof of the Residence shrieked. A hard white streak of light intersected the first of the prop-driven planes and the machine shattered in a violent burst of flame. Debris rained down, trailing smoke and flames. The other two planes broke away from their attack run, dumping their bomb loads.

Cease fire! Koshō barked on the channel. *Kill the tanks first!*

Four heavy black canisters plummeted out of the night sky and crashed through the canopy of leaves spreading over the garden. One bomb bounced up, skidded across a lawn of short-cropped grass and plowed through a clutch of scattering Jehanan soldiers. There was a bright spark in the darkness as a phosphorus igniter cooked off.

Felix flinched back, one arm thrown up by reflex to shield her eyes, even though her combat visor mirrored immediately. The bomb detonated with an ear-shattering roar, spewing liquefied flame in every direction. Three more napalm canisters exploded in succession, filling the air with a burning white-hot mist. The burning cloud rolled across the gardens, incinerating the Jehanan soldiers, consuming every scrap of vegetation and engulfing the tanks. A wave of terrific heat boiled up over the walls, shattering brick and splintering marble, granite and alabaster alike. The windows of the whole eastern side of the Residence shattered, cracked by the concussive effect of the blast and then coated with blazing jelly.

The crews of the Jehanan tanks survived a moment longer—protected from the flame and explosion by thick armor—but none of the three vehicles were secured for a zero-pressure environment and carbon monoxide flooded in through the gun aperture and air recirculators. The crewmen succumbed to paralysis and violent hallucinations within seconds, then strangled on their own blood.

Felix bolted forward, chased by a wall of fire, and hurled herself and the unconscious engineer into the secondary tower. Her combat visor sealed itself automatically as the monoxide level in the air spiked, fresh oxygen hissing into her nostrils.

On the comm, Koshō was bawling commands and Felix could hear Carlyle scream helplessly for a long drawn out second before his voice cut off. Then she was rolling down the ramp as the ceiling roared with billowing flame and everything turned red-orange from the furnace glare howling at her back.

THE COURTS OF THE MORNING ON THE BANKS OF THE PHISON, SOUTHEASTERN PARUS

Flower petals, shriveled by the queer light in the sky, fluttered down from a roseate claw. Bhāzuradeha was sitting beside an ornamental pool, her slim head bent over the waters, watching the *sicane* buds drift on the current, slowly fattening as they saturated. The pool was served by a hidden pump and the frail gray blossoms swirled away to disappear beneath mossy rocks.

"Phantom petals fall into moonlight," she whispered. "Autumn has come too soon . . ."

A crashing sound echoed through the tall pillars around the courtyard, followed by the tramp of heavy, booted feet. The Jehanan woman did not look up. The transparency and color of the water had caught her attention, curving over the rocks, capturing the morning light with a faint rainbow sheen. A multitude of tiny blue-green tendrils—a long-stemmed algae—waved on the surface of the stones, capturing invisible prey from the flow of water.

An image occluded the smooth surface of the water—a long-jawed Jehanan in a trailing cloak, jangling with iron and leather and smelling of oil, fire and bitter smoke. Bhāzuradeha looked up, enormous green eyes taking in the crowd of barbarians who had invaded her apartments. *A jeweled display box,* she corrected herself, *a stage for my skills, filled with soft, elegant things.*

One of her 'guardians' was among the tribesmen, half-paralyzed by fear, a *kalang* knife against the rough pebbled skin of her throat. Bhāzuradeha ignored the matron, attention hungrily fixed on the leader of the Arachosians arrayed before her. The common literature of the lowland cities was filled with lurid descriptions of the habit, mien, clothing and vicious temper of the highland raiders, but the poetess had never seen them before, not up close.

The Jehanan looming over her was tall, scales hard and bright, powerful chest draped with a leather harness holding knives, pistols, soft leather pouches bulging with bullets and powder, and thumb-sized cylinders of black metal thrust into fabric loops. Leather cords heavy with fore-teeth crowded his neck and upper arms. Oddly, to her eye, his broad shoulders were draped with a thick linen cloak in dull gray and brown, though the inner layer—only partially exposed—seemed to be of a softer, shinier fabric. The poetess realized temperatures among the highland mountains must be regularly chill, requiring the inhabitants to conserve warmth. Even the bone structure of his face was strange—harsher and crueler than the soft-scaled denizens of the lowland plains. His hands and forearms were scarred and chipped from rough usage on the field of war.

Humara would be apoplectic at this sight. All his glorious civilization laid to naught by one day of strife.

"This is the one we seek," the Arach war-captain said, after looking her over carefully. "Kill the others."

"How can you be sure?" Bhāzuradeha stirred, rising to her feet. The engraving on the creature's sword hilt had captured her attention for a moment—obviously the work of a woman with fine, delicate hands and skill the equal of any jeweler's shop in the city. "What if I am only an attendant? If you reach so high, do not pluck a rotten fruit by mistake!"

"You are no milkmaid," the Arach growled, turning back to face her. His snout was oddly shaped, to her eyes, almost hooked, with twin ridges of jutting scales starting above the nostrils and rising up behind the eye-shields. In contravention of the literature, his eyes did not blaze with the fires of burning cottages, but they were very, very cold. "But you are indeed the 'color of dawn.' "

There was a choked cry, and the matron crumpled to the floor, blood sluicing from her neck. The *kalang* had sheared through soft scale and bone alike, making a clean, neat incision.

No molk *was ever butchered with less thought or more skill.* Bhāzuradeha allowed her nostrils to flare slightly as the smell of urine and blood and severed bone washed over her. The Arachs did not seem to notice, or care. She considered the arrangement of the invaders, saw they had formed a loose cordon around her and their captain. Not one of them paid her the least attention, save the creature directly in front of her. The others were keeping a wary eye on the rooftops, the doors opening into the bedrooms off the courtyard and the passageway whence they had come. All of the raiders were armed with *asuchau* weapons, and Bhāzuradeha was sure the dull, efficient-looking rifles had issued from workshops tended by human hands. No Jehanan craftsman could reproduce one object with such soulless perfection.

Not a dozen times. At least once, some hint of beauty might leak in.

"I am Bhāzuradeha," she said, lifting her wrists, palms together. "Do you take me for yourself, or for another, or for ransom?"

The Arachosian hooted in amusement, adjusting his cowl. His eyes glittered in shadow. "Our master does not desire *you*," he said. "You are summoned to observe a thing of import and—in time, when the gods move your tongue to recite—to sing of what you see." He pointed to her proffered hands with his snout. "No restraint will be placed upon you."

Bhāzuradeha drew back, alarmed and insulted. "Not a properly taken captive? What kind of cruel master do you serve? Do they wish me to beg?"

The Arach snorted, nostrils flaring and shook his head. "By my eye, singer, you are a delight to look upon." He gestured sharply at his men and made a deep, respectful bow. "Bringing you home in chains or tied to the stirrups of our *sherakan* would bring *us* vast honor. No greater prize has been taken from the lowlander soft-scales in a thousand years! Even under the White Teeth, tales are told of your skill and beauty."

Well! The poetess started to smile. *He's well spoken, at least!*

"But," he continued, turning away, "you will accompany us and observe."

"I will not," Bhāzuradeha declared, irritated and growing angry with his obstinacy. "When did an Arachosian ever ask a lowlander for anything! Where is your spirit? Have the men of Ghazu lost their *kshetrae* to some malign demon?"

The Arachosian turned sharply, a low *hooooo* rumbling in his throat. "Do not insult me, singer! You are summoned and you will come—in chains and gagged, if you like—but standing upon ritual and convention is useless in this case. My master is no Jehanan, but an *asuchau* human from beyond the sky and *she* cares not at all for your propriety!"

Bhāzuradeha recoiled, fear finally seeping into her heart. "You serve the *asuchau* . . . willingly?"

"Their copper is as good as anyone's," the Arachosian captain spat, seizing her by the neck with a rough, well-calloused claw. "Now move!"

Weeping and distraught, the poetess was dragged from her courtyard and out past the bodies of the guards General Humara had set to watch over her. A truck was waiting, engine idling, stinking of half-combusted ethanol and motor oil. She was shoved into the back and the Arachosians piled aboard, glad to be moving again.

There were far too many lowlanders with guns abroad in the streets of Parus for their taste.

Crying and feeling very ill used, Bhāzuradeha started to sing under her breath, hoping old familiar words might buoy her spirits.

> *"The Night comes near and looks about,"* she wailed softly,
> *"A goddess with her many eyes, she dons shining silver glory.*
> *Immortal, she fills the limit of sight, both far and wide, both low and high;*
> *for whose approach, we seek today for rest, like the* yi, *who in the branches seek their nest.*
> *The villages have sought for rest and all that walks and all that flies.*
> *Black darkness comes, yet bright with stars, it comes to us, with brilliant hues . . ."*

She stopped, feeling the gaze of every highlander in the truck fixed upon her.

"Prettily sung," the captain said, watching her with eyes shrouded by his cowl. "You *are* a worthy prize . . ."

Bhāzuradeha turned away, delicate snout in the air, pleased someone had the wit to respect the old usages.

THE MAIN TRAIN STATION
DISTRICT OF THE IRONWRIGHTS, PARUS

The sound of hissing steam—a long, ululating wail of pressure venting from a split boiler—greeted Mrs. Petrel as she woke from an evil dream of pain and leering, sharp-toothed ogres cracking her bones with iron mallets. She found her vision obscured and the flushed, hot sensation of a medband surging painkillers and reoxygenated blood through her joints made her feel nauseated. Moving as little as possible, she tested her fingers—found them to work—and essayed raising one hand to brush matted, sticky hair away from her face.

A vision of glass panes set between wooden beams greeted her. The windows gleamed pearl with mid-morning sunlight for a moment before a drifting, translucent shape no larger than a child's marble floated directly into her field of view.

A spyeye, her muddled brain realized after patient consideration. Greta was puzzled by the provenance of the indistinct creature for a moment, but then other memories intruded, the haze clouding her mind faded and she realized she was being watched from the aether. *Oh bloody hell*, Petrel grimaced, baring her teeth at the tiny flying camera. *I'm sure this will go Empire-wide on Nightcast if the old hag has her way . . .*

"I'm getting up," she whispered to the spyeye, "just as soon as I can feel my toes."

The translucent sphere bobbed in the air once and then darted away towards the roof of the train station. Human voices approached, sharp with whispered argument, and Greta fumbled with her earrings, fingertips brushing against a particularly smooth pearl. With a twist, the earbug was snapped from its fitting and safely lodged out of sight.

A beautiful day, my dear, echoed almost immediately in her mastoid, *so much has been happening.*

"I'm sure it has," Petrel whispered, feeling dreadfully tired and numb.

"Ma'am?" A haggard, blood-streaked face appeared above her, blotting out the graceful carvings and delicate woodwork ornamenting the station roof. Sergeant Dawd peered down at her, his broad, common-born face tight with worry. Gloved fingertips turned her wrist. "Ah, thank the good Lord, you've taken no permanent hurt."

"Of course not," Greta heard herself say, clutching his hand for support. Even in such extremity, years of polite conversation amid wretched circumstances came to her rescue. "Only a little tumble. I just need to get on my feet . . ."

Petrel felt herself raised up by two sets of hands and turned to find Master Sergeant Colmuir by her side. She was momentarily taken aback by the dreadful appearance of the older Skawtsman. Then, glancing past his puffy, badly bruised face, she caught sight of the train station itself and became quite still. "Oh dear."

Despite her effort to set the brakes, the train had barreled into the station at a very decent speed. The engine had smashed through a retaining barrier at the end of the track and plowed into the side of the station itself, destroying a seating area and collapsing a washroom. The boilers, subjected to pressures and stresses far beyond their design capacity, had ruptured, venting an enormous amount of steam. Dozens of Jehanan bodies lay scattered about, hides scalded an ugly red. Burning coals smoked and sputtered on the platform. Flames licked up the broken wall, devouring the wooden timbers and charring the brick pillars holding up the roof. The train cars had jackknifed behind the engine, which was mangled beyond recognition, and crushed themselves into a huge pile of splintered wood, broken glass and tumbled iron wheels. Smoke oozed from the wreckage. Greta put a hand to her mouth, realizing she'd escaped a particularly gruesome death by no more than a hair's breadth.

The pinging sound of hot metal cooling mixed with the moaning cries of injured Jehanans unlucky enough to have taken refuge in the station. A creaking sound echoed from overhead, where the roof-beams were beginning to give way as the walls shifted. A section of green glass suddenly cracked, showering glittering debris towards the station floor. Greta clutched Colmuir's supporting hand, trying not to fall to her knees. Waves of dull pain radiated through her right leg, arm and rib-cage.

I will never complain about wearing a medband and gelsuit again, she vowed silently. *Never. Not even once.*

"You're a lucky one, mi'lady," the Skawt declared, staring in disbelief at the carnage all around them. "Must have been pitched clear on impact."

"Where . . ." Petrel cleared her throat. "Where is the prince? Has he been injured?"

Dawd shook his head. "Your pardon, ma'am, but we searched for him first—his Fleet skinsuit has a responder . . ." The Eagle Knight held up a scratched and dented but still working comp. The machine was displaying unintelligible symbols. ". . . which says he's alive, at least. We just can't find him."

"Curst jamming," Colmuir interjected. "They've taken the lad away—we're sorry, lass, but we have to find him. You stay with these other civilians—" The master sergeant pointed with his head and Petrel became aware of the bulky, inhuman shape of a Hesht kneeling beside a badly injured human male amid drifts of scattered coal, charred paper scraps and abandoned parcels.

"Who are they?" Petrel fingered her medband, summoning a cold, sharp rush of clearmyhead. The Hesht was making a growling sound as she poked and prodded the man's limbs. He was grimacing and the awkward position of his leg told Greta he'd suffered worse injury than her own.

"Never mind." She tested her own legs, finding them weak but serviceable. "The Jehanan who had the prince in his clutches is an agent of the *moktar*, the cabal behind this stupid war. We have to get Tezozómoc back as quickly as possible, before he comes to mischief."

Petrel gave the two Eagle Knights—who were staring at her with alarm—a quick smile. "The boy may believe he is of no use to anyone, but I do not agree. The *moktar*, in particular, will gain heart from his capture." She paused, thinking. Voices whispered to her from the air. "I have an idea where he might be . . ."

"Mi'lady . . ." Dawd stepped forward, extending a hand in warning. "You're in no condition to venture out into these streets—can't you hear the guns?"

Greta bound back her hair, head cocked to one side as if listening. There was a tumult of sound on the air—a hoarse droning sound filling the sky, the crash of distant bombs, the crack of rifles, screams, wailing alarms, the crackle and snap of burning buildings. She breathed in, tasting air stiff with smoke and fumes and the cloying, sweet smell of burning methanol. The whisper of her earbug was very faint, the voices of faeries and sprites darting among the hanging limbs of ancient trees.

"I've heard worse," she said, tying back the sleeves of her mantle and making sure her skirts were untangled. The absence of the antique Webley brought a keen, heartfelt pain. *Poor James gave that to me . . .* "Quickly now, if you value the oath you swore to the boy's father."

Without waiting for their response, Petrel limped across the rubble-strewn platform, heading for an arched doorway leading out into the street. Colmuir glanced at the two civilians who'd dragged him from the wreckage of the baggage car, cursed to himself and then ran after the woman. Dawd paused a moment as well, but only long enough to settle his gunrig and check the ammunition load in his spare Nambu. Then he too jogged out into the bright, humid morning.

The comp in his hand continued to flicker and whine, trying to pick up the prince's trail and failing, confused by the electronic maelstrom raging invisibly over the city.

"I don't feel so good," Parker said faintly. The pilot's face was chalk-pale and his lips were tinged with blue. Magdalena made a rumbling sound in the back of her throat, the soft pads of her fingers delicately probing the massive welting along his hip and knee. She considered his medband, which was two-thirds crimson and guessed the kit had shattered some joints.

"You're looking poorly," she allowed, searching quickly among the debris scattered around them for lengths of wood. The remains of a bench provided her with the rudiments for a splint. Maggie extended her claws, scored two of the sections lengthwise with a slash and then broke them apart by main strength. "Fur matted, can't clean yourself, nose cold as freezer-ice . . ."

Parker tried to smile, but failed to muster the strength. "Better . . . shut me down, Mags. Don't suppose . . . there's a medibot anywhere near . . ."

The Hesht shook her head, producing a roll of stickytape from her sole surviving duffel bag. The others were lost—along with thousands of quills' worth of comps, surveillance equipment and camping gear—in the wreck of the train. Working as swiftly as possible, she laid one section of wood along the human's side, then the other inside his leg. The tape drew tight, making Parker gasp. Magdalena showed him her teeth. "No stasis bag for you, my fine kit. No sharp-smelling, shiny clean medical bay. Only an old mother cat and a medband made of bark keeping you from the Peerless Hunter!"

"Oh . . ." Parker twitched painfully as she adjusted his shoulder. "Better get me . . . a fresh band, Mags. Something . . . sharp."

"All out." Magdalena fitted slats of wood around his shattered arm and went to find a board to immobilize his chest. "You'll have to share teat like everyone else."

Five minutes later, Parker was trying not to pass out as Magdalena hoisted him onto broad, ebon-furred shoulders, arm and leg taped tight to his torso. Her last duffel had been cut into a rough sling harness to carry him.

"You have to hold on," she growled, wondering if the monkey could handle the pain of being moved. "There's no medical attention here . . . we need to get you to a human hospital. Gretchen will be very displeased if you die. She will blame *me*."

"Ooooh . . ." Parker's head rolled limply to one side as his medband complained. "Don't wan' tha' . . ."

Time to go, the Hesht thought, licking her lips nervously. *He's turning gray.*

Setting her feet, Maggie adjusted her shoulders, took a step and then padded quietly out of the station house. The flames licking along the walls had reached up to brush the ceiling, and more glass was warping and cracking, adding yet more noise to the lamentations of the wounded and the dying hiss of steam.

On the steps leading down to the street, the Hesht raised her head and tasted the air. The sound of war continued to mutter and growl in the distance, leaving the avenue littered with debris—scattered bodies, abandoned runner-carts, drifts of blowing leaves and paper—and the air was tight with fumes and smoke. Far away, among the clouds, an air-breathing dragon boomed from horizon to horizon.

Looking both ways from the shadow of the door—just as her mother had taught her on the training fields of the clan-ark—Magdalena set off after the three other humans, following the clear scent of their blood drifting in the air. They had taken to the middle of the avenue, but Heshatun were drawn from warier stock and she kept to the mottled shadows under the shop awnings and broad-leafed trees lining the road.

ABOARD THE *CORNUELLE*
IN THE UPPER TROPOSPHERE
ABOVE CONTINENT THREE

A familiar vibration against his back roused Hadeishi from a drugged, placid daze. He woke with his heart racing, overcome by a feeling of near-panic. There were voices on the air, but more immediate was an overriding urgency. . . . *The ship is waking, Mitsuharu, you must be at your station!*

The metallic smell of urine and blood filled his nostrils. Hadeishi opened his eyes, took in a ceiling with two dead lighting panels and a dull emergency light and turned his head carefully to the side. The *Chu-sa* had woken up in Medical more than once and experience reminded him to move with deliberation. A handful of medical staff, haloed by portable lamps, tended an inordinate number of patients. The bay itself was in zero-g, which was one more sign of severe damage, and sticky webs of damage control spray kept loose garbage, debris and the wounded from drifting.

Hadeishi craned his neck, looking down his arm. His usual medband was gone, replaced by a cufflike unit attached to the medical bed. An amber indicator showed the medibot was running on battery power. *I'm still in my suit—odd—ah, now I remember. The ship is damaged. I am damaged.*

Everything popped back into focus. Hadeishi cleared his throat experimentally and found he could still move his tongue. *And speak, I hope.*

He clicked his teeth and felt the comm thread and earbug come alive against his cheek.

"Hadeishi to Engineering. Status?"

That was quick, Isoroku responded after a moment's delay. The engineer's voice was overlaid with a buzz of static. The *Chu-sa* heard the throttled growl of the main power plant and its attendant transformers, heat-exchangers and transmission apparatus in the background. *The* gui-ni *said you'd be out for hours while you healed . . .*

"The ship woke up," Hadeishi said, still feeling rather distant from the dark, suffocating room and his numbed body. "And so did I. Main power is on-line?"

Hai. Bottle's up, control systems are clean. We're about to start bringing up navigational control and the reaction drives. Should be able to make orbital correction in about . . . forty minutes.

"Do we have communications outside the ship?"

To the surface, you mean? Isoroku's voice faded with exhaustion, and then strengthened again. *We had a tightbeam link to the Legation about an hour ago . . . but the Residency came under attack and the comm dropped out. I think Helsdon is dead.*

"What about traffic control?"

Up here? Chu-sa, *there's no one to talk to! Only derelicts . . .*

Hadeishi convulsed with a wheezing hack. The table beeped angrily at him and sleepyhead began to leak into his blood. The *Chu-sa* felt a familiar numbness in his extremities and began breathing through his nose, slowing his heart. Sometimes the medical bay bedsensors had to be treated delicately if a man was to get his work done.

"*Thai-i*, the ship will be a danger to navigation—including our own shuttles—as long as the point defense systems have node power. So as you restore grid by grid, make sure *none* of the gatling or railgun mounts come back on-line. Route your damage control teams to disable them as soon as possible."

Hai, kyo!

"What is this?"

The *gui-ni* in charge of the bay suddenly appeared over Hadeishi, a reproving scowl on his dark brown face. "Awake despite the drugs, I see." The Mixtec leaned close, one hand on the bed-rail, and produced a sensor wand, watching the readout from the heavy-duty medband. "*Chu-sa* Hadeishi, your rib-cage is badly bruised, your lungs are half shriveled from lack of oxygen and low suit pressure, your leg muscles are badly strained and you've suffered a heavy dose of radiation poisoning."

He passed the wand over the *Chu-sa*'s forehead. "Why don't you let yourself heal? In sixteen or seventeen hours, the worst of the damage will be repaired . . ."

Hadeishi moved his head aside. "There are crewmen who need your assistance, *isha*. My condition is sufficient for duty. I am needed on the bridge before more of my men are injured or killed."

The *gui-ni* regarded him levelly for a moment. "Both medical bays are full. I've men in trauma bags hanging in the hallway like cuts of meat and there are whole compartments from bulkhead sixteen back the damage control teams haven't managed to cut into yet. I *need* this medical bed, but you're the *captain* and that means you get priority treatment—"

"I disagree." Hadeishi pointed his chin at the restraints across his chest. "Release me and you'll have the bed back."

"Your condition—"

"*Isha*, I'm giving you an order," Hadeishi said, forcing his tongue to move. "I'll sit very still once I'm on the bridge."

The Mixtec grunted noncommittally. His face was dotted with tiny green flecks of drying woundgel. "Fleet executive authority does not extend to the medical branch, save in an advisory role, *Chu-sa*. You can't order me to do anything."

Hadeishi suppressed a ghoulish laugh. "Nor can you restrict my authority, save by rendering me unconscious. This argument is pointless—here, I do nothing but take up space and your time. On the bridge, I can improve matters for all of us."

"Perhaps." The Mixtec sighed and made a hand motion indicating the acceptance of fate.

The *gui-ni* called for one of his corpsmen and keyed the bed to detach itself from the captain. "The primary bridge is either destroyed or unreachable," the Mixtec said conversationally. "Hayes and Jaguar were processed through here about six hours ago. Command and control has shifted to the secondary. I believe Smith-*tzin* is now acting duty officer."

A corpsman kicked over and took hold of the railing on the edge of the bed. "*Kyo*?"

"The *Chu-sa* needs to get to secondary control. Make sure he doesn't overexert himself while you're moving him." The doctor nodded to Hadeishi. "This man will take you there."

The *Chu-sa* nodded, still very weak and was happy to lie still, head back, while they detached the various tubes and sensors connecting him to the medical bed. He tried to muster the strength to ask if senior lieutenant Patrick Hayes and ensign Three-Jaguar had been 'processed' alive, dead, or crippled, but failed. The effort of holding back tears, of showing the dignity proper to a Fleet officer, was enough to exhaust the tiny store of energy left to him.

So many ghosts cling to your soul, the air whispered. *Like the ship herself, only a tattered hull, filled with indistinct voices. Do you hear them calling your name?*

Hadeishi curled his arm around the corpsman's shoulders and let himself be removed from the bed.

NEAR THE TRAIN STATION
THE STREETS OF PARUS

Mrs. Petrel limped to a halt, biting back an exhausted wheeze. Her thigh and hip stabbed with pain every time her foot came down on the broken concrete sidewalk. The three Imperials had come to the edge of a traffic circle where one of the grand avenues cutting through the tightly packed buildings intersected a spray of lesser streets. A jumbled pile of broken runner-carts had been pushed from the main road, making an impromptu barrier between a series of shops and one of the ancient trees lining the boulevard. There was broken glass and scattered dribs and drabs of cloth, plastic toys and sheets of charred *pypil* everywhere. Two of the shops were gutted, black holes in the face of the building.

"Ah now," Colmuir said quietly, coming up to her shoulder. "We've surely come the wrong way . . ."

The traffic circle ahead was crammed with vehicles—imported Imperial trucks; the flat, angular shapes of Jehanan troop carriers; even the hulking shape of an *Aganu* medium tank—and there were literally hundreds of native troops milling about. The rumbling engines filled the air with the stink of methanol and diesel. Most of the soldiers were squatting on the sidewalks, tails wrapped around their long feet, passing bottles and *bhang*-pipes from claw to claw. One of the troop carriers had its rear compartment open and four Jehanan mechanics were banging around in the engine, cursing and muttering at ancient machinery. Two short-horns pushed a cart past the soldiers, offering grilled spiced *zizunaga* on wooden tines. The clang of their advertising bell was nearly lost in the general murmur. None of the soldiers seemed interested.

"Do you see the building on the right?" Mrs. Petrel gasped, leaning her hands on her thighs. *Oh my god, I hurt inside. I think I've ruptured something.* "It's a hotel—a very expensive Jehanan hotel—where the *kurbardar* Humara makes his residence when he is in the city. There is a suite of rooms on the third floor . . ." She paused, coughed, hand over her mouth, listening with growing irritation to the smooth, self-satisfied voice chattering in her ear. ". . . which my husband and I once visited for a dinner party. The—*uhhh!*—commando who took the prince was wearing a regimental insignia from an elite battalion under Humara's command."

Colmuir grunted, looked askance at Dawd, who shrugged, just as worried as he. "So you think they've taken the lad in there? T' drag before the general and gain their honor for a braw captive?"

Mrs. Petrel nodded weakly and forced herself to stand up straight. The tree afforded her some support and her hands pressed against the crinkly bark with relief. "Humara will be ecstatic to have the prince in his claws. I wouldn't be surprised if he doesn't make the boy call on the Imperial troops on the planet to surrender."

"Ha!" Dawd smiled in grim amusement. "I'm sure *Tlacateccatl* Yacatolli will immediately send forth a noble envoy to the sound of drums, trumpets and whistles when he hears the news! He will have some choice words to say about such a turn of events. . . . Doesn't Humara know the Méxica don't believe in surrender, or in ransoming captives? The colonel is more likely to demand the boy be sacrificed, as was done in the old days!"

Colmuir nodded in agreement. "But we can't let the lad languish. He's our responsibility *and* he's no legal captive until the battle's doon." He pointed with the muzzle of his Macana. "There'd be a service way in from the back?"

Petrel peered at the front of the hotel, noting the garish, gilt-embossed balconies were now draped with blankets and reinforced by rows of sand-bags. Machine-gun barrels snouted from the lower windows. The main doors were wedged back, allowing entrance into the building, but again there was a redoubt of sand-bags draped with camouflage netting in the entryway. *The carpets in those dining rooms will be ruined*, she imagined. *Very pretty they were.*

Voices were whispering to her again, and Greta turned slightly to keep her earbug away from Dawd, who was staring at her in a puzzled way.

"There is a delivery entrance in the rear," she said, as if remembering. "But not directly behind the front doors of the hotel—it's offset behind that dun-colored building. There are—there will be—guards, but not so many as in front."

"Right," the master sergeant said, eyeing her with suspicion. He produced a slim little comp from a thigh pocket. The device made a creaky sound, but lit at his finger-press. Colmuir tabbed up a map of the city and popped through several views before finding the street intersection. Once he'd oriented himself, the Skawtsman peered around the corner and checked out the adjoining streets. Wisps of hazy smoke drifted among the buildings. To the right, a shop selling imported Imperial toys was still burning, spilling a cloud of dark gray ash out into the avenue. The sun had mounted past noon, but in the thick, polluted air down in the city, with the air reverberating with the distant bang and crash of explosions, the hour felt very late.

"Back a block," Colmuir announced, "and over one and we can get into that service access."

Dawd nodded, offering Mrs. Petrel a hand and then they crept back away from the barricade. As they moved, two of the spyeyes drifting above the woman darted off ahead, letting Lachlan's controllers spy their path for unseen foes.

A wide loading dock stood at the back of a particularly rundown-looking building. Three Jehanan soldiers with modern rifles slung forward at their hips stood in the shelter of an overhanging awning made of wooden slats. Coils of yellowish smoke drifted above their heads as they passed a *bhang* from claw to claw.

"That's the place . . ." Colmuir waited for the reptilian heads to turn and then signed for Dawd to leap-frog past him to a square-linteled doorway on the opposite side of the of the tiny lane. The younger Skawtsman dodged past, taking a long step over a pair of water-filled ruts worn into the cobblestones by the passage of generations of runner-carts. The master sergeant watched for any sign of alarm until Dawd was ensconced in the shadows of the doorway, automatic pistols in either hand.

"Now miss," Colmuir said, giving Petrel a worried look, "you're in no shape t' be invading the stronghold of the enemy today. You'd best stay in hiding out here somewhere. Do y' know—"

"I do." Mrs. Petrel nodded. Her face looked notably pinched and she stood only by dint of leaning into a sooty brick wall. She motioned back down the alley. "Just off that last turn is a very nice little bed and breakfast on the Court of Yellow Flagstones. The owners are friendly towards humans." She laughed bitterly. "If their avant-garde politics have not gotten them murdered, I will be safe there."

The elder Skawtsman nodded slowly, the corners of his eyes wrinkling. "Well, then. We'll be about rescuing the prince—again!—from the heathens." He paused, watching her right leg, which was trembling under her tattered, dirty festival skirts. "But we could go with you . . ."

"I will be fine, Master Sergeant." Mrs. Petrel drew herself up and wiped her hands on the bottom of her mantle. "The hotel has a small sign—three *Nēm* flowers in a triangle. I will wait for you there." She essayed a brave smile. The Eagle Knight nodded, dubious about abandoning her on the streets of the war-torn city and equally anxious to burst in amongst his enemies and recover the person of his lord from captivity. "Go on now, time may be wasting . . ."

"Aye," he said, unmoving, "it might. But we should—"

"Go on," Mrs. Petrel waved an imperious hand at him, starting to feel rather faint from standing unsupported. Without waiting for a response, she turned on her heel and strode off down the alleyway. Colmuir cursed, started to follow and then heard Dawd whistle softly behind him.

Turning, the master sergeant saw the other Eagle Knight sign *the way is clear.*

Hooting among themselves, the guards had finished their smoke and gone back inside.

"Ah, that tears it," he mumbled to himself and checked the ammunition level on his assault rifle. Colmuir signed for Dawd to advance and then ducked around the corner himself.

Finally!

Petrel watched the two Eagle Knights glide up to the loading dock, weapons at the ready, and breathed a sigh of relief. She tapped her medband awake again and sighed with relief at the cool touch of painkillers flooding into her system. Her injured leg was throbbing with each beat of her heart.

"I'm clear," she muttered, checking to make sure her earbug was firmly planted. The replacement unit didn't have the same fit and finish as her usual one. "Where to now?"

Excellent. The chittering voice of the old Náhuatl woman sounded like a cricket had crawled into her hair. *Back to the main street, but right instead of left. You'll meet an old friend within fifteen minutes—he's bringing your poetess—and some others of use . . .*

"Bhāzuradeha is here?" Petrel frowned, limping quickly along the alley. She found the emptiness of the streets unsettling—Parus was so densely populated even these back lanes were usually the scene of constant traffic and commerce—and her shoulders twitched with the sensation of being watched by hundreds of hostile eyes. "I thought you didn't approve of her!"

I've thought upon the matter, Itzpalicue said in a very smug voice. *She could be of great use to us, if properly handled.*

Petrel snorted. "You think everything and everyone is of use, *if properly handled.* Can your little friends find me a gun? I feel naked out here without my Webley."

The old Náhuatl woman chuckled. *Gehr Shahr can provide you with whatever kind of weapon you desire, as soon as you find him. He has an extensive collection to claw.*

Mrs. Petrel winced, feeling a trickle of fear at the back of her throat. "Gehr

Shahr is a murderous thug, a notorious villain and entirely untrustworthy. What is he doing here?"

Nonsense, Itzpalicue said, sounding self-satisfied. *He is a gentleman of impeccable honor, as long as the benefits of my employment outweigh his natural inclination to steal or burn everything he sees. He and his cousins have been of great use in the last several days, so you must treat him politely . . .*

"His cousins?" Mrs. Petrel started to feel faint despite the drugs and cleaning agents coursing through her bloodstream. "Just how many Arach slavers did you bring into the city?"

Only a few hundred, the old woman said in an offhand way, *just enough for all the murdering and thieving I needed done. It is always a joy to employ craftsmen.*

"Oh, Holy Mother of Tepeyac," Petrel moaned, limping out onto the street leading towards the court of Yellow Flagstones. "Hundreds of Arachosians are loose in the city? They'll—oh, hello!"

Greta stumbled to a halt, astonished to find herself face to face with the looming black shape of the Hesht female she'd glimpsed at the train station. A pasty-faced human lolled on her shoulder, grimy hands clutching the furred neck of the alien woman. Seeing them again nudged a memory loose and suddenly she realized the two refugees were, by a quirk of fate, her direct responsibility. *Oh damn.*

"*Hrrr!*" Magdalena growled in warning, long hands swinging up a length of saw-edged *lohaja.*

"Peace!" Mrs. Petrel exclaimed, drawing back. "I've no quarrel with you, *Heshak.*"

"I remember your smell . . ." the Hesht's voice trailed off into an exhausted hiss. "You were on the train." Sleek black eyebrows rose sharply and her fists tightened on the crude spear. "This stinking male needs a bone-setter and right away, or he will die. Is there a hospital or a doctor who understands the arrangement of human organs?"

"I . . . don't know. Not near here . . ." Mrs. Petrel eyed the length of razor-sharp wood with trepidation. *And me without so much as a knife in my girdle!* She frowned, a buzzing rising and falling in her hair. "Wait, I am searching for some friends—I'm sure they are nearby—come with me and we'll find help for your companion."

Itzpalicue cackled in her ear. *Yes, I'm sure Gher Shahr will take good care of some stray civilians . . .*

"This way," Mrs. Petrel said, hurrying past the Hesht and her deathly burden. "Not far, only a few blocks . . ." Under her voice, she muttered fiercely. "We're not going to dispose of these people—they're Imperial citizens and Company employees! I know their *oyabun.* Send me a doctor as quickly as you can."

Dawd set his back to a wall covered with posters of dainty Jehanan females hiding behind their tails and tucked one pistol under his wounded arm for safe-keeping. The hallway was rather dark, lit only by lamplight streaming from beneath a half-closed door. He groped in his thigh pockets and found, by touch, a pair of screw-on silencers. Only a few feet away, the master sergeant had already mounted a flash-suppressor on his assault rifle. Colmuir was taking the quiet moment to count his ammunition coils and remaining munitions.

"I've four grenades left," he said. "Do you want two?"

Dawd shook his head, the second silencer clicking into place. "I'll do the quiet work," he said, settling both pistols in his gloves. "And I'll lead. You've the longer reach."

Colmuir nodded. He started thumbing grenades into the launcher on his Macana. "Arm holding up?"

"It'll do." Dawd checked the set of his combat visor, tapped his earbug experimentally—he'd been getting some kind of interference out in the street—and sidled quietly up to the doorway. His breathing slowed appreciably with each step.

The three Jehanan soldiers from the loading dock had joined two of their friends around a low table. All of the slicks were kitted out in Vendanian uniforms; soft, campaign-style caps; leather harness for their ammunition, tools and personal effects; olive-colored baldrics front and back with heraldic symbols representing their brigade and lord. In comparison to the softness of the hand-made fittings, the gleaming metal HK-45B assault rifles seemed out of place.

Dawd nudged the door wide with his foot and stepped back a pace. Both automatics rose, bucked sharply in his hands as he fired, making a hissing *pttht!* Two of the Jehanan jerked, the sound of bullets puncturing scale sounding like a broken plate hitting a tiled floor. The other three slicks sprang to their feet. Blood dusted the far wall. Dawd shifted slightly, shot two more as they clawed for their guns and then ducked into the room, sliding to his left.

The last Jehanan has his assault rifle swinging up, an outraged *hoooo!* bursting from his throat, when Colmuir—his line of fire clear—shot him in the throat with the Macana. The flechette burst inside the slick's cranium, shredding muscles, spinal cord and brain alike. There was a choked, gurgling sound mixed with a whine of spinning metal and the Jehanan soldier toppled over.

Colmuir signed for Dawd to check the far door as he advanced, checking each body for signs of life. The younger Skawtsman drifted to the exit, slid a spyeye thread through the door and signed *all-clear*. Moving quietly, they slid out into a darkened kitchen. Colmuir's backup comp was flickering, showing an intermittent signature from the prince's skinsuit.

Five minutes later, on the third floor, Dawd darted out of the landing at the head of the servant's stairs, caught sight of two Jehanan officers in the hallway, long heads together in conversation and charged towards them. The passage was high ceilinged and filled with painted wooden panels depicting great feats of Parusian arms—most by brawny slicks wielding axes and swords of enormous size. The Skawtsman's boots raced across deep, plush carpet. A tall pair of double-doors stood closed behind the two natives.

Hissing in irritation, the taller of the two officers turned away sharply and immediately saw Dawd loping towards him, automatics raised. A wild *hoooo!* leapt from his scaled throat and he snatched for his own sidearm. Dawd dodged to one side and fired his lefthand Nambu twice. The other officer, still unawares, spun around, chest and face smashed by the bullets. Gargling, he fell in a cloud of blood.

A dozen paces behind, Colmuir calmly shot the alerted officer twice in the chest, the impact throwing the Jehanan back into the doorway with a crash. Dawd grimaced, stepped over the twitching body and tried the locking wheel.

"Shut tight," he whispered. The Jehanan under his feet groaned, trying to rise. The Eagle Knight knelt, jamming his knee into the slick's throat. The master sergeant drifted up, Macana swinging back to cover the hallway. Dawd fumbled in the remains of his gunrig. "Damn—I've lost my cutting gel."

"I've some," Colmuir said, slinging his assault rifle to clear both hands. "Cover my back."

Dawd made sure the wounded Jehanan wouldn't be getting up and stood aside while the master sergeant drew a box around the locking wheel with a tube of demolition paste. Colmuir mashed a lighter tab into the orange goo, and flattened against the wall, head turned away.

The paste ignited with a sharp bang and the locking wheel crashed to the floor. Dawd tensed, the master sergeant paused a heartbeat, hearing a chorus of alarmed warbling from inside and popped one of the grenades out of his launcher. A twist of the arming ring switched the little bomb from highex to flash mode.

For a second, nothing happened. The hallway was empty, the room was silent—save for the harsh breathing of many lizardy throats—and neither man moved.

Dawd crouched down, automatics on the floor. Colmuir set the flash grenade in his hand to the shortest possible fusing.

Inside the room, a human voice bleated "Get off of—*mmrph!*"

The master sergeant flipped the grenade through the smoking hole. There was an immediate roar of automatic rifle fire. The doors shredded and bullets whined down the long hallway, smashing lamps, paintings and chewing up the wall at the far end.

BANG!

White smoke vomited through the perforated door, strobing with the after-image of a brilliant flash. Dawd flung the panels open and rolled in on the floor, automatics snapping in both hands. He emptied both coils within five seconds, spraying the room with whining flechettes. Jehanan soldiers—there were easily twenty in the luxurious suite—staggered and howled, flayed by the bullets. Colmuir swung around the corner, his visor outlining the prince crawling underneath an enormous mound-shaped bed, and fired a grenade at each side of the room.

Heavy bullets slammed into his shoulder and chest. Colmuir grunted, flung back by the impact and felt something break in his shoulder. Twin blasts tore through the enemy, flinging scaled bodies in every direction. The master sergeant's medband swamped the injury with stabilizer and nopain. The Macana in his hands roared, ripping a stream of flechettes across three Jehanan soldiers blazing away at the door with their HK-45B's. They exploded in a cloud of red mist and their pulped bodies collapsed, shattering a thin-legged table.

Dawd sprang up, darting forward, smoking ammo coils ejecting from his pistols. His boot smashed into the face of a Jehanan soldier trying desperately to clear the action of his rifle. The slick went down squealing, and the sergeant smashed its eye socket with an empty pistol. Undaunted, the soldier twisted, tail lashing around to crack across Dawd's wounded arm. Gasping, the Skawtsman pitched to the side, losing the automatic.

The Jehanan staggered up, producing a dirk-style blade as long as Dawd's arm.

Colmuir slumped to the ground outside the doorway, teeth gritted, numb fingers managing to eject the emptied coil in his rifle. He caught the double-wrapped clip, swapped it end for end and jammed it back into the Macana.

The sword slashed down as Dawd rolled to the side, piercing carpet and the wooden floor beneath. Hissing in outrage, the Jehanan stamped down with a broad, leathery foot, catching the Skawtsman on the hip. Pinned, the Eagle Knight jerked up and a combat knife was in his hand. Dawd stabbed the slick in the stomach and a flood of entrails, half-digested noodles and blood spewed out, drenching him. Snout gaping wide in a dying hiss, the Jehanan toppled over.

Dawd rolled out of the mess, jammed a fresh coil into his Nambu and popped up.

A handful of Jehanan soldiers, stunned and disoriented by the grenade blast, blinked owlishly at him. The Eagle Knight, rather rattled himself, squeezed the trigger of his automatic in quick succession. Slicks jerked, strings cut, and more gore patterned the walls.

"Get the lad t' safety!" Colmuir shouted, managing to swing himself around. More Jehanan soldiers were storming up the main stairs into the third-floor hallway. Some of the other doors on the passage had banged open, surprised and wary slicks staring out. The master sergeant fired his last grenade through the nearest door as it slammed closed. There was a heavy thump and smoke leaked out from the sill.

A crowd of soldiers burst from the staircase. Colmuir switched his Macana to full automatic and sprayed the lot of them as they boiled up. Bodies staggered, shredded by the cloud of flechettes, and there was a cacophony of screams. The wall behind them exploded in a cloud of plaster dust and splintered wood. The flash-suppressor on the assault rifle began to glow red.

Dawd kicked the prince's foot, still exposed under the edge of the bed. "Mi'lord, come on! We've got t—"

The sound of the bathroom door opening had been drowned by the wailing of crippled and dying Jehanan soldiers. The sergeant caught a glimpse of something leaping towards him and then his head slammed around, combat visor flying askew, and he went down like a sack of meal.

Half-blinded by sparks flooding across his vision, Dawd tried to heave himself up. His medband squeaked angrily. Someone was dragging the prince out from under the bed by the foot. A horrified squealing sound penetrated the Eagle Knight's groggy daze as Tezozómoc clutched the bedlegs for dear life. Heartsick at the sound, the Skawtsman staggered up.

In the doorway, Colmuir had switched back to semi-automatic. A reckless Jehanan popped out of one of the hallway doors, automatic rifle stuttering bright yellow flashes. The master sergeant potted him with one burst, sending the creature sprawling.

With a second's breathing room, the master sergeant rolled back into the room and whistled with delight to see the nearest Jehanan corpse was festooned with old-style *Pakrit* fragmentation grenades. He snatched up the bandolier and parked himself against the wall.

Then he realized neither Dawd nor the prince was in the room.

A fresh burst of gunfire tore across the wall above his head, spilling dust into his hair. Colmuir grimaced, plucked four of the grenades from the belt and slapped them together with stickytape. More rounds whined across the room, shattering the rest of the glassware which had so far escaped the fighting.

"Good morning," he mumbled, waiting for the trample of rushing feet in the hallway, packet of grenades at the ready. He started to hum to himself. "It's a fine, fine day on the banks o' the Clyde an' I'm waiting for a bonny lass to come singing in th' sun . . . singing with her hair in braids an' bonnets, waiting for me lass t' come singing . . ." He flexed his trigger finger, poised, hearing the rustle of many native feet on the carpeted floor outside. "She's coming for me, an' I'm waiting, sun on my face, breezes in my hair, waiting by th' freshet Clyde, waiting . . ."

An armored personnel carrier rumbled past on the street, rubberized tracks grinding ancient concrete to gravel. A squad of Jehanan soldiers clung to the metal roof, peaked caps tight under their long jaws, legs hanging over the side. Mrs. Petrel shrank back into the shadow of a ruined shop front, one hand behind her to press the Hesht into the wall.

Now, the insect chittered in her hair, *step out and wave cheerfully, dear.*

"Here we go," Mrs. Petrel muttered and marched out into the thin sunlight, both hands raised. A cloud of diesel smoke drifted over her, eliciting a cough and then a short Jehanan riding in the commander's cupola of a truly enormous tank spotted her.

"Halt!" Bhrigu shouted into the driver's compartment of the *Gorond*-class heavy tank. There was a grinding sound of clashing gears and the engine belched dirty gray smoke as the machine ground to a halt. The *kujen* leaned down, taking in the unexpected sight of the Imperial Resident's wife in a tattered festival gown standing beside the street, broken shoes in her hand. He rubbed the tip of his snout. "You look lost, human."

Behind the prince, a column of tanks, armored cars, and trucks rolled to a halt amid a thick cloud of exhaust. Two columns of infantry jogged up, their sergeants bawling commands, deploying a screen of Jehanan riflemen to watch the buildings and the road ahead.

"I've come looking for you, mi'lord," Greta replied, straightening herself to stare icily up at the little Jehanan in a helmet adorned with golden horns perched on the massive turret. "It's time to put an end to this insurrection, I think."

"Do you?" Bhrigu hooted wryly. He felt itchy, sitting atop the rumbling bulk of the tank, his back exposed to so many relatives carrying guns. "Our mutual friend"—he tapped an Imperial comm tucked into the front pocket of his armored vest—"suggested I make haste to a building nearby—I understand the conspirators behind all this . . ." He waved a claw at the sky crisscrossed with gleaming contrails. ". . . are gathered to plot my overthrow."

"Yes," Mrs. Petrel said, climbing up onto the track housing. "They are only a few streets over. *Kurbardar* Humara has betrayed you, you know."

"Has he?" Bhrigu expressed great surprise. Swaying a little, Petrel laid her hand on the enormous barrel of the main gun. From the higher vantage, she was suddenly aware of many attentive ear-holes turned towards her and the prince. Quite a number of Jehanan officers had gathered unobtrusively near the tank. They were all very well armed.

"Yes," she said. "He plans to use the civil disturbance—unrest fomented, I must say, by enemies of the Empire who seek to dupe the more radical elements among your people into destroying themselves and weakening Venadan—to murder you, your loyal officers and to seize the *kujenate* himself."

Bhrigu hissed in alarm and outrage. He struck a commanding pose—slightly diminished by the nervous flutter of his right claw. "Then we will crush this nest of vipers with a swift, sure heel! All units prepare to advance!"

Mrs. Petrel hooted softly at him, trying to recapture his attention, wishing she'd hadn't lost her resonators in all the fuss. She was looking back down the road, past the columns of vehicles. A truck was barreling along the sidewalk at a dangerous speed. "Wait just a moment, mi'lord. There is someone approaching who should accompany you in this moment of victory."

"There is?" Bhrigu turned, unsettled, and bleated in outrage as the Scandia two-ton swerved, scattering his soldiers and screeched to a halt only inches from the side of the tank, dust and gravel spattering against dull gray armor. "What is this? Who are—"

The door of the truck banged open and a pale rose-colored female climbed out, stepping daintily onto the rear deck. She was immediately followed by a Jehanan of impressive size, all cloaked and cowled in the manner of the highland tribesmen. One hand, scarred and chipped, rested on the female's slim shoulder with a proprietary air. The other rested on the silver-chased hilt of a cruel-looking sword.

"You are Bhrigu," the chieftain growled, raising the hackles on back of Petrel's neck. The creature radiated undiluted menace. "I've something for you." Roughly, he shoved the female forward, drawing an outraged squeak as she fell against the turret.

Mrs. Petrel became aware of every single Jehanan within sight growing completely still. Bhrigu stared down upon the girl at his feet and turned a queer, pasty-yellow color.

"Bhāzuradeha? What—"

"The spoils of war," boomed the highland chieftain, gesturing dismissively at the poetess. "The traitor Humara is doomed, unable to even keep his choicest prize in safety. See how she cowers before you? She knows well who the victor will be . . ."

Bhrigu was struck speechless for a moment, but then he turned, snout wrinkling in furious suspicion, to Mrs. Petrel, who had been glad to catch a breath or two.

"You . . ." The *kujen* started to sputter in outrage. "You had her stolen!"

"Fairly captured, mi'lord," the girl proclaimed in a clear, carrying voice, taking the opportunity to stand up, brush herself off and kneel—as best she was able—before him on the turret ring. The crowd of Jehanan soldiers in the street had now grown quite large and every long reptilian face was turned towards the tableau atop the tank. "Taken in a sudden, daring raid by your . . . loyal vassals." She turned, inclining her slim head towards the Arachosian. "Oh, there was a terrible struggle, but they overthrew nearly a brigade of Humara's finest troops to pluck me from a perfumed, flowered garden where I languished, a cruelly kept captive!"

Gher Shahr twitched at the words *loyal vassal* but managed to keep hold of his temper.

Mrs. Petrel, gently reminded by the locust in her ear, climbed painfully down from the tank and picked her way through the rubble back into the burned out shop front. Parker was lying on the ground, a roll of cloth under his head, breathing irregularly.

Outside, Bhāzuradeha gazed adoringly up at the stunned *kujen*, hands crossed at his feet, her voice rising in a plaintive song describing her captivity and long adoration of the distant, noble prince, the only person who could possibly rescue her from such a powerful master. The entire street was perfectly silent, nearly five thousand soldiers listening keenly to her crystal-clear voice.

"Let's lift him up," Mrs. Petrel said, leaning down beside Magdalena and taking hold of Parker's hands. The Hesht blinked her eyes open, stirring from exhaustion. "There is a truck outside with medical equipment. A doctor is coming, too, but he won't be here for a bit. There's a bit of a traffic jam . . ."

Sergeant Dawd eased through a servant's doorway and found himself in a long, low hallway running behind the suite. The passage was very dimly lit—there were some small bluish lights spaced along the roof—but he could hear the prince sniffling somewhere ahead. A massive *whoomp!* boomed behind him, followed by the rattle of gunfire and faint screams.

The master sergeant is hard at work . . . I'd best be quick! He'll need my help . . .

Combat knife in one hand and his remaining Nambu in the other, the Eagle Knight crept forward, keeping his wounded shoulder to the wall. He could hear someone walking quickly, accompanied by the sound of dragging feet.

A door-wheel rattled open and light spilled into the hallway. A human silhouetted against the light pushed the hunched-over shape of Tezozómoc through the opening with a warning growl. The prince cried out, hitting his shin, and there was a cold laugh.

"You're a pitiful specimen," the creature wearing Timonen's shape declared in a heavy Finnish accent as he stepped through the door.

Dawd lunged out of the darkness, slashing his combat-knife at the man's neck.

The Finn blurred aside, reacting with incredible speed. The Eagle Knight's gray-green eyes widened as his blade clove thin air. Timonen spun, face peculiarly empty of expression and smashed a fist into Dawd's chest. The Skawtsman coughed blood, flew across the hallway and bounced from the wall. He staggered, finger clenching on the trigger of the Nambu. A double-flare of propellant blazed in the darkness, sketching the outline of the Finn lunging low, head twisted to one side at an impossible angle, one arm stiff to stab elongated needlelike fingers into the Eagle Knight's unarmored armpit. Dawd felt a rushing cold chill leach the strength from his arm.

Gasping, he looked down and saw razor-sharp fingers dripping with blood withdraw from his side. Ice flooded his chest and he slid down the wall, leaving a crimson smear. The Lengian loomed over him, cold blue eyes gleaming in the darkness. Dawd gaped, paralyzed, watching the man's head shift gelatinously, sliding back onto his neck. Unnaturally long arms coiled back into shoulder sockets and the creature flicked droplets of blood from his fingers, once more in their proper shape.

The Lengian leaned close, seizing the Eagle Knight's head with his hands, thumbs pressing into the corners of Dawd's eyes. The Skawtsman cried out in horrible pain once, and then he choked into silence. The creature crouched over his body and there was a slithering, sticky sound in the half-light.

Panting, his stomach clenching angrily, Tezozómoc managed to get to his feet. He was in some kind of dimly-lit stairwell. The smell of urine, rotten bread and ancient candle wax permeated the air.

"Hello?" The prince groped about, finding a railing and stepped back to the door he'd been so roughly pushed through. "Is . . . is anyone there?"

"Here, mi'lord," a half-familiar voice issued from the darkness, followed by the flare of a hand-lamp. Tezozómoc blinked, blinded, and raised a hand to shield his eyes. "Ah, sorry. There's a bit of a mess to clean up—just wait a moment."

The prince shuddered with relief, glad beyond measure to hear the Skawtsman's voice. "You've killed the . . . the Swede then?"

There was an affirmative grunt. "He was a Finn, I think," Dawd said, his voice hoarse and dull. "Facial structure is a little different . . ." A hissing sound cut the air and Tezozómoc flinched, his nostrils assailed by a sharp acidic smell. "But he's done for now."

The Eagle Knight turned back, lamp shining on the floor. The prince saw the young Skawtsman was drenched with blood, his gunrig in disarray, armor pocked by bullet impacts, hair haggard and awry. Dawd tucked his Nambu away and held out a hand to Tezozómoc.

"Step carefully, mi'lord, the floor is a bit . . . slippery."

The prince swallowed, nodded and hurried past the body dissolving on the ground. Dawd gestured for him to go ahead.

"Where's Master Sergeant Colmuir?" Tezozómoc asked, starting to feel ill again. He hadn't had a drink in hours and hours and he was feeling very poorly. "How will we get out of here?"

Dawd coughed wetly, but patted the young man on the shoulder. "Not to worry, I'm sure the master sergeant and I can figure something out . . . Yes, just through that door there."

Tezozómoc crept through the entry to the bathroom, tense as a rabbit on a full moon night, but was surprised at the silence pervading the wrecked suite of rooms.

His head held high, *kujen* Bhrigu stamped up a flight of grand, red-carpeted stairs and onto the third floor landing. A wall of soldiers preceded him, rifles at the ready. A young *sirdar* from the 111th Assault Brigade checked the passage, eyeing the scattered corpses with a disdainful eye and waved his king forward. Smoke clogged the air and several sections of wall were burning.

"Clear the way!" The officer barked. Two of his troopers stepped aside.

Bhrigu stepped over a drift of bodies and into a mangled, bullet-riddled doorway. Mrs. Petrel had hung back a bit as the royal presence entered the hotel—a large number of dazed mutineers were being rounded up and herded out of the building, but she was careful to keep out of the line of fire if some zealot jumped out of a closet with a gun—but now she stepped up to the *kujen*'s shoulder and took in the scene before him.

Prince Tezozómoc stood near the middle of the room, a heavy Imperial assault rifle slung over his shoulder, the muzzle—still glowing cherry red and steaming softly—covering a pack of haggard, bloody Jehanan officers kneeling against the wall. The young man was watching his captives with a fixed, grim expression, teeth clenched tight. His hands were very steady on the handgrips of the weapon. His black skinsuit did not show any smudges, gore or dust.

"Ah, superbly done!" Bhāzuradeha exclaimed, stepping past the *kujen*, who was staring very suspiciously at the wreckage, bodies and debris scattered around the room. "The prince of the air has swooped down on pinioned wings, seizing the conspirators in their very lair! Look, mi'lord, see who he has taken captive for you: the king of land and sea, the conqueror of the four quarters!"

The *kujen* tore his eyes away from the sight of two battered, exhausted Imperial Eagle Knights sitting with their backs to the wall, cleaning their weapons and reloading with numbed, trembling fingers. The younger one had a pair of darkened goggles over his eyes and half his face swathed in quickheal gel. Bhrigu glanced at Mrs. Petrel, gave her a lingering, suspicious stare and then turned back to the poetess, who had stepped to the largest of the captive officers and twisted his head around, her tiny rose-colored hand tight on his snout.

"*Kurbardar* Humara," Bhrigu said solemnly, looking down on the battered-looking officer. The scar along the Jehanan's snout twisted, but with the girl holding his mouth shut, he could say nothing. "Your treachery has cost many lives, but by the quick thinking of many loyal men . . . and women"—he nodded to Bhāzuradeha—"your foul and treasonous rebellion has been crushed."

The *kujen* made a slashing motion with his hand. "Take him away!"

The troopers from the 111th swarmed forward, binding the captured officers and dragging them roughly away. Humara was the last to disappear through the door, his eyes filled with rage.

"That one," Mrs. Petrel said quietly to the *kujen*, "will have to be killed."

"They will all be executed before nightfall," Bhrigu said, tongue flicking between his teeth. "All these *traitors* will be rounded up and shot. Their families will be exiled, their estates and properties confiscated."

Mrs. Petrel nodded, beginning to relax. She felt terribly, terribly tired. "What about the rebellious elements in the countryside, in Takshila and Gandaris?"

Bhrigu regarded her rather slyly. "I'm sure the Imperial Army can take care of such rabble as runs amuck in the other principalities. Aren't your Colonel Yacatolli's men already deployed across the length and breadth of the Five Rivers?" He wrinkled his snout. "Parus is wracked by civil unrest. There is no way my forces could essay to campaign against these other princes while my position is insecure at home!"

"I see." Mrs. Petrel forced a cold smile. "And if these mutinous lords are suppressed, then Imperial forces will be required to . . . maintain order . . . in the north. For some goodly time to come. Are you sure some Parusian regiments could not be spared to maintain civil administration in the rebellious towns? Taxes will have to be collected, the law enforced . . ."

Bhrigu clicked the point of a small claw against his teeth. "A pressing point," he admitted. "Perhaps an arrangement could reached, apportioning these *taxes* in an equitable manner . . ."

On the other side of the city, in a quiet suburb, Itzpalicue rubbed her hands together, well pleased. The darkened room around her was lit by the glow of v-displays and filled with the hum of machinery and men and women talking rapidly into their comm-threads.

"Cut!" she barked, tapping a nail on her display.

In a side-pane, Lachlan scratched his head, leaning back in his chair in relief.

"Freeze feed, scrub out the jitter from those spyeyes and post a copy to the Mirror as soon as a t-relay is available." The old Náhuatl woman opened a channel to all of her operators. "Well done, all. Very well done." She smiled, showing yellowed old teeth like a row of grainy pearls. "Once the city is secured by loyalist troops, go to half-shifts. Release time-delay on all controlled comms. Time for the army to clean up our mess. Everyone can get some sleep."

She yawned herself and sat down in a wicker chair from upstairs, completely spent. The warm feeling of a job well done, despite unexpected adversity, filled her breast. Itzpalicue turned to speak to Lachlan and saw the young man had already leaned back in his chair and was snoring softly. As she watched, one of his technicians draped a patterned blanket over his chest and arms, then reached out and shut down the v-feed.

"Well done, my boy," Itzpalicue said to the darkened screen. "Ah, I should rest myself. Tomorrow will be just as busy . . ." She consulted her chrono and bared her teeth. "Villeneuve should arrive soon and my services will be required again. Ah, this work is never done."

THE *CORNUELLE*
AT THE EDGE OF THE JAGANITE ATMOSPHERE

Wincing, Hadeishi settled himself into the command station in secondary control. Two medical orderlies assisted him, but despite their gentle hands, every nerve and muscle in his body throbbed with pain. At the navigator's station, a deathly-looking *Sho-i* Smith stared at him with haggard eyes.

"*Kyo?*" The boy's voice was a frail whisper.

"Prepare for maneuvering burn," Hadeishi gasped in response, shifting his hips in the shockchair. "Engineering—are you live on this channel?"

The *Chu-sa* had two earbugs and two comm-threads tacked in, one on each side of his face. Static and warbling interference intermittently flooded both channels.

We're here, an unfamiliar voice responded. *This is Yoyontzin. Isoroku has gone up into the drive deck access to control the engines from the maintenance panel on level two.*

"What?" Hadeishi kept his face still. Smith and the other junior officers in the secondary bridge were already on the ragged edge. All of them were injured—the communications officer had taken a bad cut on the side of his head and had one arm taped to his chest. A little less than half of the equipment was working—most of the control panels were dead—and there were signs of an explosion near the roof. A bitter taste of electrical smoke hung in the air. "What happened to the telemetry relay?"

Keeps dropping out. Yoyontzin's voice was cracking, veering into panic. *We've replaced the hard-line twice, and it just keeps dying. I have comm to the* Thai-i *on a separate channel. I'll . . . I'll just relay what you need by hand.*

"Understood. Stand by." Hadeishi muted the channel and stared at Smith. "Navigational scanners? External sensors?"

"Up and running, *kyo*." The midshipman tapped his panel. "On your pane now."

The command display curving around Hadeishi flickered to life. A set of v-panes unfolded, showing minimal altitude, position, direction and velocity data for the ship. The *Chu-sa*'s jaw tightened and he forced himself to focus. The pain in his legs was wearing away at his concentration one bite at a time. "We're deep," he said, checking the altitude of the ship. "Hull temperature?"

"Rising, but slowly." Smith crouched over his panel, working the glyphs with one hand. "A shallow descent."

"All that's kept us alive so far," Hadeishi said, reaching up to smooth his short beard. He grimaced—the Medical techs had shaved half of his face to get gel tape on his radiation burns—and switched back to the engineering channel. "We have navigational control. Stand by for burn plot. Smith-*tzin*, we're going to have do a preprogrammed maneuver—the live relay to the engines is down. Isoroku will have to fire them remotely."

"Hai, *kyo*." The boy began tapping on his display. Hadeishi opened a Navplot pane himself and searched around on the console for a stylus. They had all disappeared, despite magnetic adhesive which was supposed to keep them in place. *Somewhere there are millions of panel styli in a bucket*, he thought blackly, *millions of them.*

Remembering a trick from the Academy, he slipped a rank tab from the collar of his z-suit and twisted the retaining clip out. The metal point had the right kind of electrical signature to activate the sensor layer on the v-pane. Leaning over, he began sketching a trajectory on the display showing the round bulk of Jagan, his ship and the multiple layers of ever-thickening atmosphere.

"Burn pattern is done," Smith said a moment later, knuckling the glyph to transfer his work to the captain's station. Hadeishi leaned back a little, watching the calcs load—so slowly without main comp to supplement the display panel units!—and nodded. He meshed his own path-plot, double-checked the fuel levels last reported for the engines and tapped his comm thread awake.

"We're transferring burn parameters now," he said to Yoyontzin, whose rapid breathing sounded very loud in his ears. Hadeishi tapped the runner-glyph. The panel winked green, reporting a successful transfer.

Hadeishi tapped his other thread up and said: "All hands, prepare for maneuvering burn. Secure yourselves and your compartments. Burn will begin in . . ."

Yoyontzin was saying "Wait a moment, wait a moment . . . I've lost Isoroku's comm. Oh, there it is. I'm transferring . . ." There was unintelligible muttering on the channel. "He's loading the params now. Should be ready in about six minutes . . ."

"Stand by for maneuvering burn in eight, I say, eight minutes," Hadeishi announced. He lifted his chin at Smith and the other officers in the secondary. "Tack everything down in this space. No loose debris!"

Seven minutes later, maneuvering drives one, three and six ignited. Hadeishi felt the trembling vibration in his spine, stiffened into his shockchair and then he heard—for the first time in the six years he'd served aboard her—the *Cornuelle* groan in pain. The bulkheads twisted as the ship began to accelerate, emitting a deep basso moan. Overhead panels shivered, the lights flickered, and his command console began to evince a strange wavering effect.

He could feel the ship twisting as she surged forward, her prow biting into the upper atmosphere.

"Yoyontzin! The drives are out of balance," Hadeishi snarled, sweat seeping down the back of his neck. "Tell Isoroku to shut down the burn!"

Endless seconds passed and then the engines fluttered to silence. The hull creaked and groaned, flexing back into shape. Hadeishi slowly unclenched both hands from his armrests. He tapped the thread along his left cheekbone.

"Yoyontzin," he said very slowly and clearly, "you have to get that telemetry relay working properly. All I need is engine control live on my panel. Just patch the line from the drive access directly through to me, that's all. Don't use a relay."

But, kyo, *we'll lose comm with most of the ship—*

"You will do this right now, engineer, or you will be shot."

Hadeishi shifted in his chair, swallowing a gasp of pain. His legs were growing numb. "Smith-*tzin*, shut down your panel and reroute the Navplot to my station. Then come over here and stand secondary pilot. We'll take the ship out of atmosphere by hand."

The midshipman scrambled up, tapping the skull-glyph to kill his console. A moment later, he was squeezed in beside Hadeishi, the smell of his sweat pungent with body-toxins.

"Navplot is live," Smith said, watching a new set of v-panes unfold. "Telemetry is . . . *Kyo*, we're losing altitude again."

"I see." Hadeishi was listening to the comm from engineering. The channel clicked off. "Stand by for a second burn."

"But we can't warn—"

"I know." The *Chu-sa* forced himself forward, ignoring the throbbing in his hip. A set of engineering panes appeared. "Drive six is entirely out of synch. We're going to go to a burn with four, five, one and two." His fingers skipped across the panel, keying a fresh set of fuel metrics. He stabbed a finger at a status display, dragging the pane across the console. "Watch this reaction mass reservoir. Six is misfiring because there is a rupture in the fuel exchanger, the drive is getting too much mass. The cross-feed might be damaged as well. I'm going to go to minimal burn on the other four—if they start drawing too much fuel, override me and shut everything down."

"Hai," Smith swallowed, focusing on the status pane. His hand was poised over an override glyph of an eagle twisted around the pads of a cactus. "Ready for burn."

Out of habit, Hadeishi cleared his throat. "All hands stand by for two-minute burn."

He slid four fingers up the controls for the engine array. The ship trembled to life again. Vibrations cascaded through the hull and decking, riding up into his spine. Hadeishi closed his eyes, ignoring the readouts and graphs. His fingers moved delicately, adjusting thrust.

"Altitude stabilizing," Smith whispered, watching the captain's thin fingers making minute adjustments, altering second by second. Some of the motions were almost invisible.

"Eyes on the fuel feed!" Hadeishi snapped. *Cornuelle* began to drag against the atmosphere, against gravity, her nose coming up, prow breaking free from vanishingly thin waves of air. The *Chu-sa* began to surge more thrust to the lower drive nacelles. The ship's vibration changed pitch. A groaning sound began to shudder through the decking and the *Chu-sa* backed off a fraction. His fingers were beginning to tremble. A cramp stabbed in his left calf.

"Fuel is good," Smith said, blinking sweat out of his eyes. "Burn is clean. Fuel exchanger is holding."

"Advancing to thirty percent," Hadeishi announced. "Everyone hold on."

Two forefingers slid up, the subsonic roar of anti-matter annihilating ratcheted up into the audible range. The console began to shiver, making the rank badge dance loose from the crevice where the captain had secured it. Outside, the black hull of the ship began to glow, here and there, as atmospheric particles collided at higher and higher velocities.

"Fuel is holding," Smith declared, watching the reservoirs sink lower. Without the comp to microcontrol the reaction chambers, too much fuel was dumping into the system. "We're going to clog if we keep this up . . ." he warned.

"I know." Sweat purled down the side of Hadeishi's nose. "Twenty seconds."

The *Cornuelle* evened out. The *Chu-sa* cut to just two drives, and then feathered them back. He could feel the ship settle, the vibration in her hull idling down, bulkheads shifting and stretching. Gravity clutched at him in an infinitesimal way, tugging at his sleeve. Hadeishi glanced at the Navplot, saw the ship had reached a nominally safe orbit and breathed out.

"Engines all stop," he ordered himself. All four controls slid to zero with a careful, controlled movement. "All stop."

The ship creaked, bulkheads shifted minutely and the deck ceased to vibrate. The *Cornuelle* coasted into a new orbit.

"Get down to Engineering," Hadeishi said to Smith. "Take all six drives off-line. Main power to minimal—and make sure *someone* has pulled the plug on point defense and the shipskin!"

The *Chu-sa* stared at the Navplot with a wan, haggard face. Something was approaching. He could see the flare of engines against the curve of the world on a feed from one of the forward maneuvering cameras. Smith leaned over his shoulder, clinging to the railing.

"Go on!" Hadeishi slumped back into the stiff confines of the chair. His eyes were fixed on the burning mote speeding towards him. *At least someone survived groundside. . . . I hope it's one of ours.*

The lone Navplot v-pane emitted a warning tone. Hadeishi blinked awake and was instantly furious with himself for falling asleep. Smith had not returned from engineering and the two ratings on the bridge turned to stare at him, expecting a command response to the warning.

The *Chu-sa* stared at the plot, saw dozens of transit signatures appearing in a series of evenly spaced concentric circles and relaxed a little.

"A fleet battle group," he said, realizing neither of the ratings had an active Navplot on their consoles. "Villeneuve must be returning from Keshewān with *Tecaltan* 88. Is our point defense finally off-line?"

The midshipman at the weapons panel bobbed her head, face sheened with sweat.

"Good." He tapped his comm thread to engineering. "Yoyontzin, do we have broadband commcast capability?"

Ah, soon, kyo. *Soon. We're trying to decouple the external comm array from the power grid for the shipskin and point defense. Isoroku says . . . he says we'll be done as soon as we're done!*

Hadeishi started to laugh, relieved, then coughed, feeling his chest constrict. "Ah, that hurts!"

On his plot, the ident codes of a cloud of destroyers, cruisers and battlecruisers began to firm up. The mass of dreadnaughts, fleet tenders and troop ships in the middle of the globe were still indistinct behind a screen of countermeasures, but the *Chu-sa* could tell the Flingers-of-Stone had dropped into the system 'hot' and ready for battle.

The jarring realization reminded him of the Flower Priests and their plot. *Vil-*

leneuve knew. He knew and his operations officer knew. His fingers curled into a tight claw on the armrest. *They left us here to be expendable. So they could return—at a pre-planned time, or summoned by a relay drone waiting at the transit limit—just in time to rescue the situation on the planet. And be welcomed as heroes.*

The muscle in the side of his neck spasmed and both of the ratings on the bridge looked away, purely terrified by the expression on Hadeishi's face.

Shuttle three drifted across the starboard ventral drive cowling of the *Cornuelle*, maneuvering to mate hatch with the access door beside boat bay two. In the boat's airlock, *Sho-sa* Koshō watched the cruiser glide past, face impassive, teeth clenched tight.

She looks horrible, Susan thought. The outer hull of the light cruiser was ripped and shattered, huge gouges torn from the shipskin, revealing tangled metal and ruptured compartments. Debris tinged and clanged from the shuttle, sending a queer ringing noise through the cargo compartment. The *Sho-sa* clicked her teeth.

"Koshō to the *Cornuelle*, come in please. Anyone? Come in."

There was a sputtering echo of static. Then a voice made itself recognizable out of the distortion. Sho-sa *Koshō? Is that you? This is Yoyontzin in Engineering! Are you outside the hull?*

"I'm here with shuttle three," she replied, wondering how bad things were aboard if an engineer-second was running communications. "Are the boat bay doors working?"

No, kyo. *Nearly everything is dead. We've got a system infection. We do have power in the mains, but the* Chu-sa *says the weapons arrays and tracking are malfunctioning, so shipskin and most systems are unpowered for safety.*

"I see." Susan turned to look at Felix and Helsdon, who were standing behind her. The cargo bay itself was crowded with the enormous shape of a reinforced cargo bladder. Water shimmered inside the translucent plastic, gently sloshing from side to side. "We're not going to be unloading today," she declared, "but I'm going across. Helsdon, do you feel well enough to come with me? Isoroku could use your help on damage control."

"Of course, *kyo*." Helsdon's z-suit and gear were charred and still marked with soot, but he had managed the shuttle flight up from Parus. "With this much damage, the *Thai-i* will need another six pairs of hands."

Susan nodded. "*Heicho*, with power down and the ship chewed to ribbons, we're not finding any medical attention for the wounded here. Take this shuttle back and shift everyone to the cantonment. Regimental medical can take care of them. Just make sure no one steals their boots. Understood?"

"Hai, *kyo*." The Marine nodded dully. She was exhausted and her armor was glassy with heat damage and scored with bullet splashes and bright, metallic scars made by Jehanan sword blades.

The shuttle glided to a halt and a green light winked on over the airlock.

Sho-sa? The pilot's voice was tentative. *We're at the boat bay airlock . . . but it looks terrible out there! Are you sure you want—*

Koshō thumbed the access panel and the inner door cycled open. "Going EVA now. Stand by until I'm inside. I'll comm you."

Helsdon followed, the remains of his toolkit slung over his shoulder and a package of scavenged comps in his hand. The lock doors irised closed behind them. Felix turned away, yawning, and went to find a place to catch a nap while the shuttle was downbound.

"Do we have tightbeam to the flagship?" Hadeishi slumped in his command chair, only barely illuminated by the emergency lights on the secondary overhead.

"Yes, sir." The midshipman tapped the ident code and recog passwords for a secure channel. "We're getting the response carrier wave . . . hello, *Cornuelle* calling the *Tehuiā*, come in please." Two-Dog paused, listening. "I have a command priority call from *Chu-sa* Hadeishi, commanding the *Cornuelle*, for Admiral Villeneuve. Yes, it is urgent."

The acting communications officer turned to look at her captain. "They say only the Admiral's aide is available right now . . ."

"Put him on." Hadeishi's voice was cold and even.

Two-Dog keyed the transmission relay to the command chair. Hadeishi heard one of his comm threads warble to life. A v-pane unfolded on his console, showing Flag Captain Plamondon's broad, bearded face. The Novo French officer looked haggard and out-of-sorts.

Hadeishi! We've been calling you for at least an hour! What's your status? Long-range scan shows signs of fighting on the planet and wreckage in orbit. The officer's voice was tinged with panic. *What the devil is happening down there?*

"Put me through to Villeneuve," the *Chu-sa* said flatly. "Immediately."

Plamondon drew back at the harsh tone. *Are you well,* Chu-sa*? This v-feed is quite poor, but I don't believe you're on the command deck of an* Astronomer-*class cruiser . . .*

"I have no time for you, Plamondon. Put me through to the admiral."

Watch your tongue, Hadeishi! The flag officer looked off screen for a moment. Sweat beaded along his collar and hairline. *Has your ship been attacked? Are you injured? What happened to the freighters in orbit? Do you need combat support?*

"My ship has been severely damaged," the *Chu-sa* snarled, rising up. His mutilated face came into clearer view on the v-feed pickup and the Frenchman recoiled. "My crew slaughtered, hundreds of common spacers murdered on two independent freighters and perhaps thousands of Imperial citizens killed, wounded or driven into flight on the planet below. Now put the admiral on the comm!"

Plamondon blanched momentarily, but then he rallied, outraged by the hectoring tone in the junior officer's voice. *You do not demand things of the admiral! You will calm down and deliver a proper status report,* Chu-sa, *or you will be relieved of command!*

"Will I?" Hadeishi started to laugh, making a horrible croaking sound. "My ship is crippled, Frenchman. There's been a full-scale revolt on the planet and I doubt the Army will give you a polite greeting either! Now, put Villeneuve on the channel and he can explain to me, face to face, why seventy of my crew died for no reason at all! Why you abandoned us here with a ship in desperate need of repair to jaunt off to a planet where I'm sure there was exactly *nothing* going on, until you were told to return!"

Told? That's a lie—The flag captain's voice chilled. *You are making accusations—*

"I am," Hadeishi interrupted, voice rising steadily. "One of those freighters was a *Xochiyaotinime* covert operations ship—this entire war was a flowery excuse for certain officers to be promoted and get good marks on their combat record for bravery and expedient dispatch of the enemy! A safe way to move up!"

Plamondon turned a sickly shade of parchment white. *That is insane! What are you implying? We've no knowledge of—*

Hadeishi stabbed his hand off-screen, pointing out to spinward, beyond the indisinict frontier of the Empire. "If your curst admiral wants battle, he should go hunting Khaid or Megair in the empty systems beyond the Rim! Then he can see how real battle feels! Then he can watch the dead pile up in Medical, hanging in the hallways like sides of rotted beef! Then he can buy his precious medals with honest bl—"

A slim hand, still gloved in the matte black of a Fleet z-suit, slashed down on the *Chu-sa*'s panel, severing the connection.

"What?" Hadeishi blinked away tears, trying to force himself up from the chair. Another hand pressed into his chest, holding him prisoner. "Why did you do that?"

Susan Koshō stared at him, the corners of her mouth tight with anger, eyes fierce. "What are *you* doing? Have you lost all sense of self-preservation?"

"They betrayed us," Hadeishi whispered, feeling his last vestige of strength drain away, leaking from arms, legs, and chest like a spilled jar, leaving him hollow and spent. "We were chosen to die—as soon as we arrived, they saw our service jacket—they knew we could be cast aside without cost . . ."

Koshō leaned close, trying to catch the last of his words, but the *Chu-sa* fell silent. The lieutenant commander looked around the bridge, saw the two midshipmen were staring back at her with ashen faces and gave them both a steady, fulminating glare.

"I am taking the *Chu-sa* to Medical. Remain at your posts. If anyone calls from the *Tehuiā*, inform them we're heavily damaged, the captain is wounded and I will call them back as soon as the situation has stabilized."

Two-Dog nodded weakly and hunched over her station, concentrating fixedly on the display.

Koshō levered back the arms of the shockchair and gently eased her captain up. He seemed very small and frail. In z-g, she could carry him under one arm, kicking from stanchion to stanchion. The corridor outside was blackened with fire damage and nothing seemed to be working, but after years of service aboard she could find her way through the ship by touch if need be.

Instinctively, she moved up-ship, heading for the *Chu-sa*'s cabin, but just past bulkhead sixteen, she found the passageway blocked by a temporary pressure seal. Everything beyond the damage control barrier seemed to be in ruins. Guiding his limp body ahead of hers with one hand, Susan turned aside, descended the gangway to the portside hallway and found herself, fifteen minutes later, at the door to her own cabin.

The pressure door had lost power, but she managed to force the panel aside and drifted in, head-lamp glowing on the walls and glancing across her personal effects. For a wonder, everything seemed to be intact. The tiny pair of rooms had not lost pressure or suffered fire damage. Her collection of hand-sized paintings of Imperial Court ladies was crooked on the wall, but still intact.

Koshō bundled the *Chu-sa* onto her bed and tucked a cotton quilt around him, strapping the edges down to hold him in place. Hadeishi's eyes were still open and staring into the darkness, but he said nothing. Worried, she tacked the lamp to one wall, letting the beam shine up on a section of patterned silk covering the overhead. White-winged herons and cranes interlocked in a delicate geometric pattern. The reflected beam suffused the room with a soft, greenish light.

Her helmet came undone with a soft click and Koshō wrinkled her nose at the smell of burned plastic and electrical insulation tainting the air. Her medband said the atmosphere was breathable, though chill. Turning off her comm, she unlatched the captain's helmet as well, letting his frayed gray-black hair float loose on her pillow. The bed was very narrow, but just wide enough to sit by his side, one booted foot braced against the desk to hold her in place.

"What *happened* to you?" Susan brushed greasy hair out of his eyes, her fingertips gentle on the patches of gel covering burns on his face. "What happened to our ship?"

Slowly, Hadeishi's eyes turned towards her. They seemed empty, as if his soul had fled already, leaving only a pale, drained husk behind. Weary, he swallowed to clear his throat. "I made a terrible mistake, Susan. I thought we would be safe once the ship was home—once we were in Imperial space."

"A mistake?" Koshō's forehead wrinkled with a single sharp crease. "A saboteur rigged the satellites in orbit as mines—Helsdon and Felix found the power plants had been replaced. No one could have—"

"Months ago." Hadeishi said. "Months ago. Do you . . . do you remember the day the malfunctioning message drone reached us?"

"In the dead G-4 system beyond Kahlinkiat? Yes, radiation had damaged the—"

"I wiped the drone message store," Hadeishi said, so softly she could barely make out the words. "Or most of it, anyway. The common news, the things the men look forward to, those I left intact . . . but not the personnel and fleet orders. I erased them all."

"That is impossible." Susan pressed the back of her hand to his forehead. He was icily cold. "Only the ship's political officer has . . ." Her eyes widened and horror crept into her expression. "Hummingbird gave you the control codes when he left us at Mimixcoa?"

Hadeishi nodded, making the thin, worn linen on the pillow rustle.

"I wanted . . . the orders . . ." He stopped speaking for a moment, gathering his strength. "We were ordered home, Susan, to report to Toroson as soon as possible."

"Mitsuharu!" Koshō cupped his pale, worn face with her hands. "That was nine months ago! We've been living on dregs and scraping from system to system . . ." She drew back, comprehension slowly dawning in her face. Her expression softened minutely. "What did the orders say?"

"We had a good ship," Hadeishi said, eyes distant, staring through her at the overhead. "A good crew. All these years of training and learning how to act as one . . . moving so smoothly, so effortlessly, without the slightest hesitation . . . the best crew I've ever had. A fine ship."

"Mitsuharu," Susan tried to catch his eye. "What did the orders say?"

"They were . . . we were recalled to Toroson to decommission the *Cornuelle*, Susan. They were going to break her up, use her for maintenance parts for other *Astronomer*-class cruisers. They're . . . the whole class is being retired from service, or sold, or parted out."

"Oh." Koshō sat back, nostrils flaring, her face perfectly still. "The ship."

"You . . ." Hadeishi's face twisted and his eyes filmed with tears. "You're a captain now, Susan. A *Chu-sa* yourself. You deserve the honor, I must say, more than any officer I've ever served with. And Hayes—he . . . he . . . made lieutenant commander. And Smith . . . if they're still alive. If any of them are. You're bound for the *Naniwa*—and she's a fine, fine ship—fresh from the yards. You'll . . ." Tears began to leak up from his eyes in tiny silver droplets and Susan had to turn away.

Imperial officers did not cry. Susan herself did not remember Hadeishi ever showing such raw emotion before—oh, he was fond of laughing and making sly hints and poking fun at her when he thought no one was looking—and he treated the junior officers very gently, by Fleet standards, but this . . . this was too much for her. She held herself very still, hands white at the knuckles as they clenched on the edge of the fold-out bed.

"You were all being taken away from me," he rasped, barely able to speak. "I was left with nothing. No ship, no crew, no purpose. You see . . ." He stopped, racked by a gasping heave. "There was nothing for me. No promotion. No new ship. Only orders to proceed to Jupiter to wait on The List. Hayes . . . Hayes is for the *Taiko*, Smith for advanced school . . . Huémac and the Marines for a training cycle at Syria Planum on Mars. You will all do so well."

Susan closed her eyes, forcing herself to ignore the dreadful sound of his voice. His exhaustion was creeping into her as well, filling her heart with a cold emptiness.

"I just wanted a few more months of your company, Susan. A few more days to have a purpose."

Koshō turned, pressing her hand across his mouth. Her eyes were very bright. "Don't say anything. Nothing. No more." She shook her head slowly, appalled and anguished in turn. "We were out too long, *Chu-sa*! Worn down to nothing, spent, exhausted . . . did you think we were *ronin* in some old tale? Wandering from town to town, helping the peasants, fighting bandits . . ."

She stopped, her skin turning the color of fresh ash. "You should have told *me*. We are Imperial officers, Mitsuharu. We have an honorable duty to attend. We can't just ignore orders . . . even if . . . even if they're painful to consider. And the ship . . ." Koshō looked up at the dead lights on the overhead. "She is dying despite all you've done . . . we're badly damaged, *kyo*, they won't even bother to haul her back to Toroson."

Hadeishi closed his eyes, turning his head away.

"Oh," Susan said, the brief flare of anger dying, falling away into darkness. She put her hand on the quilt over his heart. "I don't know what will happen to you . . ."

The room remained cold and quiet, even after he had succumbed to a fitful, weary sleep.

Koshō watched him for a long time, checking his medband now and again. At last, she stirred and forced herself to stand up. The little washroom lacked water pressure or lighting, but she managed to repair her makeup, now badly streaked and smeared, and make herself look presentable.

Then *Chu-sa* Koshō let herself out and headed for the secondary control bridge. There was work to be done, and—if she could manage to placate the gods of the Fleet—save the careers of her junior officers. Those who lived, at least.

The dead will keep their honor. They will be remembered at the Feast of Spirits as heroes.

THE SOBIPURÉ BUS TERMINAL, PARUS
NEAR THE COURT OF YELLOW FLAGSTONES

Clouds of exhaust fogged Gretchen's view of the city as the *Tikikit* bus slowed to a crawl. A huge crowd of Jehanan townspeople blocked the street, voices raising a huge, frightened murmur, claws scraping alongside the vehicle and clattering against the windows. Anderssen stared out in alarm, barely able to make out the stone awnings over the bus stands through the moisture on the windows. Torrential rain poured down, turning the street into a muddy river.

"*Hoooo* . . . Taste the fear in the air!" Malakar leaned at her shoulder, long snout pressed against the glass. "Such a crowded city this is!"

"This is much worse than last time," Gretchen said, feeling the bus shake from side to side as the crowd surged against the vehicle. A clamor of hooting and warbling made it hard for her to hear. "Everyone is trying to flee—"

"Should we leave the bus?" The gardener folded one claw over the other, eyes wide. "Where will we go? How will we pass through such a throng?"

"Our hotel isn't far," Gretchen said, wondering if they *could* manage to move through such an enormous press of people. A wild face appeared momentarily at the glass, a young Jehanan trying to scramble up onto the roof of the bus. The window made a splintery sound as his clawed feet scrabbled on the sill. "What else can we try? If we stay here, they'll push the bus over."

Anderssen took a breath, readied herself to plunge into the fray and patted Malakar on the shoulder. "Come on."

Chuffing exhaust, the *Tikikit* bus inched into one of the quays in the station. Hundreds of Jehanan, nearly every one of them laden with baggage, pots and pans, bedding, and wicker baskets filled with personal effects, overflowed from the waiting ramps into the road and packed the open floor of the station itself. Gretchen pushed down the stairs from the bus, shoving aside a Jehanan matron trying to claw her away aboard while shrilling wildly in an unknown tongue. Malakar tried to apologize, but had to stiff-arm a frantic male to keep from being thrown to the ground.

A stifling blanket of heat and humidity started to choke Anderssen before she'd taken two steps into the surging, agitated crowd. Her medband squeaked an alarm before being drowned out by the booming roar of thousands of panicky townsmen. She reached back, seized hold of Malakar's harness and started plowing forward, head down, shouldering natives out of the way on either side.

Claws scraped her face, clutched at her shirt and pants, then fell away behind. Malakar hooted mournfully, hands tight on the back of Gretchen's field jacket. Intermittent blasts of some kind of alarm horn shook the air. A sea of noise rolled back and forth over them, echoing from the vaulting roof and the awnings over the buses. The stench of the crowd faded, replaced by the smell of smoke and burning plastic.

Anderssen stumbled through a wood-and-glass door at the front of the bus station. Broad flights of steps littered with discarded goods—potted plants, shoes, smashed sun-hats, broken bottles and fallen, ripped paperbacks, sections of sod, torn clothing, harness buckles and straps—led down to the curving road. The huge crowd inside petered away to a few mournful souls sitting on the sidewalk, huddled in blankets or staring sightlessly at the sky, rain sluicing from their scales.

Despite the rain, a thick pall of smoke hung over the city, hiding the upper reaches of the ancient *Khus*.

Gretchen shifted her pack, checked her jacket and pockets. Malakar was still clinging to her back, panting, snout down. Water streamed from her long head.

"You all right?" Anderssen put her arm under the old Jehanan's shoulder. The human was soaked already, shirt clinging to clammy flesh, hair plastered to her forehead. "It's not far."

"This . . . this old walnut has never seen so many people in one place in all her life."

The avenue was empty. The usual throng of runner-carts and wagons and trucks was gone. A long, low building across the street was on fire, belching smoke into the rain. The gutters were already full, flowing sluggishly and spreading into huge ponds where debris blocked the drains. Gretchen searched for a landmark, realized the burning edifice was the train station and turned right. "This way."

They hurried down the sidewalk, feet splashing through oily pools, past abandoned stands advertising sweets, grilled meat, newspapers, religious votives and icons, all the paraphernalia of a living city. The kiosks were abandoned and empty, shutters banging against empty stalls, garbage heaped in drifts across the sidewalks.

The doors of the hotel were locked, drapes drawn tight behind barred windows. Gretchen banged on the wooden panel, her shoulder pinched with the effort of keeping Malakar upright. The gardener was staring curiously back down the lane, rain spattering on her long snout.

"Hello!" Anderssen called through the mail slot. "I'm a guest here! I have a room!"

"I think," Malakar whispered in amazement, "those were actual *Araks* who passed us! I've heard they're bloody handed savages from beyond the vale of Acare! They eat the flesh of their own kind—or whatever live prey they can catch. Did you see the necklaces of teeth?"

"No. Can you ask these people to open the door?"

After Malakar had hooted and trilled and generally sounded like a reasonable, polite lizard, someone peered out at them through the drapes and then, grudgingly, opened the door to let them in out of the rain.

"Very dangerous," the desk clerk declared, shaking his stumpy triangular head in dismay. "You do not know what kind of horrific creatures have lately been here! They threatened to chop down my door and eat the yolks of my eggs raw! While I watched!"

Gretchen nodded politely and dragged the gardener away and up the stairs before Malakar fell to discussing the proclivities of the mysterious Araks. Anderssen really only wanted to lie down in a real bed. Her stomach was growling with hunger.

"Hello?" The door to the room swung open and Gretchen winkled her nose, smelling burning tabac. She held Malakar back out of caution. "Is someone here?"

"*Hrrr!*" A rumbling growl answered and a disheveled black shape appeared out of the bedroom. Anderssen felt a tight band around her heart ease and sagged against the wall, so vastly relieved she could barely comprehend the pressure which had been dragging at her. "Maggie. You're alive."

"Hunt-sister!" the Hesht yelped in delight, seizing Gretchen in an enormous, bone-crushing hug. Then Maggie held the human out at arm's length, paws gripping Anderssen's shoulders. "You are whole and undamaged? We thought a ghost was whispering to us on the comm . . ."

"I know, I know." Anderssen hugged the Hesht back, sagging into her soft, plushy fur. Magdalena felt wonderfully warm and dry. "We tried to reach the *khus*, but there were troops everywhere. . . . I'm glad you ran when you did."

"*Hoooo!*" Malakar made a pleased sound, long snout snuffling at Magdalena. "Your friend is not a human at all. Such strange, soft scales she has!"

"No," Gretchen stepped aside, wiping her eyes. "Malakar, this is Magdalena. She is a Hesht—another *asuchau* race—they live in great clan-arks which travel between the stars, but she works with me for the Company. Maggie, this is Malakar, she was a gardener at the House of Reeds; which is to say, she was a teacher-of-kits."

"Well met," Magdalena said, ears twitching forward. She bowed politely. "If you are a friend of the hunt-sister, then you are welcome to our pack."

"*Hoooo . . .*" The gardener seemed pensive, covering the tip of her snout in embarrassment. "I do not know if clever-thoughts counts me as friend or not."

Gretchen smiled crookedly. "We've chased each other over enough rooftops, I think we can say we are friends. You didn't turn me in to the Master of the Garden, though I haven't given you any answers to your questions."

Malakar nodded, emulating the Hesht's bow. Magdalena twitched her whiskers at Anderssen and winkled her plushy nose. "Parker is here too—but he has been hurt."

"Hurt?" Alarmed, Gretchen pushed past Maggie and into the bedroom, where she stopped and stared at the pilot, who was buried under a pile of quilts. "He doesn't look hurt to me," she declared. "He is smoking in *my* bed, and has plenty of colorful magazines filled with interesting pictures to entertain him."

"Hi, boss." Parker took a long drag on his tabac and offered her a pained smile. "They're for my health—the tabacs, I mean. A restorative! All these"—he gestured at the native magazines scattered on the coverlet—"are really Maggie's. I'm just trying not to move too much."

Anderssen leaned over him, eyeing the bandages taped to the side of the pilot's head, his neck and the visible part of his shoulder. "What happened to you?"

Parker grunted, his lips a little white. "The side of a train kind of, uh, hit me, boss."

"You *are* injured." Gretchen gently peeled back the top of the quilt. The pilot's chest, arm and side were a dark, angry purple under a layer of quickheal gel. She hissed, concerned. "How bad is this?"

"I can't walk," Parker said, watching her nervously. "My leg and arm are . . . uh . . . broken. The doc said I've got a concussion and I chipped some teeth." He grinned. Two of his bicuspids were jagged. "I'm kind of doped up right now, so I hope you don't need me to fly anything . . ."

Gretchen shook her head, looking pale. "You were hit by a train?"

"No." Maggie wrapped her arms around Gretchen's shoulders, holding the anguished human close. "We were *in* the train and there was a wreck. Parker can't land on his feet, so he used his side and leg and arm instead." The Hesht blew mournfully through her fangs. "We were lucky—many passengers were killed."

"Ok-kē." Anderssen patted the Hesht's furry arm and sat down in a chair beside the bed. Feeling dizzy, she put her head in her hands and closed her eyes. "Is . . . is there anything to eat?"

Malakar shifted in the doorway, looking expectant. "Even gruel would be welcome," the Jehanan said softly. "We had pies yesterday . . ."

"I will find food," Magdalena announced, bustling out. "Silly kits, going all wild and forgetting to hunt! You would all perish in a forest filled with fat juicy marmosets if I wasn't . . ." Her voice faded into the hallway.

"She doesn't even know what a *marmoset* is," Parker said from the bed in a sulky tone. "She never goes to get *me* food . . ."

Gretchen began digging in her pockets, hoping to find a threesquare but instead her fingers closed on her survey comp and she pulled the battered device out with a sigh.

"So much trouble you caused . . ." she muttered, staring at the blank-faced device. "And for what?"

Parker stirred, staring at her hopefully. "Did you find the tree of gifts, boss? Was it really a First-Sun artifact? Did you get me any presents?"

Anderssen looked up, running her hands over the comp. "Yeah, we found the *kalpataru*." She nodded at Malakar, who was now squatting in the corner, damp tail wrapped around her feet. "Malakar led me into the heart of the Garden and . . . it was real, Parker."

"What?" The pilot sat up slowly, eyes wide. "It was *real*? A real First-Sun device?"

Gretchen nodded, and then started to laugh. "All you had to do was see the thing and . . . it was so *old*, Parker. Like it had seen the first light of the first star to condense out of the birth-caul of the universe. You could just . . . feel the weight of millennia in the metal, pressing on the world around the device. It *felt* like so much time had passed, every atom had collapsed . . ."

"Oh." Parker took a drag on his tabac. "Sure, a *feeling*. Like, that time in the cave-shrine on Shimanjin when you *felt* where the little girl was, or . . . or when we were at the Resident's party and you *felt* the way to the door?"

Gretchen looked up, fixing the pilot with a sharp stare. "What do you mean?"

The pilot shrugged. "Just, you know . . . we've noticed that from time to time you can . . . um . . . you can tell where things are without seeing them, or, uh, you can find your way when there's just *no way* you could know the proper path . . ."

Anderssen made a face and avoided looking at him. In the corner, Malakar's head rose slightly, her dark eyes bright with interest.

"I'm lucky sometimes . . ."

"Sure, boss. Whatever." Parker pointed with his tabac at the comp. "So, did you get enough data on this eldest tree-thing to make the trip worthwhile?"

"No." Gretchen hefted the comp with a bitter expression. "There was so little time. I had this on broadband scan, but we were outside when the sky lit up—I'm sure this comp, and all the data, are *minging* dead. My medband went crazy with radiation warnings . . . and these little hand-helds aren't shielded against EMP flash."

"Crap." Parker stubbed out his tabac and held out a hand. "Lemme look."

Gretchen tossed him the comp and slumped back in her chair, watching the pilot wince with pain as he fiddled with the device. She was feeling worse and worse with every passing moment. *Oh, Mother Mary, I nearly got poor Parker killed. I nearly got myself killed, I ran Malakar out of her home, dragged Maggie all over the back of beyond . . . for what? For a prize beyond price I had to destroy.*

"Does look kind of fried," Parker admitted, turning the comp over. He pressed a tab on one side of the unit, popping the back cover free. The data cartridge fell out on his chest. "I've got a spare in my kit, can you hork it over here?"

"Sure." Gretchen got down on the floor and began rummaging in the filthy, oily mess of odds and ends in the pilot's spare duffel. "God, Parker, don't you ever clean this stuff up?"

"Never," he said, keying a self-test on the cartridge. "Rusts if you keep it clean. Gotta protect the tools, right?"

Anderssen found a working comp and handed it over. Malakar watched them intently, snout hidden behind crossed arms. Parker popped out the data cartridge in the new unit, swapped in the old one and thumbed the unit awake. The comp beeped, made a squeaky sound and the screen glimmered awake.

"See . . . might have something left to say." The pilot thumbed through to a diagnostic screen. "We'll just let it check itself out." He smiled wanly, tired just from using his hand. "Maybe we'll get a bonus after all!"

"We do not have *gruel*," Magdalena declared as she bustled in with a tray heavy with covered bowls. "But there are edible things to eat."

Gretchen accepted a warm plate covered with freshly cut vegetables, a bowl of murky-looking broth and hunks of brown bread. A little amazed at the Hesht's ability to produce something other than reprocessed threesquares, Anderssen made an amused face. "What, no chocolatl?"

"Do not complain, wet-nose, about the food on your plate," Maggie said testily, curling up on the end of the bed with a head-sized bowl of red meat swimming in a dark oily sauce. "Unless you have caught and skinned the prey yourself!"

"I'll bet these were hard to catch," Parker mumbled, mouth full of food. He waved something like a bright-green carrot at the Hesht. "Tasty, tho'. Is there butter for this bread?"

"No," Maggie said, lips wrinkling back from her fangs. "There is *no butter.* There are *no cows* on this planet."

"But they have cheese . . ." Parker's voice trailed away at the expression on the Hesht's face.

"*Ahhhh* . . ." Malakar breathed in the aroma of her bowl, which was filled with noodles slathered in black paste. Gretchen's nose twitched, assailed by an astringent smell of salt, pepper and garlic. "You are *kujena* of tasty foods," the Jehanan said, pressing her snout to the floor in respect. "I have not had such a delicacy in many years."

Maggie winkled her nose, watching the gardener inhale the noodles. "Gruel! Indeed."

The comp sitting beside Gretchen chirped to itself, announcing the completion of its tests. Parker and Malakar stopped eating. Anderssen put down her bowl of soup and picked up the device. The screen displayed her usual set of tools and interfaces.

Well, she thought, tabbing into the archive of sensor logs. *What did we see?*

Gretchen scrolled through the data, frowned, loaded some AI to process the raw feeds, frowned again, slid out of the chair and sat cross-legged on the floor. Without looking up, she took a notepad from her jacket pocket, found some writing pens and began making notes. Her soup grew cold. Magdalena turned onto her side, bowl empty of entrails, curled her tail over her nose and went promptly to sleep. Parker was already snoring.

Late afternoon sunlight crept across the floor, washing over Anderssen's back, and vanished as the sun passed into the clouds again. Malakar stirred after watching for a long time, picked up all the dishes and shuffled off into the kitchen. Anderssen's face remained tight with concentration, her brow furrowed. The comp hummed warmly in her hands. Her control stylus made faint squeaking sounds on the panel. At one point she took off her field jacket and carefully examined the durafiber surface for marks.

"Ahhh . . ." An hour later, Gretchen looked up with a grimace and stretched her back. She creaked and said "Ow!" before rubbing her sore muscles.

Malakar appeared at the doorway. "What did it see?"

"Nothing." Anderssen laid the comp down on the rug. She looked disappointed and relieved at the same time. "Nothing but dust."

"How can this be?" Malakar knelt beside her, leathery tail flipping around and out of the way. "I felt the air tremble with unwholesome power! Such strange lights there were in the old fane! Those technicians did not fall unconscious for no reason . . . did not your mind reach across thousands of *pan* in the blink of an eye, giving warning?"

"I did." Gretchen spread her hands on either side of the comp. Her face was impassive. "Yet, none of my instruments detected anything. All of this data just shows the *kalpataru* standing inertly in the shrine. No power fluctuations, no radiation emissions from the tree itself—nothing but the generator signatures of the *kujenate* equipment."

"Nothing?" Malakar rolled back on her heels, claws tapping her snout. "But—"

"We heard you!" Parker tapped his earbug, confused. "Both Mags and I heard you clear as day—"

"Whatever happened was beyond the capability of these sensors," Anderssen said, trying find the words to explain. "But I saw . . ." She paused, remembering something which Hummingbird had once said.

"A teacher once said to me: Every time we do something, anything—eat, sleep, read a book—we leave an impression upon the world. Usually, normally, the impressions are wiped away by new things happening—someone else comes into the room, opens the door, picks up the book—but if a solitary object has been in one place for a very long time, if the same things keep happening in its immediate presence, then that repetition leaves a mark, a memory, a shadow of substance upon the pattern of the world . . . that *pattern* can be enormously strong."

"*Hoooo . . .* " Malakar twisted her head from side to side. "You saw—experienced—what the divine tree had done in the ancient past."

Gretchen nodded, wondering how much to tell. The food she'd eaten lay in her stomach, undigested and heavy. *I can't tell them everything—that the artifact woke to life, if even for an instant—what if they told someone else? The Company would tear down the whole city just to dig out the fragments of the thing . . .*

She took a breath, and then said: "The gift of the *kalpataru* was to reveal the unseen, to reach across the abyss of space and yield up sight, sound, vision, allowing instant communication across thousands of light years. Over millions of years of use, the artifact gained such a massive pattern of repetition it began to twist the fabric of time and space around itself, even when there was no power to drive the ancient machine.

"I think . . . when the *kalpataru* first came into the hands of the Jehanan, great wonders were revealed to them, *even though* the device had failed thousands of years before they laid claw on the divine tree. So strong were those events, so much power had been loosed in its presence, the memory is immanent in the metal itself. If one of the ancient Jehanan was . . . sensitive . . . if the machine was disturbed by a power-source . . . then that Jehanan's mind would have been filled with stupendous, terrifying, ecstatic visions."

Gretchen felt a chill steal over her. *And that was the salvation of Jagan. The beacon was damaged, unable to reach across the void to touch the sleeping thoughts of its makers, summoning them to feed upon the Jeweled-Kings and then the Jehanan. Not unless a truly powerful mind blundered into the trap. Oh Holy Mother, preserve me from gaining such skill!*

"For some time—centuries? decades?—it seemed the *kalpataru* was still functioning. But there were only fragments of the past, only this . . . residue, repeating over and over. Mechanical sensors, like this comp, can't even detect the pattern. But my mind is . . . more sensitive."

"I knew it," Parker said quietly, watching her with wide eyes. "You were different after you came back from Ephesus. What . . . what did that old *nagual* do to you?"

"Nothing, Parker. Mind your own business." Gretchen glared at the pilot. "Go back to sleep."

"Wait a minute." Parker said, distressed. "What will the Company say about all this?"

"Nothing," Gretchen said, hands clasped around her knees. "I'm not going to tell them what really happened. I'll file a 'survey-found-no-evidence-to-indicate-First-Sun-artifact' and leave well enough alone. So, no bonus."

"Crap." Parker flopped back on the bed. "I break half the bones in my body for this?"

Anderssen said nothing, resting her forehead on her arms.

Oh, Sister of God, what am I going to do? The Company won't even pay us back for all the gear we lost. . . . What a black hole this was.

Parker lit a fresh tabac with an angry gesture and puffed smoke at the ceiling. No one said anything.

THE PETREL TOWNHOUSE
NEAR THE COURT OF THE KING OF HEAVEN,
CENTRAL PARUS

Leaning down, Mrs. Petrel picked up the broken half of an alabaster dish incised with tiny blue geometric figures. With a groan, she held the ancient plate up in the sunlight streaming through the porch windows. Her fingers appeared behind the translucent shell-like material, glowing pink and rose-red.

"That was a beautiful piece," a raspy voice said from behind her.

Petrel nodded, but did not turn around. Instead, she set the plate down. The terrace was scattered with debris. Broken cups and plates and statuary. Fire had charred the perfume trees in the garden and the rice-paper *shoji* between porch and the house proper were torn and ripped. Some of the panels had been wrenched from their tracks and lay askew. In some places, blood dried on the floor.

"Everything here was carefully chosen," Greta said, wondering where to start cleaning. "I was just trying to make a harmonious room . . ."

Leather sandals shuffled on the sisal-carpeted floor and a wizened old Náhuatl woman moved into her field of view. Itzpalicue leaned heavily on her cane, casting about for somewhere to sit.

"There are no chairs," Mrs. Petrel said in an empty voice. "All stolen."

"Ah." Itzpalicue hunched over a little more. "Your servants?"

"Gone. Dead." Mrs. Petrel looked out into the garden. The ground was torn up, as though the rioters who had invaded the house had been digging for buried treasure. Someone had taken an axe to the fruit trees, though the limbs and trunks lay where they had fallen. "Even old Muru, who has been with me since I was a little girl." She lifted her hand, pointing at the garden buildings at the back of the property. "The Marines found their bodies behind those sheds."

The old woman tapped her cane on the floor and shifted her feet. "You made a fine place here, but—"

"Yes, I did." Mrs. Petrel turned, fixing Itzpalicue with a steady, even stare. "I was happy here, my husband was happy. This was a planet with promise, Skirt-of-Knives, before you came meddling with your wrinkled old fingers."

The Náhuatl woman did not reply, merely returning the Anglish woman's gaze.

"Tell me one thing," Greta said. "I happened to pass a little time with your man Lachlan while Bhrigu's troops were securing the hotel, and he says all of *this* . . ." Her hand made a wide circle, encompassing the ruined house, the troubled city outside, the sky, the entire planet. ". . . was to find *something* you could not name or identify. A 'ghost of mist and shadow,' he said."

An angry hiss escaped Itzpalicue's lips and she straightened angrily, eyes flashing. "The boy should not have said *anything* about such matters!"

"Really?" Mrs. Petrel's eyebrows rose. "Did you find your quarry? Did you trap the ghost in your nets?"

Itzpalicue did not reply, her face hard and still.

"So." Greta bent down and picked up a pale green porcelain tea cup, still intact, from amid the rubble. "My husband's name is blackened, my house destroyed, my servants murdered—thousands of Jehanan civilians are killed—the Residency flattened—a Fleet cruiser wrecked—Duke Villeneuve's reputation and career smeared with undeserved charges of incompetence—for nothing." She cradled the cup in her hands. "It seems only Bhrigu benefited from all this. Humara is dead and the rebellious princes are fugitives, hunted by Marine patrols and your lovely highlander mercenaries. . . . Was this what you wanted?"

"No, but it will serve," Itzpalicue said in a whisper-soft voice. "Villeneuve needed taking down a peg—and those orders came from the Light of Heaven himself!—and he'll live longer, with such black marks on his record."

The old woman allowed herself a bit of a smile at the thought. *An ally of Green Hummingbird's is deftly removed from the game mat at the same time. And the Nisei admirals have their ruffled feathers soothed—Hadeishi is ruined, but his sacrifice will be legendary in the Fleet.*

"And there was something here—we caught a bit of the trail . . . but now it's gone cold. We know the *xochiyaotinime* priesthood is compromised—that will require some spadework to clean up—but the true enemy is gone. I can't even . . . feel it anymore."

"It?" Greta wrapped the cup in tissue paper and placed the package in a waiting cargo crate.

"Something inhuman. An alien presence." The old woman shifted her grip on the cane, her expression distant. "I am sure of it . . . Lachlan does not believe me, and I see you do not either, but I am sure in my bones of this. Not Jehanan, not human. Not any of the races we've met before."

Mrs. Petrel shook her head, making the white streak in her hair shimmer in the sunlight. "There are many alien powers which have no love for the Empire. Any of them would find it . . . amusing . . . to turn your flowery game back upon the Emperor. But do you have any proof?"

"No." Itzpalicue's lips tightened in disgust. "Nothing. Not so much as a feather."

"A waste, then." Greta made a dismissive motion. "Oh, surely the Foreign Office will be pleased—Bhrigu has sold us half the planet for a share of the taxes—the *pochteca* will have fresh markets to exploit—but those are such tiny gains to measure against our cost."

"Huh!" The old Náhuatl woman started to smirk. "The prince's reputation has been brightly burnished—he is acclaimed as a hero the length and breadth of the Empire! That, at least, went well. Better, I say, than expected."

Mrs. Petrel turned on Itzpalicue, real anger flushing her face pink. "You leave that boy alone! He meant no harm and did none. Did he ask to be a pawn, to be manipulated in this way? His heart is not tempered for this—you will twist him, force him down a path which can only lead to tears."

"And so? He is a Prince of the Imperial Household!" The old Náhuatl woman laughed hoarsely. "He was brought into this world to serve the needs of the Empire—let him! He is worth so little, otherwise. A disappointment to his family, which is not surprising given his mo—"

"Is he?" Greta interjected, giving the old woman a reproving look. "I think he behaved admirably in a terrifying situation. He is just a young man with a quiet soul, not a warrior, not a king. You should leave him be."

"Too late!" Itzpalicue grinned. "The Emperor has already seen the footage we put together and is very pleased with the results. Young Tezozómoc has a bright future before him now. This whole episode saved his reputation, just as we planned."

"As *you* planned." Mrs. Petrel resumed searching through the wreckage for more of the cups. She found only ground-up blue-white dust. "Nothing need more be said of the matter."

Itzpalicue grunted, nudging a broken table aside with her cane. "You have lost possessions before. . . . The Mirror will pay you well for your part in our little play."

"Not well enough," Greta sighed, finding the remains of a Khmer dancing

Saiva in pieces underneath one of the fallen paper screens. "I brought too many beloved things with me—do you know, I lost James's pistol in all the fuss?" She swallowed, shoulders slumping. "That was the last of his things . . . now it's rusting underneath a railway trestle somewhere between here and Takshila."

"It was just a tool," Itzpalicue said, her face softening. "Not your brother . . ."

"I suppose." Mrs. Petrel righted the screen, finding the ink-brush paintings were disfigured by crudely slashed graffiti in some local dialect. "The lack only reminds me of his death."

"The past is always filled with the dead," the old woman said, taking a breath. "I came to see you before you left on the starliner. To wish you a safe voyage and . . . to see if you were all right."

"Very kind, *Papalotl*." Mrs. Petrel grasped the next screen in line with both hands and set the wooden railing back into the floor-track. "You'll be fluttering away soon?"

Itzpalicue's lips twitched into a smile. "No one's called me 'butterfly' in years, child. Yes, a Fleet courier is waiting for me in orbit."

Greta nodded, finally turning to look at the old woman. "In future, if you are planning one of these little . . . soirées . . . do not invite me. I would take it as a great favor if you did not involve me in any more of your activities. They have acquired a bitter taste."

Itzpalicue shrank back a little, surprised, shoulders collapsing at the cold tone in the younger woman's voice. "You have always . . . *you* said they were amusing diversions. You have always had a talent—"

"I remember what I said," Greta replied softly. "But this time my husband was nearly incinerated. He is quite shaken by the whole experience."

"Ah." The old Náhuatl woman nodded, lips pursed disapprovingly. "This decision is not for yourself, then."

"It is entirely *my* decision." Mrs. Petrel stiffened. "But it is not *yours*."

Itzpalicue nodded, shrugged and went out, her cane tapping on the scarred floorboards.

Greta Petrel watched her go, keeping an eye on the old woman until she had departed the grounds, passing through mossy stone gates and climbing into a truck driven by some very disreputable-looking natives in long robes.

When the old woman was gone, Mrs. Petrel sighed, dabbed her forehead with a handkerchief and went back inside. There was a great deal of cleaning and sorting to do before she could leave this humid, damp planet. The prospect of Earth and a cool, dry vacation beckoned. *Switzerland*, she thought, trying to cheer herself up. Her husband had always liked little villages under high snowy mountains.

She pushed open the doors to the sitting room off the main foyer. Her other guest looked up from a book of photographs and woodblock prints made nearly four centuries before, showing the cities and towns of Russia as seen by the eyes of a Nisei artist named Yoshitaki.

"This is very interesting," Gretchen said, closing the antique volume. "I have never seen anything like this before. Russia seems to have been quite civilized, from the evidence of these pictures."

Greta smiled faintly. "That is because such books are forbidden to the public. That particular item was found by my brother James when he was serving on Anáhuac itself, in the Desolation, in an abandoned bunker."

"Oh." Anderssen pushed the book away and folded both hands in her lap. "I see."

Amused by Gretchen's contrite expression, Mrs. Petrel sat down in the other chair. Of all her furnishings, only these two moth-eaten settees remained intact, having been put away in storage in one of the attics. "If there were tea," she said apologetically, "we could have some, but . . ."

"No tea is fine," Gretchen said, squaring her shoulders. "May . . . may I ask a question?"

Mrs. Petrel nodded, finding the soft red velour of the chair a welcome support against her aching back. "Of course, dear. What is it?"

"Who was that old woman? I could hear her voice through the doors . . . she sounded terribly familiar."

"Really?" Greta raised an eyebrow, considering her fair-haired guest with the scarred hands and rough knuckles. "She is an old teacher of mine, from when I was attending university in Tenochtitlán. I did not realize our voices were so loud . . ."

Anderssen dimpled, offering an apologetic smile. "My hearing is sometimes distressingly good. I did not mean to pry. She just reminded me of someone else I know."

"No offense taken, though you should be more circumspect in the future." Mrs. Petrel said, mustering her concentration. "Now, what about *our* business? Was your trip successful?"

Gretchen swallowed nervously. "Well," she began, "I cannot say I set eyes upon a single *Nēm* plant, but . . . well, there was *something* in the House of Reeds, something extraordinary . . ."

Mrs. Petrel listened quietly while Anderssen related an abridged version of what had happened, her face growing stiffer and stiffer until the younger woman fell silent and then Greta sighed quietly, rubbing her brow with thin, well-manicured fingers. "You destroyed the *kalpataru.*"

Gretchen nodded, tensing herself for a furious tirade.

"You're sure?" Mrs. Petrel's complexion slowly drained of color as Anderssen nodded. "You destroyed a known, working First-Sun device! Sister bless us, child, why? The Army could have made do without comm—"

"I had to." Gretchen said flatly. "The Jehanan weren't even using a fraction of the thing's power—the *kalpataru* would have infected and overwhelmed every single computing device on this planet—I doubt the Fleet and Army could have done much with their weapons and vehicles rendered useless."

Mrs. Petrel's ashen expression did not improve. Her hands were trembling. "But you could have used the thing *yourself* . . . Loving God, what the Company could have done with . . . We'd never have to lift a finger again! The Emperor's favor alone would—"

"Mean nothing," Gretchen said, shaking her head slowly. "I understand how the Company will feel about this. I *particularly* understand what the Empire's reaction would be if they ever knew what actually happened in the House of Reeds. But, Mrs. Petrel, I also know such artifacts must *never* be allowed to fall into human hands. Never! The danger is too great!"

"What danger!" Mrs. Petrel snapped, surging up out of her chair. "There's certainly no danger now! The only danger is allowing such a thing to remain in Jehanan hands! Even the debris will need to be seized and analyzed . . ." She turned around, staring angrily at Gretchen. "Fool! You've cast aside both our futures! My god, I daren't even make a report . . ."

Gretchen's voice was very calm. "Just say there was nothing in the monastery, the initial report was only a rumor, unsubstantiated, a false lead. I'll say the same." She smiled grimly. "Don't worry—no one will ask questions—the *nauallis* will make sure of that."

"The—" Petrel stepped back, suspicion flickering in her eyes. She looked Gretchen up and down and her lip curled back in disgust. "You've been playing a double-game—you're an agent of the Judges!" Her hand made a sharp slashing motion. "Don't think I won't report *that* to the Company!"

"I'm not . . ." Gretchen paused, jaw tight, and thought: *She's right, even if I refused Hummingbird's offer two years ago. I've done just as he would have.*

"I am not a *naualli*," she continued. "Nor am I their 'agent.' But I have worked with them in the past. Some artifacts simply cannot be used. There are *traps* laid for the unwary—and the *kalpataru* was one of them. We have escaped—I hope we have escaped!—terrible calamity by only the thinnest claw-tip."

Mrs. Petrel said nothing. Anderssen gained the impression of fulminating, terrible anger roiling in the older woman—but then she raised her hands and let out a bitter sigh. "There is nothing to be done about this now," Greta said in a thin, leached voice. "Get out. Just get out."

Nodding, Anderssen stood up—almost stumbling, her legs weak with tension—and reached the door before Mrs. Petrel's voice echoed in the ruined room.

"I know what the Judges told you." Cold, clear anger permeated Greta's voice. "But you should know they *lie*. They lie constantly—even when the truth would serve—and they care *nothing* for any human alive."

Gretchen turned in the doorway and saw Petrel clutching Yoshitaki's book tightly to her chest. "Who did you—"

"That doesn't matter," Petrel said, her face filled with anguish. "Just remember, they will *sacrifice* you and anyone else—anyone!—to gain their ends. They are like sharks—without emotion, without remorse."

"And if those ends mean the survival of humanity?" Gretchen said softly, feeling the woman's pain as a hot pressure on her face. "Isn't our sacrifice *necessary* for our children to live? For the race to continue? How do you weigh that balance, Petrel-*tzin*?"

Greta put a hand on the back of the chair to steady herself and then she turned away, saying nothing.

Anderssen went out, quietly, and found the sky clearing. Hot, bright sunlight streamed down through the clouds, gilding the ruins of the Legation. Plumes of smoke were rising over the city, but the worst of the fires had died down. Her boots—worn and dirty, as always—crunched through drifts of broken glass.

Yi birds were fluting in the trees, Jehanan workers were picking through the debris, Marine guards were on every rooftop, keeping a wary eye on the surroundings. Everything seemed blessedly normal.

I'm alive, Gretchen thought, and her heart lifted to be out of the ruined house. The prospect of Petrel telling the Company what she'd done and their inevitable termination of her employment made her feel giddy. *We're all alive—my little pack of troublemakers—and now I am going home. And my babies will be waiting, and my mother and even that feckless husband of mine. Even penniless, they will be glad to see me!*

Anderssen smiled cheerfully at the guards in the Legation gateway and turned out onto the street, hands in the pockets of her field jacket. Around her, the city was beginning to stir to life again, citizens out chattering in the streets, aerocars droning overhead, the distant lonely sound of a steam-whistle hooting from the railyard.

ABOARD THE STARLINER *ASUKA*
PREPARING TO LEAVE ORBIT OVER JAGAN

A first-class cabin door hissed open and Tezozómoc stepped into a clean, sparkling room filled with inviting furniture. Soft music wafted on the cool, climate-controlled air. The young man stared around, drinking in every gram of luxury and his face brightened, looking into an adjoining bedroom.

"Oh, gods of my fathers and blessed Mother, look at the size of that bed! Four or five girls would fit easily!" The prince dropped a battered, grimy Army jacket on the floor and—before Colmuir or Dawd could say anything—stripped off his Jehanan cloak and discarded his skinsuit in an ugly, blood-and-oil-stained pile. Entirely naked, Tezozómoc padded into the bathroom adjoining the main room of the suite and began to laugh hysterically.

"A shower and a tub! And towels, look at these towels!" The prince's head appeared in the doorway for a moment, one brown hand waving a plushy, gleaming white bath-towel and then vanished again. The sound of water running followed, and a yelp of mingled pain and delight as Tezozómoc turned the taps on full hot.

Colmuir stared at the clothing discarded on the floor, dully noted the mess the boy had made of the carpet and wearily set down his duffel and gunrig on the couch. "This is a nice room," he said, on the verge of collapse himself. The Army medical staff had worked him over enough to get him aboard ship, but the master sergeant was in a bad way. He hurt from head to toe and even the resilience of his combatskin and the constant attentions of his medband couldn't overcome the bone-deep bruising and internal injuries he'd suffered. Worse, Colmuir felt unaccountably nervous and he didn't know why.

M' hackles are up, he realized, *like we're still in th' thick of it . . .*

Dawd let the door close behind him and stowed his own baggage. "We've the other bedroom, then? Better than the floor, I suppose."

The younger Skawtsman's face was bandaged and his combat goggles were still on. The lenses were dull black, as though he were standing outside in full sun. With a groan, Dawd slumped into a hugely overstuffed chair opposite Colmuir. In the bathroom, Tezozómoc had begun to sing lustily, voice muffled by the rush of water. Clouds of steam drifted through the doorway.

The master sergeant managed a smile. "Well, our lad seems happy at last."

"You're not?" Dawd asked, letting his head fall back on the chair. "We're alive, he's alive. We'll be home on Anáhuac soon. A great victory all around, I think."

"Truth." Colmuir considered the prospect. "You're right. The boy didn't embarrass himself when the shooting started or get one of us killed. The Emperor might even be *pleased* by how things turned out . . ."

Dawd tried to laugh, producing a croaking sound. "I'm sure someone will decide the prince saved the day, crushed the rebellion and saved more than one fainting maiden by the time news gets back home."

"Ah, now, you're getting cynical." Colmuir gestured at the younger man's face. "Your eyes still recovering? Didn't they give you a supplemental 'band to speed up th' healing?"

"My eyes?" Dawd touched his goggles absently and then shook his head. "I'd forgotten I had these on." The sergeant lifted his head, indicating the bathroom. "Do you suppose he'll leave any hot water for us?"

"Probably not," Colmuir snorted, forcing himself to his feet. He stared at Dawd, tight-lipped. "Let me have a look at this injury of yours—if yuir eyes are still hurting, it's best you visited the ship's medbay . . ."

"Master Sergeant, I'm fine!" Dawd lifted a hand, stopping Colmuir—who was looking rather pale—from touching his goggles. "Another day or so and they'll be good as new."

"Let me see," Colmuir said, making a sharp, beckoning gesture. "I can tell when a man's hiding something—and *you are*, Sergeant—there's no sense in being stoic about an injury."

"Of course," Dawd said, rather stiffly. He lifted both hands and slowly removed the goggles. Behind them, his eyes were closed tight, and puffy with dark red bruising. Scorch marks scarred his left socket, and his bushy black eyebrows were ashy smears.

"Ah, lad, you look terrible!" Colmuir peered closer. A queer tickling sensation at the back of his neck was making him even more nervous. "D' they work at all?"

The master sergeant gently peeled back the lid of Dawd's right eye, revealing a massively dilated pupil surrounded by the thinnest verge of green. The whites were a rough, angry red. The sergeant hissed in pain, flinching away.

"Sorry," Colmuir said, shaking his head and turning away. "Tha' looks quite bad."

"No . . . trouble, Master Sergeant." Dawd gingerly put his goggles back on. In the brief instant before the glassite lenses once more obscured them, the ruined eyes rippled and shifted, subsuming the hastily extruded skin and swollen veins. Cold watery blue irises emerged from beneath the camouflage and purpled bruises faded as the shiftskin of the Lengian <sower|teacher|adjudicator> returned to an efficient and optimal configuration.

This <protector|guardian|hound> will have to be destroyed, the creature thought, with the faintest tinge of dismay, watching Master Sergeant Colmuir sit again, his lean old face pinched with pain. *It is suspicious—heart-rate is elevated, senses are sharpened—by the Makers, its perceptual gestalt has determined I am not Sergeant Leslie Dawd at all. Now this one must be destroyed. What a waste of a superior gene-line . . .*

Dawd licked his lips, then said: "Master Sergeant, if you don't mind my asking—have you any children?"

"Me?" Colmuir was entirely taken aback by the question. He laughed, running a scarred hand through short, springy gray-black hair. "Oh, scads, I'm sure. Somewhere. Why?"

Dawd nodded to himself, pleased. "Nothing, Master Sergeant. I was just suddenly curious."

"Ah!" Tezozómoc bounded back into the main room, glistening and clean, his long hair tied back in a ponytail. The prince seemed, for once, actually happy. "Let's order room service," he declared, grinning foolishly at his two bodyguards, and snatching up a portable comm-plate emblazoned with the swan-*mon* of the liner. "Let's see just how good their liquor cabinet is!"

Colmuir grunted, but a smile was beginning to show on his lips. "Ah, I would not refuse a fine Skawts whiskey today, mi'lord, no I would not."

"Excellent!" Tezozómoc turned to the creature sitting so comfortably in the shape of a man. "Dawd, what'll you have?"

"Whatever you're having, mi'lord," the Lengian replied, making a bit of a bow towards the prince. "Whatever you're having."

THE ADVENTURES OF GRETCHEN ANDERSSEN, MITSUHARU HADEISHI, SUSAN KOSHŌ, AND GREEN HUMMINGBIRD WILL CONTINUE IN THE THIRD BOOK OF THE SIXTH SUN:

LAND OF THE DEAD.

APPENDIX

JAGANITE HISTORICAL PERIODS

Note: Jagan is a Jehanan word for "world" or "dirt."

1. Life evolves on Jagan, though no records of any indigenous civilization remain.
2. First Sun visitation, establishment of a Valkar colony. Ends in the destruction of the polar continent (and the colony) during the Hive Invasions.
3. The Six Hundred Dynasties rise from the ruins, though this is a time of nothing but war, chaos and monsters. Jagan is eventually conquered and ruled by the insectile Assakū, who exterminate the last of the Valkar colonists and their native slave-soldiers.
4. In time, Jagan is unified by the glorious, godlike civilization of the Haraphan kings (who are the descendants of the Assakū clan-lords). During this time the Haraphans conquer and/or colonize several neighboring star systems.
5. Though particularly beautiful Haraphan relics are found worldwide, and they apparently created a systematic, uniform society, all records of their rule are annihilated by the arrival of the reptilian Jehanan, who conquer all of Jagan, but immediately fall out among themselves.

6. The War of the Hundred and Six Brothers destroys the last remnants of the Haraphan civilization, leaving a totally new race and society in its place. Billions of Haraphan and Jehanans die during this conflict. All traces of the Valkar colony are lost. The Haraphans are reduced to tiny, marginalized tribes (the 'Jeweled-Kings') on the fringes of Jehanan dominions. The invaders lose their spaceflight capability.
7. After a long interval, the Jehanan king, Arthava, unifies most of the continent holding Fehrupuré and Takshila, founding his 'rule of right conduct.' Fehrupuré is made his capital and rebuilt on a grand scale (though he apparently knows nothing of the Haraphan civilization, many of Arthava's edicts—carved into various mountainsides and plinths—echo their sensibilities).
8. The Arthavan Empire collapses in the latest turn of the Wheel of Fate. Apparently, a nuclear holocaust consumes the high-point of Jehanan civilization just as they are about to resume spaceflight.
9. The 'Time of Ghosts' follows, as the Jehanan civilization slides back, losing much of the technology and science which had prospered under Arthava and his descendants. Squalid new cities rise amid the ruins of old glories. Though there are intermittent attempts by inspired kings to unify Jagan, none of the efforts last.
10. The Imperials arrive, landing at Parus and establishing the Legation. Without the knowledge of most Jehanan (now reduced to squabbling city-states), their world is placed under Méxica protection. Periodic invasions of barbarians out of the northwest cause a great deal of trouble for the kings of Gandaris and Takshila, particularly after the fall of the frontier city of Capsia to these nomads.